I0822384

PROGENY
The Complete Trilogy

by

SHAWN HOPKINS

This is a work of fiction. Names, characters, and incidents are either a work of the author's imagination or are used fictitiously.

ISBN: 979-8-9852856-2-8

For Mom and Dad

"Train up a child in the way he should go and he will not depart from it."
I hope you've seen that promise fulfilled.
Thank you for everything. I love you.

A New Author's Note

On a warm Southern Cali night in 1998, I sat in a cafeteria with the Compaq laptop my uncle had bought me as a "going-off-to-college" present and attempted to write a story. By the time I noticed that the CD playing on my discman was over, I had a prologue typed. A National Geographic team stationed on an island in the Pacific gets attacked during a tropical storm by unseen beastly creatures with long claws. When no one hears from them after the storm, one of the family members—a Navy SEAL, of course—goes to investigate. I called the story *Strange Soil.*

That's as far as I got before scrapping the whole thing. What came out of the next effort was an island story that combined every weird thing I could think of: aliens, the Bermuda Triangle, Nephilim, and ancient mythology. That book was called *Evil's Own.*

I rewrote that one too, and the same uncle who gave me my first laptop helped pay for its publication with a vanity press in 2005. It was called *Noahic.* And, just in case any of you think I'm borrowing from some of today's popular shows and themes…this was well before LOST and way before Nephilim were challenging the vampire scene. In fact, when I wrote *Noahic* the only material I had on the Nephilim was a commentary on the Book of Genesis and *Alien Encounters* by the late Chuck Missler (I once handed him a copy of *Noahic* when we crossed paths in Philadelphia) and Dr. Mark Eastman (who once examined my knee while doing a radio show on the same California campus I started this adventure on).

But as my next book *Even The Elect* was in the hands of an agent, I really had an urge to go back and make *Noahic* something better. I loved the premise of the island story and thought I could do better with it. So I started looking around for reference material related to my topic and ended up grabbing *The Nephilim and the Pyramid of the Apocalypse* from my local Barnes and Noble. And then I fell down the rabbit hole (see the bibliography at the end to see where this one book led me).

The ensuing rewrite of *Noahic*, with this new world of information I'd discovered, ended up being something far deeper than I ever expected. I tried to include as much of the information as I possibly could without turning the story into a textbook (which I may or may not have succeeded in doing—the reviews are mixed). It was the information that drove this new version of the story, and to get a sense of the mystery and wonder that so captivated me, I'd encourage you to search online for images of all the weird things mentioned. Reading about the giant stones at Baalbek can't compare to seeing an actual picture of a grown man standing beside them.

After *Progeny* was released in 2011, there were still parts of *Noahic* (and even the earlier versions) that I wished I had been able to fit into it. That, along with some of the reviews suggesting character development had been sacrificed on the altar of information, prompted me to continue the island story with two sequels. The sequels weren't as information driven (the resident archeologist was no longer around to enlighten us), rather I tried to bring out the characters of those left behind, getting into their back stories while exploring more of the island and upping the action.

And then there was that moment in *Remnant* (now re-titled *Principalities and Powers*) that I just couldn't resist, knowing some readers would enjoy the addition of a new level to the maze while others would see it as a betrayal to the "realism" I tried to establish in *Progeny*. This "shift" did serve as a sort of passageway in the overall feel of the trilogy, a route that led away from the information-based "what if" flavor and into a full-on paranormal action adventure series. And though part of me didn't like that crossover, it was the only way to get to know the rest of the island and its characters and incorporate some of the elements I'd enjoyed from the earlier versions back into the story.

It has been fun writing in this world for the last twenty years, and indeed more from the strange island is coming, so be sure to visit www.shawnhopkins.com to get on the mailing list and be alerted as soon as more tales from the Triangle are released.

I hope you enjoy the ride.

Shawn Hopkins
October, 2021
Chester County, PA.

BOOK I

NEPHILIM ISLAND

And he said unto them, I beheld Satan as lightning fall from heaven.

—Luke 10:18 (KJV)

How you have fallen from Heaven, O morning star, son of the dawn. You have been cast down to the Earth, you who once laid low the nations. For you said in your heart: "I will ascend to Heaven. I will raise my throne above the stars of God. I will sit enthroned on the mount of assembly on the utmost heights of the sacred mountain. I will ascend above the tops of the clouds. I will make myself like the Most High."

—Isaiah 14:12-14 (NIV)

And there appeared another wonder in Heaven; and behold, a great red dragon having seven heads and ten horns, and seven crowns upon his heads. And his tail drew a third part of the stars of Heaven, and did cast them to the Earth. And there was war in Heaven: Michael and his angels fought against the dragon; and the dragon fought and his angels. And the great dragon was cast out, that old serpent called the Devil, and Satan, which deceiveth the whole world: he was cast out into the earth, and his angels were cast out with him.

—Revelation 12:3,4,7,9 (KJV)

...And one from out the order of angels, having turned away with the order that was under him, conceived an impossible thought, to place his throne higher than the clouds above the earth, that he might become equal in rank to my power. And I threw him out from the height with his angels...

—The Book of Secrets of Enoch 29:3-4a

PROLOGUE

1609 Anno Domini. 28th day of July

For three days, the storm had wrapped the land in darkness, bombarding it with a violent fury that tried desperately to sink the whole island back from where it must have once come. Had there been any inhabitants, any natives of the island, they would have no doubt prayed to their heathen gods for merciful deliverance, sacrificing each other as some ill-thought means of appeasement. However, no such pleading had been lifted to the air, nor innocent blood spilled atop sacred altars. Such terror did not haunt the lonely speck of land, for never had a human being been there to exercise such fearful penance. But for the exception of the few birds that made their homes in the tall cedars and the tropical fish that skirted the pink beaches, the presence of a being self-aware was as foreign a concept to the tropical habitat as that of Julius Caesar and the present month that bears his name. And just as no one had been there to tremble before the storm's fierce judgment, there was also no one to appreciate the sun's return when it rose as savior over the battered landscape, illuminating the hook-shaped island that rested alone within a tropical void of blue.

Except...

As the sun climbed and the shadows retreated from the rock-littered sand, a single set of footprints could be seen tracing back and forth throughout the island. With the storm passing just the day before, whatever being left the evidence of his solitary presence had done so since. In even measure they circled the whole of the island, disappearing and reappearing beneath the cool undergrowth of its interior. The sand was still wet, so the prints—heel to toe—were well defined. They led down a stretch of crescent-shaped beach and disappeared at times through the encroaching surf. Whoever belonged to the feet that made them, feet that by all accounts seemed perfectly proportioned and quite fantastic as human feet go, must have either just arrived or somehow survived the three-day storm. However, if he had indeed survived nature's wrath, then the question immediately must be put forth as to just how long this person had been here and how exactly he appeared to be so, for no seafaring vessel had ever graced these peculiar shores. In fact, it wasn't just the world of mankind that this island was foreign to, but to all other worlds as well—save that of its own natural environment and the few creatures that lived off its plant life.

If the footprints, now leading out from the sand and into some tangled grass, belong to one who had been in such a desolate place for any period of time, regardless of how he might have ended up here, he would no doubt be going mad with ideas of escape.

At last, the footprints left the unkempt grass, vanished straight into the crystal tide, and led to a single man standing waist deep within the waves. He wore nothing, and his skin was so darkened by the sun that it appeared as though he had spent his entire lifetime stranded on the lonesome shores, his hair bleached blond and reaching below his shoulders. However long he had been here, though, he looked not a day beyond thirty-three. His eyes, as they stared out into the glimmering horizon, reflected a wisdom that should far exceed such a young age. His features appeared flawless—a strong, hairless body rippling with lean muscle and a face aching to be carved by ancient Greek artists.

He stood there gazing out into the beautiful nothingness once more and saw what he had always seen—emptiness, an expanse of water whose true nature hid whatever beauty might otherwise be found. Not that beauty was of any concern to the man, not anymore and never of this sort. But it was his interest in beautiful things of another kind that had proven to be his further undoing; and then his failed attempt at restoration had led him here—a place, he concluded, that was designed by God simply as a way of letting him know forevermore who it was that truly held the keys to creation's secrets.

The man looked down at his hands and flexed all ten fingers. Even after all the years, the wonder of it still struck him as something fascinating, while at the same time stirring strong feelings of regret. Without the pleasurable availabilities of what had made him choose such a state—the peculiar beauty he had pursued with its use—it had become a sacrifice in vain.

This place…

It was its own sort of hell, the never-ending question of its unique properties swirling dizzily in his head. He had constructed a vessel once and had tried on multiple occasions to escape, but every effort brought him right back where he started, as if all that existed in the universe was this little island and the water that surrounded it. And so, this was his punishment for attempting to free his brothers. Solitary confinement and the ever-present awareness of time's slow passage to nowhere.

As a wave struck his chest, salt water dripping down his torso and over his navel-less stomach, he turned away from the point where blue sky met blue water and disappeared into the limitless void in which he was imprisoned. He was about to return to his abode when, just as his head swiveled away, something caught his eye. He was so accustomed to seeing such trickery out in the rolling waves, however, that he almost refrained from looking back. But he humored himself anyway and was, for the first time, rewarded by the effort. There was surely something out there. A ship of some kind, a model whose origin he was unfamiliar with, but a ship nonetheless.

But how could that be? His mind spun in circles, searching for an explanation. But, just like everything else about this place, there simply wasn't one to be had. So he returned to the beach and sat, anxiously awaiting whoever it was that was coming to visit his lonely island.

Fascinated, he watched as the ship fixed itself on the reef just beyond the breaking waves. Even at such a great distance, because of his uncanny vision, he could see men lowering small boats into the water. The men were unfamiliar to him. White-skinned, bearded, and dressed in armor that reflected the sunlight, he had never seen the likes of such a race. They began paddling toward him.

It almost escaped him, the fact that he was naked. Wrought with hesitation, as if turning away from them could make them disappear, he got to his feet and began running to his home for clothes he had not worn in a thousand years.

Though he sprinted the distance without a moment of rest, there was no shortness of breath or any other kind of fatigue to chase after his physical frame. Entering his temple home, he proceeded quickly to a stone case that secured the clothes he had been wearing when he first arrived so long ago. Had they not been masterfully crafted from some chemical union secret to the natural order of things, the clothing would have surely disintegrated, turning to dust in his grasp. Instead, the shiny white fabric slid over his skin as if it had been fashioned just days before.

As he hurried dressing himself, a strange presence suddenly startled him. He spun around, wary of a feeling he had not known in ages—before even his arrival *here*. It was obvious that things had suddenly changed, and he was not underestimating the allowances that such changes might have created.

"Who is there?" His question was put forth with words no one would now understand, though the resonance of his voice sounded exactly as it had the first time he ever opened his mouth to speak.

A shadow materialized in front of him, though not caused by any natural blockage of light.

"You have waited a long time," a slithery voice responded in the same language.

The man squinted into the shadow. "Show yourself."

The shadow began taking shape and mysteriously formed itself into the smoky embodiment of a manlike figure.

"This is the best that I can do here," it explained as two holes of light shone forth as eyes.

"*You…*"

Bewilderment stroked the accusation.

A semblance of acknowledgement. "Yes. We have come to help you."

"I thought you had abandoned me," he said, years of anger and frustration bleeding into his words.

The smoky figure seemed to nod. "It wasn't until now that we could come to you."

"Who are those people? How did they get here?" He pointed toward the ocean.

"They are not *here* in the sense that you think."

"What do you mean?"

"I mean only that you are wasting your time putting on such coverings. They cannot see you."

A wave of confusion contorted the man's perfect face. "I don't understand."

The sound of the voice transformed from serpent-like to that of crumbling rock. "There is much you do not understand, nor could you. You have been away for so long."

"Is there a way of escape? Have you come to free me?" His tone spiked with hope.

"We do not know whether it is possible for you to leave or not. But unlike your brothers, who have *no* hope without heaven's key, *you* may be able to reverse what you have done."

The man looked stunned. "You mean—" He pointed at himself.

"No. I am afraid that is irreversible. I speak of the ill-fated journey that saw you here."

Here... The agonizing question surfaced on his lips before he could stop it. "And where is this horrid place?"

The fluttering form of encircling smoke suddenly split into another presence, again speaking through the hissing tongue of a serpent. "It is an island that is surrounded by the body of water mankind has named after Atlas."

Atlas... But he could not let such personal thoughts divert him from the sudden plausibility of escape. "Is this the first time that sons of Noah have visited this place?"

"No. It has been more than a hundred years since man has become aware of this island."

"But I have not seen anything until today. I have not seen anyone since the day I entered the device!"

"We know," they said in unison, the slippery voice choking on rock.

"How is that possible? What has changed that your presence is suddenly allowed here, that I can see *them*?"

"We will explain all of that in time. But first, do you remember how you came to be here, the plan that you followed?"

"Of course. Though clearly my plan was flawed, for it put me here instead of at the doors of my brethren."

The form on the left hissed, "Ye*ssss*, much to His amusement, I suspect. But that is beside the point. We need only to get you back to the realm of man."

"Why? What is happening?" the man asked, wondering why after so long there was finally a communal interest in freeing him.

Both voices were as one: "The end draws near, and we grow anxious."

He nodded, the prospect of again intermingling with humans making his flesh tingle. "I will need to build, but without children—"

"Do not fret. We have come to help."

"How can you? Without physically manifesting your presence, you are of no use."

Just then the two pillars of swirling smoke converged into a large and formless cloud, churning within itself. And then, just as quickly, it was gone, leaving in its stead a strange object fixed with mirrors. At first, the man caught only his own reflection and was not surprised that he still looked exactly as he had on the day he left his first estate. But then his image faded and gave way to others. People. Walking about in places he did not recognize.

"What is this?" he whispered.

The gravelly voice came back from the unseen. "We have been busy this last century. Soon you will be able to begin your work again in reestablishing his kingdom."

He let the words simmer, and as a result, hopes that he thought to be long dead once more began twinkling in his eyes. "Was I even close in my endeavor to unlock the gates?" he asked, momentarily reflective.

"Abaddon will indeed be free once more, and the earth shall yet again be ours, but not until the appointed time. Now sit, we have much to teach you."

* * * *

1687 Anno Domini. The Atlantic Ocean

Of course it didn't make any sense! None whatsoever. And though he tried to understand it, he knew it was nothing short of impossible. There was simply nothing to understand.

Standing on the main deck, he looked again to the mizzenmast and the mainmast, ignoring the lingering storm clouds. Both were without sails, reduced to bare poles stretching up into the sky, their ends splintered into jagged points. Then he turned and studied the foremast, the only sail still intact. But this observation only taunted his reason more.

Managing to tear his eyes away from it, he began moving his feet and navigated through a couple of his men, coming to the port side of the ship. Again, he leaned over her broken railing and peered down the side.

How was it possible?

The captain looked up from the passing water sloshing alongside the *Sovereignty*'s hull and fixed his gaze ahead to the portside bow—at the water it was somehow speedily cutting a path through.

"Strange."

The voice behind startled him, and he turned to see his lieutenant standing there staring out to the vast ocean as well.

The captain frowned, moving his gaze over the rest of his crew. "What are they saying?"

The lieutenant shifted his eyes to the driver, to Britain's flag flapping in the breeze. The red, white, and blue amalgamation of St. George's Cross and St. Andrew's Cross was still blowing in the wrong direction.

"They do not know what to think," he replied. "Though the storm itself is the context through which they are interpreting this odd phenomenon."

"Are they scared?"

"Of course. It has been two days since the storm overtook us. Two days since we have had any control of the ship, and now many of the men are beginning to wonder where this mysterious fate is taking them."

Looking straight into the eyes of his old friend, the captain asked, "And what is it that *you* believe?"

He shrugged. "I cannot deny that the storm seemed to be of distinct character." His eyes went back to the unknown. "It was not like anything that I have seen before."

"You think it was evil."

The lieutenant ignored the amusement that sat behind the statement because he knew it to be fabricated. He answered unashamedly, "There seemed to be a will behind it."

The captain laughed nervously, attempting to dismiss such a ludicrous idea. "Listen to us, talking as if nature were a person!"

Eyes narrowing, he responded, "Yet here we are with no sails to propel us, no means of our own by which to make a speedy retreat—"

The captain nodded in consent and finished the lieutenant's thought for him, "—moving quickly through this dead calm."

"It is not natural."

Looking up into the lingering rain clouds, the captain asked another question, this one born of simple hope. "Do you think that this could be Providence guiding us? Saving us, even?"

"Perhaps I would have been more apt to consider such a pleasant thought if it were not for the nightmare that introduced us to such circumstances in the first place."

There was no denying what his lieutenant was saying. He had seen the storm—had *felt* it—and it had not been according to the natural order of things. Maybe he would never be able to put into words what they had encountered out on the sea two days ago, but the inability to express it would never erase it or change it from being something other than what it was—a mystery, of course, but a reality nonetheless. For though they might not have seen one, they were all certain that this particular storm had a face. And it had not been the face of God. Simply recalling the way in which it had spread across the sky made his spine tingle. That cold darkness that penetrated his flesh seemed to pass right through his soul… And now, here they sat, captive to something they did not understand nor could ever hope to control. In their own power and by their own means they were but stranded in the middle of the Atlantic with half of the crew dead, most of their supplies lost, and no means of navigation whatsoever. Yet there was indeed an unseen force moving them in contradiction to nature. But what was it, and where was it taking them?

Certainly not back to England.

"It would have been better to stay and fight," the captain whispered remorsefully.

But the lieutenant shook his head in respectful disagreement. "The pirates led us into a trap, and you did all that you could to save us. No one among the living could have foreseen this. It is not your fault."

But the thought of *something* being at fault triggered another idea in his mind. "Do you suppose we could have a Jonah on board?"

"You mean someone whom God is angry with, his presence among us bringing judgment on the whole ship?" He shook his head, though his attention was still captivated by the watery horizon. "Even if we found such a person and threw him overboard, where would that leave us? Would God then tell us where we are, repair the whipstaff, and return our charts?"

The captain thought about this. "You think it best to see where this invisible hand takes us?"

"I see no other option. It is either that or we starve."

"We could eat the prisoner," the captain jested with ill humor.

The prisoner had been caught trying to reach the colonies in a small ship manned with a hired crew. It was after attaining him and upon their return to England that they ran into a horde of pirate ships. Though they were able to outrun the pirates by heading southwest and into a strange fog, they were unable to outrun the storm the fog had veiled.

"I would not care to touch that man, let alone eat him," responded the lieutenant. "But if there is a Jonah on this ship, he certainly has my vote."

After a moment of silence and watching a few scattered water drops plunge into the surface of the water, the captain mumbled, "Would it be so outlandish to credit what is happening…to our prisoner?"

"You are not suggesting that he is responsible for the storm, that he somehow plotted out this course for us?"

"No, I would not suggest all of that. I merely wonder if there could be a connection, no matter how minute. After all, he is no ordinary man, is he?"

The lieutenant finally turned to face the captain. "Other than the fact that he has six fingers on his right hand, how different can he possibly be from the rest of the depraved lunatics roaming our countryside?"

"You do not give credence to the stories, then?" The captain's previous attempt to ignore such extreme possibilities had waned quickly.

"Though I cannot explain what I have seen with more thoughts than I have already disclosed, I do have a difficult time believing the stories to be anything more than exaggerations."

The captain frowned, confused as to how their roles had so quickly become reversed. "In light of what we just witnessed and what we are witnessing now, would it seem like so great a stretch to think of the supernatural as being present with us?"

"No, I suppose not."

At that moment a cry went out from the bow, drawing their attention away from bizarre speculation and to the more immediate and tangible present.

"Land!" the voice was crying. "*Land!*"

SUMMONING

And the angels which kept not their first estate, but left their own habitation, he hath reserved in everlasting chains under darkness unto the judgment of the great day. Even as Sodom and Gomorrah, and the cities about them in like manner, giving themselves over to fornication, and going after strange flesh, are set forth for an example, suffering the vengeance of eternal fire.

—Jude 6–7 (KJV)

In like manner the Watchers also changed the order of their nature, whom the Lord cursed at the flood, on whose account He made the earth without inhabitants and fruitless.

—The Testament of Naphtali 1:27

It happened after the sons of men had multiplied in those days, that daughters were born to them, elegant and beautiful. And when the angels, the sons of heaven, beheld them, they became enamored of them, saying to each other, Come, let us select for ourselves wives from the progeny of men, and let us beget children… Their whole number was two hundred, who descended upon Ardis, which is the top of mount Armon.

—Book of Enoch 7:1–2, 7

ONE

20th day of May. Wilkinsburg, Pennsylvania

He reached into the glove compartment and pulled out a faded Pittsburgh Penguins hat, quickly fitting it onto his head before the light changed. He didn't care that his registration and insurance information had spilled onto the floor and was now hidden amongst empty coffee cups, old blueprints, tools, and a plethora of other strewn articles. The door to the glove box, like most of the truck itself, was broken, and he'd long ago grown tired of trying to keep things from falling out of it.

When the light turned green, he leaned forward over the steering wheel, the brim of his hat almost touching the windshield, and applied careful pressure to the gas pedal. He couldn't see anything through the sheets of rain falling against the glass, his view horribly distorted thanks to a pair of lazy wipers that decided to work only every three minutes or so. He had apparently delayed a day too long in seeing to their repair.

Five agonizing minutes later, he pulled into a vacant spot facing the entrance to a convenience store. Hopping out with a handful of change, and not bothering to lock the door or turn off the engine, he took six quick strides through the downpour before he was under the canopy and holding the door open for someone. He was sliding back into the truck and across the torn bench seat with a steaming hot cup of coffee and seven cents in change two minutes after that.

His T-shirt was clinging damply to his chest, and his water-logged boots were beginning to divert some of their dampness up into the legs of his jeans. Suppressing a series of chills, he switched the heat on, a feature that ironically still managed to work this far into May, though the air-conditioning did not. As he pulled back onto the road, aiming his old pickup toward Pittsburgh, all the windows began to fog up, and he had to lean forward to wipe off a small area of the windshield that he hadn't been able to see through to begin with. Taking a sip of coffee and pushing an old cassette into the tape deck, he settled in for what was usually a short drive into the Steel City.

Despite already running late, he kept to his daily routine of passing by the church. Twice in the past month he'd spotted the vulgar work of heathen pranksters splashed across the exterior walls of the white building. It was the reason he kept half a gallon of paint in the bed of his truck. As much as it frustrated him, though, when approaching the pastor about possible precautions to take, the man just smiled and humbly quoted the statement penned by Ignatius just ten years after the close of the first century: "Christianity is truly a matter of greatness as long as it is hated by the world." John figured it'd take him a bit more time to wrap his head around that one.

His trip by the church today, however, was just as futile as trying to get the pastor to condemn the local artists. It was raining so hard, and his windows were so foggy, that he couldn't even tell that the building was there. That was what his pastor called it, anyway—a building. Nothing more, nothing less. Just a place set apart for the fellowship of the saints. "The church is not a building, she's a people," he'd say. He wished he could view things as graciously. In light of how much grace had been extended to him, he should probably be more lenient toward others by now.

He stopped at another light and listened to the sound of a guitar playing through the only speaker that still worked, its volume being contested by the squeaking wheels turning within the player. He took another sip of coffee while gazing at the big red blur hanging out in front of him. The streetlights still shone down the sides of the street, and with headlights turning into streaking taillights, the whole scene looked as if it were from some underwater sci-fi film.

Guitar chords segued into the quick beat of a bass drum while the light still wavered as a shifting red stain over the street. When the song finally settled into a rhythm, and lyrics began accompanying the noise, he leaned over and retrieved the rearview mirror from the seat beside him. He held it up and stared. It was an exercise he'd taken up recently, though he wasn't entirely sure why. For some unknown reason, the last few days had introduced the strange and deeply disturbing sensation of being watched. And then there was the presence of shadowy things skittering haphazardly across the boundaries of his peripheral vision… He wondered if he could be going crazy, or if maybe some sort of delayed PTSD was finally coming to collect on his sanity.

Thunder sounded, and lightning streaked across the sky, but still the light glowed red. He sighed and leaned back, tossing the mirror beside him and rubbing his eyes. Dropping his hand down to his stubbly beard, he subconsciously traced the scars he kept hidden beneath it. He didn't know why the things that he had tried so hard to forget were suddenly coming back to him now. But he didn't want to think about it, so instead, he set his mind on something else—tomorrow, Friday. Though it was barely an improvement upon the last thought, it was one he had no choice but to deal with. *Tomorrow…* He would deal with it *then,* and for now just hope that it took its good old time in coming.

The light finally switched to green, and he was grateful to turn his attention back to navigating through the real, albeit unfocused, world of the living.

* * * *

He turned the key, shutting down the engine and the music in mid-lyric. Sitting there for a minute, intent on finishing his coffee and listening to the hypnotic sound of the rain pitter-pattering off his truck, he could just make out his partner's yellow raincoat moving back and forth on the site beneath the stormy veil.

Draining the paper cup, he tossed it onto the pile of others, further burying his driver's information. Then he reached behind the seat, grabbed his tool belt, and took a deep breath before jumping out into the mud.

"Is that you, John?" a voice called out from behind a curtain of runoff water. "If it is, you're late!"

John ducked through the waterfall that was pouring off the concrete slab above them and wiped the rain out of his eyes. "Sorry, Miles," he muttered. "Needed a coffee like you wouldn't believe."

"You pick me up one? Nah, of course not. You're never thinking of Miles. It hurts, man."

John just rubbed his thumb and first two fingers together. "Sorry. Can't exactly afford the ostentatious stuff you drink."

"Ostentatious? What is that, the word of the day?" He looked over his coworker, taking him in from head to foot. "Where's your hardhat?"

But John just gave him a knowing look that suggested how ridiculous he perceived such a notion to be.

"Man, you're gonna get in trouble! And then who's gonna help me finish this place, huh? Doesn't the Bible say something about following the rules?"

John knew it did—evidently another thing he had to work on. "Come on, let's get this done."

But Miles didn't move. "You don't look so good, man. You okay? The wife been chaining you up in the basement again? Doin' that crazy thing with the strobe light, putting Scotch tape on your eyelids and all? I mean, it's strange, but then there's a lot of strange people out there… I'm just saying I didn't peg her to be one of them—a weirdo like that. Even if I'd known you before, been your best man and everything, I still wouldn't have warned you because, like I said, I had no idea she was into that stuff. You should really call the police. It's a free country. You have rights. I mean it, man…"

Smiling, John shook his head and walked over to a stack of Sheetrock.

"You haven't been sleeping, have you?" Miles asked with more seriousness.

He shrugged. "I'm fine."

Miles walked to the other side of the stack and asked, "It's tomorrow, isn't it? You don't want to go."

"Of course I don't want to go."

They picked up four four-by-sixteen-foot sheets of drywall and moved them to a bare aluminum-studded wall.

Miles rolled his eyes under the low-hanging brim of his hardhat. "Yeah, you're right. Why would *anyone* want to go to a place like that?"

John shrugged off the sarcasm as he stood one of the pieces on end himself. "It's not like that."

"What is it, then?" Miles asked. "You don't want to leave Kristen? She'll be fine."

"It's not that either."

"It's the guys, then. You're afraid they'll make fun of you."

Sighing, John held the edge of the sheet up against a piece of 'rock they had hung the day before while Miles used his drill to drive some screws into it. "I'm not afraid of them." He pulled a ten-foot ladder over, and Miles started climbing it, driving screws into the drywall as he went.

Turning at the top of the ladder, Miles looked down and continued to probe. "You're afraid of what you'll find."

But John didn't have an answer for him. "I don't want to think about it right now. I'll worry about it on the plane." Then he looked back up to Miles. "It's not like it's a vacation, you know. It's only four days."

"Three." Miles held up three fingers. "Three days, John. In *four* days, we're here wrapping this place up, you understand? No gallivanting around, getting caught up in the moment over there. You better be back here on Monday, man."

"My return ticket's for Sunday night. Don't worry, I already can't wait to be back."

Retreating back down the ladder so that he could move it over to the next stud, Miles shook his head. "I ain't sayin' you can't have fun. I'm just sayin' don't forget about Miles."

John turned and looked back out into the rain, into the rising industrial park, the serenity of the view lulling him into a daze-like stupor.

Miles moved the ladder over and noticed John staring off. "You sure you're okay, man?"

John blinked. "Yeah, I'm sure."

"You sure you're sure? This ain't something from the war, is it?"

John's demeanor was beginning to ripen with impatience. "I'm fine." And there was a finality in his voice that warned against further inquiry.

Miles held up his hands in surrender. "Okay, fine. But whatever's going on, you just don't look right. I tried to help you, so I done my part."

"Appreciate it," John muttered, getting another sheet ready. In fact, he did appreciate it, though he didn't know how to express it without venturing through the swelling tides of what was really bothering him—something that he didn't understand himself. Maybe that was another thing he had to work on. It seemed to be a never-ending list. He knew it was a lifelong process, the changing, but that wasn't something he often found a lot of solace in.

"Yeah," Miles muttered back, frustrated. "What are friends for, right? Now if you're done sulking about tomorrow, we need to double-time it if you want me to spackle and tape all this before you get back."

TWO

5:21 p.m. 20th day of May. Wilkinsburg, Pennsylvania

Rain was still falling when John parked his truck a few doors down from their home, and as he ran down the cracked sidewalk, the cool breeze sweeping down the street of old row homes and playing every wind instrument it could find, he waved to a few neighbors that sat watching from under the dry protection of their covered porches. Struggling with the gate at the foot of their property, he added another stroke into the neat arc that was carved into the concrete below its metal post. He didn't bother to close it behind him, just ran for the steps, passing the mailbox in his haste. As soon as he got onto the porch, he pulled off his soaking wet T-shirt and tossed it on a rocking chair that sat facing the overgrown baseball field across the street. He then kicked off his boots and removed his socks before opening the squeaky storm door. He noticed in the reflection of the glass that his neighbors were still staring at him from their porches. Whether they were looking at his well-defined upper body, the scars that traced it, or the tattoos, he wasn't sure and didn't really care. Pretending not to notice, he slipped the key into the keyhole and pushed open the wooden door.

"Kristen," he called.

"Hey, babe," she responded, leaning over the banister above him. She smiled when she noticed his condition. "You're half naked." She waited for him to climb the steps and wrap her in his arms. He pressed his lips into hers before she could pull out of his slippery embrace. "And you're wet," she said, finally escaping his grasp.

"It's raining out."

"Really? Are you sure?" She smiled as thunder shook the house. "Dinner'll be ready in fifteen minutes. You should take a shower." She kissed him again and bounced gingerly down the stairs, her dark hair floating after her.

"How was work?"

"Work," she replied from what he guessed was the kitchen, "was work. You?"

"Same."

"You finish rocking the place?"

"Yeah, had to." He leaned over the balcony. "Miles would've killed me if he had to hang something by himself tomorrow." Hearing her laugh, he turned away from the stairs and headed toward the bedroom.

The scent of garlic and olive oil caught his nose as the hot water fell out of the faucet and erased another day's work from his body. He tried to relax and enjoy the moment, but his mind seemed determined to fixate only on tomorrow. On his brother. And so, his shower was a quick one.

* * * *

After eating a pleasant dinner and chasing after topics to talk about other than the following day, they retreated into the living room, where they both knew the topic would finally be raised. Kristen had held off as long as she could, but tomorrow was now on the horizon.

John sat in an armchair that faced the couch Kristen was lying on. She was leaning comfortably on her side with knees bent beneath her, her arm resting on a cushion. Her shorts, usually modest, were riding up and exposing her toned thighs. John thought she looked beautiful and told her so. She smiled and told him not to change the subject. He looked at the clock hanging above the cherry-red bookcase they'd gotten from a Salvation Army when they first moved in, and couldn't believe that it was already quarter till seven.

"So…" she stated as she wiped a long strand of hair away from her blue eyes.

He sighed, realizing just how incredibly immature he was being.

"You're leaving tomorrow," Kristen went on.

"Yeah."

She looked at him sympathetically. After being married for three years, it didn't take any great amount of sleuthing for her to know that something about this trip was bothering him, *scaring* him—that there was more to his strange silence than just a stubborn refusal to face a chore he had no desire to participate in. But she had decided not to press him for answers. Instead, she wanted to give him the time that he needed to work out whatever it was before having to actually put it into words for her. But now, with him leaving in just a matter of hours, that time had come to an end. "Still don't want to go?"

"Still don't want to go."

"Is it Henry, or his friends?"

John diverted his eyes, setting them on nothing in particular. "I don't know."

"Johnny, what is it?" Her eyes were soft and pleading, begging him to trust her.

He met her gaze. "I don't know. I don't know why they need me to go with them. It's…*strange*."

"If you're having bad feelings about the trip, Johnny, then don't go. Maybe it's the Lord's way of stopping you."

He thought of a hundred more effective ways God could tell him as much. "He's my *brother*," he stated. As much as he didn't want to go or understand why *they* wanted him to go, it was that simple fact that had predetermined his going from the start. "I don't know, maybe this is my chance to set things right between us."

She looked down at her hands and began playing with her wedding ring. "I don't know what to tell you, Johnny. You feel you need to go, yet you have all these reservations about going…"

"I don't know, babe. And I don't really want to think about it. I'm going whether I like it or not, and what happens, happens."

She got up and sat in his lap, throwing her arms around his neck and nestling her face into his chest. She sat like that for fifteen minutes while he silently ran his fingers through her hair.

She finally looked up, her eyes twinkling in the artificial light shining from a nearby lamp, and kissed him. "You've been acting a little strange over the last few days. Is it really because of the trip…or is it something else?"

He looked down at her, not realizing until now just how much his feelings had been affecting his behavior. He realized he'd been standoffish, stuck somewhere in his own head. "I don't know."

She sat up a little. "What do you mean?"

"I feel weird."

"About going?"

"Maybe." And then he shook his head. "I don't think so. Something just seems…off. I can't explain it." He sighed. "Sorry."

There was a shred of concern in her voice when she asked, "It's not war related, is it? Not the nightmares again?" Maybe she had been wrong in thinking that he didn't want to go because of the company he'd be keeping or that he wasn't ready to confront the reality of his brother's fate. Maybe it was something else entirely.

"No." But then, once more, he thought better of it. "I don't think so." He clenched his jaw. "I feel like I'm losing it."

She could see in his eyes how much whatever this was was afflicting him. She touched his face. "What do you need, Johnny?"

He shook his head. "Prayer."

They talked about it for another ten minutes before John's eyes began growing heavy with exhaustion. In the years she had known him, she had never seen him like this. She was convinced that he was scared of something but wasn't sure if saying so would make things better or worse for him. So she left him to his thoughts, praying that whatever was troubling him would eventually come to light, and that there would be some way for her to help him once it did. In the meantime, however, she was going to wash the dinner plates.

As she walked away, John let his eyes close.

* * * *

"*John.*"

Kristen's voice startled him, and his eyes snapped wide. "What?" he asked, confused and trying to find his bearings.

"It's okay," Kristen said soothingly. "I'm going to bed. I packed your bags, so unless there's something I missed, you should be all set for tomorrow. The tickets are on the dresser with your passport and cash." She leaned forward and kissed him rather passionately. "Come to bed soon."

He nodded, his senses returning, and watched her walk to the steps.

"If I'm asleep, wake me." She winked and disappeared up to the bedroom.

John looked up at the clock. 11:18. He'd been asleep there on the armchair for nearly four hours. He had to get up, had to be with Kristen. What kind of husband would he be if he spent the night sleeping downstairs? *Just five more minutes…*

* * * *

When he awoke, everything looked exactly the same, and he was sure he had only been unconscious for ten minutes at the most. However, upon testing his theory against the record of the clock, he found himself to be terribly wrong. It was pushing close to 2 a.m. The revelation squeezed a swear word out from under his breath, and he chided himself for the slip. Angry with himself for leaving Kristen to spend her last night with him in an empty bed, he went quickly for the stairs.

He had a foot on the first step when something he couldn't explain made him turn and look back at the front door, through the glass window. The mailbox, sitting lonely beneath a streetlamp at the end of the property, suddenly captured his attention. And before he knew what he was doing, he was out the front door and descending the steps. He reasoned with himself as he went, trying to convince himself that it was because he'd probably forget to check it in the morning that he was drawn to it now. He went through the open gate and pulled down the lid to the mailbox. There was a package wedged into the small space and resting atop a small stack of white envelopes. John looked up and down the vacant street just as a flash of lightning lit up the cloud-covered sky, the timing of which seemed too perfect to be blamed on mere coincidence. He spit on the ground before reaching into the box. This time, as he paused to study the darkness hiding the ball field he knew to be across from him, he made sure to close the gate.

Standing at the kitchen table, he stared at the manila envelope. There was a kind of foreboding that seemed to be emanating from within it—like the ticking sound of a clock, like some countdown to doom. Though there was no return address or any kind of postage decorating the bland package, it might as well have been covered in biohazard warnings, radiation symbols, and postmarked from the Middle East. The lack of identification, of origin and intent, seemed bizarre enough when considering the context of his recent feelings—the physical evidence of such a fact being represented by the hair standing on his forearms. Taking a deep breath, he ripped it open and dumped its contents onto the kitchen table.

A single video cassette tape, unmarked.

The tabs were snapped, so he knew it wouldn't be blank. You didn't break the tabs unless you wanted to keep the contents of the tape from being recorded over.

Suppressing a series of chills that raced up his spine and tingled his scalp, he walked to a cabinet and retrieved a flashlight. Leaving the cassette on the table, he walked quietly upstairs, past the open door leading to the bedroom, and went to the attic. Reaching up for the cord dangling above him, he pulled the stairs down and unfolded them, hoping the stretching springs wouldn't stir Kristen from her sleep. He flicked the light on and took one squeaky step at a time.

He found what he was looking for in the third dusty box, and, with the VCR in hand, he descended from the attic, quickly closing the door behind him—afraid an attic demon would leap down at him before he could reseal its cell. He was pretty sure that once demons from the attic gained access to the rest of the house, life would just get more complicated. He'd Google it later, providing the top-story terror didn't escape down the stairs after him.

He managed to close the attic door without waking up Kristen or springing free the malevolent spirits thought to be trapped in the room's cobwebbed corners.

Sitting in front of the television, the old VCR hooked up to the TV, John continued to study the black plastic cassette in his hands, flipping open the long plastic door at the top and examining the tape itself.

Suddenly feeling a presence behind him, he turned, ready to explain to Kristen what he was doing. But there was no one there.

More tingles.

Trying to ignore his shaking hands, he pushed the cassette in.

The tape dropped down into the deck, and the picture flickered on the television screen. It began playing, and the sudden image of a man in mid-sentence filled the picture. But John knew from having looked at the tape that it didn't need rewinding.

Five seconds later, the shot changed, panning back and showing two men positioned on a stage and facing each other. They were seated at their own tables, books and other reference materials strewn out in front of them. A large symbol was painted on the wall up behind them—three circles with a cross and some initials over a scripture reference. The men appeared to be facing off in front of an audience. Some kind of debate. An old one, if the video quality and the men's clothing proved a reliable indication.

John sat back and tried to pick up on the topic of discussion and why someone would want him to witness it.

"Men began to multiply on the face of the earth," stated the man on the right, removing a pair of wire-rimmed spectacles and holding them in a rather animated right hand. "What men?"

What men, indeed? thought John.

"Is it not the whole of the human race that is meant here? So, contextually, does it not make sense that the next time we see the word *men* in the narrative, it is once again referring to the same *general* humanity?" He turned and faced the audience, his short hair and dark beard glimmering in the spotlights hanging above. "If the 'men who multiplied on the earth and the daughters that were born to them' is just a commentary on the human race at that time, then it must have been the intention of the writer to distinguish the generations of Adam *from* the sons of God." At this, he stood, his chair sliding backward and out from under him. "The sons of God—*Bne-Ha-Elohim*—is an expression that occurs only four other times in the Old Testament. Job 1:6, Job 2:1, Job 38:7, and Daniel 3:25. And in every one of these cases, it is *indisputably* speaking of angels."

John frowned. Was this Pastor Brian's idea of a joke?

Back on the screen, it looked for a moment like the man's adversary was going to interject, but apparently the time for presenting his case had already expired, because he bit his tongue and remained quiet. He would have to wait for his turn to respond.

Thunder sounded outside.

The man with the beard was getting livelier. "Perhaps, though, Professor Adler is correct in his charge that no first-time reader of the verse would ever assume the phrase to be speaking of angels. Or, I should say, no first-time reader *proceeding* from a certain point in history, if my view is the correct one. You see, if he is right, which he probably is, I argue that the reason has nothing to do with the language, the context, history, or any other body of evidence other than that the notion of it is simply too far removed from our ordinary conception of reality. However, to think that a first-time reader would *just the same* know to interpret the phrase as 'the sons of Seth' is even *more* unbelievable. In fact, I am quite sure that once the reader is educated in the language and the context and sees where the phrase is used to mean angels elsewhere, he will then not only understand, but also appreciate a more satisfying explanation as to why God nearly exterminated the whole human race. Especially when seeing that the *alternative* theory for such destruction appears to be the judgment of simple marriage between ungodly women and godly men—something that still happens every day and without such bizarre results. So, though the initial reaction to the idea of angels being present in our text may be one of unbelief, it is *more* believable than the other views when we see that such marriages—" he held up his index finger "—regularly produced supernatural offspring, which no other position can account for, and—" he put up a second finger "—called for the near annihilation of every living thing on the planet. These are *two* extraordinary factors that Professor Adler, and most theologians, will *not* deny. Is it so hard to believe then that the *extraordinary* offspring and the *extraordinary* judgment were the result of an *extraordinary* circumstance?"

The man put his glasses back on, looked up at the clock, and took a sip of water from a glass that was resting on the desk in front of him. "*Bne-Ha-Elohim, Bnoth-Ha-Adam…* No other view was prevalent among Christian theologians until three or four hundred years *after* Christ. Since then, we have this view of Seth and Cain, we have the *filii-magnatum*, which claims to read 'sons of princes or rulers' and 'women of inferior station.' We have a view that suggests the sons of God are earlier descendants of Adam and Eve who intermarry with the latter. And we have the opinion that the patriarchs in chapter five are referred to as thus because of their longevity. But none of these views, as with Professor Adler's, can account for the supernatural offspring that resulted and the unprecedented judgment that followed. There is only *one* view, as ridiculous as it may be to our modernized way of thinking, that can offer an adequate explanation."

Though John's eyes were fatigued by the poor picture quality, he nonetheless found himself mesmerized and strangely fascinated by the man's words—despite still not having the proper context through which to interpret them. It wasn't until a few minutes later that he finally understood the debate to be over the meaning of a specific phrase in the book of Genesis—whether it was speaking of angels or the sons of Seth. Goosebumps were still tracing his arms when the man began making his closing statements.

"Lastly, ladies and gentlemen and Professor Adler, I ask you, is it not likely that the children of these condemned unions, the 'ancient heroes' as they are called, are none other than the originators of all the legends concerning the gods—which the legends *themselves* expressly declare? If not, and God truly did annihilate everything and everyone simply because the godly began intermarrying with the ungodly, then perhaps we should pause and wonder at such a judgment. Though, I do not know how the marrying of holy Sethites to unholy Cainites could disturb the development of mankind so much as to render the human condition utterly hopeless, requiring the extermination of all but eight people. Perhaps, along with a more intimate knowledge of who the mighty men of old truly were, there is a *reason* why the angel-view is the oldest view there is on the subject. Thank you."

The picture instantly turned to static.

John sat unmoving before the static, the subconscious awareness of an evil presence quickening his beating heart. Of course, he was as unsure about the stalking tendencies of evil presences as he was about attic demons, but he was pretty sure it wouldn't be God's holy angels stirring such feelings within him. Leaving the tape, he got to his feet and went into the kitchen, picked up the phone, and dialed Pastor Brian's number.

It rang three times before someone picked up, but it took another five seconds before that person's groggy voice fully escaped the clutches of a sound sleep. "Hello?" Brian rasped.

"Brian, it's John Carter."

"What's wrong? Is everything okay?"

"Yeah, did I wake you?"

A pause. "It's 2:30 in the morning."

John looked up at the clock, swore for not realizing the time, and then apologized, embarrassed, for the swearing.

"It's okay, John," he said, and there was a long pause as he yawned. "We all grow at different paces." Brian had been over this with him before. "It's a long uphill battle. We rarely change overnight."

"I can take some rebuke."

"If I thought rebuke was what you needed, then I'd give it to you. No, you need encouragement. You need to look back for a second and see the proof of who you're becoming, of how far you are from being who you used to be."

He was right, of course. Though his shortcomings always whispered condemnation, he was nothing at all like the man he had been three years ago. And he knew it *should* be encouraging.

"But that's not why you called, is it?" Brian asked.

"No." He paused, suddenly aware of how absurd he was about to sound. "This may sound stupid, especially at 2:30 in the morning…but is there a place in the Bible that talks about 'sons of God' and 'daughters of men'?"

Silence for a second, like he was waiting for the punch line to a bad joke. "You're right, that was probably the last thing in the world I expected someone to call my house for. Ever." He sighed over the line. "Yeah, the sixth chapter of Genesis."

John's heart fluttered. "What's your take on it?"

"On what?"

John knew he should just let the guy go back to sleep, but for some reason it was important that he know right now. "On what the verse is talking about." Even as he was asking the question, he was reaching into the next room and grabbing a Bible off a corner table.

At that point, Brian whispered something to his wife, telling her to go back to sleep—no one was about to jump off a bridge, the church wasn't burning to the ground, their children were all okay… "I hold to the orthodox view, that the sons of God are angels. What's this about, John?"

He found chapter six of Genesis and began reading it softly over the phone. "'And it came to pass, when men began to multiply on the face of the earth, and daughters were born unto them, that the sons of God saw the daughters of men that they were fair; and they took them wives of all which they chose. And the Lord said, My spirit shall not always strive with man, for that he also is flesh: yet his days shall be an hundred and twenty years. There were giants in the earth those days; and also after that…'" His voice began to tremble. "'…when the sons of God came in unto the daughters of men, and they bare children to them, the same became mighty men which were of old, men of renown.'"

Brian spoke up. "You're reading from the King James."

"Yeah," John muttered, his mind suddenly lost somewhere else. "Giants?"

"Yeah, *Han-Nephilim* and *Hag-Gibborim.* Listen, John, is everything okay?"

"It says that there were giants also after that. What does that mean?"

"Well, it depends on your interpretation of it. I understand it to mean that, even after the promise of judgment was to be fulfilled in a hundred and twenty years, angels and women were still marrying and producing giants—all the way up to the Flood."

"Could there be giants *after* the Flood?"

"Sure. We find giants mentioned all over the Old Testament as well as in other historical accounts."

"So, then this angel thing still happens?" His throat was dry, the phone shaking in his hand.

"You mean, like today? I don't think so. I believe the severity of the Flood put a stop to that. Although there are others who don't agree. Jewish tradition even holds that Og, king of Bashaan, survived the Flood as the last of the giants and was responsible for their outbreak afterward. To tell you the truth, I never really thought this a subject I had to nail down to a perfect theological argument. I guess, as you've noticed, my own view seems somewhat contradictory. Can you tell me why you're asking?" It was obvious from his tone that he was as confused by the query as was John himself.

"I'm so sorry for waking you, Brian."

"That's why I'm here. Hey, aren't you leaving in the morning?"

"Yeah." He hung up the phone without even waiting to hear Brian's next question. Standing there in the kitchen, he reread through the first part of Genesis 6 and shuddered. "Giants," he whispered. Suddenly, and somehow, all the ill-feelings he'd had over the last few days converged and attached themselves to that one word. He prayed it had nothing to do with where he was headed to in the morning. But then, how could it? He turned the television off and went upstairs, looking over his shoulder the entire way, trying to spot the movements dancing in the shadows of his vision. He got into bed just as more rain started falling on their house, his thoughts a tangled mess of insinuations all pointing to his past.

THREE

Something is leading me, showing me where to go. I can feel it pulling me. There's something I'm supposed to find. But I'm scared. I don't know where I am, where the rest of the men are. I'm not supposed to be scared, though—I'm a trained killer and better than most. I'm not afraid of anything. Except this. Whatever it is. I wander deeper into the caves, hearing bombs explode somewhere up above me. I should go back before I get lost in here. But I can't. I have to keep going…

John snapped into a sitting position, suddenly awake. He was sweating, breathing heavily. Getting out of bed, he quickly crossed the bedroom and shut himself in the bathroom. He flicked on the light and vomited in the toilet. His whole body was shaking, sweat dripping into his eyes. Sitting on the floor, he tried to regain his composure, to weed the nightmare's lasting impression out of his reality.

There was a knock on the door.

"Johnny, are you okay?" Kristen was leaning her ear against the door, her hand trying the locked handle.

John wiped his mouth. "Yeah."

"You sure? Why is the door locked?"

In fact, he didn't realize he'd locked it. "Yeah, it's nothing. You can go back to bed."

It was obvious from the ensuing pause that she was wrestling with what to do, whether to believe him. "Okay, but I'm right here if you need me." No doubt she was thinking about the dreams he'd told her about, the things that used to torment him.

He heard her footsteps evaporate away from the door, her shadow disappearing from the sliver of light beneath it. He stood, flushed the toilet, and went to the sink. He turned on the faucet and splashed handfuls of cold water into his face. Then he bent over, gripping the edges of the sink, and tried to stop himself from shaking. When he finally looked up into the mirror, he could only stare at himself. For five long minutes, he held such a position, reciting in his head what was real while trying to ignore the tattoos that covered his chest and wrapped his biceps.

John Adam Carter. He was named such after the founding father, which was in keeping with the custom held by his family. Most Carters had patriotic names and were expected to serve their country in one lifelong capacity or another. It was a legacy John had had every intention of living up to, and in 2001, he was one of the first to Afghanistan. But a rocket-propelled grenade had changed everything.

He shook his head. This wasn't the reality he was searching for, but it was the one the dream had brought back. He closed his eyes and tried to forget both.

Shutting off the water, he dried his face on a towel before glancing at an old wristwatch he kept on the sink. 3:52. His flight was at seven. The taxi would be here at 5:30. He flicked the light off and returned to bed, climbing back in beside Kristen. Whether she was really asleep or just pretending, understanding that getting into a conversation at this hour would be pointless, he didn't know or pursue. Instead, he lay there on his back, stared at the ceiling, and listened to the rain whip the side of the house. It didn't take long, however, before his thoughts were back to the video. If there was a message he was supposed to have gleaned from it, he'd failed miserably. Yet the video had led to a discussion about giants—which had triggered a dream that he hadn't had in three years... Something was at work here, he knew it way down in the deepest part of himself, a billboard advertising some vague spiritual truth he didn't understand.

He prayed silently and eventually fell asleep.

* * * *

Morning had come way too soon. Looking down at his wife, he knew she felt the same way. They were standing together—John's arm around her shoulder, her arm around his waist—staring out the window, waiting for the taxi to materialize out of the pouring rain.

"Are you sure you're going to be okay?" she asked, leaning her head against his chest.

"Yeah, I'll be fine." He hoped. In all actuality, he had no idea what would be awaiting him.

"Look at me, Johnny." She turned him so that they were standing face-to-face. "I have something to tell you. Something very important." A mist settled over her eyes, and she squeezed his hand tight enough to communicate the severity of what she was telling him. "But I'm going to wait until you get back and all of this, whatever you're going through, is behind us. That means that you have to come back to me, Johnny. You understand me?"

He smiled despite what he was really feeling. "Yes, ma'am." Then he pulled her to him, wrapped his arms around her, and kissed her head. "Sorry about last night," he whispered, the words meant to alleviate the horrible feeling that was stabbing him in the stomach.

"I guess you'll have to make it up to me on Sunday," she teased.

"I'll be here."

Because the atmosphere suddenly seemed too final for her liking, and because crying would just make it feel more so, she took his hand in hers and began dancing with him. It was something she often did to lighten a moment.

Laughing, John twirled her around, sudden flashes of him doing so on their wedding day flooding his throat with emotion. He knew now, more than ever, that he didn't deserve her—that she should have married someone else, someone that grew up in the church like she had. She didn't need his baggage to complicate her life. It didn't seem fair. "Sorry I've been out of it the last few days. I don't know what's gotten into me."

She didn't want to bring up last night, a discussion about the nightmares having possibly returned not exactly her idea of a happy parting. Not after what he told her about them, what he'd been through before meeting her. Hopefully, he would be fine when he returned. And if not, maybe she could help him deal with the dreams this time around. "Well, when I see you on Sunday, not only will you have a hot tan, but you'll be back to being my Johnny again." She stood on her tiptoes and pecked him with a kiss before being spun again.

"I promise." He stared at her as they circumnavigated the living room, keeping time with the sweet-sounding melody Kristen was humming. "So, what is this thing you have to tell me?" he poked.

"Guess you'll have to be here on Sunday to find out." She smiled, her eyes sparkling.

"I see. And there's nothing that can persuade you to spill it now, huh?"

"Not a thing."

"Really?" He picked her up and tossed her onto the couch. She landed in laughter even as he was jumping on top of her, tickling her.

"Stop it!" She was screaming, her arms and legs flailing.

"Tell me!"

She found a way to scream through her laughter. "No way!"

So he engaged the most ticklish spots on her body.

And then the sound of a horn sounded from outside.

Their laughing slowed, and they stared at each other for a second, as if holding their positions would prevent time from continuing and the moment from coming to an end. Suddenly, the weight of a thousand unspoken words fell upon them, desperately wanting to be expressed but without the time or know-how to do so.

For a moment, John spotted a certain look in Kristen's eye. The look of fear, of uncertainty and desperation. They were all wrapped up in a sole expression that came and went so fast that, had he not seen it before, he would have completely missed it. It told him more about this trip than anything else possibly could. It was the look his mother had given him the day he left for Afghanistan. It was the look in the eyes of fathers, wives, brothers, and sisters while they waved goodbye to their loved ones for perhaps the last time.

"You know what," he said, "this is crazy. I don't have to go."

She grabbed him. "We're just being stupid about this. He's your brother; of course you should go." Did she really just say that?

The horn sounded again. There was no time to argue.

"I love you."

She smiled. "I love you more."

He got up and went back to the window, saw the airport cab waiting at the curb, and picked up his bags. Taking a deep breath, he leaned forward and kissed Kristen much the same way he'd seen other couples kiss before heading off to war. But he told himself that it was a ridiculous and unwarranted comparison. "I'll see you in a few days."

"I'll be praying."

"Thanks." He turned to open the front door.

"Hey," she called after him. "You behave yourself, you hear?" And she pinched his butt with a smile.

He kissed her one last time. "Sunday night."

"I'll be waiting." She leaned against the doorframe and watched him run through the rain and to the waiting car. Her free hand rested on her stomach as the cab pulled away from the curb, her husband waving and then disappearing in a wash of glowing taillights.

* * * *

The flight from Pittsburgh to Philadelphia had taken an hour and twenty minutes, which he soundly slept through. Now he was sitting in an empty terminal, in a row of connecting chairs facing huge windows and the runway beyond. Nursing a cup of coffee, he watched the rain keep falling while another plane took off. He had an hour and forty minutes before his connecting flight was scheduled to depart, so he tried to get as comfortable as possible between the encroaching armrests. Propping his feet up on his luggage, he closed his eyes, the sound of the rain against the glass soothing his weary mind.

* * * *

When he next opened his eyes, his coffee was cold and the terminal was half full. Five minutes later, the call to board went forth over the loudspeaker. Tossing his coffee into a nearby trash can, he picked up his bags and got in line. As he watched a woman check everyone's boarding pass and ID, he couldn't help but notice a man up ahead of him who was standing head and shoulders above everyone else in line. John knew just from the way the man carried himself that he had spent time with the Special Forces. After spending ten years in that line of work himself, and spending his entire life around their kind besides, he had developed a certain kind of sense capable of profiling such specimens. Especially the ones who had actually killed. He wondered if the man could pick up such a scent from him. Not that such a sense would be needed to count his confirmed kills—they were carved into the side of his neck as rows of white scars.

He handed the woman his ticket and boarded the plane to Bermuda.

* * * *

Now en route to L. F. Wade International Airport in St. George's Parish, Bermuda, John looked out the window beside him. All that was to be seen in any direction was water—an unsettling thought considering the streaks of lightning stretching through the dark skies. Turning his attention to his right, he observed a young college girl seated next to him in seat C. Stranded from her friends, who were seated a few rows up, she had her MP3 player blasting in her ears and her eyes locked in a magazine. John reached down and pulled his Bible out from the bag he'd placed beneath the seat before takeoff. He noticed that his movement caught the girl's attention and wondered, as he always did, what she thought of him. He didn't have to wonder long.

"Didn't place you as the type," she said, pulling an earpiece out of her ear and nodding toward the holy book.

He smiled politely. "Most don't."

"My name's Gina," she said, holding out a petite hand.

He shook it gently. "John. Nice to meet you."

"Like the tat." She nodded at a flash of green ink peeking out from beneath the color of his T-shirt. Then she leaned over and lifted her own shirt, revealing a rather large display of someone's colorful artwork stretching below her pelvis and up to her black-laced bra. "What do you think?" she asked, smiling.

"It's lovely," he said, steering his eyes back to the Bible.

"Didn't know God let you get them. Thought it was a rule or something."

He shrugged. "It was a long time ago."

"Can I see?"

"I'd rather you didn't."

She frowned, and he used the pause to change the subject. "What's in Bermuda?" A horribly phrased question that only helped increase the feeling of awkwardness.

She nodded in the direction of her friends. "Just looking to have a good time. You?"

It was the natural question to ask, and he'd set himself up for it. He sighed, figuring it would be a safer conversation than where the "show-me-yours" one was heading. "Looking for my brother."

"Older or younger?"

"Ten years older."

She pondered his words before asking, "Is he lost?"

"Not sure."

She pulled the other earpiece out of her ear. "If he's in Bermuda, maybe he just doesn't want to be found."

"That's possible."

"But you don't think so."

He shrugged.

"Tell me."

There was something in her voice that seemed to encourage such a suggestion, and this quality made him look at her more closely, further evaluating her. She was attractive, and whether she was truly interested in his story or if she was just flirting with him, he wasn't sure. He wasn't about to flatter himself but made sure to tread carefully just in case. "He retired from the military not that long ago, decided he'd sail down the east coast from Maine to Florida. At least that's what people think. He didn't bother telling anyone except his platoon. That was two months ago and the last anyone saw him."

"What makes you think he's in Bermuda?"

"According to his friends, he was planning on taking a detour there, to talk with some author. They claim he made it three weeks ago, but that's all they got."

"Three weeks isn't that long to be unaccounted for in a place like Bermuda," she responded, smiling again.

"That's what I said," he muttered.

"You don't want to go?"

He shrugged again. "Don't have much choice. My brother and I, heck, my whole family and I, haven't been on the best of terms for a while. I'm hoping this might give us a fresh start, him knowing that I came looking for him and all."

"You all by yourself?"

"No, I'm meeting his old friends from Navy SEAL Team One." The manner in which he stated their designation betrayed how he felt about them. She picked up on it.

"Not a big fan?"

He shrugged. "Never met them."

"Not the military type, then?"

He shook his head. "Not anymore."

"But you were?"

"Oh, yeah. I was born a Carter. Had no choice. It was my destiny."

"So what happened?"

He held up the Bible.

She smiled, amused. "Is that why you've been on the outs with your family, because you denounced your patriotism?"

A grin spread across his face. "What are you studying anyway?"

"Psychology," she chirped matter-of-factly.

He laughed before conceding. "Yeah, something like that."

"What about your brother's friends? What do they think of you?"

"That's the million-dollar question. But my money's on an awkward and unpleasant few days."

She looked him up and down. "You look like you could take them."

Smiling from the flattery, he answered, "I don't know. They were SEALs. They'd have to be pretty out of shape. They were a force to reckon with in Desert Storm."

"Like they killed a lot of people?"

"Like this one time at the beginning of the war, they swam in the middle of the night from landing boats five hundred yards from the Kuwaiti coast, each pulling twenty pounds of explosives. Once they reached the beach, they set up the explosives right under the enemy's nose and swam back to the boats. When they set off the bombs, it made the Iraqis think the allied forces had planned an amphibious attack, making them pull two divisions off the front lines and send them to the vacant coast. And then there was Operation Restore Hope in Somalia…" He smiled and looked over at her and saw she didn't really care about *them*. "Never mind…"

"So what were you?"

"Ranger."

"What made you become a Ranger?"

"My other brother, George, named after George Washington, of course, was killed in '93 during the first battle of Mogadishu. Day of the Rangers, or *Maalintii Rangers* as the Somalis call it."

"That must have been tough."

John looked ahead, nodding. "Yeah. Joining the Rangers was my way of keeping his memory alive." He sighed again. "But enough about me. What about you?"

"You want to know about me?" she asked, narrowing her gaze.

"Sure," he answered, suddenly not so sure.

"Well, I'll be staying in the Southampton Princess Hotel, room one thirty-seven. Stop by some night, and you can learn as much about me as you'd like." She accented the offer with a seductive smile that made his heart flutter.

Recovering, he did his best to be polite. "You know, there was a time…before this—" he held up the Bible "—and before this—" he held up his left hand, showing off the wedding band "—that I would have taken you up on that offer." Though it was a statement that was intended to direct the conversation in a different direction, he wondered if it had been inappropriate to admit as much.

"You'd be missing out."

Suddenly, he felt sad for the girl, her lifestyle all too familiar. "I don't think so."

"Whatever." And just like that, she shoved the earpieces back into her ears and returned to her magazine.

Shocked by such sudden betrayal, John shook his head and turned his attention to the Bible, reading over Genesis 6 once more. As he read, he couldn't help but think back through the conversation he'd just had with the girl, the parts of it he'd left out. Like why his brother wanted to talk to the author in the first place, or how it was the ex-SEALs that had set up this whole "rescue" operation, threatening even to kidnap him if he wasn't determined to go with them on his own. And then he thought once more of his brother's teammates, rehearsing again what little he knew about them.

Paul, Nick, Hunter, Chris, and Jackson—the men waiting for him at the end of this flight. They were the remaining five SEALs from his brother's squad, which had managed to stay intact for most of their colorful careers. The other two were dead—one killed in combat, and the other uniting a Ferrari with a tree at 130 mph. His father used to talk about them all the time. Apparently, their work had earned them a certain reputation at the Pentagon and even in Washington. According to his father, their squad had once been assigned bodyguard detail for a world leader on the West Coast and had even been detached from the team to secretly work with the CIA on a few occasions.

It was going to be interesting, and he had about an hour and a half before it became his reality. Closing the Bible, he set his eyes back on the blue planet beneath him and once more reflected back on the last few weeks…on the VHS tape.

* * * *

He was jolted awake by a sudden drop in cabin pressure, the oxygen mask falling out of the ceiling above him and a hollow feeling bursting in the pit of his stomach.

"I think we were struck by lightning," Gina said in disbelief. Her knuckles were white, gripping the armrests. "I think we're falling!"

John looked around as the lights in the cabin flickered, and luggage started spilling into the aisle. A panic was indeed spreading through the plane—women screaming, men too shocked to comfort them. He looked out the window and expected to see the ocean growing terrifyingly close. But what he saw instead was something from a different sort of nightmare.

A huge cloud formation was swirling in a circular motion below, lightning flashing at its center. Out of its midst came some kind of being wrapped in churning storm clouds—thunder its armor, lightning its sword, and eyes like burning coals—emerging like some kind of Greek god. The figure ascended, reaching as it were, directly for *him.* The face it bore was horribly familiar, and John knew that he had to be dreaming. He grabbed his Bible and held it tight against his chest, squeezing his eyes shut and praying.

Slowly, the falling sensation subsided as the plane seemed to level out. And a moment later, the pilot's voice over the intercom confirmed just that, apologizing for the scare but assuring the passengers that everything was now okay. They *had* been struck by lightning, but all things were now stabilized and functioning properly.

John stole a quick glance out the window, expecting to still see the ghastly figure reaching out for the plane. But there was nothing there, just lightning in the distance and an eternal, choppy sea far below. He tilted his head back and tried to catch his breath, his heart pounding in his chest.

"Thank you, Jesus," he whispered.

"That was pretty scary, huh?"

John turned his attention back to Gina, whose face was just starting to regain color. "Yeah."

"Does it help?" she asked in a shaky voice, nodding toward the Bible still clutched against his chest.

"You should find out for yourself," he answered, handing it to her.

A moment of hesitation lingered on her part, not knowing exactly what it was he was suggesting.

"Here, take it."

Reluctantly, she accepted it, the look on her face as she touched the book illuminating a superstitious—or perhaps even a reverent—awe, like it might turn her to dust if she handled it improperly.

"It's not a bomb," John said not too loudly. "You can have it."

"That's nice of you, but—"

"I insist. Take it. Read it. Who knows, maybe the next time we meet, we'll have more in common."

She carefully opened the leather-bound book, inspecting it curiously. "Hey, what's your brother's name anyway?"

"Henry."

"Like Patrick Henry," she guessed.

"Yep." He managed to smile, and then the memory of what he'd just seen suddenly came back and erased any trace of joy from his face.

FOUR

2:04 p.m. 21st day of May. L. F. Wade International Airport, St. George's Parish, Bermuda

As John exited the plane, giving a subtle wave goodbye to Gina, he could hear the anxious crowd around him speaking of the event that had almost sentenced them to a watery grave. But he had yet to hear any mention of the sinister apparition. Not knowing what to do with that fact, with whether it suggested he was losing his mind or not, he set out after the signs pointing toward customs and immigration, anxious to put the whole flight behind him.

The customs agent asked to see his passport and his return ticket.

"My return ticket?" John asked uncertainly.

The man politely explained that anyone who planned on staying for more than three weeks needed to see the chief immigration officer at the Government Administration Building and needed to fill out an immigration form requesting an extended stay.

John complied and handed them over with a strained smile.

The agent took his time examining the documents before glancing at John's bags and finally stamping his passport. "Enjoy your stay, Mr. Carter," he said with a big smile, handing his ticket and passport back over the counter.

"Thanks." He slipped them into the front of his pants, always wary of pickpockets, and picked up his two bags before setting out to find his contacts.

Just when he was about to abandon his search and head out to the curb, he saw a giant of a man walking toward him and knew it to be the same guy he'd seen boarding the plane in Philadelphia. They made eye contact, and John immediately realized that this was one of Henry's friends. Though why he had been on his Philadelphia flight was a particularly disturbing question.

The two men approached, each quickly eyeing up the other and assessing a hundred conclusions in an instant.

"You his brother?" the man asked without wasting any time on pleasantries. He stood a good six or seven inches above John and was almost twice as wide. The man was a freak of nature, networks of veins traversing the visible terrain of his body, making him even more intimidating.

John extended his hand, seeing only his own reflection in the monster's sunglasses. "John." An awkward moment followed, his hand hanging out in front of him, the ex-SEAL towering above him and staring at him without expression. But just as John was about to pull his hand back, an enormous hand engulfed it and pumped it a single definitive time.

"Jackson."

His voice couldn't have been more perfectly matched with his physique. It held a no-nonsense tone that discouraged unnecessary talk. Just the facts, ma'am. *Or I'll break you in half.* For now, John decided to keep inquiries about the shared flight to himself. He wanted to see how Jackson was going to play it.

"Been waiting long?" he probed, eyes daring.

"Not too long," Jackson deflected.

John nodded, his suspicions confirmed, his guard up. "Well, good."

"Come on, there's a cab waiting." Jackson turned and headed toward the exit, leaving John to follow in his shadow.

If John wasn't supposed to notice Jackson signal the first taxi in a long parade of transport vehicles lining the curb, his intelligence was being grossly underestimated. He heard the trunk pop as they approached it, and Jackson reached for his bags. John handed them over and watched Jackson toss them effortlessly into the trunk, his biceps threatening to tear the sleeves off his white polo.

They both sat in the backseat of the cab, Jackson's knees pressed up against his chest.

"Where to, my friends?" the driver asked, obviously making it a point not to stare at the goliath situated in the rearview mirror.

"Grotto Bay Resort," Jackson said.

As the driver pulled away from the curb, John looked over at the man who had fought beside his brother for over twenty years. "Where's everyone else?"

"At the hotel."

"You draw the short end of the stick?"

Jackson's bald head rotated, his mirrored sunglasses continuing to cast John back down at himself. "I was the closest to Henry."

John didn't press the issue. Obviously, Jackson wasn't going to admit to being on the same flight. Which could only mean that Jackson was escorting him, making sure he got to where he needed to be—a fact that raised all kinds of questions. He turned his gaze out the window for the first time and found that they were surrounded by the bluest water he had ever seen. Boats were sprinkled throughout the water rather liberally and actually accounted for more traffic than the road they were on. A light rain was falling over the island, but the sun seemed ready to make its appearance, its face stubbornly clinging to a few straggling clouds.

A dark-skinned man in his forties, the driver began filling the sudden silence by commenting on their short journey. "We are heading over the Causeway, crossing Castle Harbor," he reported rather cheerfully. "Your hotel is just on the other side."

John looked ahead about half a mile to where the bridge ended and could indeed see the hotel nestled in the embrace of a lush hill.

"To your right is Coney Island Park," continued the driver, "and to your left, past the airstrip, is King's Castle."

There were two forts that John could see off to the right and little islands beyond Jackson's obstructing frame to the left.

"We built the airfield back in '41," Jackson started to say, staring back at the airport. "Thought Hitler might defeat Britain, so we took out a ninety-nine-year lease on a base. The Navy closed it down in '95."

The driver laughed, overhearing him. "And now we bring tourists in civilian planes, something our economy has come to depend on!"

"We left you with roads, too," Jackson said.

"You sure did, my friend. In fact, you took over an eighth of our entire island, changing forever the very landscape of our humble home."

"But like you said, the economic benefits we left you were great."

"That they were," he replied, chuckling.

At that moment, his eyes still fixated on the view, John pulled out his phone to call Kristen. As he waited for her to answer, he recalled that Bermuda was an hour ahead of eastern standard time. She would be on her way home from work now. Picking up on the last ring, she saved John from having to leave a message. But just as they started talking, Jackson and the driver ceased with their own conversation, allowing for an odd silence to erase any sense of privacy. So they didn't speak long. "Just wanted to let you know I'm here," he told her. "Is everything okay? Then I'll call you later. Love you."

They pulled off the Causeway and passed a couple of tennis courts before stopping in front of an elegant orange building that was outlined with white trim, the lawn surrounding it littered with sculpted bushes and palm trees.

"Enjoy your time in Bermuda," the driver said, accepting with thanks the tip from Jackson.

John closed the trunk and waved, following Jackson away from the curb and to the hotel's exquisite lobby.

After picking up their keys—apparently John wasn't supposed to have a problem with Jackson not having checked in yet—they headed out the rear door, following a road that cut a beautiful path through acres of gardens. They walked past some scantily clothed people lounging around a pool, and entered the lobby of another building, finding an elevator to their floor.

The doors opened and let loose a young couple armed with tennis rackets and too much caffeine.

"Watch where you're going," Jackson growled as he sidestepped them. He entered the elevator and poked a round button. The doors closed.

"You know a lot about this place?" John asked, referring to the airfield talk in the cab.

"A little." Then the doors opened again, and Jackson stepped out. He walked down the hall to John's room and then stepped aside so that John could open it.

John entered and did a quick tour of the room, impressed mostly with the balcony and its awesome view of Castle Harbor, the Causeway, a few scattered islands, the private beach and dock harboring a large sailboat below him, and half a dozen Jet Skis cutting trails of white wake through the tranquility of it all.

Jackson came up behind him. "That's St. David's Island at the other end of the Causeway, where the airport is. Over there to the left is Grotto Bay Bridge. It connects to Coney Island. You either have to take a ferry from the West End or take the Causeway and go all the way around the airport to get to St. George's Island."

"What's on St. George's Island?" John asked, figuring there was a point to the unprovoked flood of information.

"White Horse Tavern. Be there in an hour and a half." And then he turned and walked out of the room, leaving the door open behind him.

John followed him to the hallway and watched to see which room he was staying in before closing the door and returning to the bedroom. Opening the sliding glass door that led out to the balcony, he stepped into the warm breeze. He could hear the water lapping against the shore below him, but it did little to allay his growing concerns. And then there was that thing he'd seen outside the window of the plane…

Staring out at the blue-gray horizon, storm clouds drifting farther apart from each other, he began to formulate a plan.

He needed to know why he was really here.

* * * *

After acquiring a scooter from the hotel's renting center, John asked the employee how to get to the tavern.

"Take Swing Bridge over to St. George. It's on the other side of Water Street, right across from the cruise ship terminal. You can't miss it, there's a Norwegian ship docked there. Here—" the woman handed him a map "—just in case."

"Thanks," John said. He walked the bike away from the hotel before unfolding the map, matching the woman's words to it. As it turned out, St. George's Parish contained both the town of St. George and St. George's Island as well as St. David's Island. After committing a course to memory, he folded the map and tucked it into his back pocket. Then he set out for the Causeway.

John found the drive back over the Causeway and through St. George to be beautifully relaxing despite his present circumstances. There was a sense of serenity and goodwill attached to the narrow streets, a placidness covering the pastel-colored houses barely contained by the white stone walls separating them. And every Bermudian he passed waved a happy hello. If only he could forget his progressing psychosis long enough to enjoy this place.

Leaving the moped next to a dozen others, he stepped through the door of the green and white tavern. No sooner had the door closed behind him than someone was calling his name. Jackson stood near the back of the room, motioning for him to follow.

John was led outside and to a waterfront terrace lined with tables. At the end of the terrace, a set of stone steps descended to the water and a row of bobbing Jet Skis. To his left, a huge cruise ship was resting on the other side of a small islet—the Norwegian ship the woman had referred to.

"Ordnance Island," Jackson muttered. He followed his gaze while squeezing through tables.

The remains of a fortification sat on the island's east side, old stonework stretching up out of the ground and still attempting to hold its position around a cannon aimed out into the harbor. Stealing a look behind him, John saw that there was a road bridging them to the small island.

"Boys, Henry's little brother," Jackson announced as they approached a table surrounded by rather large men.

But no one stood, no one reached to shake his hand or offer him a seat, no one introduced themselves or even so much as said hello. They just continued staring at their menus as if they hadn't heard Jackson at all.

So John just stood there, sweeping his gaze over them one at a time, attempting to apply his peculiar powers of sense to all of them. Finally, and still without invitation, he reached for an empty chair and sat.

The man next to him took a long sip of something in a short glass, slammed it down on the table, and spun to face him. "So, you're Johnny, huh?"

"John'll do fine," he said icily.

"Nick." He offered him his left hand.

Only the familiar feeling of colliding flesh never came, empty air the only thing in his grasp. At first, John thought Nick had simply pulled his hand back. But upon looking down, he realized that Nick didn't, in fact, *have* a left hand.

The table erupted in laughter, but Nick's gaze narrowed threateningly on John.

John looked him over again and could immediately tell that Nick had seen better days.

"You have something to say, Johnny?" Nick asked. He seemed intent on forcing an altercation.

There were a hundred things John could say, most of which he certainly would have said a few years ago. But he let it go, looked back down at the scarred stump Nick had as a hand, and said, "That stinks."

Nick continued to hold his gaze before a modest smile cracked his lips and some of the hostility evaporated from his eyes. "Yeah, as a matter of fact, it does." He noticed the scars on John's neck, the piercing blue look in his eyes, and quickly decided to change his approach. "Don't let it scare you."

"What?"

He waved his arm. "My stump. It bothers some people."

"I think I'll be okay."

"Lost it in '98. Serbia. Ended my career."

"Sorry to hear that," John mumbled, bringing the menu up to his face and signaling an end to the charade.

"Johnny," Jackson said, "next to Nick are Hunter, Chris, and Paul."

John acknowledged them with a subtle nod of his head, again quickly sweeping his gaze over the last three men.

Hunter, sitting immediately to Nick's right, was an African American with a perfectly shaped bald head that would be devastatingly effective if used as a wrecking ball. It was supported by a muscular neck and shoulders that had a wingspan all to themselves. He was wearing a red and white Hawaiian shirt that, like Jackson's polo, seemed barely able to contain the rippling mass beneath it. He was naturally kind, though his eyes told of a sharpness that never retired, questioning and expecting everything—even while seated at a table in Bermuda. The man was, no doubt, remarkably intelligent.

As John moved his attention to Chris, he began to appreciate the reputation the squad had earned amongst its superiors.

Chris looked less like a bodybuilder and more like a stuntman—wiry, athletic, fast. He looked more like John's age than the mid-forties he had somehow managed to embrace with such rare elegance. With messy blond hair reaching his shoulders, green eyes that seemed to be amused by everything, and a white smile that beamed against his tropically tanned face, he was the one Henry had told the most amusing stories about. His brother had described him as a pure adventurer, a guy always looking for a thrill to ride out and not a care in the world to keep him from it. But along with such stories was a fierce loyalty he had to his brothers here, willing to eliminate anything that threatened even so much as one of their reputations. There was one particular incident that Henry had described (but one that John couldn't fully recall at the moment) involving racial slurs thrown at Hunter by a gang of skinhead trash, an ice cream cone, a pool stick, a hanger, and a few ambulances…

Wearing a sheer white linen shirt, sleeves rolled up to the elbows, khaki shorts, and flip-flops, Chris looked more like a surfer than a SEAL. But John knew that the man could instantly transform himself into the multimillion-dollar weapon that he had been trained to be, if the situation required it. Though, presently, he seemed more interested in a girl at the table behind them than in anything else.

And then there was Paul. Though Paul wasn't as physically intimidating as Jackson and Hunter and didn't appear as athletic as Chris, he was by far the meanest looking. His black hair was buzzed short and sat growing atop a face carved from granite—a pair of thick sideburns traveling down past his ears and ending abruptly at his jawline. A single patch of black hair grew in the shadow of a lower lip that might never have known the tug of a smile. But unlike John, who always wore at least a day's worth of stubble to conceal his facial scars, Paul seemed perfectly content in showing his off. They crisscrossed his face in angry fashion, hinting at experiences that could explain the coldness in his eyes. Tattoos ran up his forearms and disappeared beneath the sleeves of a black T-shirt. If the group had a ruthless killer among them, a man with no soul and capable of shamelessly executing whatever form of punishment a mission demanded, it was him. The time off since his retirement had apparently been without the relaxation Nick had become accustomed to. And it was John's guess that he was still actively involved in a similar line of work.

All things considered, the group sitting around him seemed more than capable of finding their missing comrade. Which once again begged the recurring question, why did they so desperately want *him* here? It went against the very fabric of how they operated, for not only did they despise him because of his political heresy, but also for being an outsider. To invite a stranger to participate in a mission, let alone a mission intent on saving one of their own, seemed like the last thing in the world they would be prone to do.

The waiter came to the table and asked for their orders, interrupting his thoughts.

Grilled wahoo, baby back ribs, fish and chips, a burger and fish chowder, ribs…

"And for you, sir?" the waiter asked John last.

Sensing that he wasn't ready and not wanting to wait for him, Jackson ordered for him. "He'll have the grilled wahoo, too."

The waiter asked what he would like to drink.

"Water, please," he answered before Jackson could.

Chris mumbled something derogatory under his breath and asked for another Rum Swizzle.

As the waiter left with their orders and menus, Jackson told John about the wahoo, that it was the local catch and surely fresh.

"Thanks." John leaned back in his chair.

"Yeah," Chris said, "if you ever need to be told what to do, just ask Jack. He thinks he knows everything. Thinks everyone should know it, too." He winked at Jackson.

Jackson took a sip of what John guessed was beer. "Didn't bother you when I told you not to wipe yourself with *Nicandra physalodes* when we were in Peru, did it?"

Chris laughed, clapping his hands. "You see. He can't just say 'that poisonous plant.' He has to let everyone know its scientific title. Like anyone cares. You better tell him now, Johnny, that you're not impressed, or you're in for a grueling few days."

Jackson shook his head and looked over to John. "Just ask Henry what the CIA's profile says of *me*, and what it says of *Chris*."

"Yeah, proof that their letter 'I' is nothing but a joke," Chris retorted as the waiter appeared and set another drink down on the table in front of him.

John accepted his water with a polite thank-you. He took a sip while eyeing the company around him once more, deciding to jump in and get it over with. "So, what's the plan?" The question earned him an unpleasant look from Paul that confirmed his theory that he was nothing but an outsider and not really wanted here at all.

But Jackson answered the question. "The author that he wanted to talk to lives in Somerset Village, all the way on the West End. Problem is, he's away until tomorrow afternoon."

"You're sure he actually met the guy?" John asked.

"As sure as I need to be."

"How do you know he even got here?"

Hunter leaned forward. "I happened to be texting back and forth with him when he arrived. He said he'd write me later, once he got settled. That was the last anyone's heard from him."

"And what makes you think he's in trouble?"

"You know *why* he wanted to talk to the guy, right? The things he was into?" Jackson asked.

"Not really."

And with that, all the trained killers seemed to fidget a little; a look passed around amongst them that John wasn't exactly sure how to interpret.

But Jackson grinned, seemingly unimpressed with John's answer. "Sure you don't."

Before John could respond, however, the food arrived, and all conversation came to an abrupt halt—or at least his participation in it. They continued talking back and forth as if he were no longer even sitting at their table. Outsider. Traitor. Unwanted… *So why am I here?*

Once the check was paid and the table cleared, Chris stood and announced, "See you tonight, boys." Then he winked at the girl behind them, walked down to the end of the terrace, his shirt blowing in the breeze, and skipped down the steps that led to the water. He slid a pair of sunglasses on and gracefully threw himself onto one of the Jet Skis, switching it on and sending a cloud of black smoke puffing into the tropical air. The water churned beneath him as he reversed away from the tavern. And once he was positioned toward the open harbor, he stood, gave a half salute, and hit the accelerator. The Jet Ski shot a stream of arching water high into the air, barely missing the tavern's waterfront guests, as Chris circled around Ordnance Island and disappeared behind the cruise ship, apparently heading out to sea.

Hunter mumbled something under his breath about his friend's apparent lunacy as he led the rest of them away from the table and back through the tavern.

John stayed by the tavern's front doors, leaning against the wall while the rest of the team hovered around their scooters in the parking lot, brushing up in private whatever their immediate plans were. Evidently, they were top secret. Once they were clear on their next move, Hunter helped Nick onto the back of his scooter while Paul sped off on his own.

"Let's take a walk," Jackson said to John as he came back toward him.

John pushed himself off the wall and followed the little bridge onto Ordnance Island. On the other side of the bridge, the road dead-ended in a circle that sat in the shadow of the huge ship. They steered right, heading toward an alcove shaded by trees and surrounded by the remains of the fortification that once stood there. In the middle of a circular stone wall, there stood the statue of a man, his arms outspread in triumph or some other gesture that John couldn't determine. Lights at his feet were waiting for the sky to grow dark so that they could honor his memory, as they did every night, with illumination.

Jackson put his sunglasses on as he sat, though with the number of clouds still lingering, there was really no need for them.

"Is this the part where you explain what I'm doing here?" John asked, sitting beside the giant.

"You don't know why you're here?"

"I know why *you* are here. I don't know why *I'm* here."

"You don't want to be here?"

An impasse. Jackson was playing his cards tight. "Why do *you* want me here?"

"Well, we certainly don't need you."

At least he admitted that much, and in doing so had committed himself to another explanation, the one John had been waiting for.

"Would you believe me if I told you that it was for Henry?"

No, in fact, he wouldn't.

But Jackson didn't wait for such a reaction. "He resented the way things had gone between you two."

"Of course he did," John said. "He resented my leaving the Rangers."

"Yeah, but that's not what I meant, not what *he* meant. He wanted another chance. He said it was his one regret, letting your differences get in the way of blood."

"Henry told you this?" Knowing Henry as he did, he had a very hard time believing that.

"Last year, after your father's funeral. So for you to be there with us when we find him would mean all the world to him. It would give you both the perfect opportunity for a new start."

John couldn't bring himself to believe a single word of it, but he nodded as if it made absolute sense. If Jackson was going to keep underestimating him, then he was going to use it to his advantage. After a short silence, he asked, "It can't be easy, can it?"

"What?"

"Keeping the company of an apostate."

Jackson stared ahead, a cloud settling over his features. "I don't let people's weaknesses affect me."

"That's what you attribute it to, weakness?"

Jackson turned and stared at him. "You lost your edge, turned to whatever would justify you getting out."

John's expression turned cold. "I didn't *lose* my edge."

Smirking, Jackson said, "Oh, that's right, the Man in the sky appeared and knocked you off your high horse, revelations in His hand."

John turned and noticed a crowd making its way back to the ship. "Yeah, something like that."

Another awkward moment of silence ensued before Jackson began fishing something out of his pocket.

"What's this?" John asked, taking a ticket and pamphlet from him.

"Bus and ferry pass."

A quick examination revealed the ticket to be valid for the length of seven days—four days longer than he would be able to use it. "Seven days?" he asked, squinting with skepticism and smelling something foul in its insinuation.

"Doesn't come in three."

John shrugged. "Thanks."

Then Jackson threw his massive arms around the back of the bench and moved his gaze to the bronze statue now green with age. "Sir George Somers," he stated. "A shareholder in the Virginia Company."

John followed his stare to the memorial.

"In 1609, he took a fleet from the English Channel and traveled straight across the North Atlantic for Virginia. A feat that hadn't been made before. But a storm separated his ship from the rest of the fleet, and they ended up right out there at St. David's Head, the *Sea Venture* stuck between two rocks. What's left of her is still out there."

John looked out over the sparkling water, wondering if this new train of thought was headed somewhere specific.

"Sir Thomas Gates was the first one to shore. He was supposed to be the new governor of Jamestown, so there was a little confusion as to who should be the leader, him or Admiral Somers. They each ended up with their own following, and as a result, two separate ships were built for the escape. Sir Thomas' *Deliverance* and Sir George's *Patience*. It took nine months before Gates and Somers finally settled their differences and set sail for Jamestown."

"They make it?" John asked flatly.

He nodded. "But by the time they got there, only sixty starving people were still alive to welcome them. They decided to abandon Jamestown, to sail up the coast in search of help. As luck would have it, though, they crossed paths with a supply fleet that was just entering the river's mouth." Jackson looked back to John. "If Somers and Gates are four days later getting to Jamestown, there's no settlement to save. And if they abandon the settlement a day earlier, the supply fleet doesn't have a settlement to supply. And so, Jamestown's destiny as America's first settlement was in fact decided by a storm nine months earlier, this island, and pure dumb luck."

John wasn't familiar enough with Jackson to know if he was prone to pointless ramblings or if he was carefully crafting each word. His first impression of him had suggested the latter, but now he was beginning to wonder. He looked back at the statue. "What happened to Somers?"

"He eventually came back here for supplies but died. His nephew took the *Patience* back to England with the body, though his heart was buried here. And when England heard the stories of Bermuda, she decided to send settlers." Jackson stood. "A replica of the *Deliverance* is just over there on the other side of the street."

John asked, "You study the brochures on the plane ride or something?"

He shook his head. "This isn't the first time I've been here." And then he ended the strange history lesson. "We're meeting at the tavern later tonight. It serves as a nightclub then."

"I'll pass."

"Then by all means, feel free to do some investigating on your own, and we'll touch base tomorrow."

"That's it?" He was slightly irritated, trying to determine why his time had been wasted on this little field trip.

John could tell from the way Jackson's eyebrows moved that his eyes had narrowed beneath the lenses of his sunglasses.

"I don't think we'll have much luck finding Henry without the author's direction, but if you got nothing better to do…"

John thought about that, superimposing it over the small size of the island…over the four SEALs. "You don't think he's on the island," he realized. Otherwise, they wouldn't be basing their next move on the "direction" the author pointed them in.

Jackson shrugged. "I don't know."

"You're hoping that Henry happened to mention where he was headed to next."

But Jackson just turned and began walking away, leaving John to stand there dumbfounded. *If Henry isn't on the island…*

Once Jackson was out of view, John walked over to the cruise ship terminal and inquired about the ticket Jackson had given him. In the process, he learned that he could get a pass for three days, two days, or whatever number of days he wanted. John thanked the nice woman and walked back to his scooter.

Five minutes later, he was back on the Causeway. It was 5:30, and another layer of mystery was beginning to descend with the approaching night.

FIVE

5:49 p.m. 21st day of May. Grotto Bay Beach Resort, Hamilton Parish, Bermuda

John entered his room and immediately began looking for something on which to write. Dumping the contents of a drawer from the bedside table onto the carpet, he sifted through menus, TV guides, and other brochures before discovering a pad of paper and a pen. He picked up the phone that sat resting upon the same table and dialed room service, placing an order for a pot of coffee. After hanging up, he took the paper and pen out onto the deck and sat before the wonderful scene exhibited below. His eyes, however, were not captivated by the island paradise, but by the blank piece of white paper resting on his lap. Slowly, and very deliberately, he began moving the pen, scribbling notes across the face of the pad. He couldn't be completely certain about what he was writing or why he was writing it, but intuitively, he knew that his subconscious, or spirit, might have a better idea of what was going on than did his analytical brain. As he wrote, an army of chills invaded his spine, the banner under which its soldiers hacked away at his nervous system bearing the image of bizarre connectedness. As his hand shook and the pen faltered, he tried to gain a sense of the image such dots would form once joined.

Afghanistan. Cave. Dream. VHS tape. Genesis 6. Henry. Bermuda. Author. Storm. Lies. 1609. 7-day pass. "You know the things he was into." Jackson…

The knock at the door was like a bowling ball thrown through a cathedral window, his thoughts fracturing into a million dislocated pictures and snapping him out of the trancelike state he'd fallen into. After composing himself and answering the door, he returned to his notes with a hot pitcher of coffee and a small porcelain tea set. The china rattled in his unsteady grasp. He poured himself a cup and took it with him back out to the balcony. The notepad was sitting on the floor, where it had landed after presumably falling off the chair, the breeze flipping through its pages. John took a sip of the coffee before bending to retrieve it, hoping the drink could bring clarity to his thought process. He bought himself a few more precious seconds, giving the caffeine a bit more time to make its way to his brain, by sitting first and taking another sip from the steaming cup. Then he picked up the bizarre notes.

Now divorced from the trance that had inspired the list, he looked back over what its influence had helped him produce and, in his present state, wasn't entirely sure why he'd included some of the things he had. Surely there couldn't possibly be a connection between his experience in Afghanistan—and the dreams that had ensued—and Henry's sailing to Bermuda. It was preposterous. Yet he couldn't deny that the emotion of the last few days did seem to find its manifestation in the video cassette tape, a tape that referenced giants and had triggered the return of his nightmares. But again, to think that his personal issues were somehow interconnected with the events that brought him to Bermuda was ridiculous—even if there was something about the face in the whirling storm clouds that wouldn't leave him alone. And whether the thing had actually been there, or if it had just been a product of his warped imagination, was irrelevant. Because neither case would change the fact that, after a three-year hiatus, the whole lurid problem was beginning to resurrect itself. The flashpoint, no matter how much sense it made, was this trip to Bermuda and the feelings of trepidation it had given birth to. But why such an apprehension about coming here existed in the first place was, in the end, both the mystery and the connection he found to be evading him.

John studied his notes—rearranging their order and connecting certain words with uneven lines—until he made three trips back inside for refills and finally finished off the pitcher. No great revelation had welcomed him, so he leaned back and lifted his gaze to the sight below. As far as Henry's friends went, he was in the midst of something he wasn't supposed to fully appreciate, his role actually that of a pawn in some greater scheme. Believing that Jackson's reason for bringing him was pure nonsense (that it was for his and Henry's sake), John decided that he would do a little investigating of his own.

Standing, he crumpled his notes in his hands and tossed them into a trash can beside the bed. Closing the door to the balcony, he left the room altogether. Entering the hallway and seeing that it was vacant, he quickly walked to Jackson's room. He put an ear against the door and listened for any sign of activity coming from the other side. Taking a breath, he knocked. No answer. He tried the handle, but, of course, it was locked. For a moment, he entertained the idea of forcing his way in. Deciding against it, he instead took the elevator down to the lobby. Spotting a big clock on the wall as he walked out the doors to his scooter, he noted the time. 7:01.

* * * *

After consulting the map that the scooter lady had given him, John planned out his route to Somerset Village. He was going to find out just how much of the truth he'd been told. Because Bermuda was shaped like a giant fishhook and their hotel sat directly across from the hook's point—the Great Sound and Dundonald Channel separating the two—he would have to drive all the way down south and then back up north on the other side. It looked like Middle Road would take him all the way to Somerset, with only a short detour onto South Road in Devonshire Parish to complicate things. Looking up from the map, he asked a passerby how long it would take him to get to the West End.

"About forty minutes," a nice gentleman in Bermuda shorts replied.

With the hiding sun peeking playfully through the obstinate clouds while coming into position for its daily descent into the Atlantic, John thanked the man for his help. He then took Middle Road on a southwest bearing, careful not to exceed the island's slow speed limit. But the drive through Bermuda's interior, which touched near the coast of the Little Sound in Southampton Parish and crossed over Somerset Bridge (which the map proclaimed to be the smallest drawbridge in the world), passed by in an unnoticed vibrant blur, his recent pensiveness erasing from vision the beauty of the British tropics.

When he reached Somerset Village, he spotted a police station sitting off Somerset Road. He parked the scooter and entered the building with a few simple questions in hand.

Five minutes later, he was back on the scooter and continuing north toward the sharp tip of Bermuda's hook, the information just gleaned confirming at least a portion of Jackson's story to be true. There was indeed an author who lived in the Village, and yes, he was presently in the States on business.

He drove over Watford Bridge, Grey's Bridge, and then the Cut Bridge before reaching the Royal Naval Dockyard on Ireland Island North, where another cruise ship sat docked on the east side and a tall clock tower stood reaching up into the sky at his left. He parked the scooter and strolled into the mall that surrounded the clock tower, looking for a small souvenir for Kristen and a replacement for what he'd given away on the plane.

Ten minutes later, he was leaving the assortment of stores with a New International Version of the Bible and more time to find his wife something. He came to an empty bench and consulted his map. It revealed a big fort standing nearby and a little beach resting in its shadow. So, with the sun aiming to fall right on top of that location, he set a leisurely pace for Snorkel Park Beach, his scalp still tingling from both mystery and a whole pitcher of coffee.

He eventually found himself mixed with a group of vacationers, following them into the Keep, which was the name of the island's largest fort. As he walked, he consulted the map again and learned that the giant structure encompassed ten acres of the Dockyard, was originally a citadel and arsenal built to protect the island from air and sea attacks, and was complete with bulwarks, ramparts, carronade cannons, and six-inch-shell guns. It was surrounded on three sides by buildings and magazines, the Commissioner's House resting comfortably on a hill in front of him. Overhearing statements from the group, he also learned that construction of the Dockyard began in 1809 and that the buildings in the Keep were constructed from native limestone. The work had apparently been undertaken by slaves at first but later became the burden of prisoners and other laborers imported from the West Indies. Someone said the Keep closed in the 1950s and had lapsed into disrepair until, in 1974, the Bermuda Maritime Museum gained control of the site.

John looked back down to the map and saw that the Keep was now indeed Bermuda's largest museum, and that the Commissioner's House now displayed exhibits ranging from defense and slavery to immigration and maritime art. There was another building within the confines of the Keep that now served as the Dolphin Quest, the Keep's pond (once used for transporting munitions) having been converted into a place where one could go frolic with dolphins.

When John lifted his gaze from the map, he found that he had drifted away from the group, which was now collectively snapping pictures of something he couldn't see. As they moved on, John curiously approached the object that had so adamantly held their interest. But as he stepped closer, realizing at once that it was a statue, he stopped. Even in the failing light there was no mistaking its resemblance. Elevators packed with prickly occupants were unloading at the base of his neck. He knew from the trident in its hand and the crown on its head that it was supposed to be some Greek or Roman god.

"Excuse me," he called after the wandering crowd.

A straggling professor-like gentleman and his skinny gray-haired wife turned, hand in hand, toward his voice.

"Who is this supposed to be?" he asked without introduction. He wondered if they could detect the desperation in his tone.

They stopped and let the rest of the group stray farther away from them. "It's Neptune," the man said. "The Roman god of the sea, brother to Jupiter and Pluto."

As John approached them, he turned his gaze back to the sculpture. "I've seen it before," he mumbled.

The woman had supersonic hearing. "You've probably seen him all over and just never noticed." She smiled. "He's depicted as representing American naval supremacy in the *Apotheosis of Washington* inside the US Capitol building. In fact, he decorates fountains all over Washington, Italy, and France. He's analogous with the Greeks' Poseidon…"

Maybe *she* was the professor. She continued rattling off one famous location after another, but John knew that it wasn't from any one of those places that he recognized the heathen god's face. And, despite his racing heartbeat, he forced a smile of his own. "Thanks."

"Where are you from?" the man asked.

"Pittsburgh."

"Oh." He smiled. "I teach at Temple University. Came over on the boat." He nodded toward the cruise ship while extending his hand and giving his name.

"John. I flew in this morning."

"Beautiful place, isn't it?" the woman asked.

He agreed, and they spent a few minutes talking Eagles and Steelers football, mentioning briefly the "Steagles"—the unofficial name given to their short merging during World War II. John thought about mentioning all the Steelers' Super Bowl rings and the Birds' lack of them but wasn't sure how fanatic the guy was about his team. Wasn't sure if he'd start belting out the Philadelphia anthem, "Fly, Eagles, Fly," while throwing his wife's shoes at him.

"Well, glad we could be of help." They shook hands and hurried after their friends, leaving John alone with Neptune—the same Roman god he swore had materialized beneath his plane earlier that morning.

It also bore an eerie similarity to something else he once saw.

* * * *

Snorkel Park closed at seven o'clock, and because it was now only minutes away from eight, he was alone. The fort's west wall was beside him and stretching out into the shallow water. Palm trees were scattered around the tiny beach behind him, doing their best to isolate his position. Standing on some rocks that took off into a long jetty, he crossed his arms against the wind blowing off the ocean. The sun was just about to make contact with the surface of the water, and it looked as if the dark clouds were actually going to allow the display to go on uninterrupted. The sun struck the water as if it were the tip of a cosmic match, the contact igniting a line of fire that ripped across the ocean, the lazy surf spreading its orange glow up and onto the beach around him.

Such a display helped turn his thoughts toward Kristen. He pulled the cell phone from his pocket and called her.

"You won't believe the view I'm standing in front of," he said as soon as she answered. He turned his gaze farther west and imagined her in their home some seven hundred miles away. It was hard to imagine that anything lay beyond the liquid horizon, and it was even stranger to think that his forsaken sense of reality was still there with Kristen, accompanying the very location from which her words were emanating. He felt worlds apart from her…from all that he had come to know over the last three years.

"So how are they treating you?" she eventually asked.

"Better than I thought." He chose not to share his growing concern regarding whatever their true intentions were and also refrained from mentioning the little incident on the plane. Instead, he tried to assure her that everything was okay. "We're going to meet with the author Henry came to see sometime tomorrow afternoon. I'll call you then."

They spoke for a few more minutes before he returned the phone to his pocket, and the ball of fire slipped completely into the water's embrace, projecting a magnificent lightshow up into the night sky. He stood there transfixed, until all that was left to be seen was a line of red highlighting the horizon. He turned his back to the twilight, his encounter with Neptune and the terror it had stirred within him making what he'd said to his wife a big, fat lie.

* * * *

An idea began to take shape while he headed south and back onto Somerset Island. He had intended to confirm the existence of such an author, and now that his mission was complete, he wanted to learn more about him—what kind of stuff he wrote about and why it would prompt Henry to sail so far out if his way. So he pulled into a gas station along Middle Road in Sandys Parish and inquired about bookstores in the area.

The dark-skinned man was in the process of wiping grease off his hands but nevertheless gave John his utmost attention. "Well," he answered, considering the question, "the biggest bookstore on the island is The Bookmart in Hamilton. I am pretty sure that they close at five o' clock, though. However, you could get lucky with the cruise ships in port."

"What's the easiest way to get there?" he asked.

"The ferry."

"Where's the nearest one?"

"Right down the road here." He pointed. "It will take twenty-five minutes, but it will take you straight into Hamilton. The store is on Reid Street. Now, if that one is closed, or you do not find what you're looking for, there is another bookstore in Hamilton on Queen Street."

"Thank you," John said sincerely.

"Enjoy your stay, my friend," the Bermudian waved after him.

John made it to the ferry just as it was about to set out for Hamilton. And, just as the gas station attendant had said, the trip across the Little Sound, Granaway Deep, and Hamilton Harbor took exactly twenty-five minutes. The crew on the ferry helped sharpen his directions, and five minutes later, he found himself standing in front of the bookstore. But, as the man at the gas station had also guessed, it was closed. So he rode over to Queen Street and found the other one. It, too, appeared to be closed.

John swung off the scooter and walked up to the storefront window. Upon peering through the glass, he could make out someone moving around inside. He knocked on the window, trying to get the person's attention. Finally, a man approached the other side of the window and pointed to a sign that read *CLOSED*. To which John removed some crisp twenty-dollar bills from his wallet and held them against the glass. "Please," he begged.

The man slowly moved over to the door, and the sound of keys jingling could be heard from the other side. The door cracked open.

"What is it you want?" the man asked.

"I'm sorry to bother you, sir, but I'm leaving early tomorrow morning, and I just heard that there's a local author who lives over in Somerset Village."

"Ronald?" He laughed. "Yeah, I carry some of his books for him."

"Wonderful. Listen, I would be forever grateful if you'd let me purchase one… It's a thing I do, pick up souvenirs native to the place I'm visiting. Local reads are a must for my collection. I'll even pay you double what it's worth."

He laughed some more, opened the door, and motioned John into the store. "Well, I am no expert, friend, but in my opinion, Ronald's books are not worth the paper they are printed on. But you will buy *all* of them for this special treatment." Then he closed the door behind them. "Come, this way."

There were three different books by Ronald sitting on the shelf. John pulled one off and turned it over. *The Bermuda Triangle and the Doorway to Hell* by Ronald Douglas. John looked up in disbelief.

"Yeah," the man said through a teasing grin.

John grabbed the next one. *Lost Bloodlines: The Gods Among Us.* And finally, there was *Journey with the Gods. Third Edition.* More than confused, he tried to match the book seller's smile. "Okay then."

"Will that be all?"

"Oh, I think this will be plenty," he answered, wondering if he was just contributing to the production of tinfoil head coverings Ronald was probably selling on eBay, paranoid masses bidding for rolls of autographed brain armor.

"The register is closed out, so…"

John doubled the price for each book and handed over the money, feeling all kinds of things while doing so. Silly and stupid, obviously. Irresponsible for supporting such things with money he couldn't afford to part with and guilty for lying to the man about why he wanted them.

"Would you like a bag?" He was still smiling, no doubt finding the whole transaction very amusing. John imagined a pegboard in the back full of security camera printouts showcasing the "suckers" leaving with Ronald's books.

"Please," he mumbled.

As he put them into a plastic bag, he commented, "I have never read them myself."

"Really?" he replied in feigned disbelief.

"I don't sell many. I think there is a bigger market for them back in Britain and in your United States. What do you call it, *New Age*?"

"I don't know *what* you call this."

"Rubbish." He laughed again. "But I hope you enjoy it."

"Yeah, thanks."

His stomach was growling, so after leaving the store, he rode around Bermuda's capital city until finding the kind of place he was looking for, one that locals would be congregated in. It was called The Spot Restaurant, and as he entered, he knew that he had guessed correctly. Sitting near the back, he put his bag of books, which he added the Bible to, on the floor under his chair, where they wouldn't be visible to any curious eyes. When the waitress came to take his order, he learned that the lower prices played a large part in attracting off-duty police officers, nurses from the hospital, and other locals, many of whom were regulars to the diner. After some chitchat, she recommended the roast turkey, but he ordered a hamburger and soda instead.

While he waited for the food, he unfolded his map across the table, combing his gaze from one side of the island to the other. He wasn't sure what he was looking for, but something caught his eye up near the airport on St. David's Island. It was labeled the Carter House, a notation stating that it was believed to be Bermuda's oldest house. Curious, John asked the waitress about it the next time she came by.

She bent over and squinted at the map before shaking her head. Then she stood, put her hands on her hips, and shouted to a man seated alone at another table across the room. "Hey, Frank!"

There was evidently only one Frank in the room. He turned around in his chair and looked back at her. "What is it, my dear?"

"This gentleman here would like to know about the Carter House. Can you help him or not?" Then she whispered to John, "He's a police officer."

"It's a museum dedicated to St. David's Island and the people who have lived there," Frank called across the room. His British accent came from a round face poised below a balding head. He looked to be about fifty-something and was somewhere just beyond medium build. Though not exactly overweight, it was still clear that he enjoyed this place more than he ought to. "There are some artifacts on display."

John crossed the diner and sat down in the empty chair across from the officer's. "But who was Carter?"

Having finished his meal, Frank was now only nursing a cup of coffee and didn't appear all that bothered by the sudden intrusion. "Christopher Carter," he responded patiently, "was the first settler to Bermuda."

John recalled the things Jackson had told him earlier. "He came with the English settlers, after Somers died?"

Frank's expression revealed a spark of interest, and he reevaluated the stranger sitting before him. "No. He was on the *Sea Venture* with Somers when they shipwrecked here in 1609."

John was confused. "I thought they all sailed to Jamestown nine months later."

"Not everyone. Carter, Robert Waters, and Edward Chard stayed behind."

"Why?"

"Well, Waters was a murderer that had been sentenced to death, and Carter, after rebelling against Gates twice, believed that he would be punished by him. I am not certain of the circumstances behind Chard's decision to stay behind, but I know that it was Carter's idea, so my guess would be that, in his case as well, it was because of a failed conspiracy to kill Gates. When Gates caught Henry Paine and had him executed, the other conspirators in Somers' camp thought Paine might have betrayed them, so they fled into the woods. All the sailors, however, did end up returning to Somers. Except, of course, Carter and Chard."

"What happened to them?"

"Waters and Chard eventually immigrated to Virginia. When the English settlers came, Carter was given Cooper's Island—actually chose it over St. David's because he thought there was treasure buried on it—and became one of the six governors left by Governor Moore."

John shook his head. "Six Governors?"

"Moore was the first governor of Bermuda, but he returned to Britain to defend himself against negative reports that had arisen from the settlers. He left six men to govern in his absence, rotating every month." He took a sip of coffee. "May I ask why this interests you, Mister…"

John ran a hand over his prickly jaw. "Carter. John Carter."

Frank's eyebrows reached upward for a head of hair that wasn't there anymore before lying back down again. "You think he may be a relative of yours?"

"I don't know. I've known about him for all of three minutes."

Frank nodded. "Well, there's an author that lives here who I believe *is* related to him."

"You guys sure get your share of authors," John remarked.

Frank smiled. "Some better than others. Thomas Moore, Mark Twain, Eugene O'Neill, Sinclair Lewis, Hervey Allen, Rudyard Kipling, C. S. Forester… And that is not to mention *Bermudian* authors. But anyway, it is commonly believed that many of Bermuda's native people are actually descendants of Christopher Carter."

John went silent, the year 1609 reaching into the future and trying to pull him back in time.

"What *really* brings you to Bermuda, Mr. Carter?" Frank asked, as if he had only just now noticed the tattoos peeking below John's sleeves and flickering up his neck.

John considered his next words very carefully but ultimately decided that asking a few questions couldn't hurt anything. At least, he didn't think it could. After all, it had been Jackson's suggestion. "My brother, Henry, sailed here a few weeks ago, and no one has heard from him since."

Frank leaned forward onto folded arms. "Has anyone reported him missing?"

"I don't think so."

"Well, I could certainly find out when he arrived and whether or not he left. What is the name of his boat?"

Shaking his head, he said, "I'm not sure."

Frank sighed. "Henry Carter, you said?" He leaned back, took out a pen and small notepad, and jotted down the name. "What is your phone number?"

John gave it to him, hoping it was a good idea. For all he knew, this guy could have Henry's head in his freezer. Probably not, though.

"Was he involved in anything that I should know about?"

He thought of the books still sitting back under his chair and didn't think mentioning them would do wonders for his image. "I don't think so."

"Fine. But lie low, okay? I will work on this for you. You just relax and try to get some enjoyment out of your stay here." He finished his coffee and began fishing through his wallet for a tip. "You know, Mark Twain once said, 'Sometimes a dose of Bermuda is just what the doctor ordered.' And in your case, Mr. Carter, I'm the doctor."

John thought that a real doctor would probably prescribe something else, like a large dose of straitjacket. "I'll try to heed the advice." Though he had no intention whatsoever of leaving his brother's fate in Frank's hands while he got friendly with the dolphins back at the Keep.

As Frank placed a few coins on the table, he narrowed his gaze on John's neck, following the ink upward until picking up the scars tracing his jaw. "How did you get those scars anyway?"

"You don't want to know." He stood, thankful that the waitress had just come out with his food. "Sorry for interrupting."

"I'll call you with what I find or don't find tomorrow. In the meantime, John, stay out of trouble. And look to take Mark Twain's advice early tomorrow. There is some nasty weather moving in."

"More?"

He nodded and stood. "Old Neptune seems to be in a bad mood lately." He turned and headed toward the door, waving to the staff as he left.

It wasn't until after the door closed behind Frank that John was finally able to regain his composure and return to his own table. Why had the officer left riding on the wings of those specific words? *Another coincidence?* He tried not to think about it while he ate, but by the end of his hamburger, he was dizzy with vertigo, his situation trapped in a vacuum of indiscernible borders.

Books in hand, he drove out of Hamilton and headed northeast back to the hotel.

* * * *

He was still wide awake when he entered his room at 10:40, so he stacked the four books beside the bed and went back out to the balcony. Leaning against the railing, he stared out over the harbor and the illuminated islands floating beyond it. He stood there for a while, enjoying the cool breeze and the gentle sound of the waves crashing below, as Mark Twain's words drifted through his mind. He wished that he *could* take pleasure in such a place, and that its antidote was compatible with his disease. But it wasn't. Finally, he retreated inside, closing the door on the still night and climbing into bed. Reaching for his new Bible, he turned to Genesis 6, wondering how the New International Version interpreted the passage.

> *When men began to increase in number on the earth and daughters were born to them, the sons of God saw that the daughters of men were beautiful, and they married any of them they chose. Then the LORD said, "My Spirit will not contend with man forever, for he is mortal; his days will be a hundred and twenty years."*
>
> *The Nephilim were on the earth in those days—and also afterward—when the sons of God went to the daughters of men and had children by them. They were the heroes of old, men of renown. The LORD saw how great man's wickedness on the earth had become, and that every inclination of the thoughts of his heart was only evil all the time. The LORD was grieved that he had made man on the earth, and his heart was filled with pain. So the LORD said, "I will wipe mankind, whom I have created, from the face of the earth—men and animals, and creatures that move along the ground, and birds of the air—for I am grieved that I have made them."*

He stopped after that and thought back to the videotape. There was a connection to be made there, but it remained just beyond his grasp. Frustrated, he turned to Ronald Douglas' strange books, wondering what in the world would make Henry want to talk to the guy. And then, spotting the title of the third book, he understood with metaphysical thunderclaps what dots his subconscious had been trying to connect.

Journey with the Gods. Neptune. Heroes of old.

But John couldn't quite remember what the man on the tape had said about these "heroes"—some kind of inference suggesting they were none other than the mythological gods of antiquity. It was a connection, though, that he couldn't do anything with at the moment. So instead, he grabbed the first book in the pile.

The Bermuda Triangle and the Doorway to Hell.

For over two hours, he read the book that attempted to define the physical boundaries of the phenomena, document the strange occurrences within them, and even bring a theological perspective to the topic—addressing creation, the ocean, demons, and why there was to be no sea in heaven.

John had always been under the impression that the entire subject was nothing but pure fabrication. But the detail Douglas included in the reports was sowing his mind with second thoughts. There were simply too many official records and too many mysteries that went unexplained by the available theories.

The story of Flight 19 especially gained his attention because it seemed to be "the event" that had first cemented the Triangle's infamous reputation throughout the world.

In December of 1945, five Navy Grumman TBM-3 Avenger torpedo bombers took off from Fort Lauderdale on a routine training mission that was to take them no further than one hundred and twenty-three miles from the base, following a triangular pattern. But the entire flight vanished on its way back. Some of the pilots' transmissions that had been picked up within the three-hour ordeal included reports of erratic compasses, unknown directional headings, low fuel, and no idea as to where they even were.

A twin-engine Martin Mariner, manned by a crew of thirteen, was sent out to look for Flight 19, and heading toward the last known position of the five bombers, it too vanished—though it had only been in the air for twenty minutes. But despite over four thousand one hundred hours of air-search time by more than three hundred planes and a small army of destroyers, submarines, Coast Guard vessels, search and rescue cutters, and private yachts and boats, not a single trace of Flight 19 was ever found, leaving a board member from the Navy Board of Inquiry to remark, "They vanished as completely as if they had flown to Mars"—a statement that only led to more bizarre theories about the area. A scientist from Miami was quoted later by the press as saying, "They are still here, but in a different dimension of a magnetic phenomenon that could have been set up by a UFO."

And then, twenty-nine years after the disappearance, a ham-radio operator that had been working during the time of the ordeal told a reporter that the lieutenant in command of the flight had actually transmitted, "*Don't come after me…they look like they are from outer space.*" But the reporter sat on this information for obvious reasons, until he was able to view, in part, the transcript from the plane's transmissions—something that was made available only after severe pressure was applied by the missing pilots' families. Though he wasn't able to see the entire thing, he did discover that, indeed, the lieutenant did transmit at least the first part of the strange command, "*Don't come after me…*"

There was also a US Army C-54 that disappeared between Bermuda and Palm Beach in 1947 and then a British South American Tudor IV passenger plane, *Star Tiger,* that disappeared in January of 1948. Even though the captain of the *Star Tiger* announced to Bermuda's control tower that weather and performance were excellent and that they expected to arrive on schedule, the *Star Tiger* was never heard from again. Even more bizarre, the Coast Guard station in Newfoundland later picked up a voice transmission pronouncing *G-A-H-N-P,* which were the *Star Tiger*'s call letters. This strange phenomenon, if not a hoax, led someone to suggest that these late transmissions could, perhaps, have been broadcasted from a great distance away…as in another dimension of time and space. A court of inquiry concluded that there was no ground for assuming radio or mechanical failure, fuel exhaustion, meteorological hazards, or that the pilots simply got lost, but instead concluded, "It may be truly said that no more baffling problem has ever been presented for investigation… What happened in this case will never be known."

The *Star Arial*, *Star Tiger*'s sister ship, disappeared during a flight from Bermuda to Jamaica almost a year later to the day. Again, the pilot reported clear weather and that their ETA was as expected. It was, as in the other cases, the last anyone ever heard from the *Star Arial*, even though a US Navy task force was already positioned within the general area the search would begin. And the reason why the task force was already present within the area was because it was looking for another plane, a chartered DC-3, that had disappeared on December 28. The search had just been called off a week prior to the *Star Arial* incident. The circumstances surrounding that incident were even more troubling than that of the *Star Arial*'s disappearance, namely because weather was calm and clear and that the last thing ever heard from them was the pilot announcing they were just fifty miles out, the lights of Miami visible. The term *dematerialized* began being used to describe the mystery.

By the time Ronald's book had concluded the accounts, such phrases as *clear air turbulence*, *wind shear*, *atmospheric anomalies*, and *electromagnetic disturbances* had become regular in use. It was true that official theories existed concerning certain disappearances, but it seemed that none could truly account for missing planes *and* boats or explain how completely such vessels could even vanish.

But more troubling to John than the thousand plus missing vessels and their passengers was a chapter on the ocean itself. He was suddenly too tired to think back through it, though. Instead, he quickly sent off a text message to his pastor, asking for his opinion on the strange theological theory Douglas had presented within the chapter.

He rubbed his eyes and swung his feet over the side of the bed, needing only to reach the light switch before committing to some much-needed sleep. But in his movement, he accidentally knocked the bizarre book to the floor. It landed awkwardly, its pages momentarily fanning open before gravity could set them back to rest. Now only the front cover remained bent open. John tilted his head as he noticed something scribbled across the inside of the cover, beneath the dust jacket. Reaching down, he removed the jacket and discovered that the author had signed the book. It took John some effort to make out the scratchy signature, but when he finally did, he picked the book up off the ground, closed it, and with trembling fingers, removed the sticker price from the front cover. It had been concealing the author's true last name—which was not Douglas.

His full name was actually...Ronald Douglas Carter.

SIX

I'm sure that I'm lost now, and quite certain that the sinister presence that is leading me will abandon me in this labyrinth once its purpose is satisfied. The thought of dying down here has my hands shaking uncontrollably. I want to turn and run. I don't care about the terrorists' booby traps. I just want to leave. But still, I can't stop moving forward and am only getting deeper and deeper into the strange network of tunnels. My night vision only intensifies the eeriness, masking everything in a ghostly glow of green and white. I swear that I can see things creeping around, hiding in the corners of my vision. I come to a split in the path and swing my MP5 submachine gun up, peering down each black hole. Everything in me says to go left, that the stone floor inclines and leads back to the surface. But I go right. Something is pulling me. I can feel it dragging me now, summoning me against my will. My screams echo around me. I curse the god of this horrid land and beg whatever other deities may be listening to just kill me.

John let himself acclimate to the foreign surroundings that were beginning to appear before his somnolent eyes. Slowly, the dream's influence began to fade, replaced instead by the seeping memory of the past day. He sat up in the bed and looked out the sliding glass door beside him. The sun was up, and there was not a cloud anywhere in the northeastern sky to encroach upon its declaration of the new day. The clock next to him read 8:39.

Noticing that his hands were still shaking, he decided it would at least take a hot shower to rid the dream's lingering aftertaste from his worldview. As he stood, he caught sight of the books stacked next to the alarm clock and remembered in an instant the things he had discovered just before falling asleep, namely the stories of the Bermuda Triangle and the author's last name. He also recalled texting Pastor Brian a question about hell's association with the ocean, if even there was one. But after checking his phone, he saw that neither Brian nor Frank had gotten back to him yet. There was, however, a text message from Jackson instructing him to meet them in the lobby at noon. He tossed the phone back onto the bed and anxiously headed for his morning therapy.

As the hot water splashed against his skin, he felt the dream—and the memory that still managed to sustain it—begin to grow fainter, evaporating into the steam that engulfed the bathroom. He bowed his head in prayer, seeking a guiding light that would lead him through the mysterious maze he was so helplessly lost in.

* * * *

After surviving the shower without incident—no drain demon trying to suck him out to sea by his toenails or Neptune disguised in a wig and brandishing a knife—John walked back into the bedroom and sat on the side of the bed. Adjusting his towel, he reached for Ronald's other book, *Lost Bloodlines: The Gods Among Us*. He had an hour before he would set out with complete disregard for Frank's advice, so he took the book out onto the balcony and sat in the morning sunshine. Cautiously opening the cover, as if by mishandling it he might release into the world a manifestation of its contents, he started reading.

He didn't get far. Chapter two was already thrusting a rather large monkey wrench into the biblical timeline with which he was familiar. The stumbling block proved to be a passage in Ezekiel chapter 28, a passage, Ronald declared, that concerned the priesthood of Satan before his damnation.

John went and got his own Bible just to make sure that Ronald wasn't rewriting the holy Scriptures.

> *The word of the LORD came to me: "Son of man, take up a lament concerning the king of Tyre and say to him: This is what the Sovereign LORD says: You were the model of perfection, full of wisdom and perfect in beauty. You were in Eden, the garden of God; every precious stone adorned you: ruby, topaz and emerald, chrysolite, onyx and jasper, sapphire, turquoise and beryl. Your settings and mountings were made of gold; on the day you were created they were prepared. You were anointed as a guardian cherub, for so I ordained you. You were on the holy mount of God; you walked among the fiery stones. You were blameless in your ways from the day you were created."*

But there were a few differences between John's NIV version and whatever version Ronald had used, so John checked the copyright information on the first page of *Bloodlines*, learning that all quoted verses had been taken from the New King James translation.

The places in which the text varied were where the NIV had "adorned" instead of "covered" and "Your settings and mountings" rather than "The workmanship of your timbrels and pipes." "You were the anointed cherub who covers" was also rendered "Anointed as a guardian cherub," and "you walked back and forth in the midst of the fiery stones" was instead translated, "you walked among the fiery stones."

John was not educated in any form of Hebrew, so any opinion he might have on the matter would be useless. Perhaps when he returned home he would inquire about the original language of the text. But for now, he was only concerned with understanding Ronald's point, a point that might or might not have brought his brother to this place.

The chapter argued that Satan "was in Eden" but that the Eden described could not be the same Eden that Adam was placed in because Satan was said to have entered this Eden as a minister of God, the Genesis account obviously painting quite a different picture. Also, in the Ezekiel text there was no mention of trees or other things commonly related to the Genesis Garden. Instead, Ezekiel confronts the reader with what appears to be some kind of palace—constructed of gold and precious stones (the "covering")—that seems peculiarly similar to the Scripture's description of the New Jerusalem. It also seemed, from a proper translation of verse 13—*the service of thy tabrets and of thy pipes was prepared with thee on the day when thou wast created*—that from the time he came into being,

Satan had been surrounded by symbols of royalty, his person and position being announced, as it were, with the very noises appointed for such a high inauguration; for indeed, God made Satan to be the wisest and most beautiful of all His creations, appointing him as the Prince of the World and the Power of the Air.

It was clear from the verses, Ronald proclaimed, that Satan's dwelling place consisted of three areas—Eden, the Garden of God, and the Holy Mountain of God. Just as the tabernacle itself contained the Outer Court, the Holy Place, and the Holy of Holies. And just as Satan was described as being "upon the Holy Mountain of God as the Anointed Cherub that covereth"—like the covering cherubim situated atop the Ark of the Covenant within the Holy of Holies—so was the Jewish High Priest fixed in Jerusalem near the Temple and the presence of God. From all of this, Ronald claimed that it was a matter of reasonable deduction to conclude that Satan had been the great high priest of his realm, perfect in all his ways and dwelling in a palace of gold and jewels that was located near the very presence of God.

John read through it again, paying special attention to the references made to the fiery stones and the parallel verses Ronald used to explain them. Compiling Ezekiel 1:26 and Exodus 24:10 and 17, he believed that the fiery stones were present before the throne of God, which suggested that when Satan was in Eden, he must have had customary access to and from God's immediate presence, even holding from such a location the exalted responsibility of leading all creation in worshiping God (as seemed to be the responsibility of the cherubim in the book of Revelation).

John closed the book and stared out over the harbor, his mind suddenly troubled by something new. And upon further reflection, he realized that the cause of his discomfort could not entirely be attributed to the things written, but rather the *manner* in which they were written. Turning to the Bible, he very briefly read the entire chapter, wanting immediately to discount Ronald's theory on the sole fact that it was not Satan being addressed at all but rather the King of Tyre. But he had to admit that even that explanation led to a host of other problems, since no mortal man could possibly be said to have met such requirements. He would have to ask Brian about this, too.

Still unable to truly lay his finger on why the words were troubling him, he went back to the book and continued to read. Two pages later, it struck him right in the face. It was the way in which Satan's apparent reign had been pronounced without an account of its end. In fact, the last verse Ronald quoted, "he was perfect in all his ways," was cut off from the rest of the verse, which stated, "till wickedness was found in you." There was simply nothing in Ronald's writing that hinted toward the *fall* of Satan. Rather, there seemed to be a sense of *sympathy* behind the carefully chosen words used to describe such a lost "Golden Age."

When he read those two words, reinforcements of terrible vibrations hurriedly rushed to join the violent assault already in progress. He didn't even know what they meant, but for some reason they fell on him like contestants from one of those reality weight-loss shows, pinning him down into the chair.

And then the sliding glass door slammed shut behind him, nearly shattering from the impact.

Once his heart sank back into its rightful place, John turned around, almost *hoping* to see someone in his room. Even a man strapped with explosives and shouting, "*Allahu Akbar!*" would have been preferable to an invisible attic stalker closing doors on him. But no one was there. Opening the door, and for some reason expecting it to be cold to the touch, he stepped back inside and looked around the hotel room, wishing *someone* would jump out at him. After not finding a single trace of anyone having been in the room, he gathered his things and left. As far as he knew, heavy glass doors thrusting themselves closed was pretty abnormal. If not completely *paranormal*.

Speeding away on his scooter, he quickly put as much distance between himself and the hotel as possible. He didn't think the invisible intruder, whether a ghost or a time traveler equipped with a cloaking device, would come after him, but he wasn't taking any chances. Besides, the timing of the door closing had corresponded too perfectly with his third reading of the words *Golden Age*. It was getting harder to ignore now that something was indeed happening. Something from some other sphere was reaching its hands across the Great Divide and beginning to muddle in the world of the living...slamming doors shut, making VHS tapes, manipulating storm clouds...

Ignoring the speed limit over the Causeway, and against all reservation, he headed into the rising sun, Bermuda's oldest home waiting for him.

* * * *

Coming down Southside Road, John was surprised to spot Jackson on a scooter pulling away from the curb that lined the Carter House. John quickly dropped his head, and Jackson passed by without noticing him. He was heading back west.

John pulled up to a stone wall that was adorned with a circular plaque announcing "Carter House: One of Bermuda's Oldest Houses." Turning on the scooter's seat, John stared after Jackson, wondering what could've possibly brought him to this place. Another improbable coincidence.

Once he was sure that Jackson was too far away to notice him in a rearview mirror, he shut down the scooter. Entering a wooden gate and passing between two signs advertising the Carter House Museum, he followed a stone path between a palm tree and some other island foliage, coming to a white stone building accented with dark green shutters. But he didn't enter the building, just stood before it, trying to appreciate its four-hundred-year history. Though he hadn't doubted its existence, he nonetheless felt he needed to see it for himself to grasp the magnitude of what its history suggested. Not that he had any idea what that could be, but there was little doubt now that whatever was going on involved not just Henry, but the whole Carter name.

He spent another quiet moment in the early morning breeze that was blowing over the grassy hills around him, trying to imagine Christopher Carter living here on the island back in the early 1600s—first as one of many shipwrecked sailors, then as a conspirator, then as one of the three men remaining on the island, and then as the owner of Cooper's Island and governor of Bermuda itself.

Trying to downplay the nagging suspicion that the old home was a piece of his own heritage, he finally turned away from the house and decided to follow Jackson to his next stop.

It turned out to be St. Catherine's Beach.

John walked out onto the pink sand and took notice of Fort St. Catherine sitting above him on the left, marking Bermuda's northernmost point. Jackson was standing just inside the turquoise tide and letting the water swallow his bare ankles, his gaze cast away from John's approach and into the ocean ahead. But as John came up beside him, Jackson turned his head, peeking knowingly over his massive shoulder.

"You following me?" he asked.

John kicked his shoes off and walked into the surf, standing next to Jackson's towering frame. "Maybe."

Jackson set his stare back out to sea. "This is where Somers and his crew first came to shore."

Despite how badly John wanted to know what Jackson was doing at the Carter House (among hundreds of other things), he decided to wait until he heard from Frank before confronting his brother's friends with what he knew—or didn't know. "Was the *Sea Venture* the first ship to the islands?"

He shook his head. "A Spaniard named Juan de Bermudez is credited with discovering the island while sailing for Hispaniola in 1505. In 1515, Gonzales Ferdinando d'Oviedo spotted the island and tried to get some pigs on it."

"Yeah, pigs…" John nodded, feigning understanding. After all, that was just what he'd do if he found an island, drop off some bacon.

Jackson explained, "So that anyone who found themselves shipwrecked would have something to eat."

"That was nice of him."

"The winds wouldn't let him get close enough, though. The Spanish never tried to settle, but the Portuguese almost did in 1527, though they didn't actually make it to the island until they were shipwrecked themselves in 1543. They didn't stay long, built another boat, and sailed to Santo Domingo. They left a rock at Spittal Pond engraved with the monogram of *Rex Portugaliae*, the Portuguese Order of Christ." He was still staring out at the blue horizon, but it was evident that his thoughts were on something more than his monologue and the seascape that must have spawned it. "The French came and went, but it was 1609 that was to be the deciding year for Bermuda, colonization beginning three years later." He turned to face John. "First person to be born on the island was the daughter of John Rolfe, the guy who later married Pocahontas."

"Really?" John didn't have to fake interest this time.

"They named her Bermuda. She was also the first person to die on the island."

"They were on the *Sea Venture* with Somers and Carter?"

Jackson's own eyes betrayed him if only for an instant, confirming to John that indeed Christopher Carter was part of this bizarre puzzle—which, again, would only make his own relationship to the sailor all the more likely.

Recovering from the shock of hearing Carter's name, Jackson continued the conversation in stride. "Yeah, along with Captain Newport."

John shrugged, unfamiliar with the name.

"The pirate hired by British businessmen to raid Spanish ships and towns in the Caribbean, brought the first fleet of settlers to Jamestown?"

John shook his head.

"He eventually became a member of Virginia's governing council. Newport News is named after him. Anyway, Stephen Hopkins was on the ship, too."

"He related to Anthony Hopkins?" If he was, and John was really the offspring of Christopher Carter, then perhaps that would be incentive enough to arrange a meeting, maybe get a role in one of his films… He imagined a blooming friendship with the knighted actor, until a scene from *The Rite* transformed all such dreams into a twisted nightmare entitled *Hannibal: Exorcist Cannibal.*

"I don't think so. He's mostly known for his arrival to America on the *Mayflower* in 1620, and not for almost getting himself shot by Gates for wanting to stay on Bermuda—a mutinous offense."

"Who was Somers?"

"Sir George Somers, the Father of Bermuda, was just a wealthy pirate who happened to earn his fame by capturing a Spanish city in Venezuela. He was knighted in 1603 for saving a ship in Sir Walter Raleigh's fleet, was the mayor of Lyme Regis, and became a major player in the English company that colonized Virginia."

"And Gates?"

"Fought in the Dutch wars and sailed with Francis Drake to the Caribbean in 1585."

After a moment of silence, and the settling impression that he was about to lose Jackson's attention, John asked the next thing that came to mind. "Why so many forts on the island?" He indicated Fort St. Catherine with his eyes.

"Richard Moore, Bermuda's first governor, thought the Spanish might try taking the island."

"Did they?"

"They had a plan to, but the closest they ever came was to sail a ship close by on its way back from South America in 1614. Moore fired two shots at it from the fort on Castle Island and drove it back out to sea."

"So were the forts ever used?"

"There was a mini-civil war in 1646 between Puritans and non-Puritans; the Puritans were eventually expelled from the island. Bermuda almost went to war with the Bahamas in 1692. The French and Spanish captured the Turks Islands and New Providence during Queen Anne's War, forcing Bermuda to guard herself against a like invasion that never came; though when the war did end in 1713, a lot of the guys who'd made a living on the warships turned pirate and began raiding Bermuda's ships. Some of the captains who returned said that Blackbeard and Major Stede Bonnet were planning an attack on the island, to turn it into their base of operations. The forts were all garrisoned in anticipation of an attack that, again, never materialized. And then, of course, the US tried capturing her in 1779, nothing coming of that either. In 1812, Bermuda played a major role in blockading the American coast, and every time it looked like we might go at it with Britain again, the forts were improved. In 1826, a major defensive military strategy was hatched that transformed a lot of the island. Prospect was turned into a military instillation, South Shore Road was built to defend the beaches, more islands were fortified, and the Royal Navy built a huge fortification at the tip of Ireland Island.

"In 1861, a week after the Civil War started, Lincoln established a blockade on all the southern ports, and blockade runners were going back and forth between the Southern states and Bermuda, maintaining the Confederates' reliance on European suppliers and Europe's dependence on Southern cotton. And then during World War II, we finally came as allies, set up all kinds of military bases, paved roads, built the airfield—which took connecting a few smaller islands to St. David's and adding about a hundred and fifty acres to it."

Finally, John turned and looked up into Jackson's face. "How do you know all this?"

Jackson tilted his face downward at him. "I told you, I've been here before."

"Lots of people have been here before, *Jack*."

But before Jackson could reply, John's cell phone rang in his pocket.

"Hello?" he answered, not recognizing the incoming number. "Yeah. Is that a fact? No. I will, thanks." He hung up and returned the phone to his pocket while a new appreciation for the man standing next to him began taking hold of his unease. Through a narrowed and icy stare, John told Jackson that the call was from a police officer he'd met the night before and that he had some information regarding Henry's stay on the island.

Jackson just waited for John to elaborate.

But instead, John shrugged toward the sunrise. "I'd better be getting back. Don't want to be late for our *meeting*." And then he turned and headed back to his waiting scooter, pausing only to slip on his shoes before driving away from the behemoth's stare.

Minutes later, just about to cross the Causeway, Jackson drove up beside him.

Over the whine of the scooters' engines, Jackson yelled, "It's supposed to be getting pretty nasty." He nodded his head forward to the western sky, where there were indeed darkening clouds congregating. "Dress appropriately." And then he throttled back, falling in behind him.

Coming off the Causeway, John headed straight for the hotel, expecting Jackson to do the same. But Jackson missed the turn, continuing west. John didn't care; he was done following him. He'd already learned more than enough for right now.

* * * *

As John loaded his backpack with an extra pair of clothes, his Bible, the map, and *Journey with the Gods*, his phone began vibrating. It was a text message from Pastor Brian, responding to the message he'd sent the night before. It read:

SOME BELIEVE HELL BENEATH OCEAN IN CENTER OF EARTH. REV 9 AND REV 20:13 TOGETHER MAY LEND CREDENCE TO VIEW.

John pulled the Bible back out of the bag and turned to the indicated passages, first reading Revelation 9.

The fifth angel sounded his trumpet, and I saw a star that had fallen from the sky to the earth. The star was given the key to the shaft of the Abyss. When he opened the Abyss, smoke rose from it like the smoke from a gigantic furnace. The sun and sky were darkened by the smoke from the Abyss. And out of the smoke locusts came down upon the earth and were given power like that of scorpions of the earth…

They had as king over them the angel of the Abyss, whose name in Hebrew is Abaddon, and in Greek, Apollyon…

He flipped the pages a few times and found chapter twenty.

And I saw an angel coming down out of heaven, having the key to the Abyss and holding in his hand a great chain. He seized the dragon, that ancient serpent, who is the devil, or Satan, and bound him for a thousand years. He threw him into the Abyss, and locked and sealed it over him, to keep him from deceiving the nations anymore until the thousand years were ended…

When the thousand years are over, Satan will be released from his prison and will go out to deceive the nations in the four corners of the earth—Gog and Magog—to gather them for battle… But fire came down from heaven and devoured them. And the devil, who deceived them, was thrown into the lake of burning sulfur…

Then I saw a great white throne and him who was seated upon it. Earth and sky fled from his presence, and there was no place for them. And I saw the dead, great and small, standing before the throne, and books were opened. Another book was opened, which is the book of life. The dead were judged according to what they had done as recorded in the books. The sea gave up the dead that were in it, and death and Hades gave up the dead that were in them, and each person was judged according to what he had done. Then death and Hades were thrown into the lake of fire…

John texted back: DONT GET IT.

A few minutes later, the phone vibrated with a message offering a further, and rather lengthy, clarification.

ABYSS IS DESCRIBED AS BEING "FIERY HOLLOW IN CENTER OF EARTH" BUT CAN ALSO BE USED FOR "DEPTHS OF THE SEA." SEPTUAGINT HAS ABYSS AS BEING THE DEEP THAT DARKNESS WAS HOVERING

> OVER IN GEN 1 AND THE GREAT DEEP OF WHOSE FOUNTAINS WERE BROKEN UP DURING FLOOD. SOME THINK THE ABYSS IN CENTER OF EARTH IS COVERED AND SECURED BY DEPTHS OF SEA—THIS BEING THE REASON THAT (AFTER PRISONERS OF ABYSS ARE THROWN INTO LAKE OF FIRE) THERE IS NO MORE SEA IN RENOVATED EARTH. ALSO TRANSLATION OF "HADES" INTO "HELL" IN REV 20 IS SUSPECT AND MAY BE MORE APPROPRTLY RENDERED AS "THE UNSEEN WORLD." IT IS

The rest was continued in another incoming text.

> COMMONLY BELIEVED THAT "SEA GIVING UP ITS DEAD" IS ONLY REFERRING TO THOSE WHO DIED IN SEA. BUT IT IS ODD THAT THERE IS NO MENTION OF EARTH GIVING UP ITS DEAD TOO. INSTEAD OF SEA BEING CONNECTED WITH LAND IN THE TEXT IT IS CONNECTED WITH DEATH AND THE UNSEEN WORLD… THUS SOME BELIEVE THEY ARE THE DISEMBODIED SPIRITS FIRST SENT TO ABYSS—WHICH WOULD BE WHY THEY ARE FIRST TO BE JUDGED.

Another text.

> MOST COMENTATORS STRESS THE INSANITY OF THE ENEMY WHEN COMENTING ON THE DEMONS POSESSING THE SWINE AND SENDING THEM OFF THE CLIFFS TO DROWN IN THE SEA. BUT WHAT IF THE SEA IS WHERE THEY WANTED TO GO? MAYBE THERE IS A CONNECTION BETWEEN THAT AND MAT 12:43 ESV.

He flipped to the verse and read, *When an impure spirit comes out of a person, it goes through arid places seeking rest and does not find it.*

He texted back that he only had an NIV handy, and Brian responded:

> WHEN THE UNCLEAN SPIRIT HAS GONE OUT OF A PERSON, IT PASSES THROUGH WATERLESS PLACES SEEKING REST, BUT FINDS NONE.

Brian then asked why the sudden interest in such things. But John didn't respond. Instead, he sent a text message to Kristen that simply told her that he loved her. And then he finished getting ready for a day that would no doubt be throwing everything it possibly could at his stained-glass construction of reality. He dressed in dark blue jeans, brown boots, and a gray T-shirt with a black windbreaker overtop before being ready to meet the SEALs in the lobby half an hour earlier than scheduled.

Sitting on the bed, leaning forward with his elbows resting on his knees, he was staring out through the glass door that some phantom had slammed shut earlier that morning. Maybe Bill Cosby. Or James Stewart's invisible bunny, Harvey. Or, if it had been a rabbit, perhaps it was the one shown in the *Donnie Darko* movie, though he hoped not. If he ever met that thing in a nightmare, he'd never risk falling asleep again. It could have been Marty McFly searching for a flux capacitor to correct the time-space continuum, though why he would be looking for it here wasn't exactly clear. Maybe it was Kevin Bacon reprising his role in *Hollow Man 4*, or even James T. Kirk coming to visit the Dolphin Quest but miss-teleporting into his room, slamming the door in frustration and cursing Scotty before beaming back to the Enterprise. Though scores of movies supplied him with faces for the formless invaders, it was Hollywood's take on exorcism that sent spiders crawling down his back. He looked past the door and to the island-riddled horizon beyond it. As his mind reeled to and fro, he caught a glimpse of the two books still sitting beside the bed.

Minutes later, he was on his scooter and looking for a post office, the books in his possession.

SEVEN

11:58 a.m. 22nd day of May. Grotto Bay Beach Resort, Hamilton Parish, Bermuda

Entering the lobby empty-handed, John found Chris, Nick, Hunter, and Paul already waiting for him. But no Jackson. John ignored them and walked toward the elevator, prompting Hunter to stand.

"Hey, where you going?"

John hit the round button and, as soon as the elevator doors opened, stepped in. "I'll be right back," he muttered. As the doors closed on the scene in the lobby, he saw Hunter look down at his wristwatch.

It was 12:04 when John walked back into the lobby with his backpack slung over his shoulder. "Where's Jackson?" he asked, taking note of his still-lingering absence.

"He's gonna meet us there. Let's go," Paul commanded, leading them out the doors and to a waiting taxi.

Once the minivan was headed southwest toward Hamilton, John decided to break the uncomfortable silence by inquiring about the afternoon.

Chris, who had been staring out the window beside him, answered, "We're taking a ferry across the Great Sound to Somerset. Find this author guy and see what he has to say."

It was impossible to miss the atmosphere surrounding the ex-SEALs. They were all staring quietly out the windows, their faces set like stone. If John didn't know any better (which he didn't), he'd assume they were mentally preparing themselves for a bank robbery or some other type of tactical mission, ski masks about to be pulled down over their faces and weapons cocked.

"Anyone gonna tell me what's really going on?" John asked, looking them over with a challenging eye.

Hunter and Paul moved their gaze from Hamilton Parish and set it, full of suspicion, on John. But they maintained their eerie silence.

"Wonderful. Thanks. No, really, I mean it. Thank you for bringing me all the way over here to play games. I love games."

They drove through the capital, taking Victoria Street west over to Parliament Street and then south toward the water. As they crossed over Church Street, they passed a white Methodist church that was fitted with a giant steeple. John's attention was captured by the crucifix atop it, a sense of comfort that he wouldn't usually associate with the instrument of torture suddenly filling him with reassurance, as if the nail-pierced hands that had once been hammered to it were now resting on his shoulders, encouraging him. *If God be for us, then who can be against us?* But then, just as quickly, another verse came crashing into his mind, this one from Paul's message to the church in Ephesus. *For we wrestle not against flesh and blood, but against principalities, against powers, against the rulers of the darkness of this world, against spiritual wickedness in high places.* And though he was assured that neither death, life, angels, principalities, powers, things present or things to come, height, depth, or any other creature could separate him from the love of God, those words—*principalities and powers* and *spiritual wickedness in high places*—continued to slither through the standing hair on his arms and neck.

As they passed the Parliament Building and crossed Reid Street, the Cabinet Building came up on their left. It seemed to be a smaller version of the White House, the Union Jack flying high from the flagpole erected in front of it. A small obelisk and cenotaph also decorated the surrounding property, but John seemed to be the only one who appreciated that little detail—perhaps because the monolith had become familiar to him through a past experience he was forever trying to forget.

They turned onto Front Street, leaving the government buildings behind, and found themselves between the water and large pale-colored buildings that stood lining the street. Tiny cars, motorcycles, and scooters stood in rows that ran up and down both sides of the road while another cruise ship loomed over the city, resting comfortably in the harbor.

John followed Chris out of the taxi and to the ferry terminal, oblivious to the multitudes of shops around him, focusing instead on the SEALs' choice of clothing and wondering if the impending weather was really to blame for it.

Hunter was wearing jeans, hiking boots, and a dark blue denim jacket over a black T-shirt. A desert bush hat hung loosely from his neck and was resting between his shoulder blades. He looked ready for some jungle hiking…if only Bermuda had a jungle.

Chris' face was hidden beneath the brim of a baseball cap, and his black ribbed tank top was mostly concealed by a gray hooded sweatshirt. Loose khakis and combat boots suggested that he was ready for some off-roading as well.

Nick and Paul were both wearing camouflage pants and zipped polyester jackets. Boots also covered their feet, black bush hats hanging from their necks.

Moving his scrutiny away from the four men walking beside him, John looked up to the darkening sky, again wondering if the forecast alone could account for their choice of attire. And then, as they approached a couple of benches, Paul stepped in front of him.

There was no mistaking the bulge positioned at the small of his back. A gun.

But just then, the ferry appeared from the west, leading a wake of churning water toward them. Shifting his eyes from the ferry back to the gun and then back to the ferry again, John sensed that the boat was bringing more than just the dark storm clouds with it. He quickly pondered Paul's pistol. It implied a more physical threat than the one he'd been fearing from the shadow stalkers. It was a development he almost welcomed. Unlike ancient gods trying to swat him out of the sky, he had been trained to survive bullets. He chose to sit on the discovery for now, unwilling to get into a confrontation with Paul until he had a better understanding of what he should be trying to get out of.

After the ferry unloaded its passengers, the five men boarded with a crowd of other tourists. Paul led the search party up to the second level, and John took a seat by the rail. When Paul sat down in front of him, he turned his attention to the crew helping an elderly couple onto the boat so as not to stare at the shape of Paul's pistol. Boring of that event, he allowed his eyes to drift away and caught Hunter staring at him from across the aisle. It was an odd look that John couldn't interpret. He held Hunter's stare until Hunter was forced to look away.

Thirty-five minutes later, they were leaving the ferry at Watford Bridge and walking up Middle Road toward the bus stop. The wait was a short one, and soon John was standing in the aisle of the crowded bus, holding on to the metal bar above him. An old dark-skinned Bermudian stood up and offered him his seat, but John politely declined.

Stepping off the bus, Hunter took a moment to look around and gather his bearings. "Okay. We follow that street into Somerset Village. His house is pink with white shutters and a white roof. Should be on the right."

With the bus pulling away from the curb behind them, Nick asked, "How far?"

"How should I know?"

They walked in single file along the road for nearly ten minutes before they came to a row of houses. The pink house with the white roof had a brick-enclosed driveway with a small black car parked in it.

"Guess this is it," Chris commented as he skipped up the steps and knocked on the door before anyone could even think to stop him.

As they waited, everyone took notice of a subtle change in the air. The leaves on the trees were beginning to rustle, pine branches gently swaying back and forth in the breeze. The bad weather was starting to fidget in its sleep.

When the door finally opened, but before John could see whoever had opened it, he was struck by a sudden thought. What if Ronald had actually killed Henry and now Henry's friends, one of which was presently armed, were about to exact vengeance on the murderer? And what if the reason they had wanted him to come so badly was for the sole purpose of getting away with it, making it look like *he* was avenging *his* brother? It was something he didn't think they'd mind pinning on a soldier turned conscientious objector.

A raindrop struck him in the forehead as Ronald appeared in the doorway, Hunter attempting to explain who they were and why they were there. Not paying attention to the exchange, John looked more closely at Ronald and noticed that he didn't appear a day older than in the picture on the back of his books.

"Come on, Johnny," Nick said, motioning him up the stairs with his handless arm.

Taking a deep breath and saying a silent prayer, John passed Nick and entered the house. He knew there was no turning back now, though he hadn't completely ruled out trying.

Ronald Douglas Carter looked to be somewhere in his mid-thirties. He had a handsome face that was decorated with black hair and a neatly trimmed beard. He was almost as tall as Jackson, and the British accent in which he spoke only made his persona all the more exquisite. He seemed to be the perfect gentleman, walking smoothly right out of a Hollywood set. He smiled at his unexpected company as they came and stood in the little foyer of his dwelling place.

"Well, you fellows are a menacing sight, aren't you?" he said, noting their own physical presence. "And just what is it that you think I can do for you?"

Hunter stepped forward. "A friend of ours sailed here a few weeks ago. Had some things he wanted to talk to you about. We're wondering if he ever showed up and if you know where he went after he left."

Ronald put a hand to his chin, his striking blue eyes narrowing with thought. "Believe it or not, quite a few people show up at my door wanting to talk about my writings. What was his name?"

"Henry," John said. "Henry Carter."

Ronald moved his head slightly to the side so that he could get a better view of who had spoken. When his eyes fell on John, a delicate grin turned the corner of his mouth. Then he turned away from them and began walking into another room. "Come in. I have some tea on."

As they all gathered around the kitchen table, some sitting and some leaning against the wall, Paul asked again if he had met with Henry.

"As a matter of fact, I do recall our conversation." He poured some tea into a few teacups and handed them to whoever was polite enough to reach out for them.

John wasn't. There was something about Ronald that he didn't like, and as he adjusted his backpack and folded his arms, he asked, "And what was that like?"

"Oh, why he had some questions about certain things he'd read in my books."

John was about to pursue the issue some more, but a picture hanging on a wall in the next room suddenly caught his attention. Without realizing it, his feet began taking him closer to the framed black-and-white photograph and away from the new conversation that another of Paul's questions had just spawned. Stealing a glance over his shoulder, it appeared that he'd escaped the kitchen unnoticed.

When he stood before the picture, his hands began shaking.

It was an old photograph of a fossilized body lying inside a wooden casket, its hands resting on its stomach. Only, the casket was standing up on its end and leaning against the back of a railroad car. Both the casket and the person within it stood taller than the car, even at such an angle. To communicate scale, there was a ladder standing straight up alongside the train car and the casket. John held out his trembling finger and touched the glass. As soon as his flesh contacted the image, a sudden voice came from behind him, nearly startling him to death. Somehow, he was able to keep himself from turning around.

"Twelve feet and two inches tall, if you believe it," Ronald commented from an awkward distance comprising of just two feet. "Discovered in Ireland in 1895 but supposedly disappeared after the picture was taken, though it was said to have made its rounds in Dublin, Manchester, and Liverpool first."

"Is it real?" he asked, still staring at it.

His large shoulders shrugged under the blue polo sweater he was wearing. "That depends on who you ask." He paused and, before taking a sip of tea, added with the faintest whisper of a smile, "There are six toes on its right foot."

Though John did the best he could to hide the surprise he felt explode in his chest, he knew he'd failed miserably.

Ronald's ghost of a smile now materialized in the flesh. "It's hard to say whether or not it's a fake. There have certainly been a few of them, fakes, that is. The Cardiff Giant, in 1869, was one of the biggest hoaxes in US history."

John managed to pry his eyes off the image, finally turning to see Ronald standing there rocking back and forth on his heels in anticipation of the next question. He was still standing just two feet away. John could actually taste him, whatever cologne he was wearing attacking the roof of his mouth. But his back was to the wall, and he wasn't sure the invasion of personal space warranted a violent separation. "Cardiff Giant?" he managed to ask, playing right into the author's rather large hands.

"I won't bore you with the details, but it concerned an atheist named George Hull who got into a discussion with a Christian minister over the Bible's literal credibility. They were speaking specifically of the sixth chapter in Genesis, on whether or not there were really giants on the earth."

The odds that this particularly obscure passage would keep coming up like this, and within such a short period of time, were absurd even without allowing into the equation what he'd seen in Afghanistan. John was beginning to get the terrible feeling that somehow things might be more about *him* than Henry.

Ronald continued, his accent polished with a sense of romanticism that made ignoring him impossible. He explained the entire hoax that had ended up involving P. T. Barnum and a court ruling.

John gave the picture one last glance and shuddered before following Ronald back into the company of the other four guests.

When they entered the kitchen, Hunter had a look waiting for John that rebuked him for wandering off. John gave him a wink.

"So," Nick said, trying again to discover what they'd come for, "do you know where he went?"

"Who?" Ronald asked, taking a seat.

"Henry."

"Ah. Henry Carter." He drew out the phonetics of the name as he crossed one leg over the other, tilting his head back and staring in thought up to the ceiling. But before the ceiling gave way and the heavens parted to reveal an answer, a knock sounded at the door.

"It seems as though I am a popular man today." He smiled. "Excuse me." He left the room.

As he left, Chris whispered, "I bet he has no problem with getting the ladies," referring to the suave sexuality that seemed to radiate from the author.

Peeking his head back around the corner, and with a strange twinkle in his eye, Ronald exclaimed rather boldly, "You have no idea."

While Ronald was busy answering the door, John stepped back into the living room and began examining the titles of books that were stacked side by side within several tall bookshelves. The subject matter Ronald was apparently interested in stretched from one end of the occult to the other end of science. Numerology, astral projection, psychokinesis...and then astrology and alchemy transitioned downward into quantum physics, wormholes, dark matter, string theory, time travel, alternate universe theories, geology, astronomy, and even underwater exploration. Turning to another bookshelf, John read even more strange titles, these encompassing more of history, philosophy, and literature than methodology and science—UFOs, secret societies, mystery religions, esoteric wisdom, ancient calendar systems, and megalithic archeology. But there was one shelf that contained only religious texts. The Book of the Dead, the Pyramid Texts, the Bible, the Apocrypha and Pseudepigrapha, the Koran, and a score of other religious accounts ranging from Roman, Greek, and Hindu mythologies to the sacred texts belonging to the Sumerians, Aztecs, Chinese, and Native Americans. There were two other bookshelves across the room, but John traded the knowledge of what they held for a specific book that caught his eye. He cautiously pulled it from the shelf, holding it in his hands. The title was in French and was perfectly handwritten, inlaid with gold. Though he couldn't be exactly certain as to what it said, he knew as much as *Giants…Civilization…and Age of Enlightenment.* John opened the hardbound book and found the crisp pages to be yellow with age, the handwritten text faded in many spots. He searched the book for a date, a publisher, and even its place of origin, but there wasn't even an author's name to which the material had been credited. The book must have been rebound, perhaps even a few times. He carefully returned it to the shelf, painfully aware of the distinct—and even *ancient*—aura it seemed to have about it, afraid that if he opened it again, he might be sucked inside and lost forever in some dark fantasy.

A commotion in the foyer drew his attention back to the aspects of reality he was accustomed to, and he went to investigate. As he entered one side of the kitchen, he was surprised to see Jackson and Ronald exchanging hugs and handshakes. Even the others seemed taken aback by this.

"You two know each other?" Hunter asked, an expression of bewilderment painted across his dark features.

Ronald smiled. "Of course! Jack and I spent many days together back in…" He looked at Jackson for help. "What year was that anyway?"

Jackson laughed. "I see you've met my friends."

"Ah, yes. They were telling me about Henry. Is it true that he is missing?"

Jackson nodded his head. "Yeah. So, you talked to him?"

"Yes, he visited me. We spent the entire day in conversation. You were very wise to send him my way. He had lots of questions."

John saw Chris and Hunter looking at each other as if this was all new information to them.

Nick held up his missing hand. "Hold on a sec. Jack, you wanna tell us just what's going on?"

"Later." It was the impatient and hushing way he spewed it that made Nick's eyes turn cold.

"Would you like some tea?" Ronald asked Jackson.

"You have a bathroom that I can use?" John interrupted before Jackson could respond.

Ronald pointed out of the kitchen. "Second door on your right side."

Once he was leaning over the sink and staring into the mirror, John began splashing cold water in his face. This just couldn't be happening. It had to be a new part to his nightmare.

Flushing the toilet, he walked back into the hallway, where he noticed that the door beside it stood slightly ajar. Not able to stifle his curiosity, he pushed it open and entered.

There were books stacked in piles from one end of the room to the other. Atlases, maps, old shipping charts… There were maps pinned up on the walls, too, lines of string dividing them up into hundreds of shapes. Some of the maps were modern while others looked to have been preserved from the earliest days of sea exploration. One map in particular caught his attention. As he moved closer to it, he accidentally bumped into a wooden desk. Looking down, he discovered pages and pages of handwritten notes scattered across its surface. After quickly leafing through them, he discovered that the handwriting was exactly the same handwriting used in the old book out in the living room. And though these notes were mostly written in English, there were also phrases penned in French and some smaller footnotes in Hebrew or Aramaic.

While sorting through the papers, he managed to catch a glimpse of what looked like a map beneath them. It seemed to cover the entire top of the desk. Quickly clearing the papers away, he saw that it was a map of the Atlantic. A red triangle was smeared over it, its sides extending from Bermuda to Miami to Puerto Rico and back up to Bermuda again. The top of the triangle was sectioned off by a line drawn parallel to its base. And, just like the reverse of the United States' Great Seal, there was an eye floating within it. Only this eye resembled more of an Egyptian hieroglyphic than that of the Masonic art he'd witnessed in his grandfather's house as a child. But even more disturbing was what was written around the triangle. Along the Bermuda-Miami line was written out, DOORWAY. Across the base was the word, TO. And following the angle of the Bermuda-Puerto Rico line, it said, HELL. At the bottom of the map, and outside its blue boundaries, were very small columns of names written in all different languages. John knew them to be the names of ships and planes. Judging from Ronald's book, he figured them to be the names of those gone missing. And then John noticed that a corner of the map was turned slightly upward, revealing more writing on its reverse. Grabbing the right end of the map, he pulled it back across the desk to reveal its blank underbelly—only it wasn't blank. From one end of the map to the other, and from top to bottom, were lists of names…thousands of them. The print, however, was so miniscule that he could hardly read it. Dates were affixed to some of the names, the list chronological.

John spotted the year 1945 and recognized the name beside it as belonging to one of the pilots from Flight 19. Strangely, though, if indeed this was a list compiled of those who had vanished along with their vessels, the rest of the pilots were nowhere to be seen. He followed his finger to the end of the last list, to the most recent date. His finger jumped off the paper as if electrocuted by the final name it touched.

Hanging there at the end of the page, in small English print and staring directly at him, was his brother's name.

HENRY REVERE CARTER.

Heart pounding in his chest and hands clenched into fists at his sides, he stared ahead, peering into the other world the old map had suddenly opened a portal to, its oceans alive with a psychic tempest bombarding his sanity.

"The seventeenth century Jesuit priest Athanasius Kircher drew that map."

Again, the sudden sound of Ronald's voice made his heart stop. Slowly, and still shaking, he turned away from the map Ronald assumed he had been looking at. "It's amazing," he whispered. He had no idea why it would be amazing but needed to keep Ronald's attention away from the desktop and the evidence of his snooping.

"The map shows the lost continent of Atlantis. Kircher claimed that it was based on a map the Romans stole from Egypt and later discovered in the cellars of the Vatican." His eyes were twinkling. "What is even stranger than Atlantis being on the map, however, is that north is pointing *downward*, to the bottom of the map."

"That *is* strange," John muttered, just wanting to get out of the room…out of the *house*.

"The one next to it is the 1531 map of Oronteus Finnaeus."

John adjusted his eyes, just playing along. "I don't recognize the area."

"That's because it isn't covered in ice. Do you notice all the mountain ranges and the rivers flowing to the sea? All these things are now covered with miles of ice."

"How is that possible?" *Keep his attention on the wall…*

"Apparently, the map was made by someone who was familiar with Antarctica a very long time ago." He pointed. "Look to your right. That is Philippe Buache's map, made in 1737. It actually shows Antarctica divided into two large islands, something that was only recently learned. His map must have been based on even earlier records than Finnaeus'." He took a step farther into the room. "But over here is the famous Piri Reis map of 1513, discovered in Istanbul in 1929." He walked beside it, motioning at its detail. "You see that it shows South America, part of West Africa, and part of the ice-free coast of Antarctica? Reis gave the credit for his map to twenty other maps he claimed dated back to the times of Alexander the Great. But we all know that, even at that time, Antarctica was already covered in ice. So the maps that he used to make this one must *also* have come from much, much older sources." He smiled. "I know what you are thinking. How is that possible when writing itself wasn't invented until the Sumerians?"

Actually, that was the furthest thing from John's mind.

"Part of his map was based off another map that was actually in the possession of Christopher Columbus. It is believed that the maps came from the Library of Alexandria and ended up in Constantinople. The center of the map, Johnny, is synchronized with the center of Upper Egypt." He turned away from the map and began walking back toward the door. "The ancient maps are accurate to within one-half of a single degree of longitude, something not achievable until the chronometer was invented in the eighteenth century. Also recorded are islands no longer existing, West Africa with an ample water supply, and lakes in the Sahara." He walked out of the room and waved for John to follow. "But come, let us rejoin your friends."

* * * *

It was a pointless trip, and now they were just wasting time. Ronald had watched Henry sail out of the harbor weeks ago and hadn't seen or heard from him since. And now they were all drinking tea. But something else wasn't right here. Invisible bunnies and fertile Antarcticas aside, John had warning bells sounding off in his gut. Though Ronald had no other information to offer, John had the distinct feeling that the author was trying to keep them there. Of course, that didn't make sense, *couldn't* make sense, yet story after story just kept rolling off the guy's tongue, more tea being poured to the persistent reassurance that Henry was probably fine.

Finally, John had had enough.

"Why did Henry want to see you?" he snapped in the middle of another boring story.

Not fazed by the interruption, Ronald answered calmly, "He was interested in my writings."

John's eyes were barely visible through the slits of his eyelids. "And which ones, exactly?"

"It would be hard to explain to someone who hasn't read them."

"Actually," John stated, "there was one question I had about your writings. You said something about demons, how they're characterized apart from fallen angels."

Jackson looked shocked, and he quickly tried to interject another thought into the building tension.

Ronald waved him off, wanting to answer the question. "Well," he began, "the New Testament describes demons as spirits, doesn't it? And angels as beings clothed with spiritual bodies, not as disembodied spirits. The Gospel of Luke and the book of Philippians attest to that. It is also clear from such passages as Acts 23:9 that the Jews believed in such distinctions. The Sadducees believed that neither angels *nor* demons existed, a clarification that seems a bit unnecessary if the two were believed to have been the same. But aside from the biblical—" he waved his hand in circles, searching for the appropriate word "*—discrimination* against demons, Homer simply applied the term to the gods. And Plato understood them to be disembodied spirits privileged with superior knowledge. In fact, he said the interaction between man and the gods was carried out through the mediation of demons, teaching that they were the interpreters of prayers and sacrifices to the gods on behalf of man and the interpreters of the commands and the rewards of sacrifice to man on behalf of the gods."

"What's he talking about?" Paul growled, wondering what ocean of weirdness John had just uncorked.

But Ronald pressed on. "It is believed that these demons are actually the spirits of men who lived during the Golden Age and, having been canonized as heroes throughout the world, are now acting as deities. In his *Works and Days*,

Hesiod wrote: 'First of all the immortals, who possess the mansions of Olympus, made a golden race of articulate-speaking men…'" Ronald closed his eyes as if he were an English professor worshipping Shakespeare and continued reciting from memory the ancient words. "'These lived in the time of Cronos. Like gods they spent their lives, with hearts void of care, apart and altogether free from toils and trouble. All blessings were theirs. And so, they occupied their cultivated lands in tranquility and peace with many goods, being rich in flocks and dear to the blessed gods. But after that earth had covered this generation, they indeed by the counsels of mighty Zeus became demons, kindly ones, haunting the earth, being guardians of mortal men…and going to and fro everywhere upon the earth, watching both the decisions of justice and harsh deeds, and are dispensers of riches. Such a royal prerogative is theirs.'"

"You believe that?" John asked.

Ronald opened his eyes and smiled patiently. "I would encourage you to read the account in Genesis, of the firmament being formed, a little more carefully. And then ask yourself, why is it that the Hebrew God did not pronounce *this* day's work to be good?"

"Why don't you just tell me now?"

But he only smiled.

John stood, his patience completely running dry. "You said you watched Henry sail away?"

"That's right."

He looked around the room, at the others. "Then there's nothing more we need from him, is there?"

"You must have been close to him," Ronald said, a mock sympathy forming on his face.

"Henry was—*is* his brother," Chris tried explaining.

Something happened to Ronald's eyes at that moment, something that John couldn't quite explain but that woke up the spiders weaving webs down his vertebrae nonetheless.

"Are you sure about that?" he asked, staring.

Jackson smiled despite the expression that floated in his eyes, one that revealed how much he loathed the situation being taken out of his control. "Yeah, he's sure. John Carter."

"Carter, huh? You know, my last name is Carter as well."

"What's your point?" John asked.

"No point. I just find it interesting, is all."

"Yeah, well, thanks for all the stories." And he walked out the front door, letting it slam shut behind him.

* * * *

He was almost to the bus stop on Mangrove Bay Road when Hunter came running up behind him.

"Hold on, John!"

John turned, light traffic and raindrops decorating his immediate surroundings. He focused on Hunter. "Let me ask you a question, Hunter. How did Jackson get you here?"

"*Get* me here? Henry's like a brother to me. No one needed to *get* me here, Johnny." He was implying that because John *did* have to be made to *get* here, he was less of a brother to Henry than were his teammates.

"Then why am *I* here?"

Hunter paused, sighing. "He said you knew about the stuff Henry was into. He thought you'd know where to look."

"Know where to look?" John blurted. "What does that even mean? Do I look like I know where to look? And even if I did, I don't recall anyone asking me!"

"You read the guy's books."

It sounded like an accusation. "I bought them last night, because I wanted to know who he was and why Henry would want to see him."

Hunter seemed to ponder his own words before speaking them. "Do you have the dreams?"

"What dreams?"

"Henry had these dreams. And, after he found your father's diary, they just kind of consumed him."

"What're you talking about?"

A pause. "You really don't know any of this?"

"I haven't spoken to Henry since my father's funeral. I don't know about any dreams or diaries. I don't know why I'm here." He lowered his voice. "You didn't know that Jackson knew this guy?"

Hunter shook his head.

"Well, I think I'm going to make my exit from this charade a little early." He turned back to the bus stop.

"Wait. Ronald said there was a thick fog over the water that day. He said Henry's boat might have struck the reef."

"I thought he said Henry was"—he pretended a British accent— "'probably just fine.'"

"Listen, just come out with us. We probably won't find anything, but if we do…he's your brother. You should be there."

John saw the others, spearheaded by Jackson, approaching them from over Hunter's shoulder. "Whatever." He went and sat on the empty bench, waiting for the bus.

A minute later, Jackson sat down beside him. "I acquired a boat. We're gonna go sail around the reefs, maybe do some diving. If we don't find anything, then you can leave. How 'bout it?"

"Fine, Jack."

A pink bus took them all back to the ferry.

* * * *

His tingling senses having turned to raging volcanoes, John slung his backpack over his shoulder and walked off the ferry. Black clouds were stretching across the sky like an insect plague, the wind pulling at his jacket and pushing whitecaps across the harbor.

"You want to dive in this?" John asked.

Though they didn't say anything, John could tell that a few of the others shared the same concern.

"Weather's supposed to be bad the next couple of days. This is the only chance we're gonna get, Johnny. We'll beat the storm and be back before it makes landfall. Don't worry."

They climbed into a taxi.

"Grotto Bay Resort," Jackson told the driver.

* * * *

They bypassed the hotel and followed Jackson straight to the private beach, making their way through lounge chairs, umbrellas, and grounded kayaks to the dock that sat stretching out into the harbor. A mega sailing yacht, over a hundred feet long, sat resting at its end, rocking gently in the waves.

"A bit excessive, isn't it, Jack?" Chris asked.

Jackson ignored him. "Come on!" He urged them to hurry as he walked briskly down the wooden planks. "Everything's ready to go."

This is apparently what Jackson had been doing in the time between the Causeway and Ronald's house. But if that were so, if he indeed had arranged for the yacht and scuba equipment, intent on sailing out to the reef ahead of the storm, *before* Ronald had even suggested checking the reef, then Jackson either had an inclination on his own about the reef, or they were going sailing for some other reason.

And then another thought struck him. Whereas his theory about Ronald being Henry's murderer and the SEALs being out for vengeance seemed silly now, John was wondering if perhaps *they* could have killed Henry. It was an outlandish thought but one that actually fit all the known facts surprisingly well. After all, they were the only ones claiming to know anything about Henry's whereabouts. So, what if they killed him (for whatever reason) and this was all just part of a ploy to wash their hands of it? What if they had taken the liberty of making reservations for him in a nice and cozy private section of coral reef, still planning on pinning Henry's murder on him after the "accident" he was sure to have?

But as the boat grew nearer and its name came into focus across its stern, John found his feet suddenly fastened to the dock, his heart lodged in his throat.

Stenciled in big blue letters was the boat's name. *Gegenes.* The name Frank had called him with earlier that morning.

Henry's boat.

Frank said that, according to the records, the boat should still be at its quay, but when he went to check for himself, there was only a vacant spot of water.

"What's the problem, John?" Paul called back to him. "Let's go!"

And then John began running down the dock. He jumped into the boat, shoved past Chris and Nick, and grabbed Jackson, spinning him around. "Where'd you get this boat?"

Jackson extended his hands into John's chest and threw him backward. "Shut up, Johnny. And sit down."

But John stood up. "Did you kill him?" He shoved him into the side of the boat and against the railing.

Jackson turned and unleashed a shot to John's head that sent him reeling to the deck. While struggling to get back to his knees, John saw another one of Jackson's punches coming straight for him…

And then darkness.

* * * *

It felt like he'd been unconscious for hours, but as he looked around, he saw that they were only just leaving Castle Harbor, sailing between a few small islands, King's Castle situated to his right. Struggling to his feet, he brought his hand up to his jaw and winced. But a surge of anger erased the pain just as quickly, and he set out to find Jackson. He was halfway to the front of the boat when Hunter came up from behind and grabbed him by the shoulder.

"Where do you think you're going?" he asked.

John shook Hunter's hand away, turned back around, and came face-to-face with Chris.

"Listen," Chris said, holding up his hands. "Just go along with him for now, okay? We don't need an incident out here."

John stared into Chris' eyes. "And just what exactly are we doing out here?"

"He wants to dive on the reef to make sure Henry didn't go down on it."

"Well, I find that *very* hard to believe…considering we're on Henry's boat right *now*."

"What're you talking about?" Hunter demanded.

John explained, "I met a police officer last night who promised to look into it for me. He called me this morning and confirmed that Henry Carter arrived on the *Gegenes* and that, although there's no record of him leaving port, both he and his boat are gone."

Chris looked at Hunter, an expression of disconcertment invading his tanned face. Then they both turned their heads toward the front of the sailing yacht as John's words sank home.

"You know we aren't out here because Ronald suggested it. Jackson was setting all this up before we even got to Ronald's," John stated. "And why does Paul have a gun?"

"Because he doesn't trust Jack," Chris whispered over the wind.

John pointed into the western sky as they approached the reef, and the islands began growing fainter off their stern. It wasn't hurricane season in Bermuda, but the sight off starboard could have fooled anyone. Menacing darkness was unrolling across the sky and charging directly at them. "You better find a way to get us back or we're gonna get caught on the reef in the middle of this thing."

"I think you're right, Johnny," Chris agreed, but before he could set out to do anything about it, the sound of banging suddenly erupted from below deck.

"You hear that?" Hunter stepped closer to the stairs that descended to the cabin. "There's someone down there."

All three of them climbed down below and discovered the banging to be coming from behind a locked door.

"Get me out of here!" a man's voice was hollering between blows.

"Get away from the door!" Hunter yelled back. And with a powerful thrust of his leg, he kicked the door in.

The room mostly comprised a large bed and some nautical decorations, but off to the side was an open closet containing a chair, a large length of rope lying on the floor around its legs. In the middle of the room stood a man with short black hair and glasses. There was a frantic look on his unshaven and weathered face, his blue eyes sweeping back and forth like darting mice.

"Who the hell are you?" Hunter demanded, still looking around the room as if it might provide the answer sooner than the stranger.

"Chadwick Aland," he answered cautiously. He wasn't sure whether to be fearful before captors about to cut him up in pieces or to be grateful for his saviors.

"What're you doing here?" Chris stepped toward him.

"I don't know. I think he drugged me. I woke up tied in the closet."

"Who drugged you?"

Just then, Paul entered the room with his own profanity-strung inquiry as to what was going on.

"Where are we?" Mr. Aland asked.

"In Bermuda, heading out to the reef in the middle of a storm," answered John tersely on his way back to the stairs.

Paul stopped him. "What're you doing?"

"Someone has to stop him before he kills us all." He stopped short of the steps. "But seeing that you're the one with the gun, it should probably be you."

Paul hissed, "You just hold on a second, Johnny." Then he looked at Chris and Hunter. "Where'd this guy come from?"

"New York," Aland answered for them. "I was supposed to meet somebody…"

Paul stepped closer to the stranger, causing him to step back.

Chadwick Aland spoke quickly, as if he only had a few seconds before the angry man with the scarred face would be on top of him and pummeling him to death. "Some author wanted to meet about a new book he was writing. I'm a freelance archeologist, and he wanted to interview me about my discoveries, some of my theories. I was waiting outside the place and then…that's it. Next thing I know, I'm tied to a chair in the closet." He pointed to the closet with one hand while reflexively bringing his other hand up to guard his face against what he thought would be an attack from Paul.

Paul didn't hit him, though, just stared at him.

John reached into his back pocket and pulled out *Journey with the Gods*. Flipping it over, he thrust it at Chadwick while asking if he'd seen the man he was supposed to meet.

Chadwick took the book without looking at it, confused. "Yeah, for a moment. He introduced himself, and we shook hands. That's all I remember. What's going on?"

"Is that him?" he asked, pointing to the book.

Looking down at the author's picture, the captive's eyes widened with even more bewilderment. "Yes. Professor Connelly."

John took the book back and spun it around so that the author's name was visible. "Or Ronald Douglas Carter."

Paul swore out loud.

"You've never seen this boat before? The *Gegenes*?" Chris asked Chadwick.

A flicker of recognition registered in his eyes. "What did you call it?"

"*Gegenes*. Do you know it? Do you know Henry Carter?"

"*Gegenes* is the Greek word the Septuagint used to translate the Hebrew word *Nephilim*. It's the same word Greek mythology used for the Titans… It's what the guy was coming to interview me about…"

"What's he talking about?" Paul asked Hunter and Chris, frustration and impatience boiling in his voice.

But John was halfway up the steps already. "We need to get out of here right now!"

They followed him back up to the deck, but what they saw when they got there halted them in their tracks.

The sky above was pitch black, branches of lightning flashing like spiderwebs throughout its sinister and seemingly unnatural transformation into something otherworldly. But the water around them was like a single sheet of endless glass, a placid electricity dancing over the eerie waters to the beat of thunderclaps.

Chris looked behind them and saw the reef fading in the distance. "We're past the reef! Where's he taking us?"

Though the sails were tied down, the boat being propelled by its motor, it was clear that there was not even the slightest breath of air whispering over the water. Everything was still, calm—except, of course, the churning darkness that was now twirling above them.

John stepped to the railing, grasping it tightly with both hands. "I saw a map of the Bermuda Triangle in Ronald's house, the boats and planes that have disappeared catalogued on it. There was a list of names written across its back."

"The Bermuda Triangle?" Paul hissed.

John ignored the skepticism that he himself shared. "Henry's name was the last one on the list."

But before anyone could comment, Nick came running at them from the front of the boat, appearing suddenly from behind the folded sails with his mouth open and about to shout something. And then he tripped and tumbled awkwardly across the deck.

"You okay?" Hunter asked, going to help him up.

"Yeah," he grunted. But his attention was aimed at the large black army bag that had caught his legs.

Paul went and pulled the mouth of it open, standing in shock after gazing inside it.

"What is it?" Chris asked, coming alongside him.

But Paul was already making his way to the bow.

Grabbing the bottom of the bag, Chris turned it upside down, dumping its contents out onto the deck.

Sprawled out at their feet was a small arsenal of submachine guns.

"May I ask one more time just what in the world is going on?" Aland's troubled voice sounded from behind them, his eyes wide at the sight of so much firepower.

"I think we're about to find out," Chris answered, chasing after Paul.

John grabbed Hunter, pointing to the unmanned wheel. "Why don't you steer us back to port, or at least try to get us back in the harbor before this thing breaks on us."

Hunter nodded and ran for the boat's controls.

* * * *

Jackson was leaning against the railing and staring out over the ocean ahead, seemingly oblivious to everything going on around them.

"Jack!" Paul yelled, coming up behind him, veins in his neck bulging with fury.

Jackson turned and faced him, a strange look on his face.

"We passed the reef! What the hell are you doing?"

The boat began to turn as Hunter spun the wheel, something that Jackson seemed to notice with complete indifference.

"He was right," Jackson muttered. "John *was* the key."

John stepped out from behind Paul. "What are you talking about?"

Jackson smiled as a bolt of lightning split the sky in half. "You didn't read the third edition, did you?"

"Third edition of what?"

"*Journey with the Gods…*" He looked up at the sky. "It's *you*, Johnny."

John moved forward. "What've you done, Jackson?"

"We're gonna get him back."

"Get who back?"

"Your brother." And then his attention switched to something else, his eyes narrowing on something behind John. "Who is that?" he asked, picking Chadwick Aland out of the group.

But at that moment, the darkness unleashed its storehouse of rain, drowning their world beneath a blinding waterfall of fury. A huge gust of wind suddenly pushed from the starboard side and almost flipped the entire yacht, sending them all flying to the deck, desperately trying to grab ahold of something.

His arms wrapped firmly around the bottom of the railing, John looked out ahead and could barely make out land. They weren't going to make it back into the harbor.

"Look!" Aland screamed from next to him, pointing up into the sky.

John followed Aland's finger with his eyes and watched as the sky split open above them. The clouds began to move against themselves, no longer traveling in one direction with the wind but folding backward and piling on top of themselves, as if they were trying to transform into something unnatural. And as the same swirling figure he had seen from the airplane the day before descended on them now, he knew that its reach would not come up short this time.

ARRIVAL

And it came to pass when the children of men began to multiply on the face of the earth and daughters were born unto them, that the angels of God saw them on a certain year of this jubilee, that they were beautiful to look upon; and they took themselves wives of all whom they chose, and they bare unto them sons and they were giants. And lawlessness increased on the earth and all flesh corrupted its way, alike men and cattle and beasts and birds and everything that walketh on the earth—all of them corrupted their ways and their orders, and they began to devour each other, and lawlessness increased on the earth and every imagination of the thoughts of all men was thus evil continuously.

—Book of Jubilees 5:1–2

Then they took wives, each choosing for himself; whom they began to approach, and with whom they cohabited; teaching them sorcery, incantations, and the dividing of roots and trees. And the women conceiving brought forth giants, whose stature was each three hundred cubits. These devoured all which the labor of men produced; until it became impossible to feed them; When they turned themselves against men, in order to devour them; And began to injure birds, beasts, reptiles, and fishes, to eat their flesh one after another, and to drink their blood.

—Book of Enoch 7:10–14

Moreover Azazyel taught men to make swords, knives, shields, breastplates, the fabrication of mirrors, and the workmanship of bracelets and ornaments, the use of paint, the beautifying of the eyebrows, the use of stones of every valuable and select kind, and all sorts of dyes, so that the world became altered. Impiety increased; fornication multiplied; and they transgressed and corrupted all their ways. And men, being destroyed, cried out; and their voice reached to heaven.

—Book of Enoch 8:1–2, 9

EIGHT

My footing is no longer sure as a steep decline speeds my disoriented journey into further darkness. I trip over piles of rubble and assume them to be pieces of the walls around me, recently dislodged by the bombs carpeting the mountains now so far above. For a second, my night vision falls away from my eyes, and I get a glimpse of pure nothingness. A horrible terror seeps all the way through my being. The blackness begins to crush my body with an incredible weight seemingly impossible for such a large expanse of nothing, but it presses in from every possible angle as if the absence of anything is itself the densest form of matter. I quickly adjust the equipment covering my eyes, and with great relief, the ghostly green and white display is reestablished, lifting the world a few inches off my shoulders. I stumble back to my feet and continue following the slope into the center of the earth, into some kind of chamber…

The *Gegenes* rocked gently in the clear shallow waters, the only sound that of small lapping waves caressing her exposed hull. The sky was gray, its clouds drifting lazily over the sun while a light breeze pushed ripples into the water and rustled through the plant life growing along the nearby shore, a lingering drizzle further complementing such a scene of serenity. But it was not the soothing sounds of his environment that awakened John.

Something was striking him on the head, its impact reverberating loud and painful against his cranium. He opened his eyes and half expected to see a sort of winged, sickle-carrying creature with horns laughing sadistically down at him while aiming black marbles between his eyes. Thankfully, there was only a broken piece of wood hanging above him, its jagged edge dripping water, not marbles. Even still, each rhythmic impact was threatening to destroy his sanity.

Managing to roll out from beneath the tormenting assault, he tried to gather whatever of his senses might have survived the dream…and the forgotten events that had led him off to sleep in the first place. Reluctantly, and with much soreness, he forced himself to a sitting position. As the seconds passed, a string of events pieced itself together and formed a timeline that he desperately wished could be dismissed as part of the dream. He got to his feet, his backpack still hanging faithfully around his shoulders, and stumbled for the railing. Sweeping a wary and consternated gaze over his brother's damaged boat, he noticed that the masts and sails were missing. Using the railing for support, he began walking shakily abaft.

"So, you're not dead."

The voice came from the stern, shattering the gentleness of the boat's surroundings.

It was Paul. He was sitting in a puddle and resting against the back of the yacht, his eyes barely open and a trail of blood dripping from beneath his short black hair.

"Where is everyone?" John asked, hobbling near.

"Saw Jackson head off into the woods with an MP5." He licked rainwater off his lips. "Think I heard voices coming from the other end."

"You okay?"

"Just a concussion."

John turned without another word and headed back portside. By the time he reached the cockpit, he could hear voices coming from the bow. "Hey!" he hollered, stopping to lean on the railing. He could hear approaching steps, the *thump, thump, thump* of heavy boots jogging across the yacht's deck.

Hunter and Chris appeared.

"You alright?" Hunter asked, looking him over.

"Yeah." He swallowed, closing his eyes. "What happened?"

Chris shook his head again. "No idea. We all blacked out when that wave hit us."

"Where's Nick and that Chadwick guy?" John only lifted his eyes, finding it an easier chore than moving his whole head.

Chris threw a thumb across the deck and toward the starboard bow. "They're fine."

"Paul said Jackson ran off into the woods with a gun." He managed to stand tall and tried stretching his back, wincing in the process.

"He's awake?" Hunter looked relieved and began moving astern.

Chris took off his baseball hat and ran fingers through his long wet hair. "Why would Jackson take off?" His green eyes reflected the blue water around them as they searched for clues.

"Why does he have so many guns?" was what John wanted to know.

But Chris just shook his head and went after Hunter, so John went the opposite way, heading instead for Nick and the archeologist.

They were standing at the bow, staring out over the water. They seemed to be worked up about something, their animated voices matching their exaggerated hand gestures.

Hearing footsteps, Chadwick Aland turned. Once he recognized John, he stepped toward him. "Did *you* see it?" There was a slight tremble in his voice.

John hesitated, not wanting to admit to himself that he knew what the guy was referring to. But then he thought it might be *good* news, not being the only one who saw it. It would mean that he wasn't crazy after all. Of course, there were things worse than being crazy…

Chadwick sighed in relief. "I was starting to think I was losing it. No one else saw it."

John recalled the incident the day before, how none of the other passengers had noticed the creature then either, something that was preposterous if it had actually been real. "You didn't see it?" he asked Nick.

Nick looked amused. "You mean the storm monster?" He spit over the side of the boat. "Sorry."

"They think I'm nuts," Aland commented while using the bottom of his expensive dress shirt to clean his glasses.

John didn't want to pursue the issue right now, so he turned and focused his gaze on the land around them instead. "Looks like we're in one of the harbors," he muttered, squinting into the rain.

"It's amazing that we made it around the reef and back through the channel," Aland explained, returning the glasses to his face. Evidently, he had properly assessed their position after having been set free from below.

He was right. But for some unknown reason, John found the miracle to be more troubling than consoling. He swiveled his head, suddenly confused by something else. "Where are all the other boats?"

Nick raised his eyebrows while pointing at the islands surrounding them—they were formed a permeable barrier against the open ocean. "We were just saying that. We're it."

And he was right, there wasn't another boat to be seen anywhere.

"We can't be in a harbor, then," John stated, his unease growing. Swinging his backpack off his shoulders, he unzipped it and pulled out the map. It was slightly damp but otherwise okay. As he unfolded it, he looked up at the relaxing sky. "How long you figure we've been out?"

"Looks like it's late afternoon. Maybe a couple of hours?"

Aland was obviously disoriented, and his facial tics were doing him no favors in hiding it. "Isn't it a little weird that we *all* blacked out?"

But John just looked up from the map, turning in a complete circle to compare what was before his eyes to what was printed on the paper in his hands. "This doesn't make sense," he whispered.

"What doesn't make sense?"

Paul's voice interrupted his thoughts. Turning to see Chris and Hunter half-carrying him to the bow, John swept his hand in a circular motion, indicating the land around them. "According to the map, the only place this could be is St. George's Harbor."

"So?" Aland asked, reminding everyone that before being freed from the closet, his last memory was that of standing somewhere in New York.

"So, this island *here*" —he pointed to the shoreline fifty yards away—"has to be St. George's Island. And that one over there"—he swung his arm to the opposite side—"should be St. David's Island. And Smith's Island, Paget Island, Higgs' and Horseshoe Islands should be those smaller islands."

Chris moved closer, peering intently over John's shoulder. "He's right," he mumbled, not a hint of amusement in his tone.

"What do you mean 'he's right'?" Paul snapped as he wiped more blood off his face. "He can't be right. If it's St. George's Harbor, then where the hell's the airport?"

"And the forts?" added Chris.

Nick frowned. "Yeah, that doesn't make sense. What about the cruise ship terminal?"

After Hunter looked at the map himself, he could only shake his head. "That *can't* be St. David's Island. It's too small."

John looked back at the map and realized that Hunter was right; the island that he had suggested on their starboard side was only half the size of St. David's. He shrugged, confused but not yet concerned. He folded up the map. "I guess we should just motor back out and follow the coast until we find a wharf or dock."

"Can't," Hunter said. "Motor doesn't work. Nothing works."

"What do you mean '*nothing* works'?"

He held up his wrist. "Not even my watch."

John reached in his pocket for his cell phone but found only his reflection in its blank face.

"None of our watches work," Nick stated.

And then a little seed of concern did sprout. "That's a little odd."

"The storm must have produced some kind of electromagnetic pulse or something," explained Hunter, though it was obvious from the look in his eye that it was nothing but a wild guess.

Paul's icy stare was fixed on the trees covering the land around them. "Where's all the hotels and pink houses?"

Whereas the skyline should have been highlighted by hills decorated with multicolored homes, big hotels, golf courses, and old military forts, all they could see in any direction and on every island were twenty-foot trees.

"The storm just pushed us to a place we haven't seen," said Nick, impatiently dismissing the tone in Paul's voice.

John quickly unfolded the map again, examining it more closely. "There's only *three* possible places we can be." He stabbed his finger at the map. "The Great Sound, Castle Harbor, or St. George's Harbor. They're the *only* spots where we can have land off portside and open ocean from the bow."

Again, Chris confirmed.

"Then what're you saying, Johnny? You saying that the airport just vanished?" Nick was pointing his handless arm toward where John was suggesting the airport should be.

"No. I'm just saying that, according to the *map*, we have to be in one of those places, and that, of the three, St. George's Harbor is the only one that works."

Hunter stared out to the island resting off starboard and repeated his original objection. "It's too small."

"It's too small?" Nick shook his head in disbelief. "How 'bout there's nothing *on* it?" He laughed, unable to comprehend what was being implied by his friends. "I'm telling you, the storm just pushed us away from all that."

"From all what?" Chris asked, taking his eyes off the map. "From the twenty-one square miles that accommodate sixty thousand people?"

"Yeah, but there's over one hundred and fifty smaller islands, and a lot of them look like this." Nick was waving his remaining hand now. "With nothing on them!"

Chris pointed back to the land that was resting off their port and stretching out a mile ahead of them. "You think that's one of the *small* islands?"

John tuned out their argument, trying instead to untangle a nagging thought that was tugging the back of his mind. Nick *had* to be right; it couldn't possibly be St. David's. Yet he still found himself searching for an explanation that might account for its smaller size. And then the thought finally pulled free and he remembered. It was something that Jackson had said in the taxi the day before. *We built the airfield in 1941*… The revelation slipped out of his mouth.

Nick sighed, his irritation growing. "What are you talking about, Johnny?"

But it was such an absurd thought that he couldn't even bring himself to say it. "Nothing."

"Maybe this isn't even Bermuda," Nick offered, finally conceding the fact that there *were* discrepancies.

Chris sneered. "Cape Hatteras, North Carolina, is the closest piece of land to Bermuda, Nick."

"Then the map's wrong."

Hunter held up his hands, bringing the discussion to an abrupt close. "Whatever, it doesn't matter. We're not gonna solve anything by just sitting here arguing. All we know is that Jackson lied to us. So we should go find out why."

Chris nodded in agreement. "You're right." And then he turned and headed back astern. Twenty seconds later, he reappeared, holding a few of the weapons the sinister wave hadn't claimed, extra clips shoved into his pockets.

Nick wagged his head in shock. "What are you doing?"

"Jackson brought these for a reason, and since he's the only one who seems to know what's going on, I'm gonna trust it's a good one." He tossed an MP5 to Hunter and another one to Paul.

Nick protested. "If you get caught with that thing, you're gonna get in a lot of trouble. And depending on what Jack's been up to, you could get us *all* in trouble."

Chris looked down over the side of the boat. "There's a couple more down there, but suit yourself." And then he hopped over the railing, landing in the water below with a gentle splash.

Cursing under his breath and shaking his head, Nick went after one of the remaining guns.

Paul moved his fingers in a circular motion over his temples for a few seconds in a futile attempt to alleviate his headache. "When we find him, I'm gonna kill him…" And then he fell backward over the side, joining Chris in the water below.

Hunter swung his own leg over the railing, intent on following Chris and Paul, but first asked Aland, "Any idea why that author guy or Jackson would want you here?"

He didn't even have to think about it. "No idea. But I got the impression that your friend didn't know who I was."

John nodded in agreement. "Ronald must've hidden him in the closet before Jackson got the boat."

"Doesn't make any sense."

John looked at Aland. "Can I call you Chad?" He spoke calmly, attempting to reassure Aland as much as himself.

He nodded.

"Okay, Chad, where's the book I handed you?"

"It's down in the cabin."

"Can you go get it?"

"Sure." Though it was obvious he didn't understand why John would want it now.

Nick brushed by Aland with a scowl as he came back carrying the remaining two guns, one tucked under his handless arm. He extended one out to John.

John declined. "I don't want it."

"I can't imagine why we'd need them, but I guess Chris is right. Jackson wouldn't have brought them for nothing." Then he jumped into the water, too.

Now standing alone with John, Hunter asked him, "Why did Jackson say that about the storm? That you *caused* it?"

"I have no idea."

Hunter swore. "None of this makes any sense." And then he joined the others.

John watched them all swim to shore as Chadwick came back to him with the book in his hand.

"Here."

John put it in his bag. "You ready?"

"For what?"

"I have no idea."

A short hesitation. "Can I take that?" he asked, pointing at the submachine gun.

"Everyone else seems to think it's a good idea."

"Yeah, well, I think it'd make me feel a little better, you know? Considering that I was kidnapped and don't really know who any of you people are. And after seeing that thing—" He squinted. "Why do you think we're the only ones that could see it?"

He said "that *could* see it" instead of "*saw* it," and John didn't care so much for what the phrasing insinuated. "Come on."

"Do you feel it?"

The way he asked raised the flesh on his arms. "What?"

"Something's not right here," Chadwick whispered, looking around at the trees. "That storm did something."

"And what do you think it did?" John moved closer to the railing, keeping an eye on the SEALs, who were just now getting to shore, disappearing into the aerial roots of a mangrove swamp.

"I don't know, but you know what I'm talking about."

"Just get in the water and try not to shoot anyone." But the truth of the matter was that he knew *exactly* what Chadwick was talking about.

He dove for the crystal water, the dark sky above inverted in its reflection. And as he descended, the clouds coming to greet him, he wondered if he was in fact plummeting to a different world. Surfacing, and making sure Chadwick was following, he began swimming after the others.

* * * *

The turquoise water slowly gave way to the shallow mangrove swamp, the plants' dense aerial roots forming a thicket that was more reminiscent of the Florida Everglades than the long stretches of pink sand Bermuda was famous for. Exhausted after laboring through the oppressive terrain, John turned back to help guide Chadwick.

"I'm fine," he said, waving him off while climbing through the last of the larger roots. "Regardless of my formal appearance, I'm more than capable of handling myself in such an environment."

And despite the dark slacks, expensive black shoes, satin shirt, and glasses—now soaking wet and looking rather silly—he did indeed maneuver through the overgrown maze with a gracefulness John found rather surprising.

"You said you're an archeologist?" John removed his backpack and took off his windbreaker.

"Well, I was," he said, bending forward with his hands on his knees, trying to catch his breath. "Not anymore. At least not officially."

"Anymore?"

"Some of my views were considered unorthodox by my peers, so I never made it through their reviews. Now I just do it as a hobby on the side while I teach history at community college. That's why I was meeting this author. I thought maybe having some of my ideas published in a bestseller would be the break I needed to establish a credible platform for my work."

Nick, Paul, Hunter, and Chris were standing nearby and pulling their own clothes off, wringing them out.

"How'd Ronald find you?" Paul asked from a few yards away.

"I don't know. I have a few published articles, a newsletter, a daily blog… I guess I never asked." And then he stood up and started unbuttoning his own shirt. "Why do you think he kidnapped me?"

Chris just laughed. "Dude, you know as much as we do."

He looked back at John, thinking. "So you're all looking for this guy Henry—that was his name, right? But your friend Jackson—"

"He said we don't know," Paul snapped.

The finality in his voice came off a little too threatening for Chadwick's liking. "I'm just trying to figure out what I'm doing here."

"At this point, we all are."

"Oh, I'm sorry. I didn't realize that you *too* were shaking hands with someone in New York one second and then locked in a yacht seven hundred miles away the next."

"Chad," Hunter called out, getting his attention, "relax."

"Whatever," he mumbled, and then hoped no one had heard the comment. Seeing these men without their shirts on was proving to be an extremely intimidating experience for him. "What are you people?" he asked. He wasn't exactly out of shape himself, but next to these people he looked like one of those weird stick insects.

"They're retired SEALs," John explained, wringing out his shirt.

That was when Chadwick noticed John's bare chest and the inked covering that wrapped his flesh. "Interesting artwork," he mumbled, eyes narrowing suspiciously.

"It was a long time ago."

"Yeah," Paul said, "once upon a time Johnny was a Ranger. And then he saw a blinding light that changed his life forever." He sneered, but even he seemed a bit taken aback by the images across John's body. It was a plethora of death, dark and twisted images ranging from skulls, sickles, and web-covered tombs to crossed M-16s and black-hooded skeletons.

"What's with the obelisk?" Chadwick wanted to know.

It started below his beltline and reached up beside his navel, capping just below the clavicle.

"I don't want to talk about it," he responded, and instead flipped the conversation back on him. "You said something about the boat's name having to do with why Ronald wanted to meet you. What did you mean?"

"The *Gegenes*." He twisted his nice shirt, draining it onto the fertile ground at his feet. "Yeah, like I said, it's the Greek translation of the Hebrew *Nephilim* and the same word for the Titans in Greek mythology."

"What's *Nephilim*?" Nick asked, inserting a rather strong expletive between the words. He was having a little trouble wringing out his shirt with just his one hand.

"It means 'fallen ones,' but it's sometimes translated as 'giants' in the Old Testament. The Titans were the offspring of gods and mortal women. Our English words 'genes' and 'genetics' come from the same root, *genea*—meaning 'breed' or 'kind.' That's what the author said he was researching, the gods' hand at eugenics."

Nick shook his head. "I met the guy twenty minutes ago and he still hasn't said a word I understand."

John asked, "Why would Henry choose that name for his boat?"

"How should I know?" He had his shirt back on, a pale blue work of silk, and was busying his fingers with buttoning it. "But just naming it *Titan* would've made more sense in a conventional way."

"What do you mean?"

"Well, the modern concept of the Titans, like the Celts and pirates in general, have been largely romanticized. I mean, you even have a professional football team named the Titans… But to use that *specific* word? It suggests a more intimate knowledge of the subject, though why someone with that knowledge would name their boat after it…" He shrugged.

Paul had his shirt and jacket back on and was adjusting the German-made Heckler & Koch MP5 submachine gun over his shoulder. "This is all fascinating my socks off, but we need to start moving." He turned and began leading them away from the shore and toward the interior of the island, the sound of light rain pitter-pattering against the tropical plant life accompanying them.

A few minutes later, they found themselves facing a wall of cedar trees, their thick trunks twisted in braids and their needled branches curving upward toward the sky. Once past the edge of the twenty-foot evergreens, they discovered a thick forest—its red soil spongy beneath an endless bed of ferns, and palmetto trees waving their shaggy, fan-shaped appendages in the breeze. There was an eerie loneliness permeating the air, a feeling that had been completely foreign to the busy island they were on just a few hours earlier.

"Can you tell which way he went?" John called up to Hunter, who was now taking the lead.

He nodded, pointing further into the forest.

A few birds suddenly flew by, letting loose an awful scream that echoed back and forth through the trees.

"This is weird, man." Chris' eyes were fixed on the dripping canopy above.

As they followed Hunter, everyone but John with weapons hanging off their shoulders, John stepped closer to Paul's back and began speaking softly over his shoulder.

"You find any diving equipment on the boat?"

Paul shook his head no.

"And none of you knew that he and Ronald were already acquainted?"

"No," he grumbled.

"Why would they lie about the boat?"

Paul smirked back over his shoulder. "I don't know, Johnny, you're *the key*, why don't you tell me?"

Not amused, he walked past Paul and approached Hunter again, setting a watchful eye on Chadwick while doing so. It was impossible that an archeologist familiar with the giants of Genesis 6 could have found himself here by random chance. As he'd begun to suspect earlier, there was a design emerging behind all this, some kind of purpose. Though whoever (or whatever) the master architect of their predicament, and whatever its intended end, John's limited realm of comprehension could draw no suspects. Considering that he'd never told anyone about the Afghan cave, it was unlikely that Jackson even knew of the subtle connections now being paraded around him. Ronald, on the other hand, somehow seemed to be right at the center of the mystery. And yet the accusation wouldn't stick, the author getting off due to the lack of any *rational* evidence.

John came alongside Hunter and asked, "You were saying something earlier about my father's diary and dreams Henry was having?"

After a moment to climb over a fallen cedar, he sighed. "You were supposed to know all this. It's why we brought you along."

"According to Jackson."

"Yeah, according to Jackson."

John navigated over the tree. "So fill me in."

Hunter shook his bald head and pushed some underbrush out of his way. "I only know what Jackson told me. I never heard it from Henry. You should ask him."

"He's not here."

Hunter swore under his breath, for some reason reluctant to divulge what little he knew. He stole a glance at the others behind them before yielding to John's request. "Ever since I knew him, he had these nightmares that would wake him up. After he read your father's journal, though, he became obsessed with trying to decipher them, convinced they meant something. Apparently, the journal indicated that the malady had been in the family for a long time. Some secret legacy he was determined to understand. But like I said, he never talked to me about it."

"But he thought this Ronald guy knew something about it?"

"Apparently."

John lapsed into silence, his mind clogged with half-digested thoughts. Was there a connection between the *Gegenes* and Henry's dreams? If so, then perhaps this "family legacy" Hunter just mentioned had tainted his branch of the tree as well. And what of Henry's name being included on the list of those who had disappeared in the Triangle? But there were simply too many dots to connect, and even the ones that seemed in tune with each other weren't creating a very sensible picture.

And then, before he could formulate more thoughts into questions, he found himself, along with the others, standing before a wide-open clearing, the rain now unimpeded by the forest's canopy. Ripping across the field of rustling grass, stretching from left to right for a hundred yards, stood a massive rock wall.

"That's interesting," Chris remarked, shaking water off his baseball hat.

The wall stood almost twenty feet high and was constructed like some sort of jigsaw puzzle—huge rocks, geometrically cut into an assortment of sharp angles, fitting precisely into one another.

"Don't remember seeing that in the tour guides," whispered John.

Chadwick took a cautious step forward, shaking his head in bewilderment, his eyes frantically sweeping back and forth. "It looks just like the fortress of Sacsayhuaman hill."

"The what?"

He whispered, "I don't understand."

"Understand what?" Paul growled.

And then Chadwick spun around, a fire suddenly burning behind his water-beaded lenses. "Are you lying to me?" he asked with such indignation that he confused them.

"About what?" John asked.

"Where we are. That this is Bermuda..."

Hunter held up his hands in an attempt to reassure him, not fully understanding what had just made him so skeptical of their location. "We're in Bermuda. I promise you." Like Chris had said, the closest piece of land was North Carolina.

"Well, excuse me if I'm just a little hesitant to believe you. This—" he pointed to the wall, wagging his head "—how do you explain *this*?" And he began backpedaling away from them. "Who are you? What do you want from me?" He brought the submachine gun up, aiming it at them.

"Chad, it's okay. Just calm down," John said.

"Calm down? I was *kidnapped*! And now here I am in the middle of *nowhere* with a bunch of... You're gonna kill me, aren't you? You're gonna shoot me and bury me out here..." He flexed his hand around the gun's handle, his face contorted with confused agony. "Why? Who sent you?"

"What are you talking about?" Paul stepped forward, his own weapon rising a few inches.

John stepped between them, holding out his empty hands. "Chad, listen! We're all in this together! We—"

"Why don't you think this is Bermuda?" Hunter interrupted.

"Because I've been to just about every known megalithic site on the planet! It's kind of my *life.* So I'm pretty sure that I'd know if there was one on Bermuda!" The gun was rattling in his hands.

"I don't understand," Hunter replied calmly.

Chadwick pointed at the wall behind him. "These rocks, if anything like the ones from the Cuzco-Machu Picchu region or Tiahuanaco or the Valley Temple at Giza, weigh around one hundred tons each!"

"It's just the ruins of an old fort," Nick shouted, not at all liking the gun being pointed at him.

Chadwick shook his head. "No. This was not built by the British, Spanish, or Portuguese."

"I don't care who built the stupid wall," Nick snapped back. "We need to keep moving!"

But Chadwick was already departing from the group, his aim a little more liberal as he moved closer to the wall. Once he was just twenty yards from it, he began skirting around its side, looking for an entrance into what turned out to be a kind of enclosure. Finding one, he disappeared through it.

"Chad!" John hollered after him as a gust of wind flattened the grass at his feet.

"Just leave him," Paul snarled, making his way out of the rain and back beneath the umbrella the forest offered.

"It does seem to defy logic," Chris observed, suddenly in awe of just how big the rocks were and how impossibly they were assembled.

And then the distinguished *crack* of a gunshot rebounded throughout the island and shattered the creepy stillness around them, dozens of birds fleeing their perches and flapping desperately into the cloud-covered sky.

Instantly, the five of them were sprinting as fast as they could around the wall and through the tall entranceway.

Standing in the middle of the enclosure, a half-completed stone building around him and the MP5 lying at his feet, was Chadwick.

"What happened?" Hunter shouted as he ran up beside him.

Chadwick slowly moved his head toward them. "I dropped it," he explained, his voice weak.

"Are you okay?" John quickly examined him for any kind of wound.

But Chadwick's gaze had already returned to something ahead of him.

"What is this place?" Chris' eyes had drifted away from Chadwick and were now taking in the whole of their surroundings.

There was a sense of awe in Chadwick's voice when he stated, "It's like Ollantaytambo."

"We don't have any idea what you're talking about," Nick reminded him.

The walls surrounding them seemed to make a perfect square, each side a hundred yards long. Within it, and now under their feet, were stone steps that descended into a valley full of monoliths.

John didn't like it and said so.

But Chadwick just descended into the valley, skirting around the stone pillars. Running a hand over the giant stone blocks that were standing twice as tall as himself, he said with astonishment, "It's just like the Osireion at Abydos."

"In Egypt?" Hunter inquired, looking down at him.

"In the House of a Million Years…The temple of Seti I, dedicated to Osiris. It's identical to it. It's unfinished, of course…but a hundred feet long, sixty feet wide, two colonnades dividing it into three naves, and cells in the four corners…" He began whispering to himself, saying repeatedly, "It doesn't make sense."

Chris called down, "What doesn't make sense?"

And Chadwick finally seemed to snap out of his internal musings. "Why this would be in Bermuda." He climbed back up the steps. "The experts want you to believe that the Osireion was built by Seti, but that's just because they can't comprehend what the evidence really suggests."

Nick looked around intolerantly. "We're looking for Jackson, remember?"

But John's interest in the strange site was growing. "And what does the evidence suggest?"

"That it was built in some distant epoch, maybe even in the time of Zep Tepi."

"What is Zep Tepi?" John had never heard of it before. None of them had.

"First Time. The period all the ancient records and traditions of Egypt claim the gods—Ptah, Ra, Shu, Geb, Orion, Set and Horus—ruled on the earth."

"Built by the gods?" Paul asked, amused. "I can see why you lost your job."

But Nick was altogether missing the wonder of their surroundings. "It's a bunch of rocks stacked on top of each other. They're probably left over from the set of a movie or something."

"You're wrong and, quite frankly, have no clue what you're talking about," Chadwick answered. "From the Pacific Islands, to Egypt, to South America and Asia, there are ancient ruins that share striking similarities to this. But no one knows who built them or for what purpose. The only thing they know is that the technology used to build them wasn't supposed to exist at the time. For instance, the Trilithon in the Roman temple of Jupiter at Baalbek contains the three largest building blocks ever used in a man-made structure. Each one weighs a thousand *tons*. They sit side by side on the fifth level of a cyclopean wall. The six stones they sit on weigh four hundred and fifty tons *each*—thirty feet long, fourteen feet high, and ten feet deep." He took a breath. "The so-called experts believe it was built by the Romans, though there's no record of it being built by anyone, or an explanation as to how the rocks were quarried, transported, or even lifted."

If his excitement was the head of the passionate report, then fear was its tail, and they were chasing each other in circles, his eyes intermittently revealing an underlying belief that, fascinated or not, all was not right with this place. He continued, "The physical magnitude itself is a mystery, but if this site is like the others…I'm almost positive you'll find that a precise measuring system was used, perhaps even one based on the megalithic yard. You'd certainly find a stellar orientation and, more than likely, a perfect alignment with the poles. A lot of these sites contain at least that much, the Great Pyramid probably being the best example."

"And no one knows how they were built?" Chris inquired, doubtful.

At which point Nick began singing the Louis Armstrong song. "*Nobody knows…*"

"Shut up, Nick," Hunter said.

Chadwick resumed, "Anyway, all we really have are the legends of the people who inherited the sites."

Chris frowned. "Inherited?"

"Most archeologists want to believe that since a certain civilization lived among such structures it must have been responsible for constructing them. The Mayan calendar is a good example of a civilization getting the credit for a body of wisdom that's a lot older than itself—either the Olmecs or a people even before them. In many cases, the records we have of certain civilizations blatantly admit to inheriting their wisdom from much older sources. But such concepts don't complement our preconceived notions of evolution, so we ignore them and label them fables."

"So what do the legends say?" And, as if in expectation of the answer, Chris tightened his grip on the submachine gun even before Chadwick opened his mouth.

"Well, in the case of Baalbek, they say that the city was built by Cain before the Great Flood and named after his son Enoch—which seems to be the same city referred to in Genesis 4:17. They say it was destroyed by the Flood and was later rebuilt by a race of giants."

"Giants?" John whispered.

"Actually, according to most of the legends, it was giants that were responsible for these anomalies. And in cases like *El Fuerte*, or 'the place of the giants,' the architecture is built to such a massive scale—down to chairs, beds, entranceways, and tunnels—that it seems they were specifically designed to accommodate *very* tall people."

Thunder rumbled through the sky.

Chadwick again wiped off his glasses. "The giant legends go back to the beginning of mankind, appearing in the earliest records we have. Jewish, Greek, Norse, Hindu, Siamese, Indian, Mongol…"

"And this is the stuff Ronald wanted to talk to you about?" Hunter wondered aloud.

"This stuff is my forte. It's how he got me to meet him."

Paul began to stray away from the group, his attention captured by something else. "What's that smell?" He was wiggling his nose.

"I don't smell anything." Hunter watched as Paul turned the corner around some more scattered blocks the size of U-hauls.

A few seconds later, he reappeared from behind the wall. "I think you should see this."

They all joined him while the sound of thunder drum-rolled across the heavens.

It was resting in the center of a circular pattern that had been manipulated into the grass, its short, round body topped with a flat surface. But rather than resembling the paler limestone rocks that made up the surrounding walls, this particular rock was black.

Chris stepped closer. "What is it?"

"An altar." Chadwick's unstable voice could hardly be heard above the increasing wind. "But this figure on the ground resembles the Neolithic henges in Britain."

"Like Stonehenge?" Chris asked.

He shook his head. "Britain has as many circles *without* stones as it does with them. Stonehenge was probably a later development on an already existing circle... They were used by astronomer priests as observatories..." His voice trailed into a whisper, his mind trying to compute for itself what was before him. "The Thornborough Henges reflect the constellation Orion, as does the pyramid complex at Giza—Orion being the manifestation of Osiris. This circle, if it is like the Neolithic ones in Britain, certainly used megalithic measurements—"

John stopped him from continuing. "What do you mean by 'megalithic' measurements?"

With great effort, Chadwick lifted his eyes from the huge circle sweeping around their feet. "It's supposedly the unit of length the builders used, what would be sixteen point three two inches to us. It's hard to explain. A pendulum clock, a three hundred and sixty-six-day year that was determined by the number of days passing between winter solstices, three point nine three minutes for a star to travel one megalithic degree—there were three hundred and sixty-six megalithic degrees—" He fell silent, realizing how futile it was to go on.

Just then, Chris felt his feet begin to sink. Looking down, he saw a red liquid bubbling up around the soles of his boots. "What the hell?" He lifted a leg and examined the dark substance stuck to his foot. "It's blood," he said, and realized that it wasn't a black stone they had been staring at after all. He took a step backward, something crunching under his heel in the process. Spinning to see what it was, he discovered bones protruding out of the ground, rotting flesh still clinging to them. The soil in which he was beginning to sink was regurgitating its buried victims. He took a few quick strides away from the circle, eager to find firmer ground. "I think we should go," he said.

But Nick still wasn't appreciating the bizarre undertone of their situation. "They're probably animal bones left over from some weird pagan ritual the local crazies get off on."

To which John responded by pointing down at Chris' footprints, at an exposed human hand that was reaching out of the ground and begging for assistance. "Animals with hands?"

And then a terrifying sound exploded from somewhere in the forest behind them, moving them all closer to each other. Suddenly, as if his life depended on it, Chadwick took off to retrieve the submachine gun he'd dropped earlier. Hugging it to his chest, he walked up to John and whispered, "I told you there was something wrong with this place."

And it was actually Chadwick Aland who then led them away from the site—it having no business being on the Bermuda they knew of.

* * * *

The cedar forest eventually gave way to a sandy clearing scattered sporadically with large clumps of grass. Jagged rocks poked up out of the ground near the clearing's end before dropping down into the tide below.

The wind was stronger at this elevation, and Chris found himself chasing after his hat, hoping to get it before it flew off the cliff and went out to sea. Paul was laughing at him.

Ignoring them, John struggled to keep the map from being torn from his hands as he tried to compare it with their location. And even though there weren't any streets or buildings to help mark his location, the geography was a near-perfect match, and he showed the others.

Not exactly ready to accept what the map implied, they chose to ignore it, instead continuing along the outskirts of the forest, each one sure that this all had to be some twisted dream.

And then came the next mystery.

A row of damaged and neglected huts stood silently in the shade of more palmetto trees, stretching across a length of deserted beach.

"Wattle and daub," Chadwick stated.

"What?" Hunter whipped rain off his smooth head with a flick of his wrist.

"It's the name of the method," he explained. "You pound wooden posts into the ground every two feet or so, forming a row." He pointed to the huts, showing him. "Then you weave branches between them, filling the spaces with a mixture of mud, clay, and animal hair. The roof is palmetto-thatched. The settlers in Jamestown used this method."

"It's some kind of preserve?" Nick asked while searching for a tourist sign that would justify such an explanation.

Chad shook his head. "No way. Hurricanes would have destroyed these a long time ago. Could be an abandoned replica, but—"

The distinct sound of a weapon being readied made them all turn, its metallic sliding and clicking clearly identifying itself above the palmettos' rustling leaves and the crashing surf behind them.

It was Paul. He was aiming his submachine gun into a hut that had collapsed on itself.

"What is it?" Hunter called to him.

But Paul just swore under his breath and turned away. "It stinks."

Curious as to what could've triggered Paul's aggressive response, they made their way to the hut.

And there, sitting on the floor, back against a wall but mostly covered by the fallen roof, was a body.

Hunter entered the hut, trying to ignore the stench of rotting flesh, and began clearing the debris off the corpse. Once he had most of it removed, the body's full condition became disturbingly clear.

It was an old man… Dark green flesh covered his bare stomach, and all other exposed skin was brown. His neck and face were swollen with gasses, his eyes sunk back into his skull.

"In the middle of putrefaction, been dead maybe two weeks." Hunter's explanation wasn't needed by anyone, being ex-Special Forces and an archeologist, they had all seen their fair share of death in one way or another. Hunter leaned over and grabbed the lifeless old man, spinning him around.

"What're you doing?" Chadwick asked.

"He's wearing Levi's."

Nick was nervously rubbing his stump, something John noticed he did when stressed. "What did you expect, a thong?"

Hunter reached into the back pocket of the guy's jeans and pulled out a wallet. He tossed it to Chris.

"How'd he die?" John asked, peeking into the hut.

"Probably the roof fell on his head. Broke his neck."

Nick nodded. "Probably exploring the island when the storm hit. Came in here to wait it out and…"

Chris was staring at the other huts while absentmindedly rubbing the black leather wallet in his hand. "You think so, Nick?"

"I don't think so." Chadwick stepped forward and entered the hut. Kneeling beside the rotting corpse, he began digging his fingers into the wall. "Look." And he uncovered a pair of feathers protruding from the mud and clay mixture. Getting a firm hold of it, he pulled the long arrow back into the hut.

A few strings of profanity escaped the lips of the ex-SEALs.

Chadwick ignored them. "That's strange," he murmured to himself, his eyes fixated on the crystal arrowhead. "Never seen one of these before."

"Come on," Chris urged, taking a step backward. "Let's just find Jackson."

"We should check the rest of them," John said.

But even with an abundance of arrows scattered about, all the other huts proved clear of bodies.

They left the huts, and the hanging sensation of death that lingered over them, behind.

Chadwick came up alongside John. "Where are we, John? This can't be Bermuda. You said so yourself." He pointed to the backpack, indicating the map that was in it.

John leaned closer so that only Chadwick could hear him. "But it *is* Bermuda. There's too many similarities with the map for it not to be."

"What are you saying?"

He sighed in surrender, not caring by now how it would sound, and related what had disturbed him back on the boat. "The first settler on Bermuda, when given a choice, chose Cooper's Island as his own *instead* of St. David's because he thought that there was treasure buried on it." He quickly retrieved the map from his bag and unfolded it. "But the map shows both Cooper's Island and St. David's as being the *same* island… Look—" he pointed to the southern perimeter of the airfield—"all of this up to Swing Bridge is *not* a natural border. The US enlarged the island when they built the airfield back in 1941. But I'm telling you, the islands we saw earlier were right *here*." He pointed to the west part of St. David's, to the airport. "Right where they *used* to be…" Then he moved his finger to the southeast of St. David's and to a road that was labeled Cooper's Road.

"The channels were filled to expand St. David's, turning all these islands into one. That's why Hunter thought the island we saw was too small to be St. David's."

Chadwick frowned. "Wait. Are you saying that the airfield was never *built*?"

"That would mean time travel, wouldn't it?" Chris asked, evidently overhearing them.

"I don't know what it means," John murmured. "Nothing makes sense." But then Ronald's history of the Bermuda Triangle began playing through his head. "I want to know why Henry's name was the last on Ronald's list of people claimed by the Triangle. And I want to know why, as he was taking us straight into the storm, Jackson said we were going to get Henry back."

"You think this was all Jackson's plan? To get us to *this* place?" Paul asked, half serious.

"What place?" Nick whined. "We're in Bermuda!" He swore, the vulgar word echoing around them.

Growing impatient with Nick's refusal to accept that something was seriously wrong with their present predicament, John threw the map at him. "Show us where." And then he turned his attention back to Paul's question. "He made sure to have the guns, didn't he?"

So caught up in his thoughts, and still half convinced that he was dreaming, Chris had forgotten about the wallet Hunter had thrown him. Ignoring the conversation unraveling around him, he began rummaging through it…until he found himself holding the man's driver's license. He held it up, curious to know who the old man was. But the image on the plastic ID was not that of the old man. Chris stopped walking. "Holy—"

The astonished perplexity in his voice made everyone stop and turn toward him.

With everyone staring at him, all he could do was lift his hand, showing them the driver's license.

Henry's driver's license.

NINE

Early evening. 22nd day of May. Bermuda, Northeast end

Following the tourist map along the coast, they came to a corner of the island that stared off into the open ocean. From this location, they were all forced to admit that the obvious geographical similarities between the map and their present position made the probability of them being anywhere other than on Bermuda's most northern point extremely unlikely—if not altogether impossible. Except that there was no Fort St. Catherine towering above them, as there had been just that morning when John stood with Jackson in the shallow surf of St. Catherine's Beach.

"Might as well stick to the coast, follow it around and back to the boat," Hunter suggested, looking down at the map John had relinquished into his care. "Sun's gonna be setting and the forest'll be dark." He looked up at the menacing sky sliding across the crystal water. "We'll take a rest when we get to the next beach. Looks like it should be about a mile."

They trekked on, skirting the rocky coast.

While he walked, John stared down at Henry's licence, turning it over and over in his fingers.

"Was it him?" Chadwick asked sensitively.

John didn't think so. "That guy was in his seventies."

Chadwick lapsed into silent contemplation. "But it at least proves that he's here."

"Or *was*," Paul said without taking his eyes off the tree line to their right. The strange feeling that John had awoken to had finally made its rounds through the others, everyone now willing to admit that something was wrong.

Chris removed his baseball hat and stuck it into his back pocket. "You think the Triangle could've done something?" It was an absurd question, but then so was their current situation.

Chadwick shook his head. "It didn't send us back in time, if that's what you're getting at. Bermuda's never had these types of megalithic structures." But then he recanted from the absoluteness that had carried his words. "Of course, I suppose there could've been anything here before the Great Flood."

"As in *Noah's* Flood?" Chris asked, blond eyebrows raised.

"Yeah."

"That was a long time ago," he said.

"Conservative accounts taken from the genealogies in Genesis place the date at around sixteen or seventeen hundred years after creation. Some scientific estimates coupled with ancient accounts—like Plato's telling of the Egyptian priest who spoke to Solon in 600 BC—place the year to be around 9600 BC. It's also the date generally given to the sinking of Atlantis."

Nick laughed. "Atlantis…"

Chadwick shrugged. "Some people think that the waters in the Bermuda Triangle cover the ruins of Atlantis, that power crystals are somehow to blame for the phenomena." Then the corner of his mouth turned upward with amusement. "In 1974, the Isis Center for Research and Study of the Esoteric Arts and Sciences took a cruise into the Triangle to run psychic tests. Trying to channel the lost Atlanteans from within the Triangle is more popular than you'd think."

John recalled Ronald's book *The Bermuda Triangle and the Doorway to Hell.* "Ronald mentioned that in his book…the Atlantis theory. Talked about the Bimini Road and all that stuff."

"Yeah, in fact, there *are* megalithic ruins off the coast of Bimini, ruins that resemble the walls in Peru and Lebanon…and the walls we just saw. The native Taino tribe even refers to Bimini as the 'Island of the Fallen Wall.' And on the Piri Reis map, there's a row of polygonal stones drawn on the center of a large island in the Bahamas, indicating that the ruins were once above water…"

"Ronald talked about that, too. Had it hanging on his wall."

"The Piri Reis map?"

"Along with a bunch of other ones that showed Antarctica without ice. He said one of them had Atlantis on it."

Nick scowled. "This when you went to the bathroom?"

He nodded. "He gave me a presentation on ancient maps."

Chadwick scratched an imaginary itch on his cheek. "What else did he have?"

"Books on the Bermuda Triangle, psychokinesis, quantum physics, string theory, time travel, megalithic cultures, UFOs…"

"Pertinent things," pondered Chadwick.

Chris asked, "What do you mean?"

"The Bermuda Triangle"—he waved his hand out to the ocean, though he realized that the traditional boundaries encompassed the waters *below* Bermuda and not the water beside them now—"megalithic sites, time travel theories…"

"And he had a picture of a giant with six toes hanging on his wall."

"Which your brother's boat was named after," Chadwick pointed out.

John nodded. "And then there's *you*, who just so happens to know all this stuff."

"There's a design…" Chadwick admitted, mystified by his own statement.

John was glad that someone other than himself realized it. He wondered if there was something in Chadwick's past that had helped lead him to such a conclusion. There certainly was in his.

Chadwick stepped closer to John. "Can I see the book?"

John reluctantly unzipped his backpack and reached inside for *Journey with the Gods.*

When he pulled it out, Chadwick caught a glimpse of the Bible that was also in the backpack. When he took the book from John's hand, he asked, "Are you a religious person?"

Though under normal circumstances he would prefer to define the question more clearly before answering, he just nodded. "Yeah."

Paul spoke up. "That would be the blinding light I was talking about."

Ignoring Paul, John flipped the question back around. "Are you?"

Chadwick shook his head. "Not really."

"Atheist, agnostic?"

"Neither. I've read most religious texts, and I've seen their sincerity materialized in the most incredible structures. I've also seen it behind the most disgusting practices the world's ever seen. I've seen the beauty of certain belief systems and the insanity in others. As for your *Bible*...God choosing one people group to reveal Himself to while the rest of the world was left to frolic in human sacrifice and animal worship? Not a very fair picture."

John figured it was a reasonable observation, though he thought he remembered hearing Pastor Brian explain how Israel failed to be the light to the world they were meant to be, instead keeping it for themselves. He kept his silence.

Chadwick's eyes turned to the book he was holding in his hands. He opened the first page and squinted, his brow furrowing. "That can't be right," he said to himself.

"What?" John looked over.

"The copyright is dated 1979." He flipped it over so that he could see the picture on the back. "He looks exactly the same..."

"It's a third edition, probably a newer picture," explained John.

Chadwick looked at him with a hint of impatience. "So you're saying he wrote this book when he was ten?"

And then John remembered the book he'd seen at Ronald's house, the one about giants and ancient civilizations, how it seemed incredibly old but somehow written by the same hand as Ronald's notes. But he decided to keep that thought to himself, the conversation already well down the rabbit hole.

Chadwick searched through the table of contents, circumnavigating around some rocks and nearly twisting an ankle.

Chadwick's fancy shoes triggered another thought in John's mind. "You guys get Jackson's instructions to dress appropriately?" he asked Hunter, Chris, Paul, and Nick.

Hunter nodded. "Told us we might have to do some hiking."

"I thought he told you we were scuba diving?"

Hunter just looked at him, no answers coming to mind—other than the one no one wanted to put in words.

"Yeah, well, I wish someone told me," Chadwick complained. "You think this guy's last name is really Carter?"

John didn't know.

"That's your last name, right? And I'm guessing your brother's, too?"

"Yeah."

"So are you *related* to this guy?"

"I don't know, ask them."

But they didn't know either, though Chris hinted that Jackson might.

Reaching the ledge of an outcropping, John hopped down and landed in the sand six feet below. Then he turned and watched the others do the same. "I saw Jackson at the Carter House this morning. Any idea why he'd go there?"

"What is it?" Nick asked while being helped down by Hunter and Chris.

"The house of Bermuda's first settler."

"Bermuda's first settler was a *Carter*?" Chadwick asked in surprise.

"Yeah."

"Are you related to *him*?"

"No idea."

Chadwick looked back down to the soggy book. "Interesting..."

It most certainly was, John thought. "When was Jackson in Bermuda before?"

"Five years ago," Hunter answered. "His honeymoon."

John hadn't placed Jackson as being the type to even take a shot at marriage. "That's how Henry discovered the guy?"

"What do you think?" Paul sneered from his elevated position atop the rock outcropping, still massaging his head with one hand while training the MP5 on the woods with the other.

John decided now was as good a time as any to bring up the whole Jackson thing. "Why is it that none of you trust Jackson?"

No one answered him.

John sighed. "Come on, I saw how apprehensive you were during the taxi ride. You knew he wasn't giving you the whole story." He pointed up at Paul. "And he was carrying a gun."

"It's not a trust issue," Hunter finally answered. "He would die for any one of us in a heartbeat, almost has a few times." He paused, choosing his words carefully. "It's just...sometimes he can get a little...strange."

"What's that supposed to mean?"

"Forget it, Johnny!" Paul yelled. "Just forget it." And then he shot a warning glare at Hunter, telling him he had no business disclosing such information to an outcast.

John understood that he had crossed an invisible line, and that by trying to turn them against one of their own, had threatened the integrity of the entire team. He was an outsider, worse than an outsider, and had no right speaking of such things. They would handle Jackson themselves as they would their own business, which was fine with John. At least they recognized what was going on with their tall friend and that he would, eventually, have to be dealt with. For now, though, he dropped the pursuit of his investigation and turned his mind back to Chadwick, who, all things considered, was holding up rather well. Not too many people could take such a string of weird events in such patient stride. Or maybe, as John suspected, there was a *reason* for such acquiescence. Maybe there was, as Chadwick had seemed to imply before they had jumped from the *Gegenes*, a reason *they* were the only ones who could see the monster in the storm.

They all lapsed back into momentary silence, their minds doing what they could to process their shared dialogue. Five minutes later, of all people, it was Nick who broke the stillness.

"Maybe it's like the Philadelphia Experiment," he suggested, suddenly willing to entertain an unconventional theory. "You know, the stories of the ship in Philadelphia they were trying to cloak from radar, transporting it instead to Norfolk."

"Those are the two choices I gotta pick from?" Paul asked dryly. "Teleportation or time travel?"

John finally inserted Henry's license into the pocket of his wet jeans. "Even if it *was* possible, it wouldn't explain where we are."

"What about space-time vertices?" Hunter cautiously suggested, mostly wanting to hear another mad idea debunked.

Chris asked, "Alternate worlds? Different dimension stuff?"

"If that's the case, if some kind of quantum theory could be applied here, then that *could* have been Henry." Hunter fell into contemplation before explaining, "At least according to some of the movies I've seen."

Chris was confused. "You mean the Triangle, or whatever, brought Henry to this place, but thirty years ago?"

"Something like that."

"Yeah," Nick said unimpressed. "I saw that movie. I like the Philadelphia Experiment better."

John took the license back out again, examining it for another reason now. According to the issue date printed on it, the piece of plastic should only be three years old. If Hunter's idea had any validity to it, then the ID would be around *thirty*-three years old and would have spent its entire life within the confines of the wallet. "Let me see the wallet." He held his hand out to Chris.

Chris tossed it to him just as a gust of wind tried to knock them down, pushing them all backward.

The wallet fell at John's feet, and he bent over to pick it up. Flipping through it, he found that it still contained one hundred and thirty-six dollars and some credit cards. None of which bore the markings of such an elapsed period. "There's no way it spent thirty years on this island," he concluded, tossing it back to Chris. He looked out to the water and watched a bolt of lightning strike the horizon. A rumble of thunder followed shortly after, elevating the eerie static buzzing in the air around them. "The doorway to hell," he whispered.

"What did you say?" Chadwick asked, looking up from the strange words still reflected in his glasses.

"That's what Ronald called the Bermuda Triangle."

And Chadwick's own eyes darted to the rolling horizon.

* * * *

The rest of the island's eastern coast was traversed in silence and without a single boat sighting. When their feet started trudging through pink sand, the terrain transitioning to that of a hotel's private beach—minus the hotel, of course—Hunter announced the map's failure to include the name of the beach, noting only that Alexandra Battery and Gates Fort should be present.

"Let's break," Paul announced, collapsing to the sand. "Ten minutes max. Come sunset, we're back on the boat."

And they all settled down, trying to get comfortable for a few seconds.

Chadwick sat and opened Ronald's book, letting the ocean breeze ruffle his hair while his eyes skimmed the mysterious text. He was in his own world, still trying to figure out where he was.

Nick was exhausted and simply rolled onto his back, closing his eyes. All he wanted to do was wake up from the nightmare…if only he could fall asleep first.

Removing his boots and rolling his khakis up to the knee, Chris walked out into the surf, his gaze locked onto where the sky touched the water so far away, wondering if there was still anything beyond it. The water felt good on his feet, and he crouched down to splash some of it on his face.

Paul sat facing the forest, the MP5 lying ready across his lap. He wasn't going to be turning his back to the woods anytime soon, not after the sounds they'd heard. So Hunter decided that he'd take advantage of his friend's alertness by lying down beside him, maneuvering the bush hat over his face and creating a retreat center of his own.

Unable to relax, John retrieved the Bible from his backpack. Turning to the creation account in Genesis, he read over the verses that Ronald had suggested he pay closer attention to.

> *And God said, "Let there be an expanse between the waters to separate water from water." So God made the expanse and separated the water under the expanse from the water above it. And it was so. God called the expanse, "sky." And there was evening, and there was morning—the second day.*

What John was supposed to glean from that, he had no idea. Ronald suggested there was a particular reason why the "Hebrew" God didn't pronounce this day's work to be "good," as He had all the others. But just how these verses could be made to fit the context of what their conversation had been—demons being the disembodied spirits of those who had lived in some remote golden age—John was equally oblivious. He recalled Ronald's other book that spoke of Satan's earthly rule, a period of time he had referred to as such a golden age, and put the idea to Chadwick. "You know anything about a golden age?"

Chadwick's eyes lifted from the otherworldly text only to find himself still trapped within the bizarre. "Sure. Most cultures have a golden-age legend."

"The reign of the gods on earth?" he recalled him saying.

Chadwick nodded. "Egypt's golden age is known as Zep Tepi, and Central America's was headed by the gods Quetzalcoatl, Viracocha, and Kukulcan."

"Are they the same?"

"Yeah, most likely Mayan and Aztec names for the same person, all meaning 'plumed serpent.'"

"No, I meant the golden age of Egypt and Central America. Were they the same?"

"Oh." He thought about it. "There are similarities. Why are you asking?"

He pointed at the book in his lap. "One of Ronald's books claims that, according to a passage in Ezekiel, Satan once ruled on earth as God's high priest, directing creation in worshipping Him. But he left out Satan's subsequent rebellion against God and just referred to the time as a lost golden age."

"And you think that Zep Tepi was that time?" Chadwick asked.

John shrugged. "That's what I'm asking you." He handed him the Bible and pointed to the section he was referring to.

"Interesting," Chadwick responded after reading it. He handed the Bible back. "Though, I'm not sure First Time is what's being referred to here. According to some sources, Zep Tepi is said to reoccur at the beginning of *every* 'Phoenix' cycle."

"What's that?"

"A cycle that rotates in thirteen-thousand-year intervals, always ending with a cataclysm. Which some believe to actually be an evolutionary agent that nature, or order or whatever, uses to propel the planet's life forms into the next stage of enlightenment. Thus the New Age craze surrounding the dawn of Aquarius."

John squinted in thought.

Picking up on John's confusion, Chadwick explained that many ancient civilizations believed the earth went through phases, each one having come to an end with a global cataclysm that humanity barely survived. The present cycle, according to the Aztecs and Mayans—or their much older predecessors, whoever they might be—is the Fifth. And it was the dawn of the Fifth Sun, after the destruction of the Fourth by a great flood, that Kukulcan, or Quetzalcoatl to the Aztecs, had supposedly ruled over in a sort of golden age. The Fifth Sun was believed by them to have its own expiration date on the winter solstice of December AD 2012, when a special planetary alignment that only occurs once every twenty-six thousand years is to accompany the end of the Great Year. He said that was why the Mayans sacrificed each other, to keep the present Sun alive with the blood of those sacrificed, trying viciously to keep the present age from dying off as the last four had. "A lot of the megalithic ruins may have been built to survive the transition of the ages, acting as an encoded system of wisdom passed from one cycle to the next. There's a hermetic text of Egyptian origin called the *Sacred Sermon* that speaks of lordly men who were devoted to the growth of wisdom before their civilization was destroyed by the Flood. 'And there shall be memorials mighty of their handiworks upon the earth, leaving dim trace behind when cycles are renewed.'"

"You're losing me. What does this have to do with a golden age?"

"It has to do with First Time, which inadvertently has to do with your golden age. Are you familiar with astronomy?"

"Not really."

"Precession of the equinoxes?" he probed.

"No." John shifted in the sand, noticing Hunter peeking at them from beneath the brim of his hat.

"Well, let's just call it a phenomenon involving the earth's rotation, supposedly discovered by Hipparchus in 100 BC, although the ancients equated it into their monuments and calendars long before him. There's also a kind of precessional code that was worked into a lot of the ancient literature." He could tell from John's silence that he was going too fast. He sighed impatiently and backed up. "The earth spins on its axis once every twenty-four hours, right? And it orbits the sun every three hundred and sixty-five days, right? Well, precession is the twenty-six-thousand-year wobble the earth makes on its axis as it spins. It's such a slow process that it takes seventy-two years for the stars to shift just a single degree along the ecliptic. Anyway, it keeps the sun rising in a particular constellation on the vernal equinox for two thousand one hundred and sixty years. For example, they say the Age of Leo lasted from 10970 BC to 8810 BC before giving way to the Age of Cancer…which gave way to Gemini and eventually to our own Pisces. The entire rotation, caused by the wobble, takes almost twenty-six thousand years to complete. It's called a Great Year. You follow?"

"Yeah, sure," John mumbled.

"It's something we can very easily calculate with computer programs today, but that was somehow figured out and observed in prehistory, too." He scratched an itch on the back of his shoulder while gathering his thoughts. "Anyway, Orion's three belt stars are believed to have reached the lowest point of their precessional slide up and down the meridian around 10500 BC, while its zenith will come around AD 2012, depending on your numbers. So for the stars to go from the top of the meridian all the way down to the bottom takes twelve thousand nine hundred and sixty years, or half of a Great Year." He was using his hands to create a visual tutor. "The Sphinx locked into place with the constellation of Leo circa 10500, near the beginning of the Age of Leo. The three pyramids and the Nile River fastened into Orion's belt stars and the Milky Way at the same time. In other words, around 10500 BC, during the Age of Leo, the Sphinx was aligned with Leo, the pyramids were aligned with Orion's belt, the Nile reflected the Milky Way, and the belt stars were at the very beginning of their precessional journey, about to head back to the top of the meridian and up through the ages." He let John try to digest what he was saying before continuing. But to his surprise, it was Hunter who responded.

"So you're saying that the pyramids were built during this First Time, which was around 10500 BC, because they reflected Orion's belt?" he asked, not trying to conceal his skepticism.

Paul just glanced at them from over his shoulder, shaking his head in disgust. "Five minutes."

Chadwick ignored him. "Well, isn't it reasonable to think that First Time would've corresponded with the start of this astronomical half cycle?"

Hunter sat forward. "You're saying that these cataclysms are actually astronomically calculated?"

"And that First Time was designated as the beginning of our present cycle circa 10500. Which will supposedly expire in 2012. At least that's the theory." He looked out to where Chris was walking through the surf, and noticed that the curtains of night were beginning to close, the sun starting to descend behind them. "The Mayan First Sun began at the beginning of the precessional cycle, which would certainly seem likely if the existence of the solar system is to be credited to a creator-god; I mean, why *wouldn't* God start things orderly and at the very *start* of a cycle rather than just throwing everything into some random point within one? Why would He create and design the precise, synchronistic *order* of the cycle and not use it? Anyway, the Fifth Sun began in 3114 BC after a flood destroyed the Fourth—which obviously doesn't add up with the 9600 BC date, especially when First Time itself was supposed to come *after* the sinking of Atlantis."

"After? How could First Time come *after* anything?" John was growing more confused.

Looking up into the darkening sky, he sifted pink sand through his fingers as he answered, "There's an ancient text called the *Emerald Tablet of Thoth the Atlantean* that eludes to Thoth as really being the god Tehuti, the supposed ruler of Atlantis. Thoth is also known as Hermes and Merlin. Anyway, it's said that he escaped Atlantis in a pyramid-shaped spaceship at the end of the previous cycle and then returned through a portal once the cataclysm was over. The Zep Tepi gods then re-created life on earth."

"At the start of the Great Year's second half?" Hunter asked.

"You guys are ridiculous," sneered Nick from behind closed eyes.

Paul smiled in response to the accusation, though his hawkish gaze never unlocked from the swaying trees.

Chadwick nodded to Hunter's question.

John's eyes fell to his feet. "But how can the Fifth Sun correspond with Egypt's First Time if—"

"They don't," Chadwick cut him off. "The Fifth Sun began in 3114 BC, which would put it around the time of the Bible's date for Noah's Flood—at least according to 'young earth' creationism. The sinking of Atlantis and First Time are said to be much older. The *First* Sun began at the beginning of the Great Year. By calculating backward, using the five thousand one hundred and twenty-six-year length of the Fifth Sun, we get twenty-five thousand six hundred and thirty years for the Great Year. Calculate 10500 BC as the date for the beginning of that cycle and you're only off by three hundred years. It's ballpark and close enough to suggest that Egypt's First Time corresponds with the First Sun and will end with the Fifth at the completion of the precessional cycle in 2012."

"Okay, so even if 10500 *is* First Time, how do you know the pyramids were built then?"

"Well, it'd be easier to build them as a reflection of the sky above rather than having to calculate what the sky either would be or had been in the past. But who knows, maybe they were built beforehand so that they were already standing when they locked into the stars, or maybe they were built much later on sites already considered sacred by ancient astronomer priests."

John asked, "You're referring to the alignment you were talking about?"

Chadwick sighed again and got to his feet. "Yeah. The Giza plateau was constructed to mirror the heavens," he said impatiently. "According to astronomical calculations, the three pyramids of Giza were perfectly aligned with Orion, Osiris' counterpart, around 10500 BC. As are most megalithic monuments, temples, and pyramids all the way from Mexico to England. Anyway, the Great Sphinx was also perfectly aligned to its counterpart, Leo. There's also a temple complex in Angkor that reflects Draco, and though it was built between AD 802 and 1220, its alignment is perfectly matched to the skies of the 10500 BC spectrum as well."

"Then couldn't the pyramids have been built afterward, too?" Nick asked, rolling onto his side. It was clear from his tone that he was barely able to keep from addressing the question with, *you idiot*.

"Yeah, I just said that," Chadwick said, stepping backward. "But there's aquatic erosion on the body of the Sphinx that some believe was caused by a great flood or some rainy climate that preceded it. And if you're to take 9600 BC to be the general time of the flood, then you're back to ballpark with 10500."

"What's the accepted date?" Hunter asked, getting to his own feet.

"Fourth Dynasty. Though there's no evidence for it. Old Kingdom texts are silent about it, and it's pretty clear that it's not Khafre's face, as the experts so adamantly claim. Like I said before, the Sphinx Temple and the Valley Temple are constructed from blocks that weigh an average of two hundred tons each, a feat that scholars like to pin on the back of slaves. But even if it could've been accomplished by mere manpower, it still doesn't explain where their astronomical knowledge came from, or how they were able to so accurately manifest it on the ground through such large structures."

After contemplating for a moment, John further inquired, "But if the new era began in the wake of the Flood, and the Sphinx predated it, how could it have been built during First Time?"

"Like I said, First Time is believed by some to be the *re*-creation of life, not necessarily the beginning of all time. The Sphinx *could've* been built before the Flood. There's a stela that's still standing between its paws that claims it marks the site of First Time, though which First Time isn't exactly clear. Who knows? In the case of the three pyramids, they align with Orion's belt at 10500, but the four star shafts of the Great Pyramid line up with their own respected stars in the sky of 2500 BC. So whether it was constructed in 10500 to look forward to 2500 or whether it was constructed in 2500 to look back at 10500, or some explanation in between, is certainly debatable."

"What star shafts?" This from Hunter.

"There's four long passageways built into the Great Pyramid. The two to the north point to *Beta Ursae Minoris* and *Alpha Draconis* in Draco, and the two facing south point at *Sirius* and *Zeta Orionis*." He turned and started walking away, saying as he went, "It's said that the gods ruled over Egypt for more than ten thousand years before the time of the demigods, while other texts credit the demigods for the re-civilizing of the land. Egypt's own records aren't consistent with each other and date First Time anywhere from eight thousand to forty thousand years before the First Dynasty. It's the similarities that are significant. I have to pee." He dropped Ronald's book and walked to the edge of the woods.

Paul watched him intently, maneuvering the submachine gun on his lap as if expecting something to burst from the forest and snatch Chadwick away.

John tried to find a place within his mind where Chadwick's information might comfortably fit, but he wasn't having any luck in quantifying such material within the library his worldview so diligently maintained. But then, thinking back to what had triggered his question in the first place, he suddenly became enraptured by a sort of relationship between Ronald's words and the things just learned. He absentmindedly began tracing an image into the sand while trying to mentally decipher the connection.

Chadwick was about to turn away from the tree line when a sparkle caught his eye, something lying five yards away and half concealed by undergrowth. He looked back at the others and saw Paul watching him. Quickly flashing a nervous smile, he laughed to himself, giggling at his frayed nerves…or because of them. "What am I doing?" And then he stepped across the boundary between beach and forest.

It was some kind of metal, the water lying on its exposed edge responsible for creating the glimmer that had captured his attention. As he bent down to brush the dirt off the object, an odd feeling swept over him from behind. He spun around. Nothing. Only the beach off in the distance, Paul standing and looking annoyed. Taking a deep breath, he waved an "it's alright" gesture to him before forcing his eyes back to the metal. He sensed something watching him, closing in on him. He needed to get out of there. But…

"What the—"

A handle.

Grabbing it with two hands, he pulled, lifting whatever it was connected to up and out of the mud.

A sword.

He stood there for a second, staring at what he had unearthed, not able to fully comprehend it. That it was a *sword* was strange enough, the fact that it was seven feet long…

Chadwick thought he heard something close by. Probably just the leaves rustling. Or maybe not. He decided to run.

When Chadwick first stepped into the woods, Paul initially thought something was wrong. But when Chadwick turned and waved to him, Paul just assumed that nature was calling for something more time consuming. He began to relax a little. At least until, seconds later, Chadwick came running out of the woods.

"Hey," Paul said over his shoulder, getting the attention of the others. Once he had it, he nodded in Chadwick's direction.

Everyone got to their feet, weapons suddenly in hand.

When Chadwick got closer, they noticed that he was dragging something through the sand, a long thin line following him from the woods.

They jogged out to meet him.

John asked, "What the heck is that?"

Breathing heavily, Chadwick answered, "What's it look like?" And then he held it up, struggling to keep its blade balanced in the air above him. "It was buried just inside the tree line."

After a moment of silence, Hunter could only state, "It's seven feet long."

Paul was already scanning the trees again, as if expecting whatever had lost the monstrous weapon to be lurking nearby.

"It's heavy." And Chadwick let its blade swing down, an audible arc slicing through the air before burying itself in the sand.

"Look at it," Nick whispered. "That didn't come from a souvenir shop."

"Just where in the hell are we?" It was Chris, back from his stroll and now standing behind them, his boots on and laced.

Hunter reached for the sword, touching it. "Look at the handle, the craftsmanship." The handle itself was about two feet long, the metal construction wrapping around itself in braids. There were little chips along the edge of the blade that indicated use.

"Wouldn't want to meet the guy who wielded that in battle," John remarked.

"What battle?" Nick responded.

"Come on," Paul interrupted. "Let's get out of here." And he marched back to collect their stuff.

Reaching down for his backpack, John noticed Chadwick standing beside him, looking strangely down at the ground. "What?" he asked.

Chadwick pointed to the design John had drawn into the sand. "What is that?"

"It was on one of Ronald's maps," he said, throwing the bag over his shoulder. "Each corner originating at a point of the Bermuda Triangle. The top of the triangle was capped off like this with…"

Chadwick's eyes narrowed in scrutiny. "The Eye of Horus. It's a pyramidion, or *benben* stone. Associated with the cult of the Phoenix. The Egyptian *Benu* bird of Heliopolis came from the place the gods were born and, when it landed, started creation—or *re*-creation—giving birth to First Time. The word *beben* indicates the seeding of a womb, and the capstone represents Osiris' seed, which created Horus from the womb of Isis."

"Really," Chris said, now joining him in studying John's artwork. "And I thought it was on the dollar bill."

Chadwick turned. "It is."

"Come on, time to go," Paul announced again, this time with a little more urgency.

John walked over to where Chadwick had dropped Ronald's book and picked it up.

Chadwick asked, "What about the sword?"

Nick smirked. "Would you rather carry the sword or the gun?"

A quick look back to the forest. "Definitely the gun." And he dropped the sword, leaving it behind in favor of the submachine gun, though deep down, he wasn't so sure even that could protect him from the presence he'd just felt in the woods.

* * * *

As they left the mysteriously empty beach and its giant sword behind, they eventually had to enter the edge of the cedar forest to avoid more mangrove swamps that had come up to engulf the coast. Paul walked out in the lead, never taking his eyes from the wildlife around them, searching for any sign of a hidden presence. All of them were on guard, the altar, the crystal arrow, and the sword resonating in the collective center of their apprehension.

John walked up closer to Chadwick, his own eyes scanning the treetops, wondering when he would begin hearing thunder again. "Ronald said that demons are actually benevolent spirits disembodied from a golden age," he said softly.

Chadwick nodded and then almost slipped on a wet rock. "Hesiod. *Works and Days*."

"Yeah, well, I think he was trying to say that those spirits were once people on the earth during Satan's reign."

"If you Google it, you'll find a similar theory about the Atlanteans."

John thought back to the books on Ronald's shelf, the map that included Atlantis, Chadwick's reference to *Thoth the Atlantean,* and the 9600 BC date for the sinking of the island. "Does Atlantis play into the golden-age scheme?"

"Oh, yeah," Chadwick answered enthusiastically. He removed his glasses and rubbed his eyes. "According to Plato's *Critias* and *Timoeus*, the gods divvied up the earth among themselves in the first ages, Poseidon being given the sea and a large island continent. He divided the continent into ten kingdoms, giving one to each of his ten sons, but made his oldest son, Atlas, ruler over all of them. He named the continent and its surrounding seas after him.

"To make a long story short, the first ten kings inscribed a code within Poseidon's temple that was to be followed by all the kings and kingdoms of Atlantis, but future generations of evil kings ignored it and tried instead to conquer the whole world. As an apparent act of judgment on the island, which had become full of evil sorcerers, Zeus sent earthquakes that sank the island."

He wiped sweat from his brow before putting his glasses back on. "The account of its sinking was passed down to Solon, the Athenian statesman who died in 558 BC, by an Egyptian priest. The priest told Solon that the earth had gone through *many* catastrophes, the most recent being a great flood around 9600 BC. The Greek philosopher Proclus reported that Plato's student Crantor visited Egypt in 300 BC and actually saw for himself two pillars that had been inscribed with the Atlantis story."

The more Chadwick talked, the more uneasy Hunter became, chills racing up and down his spine. "How's Atlantis connected to Egypt?"

"The Egyptian priest told Solon that his Greeks were only children in the realms of wisdom, because unlike them, they didn't have an ancient system of wisdom that was handed down to them, a wisdom that contained the earth's cataclysmic history and the Atlantis account."

"Wait," Nick interrupted. "Are you saying that Plato got the Atlantis story from the Egyptians?"

"Certain esoteric traditions claim that the illuminated initiates of Atlantis knew their continent was going to be destroyed and that they fled the island beforehand. They established themselves in Egypt as the land's first divine rulers and the originators of the ancient teachings Solon had been told about. The very center of the Atlantean wisdom-religion was a great pyramid temple that stood in the midst of the City of the Golden Gates. It was from that pyramid that the initiated priests of the Sacred Feather went out into the rest of the earth with the keys of universal wisdom, building pyramids and temples wherever they proselytized."

Hunter was confused. "So then all this pyramid stuff *did* originate with Atlantis?"

But before Chadwick could attempt to clarify, John asked about the Sacred Feather. "Didn't you mention something about a feather before?"

"The plumed serpent." He swatted some dangling leaves out of his face. "A civilizer, astronomer, and builder who taught religion and wisdom during Central America's golden age—the wisdom of which is detectable within the Olmec, Mayan, Chiapa, Aztec, and Inca civilizations." He shrugged. "Some believe Quetzalcoatl and Noah to be the same person described by different cultures in the re-civilization stories. Whether Noah, Xisuthrus, the great father of the Thlinkithians, Quetzalcoatl, or the Seven Sages, they all appear as the great civilizer who rebuilt the kingdom of man in the wake of global apocalypse. What's interesting is that the account of the Seven Sages leaving Atlantis and arriving in Egypt correlates with the 10500 date of First Time."

Hunter asked his question again. "And Atlantis is *the* lost civilization that all this stuff originated from?"

Chadwick raised his shoulders again. He was enjoying talking because it was taking his mind off their predicament. "It's one of the theories. The priests who fled Atlantis took their advanced wisdom and knowledge of the sciences and established themselves as deities all over the world. They marked sacred sites and built on them in ways that were recorded by the constellations some nine hundred years before the Flood. Some of the ruins may still exist, like the

Temple Valley and maybe the Great Pyramid, but probably in most, like in Angkor and Baalbek, initiates of the surviving Craft built on the sacred sites long after their original structures were wiped out by the Flood. So according to one view, Atlantis was destroyed by the cataclysmic Flood that ended the first half of the precessional cycle, but its wisdom was preserved and reestablished in specific places afterward, whether in Central America under Quetzalcoatl or Viracocha, or in Egypt by Osiris. All three of them, among plenty of others, share similar characteristics as great civilizers appearing after a flood. All of them are associated in some way or another with serpents, statues of feathered serpents appearing everywhere from Egypt to South America."

"Thus suggesting a connection between them and the Sacred Feather priest-craft from Atlantis," mumbled John. He found it rather disturbing that all these legends were crediting a *serpent* for their past golden age.

"Seems that way," Chadwick replied. His shoe slipped off and he had to go back and pick it up.

Paul turned and waited for him before continuing. He didn't trust their surroundings at all and, though Chadwick might be finding this dialogue familiar and a source of some comfort, all the talk of cataclysm was putting him on edge.

"However," Chadwick stated, hurrying to catch up, "the book of Genesis says that God gave a one-hundred-and-twenty-year warning of the Flood, not a nine-hundred-year warning."

"What are you saying?" Nick asked. The weapon was growing heavy in his one hand, and he was forced to rest its barrel in the crook of his handless arm.

"I'm saying that trying to make everything fit into one scenario will give you a migraine. But like I said, it's not the differences that are important. It's the similarities that prove there is an element of truth that propelled the stories in the first place."

John was getting the distinct feeling that all of this was somehow directly related to his present state, encompassing everything from Ronald's writings and the VHS tape to what he'd seen in Afghanistan. He wasn't exactly sure why, other than the obvious connection between Ronald's writings and this strange place he was captive in. He asked Chadwick if he thought the things they had just seen were connected to the esoteric wisdom supposedly passed down from the other side of the Flood.

"A trademark of this esoteric wisdom is the seeming obsession with the sky. It was said of Quetzalcoatl that he taught man science, showing him the way to measure time and study the revolutions of the stars. It's this intimate astronomical knowledge introduced to mankind that explains how the Mayan pyramids could be aligned with certain constellations, and the Great Pyramid could summarize the entire northern hemisphere with atomic-clock precision using methods that, *to this day*, baffle engineers, astronomers, mathematicians, and archeologists." He nodded cautiously, as if admitting it might bring it into existence. "I'm pretty sure that the site we just came from has the same astronomical characteristics."

John had one more question left, something that had been nagging the back of his consciousness throughout the length of their entire conversation. "Is it true that Poseidon is analogous to Neptune?"

Chadwick looked at him strangely, not comprehending the origin of such a question. "Yeah," he answered.

John stared down at his moving feet, watching the terrain pass beneath them. "I saw a statue of Neptune in Bermuda…" But he couldn't bring himself to finish the thought, so instead he asked, "Did Poseidon happen to father children by a human woman?"

"Of course."

"Any chance they were giants?"

"He fathered a lot of strange things, and with a lot of different creatures, but yes, he had giants as offspring."

"So the Atlantis story would fit with the giant legends, too."

"Actually, the war instigated by the evil Atlantean successors is thought to be a parallel to the story of Cain's line, the giants, and Noah's righteous family, the conflict climaxing with the Flood."

Wonderful, John thought.

"The City of the Golden Gates, Atlantis's capital, is also believed by some to be the archetype of the New Jerusalem. Man chased from the Garden of Eden by a flaming sword, the Genesis flood, and the serpent on the cross—which is an Atlantean emblem of divine wisdom—are all suspected to have arisen from the Atlantis account. A mountain in the middle of the island was supposedly the basis for the stories of Olympus, Meru, and Asgard."

John wondered if the City of the Golden Gates could be related to the Ezekiel passage, of Satan's surroundings in Eden. The VHS tape, the giants in Genesis 6, fallen angels, the Bermuda Triangle, Satan appearing to Eve in the form of a serpent…what did all of it have to do with him, with everything that was happening?

Hunter's voice interrupted his thoughts as he looked up from the map and announced that Higgs' and Horseshoe islands were just ahead of them.

But it was Nick's voice that captured their attention. "What is that?" he asked, stepping closer to the bank and peering through the mangroves. "Look, on the tip of the island, you see it?"

"I see it," Chris agreed. "Looks like a bunch of rocks."

"No." The now-familiar sense of awe had swept back over Chadwick, perplexity moving his feet toward it despite a significant channel of water standing in the way. "They're monoliths. Like the Moai of Easter Island."

"You mean that row of statues?" Chris questioned. *Why not?* he thought. Soon they'd probably be coming across a flying saucer, too.

"Actually," he whispered in response, "there are eight hundred and eighty-seven of them."

"Never understood why they called it Easter Island," Chris remarked, placing his hands on his hips and letting the wind pull at his hair.

Even as he responded, his eyes were glued to the distant piece of land. "Because Jacob Roggeveen's crew came across it on Easter Sunday in 1722.

Researchers think it might've actually been called 'eyes looking to the sky' before that." He started taking his shoes off.

"What're you doing?" Paul asked.

"I'm going over there."

"No, you're not."

"Yes, I am." He took the gun off his shoulder and handed it to John.

"No, you're not."

But it wasn't Paul's voice this time.

They all turned.

Standing there before them, chest heaving and covered with dirt, was Jackson. "You go over there, and they'll eat you."

TEN

9:13 p.m. 22nd day of May. Wilkinsburg, Pennsylvania

Curled up in John's favorite chair, Kristen sat staring through the blank television set that was positioned across from her. As if a looking glass into the deep territories of space, it provided a boundless eternity through which her thoughts could travel free. Her mind grappled ceaselessly with all the possible scenarios that might explain why John wasn't calling or answering her calls. His last text message, sent this morning, was all she could think about. Was it just her emotions getting the best of her, or did the message contain a hint of finality to it? After spending the day cleaning the house to pass the time, she now found herself exhausted and left with nothing else to distract her from such worried thoughts. The idea of watching a movie was what brought her to the chair, but upon sitting down, she found that she was too physically and emotionally drained to even reach for the remote beside her.

Finally, as her eyes focused, exchanging one world for another, the television's spell released her. And that was when she noticed the VCR. It was resting on the floor beside the TV stand, the multicolored cables reaching up and into the side of the television. *Strange*, she thought. Because she knew the old machine should be in the attic, where it had been stored ever since they moved in. How she'd missed it while cleaning was equally as puzzling. Finally, with curiosity now motivating her, she leaned forward and took the remotes from the small table next to her. She hit the play button, and the screen filled with static. So she rewound the tape, wondering why John had brought the relic down from its dusty home. After a few seconds, not waiting for the tape to reach the beginning and stop on its own, she randomly pressed the play button again.

A man wearing glasses instantly filled the screen. He was speaking rather animatedly about something she couldn't determine, but after a few moments, she realized it had to be footage from an old university debate. Her curiosity rising, she watched as the man on the television retrieved a microphone from its stand and stepped in front of the table he'd been seated behind. He walked to the front of the stage, the microphone's long wire chasing after his feet. She couldn't say why she was so captivated by the man's words, for she couldn't even siphon a droplet of meaning from them. But still she leaned closer, drawn to the mysterious message—or perhaps the lips forming it.

"Professor Adler's view *assumes* that the progeny of both Seth and Cain grew apart from one another, being segregated morally," the man was saying. "It *assumes* that Cain's descendants were universally characterized by godlessness and carnality, and it *assumes* that Cainite women were of a higher beautiful quality than those of the godly Sethites. And," he added, "the view *assumes* that these characteristics were so *universally* well-known that the writer was doubtless as to what his readers' interpretation of such a text would be. For at the time in which the author set down to describe this ancient event—many, many years later and from the other side of the Deluge—it is obvious that the universal fame surrounding the event of our passage was *still* very familiar to all and that all knew *exactly* what was meant by his specific descriptions of *Bne-Ha-Elohim* and *Bnoth-Ha-Adam*. The mighty men of old, heroes, men of renown…

"These were the ancient and legendary tales that stemmed from the unlawful unions spoken of, unions that required a *universal* flood to, in effect, return the production of the human race back to a single pure family." He frowned as if saying as much recalled pictures of what it must have been like to witness such universal death. "Again," he breathed, "the words used at the time of this writing, and at the time of Job's writing, were well-established and familiar ones that had been used to define a very *specific* class of beings. They were so familiar that the authors of both books took for granted their readers' ability to decipher the true meaning of their words, which, ironically in Job's case, there is not even a debate today as to what the interpretation of the words should be. Indeed, if the 'sons of God' should be rendered as the 'sons of holy or pious men,' then why in other places where such classifications are more than obvious does this phrase *not* appear? Psalm 37:29, Proverbs 11:28, and Ezra 9:2 are examples of where one would expect *Bne-Ha-Elohim* to appear if this is indeed its true meaning."

Kristen still had no idea what he was talking about and figured she should finish rewinding the tape if she really wanted to find out, but she couldn't seem to move. She was so entranced by the man that understanding what his words actually meant wasn't really a concern. But why? What was it that was provoking such a response from her? He was only as handsome as the poor quality of the recording allowed, so it wasn't some physical attraction that was paralyzing her. His voice, however… It carried within it the tone of authority. And the way he moved seemed almost mystical, something slightly seductive even in the way he took a sip of water from the glass on the table.

"Even if you want to look to Cain's settlement in the land of Nod, which is described as being over against Eden, you have to come up with an explanation as to how the close proximities of these two lineages managed to produce, over time, two *separate* and *distinct* races. And yes, I acknowledge the fact that Seth's genealogy is set apart from Cain's, but is it not for the simple reason of pointing out the Messiah's line? The fact of the matter is, there is no scriptural evidence that Cain's line was more wicked than any other line, either at the time of the Flood or some other point prior. And, on the other hand, if the sons of Seth were as godly as some would have you believe, how then did they come to be enamored by women who represented the very opposite of everything they held dear? That 'they were fair' is the only reason we are given as to why the sons of God took wives from the daughters of men. Are we really to believe that the females in Cain's line were the only fair women in the world?"

The back of the moderator's head suddenly appeared just above the bottom of the picture, informing the bearded man that he had five minutes left before his rival received the floor again. The man nodded his acknowledgement without pause.

Kristen's heartbeat accelerated.

"Allow me to quote the Reverend Fleming," he continued, turning to pick up a piece of paper from the desk. He held it up but didn't seem to need it, the words rolling off his tongue unashamedly. "'When we find that, in the four passages in which it occurs, the expression *sons of God* meets us without any explanation of its meaning—this, at least, in the time of the writer, being well understood—and that, in three of these, it can designate only angels: when we see that to assign to it, in the remaining passage, the same signification, is consistent at once with the facts which are there related, and with the connection in which the passage stands—that it accords with all the circumstances, and meets the requirements, of the case—and that, only when we thus understand the term, can these ends be attained—we cannot but think that, to reject this signification, and substitute for it that of *pious men*, is, not merely to set aside the true and natural meaning, but it is, further, to propose an interpretation, which is not supported by the *usus loquendi,* and which, moreover, involves not only improbabilities, but even some absurdities.'" He then walked back around the table and sat down, replacing the microphone in its stand.

As soon as the man sat, the spell that had enraptured Kristen to his strange aura, felt through both time and space via the recording, was shattered. She quickly threw her finger at the stop button, immediately sending the picture to a sheet of blackness that stood reflecting her position before it. The series of chills trembling through her body was almost a welcome response simply because they spoke on behalf of her true purity, evidence that whatever had just happened to her was something that her soul did not welcome but, in fact, despised.

She ejected the tape and turned it over in her hands. Somehow, captured within the plastic box, was a sense of lingering sexuality, a primitive instinct cloaked within a body of sophistication that had drawn some part of her toward the mysterious speaker. She dropped the unmarked cassette tape on the floor, suddenly afraid that even touching it might welcome back the overtaking of her senses. More than just her senses…her very *body.*

Standing up, she went to the small table and fumbled with the remotes until she found the one that would shut the television off. As she began longing for the safety of her bed, wishing even more desperately that John would call, the tape stared up at her from its position on the floor, its two white-spoked wheels the eyes taunting her, asking questions she had no way of answering.

She fled the room, heading for the steps that would lead to the bedroom. But as soon as her foot touched the first step, the radio in the kitchen turned on, and the house suddenly filled with music. It stopped her in mid-motion. Slowly, she removed her foot from the bottom step and placed it gently back on the wooden floor, as if the music itself might detect her presence. She walked carefully toward the kitchen, her fingers tracing the wall beside her and offering some semblance of balance. As she grew nearer, she was able to identify the song echoing throughout the house.

"Kokomo" by the Beach Boys.

Her mind snapped at the song's audacity, its significance allusive but not so much so as to prevent her from applying it to her situation. Standing in front of the radio, she listened shakily to the message it sought to communicate—from where or from whom, she didn't know. Though the hair on her neck standing to attention suggested she had at least *some* idea.

The Boys wanted to take her to Bermuda.

She wanted to believe that it was just some fluke, a coincidence targeting an emotional overreaction already in progress.

And then the song, though it was playing from the radio, began to skip.

Kristen reached out to turn it off.

But it *was* off.

Gasping, she yanked the cord out of the wall.

The music kept playing.

And then her hands went to her mouth as she further realized that the skipping was rearranging the words of the song.

> *"Bodies in the sand, I wanna take you…bodies in the sand, in the sand, that's where you wanna go…falling bodies in the sand, out to sea…falling out to sea, that's where we wanna go…way down to a little place like…a place like…Bermuda… Bermuda… Falling bodies in the sea, out to sea, in—to the sea…Bermuda…Bermuda…"*

She grabbed the radio and flung it across the room, smashing it into the wall. Pieces of plastic bounced and skipped across the floor. But the Beach Boys just wouldn't shut up. Kristen covered her ears with her shaking hands, crying, prayer-filled tears streaking wet lines down her face. A few seconds later, the music came to a sudden stop, plunging the room into eerie silence.

Her cell phone rang.

The sudden loudness of the digitized tone destroyed the creepy silence, and she screamed in surprise. Trying to recover by placing a hand over the drum solo her heart was pounding out, she answered the incoming call with the other.

Her hope that it was John finally calling was dashed when the sound of Pastor Brian's voice came over the line. But at least it wasn't the hard and steady breathing of some masked villain wordlessly claiming responsibility for both the movie and song.

"Are you okay?" he asked, hearing the tremble in her voice.

"No," she blurted out, sobbing into the mouthpiece.

"What happened?"

She put a hand to her head. "I don't know," she cried.

"Are you alone?"

"Yes."

"Do you want me to send Tabitha over?"

A pause to compose herself. "Can you both come over?" She wasn't in a condition to care how presumptuous the request might sound.

But there was no hesitation on Brian's end as he assured her that they'd be right there.

* * * *

It was only fifteen minutes before Brian and his wife arrived at her front door, but those fifteen minutes proved to be enough time for Kristen to at least begin reacquainting herself with the reality she was used to. After hugs were exchanged, she explained John's failure to call (which had caused Brian to frown rather deeply) and then she showed them the cassette tape, trying to explain its contents while refraining from divulging the strange effect the movie had had on her. Next, she took them into the kitchen, to the radio she had thrown against the wall.

Brian studied the shattered remains, his mind trying desperately to appreciate what Kristen told him had happened. Was she mad? Had she imagined the song? Was there something else going on here? He had to consider the possibility. But then…

"You believe me, don't you?" Kristen asked, suddenly wondering if she'd made a mistake calling him.

The look in her eyes was all the convincing that Brian needed. Of course *she* believed her story about the Beach Boys' remix, but something told him that there was more to it than just a psychological fracture, that it *had* been real. There was an electricity in the air he could just sense fluttering on the periphery of their realm. "Yeah, I believe you." He moved a speaker with his foot, half expecting it to blast music at him. It didn't. "You know," he said, looking up at her, "John called me the other night. Late."

She shook her head. She hadn't known that.

"He had some interesting questions that seemed particularly weird at 2:30 in the morning." He put an arm around his wife. "Do you mind if I take a look at the tape?"

"No." And she led them back to the TV. "What was John calling about?"

"I think that whatever was on the tape stirred a curiosity. Not sure why, though."

She pointed to the VCR and the tape. "I'd like to leave the room while you watch it. There's something about the man in the video that's…" But she didn't finish the statement, just turned out of the room. Tabitha followed her.

Brian picked up the cassette and pushed it back into the machine, rewinding it to the beginning. With great curiosity, and picking up a strange vibration from some otherworldly sphere, he hit PLAY. He sat down in the chair facing the TV and settled in for whatever was to come.

When the tape ended, he found himself glued to the chair, deep in thought.

Once she knew the tape was over, Kristen brought a cup of coffee into the room for him. "So, what was it?" Try as she might, she couldn't hide the anxiety from her face. She was still shaken.

"It's an old debate on the sixth chapter of Genesis, on whether the phrase *sons of God* should be taken to mean 'angels' or 'sons of Seth.'"

"Oh."

"It's all the stuff John was asking me about. He even texted me from Bermuda last night and this morning. I called you to see if you've heard from him because he isn't texting me back."

"Do you think he's okay?" A hand reached to intercept a tear.

"I can't see why he wouldn't be." He left it at that, at a *logical* assessment.

She sat on the sofa next to Tabitha. "What about the guy in the video?"

"What about him?"

"Did he seem…*strange* to you?"

But the look that crossed his face made it clear that he didn't know what she meant. "No, why?"

Her eyes went to her feet as she whispered dismissively, "I did." But then she looked up, eager to change the subject. "What about the radio? That's weird, isn't it?"

He nodded, not knowing what to say. Yeah, it was *very* weird. Horror-movie weird. But he put the cup hastily to his mouth to escape such a need to clarify.

"Well, what should we do?"

"I think we should pray and keep you company until you feel you're okay to be alone."

She sighed. She didn't know if she'd *ever* feel like being alone again.

He set down the coffee. "Do you mind if I use the restroom?"

She shook her head, of course not.

He used the short walk to clear his mind. This was an odd situation that required a different approach than anything he was accustomed to dealing with. When he flicked the light on in the little bathroom, he found himself staring at the mirror across from him.

At what was written on it.

Two words took up the entirety of the glass.

SILLY WOMAN

The accelerator to his heart was thrust to the floor as he reached out to touch the letters. There was no substance he could detect beneath his fingertips, as if the words had been seared into the glass. He knew exactly what the phrase inferred—Paul's second epistle to Timothy, chapter three, verse six. *For of this sort are they which creep into houses, and lead captive silly women laden with sins, led away with divers lusts.*

And then he noticed something else in the mirror. The reflection of the wall behind him, above the toilet. It, too, had something written across it.

COVER THY HEAD,

It was a reference to Second Corinthians 11:5–10. *And every woman who prays or prophesies with her head uncovered dishonors her head…for this reason, and because of the angels, the woman ought to have a sign of authority on her head.*

His heart in his throat, and his skin on fire with trepidation, Brian spun back around to the mirror and took in all the words together, taking special notice of the comma after "head." In this case, it was a grammatical mark indicating who was being addressed. And so it read, *COVER THY HEAD, SILLY WOMAN.*

Brian knew this was no theological attempt at defining a woman's role in the church (he had settled that issue in his own mind a long time ago with Galatians

3:28 and a closer contextual study of the few so-called 'problem' passages). No, this was something sinister and twisted, meant to threaten and to divide. Much like the way man had misused Paul's letters to subjugate women and render half of Christ's body expressionless for nearly two thousand years. This writing here on the walls of the Carter house was the work of the author of such lies. Of such deception and destruction. He could feel it, radiating from the letters themselves, the taloned finger that penned them still near.

Without using the bathroom, Brian walked as calmly as he could back into the living room. He motioned for Kristen and Tabitha to get up, and then looked into Kristen's swollen eyes. "I think you should spend the night at our house."

ELEVEN

There's more rubble piled up at my feet, spilled both from the adjacent wall and the roof above. It stretches to the ceiling, almost completely concealing that whole side of the room—if it can be called that. As I begin to climb up the hill, loose rocks shifting underneath my weight and bouncing down to the floor, I notice an entranceway buried behind the debris. I don't know what I'm doing, why I need to get through the rocks. I can hear voices in my head coming from the other side, encouraging me to enter. I'm at the peak of the pile, just two feet from the top of the chamber, and I'm clearing away as many of the rocks as I can, tossing them one by one to the stone floor below. Finally, I have enough of the blocks cleared to make out the top of what can only be a giant door. Made of iron, it must be almost twenty feet high and up to six feet wide. I detect through my night vision strange markings on the stone surrounding the door, some kind of hieroglyph. It certainly isn't Arab. I can't stop myself from digging out the entire door. I need to know what's behind it.

John awoke to someone shaking him. "Time to move," the voice said. But the words slipped in and out of his cognizant grasp until the hands of comprehension could finally snatch them out of the air. He sat up and stared into the fire before him, but its dancing flames only entranced him more. A tall, shadowy figure was moving around the small fire, and for a second, John didn't know what it was. Indeed, he didn't know where he was or even *who* he was. With great effort, he turned his eyes away from the crackling spellbinder and tried to focus.

He saw his backpack resting beside him in the flickering light, and the familiar sight proved to be his first step back to reality. Slowly, the steps compounded, and past events began to catch up with him. Until they mercilessly ran him over, the shape of a million mysteries speeding away behind mystical taillights and a license plate shouting vulgarities that further mocked his confusion. He pressed his palms into his eyes and moaned, wishing that, nightmare aside, he could simply return to sleep's delightful state of ignorance. Even dreamworld wasn't as bizarre as the place he was currently drawing his breath.

It was Jackson who was going around the fire, shuffling everyone else awake, prodding them urgently toward the forest. And, judging from the moans that resulted, John was not the only one who had trouble making the transition back to the tropical Oz.

A silhouette appeared in front of the fire, kicking dirt at it. "You okay?" It was Paul's voice.

John wasn't sure if he was the intended recipient of such concern, so he didn't respond, just stood up to stretch. With his head tilted back and his eyes facing the sky, he could tell immediately that the angry cloud covering was still above them, blocking out any light the night sky might otherwise have had to offer. And then a raindrop struck him on the forehead and detonated all the weary trappings still imprisoning his senses.

Hours ago, Jackson had instructed them to get some sleep before nightfall, because for reasons he wouldn't specify, they were going to be traveling through the night. And because Jackson had seemed rather eager to get to wherever it was they were headed, John figured it couldn't have gotten dark all that long ago. He guessed it was probably ten or eleven o'clock.

By the time Paul finished quenching the fire, they found themselves surrounded by such a near-perfect blackness that their quiet voices and the earth beneath their feet became a source of surprising consolation, letting them know that a physical world still existed and hadn't really fizzled out with the fire. And then a beam of light pierced the darkness, sweeping back and forth and illuminating their surroundings.

"Let's go," Jackson's voice commanded from behind the brightness.

They could hear him walking away, the flashlight's glowing head moving with him.

The location Jackson had approved for their campfire rested some thirty yards into the tall cedar forest. He had warned against fires on the beach that might signal to the others their presence, something Chadwick received a scolding for—the needless discharge of his firearm (which was how Jackson tracked them after returning to the *Gegenes* and finding it deserted). But as to who or *what* it was that might discover their presence, he offered no such clarity. His silence, however, had not been taken to kindly, and it prompted a confrontation among the ex-SEALs that, for the most part, concluded with Jackson still not having to divulge much of anything.

Even as he moved farther into the darkness, John began reciting what had been revealed in the confrontation. One—they were, in fact, on the same land mass as that of the Bermuda islands, though there were obvious differences that Jackson didn't attempt to explain. Two—Henry was here somewhere, and they were going to find him. Three—Jackson had worked with Ronald to get them here, though he didn't seem to completely trust Ronald and was slightly bothered by Chadwick's presence. Four—Jackson was sorry for deceiving his teammates but didn't think they would have taken him seriously if he'd disclosed everything from the start. Five—there were things on the island that would be looking for them, specifically "Johnny." And six—they couldn't return to the *Gegenes* because "they" had already taken it.

These were the useable pieces that had spilled out of all the pushing and shoving, everyone seemingly resigned to the fact that it was all the information they were going to get for a while. But now, walking through the darkness and trying to avoid a thousand different unseen obstacles, John could sense the men around him growing impatient once more. And it was Chris who finally served as the mouthpiece for their fuming frustration. He began asking questions about the village, Henry's license, the wall that Chadwick claimed to be from some unknown but advanced era, the sword… But Jackson didn't respond. Not with shock at hearing such fantastic things, or with an explanation that might explain them.

John kept his eyes on the flashlight's beam as it picked up the terrain ahead, trying uselessly to remember what it revealed for when he finally reached it. But he just continued walking into trees and banging his shins on fallen branches. He was growing extremely impatient with the quick pace Jackson was setting and was about to call out to him when Chadwick whispered a question from the darkness behind him.

"Why did Jackson say that 'they' would be looking specifically for *you*?"

To which John simply replied, "Why do you think Ronald wanted *you* on the boat?"

The simple fact of the matter was that neither of them had a clue as to why they were here, or what role they had been destined to play in the place.

Wanting something to take his mind off both the agonizing journey and the ravenous thoughts of what his wife must be going through after not hearing from him, he further inquired about the monuments Chadwick had suggested had been built to reflect First Time.

It was obvious to Chadwick that John was trying to find a connection between First Time and the Golden Age Ronald had suggested belonged to Satan before his fall, and though he couldn't bring himself to care personally—not seeing what it had to do with their situation—he humored the request, explaining further the reason for the ground plan at Giza.

John had already forgotten most of the ancient Egyptian texts Chadwick was referring to, but he retained an understanding concerning the layout of the ancient sites, that it was supposed to play a pivotal role in the afterlife journey of the pharaoh, somehow directing him to the place where Osiris dwelt.

They continued to follow Jackson's beam of light through the falling rain, stumbling and falling and stumbling again. And as they walked with their hands stretched out in front of them, Chadwick attempted to further explain. The last thing John heard him say, however, was that the monuments of the Giza necropolis were part of a long-forgotten scheme used to initiate certain individuals into an esoteric cosmic wisdom linking earth to heaven and offering immortality to the traveler.

After that, Chadwick's voice had faded into the backdrop of John's own inner thoughts, further soothed away by the rain falling through the forest around them. When he finally tuned back into Chadwick's dialogue, he caught him saying something about the Egyptians being obsessed, not with the afterlife, as many supposed, but rather with creating a higher form of man through genetic engineering and other means. He started to relate it to the name of Henry's boat when the flashlight's beam spun around and landed right in his face.

"No more talking from here on out," Jackson ordered, shifting the bag of ammunition he'd taken from the boat.

"Where we going?" Chris' voice sounded from somewhere within the indiscernible obstacle course.

"You'll see."

And thunder erupted above them as they continued westward through the most troubling of dreams.

* * * *

The first trace of light broke over two pinnacles that were standing above the forest and piercing the coming dawn with their silhouettes. Which meant they were again heading eastward, into the rising sun. The two towers were standing about a quarter of a mile away, and even though three-quarters of each monument's body was hidden below the tree line, there was certainly no mistaking what they were. Suddenly, Chadwick's obscure and whispered lectures on Egyptology, prompted by John's search for a common denominator linking this place to Ronald's writings (and even more so, his own past), seemed all the more practical.

Chris squinted at the graying skyline. "Is that what I think it is?"

"The Washington Monument?" Hunter shook his head. "No."

"Obelisks," Chadwick stated with that familiar wonder woven into his voice. The sight made him forget about the body of water they'd had to swim across to get here and that his clothes were still soaking wet because of it.

"Come on," Jackson ordered, completely ignoring what everyone else was feeling. "We're not going that way." And he redirected his steps to the right, aiming instead for the beach.

But Chadwick's eyes were so captivated by the monoliths that he couldn't bring himself to move. "Where *are* we?" his voice whispered, echoing the same question Chris had asked earlier.

It was a question that everyone, Nick included, now found completely rational, for all notions of them being in present-day Bermuda had vanished with the night.

John, too, was mesmerized by the obelisks, electrocuted with an even stronger dose of the trepid feelings the smaller obelisk at the Cabinet Building had generated. And then he found Chadwick no longer staring at the monument, but at his chest, no doubt imagining his bare skin and the tattoo he'd seen on it earlier. John just shrugged and kept moving.

"Hey, Dr. Jones," Chris called back to Chadwick, "you wanna tell us what *they* mean, too?" Then he swore rather loudly as he walked into a tree.

Chadwick took his eyes off the flashlight's illuminating beam and put them back on the monoliths, staring at them again as if trying to decipher a meaning from some obscene riddle. "I already did. The pyramidion, or *benben* stone, that I said was associated with the cult of the Phoenix… I said that *benben* indicated the seeding of a womb and that the capstone represented Osiris' seed…"

"You were talking about the hovering capstone on the dollar bill," Chris remembered.

"Actually, I was commenting on Ronald's drawing of the Bermuda Triangle, but yeah, the capstone's represented at the top of the pyramid as well as at the top of the obelisk."

"Wait a second," Paul snorted from the growing shadows. "You're saying that Osiris' seed is sitting on top of the Washington Monument?"

"And in Vatican City. It's a phallic symbol," he clarified.

"But why would Osiris' winkle be made into a monument dedicated to our first president?" Chris asked, confused. It was a strange question because it seemed so foreign to the issues at hand…or did it?

"Washington, DC's filled with Egyptian symbology."

The statement prompted John to recall his conversation with the people from the cruise ship, the couple at the Keep who told him about the painting of Neptune in Washington.

Chadwick leaned closer to John, letting him know that he was the intended recipient of the coming statement. "During First Time, Osiris left Egypt to spread his wisdom to the rest of the world, but when he returned, his brother Seth killed him. Chopped him up in pieces and hid him. Isis, his wife, was able to find all the pieces but one." He pointed at the obelisks. "So she made one of gold and reassembled him, bringing him back to life long enough to conceive a son, Horus."

Chris overheard and chuckled despite himself. "An interesting twist to 'all the king's horses and all the king's men…'"

"It's where the practice of mummification was said to come from," Chadwick added before falling silent to his own thoughts. "The knowledge of Zep Tepi is believed to be stored in the golden capstone that once sat on the Great Pyramid…"

Jackson held a fist up in the air, suddenly signaling everyone to stop. He clicked the flashlight off and crouched to the ground.

"What is it?" Hunter whispered in Jackson's ear. The urgency in Jackson's actions had his own finger caressing the MP5's trigger.

Jackson whispered back, "We're at Tucker's Town Bay in Castle Harbor."

Hunter opened John's map, and Jackson obliged him by carefully shining the light on it. If Jackson was right, then they had trekked the entire length of St. David's Island, swam across to Hamilton Parish, and then traveled all the way south to their present position, the coast to their right and the bay directly ahead.

After Jackson turned the light off, Hunter asked in the blackness, "What are we doing here?"

"There's something I want you to see." Then he looked back in the general direction of the others. "Keep your heads down and be as silent as you possibly can. We're going in and out quickly." And then he crawled forward through the underbrush, leaving the rest of them to follow carefully in his wake.

The dense ferns eventually gave way to the bay and the large rocks piled high along its coast. Now that they were out of the forest and the sky was growing brighter, they could make out their surroundings without the aid of Jackson's flashlight.

"What the hell?"

It didn't matter who said it. They were all thinking the same thing.

Resting in front of them and littering the shallow water of the bay as far as they could see was an enormous fleet of boats and planes.

Jackson motioned for them to follow him, and they entered the lazy water, boats of every size surrounding them. There were small private motor boats, a huge tanker that sat stretching across the mouth of the bay three hundred yards away, and everything in between. Rows and rows of airplanes were also present, keeping the aquatic vehicles company.

Moving quietly through the water, Jackson gathered them all together beneath the one hundred and eighty-six-foot wingspan of a B-52 that was providing shelter for fifteen smaller Cessnas, Apaches, and Cherokees, their lightweight bodies rocking gently back and forth in the sloshing tide. Jackson pointed to the huge ship and whispered, "USS Cyclops."

The ex-SEALs muttered a string of profane disbelief.

But Chadwick didn't understand.

Chris explained, "The Navy considers her the greatest mystery of the sea. Vanished in March of 1908 with over three hundred men aboard." Then he fell into a whispered wonder of his own. "It's five hundred and forty-two feet long with a displacement of nineteen thousand three hundred and sixty tons."

"What is this, Jack? What's going on?" Hunter demanded. "Tell us where we are!"

But by now, John was already beginning to recognize some of the names around them. *Santa Rita. Timandra. Southern Districts. Sandra. Bounty. Witchcraft...* He started drifting away from the group, moving quietly through the clear water, its shapeless fingers reaching up and caressing his stomach. More familiar names. *Real Fine. Intrepid. Polymer III.* Then he spun back toward Jackson, pointing at the old vessels. "These are all boats and planes that vanished in the Triangle!"

Hunter, Paul, Chris, and Chadwick all stared at Jackson in anticipation, their eyes begging for an explanation that would make more sense than John's ridiculous announcement.

But none came.

"Come on," Jackson only whispered. And he led them out of the water and back south across the land, his eyes surveying their surroundings with an intensity that had everyone else doing the same.

They cleared the small stretch of land and found themselves staring out across a long beach that was littered with more vehicles. A lot more vehicles.

Chadwick gasped.

Huge cargo ships, like buildings, were stretching up into the sky, their massive propellers turning slowly in the wind like giant fans. Other freighters, five football fields in length, were lying on their sides. Small yachts were sprinkled about as if they'd simply fallen out of the sky one day. While some were completely buried, others looked ready to escape if only the tide would come in, take their hands, and carry them over the reef and the large rocks that separated them from the sea. And then there were the older vessels that time had eroded, ships made of wood, their sails now absent from rotting masts. Some were seventeenth and eighteenth-century warships; others most likely the floating prisons that had been hell on earth for a number of slaves.

Jackson led them down into the sand and continued guiding them through the museum of lost vessels. After skirting around a KC-135 Stratotanker, they came face-to-face with a submarine.

Its head was buried in the sand, its tubular body stretching upward at a seventy-degree angle as if it, too, had fallen from the sky. Beyond it were sitting rows of military planes dating from the 1940s: Avengers, PV-1 Venturas, Catalinas, PB4Y-2 Privateers, a C-54, C-133 Cargomasters... They were all rocking beneath the wind's gentle touch, standing ready as if waiting for their ghostly crews to take them out of here on one last mission. Farther away, there were some jets half buried in the sand—a Grumman Cougar, Fighting Tiger 524, and a Phantom II F-4E.

Chadwick held his head in his hands, trying to compute such an impossible equation. "This isn't possible," he repeated to himself.

John stepped past him, briefly laying a hand on his shoulder before noticing five TBM Avengers resting close to each other, bleached and rusted beneath cracked or missing canopies. "Flight 19," he said in disbelief, recalling Ronald's detailed account of the famous incident.

Even Jackson seemed taken aback by the presence of the lost flight, walking past them and reverently running his fingertips underneath their eroding wings before continuing to lead them all through more aisles of twentieth-century avionic technology. There were even a few representatives from the present century scattered throughout the crowd, letting them know how recently their world had been bridged by this one.

Thunder sounded, and they all jumped. The storm that had held off all night was about to unleash itself.

"Okay, let's get out of here," Jackson ordered, moving for the trees.

As John followed, he noticed a Tudor IV resting a few yards away, its paint faded, and its name peeled almost beyond recognition, but there was enough of it remaining for him to make a positive identification. The *Star Tiger*, another of the planes Ronald had described in detail. And then a thought smacked him in the brain. "Wait," he called out to Jackson.

He turned, a slight impatience flickering in his eyes.

"Where's Henry's boat?"

Jackson nodded. "That's why we need to get out of here right now."

"What do you mean?" Chadwick asked, Jackson's voice making him maneuver the submachine gun off his shoulder.

"They'll be showing up with it soon. We don't want to be here when they do."

But before anyone could even try to wrestle with another of Jackson's cryptic messages, he stood up straight and began looking around, his face suddenly distorted with concern.

"Where's Nick?" he asked.

Everyone looked around, realizing with dismay that he was suddenly missing.

And then, as they were searching their surroundings, sweeping their concerned gaze like radar designed to detect lingering clues, John's started pinging. He stepped away and turned around, taking note of the footprints they had all left behind in the wet sand. The line disappeared behind the swaying hangar of ghost-craft. Following the tracks back the way they had come, he stopped when he came across a different set of tracks. They were stretching from another direction before disappearing into the woods. At first, he thought they had to be Nick's. But then he finally got close enough to see just how *large* they were.

Chris cursed out loud, coming up behind him and seeing the prints for himself. "So now it's Sasquatch? Give me a break, man!"

Chadwick shook his head. It was clear what they were all thinking, but it was absurd. More than absurd, it was *insane*. And the insanity of it so disturbed them that nobody said another word.

At least not until John counted the number of toes belonging to the footprints.

Six toes.

And John's nightmares had become a reality once more.

TWELVE

7:08 a.m. 23rd day of May. Wilkinsburg, Pennsylvania

Kristen rolled over beneath the crisp sheets of the guest bed and stared intently at the cell phone that was resting dumb in her hand. Though it informed her that it was Sunday morning and that John hadn't called during the night, it still wasn't offering any explanation as to why. Her thumb danced desperately over the number keys again, and soon John's automated voice was telling her to leave a message. The helpless frustration was maddening, and she slammed the phone into the pillow beside her. After a moment to gather some composure and whisper a prayer, she swung her feet onto the floor and set about getting dressed.

When Kristen walked into the kitchen, Brian was standing there with his back to her, looking out the window. He had a steaming mug in his left hand and a phone pressed against his ear in the other. He was nodding to whatever was being said on the other end of the line and then tilting his head to see the watch on his wrist. "Yeah, that's fine," he said. "Just have him call me when he gets in. Thanks, I will. Bye." He hung up the phone and sighed deeply, turning around and coming face-to-face with Kristen. "Shhhugar!" he hollered, spilling some coffee on the floor.

"I'm sorry," Kristen said, running for the paper towels above the sink.

"It's okay," Brian reassured her, chuckling. "Don't worry about it." He had his free hand over his chest, trying to catch his breath.

But she wiped it up off the floor anyway.

"Thanks, you didn't have to do that."

She dropped the wet paper towel into the trash can beneath the window and looked outside. It was a typical scene that anyone in the country would be familiar with, nothing extraordinary or alarming, just a regular side street splitting rows of modest houses. But something about it did seem different. And she realized that the world itself was beginning to feel foreign to her, its everyday sights somehow altered. When she looked back to Brian, she saw that he was sitting at the table with his hands folded around the cup, his eyes glued to the steam whisking up out of it. She knew from his expression that something was wrong. "What is it?" she asked.

He looked up at her and almost started to say something, but instead dropped his gaze back to the dark contents of the mug.

"Brian…"

And then Tabitha walked into the room. "Good morning, Kristen," she said as politely as she could. But it was clear that she, too, was troubled. She circled around her husband and came up behind him, resting her hands on his shoulders. "Did you tell her?" she asked gently.

Brian shook his head.

"Tell me what?" Kristen stepped forward.

Finally, Brian leaned back away from the table and nervously rubbed his brow. "Kristen," he began, "you know that we're in a constant spiritual war, right? That our true enemies are not of flesh and blood…"

She narrowed her eyes and pursed her lips. "Is this about the radio?"

A pause. "I think so." And then his mouth fell shut again, still reluctant to put words to his thoughts. Sighing, he stood. "There's something else I think you should see."

Now Kristen was starting to panic. She had never seen Brian and Tabitha so uneasy before. "What?"

Brian led her out of the kitchen and up the stairs. Standing off to the side of the doorway, he invited her into his bedroom by motioning her past him.

Thoroughly confused, Kristen timidly stepped forward, eyes sweeping back and forth, trying to discern whatever had rattled her hosts. But she didn't detect anything strange. She turned back to face them, shrugging. "I don't…"

Then Brian pointed a finger up to the ceiling, above the bed.

When she lifted her eyes to where he'd pointed, a cold chill swept through her body. "What is it?" she whispered while stepping back and away from it.

The entire section of ceiling above the bed was covered in writing, though made up of characters she didn't recognize. Dark, hard strokes against the white ceiling paint had formed a grid of alien symbols.

"I don't know," Brian said. "But it wasn't there when we went to bed last night."

She shook her head. "I don't understand what… You think I have something to do with this?" Tears began dripping down her cheeks.

Brian sighed, his face sympathetic and pitiful. "I saw something like this in your bathroom."

Kristen studied him while letting the magnitude of his words sink in.

"I didn't want to tell you, because I didn't want you to be worried or scared," he explained.

"That's why you wanted me to stay here with you."

He nodded, and Tabitha put an arm around his waist, leaning against him.

Kristen forced herself to look back up at the ceiling. "What does it say?" She hadn't meant to whisper, but her throat seemed to be closing.

"I don't know. I think it's Sumerian. I have someone coming to translate it later today."

"Sumerian? As in the inventors of writing?"

But Brian could only shrug, helpless. "I have to get over to the building." He never called it "church" because the church was supposed to define a body of people and not a physical location. Referring to the church as a mere building, as far as he was concerned, always led to a host of false priorities. It was something he had to explain to John not that long ago. "You can come if you'd like, or Tabitha can stay here with you. Whatever you need to do."

But she wasn't hearing him. "Why would this be happening? I don't understand. Why now?"

Brian bit his bottom lip and exchanged a quick glance with his wife. "I think it may have to do with John."

THIRTEEN

Sunrise. 23rd day of May. Bermuda, Harrington Sound area

Paul was following closely on Jackson's heels, demanding to know just how, exactly, he'd learned of the lost vessels. The rest of them listened while simply trying to compute the obvious meaning the collection suggested.

"I knew about it," Jackson snapped, "because Ronald talked about it in his book."

"Wait." Chris spoke up. "You and Ronald knew about this place?"

"In theory."

Jackson was walking cautiously through the forest's undergrowth, weapon held firmly against his shoulder. They were backtracking, looking for signs of Nick, while wary of anything with six toes that might be hiding in the woods around them. The sound they'd heard coming from within the forest while at the wall was still very fresh in their minds, giant footprints and a seven-foot sword only compounding their alarm.

"And you just didn't think it was worth mentioning, is that it?" Hunter demanded, almost shouting he was so angry.

"If I told you, you wouldn't have believed me."

"Yeah, or maybe we wouldn't have come."

"For a chance to save Henry, you'd have come," Jackson retaliated.

Trying ever so hard to push the six *huge* piggies from his mind, John took Ronald's book out of his backpack as he asked, "How did you know Henry was here?"

But before Jackson could refuse to answer, Chadwick blurted out, "How did you *get* us here?"

To that, Jackson turned and pointed at John. "Him."

"Him what?" Chadwick persisted.

"He's got the same blood as Henry. I knew he'd open the door."

"What are you talking about?"

Before anything else could be said, however, a faint cloud of smoke came floating across their path, climbing whimsically through the evergreens.

They stood still, studying the shapeless tendrils dancing toward them, until Paul pointed to their left.

"Over there." And he followed the serpent-like trail, its floating body leading them to a patch of glowing embers.

Squatting to the wet ground, they all fell silent, the wind stroking the fire's remains some twenty yards ahead of them. Slowly, they began moving forward, their weapons sweeping back and forth and searching for movement.

Upon reaching the fire and completing a reconnaissance sweep of the area, Paul announced, "It's clear." And he let the MP5 drop idle to his side.

"That's Church Bay in Harrington Sound," Hunter said, pointing to a break in the trees.

Jackson was kicking at the ashes around the fire, quenching the glowing remains of what smelled like a recent steak dinner—or breakfast. And then Chadwick's voice hollered a loud expletive that rebounded off the trees and brought everyone running toward him.

"What is it?" yelled Chris, coming up beside him.

But Chadwick was standing motionless, his eyes wide and focused on something down on the ground in front of him. Whatever it was, it had him covering his mouth with one hand and pointing shakily with the other.

Paul stepped forward, disdain rippling through the muscles in his neck. "What the—"

Piled before them was a heap of gore, broken bones and torn flesh protruding from tattered and blood-soaked clothes.

Paul reluctantly poked it with his boot, hoping that spreading it out would help identify what it was. It looked like washed-up carnage left over from a shark attack. When he nudged the pile, intestines came spilling out through the sleeve of a shirt. "Looks like it was attacked by a wood chipper."

But Hunter was the only one to appreciate the most horrible aspect of Chadwick's discovery. "Those are Nick's clothes."

Chadwick puked all over the ground behind him.

"No," Jackson whispered. "No, no, no…" And he began looking around for something.

A mist covered Chris' eyes as he came to understand the situation, emotionally if not yet rationally. "What're you looking for?"

"The head."

It was true, there was no head present within the mess.

"Look." Paul was pulling a long bone out of the clothes, tendons, muscles, and strings of flesh tearing away from it in the process. He tossed it to Jackson.

Chadwick threw up some more.

Examining what was obviously a femur, Jackson suddenly swore, dropping it to the ground.

"You knew about that, too, didn't you?" Paul growled at him.

But Jackson just turned his head toward Hunter. "Are you *sure* they're the same?" He pointed at the clothes.

Hunter bent over the gruesome pile of remains and carefully pulled out a black, blood-soaked bush hat. Setting it aside, he put his hands back in the butchered mess and retrieved a piece of camouflage. "His hat and his pants." He let them fall back to the ground.

That was when John bent over and picked up the femur, examining it for himself. As he studied it, a sense of horror wrapped itself around his body and began squeezing so hard that he suddenly couldn't breathe. He dropped the bone, taking a step back.

"What?" Chris wiped a tear from his face.

"Teeth marks."

Chris' mind reeled, his head moving back and forth between the fire and the human remains. "No," he protested.

"You saying something *ate* him?" Hunter yelled. "*Cooked* him over a fire?" He was losing it.

Lightning tore through the sky, and a blast of thunder shook the ground beneath their feet just half a second later. They all looked up in time to see the floodgates finally open, the timing of which seemed appropriately fitting.

But then a great rushing wind exploded from the trees around them, the air filling with a hideous, high-pitched whistle.

"What is that?" Hunter called out, frantically aiming the MP5 up into the trees. But the rain was falling too hard, building liquid walls they couldn't see through.

And then things were flying into them, grabbing at their clothes.

John covered his face, swiping blindly at the air around him. At first, he thought they were bats, but the demonic laughter seemed to suggest otherwise.

Both Paul and Chris opened fire on the skies above them, their anguished screams echoing along with the blasts.

"Stop shooting!" Jackson was shouting.

But still they kept channeling their pain into an attack on the unknown, at what had taken Nick from them.

When they did stop, their chests heaving from exhaustion, they could hear that the awful screaming had stopped, the forest now eerily silent beneath the downpour.

"They were just *birds*!" Jackson hollered at them, throwing half of one in their direction. "They're cahows!" He cursed loudly. "We need to get out of here! *Now!*"

"If that's Nick," Chris said, the barrel of the weapon sizzling under the cold rain, "then we need to bury him." Emotion pinched his words.

Jackson's jaw tightened. "Then do it *fast*."

Paul kicked one of the dead birds and reached into his pocket to replace the spent clip.

Jackson, however, had turned his attention to the surrounding trees the water fall was attempting to conceal. He was standing completely still, hardly breathing. "They're nocturnal, used to thrive here before the settlers ate them into near extinction," he whispered, his mind spinning. And then he turned away from whatever he was listening for and snapped impatiently at the others, "Let's go! You wanna bury him, then do it!"

John, Chris, and Hunter dropped to their knees and started digging frantically through the mud. Chadwick simply collapsed against a tree, his eyes closed, his breathing labored. The rain was mixing his vomit with the river of blood now flowing from Nick's remaining anatomy, and he tried not to look at it. "That was the noise we heard yesterday at the wall," he managed to say.

"Shearwater," Jackson said. "Another bird. Must've been up in the trees with them. Sounded to the Spanish like, *diselo, diselo*—which is 'tell them' in English. They thought they were being laughed at by witches, believed that devils haunted the islands." His voice now seemed strangely detached from their situation and Nick's death.

Chadwick opened his eyes. "Bermuda was *haunted*?"

Jackson slowly began removing the MP5 from his shoulder. "Used to be called Devil Islands—the sailors' most feared and avoided place… The shearwater, though, were gone by 1985."

Hunter looked up from their muddy hole and shouted through the rain, "You do realize that Nick is dead, don't you, *Jack*?"

But Jackson was in a world all his own. "There should only be a few cedars left, too. An insect pest destroyed most of them back in the '40s."

Not able to take any more commentary on the supposed impossibilities of their surroundings, Paul stepped toward him and grabbed him by the jacket. "Nick's dead! You tricked him into coming here and now he's *dead*!"

But Jackson shook his head. "We came to save Henry."

"And now Nick is dead!"

"It was a risk—"

In a flash of anger, Paul whipped out the pistol he had tucked in the back of his pants and thrust it up into Jackson's mouth, pushing him back against a palmetto. "You're gonna tell us everything *right* now, or I swear I'll put your brain all over this tree."

At that, the faraway look in Jackson's eyes seemed to disappear, comprehension returning beneath a squinted expression of intolerance. He saw immediately that Paul had his trigger finger resting on the outside of the trigger guard, and he quickly grabbed Paul's gun hand, twisting his wrist while, with his long reach, grabbing his throat with his other hand.

Paul countered by letting go of the pistol and throwing himself backward, grabbing Jackson's wrist with both his hands while twisting his own body toward the ground. The move took Jackson by surprise and he lost his footing, lurching forward and landing on his back with Paul on top of him. Paul struggled to his knees in the mud, throwing a ferocious blow at Jackson's face, but Jackson turned away from it, the attack simply glancing off a cheekbone.

"What did you do?" Paul screamed, taking another attempt at his face.

By now, Hunter was pulling him away from Jackson, dragging his flailing body through the gathering puddles.

"Knock it off!" yelled Hunter.

Jackson got to his feet. "Touch me again, and I'll kill you." He threw the pistol back at Paul.

Paul tried to get to his feet again and lunge one more time, but Hunter held him tight, wrestling him back to the ground. "Stop, Paul!"

John and Chris did their best to ignore the confrontation as they carefully lowered what was left of Nick into the shallow hole.

"Should we say something?" Chris asked.

Hunter turned away from Paul, who seemed to be getting a handle on himself, and looked at John. "Shouldn't you pray or something?"

"He's your friend," he responded. "You want to say something, go ahead." John didn't have anything to say on behalf of Nick and didn't think that praying for a dead person did any good anyway.

"We don't have time for this," Jackson said. "We need to go, *now*."

But it was too late.

Chadwick was the first to see it. He struggled to stand up, leaning against the tree for support while his hands fumbled clumsily with the gun. He fired a round into the ground at his feet.

Everyone spun toward the blast and saw Chadwick standing there shaking, his eyes fixated on something above him, through the rain and up in the trees. But whatever it was, the thick sheets of water prevented them from seeing it. And then a dark shadow appeared behind the moving veil.

Paul quickly got to his feet and joined the others in backing away from the towering presence now poking its head through the falling rain.

John felt his heart stop as the manifestation now towering above him married his nightmares to his past.

Six toes. Seven-foot sword… It was the answer to the equation everyone knew but couldn't bring themselves to actually believe. Now they had no choice.

The giant stood over fifteen feet tall, its head ridiculously close to the forest's dripping canopy. Mountains of muscles traversed its body. It was holding an enormous sword in one hand, the six fingers on the other opening and closing in seeming anticipation of some head popping.

It wore nothing but strange markings that wrapped every inch of its flesh, and a rope that traveled over its shoulder and across its massive, scarred chest. Hanging from the rope, like some kind of ornament, was Nick's head.

The retired SEAL's mouth hung open in a twisted scream, but his tongue was no longer present to articulate whatever pain he'd experienced before leaving earth. Or wherever this place was. The severed neck was still dripping blood down the monster's body.

Eyes frozen open in shock, the six men stared upward at the mangled face as it bounced off the giant's chest with each of its steps.

Finally, its dark eyes fell on them and registered their presence beneath it. Lifting its head up to the sky and opening its mouth—revealing sets of teeth stacked row upon row—it let out a hellish roar that shook the ground. Leaving the demonic howl to echo throughout the forest, the giant's soulless eyes then settled back on the intruders. Stepping forward, it raised the sword high into the air, its razor-sharp blade sending cedar branches dropping to the forest floor around it.

The movement jolted the six men from their terror-induced stupor, and they simultaneously lifted their weapons. They opened fire with agony-stricken battle cries of their own, John (the only one without a weapon) watching the giant's body recoil from the holes punching through it. The rain turned to red mist until, a moment later, the giant finally fell backward. It landed hard, shaking the ground and disappearing beneath an explosion of mud.

It was still, unmoving.

A second of stunned silence passed with nobody moving. Nobody breathing. Hands shaking, gun barrels steaming.

The giant moved.

"*Run!*" Jackson hollered, and he turned to take off through the trees, bursting through waves of blinding water.

They ran with such fear-fueled adrenaline that it took nearly ten minutes before exhaustion hit home, and they finally allowed themselves a glance over their shoulders. They had expected to see Nick's terrible face swinging after them, but there was only the blank forest and the rain. They stopped, their lungs burning.

But then Jackson pressed a finger to his lips. "Shhh." He squinted into the trees ahead of them.

And then a person appeared from behind a tree just ten yards away.

And then another.

Within seconds, they found themselves surrounded by men dressed in all manner of clothing and carrying old M1 carbines, AK-47s, M16s, double-barrel shotguns, and hunting rifles.

"Follow them," a man ordered as he stepped forward. He was wearing dirty bell-bottoms and a coat made from animal skins. He spoke with a British accent while pointing to a group of men falling out of rank and forming a line away from their position. Meeting curious eyes with Jackson, he said, "We'll take care of the giant." And he raised a rifle, signaling the rest of the men to follow him.

Without a word spoken between them, perhaps because the last twenty minutes had simply overridden their sense of…everything, they followed five of the mystery men northeast and into the depths of the extinct cedar forests. Behind them, the armed men disappeared into the rain, intent on making sure the wounded giant wouldn't be following them back to their secret hideaway.

FOURTEEN

3:42 p.m. 23rd day of May. Wilkinsburg, Pennsylvania

Yesterday was already beginning to seem like a dream, and Kristen wanted nothing more than to wash the taste of it from her mind. But proving whether the day had been a dream or not wouldn't introduce John back to her present reality. So her only hope was that she was *still* dreaming, that she'd fallen asleep while waiting for John to come to bed, and all of this was just some twisted concoction invented by her imagination.

Her eyes drifted shut again, and she quickly prayed that her hope would be realized when next they opened. Instead, however, the next image she saw was that of *Brian*—not John—going to open the front door of *his* house—not hers.

"Hi, Dr. Grigori?" Brian asked, leaning forward and extending his arm outside. He shook hands with someone still concealed from Kristen's position on the couch. Despite her physical appearance, which she really couldn't bring herself to care about, she got to her feet and stepped diffidently into the hallway. Hands tucked behind her back, she tilted her head to catch a glimpse of the person standing in the doorway, curious about him.

Brian closed the door and started with the introductions just as Tabitha was coming down the steps. "This is my wife, Tabitha—"

The man shook her hand, smiling at her peculiarly. It was a smile that made Tabitha's face blush, and she quickly withdrew her hand.

Brian didn't notice. "And this is Kristen Carter, a friend of the family."

Kristen was glad that was all the information Brian offered. After all, the fewer people trying to get her into a nuthouse, the better. There was also something about the man she didn't trust.

Dr. Grigori reached out to take her hand next, but Kristen refused to reciprocate the gesture, plunging the moment into sudden awkwardness.

"Uh," Brian interjected, not understanding the tension, "Dr. Grigori is a friend of a friend. He's an expert on ancient languages."

Grigori nodded and turned away from Kristen's piercing gaze. "I cannot wait to see what it is you would like me to interpret for you. From what Thomas was telling me, it sounds rather intriguing."

There was something Kristen found eerily familiar about the good doctor, but she couldn't place it. She didn't like him, that was for sure. Maybe it was the way he'd looked at her that had a whirlpool of unease swirling in the pit of her stomach. Yet, at the same time, there was a strange, forbidden flutter in her chest. "You just happened to be in the area?" she asked, suspicious without knowing why.

"Yes, that's right. I flew in from Europe last night. I am scheduled to lecture at the university a few days this week."

"Fancy that," she muttered.

Brian looked at her questioningly, wondering why the coldness toward their guest. "Well," he said, turning him by the shoulder, "how about we take a look at it?" He led them up the steps. "Would you like coffee or anything, Doctor?"

"No, thank you. I don't really have much time." He stepped into the bedroom and walked beside the bed. "Where is it?"

Brian pointed to the ceiling.

"Oh." And he pulled out a pair of glasses, sliding them over his bright blue eyes. "Interesting." He smiled at Kristen. "How did this get here, I wonder?"

It seemed to Kristen like he was toying with her somehow.

"Can you read it?" Brian asked.

"Oh, yes."

"What does it say?" Tabitha stepped forward.

"Well, you were right. It's an excerpt from a Sumerian text.

> "'To the one who is alone,
> To the Lady of Life, mistress of the land,
> Enki came unto the wise Lady of Life…
> He poured his seed into the great lady of Anunnaki,
> poured the seed into the womb of Ninharsag;
> She took the seed into the womb, the seed of Enki.'"

He removed his glasses and smiled again. "I left out some of the more *graphic* lines, in courtesy of the lovely women present."

Brian, Tabitha, and Kristen all stood motionless, staring at the doctor with blank expressions, waiting for him to start laughing and finally become serious. Instead, he just stared at Kristen.

"What does it mean?" Brian asked, his eyes still lifted by the writing. "Who is Enki?"

"Enki is the name Ea took when he came to earth. Ninharsag, or Sud, is his half-sister. The Anunnaki were a specific class of…*astronauts*, we'll say—since the name means 'those who from heaven to earth came.' One of the Sumerian texts tells that they came in groups of fifty to the earth, and that Ea's firstborn son, Marduk, was the leader of one of them." He scratched his beard. "Sumerian texts are clear that those whom the Egyptians and Greeks would come to call 'gods' actually came to earth four hundred and thirty-two thousand years before the biblical Flood. The leader of these gods was Ea, who, as I said, changed his name to Enki—Lord of Earth."

"Marduk…" Brian recognized the name but couldn't place its origin.

Grigori nodded and began circling the bed, tracing his fingers over the covers as he moved. It was a gesture that Brian didn't welcome, and he motioned for the doctor to remove his hand from the bed.

"Apparently," Grigori answered, lifting his fingers, "the tale is set during a period of time in which the whole earth was apportioned among the Anunnaki. Enki's clan ruled over Egypt, while the Sinai Peninsula belonged to Ninharsag. The excerpt written on the ceiling tells of Enki's attempt at producing a son with his half-sister. However, she brought forth a girl. Enki would then sleep with his daughter and even with his granddaughter. Eight gods, two male and six female, resulted from this mischief." He shrugged. "But to get to the point, Enki suggested to Ninharsag that they should rule Egypt and the Sinai together, assigning portions of the land to their eight gods.

"The Egyptian Memphite religion seems to have much in common with this tale, as Ptah is said to have produced eight gods and to 'put the gods in their secret abodes, build their shrines and establish their offerings in order that the Mistress of Life would rejoice.' The conflict in the Sumerian text is a lot like the conflict between Osiris and Seth, also a product of Ra's sexual mischief—of which emerged an uncertainty as to whether Osiris was, in fact, the son of Geb, or if Ra had slept with his own granddaughter. Anyway, Geb gave Seth Upper Egypt and Osiris Lower Egypt, but Seth wanted Lower Egypt for himself and thus sought to kill Osiris. Probably because he wanted control over the pyramid complex, which somehow controlled the gods' pathway to and from earth."

"Right…" If that was really what the grid of writing was supposed to be, then Brian was even more at a loss as to why it should be on his ceiling. Or *any* ceiling for that matter.

"But," Grigori continued, coming up beside Kristen and gently laying a hand across her stomach, "I would imagine the words here are meant to have a more *personal* application."

At his touch, the hurricane in Kristen's stomach intensified, overriding the more sensual feelings his touch had stirred within her. She threw his hand away and stepped back, her arms immediately wrapping her midsection in a protective embrace.

"Rest easy, Mrs. Carter, I mean you no harm."

But she ran past him and out of the room.

Brian stepped toward him, finally picking up that something was askew. "What are you doing, Mr. Grigori?"

He turned and looked at Brian, smiling. "Oh, I'm sorry." He scratched his beard again. "I was just saying that it might not be some Sumerian text scribbled at random, but rather a sort of message with perhaps a dual meaning."

Brian squinted into those brilliant azure eyes, searching for some inkling of intent… But all he saw was his own reflection. "I'd like you to leave now, Mr. Grigori. I believe you're making us all uncomfortable."

"I apologize if that is the case. Certainly, I do not mean to make anyone uncomfortable." He smiled again, this time at Tabitha. "On the contrary."

She gasped, rising to her toes.

"But I understand. I have to prepare for my lecture tonight anyway." He walked out of the room and down the stairs. "Pleasure making your acquaintances."

Brian and Tabitha didn't follow. Instead, they stood there staring at each other, only slightly conscious of the door opening and closing downstairs, the sound of a car door, and an engine starting.

"That was strange," Brian muttered, looking again at the ceiling. Then he followed his wife out into the hallway and to the guest bedroom, where Kristen was sitting on the floor with her hands over her stomach—where Grigori had touched her.

"How did he know?" she asked, tears rolling delicately down her face.

"Know what, dear?" Tabitha inquired, doing her best to shake off the lingering feeling that had so mysteriously and sexually shocked her. She knelt on wobbly knees and wrapped her arms around Kristen, seeking comfort just as much as she was trying to give it.

"No one knows," she whispered. "Not even John."

Brian's confusion turned to a slow realization even as she said it.

"I'm pregnant."

* * * *

Brian was leaning over the computer, his face awash in its electronic glow. "Here it is."

Kristen and Tabitha leaned forward on the couch behind him, neither one having said anything more about how the so-called expert of ancient languages had made them feel.

"Marduk. Jeremiah fifty, verse two. 'Announce and proclaim among the nations, lift up a banner and proclaim it; keep nothing back, but say, Babylon will be captured; Bel will be put to shame, Marduk filled with terror. Her images will be put to shame and her idols filled with terror.'"

"What does that mean?" Kristen looked at the clock. It was almost six. She had just one hour before she needed to leave for the airport. She kept telling herself that John would be there, that he would walk right off the plane, embrace her, and explain all the unfortunate things that had prevented him from calling. She imagined the last couple of days fading away into some unexplainable but irrelevant past, erased by John's tender and protective kiss.

"Marduk and Baal were Babylon's primary deities. God was going to bring judgment to them." He paused, reading more. "Marduk means 'thy rebellion' and was probably related to the planet Mars. It says here that it could be the god the Arabs called *Mirrikh*. He was apparently worshipped by the Assyrians, too. 'The author of bloodshed and slaughter,' like Saturn—the god the Shemites worshipped." He hit more keys and clicked a button on the mouse. "Let's see what we get for Anunnaki… Ah, aliens from the Twelfth Planet."

"Wonderful." Tabitha sighed.

"Wait." Brian hit some more keys and then fell strangely silent, enthralled—or horrified—by whatever he was facing on the screen. "This says that Anunnaki are the Anakim."

"What's Anakim?" Kristen asked.

Brian swallowed. "A race of giants that the Israelites fought in the Old Testament." Deep in thought, he quoted from the book of Numbers. "'And there we saw the giants, the sons of Anak, which come of the giants: and we were in our own sight as grasshoppers, and so we were in their sight.'"

Kristen asked, "Isn't that what the videotape was about?"

"Yeah," Brian whispered. And then he got up from the computer and crossed the room, stopping beside a bookshelf. He pulled a big hardback off the shelf and began silently flipping through its yellow pages. His face was pinched with intensity until, finally, he began tracing a single page with his forefinger. Suddenly, he lifted his gaze from the pages and set it on the world outside the living room window.

"What is it?" his wife asked, the concern in her voice instigated by the look on his face.

But he closed the book and slid it back onto the shelf. "Nothing…" And he quickly walked out of the room, reciting in his head as he went the words from the pseudepigraphal book of Second Enoch—or the Book of the Secrets of Enoch.

> *…The men took me on to the fifth heaven and placed me, and there I saw many and countless soldiers, called Grigori, of human appearance, and their size was greater than that of great giants…*

And:

> *…These are the Grigori… who broke through their vows on the shoulder of the hill Ermon and saw the daughters of men how good they are, and took to themselves wives, and befouled the earth with their deeds, and giants are born and marvelous big men. And therefore God judged them with great judgment, and they weep for their brethren…*

FIFTEEN

Questions can't form fast enough in my mind as the dirt begins to settle around me, and I'm confronted by the ancient secret resting on the other side of the mysterious door. There are massive stone pillars all around me, strange symbols inscribed into them and covered by layers of dust. In the center of the room is a stone sarcophagus surrounded by skeletons. My heart is beating out of control, a sense of impending doom violently shaking my hands. The stone tomb is extremely large, and I wonder if it could be something else. A stone slab almost a foot in thickness rests perfectly on top, not even a fraction of which is either inset or overhanging. I run my hands over it and remove inches of sediment, not caring that my feet are ensnared by ribcages. The two pieces feel as if they are one beneath my fingertips—I can't even slip my fingernail into the line that separates the lid from the coffin. Without knowing why, as if whatever is inside it is summoning me to do so, I push with all my might against the slab, and it moves an inch. I figure it must weigh a few hundred pounds, and push again, moving it another two inches. Sweat is splashing onto the ancient stonework and dripping down my back. I push again, grunting with exertion, and manage to move it another few inches. Panting, I bend over and rip a femur from an ancient hip socket and stick it into the coffin, using it as a wedge. The lid slides crooked across the smooth corners, and I have to move back to the center for better leverage. From there, I pull down on the human bone, and the lid finally slides off and smashes onto the floor, shattering skeletons into hundreds of fragments and filling the room with dust again. When the air clears, I can see into the coffin. My knees go weak. Staring up at me—from out of another time, I am certain—is a face that belongs to a monster nearly twenty feet tall. But more disturbing than this is the realization that I have seen the face before. In a forgotten childhood nightmare. I take a step backward, stumbling through the piles of bones, and become overwhelmed with the sense that this thing has been resting here from the beginning of time, waiting for me to discover it. This horrible giant has summoned me…and not from when I entered the cave, or even when I arrived in this godforsaken country, but from my very birth.

When John opened his eyes, he saw Chadwick leaning over him. His mouth was moving, but John couldn't hear what he was saying. And then the sound of the world around him began to creep into his consciousness, and Chadwick's lips began making sense.

"Are you with us?" he was asking.

John sat up on his elbows and realized he was soaking wet with sweat. Running a hand through his hair, he tried to swallow. His throat was as dry as it had ever been in Afghanistan or Iraq.

"Here." Chadwick handed him a sports bottle. "Water."

John took it greedily, savoring the cold liquid as it caressed his throat. "Thanks," he gasped. He handed the bottle back, not caring where it came from.

"Are you okay?"

"Yeah, just give me a minute." He sat up and leaned back against the limestone wall. Closing his eyes, he tried intently to untangle all the different worlds his mind wanted to engage simultaneously. He could tell that his sense of reality was slipping, that all its different tiers were collapsing onto each other. The dream and the memory of the cave were flirting too closely with what he'd seen out in the forest earlier, making it difficult for him to authenticate the encounter. "Did we really see that thing?" he asked, his eyes still closed.

"The giant?"

He opened his eyes, taking in his surroundings while letting his mind fill the time gaps. "Where are we?"

"The Crystal Caves," Hunter said from somewhere beside him.

There were torches hanging on the walls, filling the dark room with flickering light.

"According to your tourist map, we're a hundred and twenty feet under the ground."

"How long have I been out?"

"Who knows," Chris said from within another shadow. "We've been in this room since we got here. Seems like days."

"Where's Jackson and Paul?"

"I'm right here, Johnny," came Paul's ticked-off voice. "Jack's off *mingling* with the natives."

"So"—Hunter's voice sounded again—"you *do* have the nightmares."

It sounded to John like an accusation. "I never said that I didn't."

"Is it always the same?"

"Every time," John answered. And then he said, "I'm sorry about Nick."

The simple mention of their friend brought back the image of his head hanging from the giant's neck. The room plummeted back into silence, the flickering torches perfectly representing their own fleeting thoughts as the shadows chased each other throughout the ghostly room.

Finally, Chadwick focused their attention by exclaiming, "He wrote all about this place!" An ample level of disbelief came resounding through the statement.

"What are you talking about?" Paul moaned.

"Ronald." He held up John's copy of *Journey with the Gods*, which he had apparently been reading while everyone else was mourning. "He claims he was *here*. In *this* place. Says that the *gods* took him here through a gateway in the Bermuda Triangle."

"What?" Paul's outcry was a mixture of both anger and ridicule.

But as ridiculous as it was, it was a puzzle piece that fit. "That's how Jackson knew," John breathed.

Chadwick nodded, flipping a page. "He talks about all the ships and planes in the bay, calls it 'the graveyard.' Even mentions giants." Now he had everyone's complete attention, a book in his hands with answers.

"Giant*s*?" Chris asked. "Plural?"

"What else does it say?" Paul moved closer.

"It says that the gateway can only be opened by a special person." He looked over at John and anxiously adjusted his glasses. "Your friend Jackson must've had reason to think you fit the bill."

A string of dazed profanity echoed off the walls around them.

Hunter stood as the picture began to focus. "Why were they lying about Henry's boat?"

But John was already realizing why Jackson had gotten him a week-long pass. "He didn't know when the storm would come." He hit the wall with the palm of his hand, his blood pumping. "I *knew* Ronald was stalling with all those stupid stories."

"The storm must've been part of the equation," Chris muttered.

But Chadwick shook his head. "If so, he isn't saying so in the book."

"So apart from your recurring dreams, what makes you and Henry so *special?*" Paul demanded.

John stared at his scarred face. The shifting torchlight dancing in those eyes created a menacing image that John would rather not upset any further. "I didn't even know Henry had dreams until Hunter told me yesterday."

"Does he say who *these* people are?" Chris asked Chadwick, waving at the walls around them.

He flipped through more pages. "He just says that there are two groups of people. One divine, brought to the island by the gods themselves—like him, of course—and the other, a sort of lesser, weaker species summoned incidentally."

John thought back to everything he'd seen at Ronald's house and tried filtering it all through this new knowledge. "The lists of names on his map included every missing boat and plane, but only the names of certain people… The people who opened the doorway," he realized. "That's why Henry's name was the last entry… Ronald knew."

Chadwick closed the book. "And you said he called the Triangle a 'doorway to hell'?"

"Yeah."

"That's odd," Chadwick said, "because he doesn't describe this place as anything other than a benevolent place where the gods gather. Almost makes it sound like a sort of paradise."

"Yeah, well, he also thinks Satan was the ruler of a golden age and that demons are kind, disembodied spirits from his kingdom."

Just then, a sound came from the other end of the dark room, and a flaming torch floated toward them. "He's awake now," came Jackson's tired voice accompanying the moving light. "Let's go see him."

"Who?"

"Henry."

* * * *

They followed two men wearing torn jeans and dirty T-shirts, rifles slung over their shoulders, across a makeshift catwalk that extended out over a pool of crystal water. More torches hung from the walls around them.

"There are a lot of caves on the islands," the one on the left was saying. He sounded like he was from Texas and looked to be in his early forties, while the person beside him was just a teenager. "But this is the biggest." He pointed at the limestone ceiling. "Used to be full of stalactites, but we cut them down when we started building."

"How long have you been here?" Chris wondered aloud, surveying their cavernous surroundings.

"I've been here since I was seven. Philip was born here." Then he pointed down some other walkways that crossed their path. "We dug all this out by hand and with whatever explosives were left in the graveyard. Of course, when I say 'we,' I don't necessarily mean to include myself. They started all this before I got here."

Jackson ducked under an outcropping. "What do you mean, '*left* in the graveyard'?"

"Whatever they didn't take."

John had seen pictures of the Crystal Caves and Fantasy Cave in the brochures at the hotel room, and what it looked like now was completely different. Rather than stalactites stretching down from the ceiling like organ pipes, there was instead a small city.

"How many people live here?" John still hoped he was dreaming, that Kristen was washing dishes in the kitchen and just about to wake him up.

"We have people in most of the caves, but in this one…forty."

Hunter was staring down at the stalagmites beneath the water. "And you all came through the Triangle?"

"No. By now half of us are second or third, even fourth generation."

Paul asked, "No one lives on the surface?" He was thinking of the village they'd seen.

"Not unless they're banished from the caves."

Chadwick excitedly scooted up past Hunter and Chris as they left the catwalk and entered a stone corridor. "What about the monuments?"

The man turned slightly as he came to another tunnel. "They build them."

Chris shook his head. "They?"

But then the group was standing before a door constructed from cedar planks and vine.

"Your friend is very weak. We're not even sure how he managed to escape. No one ever escapes." He pushed the door open and stepped to the side. "When you're finished, take this corridor to the end. We'll be waiting for you. We have a lot to talk about."

Jackson ducked into the room first, followed by John, Hunter, Chris, Paul, and then Chadwick.

There was a bed made of palmetto leaves lying in the center of the room, two flickering candles beside it illuminating the fragile figure resting in front of them. They circled around the bed, an overwhelming sense of relief suddenly present to combat their recent grief.

Henry's hard, angular face was crudely stitched closed across the forehead, and purple bruises were stretching out from beneath days of gray stubble. His left arm and chest were bandaged, too, indicating the reason his breathing was labored and rasping in the silence.

John was immediately taken aback by the sight of his older brother, and a tear glided down his cheek. Even considering their broken history, he was elated to discover Henry still alive. It was something he hadn't believed possible from day one.

The blue of Henry's eyes flickered forth from his swollen face before a painful smile pulled at his bloody lips. He tried mumbling something, but it was unintelligible.

"Hi, Henry," Jackson said, shifting the MP5 across his back as he stepped closer.

Henry started laughing but ended up coughing and clutching his chest with his good hand.

Broken ribs, John realized. "Take it easy."

At the sound of John's voice, Henry's smile vanished, his eyes swinging like lightning over to his younger brother. He tried to sit up.

"Hey!" both Chris and Hunter yelled, keeping him from moving and further damaging himself. "Relax."

"I'm dreaming," Henry muttered; and then he went around the room, acknowledging each one of his visitors. "Jack, Hunter, Chris, Paul, whoever *you* are…" He chuckled. "Where's Nick? Still out looking for his hand?" But then his eyes fell back on John, and his expression turned cynical.

"Nick's dead," Paul said.

Henry closed his eyes. "And just how did you get here?"

"Ronald," Jackson answered.

Henry's eyes appeared again, but this time they were flashing with anger as he tried once more to get up. He reached for Jackson. "You *brought* them here?" he yelled hoarsely.

"You knew we'd come for you," he deflected.

"What's *Johnny* doing here?"

John felt a pit form in his stomach. At that moment, he realized that he'd subconsciously let Jackson's words, of Henry regretting how things had gone between them, take root in his heart.

"Ronald told me how to get here, about the bloodline." He looked at John and nodded. "He opened the gateway, just like you did. It was the only way."

Henry cursed at him. "You shouldn't have brought him to this place."

Such protective posturing was something that John hadn't experienced from Henry since grade school, and, just like that, more tears began to fall down his face. He grabbed Henry's hand. "It's okay," he whispered. Henry squeezed back. It was a strange feeling, his brother's hand in his, and one he never expected to be overwhelmed by. He suddenly realized just how much he'd been starving for Henry's acceptance.

But Henry was shaking his head, his eyes sharply glaring at Jackson. "Your first mistake was believing anything that came out of Ronald's mouth."

"What're you talking about?"

He sighed. "It wasn't John that opened the doorway."

"Sure it was," Jackson argued. "It worked just like he said it would."

Henry looked up at John, his face twisted with an expression of sadness that was able to transcend his injuries. He shook his head. "John doesn't have the genetic code."

A moment of silence ensued as everyone attempted to interpret the meaning of his words.

"What do you mean?" John asked. He could already feel what little stability was left in his world start to slip away. Was it just another reference to not having what it took to be a Carter, or did he mean something else?

"Johnny," he said softly, "you're adopted."

And John's entire world crumbled into a million pieces.

"I'm sorry you had to find out this way," Henry said.

John stumbled backward until he hit the wall. He couldn't think straight, his entire life suddenly something else.

Jackson shook his head. "I don't understand. Why would Ronald—"

"He knew," Paul realized.

And John remembered, too. Remembered Ronald's reaction to learning that he was Henry's brother. But his brain was in a fiery tailspin, a bottomless pit of ambiguity its fate. Nothing was certain anymore, and all he could do was hold his head in his hands.

"But why would he want me to think…" Jackson stopped in mid-thought. "Then who opened the portal?"

And all eyes drifted to Chadwick.

"Hold on," Chadwick stammered, holding up his hands.

"That's why Ronald kidnapped you and locked you in Henry's boat," said Chris. The pieces were coming together fast now. "*You* were the key."

"What's your name?" Henry asked him.

"Chadwick Aland."

"Well, Chadwick Aland, it would appear as though you and I are somehow related."

"I don't understand."

Henry laid his head back down and stared up at the ceiling. "They'll explain it to you."

"Who? Explain what?"

Hunter took a step toward the candlelight. "How did you get here, Henry?"

He gritted his teeth, sighing through the pain. "I don't remember. I was with Ronald and then…I was lying here on the beach." The little energy that had sparked his vigilance was draining fast, and he was now having trouble keeping his eyes open. "The giants found me…" He stopped, let his eyes shut. "Give John and me a moment, will you?" And he motioned for John to come over to the bed.

"Are you okay?" Jackson asked him before honoring the request.

"Yeah. Beat up, is all. Just need to rest."

"What happened?"

"Later," he whispered. "Go talk to them. They'll let you know what you got everyone into. Let me talk to John for a while."

As they all walked out of the room, John forced his own feet to move.

"I can't believe you're here," Henry mumbled.

He didn't know what to say to that; he couldn't believe it either. "What is this place?"

He exhaled a deep breath and changed the subject. "Don't trust Jackson; he probably has his own agenda. Hunter and Chris'll be the ones you want by your side when the time comes. Be careful around the Chadwick guy, too. He's gonna attract a lot of attention from them."

"Who?"

"The others…the giants, their people, whatever."

"Why?"

"Same reason they want me. I have their blood in my veins."

"What are you talking about?" John simply couldn't keep up with all the vague insinuations.

Henry took another deep, painful breath and closed his eyes. "After Dad died, I found some of his journals up in the attic. They were filled with dreams, visions, weird stuff like that. Especially from when he was in Vietnam." He paused. "Things I experienced, too. Things that were making me crazy. In one of the entries, he spoke of letters that Grandpa gave him right before he died. The letters alluded to an entire secret history that had been passed down throughout the generations. And after spending his whole life searching for it, Grandpa believed the record to be lost."

"An ancient record of bloodlines?" It sounded like a Dan Brown novel.

"I didn't believe it either, but the similarities between what Dad described and my own experiences opened my mind to the possibility. I started investigating our family heritage, tracking down anyone in our tree." His eyes opened, chasing after fleeting shadows on the ceiling. "I found a book." He seemed to be slowly opening the pages of it in his mind. "In England. Some distant cousin. She didn't even know what it was. Her father died without explaining it to her." He looked back to John. "You should've seen this book, Johnny. You can't even imagine…"

"What did it say?" He wasn't sure he really wanted to know.

"It was a book of genealogies, tracing our ancestors all the way back to the Table of Nations in Genesis 10."

Chills climbed the steps of John's spine. "What'd you find, Henry?"

"I found that our blood, the Carter line, comes straight from the Titans."

"Your boat… the Nephilim…"

He sounded surprised. "You know what it means?"

"Chadwick happens to be an expert in the field."

He nodded as if he should have figured that. "Those with angelic DNA seem to be drawn to the stuff."

"Angelic DNA?" Maybe the doctor *had* prescribed a straitjacket, and this was all some drug-induced hallucination after all.

"I know what you must be thinking, of how confused you must be, but this place confirms it."

"This place where Ronald sent you…"

"I was drunk one night and said something to Jackson about all this stuff, the journal, my dreams… He told me about this guy he'd met in Bermuda while he was on his honeymoon and gave me one of his books to read."

John squeezed his eyes shut, trying to will away the headache that was banging on the door to his brain. "Kind of a strange coincidence, isn't it?"

"I thought so at the time. But now I know better." He began coughing again. "Man, it hurts."

"You want water?"

"No, let me finish." And then his eyes opened wider, a sort of fanatical intensity filling them. "It's how they do it. They get us to gravitate toward each other, interconnect us. It's the bloodline. It's the only way he can escape…"

John could tell that he was losing him. His thoughts were quickly becoming unfocused and rambling together nonsensically. "Who? What are you talking about?"

"Talk to the others; they'll tell you. His seed is magnetic, attracts itself. The more that are together, the wider the portal, the greater his power…" His eyes began to flutter, his voice growing fainter. "He needs giants to build…"

"Build?"

And then Henry grabbed John's arm, using it to pull himself up. "The summer solstice. You have to stop them from completing it before the solstice." And then he lay back down and whispered, "But then…that might be our only way back…"

"Shhh…" John gave up on anything more useful coming from the reunion. "Just rest." He sat there for a few minutes, just staring at his older brother, trying to let the revelation so elegantly dropped on his head sink in and interpret his whole life. But it was too large a meal to consume all in one sitting. He pulled the driver's license out of his pocket and handed it to Henry, wanting to know one last thing before leaving. "We found this on a dead body in an abandoned village."

Henry looked at it and sadly shook his head. "He wasn't too bright, if you know what I mean. He thought he could trick them into thinking that he was me. Thought it would give me more time to get away." And then after another moment of silence, he said, "Johnny?"

"Yeah, Henry?"

"Why'd you leave the Rangers?" His voice was barely audible, and it was clear that he was fading.

John collapsed beside the palmetto bed. It was a question no one in his family had ever cared to ask, and in some ways, he was thankful for not having to tell them. He didn't like thinking about it, yet the greatest thing that ever happened to him had come because of it. "In Afghanistan," he began, "my jeep got hit by an RPG. I was the only one who lived." He lapsed into silence for a moment.

"And?" Henry whispered, still conscious.

"And something snapped inside. I lost it, Henry. Turned into—" he swallowed the word "—a murderer."

"It's war, Johnny. Everything's justified in war."

"That's what I used to think. Got in trouble a few times for opening fire on crowds of people we were driving past." The memory of a screaming woman holding a dead child in her arms choked him, and he wiped tears from his face. "And then—" He was going to tell him about the cave, about the giant, but for some reason decided not to. "I only became more unstable in Iraq. I pulled a guy from his bed one night. Just chose his house at random, because I was drunk and angry. Started interrogating him. As far as I was concerned, he was the one who fired the RPG that killed all my friends. Anyway, as I tortured him, he began praying for me in English. The more he prayed, the more I hurt him. But the more I hurt him, the harder he prayed." More tears dripped down his cheeks. "But he wasn't praying for himself. He was praying for me. He kept saying, 'Father, forgive him, he doesn't know what he's doing.' Turns out, the guy was a Christian, had been for a few years. His wife had been killed by her own parents for converting…" He wiped the tears away, wondering what Henry thought of the story. "Just before another soldier came over and shot him through the head, an act of mercy considering what I'd done to him, God answered his prayers. And just like that, I was different."

"That's why you left?"

"You wouldn't believe the things I did in those years, Henry. And then to have an Arab convert me to Christianity in Iraq… Everything changed." *The nightmares stopped.* "I promised God I would never raise my hand against another human being again."

There was silence in the small room for a long moment, and John thought Henry had finally fallen back asleep.

But then his voice broke the stillness. "Well, then I guess it's a good thing they're not human."

"Who?"

"Are you familiar with the Book of Enoch?" He coughed.

"Not really, no."

"Well, it seems to imply that both the giants and their offspring are beyond redemption." He turned his head toward John. "What do you think, Johnny?"

"It's not an authorized book."

"The early church considered it inspired, and Jesus, Peter, and Jude all referenced it. The book wasn't banned by the establishment church until it decided that belief in the physicality of angels should be a heresy."

"What do you want to know, Henry?"

"I had to come here, to this place. I had to know if it was real, what my heritage is. At first, I rather liked the idea of being a descendant of the Titans, from the 'heroes of old.' But after what I've seen here, what he showed me…

John, I need to know if it's possible for the offspring of angels to find salvation."

"All things are possible with God, Henry," John responded out of habit. But something was nagging at the back of his head, tickling his subconscious. Ignoring it, he asked his brother if he *wanted* to be saved.

But he was already asleep.

SIXTEEN

Nightfall. 23rd day of May. Bermuda, Crystal Caves

By the time John joined the others in the aforementioned room, he found them sitting amidst a circle of fifteen other men, some of whom he recognized from the forest. He could tell immediately that whatever the topic of conversation was, it had Paul, Hunter, and Chris wearing expressions of bewilderment. Then he noticed Chadwick sitting a slight distance away from the circle, staring blankly into empty space. Jackson, however, seemed slightly removed from the discussion; perhaps it was Nick's death weighing on his conscience that was distracting him. John could only guess as to what revelations had been shared with them and how much of their conceived notion of reality had survived the experience.

"What'd I miss?" John asked, taking in all the new and unshaven faces.

"These people think that God sent us to save them," Paul sneered.

"Save them from what?"

The oldest man present stood slowly.

Hunter quickly leaned over and whispered into John's ear, "His name's Samuel."

"We will show you." Samuel's voice was as uneven as his shaking hands, but there was a passionate purpose still projecting it. And though a fragile man now, many hard years were etched into his sun-darkened features.

But John was still trying to equate what Henry just told him with what he was seeing in front of him now. "Are all of you from the bloodline…"

The man shook his head. "No. We are simply the ones who were unfortunate enough to be in their company."

"Henry said they'd be looking for him." John pointed at Chadwick, who was still sitting motionless, trapped somewhere inside his own tortured mind and combating his newly discovered lineage.

"Yes. If he has his blood. But we'll protect him…or kill him before he can be captured."

Chadwick's eyes flicked up in surprise.

"Believe me," Samuel said, "you'd want to die before being turned into one of his slaves."

"Slaves?" John maneuvered his backpack, suddenly realizing its presence.

"His bloodline opens the gateway. The more of them"—he tilted his head toward Chadwick—"he can get here, the more powerful he becomes. But it's what they come *with* that he really wants. Men that he can use as slaves, women that he can use to breed giants, and the cargo that he can use to construct his network of sites. Of course, most of us resist…despite what he promises. The women, however, seem incapable of resistance. So we hide them away." He walked closely by a hanging torch, and John could see even more clearly the effects of his unfortunate lifestyle. "Most of us are hunted down and killed, though more for their amusement than for any threat we might pose to them. For some reason, they leave us alone in the caves. Miraculously, we have been able to exist apart from his experiments for almost four hundred years."

"Four *hundred* years?"

He nodded, his weary eyes half closing. "After the settlement of Bermuda, when he first began bringing his offspring. But we are not all descendants of those old ships. There are only a few relatives left from those who came before the nineteenth century." He reached out and placed a hand against the wall to steady himself. "We don't feel the need to bring life into this horrible place, to watch it squashed under their feet and eaten over their fires. However, we get lonely and occasionally seek companionship, which sometimes results in added life. Those that are then born here are brought up as survivor warriors in the only reality they'll ever know.

"Whenever another ship or plane appears, we try to get to the passengers before they do, hide them in the caves before he can get to them. Sometimes we're successful." He nodded again at his new guests. "And sometimes we are not. But the pace at which he brings his offspring has lessened greatly. Which tells us that he's close to completing what he has been constructing for the last four hundred years."

"Which is what?"

"It is difficult to explain, and truthfully, we have no idea how it might work, but think of it as a kind of escape mechanism."

John paused in thought, wondering again why everything had to be so elusively vague. "So this 'he' that you keep talking about has been *trapped* here for four hundred years?"

"No," he answered. "Much longer than that."

"I don't understand."

Samuel walked over to John and handed him a small leather-bound book. "The Book of Enoch. One of his offspring had it on him. He passed it into our care before he was taken. It has shed much light on our otherwise uncertain and mysterious existence. It is a tragedy that so many of us have lived and died here with no clue as to why. But I'm sure your friend Chadwick can fill you in on what mysteries the ancient book contains." He looked at the troubled man. "Can't you?"

"Sure," he whispered.

"We're not sure how or why, but most of his seed arrives with some prior knowledge of these things. Some kind of genetic bend toward them." He sighed while taking the book back from him and looking around the room. "I know this is a lot to take in all at once and that you, no doubt, believe it all to be some strange dream that you can simply wake up from. I assure you that this place is real." He shuffled back to his seat at the circle. "We usually take more time to acclimate our new arrivals, but in your case, we simply do not have the time. God has finally sent salvation to us." And then he paused. Folding his hands behind his back like he had been a general in some other lifetime, he issued some feeble orders. "You will accompany some of our men on a mission tonight. It won't be an easy thing to witness, what they have to do, but it'll give you an idea of just what this place is."

Though Jackson, Paul, Hunter, and Chris were not prone to taking orders from anyone, they realized just how fragile their situation was, that their *own* salvation might just depend on these people who were acclimated to life within this inexplicable world.

John held up his hand, wondering if the question had already been posed before his arrival. "Who is this man that you keep referring to?"

The old man's lips twitched at the corners of his mouth, and he pulled some of his white hair behind an ear as he sat heavily into his chair. "Our predecessors called him…Osiris."

* * * *

The twelve of them were divided evenly between the two boats. John, Chadwick, and Paul were in the lead boat and sharing the company of three islanders, while Hunter, Jackson, and Chris were with three others trailing behind. They were paddling ferociously through the pouring rain, flashes of lightning exposing the reef and open ocean to their right and the coast lingering at a distance on their left. Following the coast into the sound, they would take refuge on a small island lying just off what should be the city of Hamilton.

If they made it there alive.

The rowboats salvaged from the graveyard were being lifted fifteen feet into the air, the waves threatening to flip them upside down and thrust them into oblivion.

The sky lit up with four branches of lightning, and John was able to make out Paul pointing to something back on the island. But another huge wave was coming, forcing them to position the boat's bow into the wave. Once the wave passed by beneath them, and after a few more moments of its rolling form blocking the entire island from sight, John was finally able to get a glimpse of what had captured Paul's attention. "What is that?" he screamed over the weather.

Another streak of lightning lingered in the sky and turned night into day for a few seconds.

There was no mistaking what it was.

It glowed like a diamond in the midst of the storm, an ancient lighthouse from another world.

Once the sky returned to blackness, and the image faded from the moving horizon, Chadwick's voice tried breaking through the storm's wrath. But the wind stole his words before they could be heard, casting them furiously into the rocks that guarded the island.

* * * *

Defying the odds, they actually made it to the tiny island unscathed—an island that, just the other day, had resided within Hamilton Harbor. Now they were huddled together in a small cave that flooded every time a huge wave was hurled high enough to reach its entranceway. It was going to be a long, miserable night.

Chadwick was shaking from the cold, cursing this field trip and the old man who had sent them on it. He thought he should be back in the Crystal Caves, hiding from the creatures that were supposedly looking for him. He was twirling his beard with bone-white, shaking fingers, mumbling about the thing they'd seen from the boat.

Knowing that Chadwick was on the verge of slipping into despair, John tried distracting him from their situation by asking how the megalithic sites might be used as an escape mechanism and what the summer solstice could have to do with it.

It seemed to be working so far in stimulating Chadwick's mind with things not directly connected to their physical condition. "The Egyptians' entire sky religion was a manifestation of the Hermetic axiom 'As above, so below; as below, so above,'" he orated through chattering teeth. "The entire Giza necropolis is a reflection of the sky where Osiris is said to dwell. Even Arab chroniclers in the Middle Ages described the Great Pyramid as being a temple to the stars... Their religion was very dualistic—what happened on earth mirrored by what happened in the heavens and vice-versa."

Only half interested in what he was saying, because his own mind was approaching sanity's drop off, John nodded just to keep Chadwick talking.

"Sumerian texts tell of an everlasting ground plan that post-flood kings followed in reestablishing the cities of Sumer. In the original Akkadian, *Bab-Ili*—or Babel—meant 'gateway of the gods' and was supposed to be a ziggurat through which the gods were able to enter and leave Sumer. There's a lot of talk about Ekur—a pointed-peaked house of the gods that was used to bring the Anunnaki to earth—in old Sumerian poems."

"Anunnaki?" Hunter asked from somewhere in the darkness.

"Aliens. Or gods or angels...they're all probably the same. Anyway—" his teeth clattered "—some think the Great Pyramid was built in place of Ekur after Ekur was destroyed by the Flood."

John rubbed his freezing hands together, blowing warm breath into them. "And how is it supposed to be used as a gateway?"

"Mentioned in the Coffin Texts is a formula that was used to access the heavens, somehow enabling the initiate the ability to work out or visualize the correct position of the stars from any epoch. There are other texts that describe the pyramid as being a gateway to another world, too." His words were growing slower, beginning to slur from the cold. "The whole system was designed as a transporter used to send the pharaohs back in time to Osiris' reign. Or, as in the case of the Edfu texts, the development of the sites was supposed to *resurrect* the former world of the gods." He paused. "Religious texts regard the area as a sacred landscape inherited from the gods—Osiris' cosmic kingdom during First Time was passed down to his son Horus and on to an era of demigods that maintained the sacred body of knowledge—even the Greeks and Romans believed the pharaohs were guardians of earth's past ages…"

And then Chadwick fell silent, presumably falling asleep. No one asked. They just sat staring into the void around them, listening to the crashing waves outside while trying to let Chadwick's words define what they had just seen.

* * * *

The storm finally seemed to exhaust itself, leaving only the choppy waves beyond the row of small islands to greet the faint glow now rising against the horizon. But though the storm was over, the sun's soon arrival presented its own challenge—the need to get to the mainland before the morning light could betray their presence.

"—small pyramid in Brewsterville, Indiana, was found in 1879…skeletal remains of a person nine and a half feet tall…" Chadwick was mumbling, his eyes staring into nothingness. It didn't look like he got any sleep, the deep mysteries of this place running like a hamster to nowhere on the wheel that was his brain.

"You think he's gonna be alright?" Chris asked Hunter as he prepared to slip off the rocks and enter the dark water.

"—in 1925, in Walkerton, Indiana, archeologists dug up eight people that were between eight and ten feet tall, all dressed in copper armor…"

A big man with an Australian accent grabbed Jackson by the shoulder. "He stays here," he stated while manipulating a rifle across his back. "He'll be safe in the cave."

Jackson nodded to the man and then looked over to John. "Tell him he's staying here."

"—the Aztec's capital was built to replicate the island their ancestors came from, yet only Plato's Atlantis can offer us such an island…"

"Chad," John said, resting a hand on his shoulder. There was no way the archeologist could make the long swim to shore, angel blood in his veins or not.

Chadwick looked at John as lingering moonlight slipped through the clouds and reflected off the water facing them. "Did you know that the Great Pyramid was made with two and a half *million* stone blocks, each weighing an average of two point six tons—some even *fifty* tons?"

"I didn't know that," John answered shortly, turning him by the shoulder so that he was facing the cave's entrance again.

"Its total mass is six point three *million* tons… Its base is a perfect square to within one-twentieth of a *single* degree, even though it sits on a raised mound thirty feet high… The sides are equilateral triangles that are locked into the cardinal axes of the planet. Its meridian axis aligns within one-twentieth of a single degree to true north and south—"

"Chad, we need you to stay here."

"—the blocks are cut to a point zero one tolerance, and the length of each side is the length of a solar year in cubits. The exact distance, John, from the earth to the sun is geometrically programmed into its architecture, and when adding up the diagonals of the pyramid's base in inches, you get the number of years in the precessional cycle."

John started pushing him toward the cave, hearing the others start to swim away behind him. "Stay here in the cave, Chad."

Chadwick grabbed John's shoulder and squeezed it tight. "Do you understand what I'm saying, John? It's a model of the northern hemisphere built with a relatively new and intricate knowledge of our solar system. Its measurements represent the circumference of the entire Earth and stands at exactly one-third of the way between the equator and the North Pole—or at least where the North Pole is now—sitting on latitude thirty. John, the value of *pi, phi*, and Pythagoras' theorem were known and used by its builders—"

"Come on, John!" Paul snapped from the rocky shore.

"Chad, please, look at me. Stay inside the cave until we come back, okay?" He handed him one of the MP5s.

"Okay, John," he said, taking the weapon. "But before you go, did you know that the Great Pyramid was originally covered with a polished limestone face that reflected the sun? It was mostly destroyed by an earthquake in AD 1301. The *benben* stone, which is still missing—the reason it's detached on the dollar bill—was supposedly gold." And then he turned away from John and climbed up into the cave, again muttering something about the Atlantean wisdom-religion and its great pyramid temple that the initiated priests of the Sacred Feather went out from, building pyramids and temples wherever they went.

John took one last look at the cave before wading out into the water and swimming after his fellow intruders. As he swam, one stroke after the next, the glowing pinnacle that was reaching up above the tree line and into the early morning sky grew closer and closer. Considering the sheer terror it seemed to induce within him, John began wondering if he'd ever see his wife again.

* * * *

They travelled up a high hill and found concealment within its thick tropical plant life. Though Jackson said there were very few plants and animals that were native to Bermuda, it was clear, especially here, that whatever life forms made it to the graveyard had found a way to survive in their new environment. All kinds of trees were spread out around them, huge flowers the size of a man's head wrapping around their trunks.

As they quietly followed their guides through the wide assortment of colorful plants, Chris spotted an animal in the thicket some twenty yards away. "Look," he whispered, pointing.

"A horse," Jackson replied.

"Yeah, but what's it eating?"

Hunter, Paul, and John moved closer to Chris, peering through the early light to see what had Chris so fascinated.

"What the—"

It was an apple tree. Only the apples were as big as bowling balls.

The horse turned away from them, waving *two* shaggy tails as it trotted away.

Before anyone could comment on the sight, one of their guides snapped his fingers at them. "Come on."

They hurried to catch up.

A few moments later, the "natives"—as Paul called them—were on their stomachs and crawling through the underbrush, approaching the edge of the hill. John was the last to reach them, and by the time he came up beside the retired soldiers, the fascination of the sight below had already immobilized their reason.

The hill they were on proved to be a lot larger than they originally figured, and the harbor could be seen down off to their right. But it was what lay at the base of the hill that had everyone staring in bewilderment.

A huge clearing spanned the ground below, a vast temple complex standing within it. A seemingly random pattern of ziggurats that all led to courtyards housing strangely arranged monoliths stared up at them. Surrounding the site were more stone faces like the ones they'd seen before. But it was the enormous pyramid they'd seen from the rowboats the night before that really stood taunting their feeble minds. It overshadowed the entire complex, reaching up and poking through the low cloud coverage. Its smooth surface held a reflection of the rising sun that illuminated the surreal structure like a colossal pillar of fire, its capstone shining light like a brilliant diamond, sparkling and refracting rainbows of color in every direction.

Finally able to avert his eyes, John saw that directly below them was a courtyard, a tall obelisk piercing its center. Connected to the courtyard by stone steps was a temple serving as the center of the overall ground scheme, linking the whole complex together in a design that would be noticeable only from space. Or by the gods.

"What are we doing here?" Chris mumbled in sheer awe.

"We're waiting for them to come out into the courtyard," the man beside him responded coolly. But there was something in his voice that suggested a concealed apprehension.

"Who?"

But he didn't respond. Instead, he clenched his jaw and poked the barrel of his rifle through the row of large ferns fanning out in front of them. All five of his comrades did the same, aiming down at the empty courtyard below.

John was on the ground next to Hunter. When he turned to whisper something in his ear, he noticed, over his shoulder, Jackson standing fifteen yards away, his back turned toward the temple complex. "What's Jackson doing?"

Hunter turned away from what should have been either ancient ruins or the city of Hamilton and noticed what had spawned John's query. Jackson seemed to be conversing with someone. He strained to see who, but a large tree was blocking the other half of the conversation.

"Who's he talking to?" John whispered, looking around. Everyone in their party was accounted for.

"I don't know." And Hunter began crawling on his stomach, moving toward Jackson.

Hunter caught Paul's attention as he crossed behind him, causing him to look up and notice Jackson for himself. Because he was the closest to him, Paul whispered, "*Psst!* Get down." But Jackson didn't respond.

Army crawling past Paul and reaching Jackson, Hunter grabbed his ankle.

Jackson's eyes shifted down to what had grabbed him.

"Get down," Hunter ordered, tugging on Jackson's pant leg.

Jackson shrank to his knees and looked around, a befuddled expression contorting his face.

"Who were you talking to?" Hunter looked through the trees around them, but there was no sign of anyone else.

"No one," he answered, his voice strangely detached.

But there was no time to pursue it now. "Just stay down." And he crawled back to John. "He says he wasn't talking to anyone," he reported once beside him.

Taking another peek at Jackson over Hunter's shoulder, John recalled Henry's warning.

Hunter shook his head. "What're we doing here, man?"

John wiped sweat out of his eyes. "I have no idea."

And then four women suddenly appeared, emerging from one of the ziggurats.

"What the—"

At the sight of the women, the six natives immediately became alert, raising their weapons and moving their fingers over the triggers.

Even from fifty yards away, it was obvious just how attractive the women were. They were adorned in sheer white dresses that hung loosely to the ground, their left shoulders exposed as if on display. The jewelry they wore sparkled remarkably, catching the early sunlight in diamond-studded bracelets, gold necklaces, earrings, and peculiar armbands. Their faces, though too distant to appreciate any exquisite detail, were painted with makeup. Walking gingerly down the steps and following the path into the courtyard, their bare feet gracefully tiptoed forward. Ten men carrying spears prodded them on.

John exchanged a quick glance with the retired SEALs, satisfied that they were as perplexed as he was, and remembered what the older man back in the cave had said about the women here.

A giant emerged from the shadows of the temple's entranceway. It looked as tall as the giant they'd seen wearing Nick's head, but this goliath wasn't naked. Instead, it was clothed in ceremonial garb, a feathered head garment and a shining robe marrying it to some twisted priesthood.

The women were led toward it.

"Who are they?" Chris asked, taken by their beauty.

Even as the first woman approached the giant, slipping her dress off her shoulders and letting it sink to her ankles, the man with the Australian accent whispered, "Family."

Because his head spun toward the Australian, Chris missed the giant's nodded approval and the woman's subsequent ascent up the temple stairs, her blond hair braided down her bare back sweeping side to side with each step. What he did see, however, was a tear slide down the Australian's face as he pulled the trigger.

The blast rocketed through the early morning stillness and replaced the woman's head with a cloud of blood, bone, and tissue, her lifeless body sent flopping awkwardly down the steps.

Two more shots rang out.

John stared in horror as three of the four beautiful women were gunned down by the men around him—the one who had removed her clothes lying crumpled at the bottom of the temple steps, the two others suffering from mortal wounds and crying out in agony before the giant. Just one girl remained unscathed. And, as she turned her young face up into the woods, as if able to see the pureblooded assassins, tears rolled over her trembling lips.

John looked to the man beside him and saw that he was shaking uncontrollably, his swollen eyes trying to aim the rifle at the young girl. But with the way he was convulsing, he was more likely to shoot the crystal capstone atop the pyramid than his helpless target.

One of the two men who hadn't yet fired a shot said to him, "Come on, Stephen."

He started sobbing and dropped the rifle. "No…" he cried, reaching his hands out toward the girl.

With a professional coldness that startled even Paul, the man who had tried to urge Stephen to fire suddenly stood, raised the rifle to his shoulder, and squeezed off a single shot. The young girl's head whipped back, and she fell flat onto her back, arms outstretched, blood staining her white dress and covering the grass around her.

By now, the ten soldiers carrying spears were almost out of the courtyard and ascending the hills. The giant also started signaling an alarm, blowing into a horn that had been hanging from its golden belt.

"Come on!" the Australian hollered through his tears. He got to his feet and fired three shots at the men coming after them. Two of them fell backward.

Then they all started shooting—Chris, Jackson, Paul, and Hunter joining in with their submachine guns—and the remaining eight attackers were quickly eliminated. They moved their aim to the giant, riddling it with bullets that punctured its body but seemed to do little in the way of stopping it. A bullet, however, did pierce its throat, putting an end to the sounding trumpet.

"Move! Move! Move!" They were sprinting through the woods as fast as they could, branches and huge clusters of fruit smacking them in the face. Behind them, the temple complex began filling with men and giants desperate to seek out and kill the assassins.

A few minutes later, they could hear something following them from above the forest's canopy. Apparently, the six natives had a pretty good idea of what it was, because they kept turning and firing blindly up through the trees.

And then, accompanied by a horrible screaming sound blasting through the air, the Australian was ripped off his feet, plucked from the planet and flying up through the cedar trees. A few screams later, pieces of him were falling back to the ground around them.

Paul cursed when a length of slimy Australian struck him on the back of the neck and stayed there. As he struggled to remove it, another of their island hosts was plucked off his feet and thrown forward with such incredible force that he splattered against a palmetto like rotten fruit.

And then three giants, with long swords held firmly in their six-fingered grasps, stepped out in front of them and cut the lead runner in half, his body spinning off in two separate directions.

Paul screamed and held the trigger down, removing most of the massive head charging toward him. The giant fell heavily to the ground and slid beneath Paul's feet as he jumped over it and kept running.

Chris was running alongside John when something struck him in the back and lifted him off his feet. Whatever it was, it threw him face-forward into a tree. He screamed out in agony as an enormous amount of pain burst like a blossoming flower in his back and chest. He couldn't move. And then, with terror, he realized that both his feet were dangling freely in the air.

Both John and Hunter witnessed what happened. One of the giants had thrown its sword underhanded, its blade swinging upward, end over end. It caught Chris in the back, lifted him up into the air, and pinned him to a tree. Running to his aid, they tried desperately to reach up and pull the sword from his body. But it was buried deep into the tree, and they didn't have the leverage needed to budge it. Hunter fired his weapon, trying to keep the two remaining monsters at bay while John tried to come up with another way to free the screaming SEAL.

Looking back over his shoulder to see just how much time he had before the creatures were upon them, or something else swooped down to grab him, John saw that there simply wasn't any time to take Chris' comfort level into consideration. If he had any chance of freeing him at all, he was going to have to shimmy the sword loose. It would cause greater injury to Chris, possibly irrevocably, but there was no other choice.

When Chris roared out in pain as John began to work the blade up and down in his back, his distress finally drew Jackson and Paul's attention. They both turned, realized what had happened, and came running back with guns blazing, managing to send another giant toppling to the ground in the process.

The sole remaining giant, perhaps less confident now that it was alone, slipped into the density of the forest and disappeared.

"Get me out of here," Chris yelled, praying for unconsciousness.

They all pulled on the sword, and it finally came free. But just as Chris fell to the ground, something from above came diving through the air and grabbed him. Chris shouted out in hideous anguish as the strange creature stung him repeatedly with its tail and ripped his left arm off with its bare hands. Its wings beat the air, elevating it up through the forest's canopy, where it disappeared from sight. Then it released Chris from its grasp, leaving him to scream all the way back down.

They had seen Chris vanish through the treetops and watched as fluttering leaves and falling branches floated down on them in his wake. And then he reappeared, suddenly plummeting back through the canopy and flailing awkwardly against every gravitational force in the universe. He landed on his head, his vertebrae crunching loudly upon impact right in front of them.

With uncontrolled fury, they let loose a volley of deadly fire that filled the air around them with more falling debris. Leaves, branches, and small trees were turned into mere clouds whirling through the air. And then their weapons clicked empty.

And they ran.

* * * *

Paul was screaming obscenities at the three natives who had survived the attack, threatening to kill them himself. Hunter and John had to hold him back and subdue him. John could feel the rage coursing through Paul's body and wondered if anyone would be able to stop him from ripping these people apart if it was what he really wanted to do.

"One of them was my daughter," the man named Stephen whispered. His eyes were captured by a tractor beam pulling him into nothingness. He was the one who couldn't take that last shot at the young girl.

"Your *daughter*?" Hunter repeated with shocked disgust.

The man crumpled to his knees, convulsing.

Paul was screaming into the empty cave that they had stumbled across during their escape, the fury in his voice echoing back and forth. All he could think about were his two friends, now dead.

One of the others said to Jackson, "We thought God sent you to save us. We thought we had His protection."

But Jackson didn't respond, just kept staring blankly at the wall.

Because they needed the cover of night to conceal their swim back to the cave Chadwick was still waiting for them in, they had plenty of time to face their unbridled grief.

In addition to grief, however, Stephen and the other two surviving islanders sobbed with the added guilt and despair of having killed their own wives and daughters.

John closed his eyes, asking God once more to wake him from this nightmare.

SUMMONING

You have seen what Azazyel has done, how he has taught every species of iniquity upon earth, and has disclosed to the world all the secret things which are done in the heavens. Samyaza also has taught sorcery, to whom you have given authority over those who are associated with him. They have gone together to the daughters of men; have lain with them; have become polluted; And have discovered crimes to them. The women likewise have brought forth giants. Thus has the whole earth been filled with blood and with iniquity. And now behold the souls of those who are dead, cry out. And complain even to the gate of heaven.

—Book of Enoch 9:6–10

...By which also he went and preached unto the spirits in prison; Which sometime were disobedient, when once the longsuffering of God waited in the days of Noah, while the ark was a preparing, wherein few, that is, eight souls were saved by water...

—1 Peter 3:19–20 (KJV)

Here the angels, who cohabited with women, appointed their leaders; And being numerous in appearance, made men profane, and caused them to err; so that they sacrificed to devils as to gods. For in the great day there shall be a judgment, with which they shall be judged, until they are consumed; and their wives also shall be judged, who led astray the angels of heaven that they might salute them.

—Book of Enoch 19:1, 2

A commandment has gone forth from the Lord against those who dwell on the earth, that they may be destroyed; for they know every secret of the angels, every oppressive and secret power of the devils, and every power of those who commit sorcery, as well as of those who make molten images in the whole earth.

—Book of Enoch 64:6

SEVENTEEN

12:18 p.m. 28th day of May. Wilkinsburg, Pennsylvania

It had been five days now since the airport...since John hadn't come home. And getting out of bed was growing harder with every new morning. Positive that something had happened to him, she was simply helpless to do anything about it. Discovering her husband's whereabouts belonged to the ability of others. There was nothing for her to do but stare endlessly at the wall and wait for a miracle.

The will it took to function in any normal capacity had waned rather quickly. At first, there was misery and shock. But when the tears ran dry, the emotion metamorphosed into a sort of bland and hopeless coma. She saw things without seeing them, her eyes bloodshot and constantly staring off, wondering how her life could have become so disoriented so quickly and with no explanation as to how or why. It was the desire to know what had happened in Bermuda that kept her waiting for an official report, and the life growing inside her that kept her holding on to life itself. She knew she should be clinging to God, but her objectiveness had been hijacked by pain and immersed in clouds of disorientation and confusion. She hoped God would forgive her for it, but even more so, she hoped that He would still grant a miracle in the face of her waning faith.

Over the past few days, Pastor Brian and some of the other men from the church had contacted Bermudian officials and talked to airport personnel in Bermuda, Philadelphia and Pittsburgh, the police, FBI, customs, the American embassy, and Interpol. But no one had any answers, just offhanded promises that they'd look into it.

But then yesterday, a police officer from Bermuda had called and informed her that he'd met John about a week ago. He related to her their conversation, his interest in Christopher Carter (of whom he had to give a brief history), and what he'd discovered about Henry's boat. And, because John and the other Americans were now missing along with the boat, he was hoping she might have some information that could assist him in finding them.

But all Kristen could offer was a few insignificant details concerning Henry's background and SEAL Team One. However, the police officer seemed rather surprised when she said that Henry had initially gone to Bermuda to talk with some local author, and that John and the other Americans had planned on meeting him, too. He asked her if she knew the name of the author, if it happened to be Ronald Carter. She told him she had no idea, and he suddenly wanted to get off the phone. He promised he would call with anything new and asked her to call him if she remembered anything else or if John happened to call her—which, of course, he told her was his hope.

Kristen escaped the clutches of the bed and walked to the bathroom, understanding that, with the growing difficulty of getting out of bed, she was waking up later and later each day. It was already early afternoon.

She turned on the faucet and stared at the mirror. Still barely visible were the faint remains of yet another message that had mysteriously appeared across it. But she didn't bother telling Brian about this one, didn't even care what it said. She knew Brian had some idea of what was going on but that he was trying to protect her by keeping it to himself. He told her about the "silly woman" passage and its connection with angels—which she was able to relate to the VHS tape herself—but he didn't seem willing to expound any further. She didn't see what good it would do to keep calling whenever a new message appeared. Besides, if the Devil wanted to scare her, he could do it in English. She was too emotionally drained to be scared, and any reaction to such things now came filtered through a bored sense of contempt.

While she was drying her hands, she heard the mailman pull away from the curb outside. Grabbing a robe, and not caring in the least about her appearance, she pulled it on and tied it at the waist while already on her way to the mailbox.

Among some white envelopes there were two packages wedged tightly into the confines of the old, rusted box. Curiosity flared as she took them into the house. Setting them on the table, she went to work tearing them open.

She froze.

It was postmarked from Bermuda. And the handwriting…

They were from John.

She tore the first one open in a frenzy, extracting its contents. And stood confused.

A book.

No note, no postcard, no explanation whatsoever. Just a book.

The Bermuda Triangle and the Doorway to Hell.

Without taking the time to contemplate the title and whether it could be relevant at all to John's whereabouts, she ripped open the other one. But she was rewarded with only the same sense of confusion…of false hope. It was another book, this one titled *Lost Bloodlines: The Gods Among Us*. She set both books down on the table and sat. Resting her head in her hands, she began to sob.

Finally, she lifted her puffy eyes and stared at the books, finally noticing the author's name on their spines. Ronald Douglas Carter—the man the police officer had asked about. It *was* the same author Henry had gone to see. She flipped the book over in her hands.

She shot to her feet.

Gasping, she knocked over the chair and dropped the book. Her heart was beating ferociously, trying to escape her chest. She couldn't catch her breath, her hands shaking violently at her sides. "Oh, Jesus…" she whispered.

The back of the book was comprised entirely of the author's picture. And the man staring up at her was someone that she knew, though not as Ronald Douglas Carter.

But as Dr. Grigori.

And, though she hadn't realized it at the time, she now knew why the doctor seemed so familiar to her. There were subtle differences, such as hairstyle and the presence of a tan, but she had no doubt that this man, whatever his name really was, was in fact the same man she had seen on the VHS tape—the one that had made her feel so peculiarly violated. Only the tape was old, at least from the early '80s, and the *Lost Bloodlines* book, as she forced herself to touch it again, was copyrighted 1976. How then was it possible that this man looked exactly the same in all three instances?

She placed a hand on her stomach, over the spot his touch had landed, and was overcome by a sudden, immense fear sweeping through her.

She ran for the phone.

EIGHTEEN

Midday. 29th day of May. Bermuda, Northeast end

Despite a week having passed, acclimation had still not set into place yet. They all assumed there had to be some level of transition experienced, if even to some miniscule degree, but so far things just seemed to be getting stranger. In fact, with every new day that passed, John, Hunter, Paul, and Chadwick only grew more certain that they were dreaming. At least until Henry, who had improved greatly from his wounds, would lecture on the likelihood of everyone having the same dream at the same time. He kept reassuring them that adjustment would indeed run its course, and that soon mystery would be drowned by normalcy—as bizarre as that normalcy might be. But they weren't so sure.

Jackson was another matter. Whereas he had once taken every opportunity to communicate some factually based diatribe about whatever was crossing his mind, he had recently grown silent, communicating in short sentences and only whenever it was absolutely necessary to speak at all. He was growing further and further away from the group, and Henry's advice not to trust him was now being instinctively adhered to by everyone.

The deaths of Nick and Chris proved to be somewhat blunted in the face of a world full of megalithic architecture, giants, flying scorpion-men, and a ruler that the natives called Osiris. Though they were certainly sad, the impact of its finality, of its true appreciation, was kept at a distance. Whether it was a psychological mechanism enacted to avoid the reality, or whether they were simply too distracted to dwell on it, no one bothered to figure out. Only when a night afforded some time to relax did John notice tears sparkle in the eyes of his brother and Hunter, even Paul. But never Jackson.

Chadwick, on the other hand (and rather surprisingly), was probably adapting the quickest. After being so close to a breakdown, he had rebounded swiftly, regaining his composure and entering an ongoing discussion with Henry about their shared heritage and what the peculiar ramifications of such a lineage might entail.

The "pureblooded" people, as they referred to themselves—like Noah's family in the biblical Flood account—were grieving the loss of Stephen, who killed himself the day after the so-called "mission" had claimed his daughter's life. As the story went, after giving birth to their daughter, his wife was taken by the giants and seduced by Osiris. She subsequently gave birth to four giants that ended up slaughtering a dozen of the pureblooded. Stephen, on a mission like the one that killed his daughter, had executed her before she could bear more. His daughter then became the only thing capable of holding back the tsunamis of shame and despair that threatened to sweep him away every day since. Once she was removed, and not just removed but also reincarnated as another world of guilt leaning against his soul, the tidal waves finally came down unimpeded.

It was related to the new arrivals that on such missions the relative was given the chance to perform the act if they so desired, but that there was always backup in case they couldn't follow through with it when the time came.

Stephen couldn't.

But despite the sorrow that accompanied the recent deaths, a sparkle of hope continued to shine in the eyes of their hosts. They still believed that John and company had been sent by God to stop Osiris from putting to use what he'd spent four hundred years constructing—something they believed was going to be *activated* in just three weeks' time on the summer solstice.

When John asked Chadwick why the summer solstice was so important, he'd simply responded by stating that there were four high points in the year on which ancient and sacred ceremonies were conducted all over the world: the solstices and the equinoxes. But that was the extent of his explanation.

In the meantime, their hosts had done their best to acclimate them with the island, taking them to some of the other caves and introducing them to more of their pureblooded comrades. They had even shown them the secret chambers used to hide their women. Such was the extent of the trust John and the others earned by simply appearing a month before the solstice.

When asked about the women, the old man, Samuel, explained why their women were the most unfortunate components within the whole demonic scheme. Once captured, females were unable to resist the seduction of Osiris and were then destined to become part of his harem, producing as many children for him as possible. Half of these children grew to be giants and performed most of the labor in constructing his sites. The others were used as foot soldiers and servants; any females were used for breeding more children. Both the men and the giants had their own harems, and both were known to produce giants of their own, the genetic anomalies apparently able to skip around from generation to generation. That was why, explained the man, they had to either keep the women hidden from them…or kill them. Their very survival depended on it.

* * * *

Even now, as they followed their guides through the forest—they'd taken a boat across to St. George's Island and had been trekking northeast for over an hour—John thought back to what Chadwick had said about the Book of Enoch. According to Chadwick's interpretation of the pseudepigraphal work, certain of the fallen angels had developed a lust for women, desiring to have children by them. Two hundred angels then irreversibly changed their form in a way that somehow allowed them the ability to participate on the physical plane and thus realize their outlawed desires. The book said they descended together upon a mountain in the times of Jared. They took women, any of whom they chose, to be their wives. They taught them sorcery, incantation, and divination; taught them the practice of applying makeup to enhance their sexual attractiveness. They taught men how to make weapons and armor, mirrors, and jewelry. They introduced astronomy, signs in the heavens and the motion of the moon; they caused men to sacrifice to devils as to gods, taught men to read and write, and even how to terminate a fetus in the womb. Indeed, Chadwick said they taught every species of iniquity upon the earth and disclosed to man all the secret things of heaven. So much so, that the world itself became "altered" with impiety and fornication as mankind corrupted all of his ways.

And, of course, giants were born to the wives of these rebel angels. The stature of these giants was three hundred cubits, and they devoured all that man had produced until they even began eating man, drinking his blood. At which point God sent Gabriel to turn the offspring of the angels against each other, that they might destroy one another. But the teachings of the angels had already infected humankind, making all their secrets and every power of the Devil common knowledge among them. So God judged both the angels and the world, intent on restoring and reviving the earth through a single righteous family. He destroyed the earth and all that was in it, causing sinners to disappear off its face and erase all of the forbidden wisdom that had corrupted man. The angels were imprisoned and cast into darkness, where they await the Great Day of Judgment and the fire intended for them…

It was a story that Henry, of all people, believed to compliment Scripture. Much to John's surprise, Henry told him that in the book of Jude, when it spoke of the angels leaving their first estate, the Greek word *oiketerion* was used—a word seen only in Second Corinthians 5:2 as referring to the "spiritual body." He believed it was describing the change the fallen angels had undergone to marry women and produce offspring, exchanging a spiritual body for a physical one, or, as the Book of Enoch described it, "laying aside their class" or "deserting the lofty sky and their holy everlasting station." For this act, God had "reserved these angels in everlasting chains under darkness until the judgment of the great day."

And then there was Second Peter 2:4 and 5, which was the only place in the entire Bible that the Greek word *Tarturus* was used. It was a place that Homer described as being a subterranean prison inhabited by the Titans who rebelled against Zeus. John recalled the verse from memory.

> *For if God spared not the angels that sinned, but cast them down to Tarturus, and delivered them into chains of darkness, to be reserved for judgment; and spared not the old world, but saved Noah…*

In First Peter 3:18 and 19, Henry had explained, it said that Christ, after dying on the cross, went and "preached" to the spirits in prison that disobeyed while Noah was building the ark. The Greek word for "preached" meant "to herald," thus signifying Christ's announcement of victory over the angels who had committed such an atrocious sin (some theologians believed that Satan's plan in sending the angels to marry women was actually to contaminate the human gene pool and prevent the birth of the Messiah, of whom it had already been prophesied would crush Satan's head).

There was, of course, the most obvious correlation in Genesis 6, a section of the Bible that had recently become unavoidable to John. In fact, the more he pondered the revelation of his adoption, that he wasn't of the Carter bloodline, the more difficult it was for him to accept his freedom from such an association. The VHS tape, his childhood dreams, the giant in Afghanistan, the Poseidon-like figure that only he and Chadwick had seen…

"The heroes of old," both Chadwick and Henry said (as did the man on the VHS tape) "are none other than the mythological gods and their offspring, most of which were produced from their mating with human women. The gods were these two hundred fallen angels; their offspring, the demigods. All the different stories all come from the same source; only the names are changed depending on which cultures are telling it." They told him about Japanese, Korean, Sumerian, and Persian traditions that contained the idea of godlike figures descending to earth and producing supermen via human women.

But as John thought about all this, he found himself still strangely bothered by Henry's question: *John, I want to know if it's possible for the offspring of angels to find salvation.* The fact of the matter was, he *didn't* know. According to Enoch, the angels who sinned in this manner, and the giants born to them, were never to obtain peace or remission of sins. The question then became: *Was it possible to be far enough removed from the purity of the cursed seed to be free from its damnation?*

"Where we going?" Hunter asked, bringing John out of his thoughts. Hunter had his eyes fixed intently on the canopy above them, ready for more flying creatures to sweep down at them—something they'd seen more of since Chris' death.

John recognized the area, too. They were heading back toward the giant wall they'd seen their first day here.

"There's something else we want you to see," a middle-aged black man named Charles answered. In addition to Charles, there was a balding Irishman named Patrick and a scrawny teenager named George traveling with them.

"Are you taking us to that wall?" Chadwick was still a little wary of their hosts, wondering if they would just turn and shoot him the second he became a conflict of interest. Though they seemed to be viewing him as a savior rather than as a threat so far, believing he shared the same divine protection as his friends, it was a view that could change in a moment—which was why he'd rather be in the caves with the women.

"Past the wall."

"To the unfinished temple?"

Charles looked back and nodded. "We want you to see it for yourselves."

"We've already seen it. It's almost identical to the Osireion at Abydos."

"I don't know what that is. But it's the altar we want you to see."

"We saw that, too. And the body parts buried around it." Chadwick was growing weary of following these people. Walking for hours without knowing why or to where was a method that hadn't ended well before.

Patrick began speaking, taking over the conversation with his thick Irish accent. "The Book of Enoch says that the giants shall be called evil spirits and that evil spirits shall proceed from their flesh. It says that the habitation of terrestrial spirits born on earth shall be earth and that the spirits of the giants shall be like clouds, which oppress and corrupt upon the earth."

"Meaning?" Paul asked, his eyes with Hunter's still up in the trees. Images of Chris falling back to the earth were playing on a continuous loop in both their minds.

"It means," Henry said, limping alongside them and armed with an MP5, "that when the Nephilim died in the Flood, the angelic part of them became disembodied spirits."

John thought immediately back to what Ronald had said about the destruction of the Golden Age and the souls of its inhabitants becoming demons.

Patrick nodded.

Chadwick contemplated this. "But according to Genesis, there were giants *after* the flood, too. What happened to them?"

Paul held up a hand. "What do you mean there were giants *after* the flood? I thought the whole point was to destroy the giants once and for all. You telling me that it didn't work? That God destroyed the world for nothing?"

Henry shook his head, forgetting that so many of their conversations had excluded Paul and Hunter. So he started from the beginning. "Satan's original rebellion resulted in his fall, as well as a third of the angels that, for some unknown reason, decided to follow him. Then, in the time of Jared, certain of these fallen angels committed an even greater sin by defying the laws of nature and putting on some sort of human physicality in order to comingle with humanity. The Flood destroyed all of that. But we know from both the Bible and history that there were giants after the Flood as well. That can only mean one of two things. Either one of Noah's sons was corrupted, or there was a second event in which fallen angels descended to earth and had sexual relations with women."

Paul sneered. "Must've been sick the day they covered this crap in school."

Chadwick smiled. "You wouldn't get this in school. Not unless you were raised in the 1800s. In which case you'd have known that Pliny spoke of two giants, Pusio and Secundilla, who led Augustus' armies into battle. Maybe you'd have heard of the Patagonian Giants in the San Julian region that were seen by Magellan, Sir Francis Drake, and Anthony Knyvett. Or that later, the crew of a Dutch schooner found several skeletons between ten and eleven feet tall—Commodore Byron, in 1764, writing that he, too, found giants there. Maybe you'd have had a test on the story of the Pawnee coming into Wild Bill's camp with a giant thigh bone and telling him that a race of giants had lived in the area, their denial of a Great Spirit bringing a flood that destroyed them."

"Yeah, right," Paul replied.

Chadwick shrugged. "The Piute Indians of Nevada had a legend of red-haired, freckled giants that roamed the Humboldt Sink area of northern Nevada. They were cannibals."

Hunter looked skeptical. "How would red-haired, freckled giants get to North America?"

"Actually, the DNA of some Native Americans shows close ties to Europeans. Seems they had contact with each other at some point. Some of the Native American tribes claimed to have descended from light-skinned people that lived on an island east of America. They called it 'White Man's Island' and claimed a race of white giants lived there, that before the island sank, they were able to build a canoe and reach the mainland. Quetzalcoatl was white with European features, too." He adjusted his glasses and wiped the sweat from his brow. "Anyway, the Celtic Benedigeidfran was supposedly a giant that no ship was large enough to carry—"

"The Celtic what?" George interrupted.

Chadwick smiled again. "The Scandinavian city of Jotunheim was said to be full of giants…"

"What about the *Chronicle of Akakor*?" Henry asked.

"Yeah, that too."

"Which is?" Patrick urged, spreading cedar branches out of his way.

Henry replied, "It told of golden airships that arrived in the New World. The occupants had white skin, black hair, and six fingers on each hand and foot. They supposedly built massive stone cities and could fling lightning and melt stone. The cities were destroyed by a flood. And ancient statues still standing in the Amazon's city of Tiahuanaco have six fingers and toes."

Chadwick adjusted the MP5 as they climbed over a rock formation, something about what Henry said tickling the back of his mind.

"The Chippewas were said to hack giants into smaller pieces," Henry was saying as John helped him up the rocky slope.

"Okay." Paul stopped him. "I get the point."

"Wait," George pleaded in his pubescent voice. "Are there more?"

Paul sighed.

Chadwick managed to pull himself away from whatever was nagging in his brain and nod. "Yeah, DeSoto's expeditions encountered giants. Narvaez found giants along the Mississippi, one of his men writing that they were excellent archers, incapable of missing anything within two hundred paces and with such force that red oaks could be pierced straight through."

"I've seen that," mumbled Patrick. And whatever the memory, it caused him to tighten his grip on the 12-guage shotgun he was carrying.

Then Hunter leaned in and whispered to Chadwick, "You know the kid has no idea what you're talking about. None of us do. Ever."

Chadwick realized that he was probably right. The kid was no doubt born in this place and wouldn't know *anything* about world history, let alone who Narvaez was.

John frowned as he remembered something from Ronald's house. "Ronald had an old book about giants and an age of enlightenment. And I swear it was written in the same handwriting as his list of names on the map."

Henry shook his head and looked over at Jackson. "Should've never trusted him."

Jackson just looked away.

"Here we are," muttered Patrick as they approached the edge of the forest, the giant wall still standing in the middle of the clearing.

Jackson, who hadn't uttered a word the entire trip, began walking into the clearing ahead of everyone.

"Strange character, your friend is," Patrick remarked to Hunter while nodding ahead to Jackson.

Hunter didn't comment.

Chadwick was still amazed by the wall's scale and the impossibility of its construction. "You have any idea how these were built?" he asked the three residents as they approached the tall entranceway.

Paul spit on the ground. "You just said giants built them."

"Well…" He'd never actually given much credence to those stories. He figured they were simply romanticized accounts of the "builder gods" spun by the primitive populations under their rule. But now he wasn't so sure. That there were giants was indisputable; however, what these giants were or could do…well, that had been a more clouded issue—even for someone as "fringe" as himself. "It's true that the legends of Viracocha and the myths of the Andes tell how 'shining ones' built them by magic, that Viracocha created giant men to build his temples. Pedro de Castaneda wrote that the Cocopa Indians were giants that could carry logs six ordinary men couldn't budge."

Charles shrugged as he lifted his eyes to the rock geometry and the conundrum he simply knew to be a wall. "Sometimes we hear strange sounds, and then the next day there's a pillar of stone standing in the middle of an empty field."

"Strange sounds?" Jackson asked, startling everyone. He was staring at the wall.

"Actually," Chadwick said, "ancient legends, like those of the Pyramid of the Magician in Central America and the Andean city of Tiahuanaco, do tell of strange sounds that could elevate huge stones."

"*Sound?*" John asked, skeptical.

"Hey, trumpets made the walls of Jericho come down, right?" he retorted, appealing to John's faith. "In fact—" he whispered while running a hand over the impossible seam separating a rock standing twice as tall as him from others stacked up alongside it. He couldn't even get his fingernail into the crack, yet there was no mortar of any kind, just huge rocks cut in perfect synchronicity with each other. As with the stones in the Great Pyramid, the tolerances would leave modern stonecutters incredulous. "—the acoustics of the Great Pyramid are perfect, like a concert hall. It's said that F-sharp, which Egyptian texts say is the harmonic of the planet, is sounded by the wind blowing across the ends of the star chambers. Sacred flutes of Native Americans were tuned to F-sharp, too. Anyway, the whole pyramid is designed like the Whispering Gallery in St. Paul's Cathedral in London."

Hunter stepped away from the wall, an eerie feeling making him want to distance himself from it. "What're you saying, Chad?"

"Just that sound is an element included within the literature. A kind of sonic purpose incorporated into the system. Maybe, if what Charles said is accurate, the sounds they hear somehow play a part in the building of these impossible structures. I mean, what's more implausible, that some sonic technology exists that can move two-thousand-ton stones, or that, as is believed to be the case in

Peru, they were quarried over two hundred miles away from the site and rolled on stones or wooden poles up and down the sides of mountains?"

"Or maybe *technology* is the wrong word," John suggested. "Perhaps it was just the same demonic power that allowed the pharaoh's sorcerers to imitate God's miracles. The same power that allowed demon-possessed men to break through chains of iron, or how Satan was able to show all the kingdoms of the world to Jesus in one instant."

"Or," Henry stated soberly, "maybe the two are a lot more closely related than we'd like to think."

As they walked away from the wall and toward the temple, John asked if anyone knew the purpose of the wall, since it seemed unlikely that such a fortification would be needed on an island ruled by giants.

"We think the walls are built to separate certain classes of giants," Patrick explained.

Henry nodded. "The Book of Enoch indicates three different species of giants. And, like in the mythology accounts, they started warring with each other—"

"What the…" Chadwick cut him off.

The temple area looked remarkably different than it had just a week ago. The strange henge-like circle that surrounded the altar was now covered in what Chadwick knew to be white gypsum. It was glowing under the midday sky in a ring of light, just as they were said to do in Neolithic Britain. However, even more startling was the assortment of monoliths stacked upon one another inside the circle and around the altar.

"It's like Stonehenge," Paul whispered, looking back and forth. "There's more over there."

They followed his gaze and saw that, indeed, all around the temple structure were circles covered in reflective gypsum. Each circle had two opposing entrances, some containing monoliths and some not.

"Where'd they get the stone?" Hunter wondered.

Jackson answered flatly, "The island consists of volcanic material that's covered with a layer of limestone two hundred and fifty feet thick."

"There must be a dozen of them," John stated, sweeping his gaze over the landscape.

"Look." Henry pointed. "There's one huge avenue that goes through all of them."

Chadwick whispered, "I wouldn't be surprised if from above it formed some sort of pattern."

"Like the Nazca Lines?" Henry asked.

"No, I was thinking more like the pyramids or the temple of Angkor. Maybe a reflection of a constellation. Though the Nazca Lines have a stellar orientation to Orion, too."

"What are the Nazca Lines?" Hunter asked as they slowly approached the brown-red altar now resting beneath the shadows of large standing stones.

Chadwick answered offhandedly, his mind concentrating on something else. "The Nazca plateau in southern Peru is two hundred square miles of barren planes. Once aviation began, people flying over the region noticed hundreds of huge drawings on the ground—birds, animals, geometric shapes…an accurate portrayal of a spider species found only in remote parts of the Amazon rainforest…"

"This is in Peru?" asked Charles.

"Yeah. There's a whale and monkey, too. A little out of place considering it's one of the driest places on earth. Strange-looking men in big boots…"

"How big are these drawings?" Patrick turned and cast a curious face at the archeologist.

"They vary. Some of the lines run perfectly straight for five miles. The hummingbird is one hundred and fifty feet long, the condor four hundred feet, the lizard—whose tail is now divided by the Pan-American highway—is over six hundred feet long."

"Where'd they come from?"

"Local traditions credit the god Viracocha."

But they all fell silent as they came upon the altar, everyone watching rather carefully where they placed their feet.

"What did you want us to see?" John asked, noticing that the breeze had suddenly ceased.

Patrick nodded to George, and George began walking around in a circle, his eyes concentrating on the ground. Then he bent over and began digging in the soft soil with his hands. A moment later, he stood with a giant skull in his hands.

"There's more," Patrick stated.

"It's a giant," Jackson mumbled, a bit surprised.

"Yeah, they sacrifice them."

Hunter examined the skull. "Why would they do that?"

"To free their spirits. We think they can leave this place once they're disembodied."

"Why?"

Henry saw it immediately. "To help assist his effort from the other side."

"And they *willingly* do this?" asked John.

"No, they usually end up killing a few of the men performing the sacrifice before they can be killed themselves."

"Men?"

"Yeah, the giants don't sacrifice each other. As far as we can tell, they don't even seem to be aware of these spirit-freeing sacrifices. When Osiris summons, the men go and capture a giant, drag it to the altar, and sacrifice it, releasing its spiritual energy. On a few occasions, we've witnessed other giants intervening and wiping out an entire priesthood." He shook his head. "The environment here is very unstable. That's one of the reasons we're able to survive, because they spend just as much time killing each other as they do searching for us."

Chadwick crossed his arms, staring at the altar. "The only things that still remain of this old pagan sorcery are the Druid altars. Once the Celtae giants died off, because Ireland was never successfully invaded by the Romans, the Druids were the last to practice this stuff." He paused. "According to Julius Caesar, the

Gauls claimed to be descendants of Pluto. Other Romans recorded instances in which legions fought Celtic giants seventeen feet tall…"

John asked, "Pluto being a fallen angel?"

Chadwick shrugged. "Fallen angel, alien, god… Like I said, I think they're all titles for the same thing. All three of them are known for conducting sexual *experiments*…" He tilted his head, noticing something lying next to the altar. He stepped forward through the bloodstained grass and picked it up.

Hunter stepped closer, until blood began to bubble up around his boots. "What is it?"

"A necklace," he said in stunned fascination. He held it up to the light, examining the golden loop with puzzlement.

"The Anakim," Henry said. "A race of giants in the Old Testament. In certain contexts, the word *Anaq* refers to a tight necklace."

Chadwick nodded slowly, seeing the connection for himself. "The Celts wore them, too."

"The Anakim were pushed out of Canaan by the Israelites. They then traveled through Europe, settling in Celtic territory."

Chadwick handed the gold necklace to Patrick. "The Celts scalped their victims and made garments from their skins, prompting some to suggest a relationship between the Celts and the Native Americans." He looked in Paul's direction. "Like the red-haired, freckled giants."

"They cherished the heads of their victims," Henry continued, "making many of them into drinking bowls."

A look of horror passed over Paul's face. "Is that why that thing had Nick's head hanging around its neck?"

Patrick looked up from the necklace, his eyes suddenly saddened. "We've seen them do that." And then he held the necklace up to eye level, his gaze focusing on it. "I'm Irish, from Ireland. My great-grandparents spoke Gaelic. Do you think it's possible that I'm one of his descendants, too?"

At such a suggestion, Jackson turned and looked him over curiously.

Chadwick answered, "Or maybe you're descended from St. Patrick and, like your namesake, will play a similar role in eradicating such evils, 'chasing the snakes into the sea.'"

Patrick smiled and dropped the necklace, crushing it under the heel of an old Converse sneaker.

But Paul was suspicious, not believing that the sole reason for the two-hour journey was so that they could stare at an altar they'd already seen. They could've just told them that giants were being sacrificed. "Why'd you bring us here, *Pat*?"

Patrick stood back and paused. He spread his arms out at the design surrounding them. "Do you have any idea how it works?" There was a kind of hopeful anticipation in his eyes, as if maybe God *did* have a role for him to play in some coming intervention.

"How *what* works?"

"This, the complex."

"What're you talking about?" Chadwick whispered through a sea of spreading chills.

But before he could explain, a small army of men appeared before them, suddenly materializing out of thin air and occupying the center of the henge. The stunned looks on their twisted faces made it clear that they weren't expecting the eight trespassers to be standing in their way. Their surprise faded quickly, however, as they raised an assortment of razor-sharp weapons…

And charged.

NINETEEN

Midday. 29th day of May. Bermuda, Northwest end. The Henges

Only those with their weapons already poised were able to fire immediately at the genetically damned, and the tropical air suddenly filled with impure blood.

One of the charging men leaped at Patrick, his sword held back and ready to swing. Patrick unloaded a barrel from the 12-gauge point-blank into his face. The headless, loinclothed body landed a few feet away before rolling to a stop against his leg. But before Patrick could slip his finger over the second trigger, another half-naked soldier jumped on him. The possessed man lifted his sword with a demonic shriek and was about to sever Patrick's head in two, when Patrick's finger finally found the trigger. The second barrel emptied into the attacker's chest and blew him backward through the air, slamming him off a monolith. With no time to reload, Patrick tossed the shotgun aside and pulled an old revolver from his belt, backpedaling away from the attackers.

Paul was yelling, the veins in his neck and arms bulging beneath his tattoos as he held the trigger down and sprayed the MP5 back and forth. Hunter was standing beside him doing the same, but there were just too many of them. Eventually, their weapons ran empty, and they were forced to make a run for it.

John, Henry, and Chadwick started running immediately. They heard the gunfire behind them but weren't about to risk slowing down to observe its outcome. Instead, they ran straight for another circle, this one void of monoliths. And then, suddenly, it wasn't so empty anymore.

More men materialized, this group struggling with a giant.

Henry realized at once what was happening and veered to the right, limping as fast as he could for another circle. John and Chadwick were following behind and encouraging him to hurry.

Charles was leaning out from behind one of the massive stone monoliths, staring through the scope of a rifle and taking out one impure abomination at a time, working the bolt action as fast as he could. Then he heard a noise behind him and turned, seeing another group of savages standing in an adjacent circle. He swung the rifle around even as he watched a man with only one eye and seven fingers step out of the crowd and release a shining arrow at him. It pierced his heart before he could move out of its way. He managed to fire a few more shots even with the crystal arrowhead protruding from his back…until a silvery flash sent his head tumbling to the ground.

The giant managed to break free from its captors, picking up the man nearest it and ripping him in half. In blind fury, it opened its mouth and revealed multiple rows of teeth while letting out a ground-shaking roar. The awful sound got the attention of the genetically tainted army, and the impure turned their attention away from the trespassers, instead attacking the giant. They wanted to put it down before it could summon others of its kind.

Once in the cover of the cedar forest, Paul and Hunter turned and watched the giant effortlessly crush the heads of its subjugators with one hand while skewering multiple others with a stolen sword in the other. It wore a gold band around its neck.

"Where's Henry?" Paul whispered while quickly replacing the empty clip with a full one from his pocket.

"Over there." Hunter pointed.

They watched as Henry, John, and Chadwick attempted to flee from a group of men brandishing spears.

Paul swore and was about to run after them when Patrick grabbed him by the shoulder and held him back. Looking up, Paul saw Henry run into the center of a gypsum-covered circle…

And disappear.

John and Chadwick, following half a step behind Henry, disappeared, too.

"What the—"

"Where'd they go?" Hunter asked, standing straight.

"We need to get out of here, now." Patrick started to run, pulling George along with him.

"We're not leaving them!" Paul yelled.

"They're not here!" Patrick screamed. "Run!"

After watching the giant throw a man about twenty yards through the air, his back breaking against a monolith standing erect in another circle, they swore and chased after the Irishman.

* * * *

They tripped and fell forward onto the ground. Scrambling quickly to get up, John turned to help Henry and Chadwick. "Come on, get up!" But neither of them was moving, just staring out past him, their bodies limp and unresponsive to John's tugging. "Get up! They're…" He looked up and expected to see a blade of some sort spinning toward his head, but there was only empty forest. He spun around. A beach rested just fifty yards away.

Chadwick forced himself to his feet. "Unbelievable," he whispered. He turned, looking up above and all around them, taking note of the circle they were now standing in.

"It's a sort of transporter?" Henry asked in astonishment.

John didn't understand. "What do you mean, '*transporter*?"

"Ley lines?" Chadwick guessed.

"You're kidding."

John had no idea what they were talking about, but a week in this place should have prepared him for something like this. It hadn't. *Teleporting* from one place on the island to another? But before the question could further assault his reason, he noticed something closer to the beach. A grove of trees. "What is that?" He began walking to it, leaving the ancient and mind-shattering mechanism behind.

"Wait," Chadwick called out after him.

But John was already there, holding a hand over his mouth.

Henry walked up behind him. "'And Ahaz burnt his children in the fire, after the abominations of the heathen whom the Lord had cast out before the children of Israel…' Second Chronicles," he whispered. "Sacrificed to every green tree."

John turned away from similar sacrifices still hanging bound to the palmettos. It was too much, and his own memories of dead children were beginning to creep up on him. Bombs, gunfire… He'd seen kids crying on their dead parents, had seen parents holding their dead children. This, however, was different. Though "collateral damage" was hardly excusable—people pushing buttons miles away and instantly creating widows, orphans, and blowing to pieces precious little ones—this revealed a whole other level of cruelty. This was the intentional torture—the *sacrifice*—of one's own children.

Chadwick walked past them and continued down to the surf. "I'm guessing we're on the complete opposite side of the island now." He had studied John's map rather intensely over the last few days, so John had every reason to believe him.

"We have to go back," John said, his voice breaking over the sight and the memories it induced. "We have to help them."

"There's nothing we can do for them, Johnny."

And then a horror-filled, "Guys…" escaped Chadwick's lips.

They spun around.

Walking lazily along the beach toward them was one of the flying creatures that had killed Chris. It was moving on insect-like legs, its wings folded back, its tail curled up over its shoulders, and a massive stinger rocking back and forth with each step. But it was its face that was most horrifying.

Peeking out from beneath long blond hair…was a man.

John and Henry started backing away from the grove of desecrated palmettos, urging Chadwick with frantic hand gestures to follow them. But Chadwick seemed too stunned to move, too horrified to run.

And then the creature stopped and looked up. A pointed, scorpion-like leg brushed blond hair out of its face, its blue eyes coming to settle on Chadwick. Its mouth turned slowly upward in a twisted grin, showing a massive set of lion's teeth. And as it stood up, stretching out its wings, it unleashed a shrieking cry, snapping its long tail in the air like a whip.

"Move!" John screamed to Chadwick.

Summoned by his voice, the monster snapped its head around toward John, seeing both him and Henry for the first time, and launched itself straight into the air with a powerful downstroke of its wings.

Henry started firing the MP5, and the sound of it finally snapped Chadwick out of his stupor. He ran as fast as he could, firing his own submachine gun up into the air as he joined John and Henry in trying to find cover in the forest. They ran back the way they'd come and straight through the henge, the scorpion tail plunging into the ground a mere second after they disappeared.

* * * *

Their momentum carried them a few strides out of the circle and into some other part of the island. Spinning back around to face the henge, six stone monoliths decorating this particular site, Chadwick and Henry raised their weapons in anticipation of the creature's pursuit. But nothing else materialized between the standing stone slabs.

Nearby palmettos and cedars rocked gently in the breeze while small birds chirped casually from their branches. It was still here, peaceful.

But maybe the creature had transported somewhere else, hunting them from another direction…

They took the time to catch their breath.

"Where are we now?" John asked, bent over, hands on his knees.

Chadwick consulted the map he'd stored within his photographic memory. "We're in the interior…"

"Should we go back in?" John asked, studying the mysterious circle.

Henry shook his head, not liking the idea. "What if it takes us right back to that thing?"

"Or to the altar," Chadwick added.

Henry nodded. "I think I like our chances here better."

"You sure you know where 'here' is?" John was still looking around. But it was quiet, no sign of anything hunting them.

"Doesn't matter," he replied. "As long as we can't see that pyramid and don't have giants chasing us…"

Chadwick agreed.

"Alright," muttered John, not thrilled with either option. And Chadwick began leading them toward the coast, where they figured they'd have a better chance at pinpointing their exact location.

As they traversed the tropical terrain, John thought this part of the island must resemble what it had looked like four hundred years ago when the *Sea Venture* showed up. He mentioned the thought to Henry, but Henry was too worried about his friends to care about anything else. He was moving quickly, as if hurrying somewhere might bring about news of the other SEALs. And though

Chadwick was keeping stride, he had once again become wrapped up in some internal dialogue, debating with himself the impossibilities of this reality.

As they continued, John began replaying the conversation he'd had with Henry a week ago, about his conviction regarding the taking of lives and his promise to God. All of that was beginning to cloud now. Where did Old Testament slaughter and New Testament love intersect for the Christian? Did it? He never thought it could. A Christian by definition, after all, was one who followed the teachings of Christ, so his entire belief system was founded on *that* example and not on the practices of King David or any other Old Covenant warrior. Jesus said that those who lived by the sword would die by the sword, to turn the other cheek, to love your enemies. He said that His kingdom wasn't of this world or else His servants *would* fight.

But the *things* in this place… Were they even capable of being loved? The Nephilim, the fallen ones, the heroes of old, the objects of God's divine wrath in a past age… Were they even redeemable, these monsters? Or, as in the Old Testament, was the only way to deal with them through bloodshed? Would John be justified in killing these *impure* men? Certainly, he wouldn't have thought so on the other side of this bizarre dimension, but here, now… He wasn't so sure anymore. The line was blurring. Yet, regardless of whether the extermination of an evil people was justified in the age of grace (which certainly it wasn't, though it could be possible that this place was under some other set of God rules), there was the issue of his own personal spirituality. If blowing the heads off people was deemed permissible, or even God-honoring, as it had been in the Old Testament, where would that leave him as the last man standing and heading back home to his wife in Pennsylvania? The psychosis of violence was something he had buried at the foot of the cross, and if he were to resurrect it now, if even for some righteous cause, he knew there was little chance of being able to bury it again. He would be raising the beast, summoning it to help him now and trusting that it would kill itself once no longer needed. Unlikely. Instead, as his nightmares were suggesting, he might just be one kill away from reacquainting himself with John Carter, Army Ranger and murderer of innocent children. He didn't know if he would ever see Kristen again in this lifetime, but if so, he wanted to be sure which John Carter she would be welcoming home.

Bermuda's typical plant life, or what it must have been before settlers introduced foreign species to it, suddenly began giving way to strange fruits and vegetables that, as far as they knew, weren't home to *any* place on earth. More beach-ball-sized melons, grapes the size of baseballs, vegetables protruding from the ground in rainbows of colors… And then they stumbled upon gardens, rows upon rows of meticulously planted food.

"You hear that?" Henry asked, freezing.

They listened.

"People," John whispered.

"Come on."

They walked around the gardens, following the sounds of activity until they were amongst ferns twice the size of themselves and facing an expanse of huts identical to the ones John and Chadwick had seen their first day here. These, however, were not deserted.

Just fifty yards from their position, between them and the scattered huts, was a group of children playing some kind of game with a ball. An audience of older kids and men had formed loosely around the boundaries of the game. They were cheering, screaming, and hopping up and down.

It was impossible to determine what the object of the game was, but apparently a loser was picked rather than a winner. Or maybe it was a king of the hill-type game where the last one remaining proved to be the victor, because the smallest of the children was suddenly being attacked by the other four boys. It was either punishment for losing, the stakes high, or this was how they honored the winner. Maybe they thought he cheated. In any case, the three intruders watched in total disbelief and horror as the crowd became elated by what must have been the alluring aspect of the game. Despite the young boy's pleading, the other four mercilessly twisted his head right off his shoulders.

"Oh, God…" Chadwick turned away, covering his mouth.

The blood-covered boys tossed the corpse into the gathered crowd like it was a football thrown to eager fans after a touchdown. What the mass of people started to do with the young boy's body, John couldn't tell. But what the kids did next was even more atrocious. They kicked the ball they'd been playing with out of the playing field and instead began using the boy's head. Now it seemed like the only point to playing was to do as much damage to the adolescent face as possible, eliciting the loudest and most frenzied cheers from those gathered around them.

There were other people walking nearby and attending to everyday chores, but none of them seemed the least bit concerned with the murderous game being played, or the gathering of adults cheering it on.

And then a near-naked woman came running onto the playing field, picked up the head, and tried to make a break with it. But one of the players, only four feet tall, grabbed her by the back of her hair and yanked her off her feet. He spun her around and flung her through the air. She flew sixty feet before striking her back against the corner of a nearby hut. It was clear that she'd broken something because she couldn't move, just screamed in agony, cursing the boys who had killed her son.

That was when the boys gave up the game and moved on to their next challenge. Her.

Now even Henry looked away as the woman's cries of pain reached new boundaries.

The crowd applauded louder.

John rose to his feet, unable to just sit and watch.

"What are you doing?" Henry asked, reaching up and grabbing his adopted brother.

"I have to help her." And he shrugged Henry's hand off him.

Henry protested, "No. It's not what you think."

"No one should have to suffer like that."

"John!"

But it was too late. He was already out of the ferns and sprinting empty-handed through the open grass.

When the first savages saw him, they were simply too shocked to react, and John was able to make it all the way to the woman before a single person began moving to stop him. But then he realized that they didn't *want* to stop him, that he was just a bonus in their sick halftime show. He grabbed the first boy off the woman and threw him to the ground. Then he moved in to pull the other three off. By the time he had the boys sprawled in the grass behind him, he realized that the woman's screams were not, in fact, the screams of hopeless anguish he thought they were.

She licked her lips.

And then one of the boys was on his back, clawing at his face. John spun and backed into the hut to knock him off. But the kid wouldn't let go, trying instead to bite into his jugular.

The crowd of people did not come to the aid of the children but continued to watch as spectators only, rooting for whoever might first deliver a lethal blow—whether John or one of their own, they didn't seem to care.

John grabbed the kid's face and flipped him onto the ground. The child landed hard, and the air escaped his lungs. Before John could begin to feel bad about it, however, two of the other kids were rushing him, a crazy, bloodthirsty light in their eyes. John kicked the first in the head, but the other one leaped off his feet and struck John with a tackle that an NFL linebacker would've envied. They both went flying backward.

The crowd erupted.

Straddling John's chest, the boy howled with euphoria, certain he was about to taste the stranger's blood in his mouth.

And then there was a loud *crack*, and his head disappeared.

Henry and Chadwick were charging the scene with guns blazing, the crowd instantly reduced to twitching casualties, the demon-crazed boys finally silenced.

John pushed the headless corpse off him, half afraid it might still try to strangle him. He ran toward the woman, hoping that his most recent evaluation of her had been wrong. She was lying still on her back, her eyes closed, her son's head having rolled to within an arm's reach of her.

"No! John!" Henry called, trying to get there in time.

But John leaned forward, checking to see if she was still breathing. She wasn't. He sighed in defeat and turned back to Henry and Chadwick.

"Johnny!" Henry screamed, raising his MP5.

John spun around.

She was standing, eyes wide with unnatural hunger. She roared.

John tried scrambling away, but she was too close. All he could do was cover his face as she landed on him, her sweating, stinking skin rubbing all over him. He could feel her fingernails, like razorblades, searching for arteries, her teeth clamping on his throat. Trying to push her off just seemed to excite her more. She leaned back and smacked him across the face so hard that he nearly lost consciousness.

Henry grabbed the woman by the hair and pulled her off him. He swung her around and let go of her, raising the submachine gun and emptying the remainder of the clip into her chest as she stumbled backward. She collapsed, staring up at him through a crooked grin.

"Come on!" Chadwick was helping John to his feet, but his eyes were on the gathering population stepping out of their homes, leaving their chores, picking up rocks, sticks, tools…

Henry ejected the empty clip and stuck it in his pocket, pulling out his last one and ramming it in. He fired indiscriminately at the mass of people walking their way. And then he joined Chadwick and John in heading back to the forest.

A skinny man leaped down from a tree, cutting off their path. Chadwick sprayed him with a cloud of bullets, striking him in the foot, thigh, stomach, and neck.

"Where we going?" Henry called up to them, feeling the strain of his injuries.

They didn't answer, fear that the demonic villagers might actually catch them blinding them to everything but the steady pumping of their legs.

Henry turned and saw that their pursuers were gaining on them. He swore.

"Up there!" John called out, pointing to a tall obelisk that stood piercing a grove of trees a hundred yards away. Of course, it was only a hope that they would find it standing in the center of a "teleporting" circle.

An arrow screamed by Henry's head and buried itself into a tree ahead of him. And then another flew by, taking a centimeter of his scalp with it. He risked one look back over his shoulder and saw, to his dismay, the forest crawling with more white-skinned, loinclothed warriors, swords and other weapons gleaming in their hands. He willed his legs to move even faster.

The monolith, which was a phallic symbol representing the Cult of the Phoenix and the seed of Osiris, did rest in the midst of a gypsum-coated henge. And as John pushed himself to get there sooner, the forest around them suddenly crawling with an impure army ascending like cockroaches out of rotten woodwork, he called out, "Oh, Jesus, please—"

And he was gone.

TWENTY

Zodiacal imagery is all around me. Like holograms, the celestial symbols circle my head. I reach out to touch Virgo, but my hand passes through it. Light is shining from somewhere, touching the shapes and smearing their dimensions into rainbows of different colors. I look around the cave and notice that dust no longer covers the ancient markings on the pillars. In fact, glancing down at the floor, I don't see any dirt at all, just polished stone. I raise my weapon only to find it missing from my hands. Did I drop it? I look around for it but don't see it anywhere. But in looking for it, I'm also made aware that the stone sarcophagus, along with all the skeletons that surrounded it, is gone. Lifting my hand to remove the night vision from my eyes, I discover that it, too, has disappeared. What's happening? I turn to leave the chamber but find a solid stone wall where the hole had been. I reach instinctively for a grenade, too scared to worry about the explosion bringing the desert down on top of me. And, of course, they're missing, too. I look down at myself, and confusion sweeps through me like a tidal wave, almost knocking me off my feet. Where are my fatigues? I don't understand. I'm wearing dark jeans, brown boots, and a ragged gray T-shirt under a black windbreaker. How is this possible? What's happening? A voice sounds from behind me, asking me if I'm okay. I spin around, fear gripping my heart as I half expect to find a terrorist aiming an AK-47 at me; but the other half of me recognizes that the accent doesn't belong in this part of the world. And then, when I see him—as if the spell is suddenly broken—I realize that I'm not really dreaming.

Are you okay, Johnny?" he asked again, walking out of the shadows.

John looked back behind him, realizing now that he must've been transported to this place when he ran through the circle. But—

"You're looking for Henry and Mr. Aland." He smiled, stepping closer. "Sorry, I wanted some privacy. I have already spoken to Henry anyway."

John examined the mysterious figure with clear apprehension. He was wearing a white linen shirt that seemed to reflect the spinning display of the zodiac still circling around the room.

The man noticed John trying to peer through the colorful images. "My apologies," he stated, and waved his hand. The zodiac vanished, and the colorful lights evaporated.

John could make out his surroundings more clearly now and noticed that the man was wearing loose pants made from the same material as his shirt. His feet were bare, his long curly hair golden around a perfectly tanned face. His white teeth shone brilliantly when he smiled, and his blue eyes looked as if they contained the oceans themselves. He looked to be about John's age, though there was something in his expression that hinted at an arrogance much older than that.

The room around them was large and constructed of smooth limestone blocks, massive pillars holding up the tall ceiling. Over the man's shoulder,

John could see a mirrored device of sorts standing beside an entranceway. Other than that, the room was empty.

The man smiled again as he turned and looked at the mirrors, acknowledging John's interest in them. "We'll get to that," he said.

"Where am I?"

"My abode, of course." He took a step back and bowed.

"How'd I get here?"

"You tell me."

John's eyes narrowed with accusation. "You're Osiris."

The man chuckled. "Ah." He held up a finger and stepped closer, strands of his hair floating whimsically through the air as he moved.

"You're a fallen angel," John whispered, only half conscious of how ridiculous such a statement was…or *should* be.

He chuckled. "That is what they call me, though the true Osiris currently resides in chains much more restricting than my own. I found using his name to be incredibly helpful in continuing his work in Egypt all those years ago. Why work to create my own legacy when I could just borrow one already established? It saved me a lot of time." He cocked his head to the side. "But what gave it away? Was it the giants or the dreams? No—" he snapped his fingers "—it was the tape, wasn't it?"

John's heart began thumping. He felt the color drain from his face.

"Oh, you thought that because you were *adopted*—" He shook his head. "Now, Johnny, you know better than that."

John clenched his fists.

Waving his hand, Osiris dismissed the angry response and walked toward the mirrored mechanism. "Come here, Johnny."

John cautiously approached the mirrors, his own reflection walking to greet him. And then it disappeared, replaced by images of strangers.

John counted six mirrors, and each one held within its properties an active view of someone different. It was like watching six televisions, each one set on some reality show.

"What is this?"

"This is the instrument by which I have united my lost family."

John watched the closest mirror and saw a man sitting at a desk working on a computer. "These are your—"

"My progeny, yes. My genetic code is written in their DNA. It's become diluted over the years, of course…"

Stepping closer, John slowly reached out a finger and touched the glass. "You were watching *me*?" he breathed.

"From the moment you were conceived." He crossed his arms. "I'll let you in on a little secret, though. It is not like it used to be when our seed filled the whole earth. Now our offspring is rather limited. Especially mine, since I have been trapped *here*. Anyway, I have found that manipulating the environment around my kin, introducing them to each other, helps tremendously in getting them to me. To get just one person to this place without having to build a 'support group' around him is very difficult and time consuming. But—" he held up a finger again "—if you intertwine a few lives together, they just about get here themselves. It is a fascinating thing to watch."

John swallowed the lump in his throat, realizing what he was being told.

"Your last name may not be Carter, but you were adopted by Carters for a reason."

He knew it was true. He'd wanted to believe what Henry told him, that this had nothing to do with him, but deep down he always knew that it did. And now Henry's question became his own. Was redemption possible with this fallen creature's blood running through his veins? The conversation he'd had with Pastor Brian the day before he left suddenly flashed through his head—the difficulty he had trying to live a holy life. But whereas he doubted before whether he had actually been redeemed, he was now wondering if that redemption was even possible at all. He began to pray as the floor moved beneath his feet.

"See! You know it's true. Look at your face! No doubt in your eyes at all." Osiris walked away from the mirrors, his hands folded behind his back. He looked thoughtfully up at the ceiling—which suddenly wasn't there, a huge section of block somehow retracting and revealing the sunny sky above. "But something happened, Johnny. While you were in Iraq. I mean, I was watching you beat the hell out of that poor Iraqi, and then suddenly—" He spun on his heel and threw his hands out in the air. "Nothing! Just like that, you were gone." He squinted like he was thinking really hard, making some kind of dramatic production out of it. "I didn't know what happened, Johnny. Where did you go? Did you die? That's what I thought. But then I saw you in Henry's mirror, and in your adopted father's mirror. But how was that possible, Johnny? That had never happened before." And then he raised his voice, suddenly angry. "What made you disappear from my vision, Johnny?" He settled back into a whisper, his fingers dancing in exaggerated animation. "I thought about it for a long time and finally determined that there could be only one explanation." He lifted his eyes, which were now shining intensely, and smirked evilly. "The *Messssiah*," he whispered with serpent-like disdain. "You must have been taken from me by the Messiah, my DNA destroyed by the infusion of His Spirit."

John stepped back as the fallen angel leaned toward him so closely that their noses were almost touching. Osiris stared into his eyes, unblinking. Tilting his head to the side, he looked up and down John's body, circling around him. John held his breath.

"I didn't think that my seed was redeemable," he said softly, his voice growing more and more eerie. "I had to bring you here to see for myself."

"That's why you brought me here?"

"I've been working to bring you here from the moment you appeared in my mirror. It would've been an awful waste to just abandon you. You should think of yourself as an…*experiment*."

"An experiment?" His stability was slowly returning, but now in the form of anger.

"Ye*ssss*. I wanted to know if I *could* still bring you here. And if I could, then maybe I could win you back. Turn you."

John laughed. "I don't think so."

The angel sighed. "Yeah, me neither. But, nonetheless, here you are." He shrugged. "Granted, I needed two others on the boat and Ronald's help to make it happen."

He blinked. *Two* others?

But Osiris just smiled and changed the subject. "Your friends interrupted a ceremony, and it has proven to be a rather large setback for me. I'm running out of time, Johnny."

"You needed to release its spirit…"

He smiled. "Ah, someone's been reading Enoch."

"Why not just kill it?"

"I don't make up the rules," he looked up into the sky and yelled, "as I have so *adequately* learned!" His voice echoed.

"I don't understand."

"Neither do I, Johnny, neither do I. Though my demon friends can visit me now"—he waved at the mirrors—"deliver such instruments and nudge my offspring toward me, it seems that the spirits born here don't have the liberty to travel back and forth as the others do. So I have to send them in a very precise and rather complicated way."

"The henges," John realized.

"Yes, the henges."

"Is that how you're planning on escaping this place?"

He sighed again, and his shoulders slumped. "Johnny, I've been on this island for about four *thousand* years. And for all but the last four hundred of them, I've been completely alone."

"Until Christopher Carter showed up."

"You're rather good at putting the pieces together, aren't you? Yes. When Christopher Carter arrived on the island in the year of *our Lord*—" he rolled his gleaming eyes in disgust "—1609, I was given my eye*ssss* back," he hissed. "I could suddenly see out from my cell, but I could not interact with what I was seeing. One offspring was not enough to cross me over, though his presence on the island did provide a way for demons to visit me in my lonely world. And they came bearing plans of escape."

By now, John's fear had transitioned into curiosity and righteous indignation. "How?"

"How do I escape? By reconstructing what got me here in the first place. But I couldn't do it myself. I needed the materials, I needed my giants, and, of course, I needed Christopher Carter to stay on the island."

Pieces of Frank's story came back to him. "You *made* him stay?"

He grinned diabolically. "I could whi*ssss*per in his ear." He arrogantly walked a wide circle around John as he continued. "His presence created a doorway out in the water, but I couldn't pull him through it because I needed him to sustain its opening. I needed others that I could bring through the gateway. And in your year of 1687, a very *special* relative was brought to me."

"Sounds pretty complicated," John mocked.

"Oh, it is. You see, that's where He got me." He put his head back and quoted from Enoch like he was some Southern preacher. "'Hear, Enoch, and take in these my words, for not to My angels have I told My secret, and I have not told them their rise, nor My endless realm, nor have they understood My creating, which I tell you today… And now to the Watchers say, In heaven have you been; secret things, however, have not been manifested to you; yet have you known a reprobated mystery.' He tricked us, Johnny. God tricked us into thinking that we did know the secrets of creation. And so I used my knowledge of such secrets, the mysteries of the universe that your scientists can't even begin to understand, to try to open the gates of Tarturus and free my condemned brethren. Only the joke was on me. Instead of freeing those in chains, I ended up trapped between the two worlds. This…*sub*-reality."

"So then you did transform yourself *after* the flood."

He feigned a look of humble shame and nodded. "After my brothers had been condemned in the abyss, and their work had been erased from the face of the earth, we decided to try once more. But it was obvious right away that things were different. God had already taken *precautions*."

"Israel."

"Yeah. The Jews. The Law. So freeing the two hundred that had first descended was the only way to overcome His *ssss*afeguard."

Something that Henry and Chadwick just told him pricked his memory. "You were trying to prevent the birth of the Messiah."

"Well, of course we were. But so much more than that, Johnny. We were trying to reestablish the *true* high priest, the *true* prophet and king back to his rightful throne."

"Satan…"

Another laugh rebounded off the stone walls. "My brother, who you would probably know as Apollo, will be free once again, once earth's cycle is complete. And I'll be waiting for him and all his hosts. And then…*then* Lucifer will once again rule over that which has been taken from him and destroyed so many times."

John shook his head. "You see, now you've lost me."

Osiris smiled. "I fear I have divulged too much anyway. But one more thing before I kill you." His appearance seemed to alter ever so slightly, the graceful fluidity of his movement suddenly becoming dark and chilling. "Did you know that women cannot resist us? And nor can we resist them. Reproducing with them is what brought this world to near extinction." He smiled and walked back to the mirrors. "I told you, Johnny, that you disappeared from my device after your little epiphany. But three weeks ago—" he waved his hand over the glass "—*this* appeared."

It was his house in Pennsylvania.

John gasped, the coolness he'd managed to maintain throughout the whole show shattering into a million pieces. His heart stopped in his chest, and he couldn't breathe. He saw Kristen walk through the front door, the display following her into the house.

The angel began a haunting laugh, clapping his hands.

"You brought us together? She's—"

He waved impatiently at the suggestion. "No, no, no. Your similar experiences with the Messiah did that. Besides, the seed, like sin, is passed down through man. Thus the whole *virgin* birth…" He was waving his hands around, waiting for him to get it.

"Then how—"

"Come on, Johnny. You've been an A student so far."

Three weeks ago…that was when the strange feelings began coming back, when the dreams started again. He quickly replayed everything through his head, trying to keep it in chronological order. The dreams, the feelings, the apprehension about the trip, the tape, the apparition…"

And then he and Kristen were suddenly framed within a mirror, looking at each other.

The day he left.

"Are you sure you're going to be okay?"

"*Yeah, I'll be fine,*" he watched himself say.

"*Look at me, Johnny. I have something to tell you. Something very important. But I'm going to wait until you get back and all of this, whatever you're going through, is behind us. That means that you have to come back to me, Johnny. You understand me?*"

He watched himself smile and remembered how hard it had been to make his lips form it. "*Yes, ma'am. Sorry about last night.*"

"*I guess you'll have to make it up to me on Sunday.*"

"*I'll be here.*"

The image faded away.

"You're not crying, are you, Johnny? Oh, for god's sake."

He realized that he *was* crying and promptly wiped the tears from his face, sadness quickly replaced by more potent doses of anger.

The angel stood back and crossed his arms again, staring at John in shock. "You still aren't getting it, are you?" He sighed. "There goes your A." He snapped his fingers, and an image of Kristen leaning against the doorframe appeared on the glass. She was waving goodbye, a hand resting on her stomach.

John didn't remember seeing her do that. It was a strange gesture, like…

And it clicked.

Collapsing to his knees, he hugged himself against the shock. But it was an internal sensation, and such a position did nothing to alleviate the realization. He couldn't catch his breath.

The angel ran to him, pretending to be concerned, and tried helping him to his feet.

"Get off me," John growled, shrugging him off and getting to his feet on his own. He grabbed the angel by the throat and pushed him all the way across the room and into the stone wall, squeezing his neck with every bit of strength he could muster.

"Now, if I'm not mistaken," the angel said without the slightest sense of pain or discomfort in his voice, "you vowed to God that you'd never raise a hand against anyone ever again."

"You're not anyone," he seethed.

The angel sighed, suddenly bored. He lifted a finger, and John was instantly thrown across the room and slammed into a stone pillar. He crumpled to the floor.

"So, obviously it's a boy. Congratulations." Osiris walked slowly and methodically around the room, keeping a narrow eye on John.

"What do you want?" John snapped, stumbling back to his feet and trying to bring his breathing under control.

"A deal." He stopped and sat down in a chair that had just materialized beneath him. He crossed his legs. "You see, I am very close to getting out of here. Unfortunately, I was sort of depending on that giant's spirit entering your world. There is just one last thing that I need, and the pureblooded people on this island somehow seem to know it."

John spit blood onto the floor. "And you need it before the solstice."

He clenched his jaw. "You see, that's what happens when I delay too long in bringing my offspring to me. They intermingle with the purebloods and *tell them everything*!" He took a breath, continuing to make a performance of it. "It doesn't matter. In exchange for your life *and* your son's, you will simply prevent any further interruptions so that I can finish my work."

"So that you can escape and await Apollo's rise from the deep and the resurrection of Satan's reign on earth? I don't think I can do that. Besides, my life, or any son I may have, is not yours to control."

A conceited shadow fell across his face, and for the first time, John got the impression that this was indeed one of the deities the Egyptians had worshipped at the dawn of civilization (or post-Flood re-civilization, as he'd indicated). "Are you sure about that, Johnny?"

And then he disappeared.

John looked around the room, but he was alone. The mirrors had vanished as well. He was sweating, adrenaline fueling his pounding heart. He needed to find a way out of this place, to get back to Kristen. As he ran back and forth through the room, he began praying, tears running down his face. The entranceway that had stood next to the mirrors was gone, too. Sprinting from one end of the long room to the other, he ran his hands over the smooth stone blocks, barely feeling the grooves where they were joined. "Come on!" he screamed. And then his hand suddenly plunged into the wall and disappeared up to his elbow. He quickly retracted his arm, stepping back from the wall. A dark circle swam in the stone. He touched it again and watched it erase his fingers. Closing his eyes and taking a deep breath, he threw his whole body into the wall, not having any idea of what doing so might introduce next.

* * * *

He found himself in another room, this one with heavy curtains hanging from the ceiling and flickering ceremonial candles stacked throughout. But the main source of light seemed to be emanating from elongated glass tubes that were mysteriously fixed to the limestone walls. Wires of some sort were going out from them and entering straight into the limestone. There was also a long rectangular pool in the center of the room with columns all around it reaching up to the ceiling. Lounging on the pool's ledge and swimming carefree in the water were naked women.

John turned his head to the left and right, taking in the enormous surroundings. He could hear the girls giggling and splashing and was able to see a few of them caressing each other. And suddenly there was a giant standing beside the pool. Where it came from, John didn't know; he figured it could have walked right out of the wall. It grabbed one of the women by the hair and, as if she were a rag doll, carried her away, dragging her across the floor behind it. He could hear the girl's laughter echoing off the walls as she struggled, thrashing her legs and sliding wet across the stone surface.

John ran to a pillar, looking around the room for another way out. There was a doorway on the other side of the room, but it was all the way behind the pool. He began to skirt around the outside of the columns. When he reached the far wall, he saw that there was another giant present. It was engaged with a whole handful of women. John spun his back up against the pillar, hoping he hadn't been seen.

A woman's voice made him jump.

"Ah, the master has brought us another one of his relatives, has he?" She grabbed him by the shoulders and pushed him up against the pillar. "Don't be shy, dear." She leaned up and kissed him vehemently on the lips.

John didn't know where she came from, but he was amazed at how strong she was. He could feel her pressing into him, almost crushing him with her force. He tried to pull away, but she reached up and held his face with her hands. She bit his lip, and he tasted blood. He tried to pull away again, but this time she put her palm on his forehead and smashed his skull into the stone. He squeezed his eyes shut, seeing stars. He felt her hands navigating across his body. He tried to grab her wrists, but then she lunged upward and bit his neck. She kept pressing her body against him, grunting in lustful anticipation.

"You want to give me a child?" she asked. "Give me a child!" And she tore at his belt.

While both her hands were at his waist, John grabbed the back of her head and pulled it into his own, using the muscles in his neck to deliver a wrecking-ball blow to her forehead. Not waiting to find out if the impact knocked her out or just excited her more, he swung her around and slammed her into the stone. Then he pulled her forward and twisted her so that he was behind her, his arms around her neck in a sleeper hold. But she bent forward, lifting him off his feet, and carried him out of the shadows and closer to the busy giant.

He swiftly grabbed her long hair and wrapped it around her neck, pulling it tight. She let go of his legs, trying instead to loosen the hair around her throat. Hopping down off her back, he spun and flipped her by her hair, slamming her into the ground. He knelt over her, grabbed a tuft of hair from the center of her head, and lifted her face right into a vicious blow that sent her skull rebounding off the limestone floor. She lay sprawled beneath him, finally unconscious. Or perhaps dead.

He stood and ran as fast as he could, not caring now that his footsteps were echoing throughout the hall. But the loud sounds of corruption emanating from within the pool proved too loud for anyone to hear him anyway.

He slipped back through the wall.

TWENTY-ONE

Midday. 29th day of May. Bermuda, Northwest end. The henges

John found himself back at the huge fortress wall where all his "jumping" had started, the Neolithic circles sprawled out all around him. By now there were no signs of anything living, only piles of dismembered corpses. Hurrying away from the circle before something else could come out of it, he began searching the gruesome remains for a weapon. Finding a sword lodged in the head of a man that had been riddled with genetic defects—three thumbs, three eyes, one ear, and something growing from his neck—he pressed his foot against the mutated face and yanked the sword free.

With no idea how the network of circles worked, he was very fortunate to be sent here…to the only place on the island he knew how to get back to the caves from.

As he navigated through the terrain, his mind kept replaying the encounter with Osiris, examining it from every possible angle. And a couple of things stood out. For one, Patrick, Charles, and George didn't lead them to the altar just so they could have a look at it. They had taken them there to intervene with the sacrifice, to keep the spirit of the Nephilim from making the journey into the real world. Another key point was Osiris' reference to needing *two* relatives to get him here, Chadwick only making one. But the biggest thing the encounter introduced to his personal world was the news that he and Kristen were having a baby, making him all the more eager to leave this place.

And he now had an idea how.

But it entailed letting the angel finish his project, and he wasn't so sure the pureblooded folks back in the caves would be too supportive of that.

He had to find Henry and Chadwick.

* * * *

When he finally showed up at the entrance of the cave, he was greeted by a young, armed guard named James.

"You're alive!" he exclaimed.

Feeling as though he might collapse, he barely managed to reply, "Yeah, I'm alive. Where are the others?"

"Which others?"

"Henry, Chadwick, Paul—"

"They're inside. Everyone but Charles and that tall guy made it back already."

"Jackson?"

He nodded. "He didn't come back yet."

John sighed and patted him reassuringly on the arm as he entered the cave.

* * * *

He was immediately intercepted by a group of men walking down the corridor. They all began talking to him at the same time, excited about something John didn't have time to care about. He held up his hands, waving the sword.

"Shut up and listen."

They fell silent.

"Osiris knows you know about the solstice, and I think he finally sees you as a threat." He took a deep breath. "So go tell whoever you need to tell…"

The two African Americans, the Italian, and the Brit turned without another word, running frantically down the corridor and disappearing around the bend.

"John!"

He turned toward the sound of his name and saw Henry coming at him with outspread arms.

"Where'd you go?" Henry embraced him tightly. "I was so worried."

John stepped back, keeping his own emotions at bay. There wasn't any time for that right now. "How'd you get back here?"

"When we went through the circle, we ended up just west of here. Thankfully, nothing was there waiting for us."

"Is it true that Jackson didn't come back?"

Henry nodded.

"I think we're in danger here."

"What do you mean?"

Some people were walking close by, and John whispered, "Is there somewhere we can talk?"

Henry put a hand on his back and urged him forward. "Come with me." He took him to the room he'd recovered in and closed the palmetto door behind them. "What is it?"

"I met him."

Henry's eyes narrowed. "Who?"

"The angel. That's where *I* went."

Henry looked confused. "That doesn't make sense. You aren't—"

"I am. Or was." And he explained the dreams, the giant, the tape, everything that proved he was somehow at the center of all this madness. He told him what the angel had said about bringing his offspring into each other's lives and how they seem to push each other to this place. "That's why I was adopted into your family."

The look of stunned understanding settled across Henry's face, and he sat down on the bed of palmetto leaves. "That's how I ended up in SEAL Team One with Jackson, and he ended up running into Ronald in Bermuda."

"Henry, he told me that he needed *two* people on the boat to get me here."

Henry nodded slowly. "It all makes sense," he whispered, staring at the floor.

"What does?"

When he looked up again, his eyes were heavy with sadness. "Jackson."

And it *did* make sense.

Jackson had been on the plane *and* the boat when the apparition appeared…

"What did he tell *you*? He said you talked."

Henry shrugged and told him mostly the same things he'd heard for himself…until he got into the angel's plan of escape.

"He's using an ancient ground plan that's designed to interlock with the stars, creating a gateway out of this reality and into another."

"He said he's only missing one piece now," John said.

"Did he tell you what it was?"

"No."

Henry sat back in silence.

"Did you have dreams, Henry, while you were growing up?"

"Yeah. So did Dad and Grandpa. It's one of the ways he drew us in, sparked a mystery we just couldn't leave alone. It's how he gets us here. You think it's a coincidence that Chad's obsessed with megalithic archeology? It's in our DNA somewhere, attracting us to our heritage."

John sat beside Henry on the soft leaves, suddenly feeling the full effects of physical exhaustion. "He wants me to try to stop them from compromising his last move."

"What did he offer you in exchange?"

"My life." A pause. "And my son's."

Shocked swept over Henry's face. "You have a son?"

"Kristen's pregnant."

"I had no idea."

"Neither did I…until he told me."

"The mirrors?"

John nodded. "What are they?"

"I don't know. Legend has it that Tezcatlipoca, Quetzalcoatl's archenemy, had a mirrored object that he watched men and gods in from afar. But scholars believe it was an obsidian stone used by wizards as an instrument of divination."

"So is this Quetzal-whatever guy supposed to be good?"

He shrugged. "He supposedly taught love and condemned human sacrifice, but in some cases, he appears to be interchangeable with the Babylonian god Marduk."

John looked at his brother and began to wonder at the change in him. He seemed different, gentler somehow. "How do you know all this?"

"Dad's journal got me reading as much as I could, trying to connect all the dots."

"And did you?"

"Enough of them, I think."

A moment of flickering torchlight popped in the silence.

"What were you and Chadwick saying about ley lines? What are they?"

"It's believed there's a series of great circles that encompass the earth. They're referred to as ley lines or lines of power. The alignments of ancient cities—the pyramids, Easter Island, Mayan and Inca cities—are all said to be built in relation to them, serving as portals connecting the different sites and allowing spirits the ability to travel back and forth between them."

John pondered this. "You're saying the circles are *connected* by these lines of power?"

"Whether they built the circles according to the lines of power or whether the sites created them, I don't know. I'm just saying there's an esoteric tradition that claims these megalithic sites are interconnected by a spiritual force acting as a gateway for spirits."

"When were you confronted by Osiris?"

"A week ago."

"How'd you escape?"

"I don't know. I just remember running down the steps of a ziggurat."

"You weren't in the temple?"

"No."

"I saw the giants taking women…" John said. "One of them tried to rape me."

A look of concern rose on Henry's face. "A giant?"

"No." John chuckled. "One of the girls."

The tremendous strain squeezing their circumstance somehow twisted the idea into something hysterical, and they erupted with exhausted laughter.

A minute later, as they were wiping tears from their eyes, John said, "Chad talked about the pyramid complex being a gateway."

Henry gingerly touched his injured ribs as he nodded, the amount of laughter not helping them heal any faster.

"Do you think that's how Osiris is planning to escape?" John asked.

Nodding again, he answered, "He must've thought he was building a gateway to Tarturus, but the secret knowledge he used created this in-between instead."

"And the summer solstice will activate a portal back? How?"

Henry wagged his head. "I have no idea. I doubt even he knows for sure, but I'm guessing the door, if it works, will be in the pyramid. I think that's its only true function."

"As a transporter?"

"Chadwick thinks that it'll draw power from all the other sites and link to a specific celestial position that'll then act as a sort of relay station."

"This is ridiculous. You know that, right?"

"We're dealing with the spirit world, of course it's ridiculous."

And then John told him his plan.

Henry sat still for a long moment as his eyes stared through the wall. Finally, he shook his head. "There are a lot of unknowns, Johnny."

"I understand that, but are you ready to spend the rest of your life in this place?"

"No, but if we don't succeed, and we allow him to escape—"

"Then this place could fold up and disappear altogether."

Henry nodded solemnly. "Which could either translate us back to our world or take us with it into nonexistence."

"But if he *doesn't* complete it, then we're all stuck here anyway. We'll have to fight. Or try sailing."

"There's nothing to sail to. According to those who've tried, there isn't anything outside the Triangle." He stood. "I think we should go get the others now."

But John stopped him from opening the door. "Henry, the question you asked me, about whether or not it's possible for his seed to be redeemed… I disappeared from his mirrors the same time that my dreams stopped."

A small smile tugged the corner of Henry's mouth. "Come on," he said. And he opened the door.

* * * *

Chadwick shook his head in utter fascination. "I just can't believe it," he said to John. "What you're describing…it's like the Dendera Zodiac in the Hathor Temple." He was responding to John's description of the holographic zodiac in Osiris' temple.

John leaned back against the wall, his eyes growing weary and longing for relief. "There were these strange lights… If I didn't know better, I'd say they were lightbulbs, wires going into the walls."

Chadwick looked up from whatever invisible analytic exercise his mind was enraptured by and looked at John with yet another expression of disbelief. "That is *exactly* what you saw," he stated.

Paul leaned forward. "What do you mean? It's a stone temple; there's no electricity."

"Egyptian drawings show men holding glass-like bulbs with wires connected to a box on the ground, like glow sticks or primeval flashlights. Some believe it's how hieroglyphics were able to be made inside small dark places without torches leaving behind burn marks on the walls and ceilings."

Henry gingerly touched the stitches on his forehead. "The mysterious technologies of prehistory…"

Paul snickered.

Hunter leaned over onto his side and yawned. They were all tired, and the revelation that Jackson was one of Osiris' offspring—something that could finally explain his strange behavior—was taking its time settling within their fragile sense of understanding. Sleep offered the only relief from this nightmare, and it was coveted by all of them.

"I saw a show on the History Channel about ancient technologies," Hunter whispered, rubbing his eyes. "Analogue computers, batteries, microscopic engraving, mechanical clocks, surgical equipment…"

Paul laughed condescendingly. "So the circles are actually transporters run on batteries and operated by a surgeon stationed at a computer!"

Hunter's yawn passed to Henry. "We know the ancients had a way to make aluminum because we've found ancient artifacts composed of it—the aluminum girdle Chow Chu was buried in."

"Gesundheit," Paul replied flatly while rolling onto his back and closing his eyes.

Henry smiled. "Unless you have a way to generate electricity, you can't refine the ore that contains aluminum."

"Okay, so they have electricity."

Chadwick took his glasses off and wiped the lenses on his shirt before holding them up to the burning flame and examining his work. "In 1991, a mummified man found in the Italian Alps was dated over five thousand years old. And not only was he found covered in tattoos that were located near the precise acupuncture points treating his osteoarthrosis, but he also had a ninety-nine percent pure copper axe—thousands of years *before* the Bronze Age." He slid his glasses back on. "Other ancient pictures suggest medically advanced procedures like heart transplants."

"I saw that," said Hunter.

"Stone blocks in the Valley Temple were hollowed out by what could only be some kind of ultrasonic drill, the marks in the hole showing a rate of 1/10th of an inch per revolution, which would obviously be impossible to perform by hand. There're vitrified sand deposits in India that were produced from an unknown source of extreme heat, though Indian mythology says huge explosions erupted from a battle that was fought there. It seems the Egyptians knew how to electroplate, since the gold on many of their statues is too fine to have been beaten or glued—"

"What's your point?" Paul interrupted.

"My point is that if we go to war with these people, we can't simply plan on being shot at with arrows. We have no idea what kind of technology or magic they have at their disposal. God only knows what they're capable of."

"All the forbidden secrets of heaven," John mumbled, his eyes ensnared by a dancing flame.

Paul put his hands behind his head. "And what's supposed to have happened to all this 'advanced' technology?"

"It was destroyed by the Flood, kept at bay ever since," Henry answered.

"What do you mean, 'kept at bay'?"

"Well, let's assume that the center of this advanced civilization was an island like the legends say. Whether Mu or Atlantis or whether Antarctica or one of the underwater sites in the Pacific or Atlantic, the island itself is obviously inaccessible. If it's Antarctica, which a lot of research suggest was Atlantis—at one point higher north, before the end of the ice age shifted the poles and caused the earth's crust to move—then whatever secrets it holds, whatever forbidden wisdom the angels had taught mankind, is buried under miles of ice and sealed from prying eyes."

John rubbed his forehead. "But what about the maps? They would've had to have been made before the Flood."

"Exactly," Chadwick interjected. "It seems that some unknown people in the distant past were actually more advanced in geodesy, natural sciences, and mapmaking than any known culture that existed before the eighteenth century. The Vedic hymns suggest a familiarity with the geography of polar regions, and so do the scriptures of India, Persia, and Zend-Avesta. Just like Jason and the Argonauts, it appears there were ancient navigators sailing the seas and charting the world in prehistoric times."

Henry added, "Some of the maps have Antarctica at their center, meaning that, to those who drew the maps, it was the navel of the world at the time."

Chadwick began thinking aloud. "God sank it and buried the secrets of heaven from the world for the rest of time. The only traces of it are found in whatever the Atlantis priests were able to plant in other civilizations, hidden in their mythologies and monuments." The statement was delivered with a sense of puzzlement, like it was a conclusion just arrived at. "It fits," he said, looking up. "The Book of Enoch and the story of the fallen angels is the perfect commentary on prehistory. It explains where and how such a body of knowledge came into man's possession. It was always the big mystery, why we couldn't find any evidence of technological evolution, of a progression within the texts. The math, the astronomy, the calendars, the systems of worship—they all just appeared on man's timeline fully formed..."

After a quiet moment, Henry shifted. "And it makes you wonder what's been behind many of our own technological advances. Especially when you consider how many of our greatest scientists and inventors were involved in the occult."

"Okay," Paul said, moving to an elbow. "So God destroys the world and everything the angels did with a flood. But Johnny said that this Osiris guy claims to be from *after* the flood. So why didn't things get as bad the second time around?"

"They will," John said calmly. "God'll destroy the world again."

"Whatever. I'm saying, why didn't it work the second time like it did the first?"

John recalled his conversation with Osiris. "Because God established the Law, which prevented Israel from being contaminated by that stuff."

"And the wars," Chadwick added.

"You mean like David and Goliath?" Hunter asked.

"Yeah," Henry said, "like Goliath. By the time of Abraham, giants had already populated large portions of the Middle East. And it wasn't until nine hundred years later that Moses and Joshua finally managed to defeat most of them. But a remnant survived, showing up five hundred years later in the time of David."

"Can I see your Bible?" Chadwick asked John.

"Sure." He took it out of his faithful bag and tossed it to him.

Beneath the flame's shifting light, he paged through the water-stained Book, his finger tracing downward over the sacred text. "'The Emites used to live there—a people strong and numerous, and as tall as the Anakites. Like the Anakites, they too were considered Rephaite...' Deuteronomy, chapter two."

He flipped to another verse. "'In still another battle, which took place at Gath, there was a huge man with six fingers on each hand and six toes on each foot—twenty-four in all. He also was descended from Rapha…' Second Samuel twenty-one.

"And then there's Deuteronomy three—" he turned to it as he talked "—and the King of Bashan's sixty giant cities. 'We completely destroyed them, as we had done with Sihon king of Heshbon, destroying every city—men, women and children… Only Og king of Bashan was left of the remnant of the Rephaites. His bed was made of iron and was more than thirteen feet long and six feet wide. It is still in Rabbah of the Ammonites…' The whole region of Argob in Bashan used to be known as a land of the Rephaites. The ruins of the Giant Cities of Bashan are still viewable today," Chadwick said. "I've seen them myself." He closed the Bible and sat forward. "I've seen the Valley of the Rephaim, too—a three-mile-long valley along the road to Bethlehem. And the ruins in Baalbek.

"Archeological evidence is clear that giants roamed free in the Promised Land, just as the Ras Samra texts that were discovered in 1928 had suggested. Even the Jewish historian, Josephus, tells of the war the Israelites fought to wipe the giants out of the Promised Land. But after seven years of fighting, Joshua became content with ridding the Anakim from only *most* of the land. Some remained in Gaza, Gath, and Ashdod and later joined with the Philistines. Some think they were the giants that would eventually migrate north and into Europe."

"This is all in the Bible?" Hunter asked.

Chadwick nodded. "There's plenty more. The Old Testament is filled with references of Israel's conflict with the Anakim and Rephaim."

John had to admit that he'd never paid much attention to such references and, as the Christian in the group, was a little embarrassed that he was just as lost on the subject as Hunter and Paul. In light of his experience in this place and the revelation that Israel's wars were fought against the offspring of angels, he found himself developing an entirely new perspective on the Old Testament.

Hunter shifted on the palmetto-thatched mat. "So the angels began teaching mankind their secret arts again, but this time God used Israel as a means of containing and eradicating it?"

Henry said, "Yeah. It wasn't just the giants that were killed, but the Law of God forbade the Jewish people from any interaction with the practices of the heathens, practices apparently handed down from the fallen angels. So rather than eight people on the planet being found righteous within their genealogy, God was now working with an entire nation. For example—" he motioned for Chadwick to toss him the Bible, and he opened it up to the book of Leviticus "—God tells Moses here that if anyone sacrifices their children to Molech, then they should be stoned to death. And if anyone turns a blind eye to the practice, then that person and all his family was to be cut off from His people. Then he says, 'I will set my face against the person who turns to mediums and spiritists to prostitute himself by following them, and I will cut him off from his people.'" He went to the back of the Bible, found something in the concordance, and flipped to a section in Deuteronomy. "'Let no one be found among you who sacrifices his son or daughter in the fire, who practices divination or sorcery, interprets omens, engages in witchcraft, or casts spells, or who is a medium or spiritist or who consults the dead. Anyone who does these things is detestable to the Lord.'

"In Second Kings, there's the record of how Manasseh followed the 'detestable' practices of pagan nations. He rebuilt the 'high places' his father had destroyed, erected altars to Baal and made an Asherah pole. He built altars to all the starry hosts and worshipped them, sacrificed his own son, practiced sorcery and divination, consulted mediums and spiritists, and even placed the Asherah pole in the temple. So God told the prophets that He was going to wipe Israel clean with such great disaster that the ears of all who heard of it would tingle."

"So even Israel needed purging from the secret arts?" Hunter asked.

But Chadwick was still trying to figure things out for himself, arranging puzzle pieces in his mind. "The Asherah pole, the high places, altars to starry hosts—all probably megalithic monuments. The 'sacred stone of Baal' that Ahab made was an obelisk." He asked for the Bible back and took a minute to find a verse of his own. "'Do not set up any wooden Asherah pole and do not erect a sacred stone, for these the Lord your God hates.' I forget where, I think in First Kings somewhere, it talks about Judah setting up high places and sacred stones." He was flipping through the pages frantically, his words coming out rapid and intense. "The Hebrew word that's used—*matstsebah*—indicates a pillar, a monolith. Here, Isaiah twenty-seven. 'When he makes all the altar stones to be like chalk stones crushed to pieces, no Asherah poles or incense altars will be left standing.' And in Second Chronicles…" He turned as fast as he could, his eyes moving back and forth. "'Under his direction the altars of Baal were torn down; he cut to pieces the incense altars that were above them, and smashed the Asherah poles, the idols and the images. These he broke to pieces and scattered over the graves of those who had sacrificed to them. He burned the bones of the priests on their altars, and so he purged Judah and Jerusalem.'" He paused. "I never made the connection before, the Old Testament and God's command to destroy the Zep Tepi monuments."

More silent moments passed before John recalled something interesting that Osiris had told him. He decided to try it on Chadwick, to see what it might mean, if anything. "The angel told me that his name isn't really Osiris, that he just borrowed the name from the real pre-Flood deity in order to continue his work in Egypt."

Chadwick stared at him, thinking.

"He said it saved him a lot of time, building off the real Osiris' legacy rather than having to begin a brand new one himself."

Chadwick nodded slowly. "It makes things a little less complicated, actually. Two fallen angels representing the same deity from both sides of the Flood… That would explain some of the discrepancies in the accounts of Osiris and First Time, whether the Sages built after the Flood to reflect *back* on First Time and the reign of Osiris, or whether Osiris re-established First Time *after* the Flood…" He fell into silence.

John began thinking through some other New Testament passages that he was more familiar with, about demons and evil spirits. "What if the spirits of the Nephilim are the ones the New Agers are channeling? What if that's how all this forbidden knowledge is starting to make a comeback, why the occult is growing so popular?" He grew silent, mulling through the idea. "The end of the age, the dawn of Aquarius, the New Order of the Ages…"

"What are you talking about?" Paul moaned.

"I'm talking about the book of Revelation. I'm talking about the end times being just like the days of Noah." He maneuvered onto his back as his words hung suspended in the silent air above them.

* * * *

What makes you think there'll be a war?" Chadwick asked.

It was morning now, and they were still in the cave.

"Because," John explained, "Osiris feels threatened by us. We know the exact date he's planning to escape. These people were left alone in the caves because attacking them would mean a lot of casualties. He couldn't afford casualties; he needed his giants busy building, not fighting. But now his sites are nearly complete, and he's about to get out of here. And he has an army of creatures that he can't take with him…"

Chadwick swore under his breath. "What do we do?"

"We need to talk to them, make sure they understand what's coming."

"How long do you think we could hold them off from here?" Hunter wondered.

Paul shook his head. "Not long enough. If they break through, we'll use all our ammo in the first twenty minutes. And, from what they told me, there's no way out of here. The water's over fifty feet deep, and the passageway to the ocean is three miles long. We'll be trapped."

"So then this is it for them. There's nowhere to hide. They have to fight." Henry looked saddened by this. "A lot of them are going to die."

"He'll be coming soon. He'll want us out of the way well before the solstice." John pulled his windbreaker on. "So we have two choices. We destroy his site and condemn him to this place for another few hundred years, possibly condemning ourselves here at the same time, or we let him finish his site and find a way to use it ourselves."

"Assuming it works," Henry replied. "I'm not sure the angel even knows what'll happen. He sure didn't think using it the first time would send him here. We could end up…" He shrugged. "Who knows?"

John looked him in the eye and asked him again, "Would you rather spend the rest of your life here?"

"Fine," he said in surrender, "I'll go get the leaders." And he left the room.

Hunter sighed. "What do you think the last piece of his puzzle is?"

"I have no idea," said Chadwick.

John zipped his jacket. "Maybe we should keep a lookout, patrol the coasts. See what he's planning."

Paul smiled as he stretched. "First we need to find out how we're going to win this war."

* * * *

John was sitting alone about thirty yards from the cave, his mind twisted in knots. He was staring up through the swaying trees, the Bible open on his lap. There was a war that was coming, and he was once again faced with the moral dilemma it presented. He had promised God that he would never raise a hand against another human being again, his understanding of New Testament Christianity completely opposed to force of any kind. But this place… Was redemption possible for this enemy, or was it God's will for them to wipe out such wickedness, as it had been during the days of Abraham, Moses, and David?

But he kept thinking back to the annihilation of the Native Americans, to the "Christians" who believed the land was their own, granted to them by God, that the Indians were just Canaanites occupying their "Promised Land" and begging for extermination. And perhaps the eradication of the indigenous species *could* be seen as a form of judgment on a people engaged in such pagan rituals as had been condemned by God in the Old Testament, but John also knew that missionaries led many Indians to Christ, which showed they were not unredeemable and that Christ did wish to save them (as 2 Peter 3:9 states).

The "church" wiped out most of the Central Americans, too, giving them the choice of conversion, slavery, or death. And again, even if such methods were to eradicate the revival of demonic doctrines, John certainly couldn't think of a New Testament principle that would justify slaughtering people of *any* kind. And so, his dilemma stood as such: was his belief in the teachings of Christ and the strict purity of God's standard prior to Christ able to coexist within such a world as this? He couldn't seem to find an excuse to kill again. Even if it was Goliath he would be slaying.

A gust of wind blew through the trees and rustled the pages of the Bible. When he looked back down, he found that the pages had come to settle in the book of Amos.

> *I destroyed the Amorite before them, though he was tall as the cedars and strong as the oaks. I destroyed his fruit above and his roots below. I brought you up out of Egypt…*

He felt a series of chills travel up his body. The wind blew the pages again, this time resting them in Numbers, to the account of Caleb and the other spies who had been sent into the Promised Land.

> *They came back to Moses and Aaron and the whole Israelite community at Kadesh in the Desert of Paran. There they reported to them and to the whole*

> *assembly and showed them the fruit of the land. They gave Moses this account: "We went into the land to which you sent us, and it does flow with milk and honey! Here is its fruit. But the people who live there are powerful, and the cities are fortified and very large. We even saw descendants of Anak there. The Amalikites live in the Negev; the Hittites, Jebusites and Amorites live in the hill country; and the Canaanites live near the sea and along the Jordan." Then Caleb silenced the people before Moses and said, "We should go up and take possession of the land, for we can certainly do it." But the men who had gone up with him said, "We can't attack those people; they are stronger than we are. The land devours those living in it. All the people we saw there are of great size. We saw the Nephilim there (the descendants of Anak come from the Nephilim). We seemed like grasshoppers in our own eyes, and we looked the same to them."*

Now John was even more confused. Was God trying to tell him that He wanted him to attack the giants? Or were these demons turning the pages, trying to lead him into a trap? How was he supposed to apply the instructions of Jesus, to love your enemies, while also adhering to this apparent green light for war? Was he supposed to be a Caleb, believing by faith that God was going to grant them victory over his enemies, or was he supposed to be a Stephen, lifting his hands to heaven while being martyred? It was too great a struggle for his weary soul, and he bowed his head. He asked that, whatever was to happen, God would be merciful and forgive the actions, or inactions, that would result from his choice.

TWENTY-TWO

Early evening. 18th day of June. Bermuda, North coast

Beneath the shade of a large cedar tree, John lay on his back, his hands folded behind his head. He was preoccupied with thoughts of Kristen and their unborn baby, praying fervently that he would be reunited with them again.

Three weeks had passed since his little visit with Osiris, since the fallen angel had claimed to be just one puzzle piece short of completing his preparations. Ever since then, and since Jackson had disappeared, the pureblooded casualties of the Triangle had been regularly patrolling the coasts, searching for the arrival of a new vessel. So far, they hadn't found anything. And now John was beginning to wonder if maybe Osiris had just invented the story to keep them focused on the coasts, allowing him to put the finishing touches on his devices unimpeded. The summer solstice was only three days away, and much to their surprise, the giants had not yet attacked. John realized that it would be equally reasonable for Osiris to pull all of his minions back into a protective ring surrounding his network of megalithic sites and just wait for the solstice to come, deciding on a plan of defense rather than instigating a war that could leave gaping holes in his security. One carefully placed explosive might be enough to render the whole scheme inoperable. It was a notion the natives had been debating over the last few days.

Most of the two hundred untainted men met in council to decide what course of action should be taken regarding the 21st of June. And once the theories started forming, the issue proved to be a rather complicated one. Most of the men born on the island, having never experienced another reality besides the one the island offered, wanted to fight, to avenge all the friends and family they'd lost over the years and to rid the land of its satanic pestilence. Others, however, didn't want to chance the angel's escape and thought it best to destroy the sites. But some suggested they do nothing at all, to let the angel escape, reasoning that without any leader and with no more offspring coming to the island, the impure armies would just kill each other off. And then there were those who happened to agree with John, that rather than *destroying* the mechanism, it might actually be worth trying to use themselves. But most of these people were newer arrivals that still maintained a fresh memory of their former lives, and their voices didn't hold as much authority as those who had been here their whole lives.

And then grew an entirely different aspect of the debate. What would happen if the gateway *was* used? If Osiris' ill-conceived plan at freeing his condemned brethren had created this place, was it then possible that his very *presence* was sustaining its reality? If so, would the island's existence simply fold up and vanish without him, leaving them all to disappear along with it? And, if they used the gateway, what assurance was there that they would end up back in the real world? What if the portal transported them to the far side of the moon? The angel was planning on escaping *this* place, but no one knew where he was planning on escaping *to.* Assuming that he was building the complex to align with a certain destination, no one was quite sure where a spiritual being—though with a physical form—would even want to go. Chadwick said that the pyramid complex was seen as a gateway to the stars, to a specific place within Orion, or back in time to Zep Tepi. Surely, none of them wanted to end up there, floating through space or walking the desert sands of Egypt twelve thousand years ago (depending on which Phoenix Cycle it was programmed to). One person had even suggested that—if the whole scheme was a forbidden art, whether science could explain it or not—using it might bring God's judgment on them just as it had for Osiris. "What if," he asked, "it sends us straight to hell?"

And round and round it went. And in the end, they had agreed to do nothing; because whether the angel sent himself to hell or he entered the real world, it would mean that he wouldn't be *here,* and that his offspring would quickly lose control of the island. But to appease some of the others who had supported a different decision, they promised not to damage the gateway so that those who wanted to use it could still do so at a later date. It was a decision that John didn't like, but one that he admitted had the highest chance of success—rather than engaging in a war they couldn't possibly win. However, that didn't mean he was satisfied with the idea of waiting until another solstice or equinox to get out of here.

"You want some, Johnny?" Paul asked from the fire beside him.

"No, thanks," he replied, steeling a glance at the charred piece of sea turtle he was holding up. Since *this* Bermuda had never been settled by the British, the ecosystem had evolved differently, sea turtles not having been eaten into nonexistence being one of the differences. Most of Bermuda's wildlife had been introduced by settlers and shipwrecks, no mammals or reptiles other than one small lizard being native to the island. And the same was true within this sphere, too, though the giants' all-encompassing appetite made it hard for any species to thrive here. But their appetite seemed to extend even beyond the "natural" realm and enter far into the profane. It was something Henry believed was hinted at in the words of Enoch: *And they sinned against birds, beasts, reptiles, and fishes.* Chadwick told of a Canaanite tablet that recorded Baal mating with a heifer and the heifer conceiving and bearing a child in his image. Chadwick then suggested that a truth might stand behind the hybrid creatures of the Greek Pan, centaurs, Minotaur, the Egyptian Horus, Anubis, Sobek, Seth, and the countless other engravings found in Egypt, Assyria, and Italy. He said that the Egyptian historian Manetho wrote extensively of such genetic anomalies that were concocted by the gods. And perhaps this was the real reason why Leviticus 19 forbade the crossbreeding of animals and plants.

Of course, John wanted to believe the idea was ludicrous, but he couldn't shake the feeling that maybe there *was* a connection between the mythology stories and God's commandment in Leviticus to kill the person *and* the beast caught in such degenerate behavior. And why had God made it a point to destroy all the animals along with man and Nephilim in the Flood? He thought of Osiris' armies, their height, fingers and toes, teeth, the genetic defects evident in the men he'd seen, and the scorpion-like creatures that seemed to bear a close resemblance to the locusts that Apollyon was to lead out of the abyss after the sounding of the fifth trumpet in Revelation 9. He remembered the enormous fruit trees and plants that he'd seen, all sure to rival the clusters of grapes that the Hebrew spies brought back from the Nephilim-infested Canaan. Surely, some kind of genetic *change* had taken place with the fall of man, i.e., the growth of thorns, the talking serpent being condemned to crawl on its stomach, etc. And since God had originally intended man and animal to eat only fruits and vegetables, forbidding the slaying of animals, John wondered if the physiology of the dinosaurs and other predators had also been altered somehow, perhaps offering a clue as to why Satan is so often associated with serpents, the leviathan, and dragons. Since the Flood was a judgment against the works of the fallen angels, was it a coincidence that only the fossilized bones of such creatures remained? The Bible spoke of a day when the lion would again lay beside the lamb, implying a reversal of the natural order that was now familiar to earth.

And then Henry's boat, the *Gegenes*, came rocking back and forth on his sea of thoughts. *Gegenes*…the Greek word for Titan, where the English word *genetics* comes from.

John combed his fingers through his growing beard as he set his eyes out over the beach and to the crystal blue water that stretched out into nothing. The pureblooded castaways' insistence that every attempt to escape had just brought them back to the island only further cemented his resolve to use the angel's mechanism.

John, Paul, and Hunter made up the patrol, their designated area of the coast being the northern district above the henge site. This time, John brought a weapon with him, though the feel of it in his hands had been awkward, bringing with it the memories that scarred his soul just as much as they had scarred his body. He hoped to escape this world without having to dip his hands in more blood, but the verses the wind had selected for him seemed to suggest otherwise.

Hunter sat back against a tree and buried his feet in the sand. "It's kind of weird that we haven't seen any of them in the last few days." He was referring to the genetically damned.

Paul said, "They're guarding the sites."

"Which ones?" John wondered, because if that were true then it meant some sites were relevant to the escape scheme while others weren't. "The henges here aren't guarded."

"Yeah, sure they aren't," Paul sneered. "Why don't you go walk up to one and see what happens?"

He was right, John realized. With the ability to transport themselves, there was no way to know for sure whether the sites were left unguarded or not.

"They could be hiding up in the trees," Hunter said, poking at the sand between his feet with a knife. "Wanting to draw us in."

And then, suddenly, the sound of crashing foliage erupted behind them.

Moving quickly to their feet, they brought their weapons up and ready to fire, not sure of what could be headed toward them. According to their hosts, they'd only seen a small fraction of the island's abominations.

But what stumbled out of the undergrowth proved to be even more surprising than any crossbred mutation.

"Don't shoot!" Jackson yelled, staggering wildly onto the sand and ultimately collapsing at their feet.

John and Hunter lowered their weapons in surprise, but Paul's aim remained unwavering.

"Well, well, well…" he quipped.

Jackson looked up from his knees and, between gasps of air, held up a hand. "Please," he choked. His face was horribly bruised, one eye swollen shut, the other bloodshot. His clothes were torn to shreds and soaked with blood, whether his own or someone else's, they couldn't tell.

"Listen to me," he whispered, getting to all fours and letting blood drip from his open mouth. "You need to stop them." He collapsed onto his side, revealing in part what had happened to him. The back of his shirt had been cut off, and his entire left side appeared to have undergone some type of surgical procedure, only the operation hadn't been repaired. Flaps of skin were hanging loose from the methodical slices of an incredibly sharp object, and hints of white were glistening beneath the muscle.

"What happened to you?" Hunter asked, running to his side.

"Started removing organs…" He pinched his eyes shut and growled in agony, his whole body sweating and shaking.

Paul was searching the woods, wary of Jackson's sudden appearance. "How'd you get here?"

"Portal. Smelled your fire…"

"How'd you know it was us?"

"Didn't know it was you," he snapped. "Just knew it wasn't them." He swore. "I think they took a kidney."

"We need to get him back," John said to Hunter, shouldering an old M16 and stepping closer to Jackson.

But Paul stopped him. "I want to know how he escaped."

Jackson kept his eyes closed. "Same way as Henry."

"Henry doesn't remember how he escaped," John answered.

Jackson's eyes opened. "Yeah, he does." And then he started coughing up more blood. "Just stop them."

"Who?"

"He's not planning on leaving his armies here…" He rolled onto his back, gasping in pain. "He's taking the entire family with him."

* * * *

By the time they got Jackson to a palmetto bed back in the caves, an absurd idea had been born in John's mind. Osiris had become trapped here just as the earlier angels that had left their first estate (in order to intermingle with women) had become trapped in Tarturus, a premature judgment exclusively reserved for such actions. In the Gospel of Matthew, demon-possessed men begged Jesus to cast them into a herd of swine instead of condemning them to the abyss before "the appointed time." But John knew from both Pastor Brian's text message and from his own recent reading of the Bible (which all the SEALs now had an interest in) that Revelation 9 indicated the abyss would be opened, releasing the angel of the pit, Apollyon. But was it the same "Apollo" of Greek lore that seemed to personify the very perfection of man, the same perfection of man that the *Masonic* Christ was supposed to embody? John's crazy thought was that maybe this fallen angel was not Osiris (as the angel had readily admitted), but Apollo himself, and that what was described by the Apostle was his escape from *here*, initiated by the blast of a trumpet. Again, *sound* being the activating component. And that, as Revelation 17 might suggest, the people of earth would be astonished by the beast from the abyss because, as the near two-thousand-year-old text said of him, he "once was, now is not, and yet will come." Was this the return of Apollo, of one of the fallen angels who had helped "alter" the earth in Noah's day and of whom Moses wrote about when penning the phrase "heroes of old"? And then he recalled Jesus' words from the Gospel of Matthew… *As it was in the days of Noah, so it will be at the coming of the Son of Man.*

Samuel looked at John through his aged eyes and tiredly shook his head, apparently not impressed with his theory. But John thrust the open Bible at him and told him to read it.

Momentarily scratching his white beard, Samuel finally obliged.

> *And the fifth angel sounded, and I saw a star fall from heaven unto the earth: and to him was given the key of the bottomless pit. And he opened the bottomless pit; and there arose a smoke out of the pit, as the smoke of a great furnace; and the sun and the air were darkened by reason of the smoke of the pit. And there came out of the smoke locusts upon the earth: and unto them was given power, as the scorpions of the earth have power. And it was commanded them that they should not hurt the grass of the earth, neither any green thing, neither any tree; but only those men which have not the seal of God in their foreheads… And the shapes of the locusts were like unto horses prepared unto battle; and on their heads were as it were crowns like gold, and their faces were as the faces of men. And they had hair as the hair of women, and their teeth were as the teeth of lions. And they had breastplates, as it were breastplates of iron; and the sound of their wings was as the sound of chariots of many horses running to battle. And they had tails like unto scorpions, and there were stings in their tails: and their power was to hurt men five months. And they had a king over them, which is the angel of the bottomless pit, whose name in the Hebrew tongue is Abaddon, but in the Greek tongue hath his name Apollyon.*

Samuel slowly closed the Bible. "You think that Osiris is this Apollyon, that this place is the abyss from which he'll ascend and lead his army of abominations into the realm of man?"

John cringed when he heard it put that way. It was true, there were correlations that didn't match up, this not being the abyss in which the fallen angels were chained being the most obvious. "No, I guess he's not Apollo…" And then the scenario suddenly became more sensible. "But he tried to *free* Apollo. He wants to instigate the apocalypse…to reestablish Satan's reign on earth… But he didn't have the key. He called it a joke, that God let the fallen angels think they knew all the mysteries of creation. So, Osiris transports himself to this other plane of reality, this interpretation of Bermuda, and…"

"What are you saying?" Samuel interrupted.

"Is it possible that he isn't just trying to escape, that he's still planning on doing his part in ushering in another golden age by freeing Apollyon from the pit, something that's prophesied to happen anyway?"

"How?"

"I have no idea. But if that's been their agenda throughout the millennia, the reason for all the megalithic sites across the world—" he looked back to Henry and Chadwick "—if the agenda has been to communicate the lost wisdom of Satan's reign, the spirits being channeled really the spirits of his agents…"

Henry nodded solemnly. "With the explosion of the New Age movement and the popularity of the occult, the New World Order could be just around the corner."

Chadwick cleared his throat. "The New Age of enlightenment heralded by the return of the capstone to the Great Pyramid. *Annuit Coeptis Novus Ordo Seclurum…*"

John's gaze narrowed on a thought. "The dollar bill?"

"The Eye of Horus is housed in the disconnected capstone, the light of *Sirius* that the southern star shaft points to shining behind it. 1776 is the date written at the base of the pyramid…the date the Illuminati was formed."

Backing up a few steps, Samuel sat heavily on a chair, the torches' shifting light casting thick and dark shadows across his tired face.

Chadwick's eyes flashed with revelation. He looked around the stone room, wondering silently if this was all possible. "The initiation into Freemasonry's three degrees are astronomically structured. The Worshipful Master marks the sun rising on the equinox, the Senior Warden marks the sun at its meridian, and the Junior Warden marks its setting. The two pillars on either side of the Worshipful Master, representing Boaz and Jachin from Solomon's Temple, mark both the summer and winter solstices. In the first degree, information is conveyed to the initiate while he's standing in the shadow cast by the northeast pillar, the second degree in the shadow of the southeast. The third degree, when the candidate becomes a 'Master Mason,' takes place in a dark room after he's symbolically killed and resurrected under the light of Venus rising at the equinox…"

"I'm not following," John stated.

"It's the same layout that's used in Newgrange and other megalithic sites. And, as far as Scottish Rite Freemasonry's concerned, the very core of Freemasonry is based on the premise that a scientifically advanced civilization existed before the time of the Flood. The Delta of Enoch, an ancient triangle of gold forming the centerpiece of a temple that Enoch built, supposedly contained the secret antediluvian knowledge. According to tradition, God gave Enoch the gifts of wisdom and knowledge and sent him thirty books filled with scientific mysteries; even the Babylonians credit him with introducing astronomy. Masonic tradition states that Enoch had his son, Methuselah, constructed a subterranean building that could survive the coming flood and preserve the secret knowledge. Apparently, while Solomon's workers were clearing the site for the temple grounds, they discovered the underground chamber and recovered Enoch's preserved secrets. In AD 1128, after the Babylonians and the Romans had their way with the holy site, the Templar Knights reportedly rediscovered the body of ancient wisdom. Freemasonry still claims to be the guardian of such antediluvian knowledge. The thirteenth degree of Scottish Rite Freemasonry, the Royal Arch of Enoch, is focused on the hiding and rediscovering of Enoch's subterranean chamber. And you know that Washington, DC, was built by Freemasons, right?"

John nodded. By now, who didn't?

"So all of this stuff was incorporated into the city's design and layout." He sighed as he placed the back of his hand against his forehead. "Never mind…" He took a deep breath, forcing himself to part with all the implications such a revelation demanded. "It doesn't concern us right now. The main point is that there's a connection between what's happening both politically and spiritually in our world, and the secret wisdom that, according to the Book of Enoch, was introduced by fallen angels in the days of Jared."

Henry nodded his concession. "The Bible talks about Satan being the king of this world order, right? The prince and the power of the air? Well, isn't it obvious? Just look around. If the world's mythologies do find their roots in the antediluvian world, in the Book of Enoch and Genesis 6, then they're more than just harmless stories handed down over the generations. They're the stories of fallen angels, of what brought God's judgment on earth." He became animated, waving his hands. "How many scientific breakthroughs came by men communicating with spirits? Yeah, we call it science today because we can back it up with mathematical formulas, but where did the knowledge come from? Take Pythagoras, for example. Along with Herodotus and Solon, he was shown Egypt's secret wisdom by a priest, Solon's impression of whatever he saw prompting Plato to proclaim that the Egyptians had a divine heritage that stemmed from the gods' reign on earth. What's even more interesting is that the Pythagorean theorem was used in the construction of the pyramids. Is it possible then that Pythagoras picked up on this formula while examining Egypt's sacred texts?" He shook his head. "Think about it, we have Sirius Radio—Sirius being the Egyptian Dog Star, its logo a dog with a star for an eye… If you look around, you'll find the esoteric attached to almost everything science produces and markets."

"Like cars," John muttered. He was referring to all the gods, stars, and planets that named them. "Or all the cities across the world…"

Chadwick tugged at a phantom itch on his earlobe. "Who do you think is behind all this, running the show?"

Henry's blue eyes were ablaze with conviction. "Satan's New World Order is spelled out on the most common piece of currency in the world, going through the hands of millions of people every second of every day. But no one stops to consider its implications, how it got there, what it means, what the strange symbols are doing on the currency of a supposedly Christian nation. Obelisks in DC, the Vatican, *Bermuda*…"

As John listened, another moral dilemma began peeking out of his exhausted soul. If the fallen angel thought that in freeing his brothers from the abyss, he could usher in the apocalypse described by the book of Revelation, then he obviously thought it was possible to construct a different ending than the one prophesied—Satan's everlasting sentence with the Beast and False Prophet within the lake of fire. But then, John wondered—and this was the quandary—was he doing the *same* thing, trying to prevent a prophecy from coming about? If God foretold the events in Revelation, then certainly John couldn't change them from occurring any more than Osiris could. It reminded him of a Christian politician he'd once heard speaking about Iran's prophesied attack on Israel, how God was going to intervene and defend Israel Himself but that America needed to defend Israel by preemptively attacking Iran so that they couldn't attack Israel. John saw it as an illogical absurdity contradicting the very belief the speaker claimed was at the center of his faith, nothing more than a political ploy designed to get Christian conservatives excited about going to war.

If Osiris *was* supposed to free Apollo, then he would need the key… The last puzzle piece.

"Do you still want to try to use it?" Chadwick asked him.

"Use what?"

"The pyramid."

Samuel, overwhelmed by the speed in which things had so quickly changed, said, "It's the only thing we haven't tried ourselves."

"Okay," Chadwick said, stepping close to John, "then there's a few things we should go over first. They may be completely irrelevant, but—"

John held up his hand. "Hold on." He turned back to Samuel. "What do *you* want to do?"

Samuel did his best to lift his tired and weary eyes, blinking away a tear. "Do we have a choice?" He dropped his gaze again, seeing in his mind's eye all the family and friends that would soon be slaughtered around him. "Now we can only hope that God really did send you here, because if He didn't…we'll all die."

John swallowed the finality of the statement like broken glass. He asked his brother, "Is this what *you* want?"

Henry nodded. "Let's get out of here."

"Alright, then you'd better start coming up with a game plan."

Henry asked Samuel to gather any men who knew about the temple complex and then followed him to the door. Looking back before leaving, he said to John, "Thanks for coming for me. And thanks for instilling some hope. I didn't think I had a chance." And then he went to find Hunter and Paul.

John clenched a trembling hand as he faced Chadwick. "Okay, what do we need to know?"

Taking a breath, he began, "If the Great Pyramid was built by Khufu, then one of the two and a half million blocks, each weighing an average of two point six tons, would've been moved into place every five minutes throughout the length of his entire reign. That didn't happen." He shook his head, "My point is, it's still a mystery and should be treated as one."

John agreed.

Chadwick then began going over the Edfu texts and their telling of how the Seven Sages (just as in the Babylonian and Indian traditions) supposedly survived the Flood and passed down the knowledge of the antediluvian world to future generations. Coming from an island—"the Homeland of the Primeval Ones"—that was destroyed by a flood, they came to Egypt as the builder gods who illuminated the land with the wisdom of the past epoch. The Temple of Dendera was inscribed with building texts crediting the architectural plan as being handed down from the demigods who ruled after Osiris. The new world that the Sages created was designed to resurrect the former world of the gods, perhaps from prior First Times. So, whether or not the pyramid complex remained from a *previous* First Time or had been rebuilt by the Sages, Chadwick didn't know because the mythologies seemed somewhat contradictory. The pyramid's mysteries were supposedly known only by Thoth. But what little Chadwick did know, he began explaining to John. The journey to the Duat, the translation from earth to heaven and from mortality to immortality… How the whole ground scheme functioned as a ceremonial gateway, and what was left of the internal construction of the Great Pyramid.

TWENTY-THREE

Morning. 21st day of June. Bermuda, Northeast of temple complex

No one knew when the sun was supposed to stand still at its northernmost point, but it was at this precise moment of the solstice that the pureblooded army suspected the pyramid would mysteriously "activate" and establish a portal to some unknown location—hell, Orion's belt, First Time… It was anyone's guess.

John looked up at the rising fireball quickly approaching its zenith and figured they only had a few hours remaining. It was going to be close.

Knowing they couldn't win an actual war, the plan was simply to gain access to the pyramid *before* Osiris' armies did and try to hold them off from within it. But if they were to attack the complex too soon, then they'd be left with the impossible task of defending the pyramid for *hours* rather than mere minutes. If they proved unable to keep the giants out of the pyramid or if the giants managed to enter the pyramid before them, then they would have no choice but to destroy the site, possibly trapping themselves on the island forever.

"They should all be in position by now," Paul growled. He was still angry with the mission, that it was based on nothing but ludicrous speculation and sure to get a lot of them killed.

Henry nodded as he stole a quick glance at the two dozen islanders surrounding them at the edge of the mangrove swamp. He wished Jackson was with them. But even after three weeks, Jackson's injuries proved too great to allow him anything more than sentry duty back at the cave. Most of the pureblooded that Henry observed around them seemed to be from the States, though he was sure at least a few were European. Their white eyes were shining with nervous tension through the mud coverings applied to their faces. Even though they still seemed to believe that God was somehow going to deliver them as a *people*, it was less of a certainty as to which of them would survive to realize the victory. Their shaking hands held weapons that ranged from AK-47s and grenades to revolvers and axes, their clothes an assortment of animal skins and whatever they had been able to salvage from the graveyard over the years. Henry knew, even more so than they did, that most of them weren't going to make it through the day. He rested a hand on the hilt of the sword that was given to him and sighed.

The rest of the pureblooded men were organized into similar divisions and were all poised to attack the temple grounds from various entrance points. Dividing and scattering the giants was their only hope of sneaking past them and gaining access to the pyramid. The men who had been designated to take possession of the pyramid were the men who desired to leave the island, hoping, like John, that the sun's position in the sky would activate the gateway while they were inside it. Those who didn't wish to be transported into the unknown, risking staying here rather than ending up in Tartarus with Zeus' condemned Titans (or worse), would be attacking from the cover of the woods, seeking to draw the giants away from the megalithic site.

"What're you gonna do, Dr. Jones, when we're all running around like grasshoppers, and the sun doesn't activate a thing?" Paul asked Chadwick.

He squinted. "I don't think these people care one way or the other. They just want us to fight."

"They still believe we're gonna deliver them." Hunter stood. "Let's go."

As John followed behind the zigzagging platoon, squeezing tightly the handle of the M16, he thought about the women they were leaving behind in the caves. Their only chance at returning to reality was in using the complex at the next solstice. Many of them wanted to leave with them now or to fight alongside their brothers and husbands, but the chance of them being captured was too great. If the attack turned out to be a total disaster, then the purebloods' very survival would depend on the impure not being able to quickly replace their casualties through more breeders filling their harems. Stuck in John's head was the image of the women being handed a couple of revolvers in case no one came back for them. He prayed as he ran, asking God to forgive him for the promise he was surely about to break.

* * * *

They first heard gunfire erupting from somewhere westward of their position, indicating that at least one of the groups had encountered resistance before being able to reach the temple site.

Paul hoped the sound of battle would pull the enemy forces away from the complex and farther into the forest. "Come on!" he urged the platoon.

But half a mile before they reached the site, they also found themselves being attacked from above, a great assortment of winged creatures sweeping down at them. They were screaming and clawing, their tails snapping the air. The youngest of the platoon was snatched off his feet and pulled up into the air, screaming as the face of a man sank lion's teeth into his chest. The boy's body disappeared up through the trees before landing in several pieces in front of them.

John and Hunter unloaded a deadly wave of fire up into the cedar trees as the rest of the platoon sought cover.

"Stop wasting your ammo!" Paul screamed.

And then one of the creatures came crashing down through the branches, landing on its head with a sickening *crack*. Bloody holes lined its torso, and its wings were mangled around its body. But then it began to move, ferociously sweeping its tail back and forth.

Chadwick ducked under the powerful death throes and stepped close, yelling savagely as he shot the demon creature in the forehead. A few men, following closely on his heels, chopped the head off, long blond hair wrapping around its face as it rolled down a small decline and disappeared into a sea of ferns.

"Come on!" Paul yelled, hearing more wings flapping above them.

As they ran, more gunfire and screaming echoed in the forest around them, the flying abominations having descended on another platoon of islanders positioned nearby.

Just when they were about to reach the edge of the forest, a handful of giants cut off their path, swords drawn and eyes ablaze.

"Fire!" Hunter screamed out in surprise, unloading a series of shots into the nearest Nephilim. But the 9 mm rounds from the MP5 barely impaired the giant's progress.

The rest of the men who were armed with guns unleashed a deafening symphony of lead that splashed into the ranks of giants and coated tropical trees with their defiled blood. But the giants continued to press forward, and they were forced to step back.

John and Paul were firing from their shoulders, aiming carefully for the monsters' heads, while Chadwick was simply sweeping his recoiling weapon back and forth from his hip.

"Fall back!" Paul called out as the rounds from his submachine gun emptied the eye sockets of the closest Nephilim.

Leaping at them from behind, a giant snapped its long blade and cut two of the retreating soldiers in half. Then it turned and swung back at John, sending John diving out of the way. Instead of his body catching the blow, a tree took it at center mass and toppled to the ground. John scrambled to his feet, running as fast as he could, feeling another *swoosh* barely miss his back.

"Come on!" Paul was leading them away from the bleeding giants and farther into the woods, intent on leading them back to the pyramid via some other route. After giving chase initially, the giants eventually gave into their injuries and surrendered their pursuit.

By now, however, gunfire was shaking the entire forest.

The war had begun.

* * * *

The sun was still rising, but dark clouds had materialized out of the west and were now stretching toward them like long oily fingers. The eerie stillness they had come to know so well on the island was now put to shame by a strange new wind that came accompanying the darkening sky.

John ran after Paul, descending a steep hill and coming into the empty courtyard of one of the ziggurats. He could see the temple standing beyond, the pyramid like a mountain in the background. The sun was almost perfectly positioned above the pyramid's pinnacle, its light reflecting brilliantly off the polished limestone and the crystal capstone. It was so bright that it was almost unbearable to look at.

"We need to get into the pyramid," John said as another platoon entered the strangely deserted courtyard.

Paul was skeptical. "I don't like this."

The other group ran over to them and reported that they'd just come from the pyramid. They said that there was no way into it.

Chadwick stepped forward while the two platoons joined in turning their weapons outward and to the forest that surrounded them. "If it's like the Great Pyramid, its entrance might be sealed shut."

"So how do we get in?" Hunter asked.

"Some think the literature indicates a tunnel system connecting the Sphinx and Valley Temple to the Great Pyramid. It could be the same here."

"*Could?*" Paul asked as the wind hissed through the grass around their feet.

"How much ammo's left?" Hunter inquired of the group.

They had used half of their supply in getting here. It wouldn't be long before they had to resort to hand-to-hand combat.

"Come on," Chadwick said, leading them past the tall ziggurats and toward the massive temple.

As the ascending steps leading into the temple's immense entranceway came into view, they saw that two giants were standing guard on either side. They were dressed in a kind of reflective, glass-like armor that mirrored everything before them. Almost invisible behind the reflection of the temple's steps and the complex beyond, their six-fingered grasps held spears longer than any normal man.

Hunter led the charge up the steps, his submachine gun echoing off the enormous buildings surrounding them and striking the guard on the right. John followed close behind, firing the more powerful assault rifle at the opposite giant. Neither of the monsters even flinched beneath the sparks showering off their armor.

And then the giant on the left raised its spear, took one step forward, and launched it through the air. It flew straight past Hunter's head, nearly taking off an ear, and picked up a pureblooded islander behind him. The force of the throw skewered the man and took him all the way to the bottom of the steps, the spear's bloody point pinning his dead body to the ground.

Henry picked up the man's weapon and slung it over his shoulder as he continued racing upward after Hunter and his adopted brother.

The giant that had thrown its spear took a step away from its position, beginning to descend the stairs en route to a confrontation with the invaders. John peppered its chest with bullets while Hunter ran a wide path around it. He turned when he was a few steps above and fired at its back until his weapon clicked empty. The giant spun back around, pulling a long diamond-like dagger from somewhere within its shining armor, and threw it in Hunter's direction. Hunter dropped the empty MP5, not bothering to load it with his last remaining magazine and pulled an old German Luger from the back of his pants just as the blade of the giant's knife flashed by his face and sliced a deep gash across his temple. Stumbling backward, Hunter raised the pistol and fired it repeatedly into the giant's face as it climbed the steps after him.

Stumbling blindly on the steps, the giant opened its mouth and roared, reaching out for Hunter.

Hunter dropped the pistol and pulled the sword off his back, raising it above his head even as blood flowed like a river down his face. But before he could deliver the strike, he noticed Henry and Paul screaming a warning to him. Turning, he saw the other giant running down the steps at him. Henry and Paul were firing relentlessly at it, but to no avail. The giant was on top of him before he could even get his sword around, its spear plunging into his chest and exiting through his back. He cried out in pain, trying to hack at the giant's hands with the sword. But the giant simply cocked the spear back and lifted Hunter off his feet. Then, with a snap of its wrists, it whipped the spear forward and sent Hunter's body sliding off the long pole and flying freely through the air. He almost cleared the entire temple but caught the first step against the small of his back.

With blind fury that was reflected right back at him in the giant's armor, Paul threw himself at the beast. But the Nephilim simply backhanded him away, sending him toppling down the steep stairs.

Henry ignored Paul bouncing past him and fired the shotgun he'd taken from the dead islander. The shot struck the giant's exposed kneecap. It buckled, bringing the giant down awkwardly across the steps. Before it could recover, John ran up behind it and plunged his own sword into the base of its neck. It unleashed a horrendous cry and, unbelievably, got back to its feet, knocking John off.

Henry aimed for the sword that was still sticking out of its neck and unloaded the other barrel. The cloud of buckshot tore away what flesh remained, and its head peeled away from its body, bouncing all the way down the steps and across the courtyard.

By now, the other Nephilim had turned on the rest of the platoon, barely noticing the bullets that were finding gaps in its armor. It reached out and grabbed one man after another, tearing them in half and tossing them down the temple steps.

John retrieved his sword and shook the carnage off it before charging the other giant's blind side. Taking a few steps up so that he was higher than the giant, he hurled himself through the air, bringing the sword crashing down into its head as it was chasing after a screaming pureblood. Knowing that he wouldn't be able to dislodge it, John leaned all his weight into the reflective body armor, pushing the "mighty man of renown" until it lost its footing. It crashed down on the steps so hard that a few corners of the steps broke off. As it began to slide down the steps on its back like some freak show amusement ride, it held John tightly in its grasp, threatening to snap his spine. The repeated blows to its head from each descending step, however, proved to be John's salvation. By the time it reached the bottom of the temple, its head was smeared all the way down the limestone, chunks of Nephilim brain matter clinging to the staggered steps.

Chadwick looked up to the sky and saw just how close the sun was to locking into position with the pyramid. He urged them all onward.

After stealing one last glance at Hunter's unmoving body, Paul and Henry turned and entered the temple. John, Chadwick, and those who remained from the two platoons followed in after them.

* * * *

They ran down a stone corridor, searching for a passageway that would lead them underground and to what Chadwick hoped was a tunnel system leading to the pyramid. But the corridor seemed to stretch on forever, no detail marking the walls or floor to signal whether their journey was even progressing. For all they knew, the floor was moving toward them and they were running in place.

John began to share Paul's cynicism about the temple complex being left guarded by only two giants. It didn't seem very likely that *all* of Osiris' armies had been drawn away from the site. And then, materializing from nowhere, a group of white men in loincloths and covered in tattoos were suddenly running down the hall toward them. But a short burst of firepower sent them all to the cold floor, writhing in pain and blood.

They hopped over them and kept running.

A minute later, however, they came to scattered corpses lying in the corridor. White, tattooed men in loincloths, blood dripping from bullet holes.

They stared for a second, confused.

"Didn't we just kill these guys?" Paul asked.

Chadwick looked down the hall. "We're running in circles."

Just then, two men fell from the ceiling and landed on Paul's back, swinging knives at his throat. Paul blocked the attacks with his forearms and threw one of the men to the floor. The other attacker started clawing savagely at his eyes, and Paul slammed him into the wall, too. Grabbing the man's arms, Paul flipped him off his back, using all the man's momentum to break both his arms at the elbows. The man howled in agony as Paul swung him around by the hands and threw him into the opposite wall...where he vanished.

Paul stood still for a second, staring at the blank wall, panting.

"It's some kind of portal," John explained, able to draw from his own experience with such things.

"Great," Paul muttered. And then he stepped into the wall, disappearing, too.

There was a moment of hesitation before the rest of them followed.

* * * *

"We're on the southwest corner of the island!" exclaimed a man with a Texas drawl. There was nothing around them but palmettos sprinkled across the shoreline, waves crashing off the reef in the distance.

John looked up at the sky. "We're running out of time." He stepped out of the circle and walked beyond the large staggered monoliths. "Come on, get out of there."

They walked away from the henge's center.

"What is *that*?" one of the men asked, pointing up into the sky.

They turned their attention upward to the encroaching darkness, and to what initially looked like storm clouds. Now, however, the shapeless black clouds were filled with ghostlike figures flying back and forth within them.

"Come on," John said, turning away from the coming nightmare apocalypse. He hurried back into the circle.

* * * *

They were back in what they could only assume to be the temple, though in a room they hadn't been able to access from within the long corridor. Huge pillars were stretched upward and held a ceiling that they could barely see.

"Are we beneath the temple?" Paul asked.

Chadwick shook his head. "No," Chadwick said, "I think we're on the outskirts of the temple's center. Look." He pointed at an enormous entranceway that stood half concealed by red curtains. He ran across the stone floor and led them through it.

John recognized the room immediately. "This is where I was," he whispered, looking up and seeing the opening in the ceiling. The sun was almost positioned at its center. Spinning around, he saw the mirrors positioned against the wall, just where they had been before.

"Mirror, mirror on the wall," Paul mumbled. "Is that the thing you—"

But John was already halfway there.

"John, we need to find the passageway to the pyramid!" Chadwick shouted.

As John approached the instrument, images began appearing within the glass. His heart jumped. He recognized them.

Henry ran up beside him, about to pull him away, when he, too, noticed what was being displayed in the mirrors. "Johnny," he whispered, gently tugging him.

It was Kristen. She was sitting in his chair, asleep.

"Johnny," Henry said again, "if you want to see her again—"

"Yeah," John whispered. And then, in a sudden flash of anger, he grabbed Henry's sword from his back and swung it into the instrument that had been watching his family. The panes of glass shattered and fell to the floor, exploding into hundreds of pieces that were sent bouncing and rolling at his feet. He continued to swing at the contraption, and once there was no longer any glass intact, he pushed the frame over and began stomping on it, twisting the metal.

"John!" Henry was screaming now, pulling him away. "Let's go!"

Panting heavily, his face red and veins bulging in his neck, John finally let himself be pulled away from the angel's spyglass.

"Come on!" Chadwick shouted. He was standing beside a section of the wall that seemed to be moving, swimming in dark circles like some fantasy out of a video game. He stepped in.

* * * *

It was the enormous room that contained the pool full of women, except that now there weren't any giants in their company.

Chadwick swore loudly and began looking for another portal when one of the men cried out, "Jennifer!" and began running to the pool.

"No, Peter!" another called after him, running to restrain him.

The women turned and watched, unmoving, as the two men approached.

Peter ran to one that must have been either his sister or wife and grabbed her, trying desperately to drag her back with him and away from the pool. But she was resisting, lashing out with her nails and raking his face. He was pleading with her, tears running from his eyes, but she seemed numb to his concern.

The rest of the women congregated in the pool and were now slowly approaching the struggle. And a moment later, Peter disappeared beneath a tide of hording flesh and splashing water, a lustful frenzy overtaking him like sharks to a bleeding wound. Trying desperately to pull the women off him, his friend, too, was pulled down beneath the writhing sea of skin.

The sounds coming from the water were too much for John, and he had to turn away. "We should leave before…"

Already finished with the two men, or simply saving them for later, the naked women stood, one by one, and turned toward them.

"Let's go," Paul said, beginning to backpedal.

As the girls began stepping out of the water, the platoon could see their friends floating facedown in the water behind them and knew there was no use in trying to save them. They all turned and ran back through the portal.

The next thing John knew, he was standing in the center of a henge, the same one he'd been transported to before. He led the shrinking platoon into another circle and vanished again.

This time, they found themselves standing at the base of the pyramid, an army of angry giants surrounding them, dead bodies of the pureblooded scattered beneath six-toed feet.

Though the sounds of battle were still echoing through the forest, it was evident from the scene before them that things had not gone well at all.

The giants began beating their bare, tattooed chests with six, seven, and even eight-fingered fists, waving swords and axes in the air while hissing at them. The eyes of those closest to them were glowing molten red.

"Why aren't they attacking?" Chadwick asked. There had to be a hundred of them, every one ready to tear them to pieces if not for whatever was restraining them.

"Look!" John pointed to the sun. It was only minutes away from moving into its final position.

"They're waiting to be transported," Henry realized.

And then explosions began blowing handfuls of the Nephilim into pieces, whipping their cursed anatomy across the grass. Volleys of gunfire swept through their ranks from the forest around them, but still the Nephilim refused to retaliate, waiting only for the sun to move into place and activate the pyramid.

A combined force of the remaining pureblooded inhabitants suddenly burst from the trees and began charging the ranks of giants even as the sound of flapping wings settled over the complex.

"We're out of time!" Henry yelled.

The churning black clouds had begun forming a circle in the sky right above the pyramid, sucking in the brightness of midday as if it were a black hole. Skinny black creatures with horns protruding from their elongated skulls beat their bat-like wings as they swam through the rolling clouds. The sun was standing as the eye of the swirling evil, its center poised above the pyramid's diamond capstone. There was no doubt that these demons had come to aid in the fallen angel's departure.

Even as more hellish creatures appeared gliding around the darkening vortex that was closing in on the sun, the pureblooded army was effectively cutting their way through the ranks of motionless giants, attacking with swords and grenades.

Branches of lightning began flashing, and gusts of wind whipped through the forest.

Paul grabbed John and pulled him back into the circle beneath the pyramid, sending them to yet another location.

* * * *

"This is it!" Chadwick exclaimed. "The tunnel system beneath the complex!" He began running down the stone corridor, glowing bulbs tracing the ceiling above them.

Another group of Osiris' soldiers appeared at the end of the hall, blocking their entrance into an ascending passageway that Chadwick could only hope led up into the pyramid.

"Is that it?" Paul asked Chadwick.

"I think so."

Paul took the submachine gun from him. "Then go."

"What are you doing?" shouted Henry.

"If you don't leave this place, then Nick and Chris died for nothing!"

"What are you talking about?"

"Someone has to look after Jackson and Hunter and keep these people"—he nodded toward the remaining platoon—"from destroying the site." A crystal arrow went streaking by his face. "If this thing even works, then I'll see you at the winter solstice." Then he turned and ran down the corridor, screaming while holding down the trigger of the submachine gun. Once it ran dry, he tossed it aside and took the sword off his back. He entered the midst of the remaining demon-possessed soldiers with a brutal savagery of his own.

"Come on!" Chadwick navigated through Paul's bloody assault and to the mouth of the ascending passageway. But then arrows began sinking into the bodies of the pureblooded men around them, four of them falling immediately.

Looking back beyond Paul, they saw another procession of evil soldiers making their way after them, two giants and one of the flying creatures accompanying them.

Another barrage of arrows flew past, finding their targets in three more of the islanders.

Paul, now finished with the evil men piled at his feet, stood between the pure and the damned. He faced the charging host of corruption with swords in each hand, blood dripping from their blades. Without looking back, he took off for Osiris' playthings with a savage battle cry that echoed off the walls and chased after him. Until it was drowned by the sound of clashing metal, beastly roars, and splashing blood.

As Chadwick led them up the ascending passageway, he knew immediately that the layout of this pyramid was different from that of the Great Pyramid, which would make sense if it were astronomically aligned—it being positioned in a different part of the world. He kept running, light from more of the bulbous objects illuminating their blank surroundings as a strange low-frequency hum began reverberating all around them.

"What is that sound?" John yelled up to Chadwick. He immediately thought of all that F-sharp stuff Chadwick had talked about—the perfect acoustics of the Great Pyramid and it being designed like the Whispering Hall in London. But Chadwick didn't answer him.

One after another, the person trailing in the back of the line was instantly and violently sucked off his feet by some invisible force and dragged, screaming, back down the corridor and into the darkness.

The passageway finally leveled out and led them into a chamber, and all the stories Chadwick had told John about Egypt's pyramids suddenly seemed ridiculously irrelevant—the stories of the pyramid's prisoner, of the war that had disabled it, of the granite plugs that were placed in the passageways, the ceremonial journey to the stars… Nothing about those stories offered any sort of clarity now.

With only a handful of the pureblooded islanders remaining with them, John, Henry, and Chadwick all stood motionless within the empty room. There were no other exits, just huge smooth black blocks surrounding them on all sides. The room was gigantic, its ceiling much higher than the passageway that led them there, its width and length forming a perfect square fifty yards by fifty yards. There were open shafts in the walls, but only large enough to fit a man's arm into.

"Star shafts," Chadwick whispered, wiping sweat from his face, "locking us into a celestial configuration."

"What now?" Henry asked, his head pivoting anxiously.

The humming was growing louder, the limestone vibrating, tickling their feet.

And then a voice cut through the hypnotic tune.

"Ah, my three children… I was starting to think you wouldn't make it." Osiris suddenly materialized in the corner of the room. "I was beginning to worry."

John flexed his empty hands, his heart pounding in his chest.

The fallen angel approached them, only now his hair was cut, and he was wearing an expensive, twenty-first-century black suit. Ignoring the five remaining islanders, he smiled. "The time has finally come for my release."

They hadn't envisioned a scenario like this.

John hesitated. "What about the last piece of your puzzle?"

An evil grin stretched across his face. "It was you, Johnny. You were the last piece."

They froze.

"I wasn't about to use this device again, not after what happened the first time." He indicated his surroundings. "At least not without a failsafe in place."

"I don't understand," John whispered against the sinking feeling burning in the pit of his stomach.

"You're one of *Hisss*," he stated. "The blood of the Messiah has cleansed you of my corrupting influence. It has also ensured your place within His kingdom."

John's head began to spin. He sensed Chadwick step closer.

"God can't condemn me to Tarturus if you're with me, Johnny."

Everything seemed to be moving around him, and his sense of stability was evaporating faster than these new dots could be connected.

"That's why you brought him here?" Henry asked.

"Ah, Henry, I appreciate you keeping your end of the bargain."

John turned his eyes to Henry. "Bargain?" And he remembered Jackson's words, that Henry remembered *exactly* how he had escaped the angel's possession.

Henry looked at John, his eyes expressing a remorse that made John shudder.

"What did you do?" John breathed.

"He wanted me to get you here for the solstice. He promised that he would let us leave with him, that we could go home."

"And what about Jackson?" John demanded.

The angel smiled slightly. "He's my backup plan…in case this doesn't work."

"He's one of your offspring, too, isn't he?"

"Of course. Without him, Ronald would never have been able to get Henry here. And then I would never have been able to get *you* here."

Henry stammered, "I'm sorry, Johnny, but there was no other way to leave."

"Ye*sss*," Osiris said. "This way everybody's a winner." And then he waved his hands at the ceiling, and a long narrow shaft stretching all the way up to the crystal apex formed before their eyes.

By now, John knew that Osiris hadn't planned on transporting his entire army into the real world, and that Jackson's warning was only to create a precedent for ensuring his own presence within the pyramid. But there was still one thing that John didn't get. "Why'd you need to sacrifice one last giant if you already had everything you needed?"

"Travel arrangements. But don't worry, everything worked out."

Just then, the sun reached its zenith and came to a stop, every megalithic structure that had been erected on the island housing the sun perfectly within its astronomical design, linking the sites not only with celestial coordinates but also with a perfect solar alignment. The sun sat in the center of every henge, setting their gypsum-covered perimeters on fire. It rested within the center of staggered monoliths, its bottom arc kissing the massive stone blocks as if resting on them. The ziggurats in the temple complex were all standing directly beneath the massive fireball of energy, its light sending strange serpent-like shadows slithering up and down their many steps.

The swirling clouds began crashing with thunder and closing in on the sun, lightning branching through them.

Giants stood staring up at the opening portal, believing it to be their salvation, while the surviving platoons of the pureblooded hurried as quickly as they could back to the caves.

The vibrations in the pyramid were growing stronger, the strange frequency elevating with them…if not causing them. They all watched the sun stand still above the diamond capstone as hundreds of rays of refracted light were beamed out from its crystalline essence and sent in every direction.

Osiris' laughter mixed with the resonating frequency that was filling the pyramid, and John, Chadwick, Henry, and the five others braced themselves for whatever was about to happen. They could see up through the rainbow of dancing colors and to the swirling clouds wrapping around the sun, darkening the intensity of the capstone.

A blinding light began spreading throughout the room, washing everything away in its brilliance.

The sound was deafening.

For a split second, John could see right through the pyramid's walls and out into the complex. Only instead of seeing stepped pyramids, there were lines of buildings standing beyond the Nephilim-infested courtyard.

But then the image flickered, and the pyramids were back, the buildings gone.

The capstone seemed to be maneuvering reality's antenna, searching for reception.

And then the brightness swallowed everything, and John had to close his eyes.

He couldn't even hear himself scream.

* * * *

The first thing John saw when he opened his eyes was the point of an obelisk piercing storm clouds. Realizing he was lying on his back, he tried to roll over, sensing with deep despair that the pyramid had simply sent them to one of the two obelisks by the graveyard. As he shifted his position, the thought that he would never see Kristen again settled horribly in the forefront of his mind. He was trapped in this hell.

Rain began to fall on him, and he closed his eyes again, not wanting to face the reality of his hopeless future. But then a strange noise registered in his ears. Turning his head to the right, he saw Chadwick standing beside him, his gaze set out at something beyond their immediate location. "What's that noise?" he asked, coughing. It sounded like a siren of some kind.

"Get up, John," Chadwick said.

John shook the cobwebs from his head and turned to see where the piercing noise was coming from, but what he saw left him utterly stunned.

Paved streets, tall pastel-colored buildings, palm trees, metal gates, cars parked along curbs, mopeds…

He looked back to the obelisk next to him and noticed the cenotaph standing beside it, the Cabinet Building in the background. Across Front Street, a cruise ship was docked in Hamilton Harbor. "I can't believe it…"

But Henry was on the other side of him and pointing to Parliament Street.

At Osiris.

The sound of sirens grew louder as a line of police cars came screeching around the corner. Their doors flew open, and police with submachine guns exited the vehicles, charging the grounds of the Cabinet Building.

At that exact moment, a black car pulled up along the curb on Parliament Street. Osiris, in his black suave suit, opened an umbrella and walked smoothly to the passenger-side door. For a mere second, John had an unobstructed view of the driver, and there was no doubting who it was.

Ronald Douglas Carter.

Looking back at John, Osiris gave a half salute, folded the umbrella, and winked. "Take care of that boy of yours!" And then he shouted something about "forsaking the God of his fathers," but the sound of the sirens had made it practically unintelligible. He slipped into the car and closed the door.

As the car pulled away from the curb and turned down Front Street, the small army of police officers stormed the obelisk with weapons raised. "Put your hands on your heads and lie down on your stomachs!" they were shouting through British accents.

They began to oblige when another voice suddenly began shouting for the police officers to stand down.

John felt someone grab his arm and pull him to his feet.

"Hi there," a familiar face said.

"Frank," John said in bewilderment. He was so confused that all he could do was stand there, speechless.

"Where is he?" Frank asked, sweeping a curious eye over John's company.

"Who?"

He leaned in close and whispered, "The fallen angel."

All John could do was point in the direction the car had driven off in. "He just took off with—"

"Ronald Carter," Frank spat.

"How did you—"

But Frank held up a hand, pulling out a cell phone. "It was all in his books." He shook his head. "How the heck am I going to explain this to anyone?" He handed John the phone. "Call your wife. She's worried to death." And then he began shouting orders to his men, sending them in pursuit of *two* fallen angels.

Henry was embracing Chadwick, while the five surviving islanders were staring wide-eyed at a world they hadn't seen in a long, long time.

Stepping away from the obelisk, and completely indifferent to the falling rain, John dialed his wife with clumsy fingers, tears of joy mixing with the rain.

"Hello?" she answered. "Is that you, Frank?"

"Actually," John responded, emotion choking him, "it's me."

There was a moment of silence on the other end, and John checked to see if the connection had dropped. "Hello?"

"*Johnny*?"

"Yeah, baby, it's me. I'm back."

"Johnny!" she screamed, and then fell into hysteria.

John could tell that she was jumping up and down. "I love you so much," he struggled to say, wiping tears from his eyes.

"I love you, Johnny! Where the heck have you been? What—" An unintelligible string of questions followed until she managed to settle down. "Are you in Bermuda?"

"Yeah, but I'll be on the first flight out, I promise."

"Are you okay? Pastor Brian watched that tape and thought maybe—"

"I'm okay, baby." He sighed. "I didn't think I'd ever see you again…" He saw Frank running over to him, and against every impulse he had, he forced himself to say goodbye. "I have to go now, but I promise I'll call you right back."

"Johnny, wait. I need to tell you something now, before I lose another chance."

"I know," he said. "We're having a baby boy."

"How did you…wait, what do you mean a *boy*?" She laughed, thinking that he was only joking.

He blinked more tears from his eyes.

EPILOGUE

21st day of December. Wilkinsburg, Pennsylvania

Voices from the television drifted into the room, distracting him from the passage of Scripture Osiris had referenced exactly six months ago, right before driving away in the car with Ronald. Though John hadn't heard the entirety of what had been said, he now knew that the phrase from the book of Daniel was generally attributed to the antichrist—a fact that occasionally kept him up at night.

Kristen's round belly made an entrance into the room before the rest of her, and she saw that her husband's Bible was resting open beneath a familiar furrowed brow. "Are you studying that passage again?" She wrapped her arms around his neck, kissing his cheek.

He nodded. He'd also discovered that there were as many theories surrounding the meaning of the words as there were theories of whom (or what) the antichrist would actually be.

"I wish you'd forget about it," she said.

And, in fact, he wished that he could. But, for some reason, the words wouldn't leave his head. A persistent tide, they repeatedly and consistently lapsed over his brain. Had the fallen angel just meant to play games with him? Driving one last thorn into his otherwise firm faith before riding off into the sunset of some new conspiracy to free Apollo from Tartarus? If not, if there was some cunning truth to his parting words, then John could only guess what it might be.

"I don't even like thinking about him," she added. The "him" was Ronald…or rather, *Doctor* Grigori.

No one had seen the doctor-professor-author or Osiris since the 21st of June. Frank said it was as though they'd just vanished into thin air. But because he wasn't looking to find himself condemned to a straitjacket for using taxpayer money in tracking down a fallen angel (who had borrowed the name of the famous Egyptian deity now imprisoned in Tartarus with two hundred other angels), his range of investigation was confined to a bed of very limited resources. That Osiris had used the disembodied spirits of his Nephilim offspring to communicate with Ronald was a story that even Chadwick didn't want attached to his name—and the reason he didn't want anything to do with an investigation into his kidnapping.

"I don't like thinking about them, either," he answered. And though his nightmares had once again fallen back into remission (the experience in Afghanistan nearly forgotten, and the attic demons staying put in their respective shadows), the memories of what he had seen on the island would be with him for the rest of his life. The Nephilim, the creatures like those in Revelation, the pyramid, the henges, the possessed women assassinated by their own husbands and fathers, the children in the village… Those things would never leave him, but thus far God was merciful in that they weren't making cameo appearances in his dreams. For the most part, his dream state had returned to normal save the occasional nightmare of impending apocalypse; but he figured that dreams of navigating loved ones through the barren landscapes of Hollywood's most haunting portrayals of postapocalyptic worlds were probably common ones.

He thought of the island often, about what might have happened to it once they left, whose theory had been correct. Had it folded up into nothingness, or did Osiris' offspring set out exterminating each other as the survivors of the Triangle had hoped? What of Jackson, Paul, and Hunter? Had they survived? Had Jackson gotten to read the Bible he'd left in his care? How many of the pureblooded survived the war? His heart ached for them, for the women that had been waiting anxiously in the caves.

John's own spiritual life had finally begun to thrive despite the nagging foreboding of Osiris' undefined innuendo. He felt no shame for killing the giant, and he honestly didn't know if he'd killed more than that. He simply couldn't remember. If he had killed more, then the thing he most feared about breaking his promise to God, relapsing into who he once was, had failed to materialize. Instead, the community had become his new mission field, and he was finally feeling like he had a holy purpose in life.

And Henry had moved nearby and joined the same community church, partnering with them to meet the needs of those less fortunate. Like John, he had finally come to believe that his tainted genealogy no longer mattered. The cross had indeed proven to be the antidote, not only for the polluted gene pool he'd been born from, but from every vice he'd struggled with throughout the years. And this new spiritual bond between him and John had forced the rest of the Carter family to reevaluate their view of Johnny's patriotic apostasy. And, if not approving of his choices, they at least began to tolerate them.

Of course, the brothers hadn't disclosed to their family all that had *really* happened in "Bermuda." And neither did they reveal the discovery of John's own adoption, his knowledge of the fact a secret shared with only Henry and Kristen. He'd been a Carter his entire life and didn't see any reason why he should make everyone feel weird about it now. After a few weeks of reevaluating almost every assumption he ever had about himself, he had eventually come to accept his unknown heritage.

John kissed Kristen's lips and then her stomach before she turned to leave the room. He followed her with his eyes, wondering again as to how long they might get to actually be parents in this lifetime. Would they even get to witness their son's second birthday, or would all the hopes and dreams that any person had for a child be found well outside the reach of time? She blew him a kiss before descending the stairs, and he snapped out of his musing.

He looked out the window and down across the snow-covered street, his mind set on nothing, barely noticing the flurries floating past him. And then his eyes fell across a notepad that rested beneath the window. It was open to the last entry, which recorded fragments of another obsession that his experience had spawned, a theological theory that believed certain verses in Genesis, Ezekiel, Jeremiah, and Isaiah suggested the presence of a time gap between Genesis 1:1

and Genesis 1:2. Basically, in opposition to the Chaos theory, it held that God created the heavens and the earth perfectly and all at once, and that the first verse of the Bible was the account of this (which seemed to be in perfect keeping with His nature, the idea of God creating anything "void and without form" somewhat foreign to His creative ways). The verses following, according to the theory, didn't offer a *further* description of the initial (and complete) act of creation, but rather described a *re*-making or remolding of the earth *after* cataclysmic events had turned Satan's reign to ruin.

After listening to every debate he could get his hands on concerning the theory, John found that it actually answered a lot of his questions concerning the things he'd learned while on the island—a distant self-proclaimed golden age over which Satan ruled, the long astronomical and planetary cycles, the evidence of cataclysm both on earth *and* other planets, the ancient maps revealing Antarctica without ice, the megalithic sites astronomically aligned to much older skies, all the ancient texts... In fact, John was surprised at how often creationists referenced the ancient writings to prove that there *had* been a universal flood, while at the same time (and in complete disregard of the same logic), writing off all other details as mere pagan mythology.

However, the theory did raise as many questions as it did answers, and though Brian said the Hebrew of the text did *allow* for such an interpretation, he cautiously added that it was by no means a necessary one. Though, when considering the Scriptural evidence supporting the theory, it became very compelling. In fact, despite all the unmarked doors such an idea opened, John couldn't find another Scriptural basis that would explain what he'd seen, of the Google images he had printed out and tacked up on the wall above the computer—images of the ruins at Baalbek, the Great Pyramid, the Valley Temple, Tiahuanaco, Sacsayhuaman hill, Easter Island, Stonehenge, and scores of other mysteries all pointing to some unknown but highly advanced civilization that existed at a time when Earth's magnetic poles were supposedly occupying very different areas of the globe.

And by now, John also knew what Ronald had implied when suggesting he take a closer look at the passage in Genesis where God separated the waters above from the waters below, the reason God refused to claim it "good," as He had His other acts. He learned from a book that the spirits of the people that had lived under Satan's reign (benevolent demons, according to Hesiod) had been trapped beneath the face of the deep, but that when God recreated the world, separating the waters, their spirits were let loose from the deep and thus gained free rein of the atmosphere. Only the author, being a Christian man, didn't claim (as Hesiod and Ronald did) that these spirits were benevolent, but were instead very much in keeping with the biblical concept of demons. It was a theory very similar to what the Book of Enoch suggested happened to the spirits of the Nephilim in the Flood, and something that John sneered at when he'd first read about it. But the closer he looked at the Bible verses, the harder it was to find some other meaning in them, and the more he wondered...

Unable to stop himself, he leaned forward and snatched the notepad off the windowsill and began flipping through it. It was unbelievable how much information there was on all this stuff. Chadwick hadn't even scratched the surface of it while attempting to educate them on the island. And, of course, *seeing* the monuments he'd mentioned only made everything that much more intriguing. It was one thing to *hear* of a stone monolith weighing a thousand tons, but it was something entirely different to see a man standing beside one. Such images pulled off the internet and photocopied from archeology books left the mind numb with incomprehension, begging to know how, why, when, and who.

And then there was the Book of Enoch, which John found to be more than interesting. Indeed, the book did wonders in filling many of the gaps found in Genesis, specifically regarding the fallen angels and their shenanigans. Enoch, being Noah's grandfather, is said in 68:1 to have passed his books of knowledge to his grandson, thus explaining how the record hadn't been lost in the Flood. It was also the only Christian text that John knew of that could explain all the advanced mysteries found in prehistory. Not only did the mythologies themselves credit giants for such anomalies, the mingling of men and gods (or fallen angels and women) permeating these accounts, but the Book of Enoch (along with Genesis 6, Jude, and Peter) seemed to reinforce such explanations, recording how the fallen angels taught men all the secrets of heaven—from astronomy and math to warfare and abortion. And what other biblical explanation was there for such an infusion of advanced technology, the impossible building of the pyramids, Britain's henges, the ruins at Baalbek, the giant Olmec heads… As far as John was concerned, the technology needed to accomplish these feats either had to be credited to aliens or angels. After all, most experts believed that all this esoteric knowledge had been delivered to man in complete form, originating from a single outside source. But then Chadwick said that, for the most part, aliens, gods, and angels were probably just different names for the same fallen entities.

He skimmed the notes for the thousandth time, rehearsing to himself that the book was rediscovered in Abyssinia in 1773 by a Freemason and eventually translated in 1821. Jude and James both quoted Enoch in their epistles, and until the Council of Laodicea in AD 364, it was widely regarded by the church as part of Holy Scripture. Once condemned, however, it faded into history, promising an anathema on anyone who decided to read it. After its discovery in 1773, its first publication in 1821, and the popular 1912 edition published by R. H. Charles, portions of the Greek text began to surface, and then seven Aramaic fragments were discovered with the Dead Sea Scrolls. With all the strange things that Scripture had to say about the antediluvian world, and the words of Jesus that His return would be marked by a relapse into such days, it made more intriguing the Book of Enoch's proclamation that it was, itself, written for some future generation—especially considering its stunning parallels to the book of Revelation. Included in John's notes were lists of books that had been written on the Nephilim, Satan, and fallen angels. He was surprised how popular the topic had been among theologians throughout the 1800s.

And then there were the more bizarre theories about Enoch. That, according to the Book of Heavenly Luminaries (a part of Enoch), the angel Uriel had communicated to him the knowledge of how to construct these megalithic sites, and that he used the sites as observatories, which enabled him to both predict and monitor the happenings in the heavens as well as the geological changes on earth…which was how he predicted the cataclysm that brought Noah's Flood.

His laptop chimed and freed his attention from the notepad. He tossed it back on the windowsill and spun in his chair to open the new email. It was from Chadwick.

Currently in Oregon investigating a vitrified tunnel that had mysteriously been carved forty feet above the ground and into the solid rock face of a mountainside in Vail, Chadwick was attempting to uncover the true reason why the government had sealed off its entrance the night of its discovery. Of course, he was convinced that Nephilim had to be involved somehow, and he was determined to prove it. His next book depended on it.

The Masonic elements of Enochian tradition had begun to *really* intrigue Chadwick when he learned that the book of Genesis actually recorded two *different* Enochs, the Enoch who walked with God for three hundred years and was the son of Jared and the father of Methuselah, and the Enoch who was born to Cain and had a city named after him—the same city whose ruins were said to be in Baalbek, destroyed by a flood and later rebuilt by a race of giants. Whereas before he had associated all Enochian tradition—from the Bible to the Pseudepigrapha and from witchcraft to Freemasonry—with one Enoch, now there were two candidates. And that fascinated him, especially since the legends seemed to branch off and run in separate directions, the occult in one and Christian sainthood in the other.

John absentmindedly glanced at the dollar bill pinned to his wall that Chadwick had sent him in the mail, all of its secret esoteric symbols and meanings highlighted in red marker. But even more disturbing to him than the presence of the tiny Moloch owl was the hovering capstone on the reverse of the nation's Great Seal itself. It was an image that gave him the creeps ever since seeing it drawn on Ronald's map of the Bermuda Triangle… *The Doorway to Hell.*

He clicked on the message. It read:

> *I channeled Apollyon last night and got him to grant us a hundred-year reprieve! Just kidding. I'm not really channeling my chained relatives! Actually, I was thinking we could all get together for a Rapture party…*
>
> *Enjoy the latest! —Chad*

John smiled despite himself. It was the theme of Chadwick's debut work, *Hijacked By An Angel,* a book claiming that fallen angels were now occupying seats of power throughout the globe, masquerading as diplomats, presidents, kings… He believed, or at least for his *book's* sake he believed (John could never quite tell), that they were nothing short of the puppet-masters sitting behind the scenes and orchestrating the emerging New World Order.

There was an attachment with the cute note, and it was titled, PENTAGON. John saved it to his computer, to the folder with all the others and, despite knowing that he wouldn't read the whole thing now, opened it once the download was complete.

Somehow, Chadwick's experience on the island sparked an obsessive investigation into the esoteric origins of Washington, DC's architecture. He was going to have a whole section of his new book dedicated to it. And, whatever he discovered he felt the need to pass on to John and Henry. There were already around forty documents in a folder that John named CHAD_MASON.

Most recently he'd written about the Ellipse in Washington—the Meridian Stone, Jefferson Stone, the Washington Meridian, Meridian Park… He told how DC's major sites were connected within a grid that was measured out in megalithic degrees, and that the secret ground plan beneath the streets was a pure example of megalithic geometry. In fact, he had written, the entire layout of DC revealed a very special relationship with astronomy and astrology, specifically to the zodiacal sign of Virgo and the planet Venus. Of course, he hadn't found this *too* surprising since he'd already known that the entire framework of Freemasonry rested on astrology. But John *had been* surprised to learn that the blessed Constitution was signed right when the sun, Mercury, and Venus were all on Virgo and that Mercury and Venus had been directly overhead at the exact moment the signatures were applied to the sacred document. He also hadn't been aware that in 1793, when George Washington laid the cornerstone of the Capitol building dressed in his Masonic apron, the sun and Mercury were again in Virgo, and Venus was rising as the morning star. He'd never learned that the Washington Monument was erected to be the sun's setting point on the spring and autumn equinoxes whenever the sun occupied Virgo. It was a link that Chad insisted connected its function with the properties of the Thornborough henges, Stonehenge, the pyramids, Rosslyn Chapel, and all the other astronomically aligned megalithic sites.

And then there was Chadwick's further explanation of Washington's relationship with the constellation Virgo. Virgo being the immortalization of the virgin goddess Isis—the World Mother often used as a symbol of justice and found standing between the pillars of Freemasonry's Jachin and Boaz. Isis, being the "mother of the gods," was also one of the names given to Venus and, when rising as the morning star, had been revered by and named "Lucifer" by the followers of Pythagoras.

But it was Chadwick's associating the Roman *Libertas* (revered as the Statue of Liberty) and Columbia (the district in which the nation's capital resides, and most commonly recognized today as the icon for Columbia Pictures) with the virgin goddess of Virgo that John was most disturbed by. There was another document that Chad had sent detailing the Jesuits' role in establishing the country and how the Catholic perception of the Virgin Mary was eerily similar to that of Isis, causing many in the esoteric arts to think of them as the same. Was it then a coincidence, he had asked, that the capital was built right between and occupying both *Virginia* and *Mary-land*? Or that the shape of DC was a diamond with its four sides aligning with the cardinal points—the diamond, according to esoteric tradition, representing female divinity and the anatomy through which life is both created and born?

There was a lot more written about the Federal Triangle, Sirius, the street plan of DC, the Capitol building, and the founding fathers, but John couldn't remember half of it. It didn't really surprise him once he sat back and thought about it. In a way, it was obvious. Like Henry had said on the island, Satan was the one running the show; he was the current prince and power of the air, the ruler of this age. And a simple Google search revealed just how many of the world's cities (let alone countless other things) were named after mythological gods and goddesses (or fallen angels and their progeny).

He clicked on "PENTAGON," wondering what more Chad could possibly add to his already overwhelmed sense of reality, and began skimming its contents. Right away he learned that the Pentagon was a perfectly built, modern-day megalithic structure and that the circle surrounding it was a scale model of Stonehenge.

Now *that* was something John wasn't expecting.

He read on and further learned that it was also two and a half times the size of the Thornborough henge. From there, Chad noted FDR's personal involvement in its construction—his cousin the chairman of the National Resource Planning Commission and running the DC Fine Arts Commission. As a side note, he stated that FDR was a thirty-third-degree Mason and that his New Deal was probably meant to be the fulfillment of the reverse seal on the dollar bill (which he had also been involved with). Then the document got even more interesting when Chad began laying out the initiation ceremony for the thirty-second degree of Freemasonry, explaining how it focused primarily on the military importance of a pentagon, its purpose for each of the five corners clarified—and, of course, the US Armed Forces was comprised of five components. The ritual stated that there was a triangle in the center of the pentagon, and amazingly, an equilateral triangle fit precisely within the Pentagon. He finished the section by recording that the ground for the Pentagon was broken on September 11, 1941.

John rubbed his eyes, the bright light from the monitor straining them. He knew from Chadwick's previous emails that the Masons believed America to be a type of New Jerusalem that would herald in the New Order, and he found it just a little disturbing that this arcane knowledge that had presumably been practiced before the Flood and had been taught by fallen angels (one of the reasons for the Flood, according to Enoch) was still in use today, marking the most elite places in world government. And, as Chadwick said, it was Freemasonry's Royal Arch of Enoch that claimed the Order to be the caretakers of such antediluvian knowledge. Was it then just another coincidence that Freemasonry had always been suspected of trying to bring about a New World Order, one that their enlightened Masonic Christ would reign over? That the five Revolutionary War cities—Boston, New York, Philadelphia, Baltimore, and Washington—shared the same ley line as Stonehenge? Again, the words of Jesus came to mind. *As it was in the days of Noah, so it will be at the coming of the Son of Man…*

But then Chadwick started talking about a stone that marked the center of DC and served as the point of a thirty-three-degree triangle connecting it with the Pentagon and the Capitol. He said that whatever was in the chamber beneath the stone had come from Rosslyn Chapel and could be something that pertained to Enoch's secrets, about the astronomical observances that told of the world's next cataclysm…

John closed the document, unable to digest all of it at once. When it came to Chadwick's emails, it usually took him a few days to get through them—as would be the case this time as well.

Suppressing a series of chills, John moved his gaze up past the picture of him and Henry holding a large tuna they'd caught in August, and set it on the calendar, to the box outlining the present day. He had drawn an obelisk within its frame six months ago. The winter solstice.

John reached for his cup of coffee as the image of the Mayan calendar wheel suddenly took over the monitor in the form of a screen saver.

Apocalypse…

Did the earth really go through this precessional cycle that the ancients somehow knew how to measure, incorporating its code into their literature and architecture? Evidently, even mainstream science said that it did. And then, as Chadwick asked, would it not make sense for the Creator-God to set His creation in motion at the start of such a cycle rather than at some random point between? After all, He created such cycles as a component of universal order. Why then create a starting and finishing point if neither were ever to be exercised? And why set the zodiac in the sky but not let the earth witness the completion of its ages? It was speculation, of course, but reason enough to at least comprise another puzzle piece.

Could the winter solstice of 2012, the expiration date of the Mayan's five-thousand-one-hundred-and-sixty-year Fifth Sun, as well as the end of the near twenty-six-thousand-year precessional cycle, serve as the beginning of the Apostle's apocalypse? Was it just coincidence that Hollywood had been capitalizing on a world consciousness that seemed to be expecting such an approaching doom? Had Noah's Flood been the melting of the Ice Age, the poles shifting and displacing the earth's crust, and now the synergy of creation was about to swing full circle for another scheduled transition? Could 2012 be the date the angel would open the bottomless pit and release havoc on the earth? And what of all the apocalyptic rhetoric in the Bible that John had jotted down in his notepad? The mighty storm rising from the ends of the earth, the sun given power to scorch people with fire, people being seared by intense heat, the moon shining like the sun, sunlight becoming seven times brighter than normal, the heavens and earth once more being shaken, great distress unequaled from the beginning of the world, flashes of lightning, rumbling, thunder, an earthquake like none other since man has been on the earth, men fleeing to caves in the rocks when the earth shakes…

And then there were the Trumpets.

> *The first angel sounded his trumpet, and there came hail and fire mixed with blood, and it was hurled down upon the earth. A third of the earth was burned up, a third of the trees was burned up, and all the green grass was burned up. The second angel sounded his trumpet, and something like a huge mountain, all ablaze, was thrown into the sea. A third of the sea turned into blood, a third of the living creatures in the sea died, and a third of the ships were destroyed. The third angel sounded his trumpet—a great star, blazing like a torch, fell from the sky on a*

> *third of the rivers and on the springs of water—the name of the star is Wormwood. A third of the waters turned bitter, and many people died from the waters that had become bitter. The fourth angel sounded his trumpet, and a third of the sun was struck, a third of the moon, and a third of the stars, so that a third of them turned dark. A third of the day was without light, and also a third of the night. The fifth angel sounded his trumpet, and I saw a star that had fallen from the sky to the earth. The star was given the key to the shaft of the Abyss.... The sixth angel sounded his trumpet, and I heard a voice coming from the horns of the golden altar that is before God. It said to the sixth angel who had the trumpet, "Release the four angels who are bound at the great river Euphrates." And the four angels who had been kept ready for this very hour and day and month and year were released to kill a third of mankind...*

More apocalyptic imagery was wrapped up in such descriptions as, *the earth giving way and the mountains falling into the heart of the sea, the waters roaring and foaming and the mountains quaking with their surging, the heavens vanishing like smoke, the earth wearing out like a garment*, its inhabitants *dying like flies, the heavens disappearing with a roar, the elements destroyed by fire, the earth and everything in it being laid bare, the stars of heaven and their constellations no longer showing their light, the sun being darkened and the moon not giving its light, the earth reeling to and fro like a drunkard, the heavens trembling and the earth shaking from its place...*

And while God had given Enoch a precise timeframe for when he could expect the floodgates to open on the earth, He seemed content leaving the people of this age with only general hints.

John would be lying if he said that the 2012 date (or if not that specific date then the future in general) didn't send tingles up his neck, things like Planet X leading the parade to his sleeplessness. The planet was supposedly scheduled to be dropping by sometime soon. Apparently, the tenth planet, named Eris, was really the Twelfth Planet that the Sumerians had called "Nibiru" five thousand years ago. That it was home to the Anunnaki (or the Anakim Nephilim that the Israelites fought) was just another ingredient in the whole end-of-days hype that seemed to reach back and touch the days of Noah. Coincidence? The leader of the Anunnaki, Marduk, was also sometimes thought to be interchangeable with Quetzalcoatl... Everything seemed to come full circle. The name the Sumerians gave the planet meant "planet of the crossing" because every three thousand six hundred years it crossed Earth's orbit. Reportedly five times the size of Earth and one hundred times its mass, its magnetic core was said to be so potent that it interfered with other planets' electromagnetic fields. Indeed, according to John's research, its influence on other planets was how astronomers even knew to look for it, NASA acknowledging its existence in 1982 (only thousands of years after the Sumerians). The planet supposedly had its own orbiting moons and a tail that stretched for millions of miles across space. Some believed that the planet would be passing between Earth and Mercury and that its effect on the smaller planet might cause it to explode. Ironically, and according to *some*, the Earth was supposed to travel through the tail of Eris once a year for seven years...the length of the biblical Tribulation.

Internet sites claimed that the planet's elite had been preparing for this encounter with the Anunnaki's home planet ever since modern science discovered it to be on an inbound course. Expecting earthquakes, volcanoes, tidal waves, major climate changes, even a shift in the polar axis of the planet, the governments of the world set out to silence the discovery, fearing that such information would lead to anarchy and the collapse of the world economy, "man-made global warming" just a disinformation campaign aimed at deflecting the warning signs of the inevitable planetary cataclysm. John didn't know about any of that, though he wasn't naïve enough to believe that the rulers of the world, if they had gained such information, would be going around announcing it. Some of the sites even suggested that the elite were preparing underground shelters in which they could ride out the cataclysm in order to birth their New World Order in its aftermath.

But John wasn't concerned with that stuff. It was the things on the news that stole his rapt attention, stuff about the New Madrid Fault coming to life, the Yellowstone caldera, solar storms, unprecedented seismic activity, birds falling dead from the sky, dead fish and other sea life washing ashore in astronomical quantities for reasons no one could determine…

According to Pastor Brian, the Masonic Christ would lead the world into a New Age, proclaiming himself to be God. But John couldn't see that happening without utter chaos setting the stage for its acceptance—the means by which the world would enter such a crisis the mystery. Would it be December 21, 2012?

He looked at a verse he kept tacked to his pegboard. It was from the book of Isaiah.

> *…They are full of superstitions from the East; they practice divination like the Philistines and clasp hands with the pagans…*

And resting above Ronald's two books that he'd kept was also printed out the damnation of all those who practiced magic arts, condemning any involvement with the occult.

There was a reason why God had wiped the so-called "Golden Age" or "First Time(s)" and all its marvelous wonders off the face of the earth—whether it had thrived between the first two verses of Genesis or had been destroyed by the Flood of Noah or quenched by the Israelites (or all three, since Zep Tepi was seen many times as a *re*-creation)—and there was a reason the prophecies of doom, no matter how sophisticated, were etched into stone by savages that had practiced slaughtering each other in their ceremonial worship to demons. Were all the megalithic workings, whether constructed before the Flood or after it, an attempt at resurrecting Satan's long-lost reign? And what of the esoteric doctrine that believed the New Age would be ushered in by the return of the Great Pyramid's missing capstone, the capstone said to hold the secrets of First Time?

All John knew was that time was short, whether due to planetary apocalypse, nuclear annihilation, the iron fist of a New World Order, or the relatively quick life of man in general. Someday, the billions of people on the planet would die, either realized all at once or gradually over the natural timeline of unfolding history. And it was with that certainty in mind that he and Henry had decided to dedicate themselves to things beyond this temporary world, a world that would one day (in some way or another) pass away.

John finished his coffee, anxious to return to his wife and forget everything for just five minutes, just long enough to stabilize his perception of reality within his own, practical world. He was about to get up when the phone rang. He heard Kristen answer it from another room.

She walked in and handed him his cell phone. "It's Henry."

John held the phone to his ear while reaching for Kristen's hand. "Hey."

"Johnny?" Henry's voice was shaking.

"Yeah?" John asked, sitting forward, his hand falling away from Kristen's.

"You know what today is, right?"

"Yeah…"

"The solstice?"

"I know what it is, Henry. What about it?"

There was a short pause. "I just got a phone call…from Bermuda."

John slowly rose to his feet, chills tingling his scalp. "And?"

"It was from Paul."

BOOK II

PRINCIPALITIES

AND

POWERS

AFTERMATH

"The men took me on to the fifth heaven and placed me, and there I saw many and countless soldiers, called Grigori, of human appearance, and their size was greater than that of great giants…"

—The Book of the Secrets of Enoch 18:1a

"And he testified to the Watchers, who had sinned with the daughters of men; for these have begun to unite themselves, so as to be defiled, with the daughters of men, and Enoch testified against all."

—Book of Jubilees 4:22

"Flee, therefore, fornication, my children, and command your wives and daughters, that they adorn not their heads and faces to deceive the mind…For thus they allured the Watchers who were before the flood; for as these continually beheld them, they lusted after them, and they conceived the act in their mind; for they changed themselves into the shape of men, and appeared to them when they were with their husbands. And the women lusting in their minds after their forms, gave birth to giants, for the Watchers appeared to them as reaching even to heaven."

—The Testament of Reuben 2:17a, 18, 19

"And there we saw the giants, the sons of Anak, which come of the giants: and we were in our own sight as grasshoppers, and so we were in their sight."

—Numbers 13:33 (KJV)

ONE

21st day of June. Bermuda, Crystal Caves

His eyes snapped open, and he shot upright. He cried out, the sudden movement sending exploding pain ripping across his torso and into his stomach, wrenching his bowels. He brought a hand to his side, almost expecting to find parts of his anatomy fleeing his body—slippery, wet things that were better off staying inside. But there was just the mending texture of flesh healing as well it could. No blood, no slimy ropes, just hot, burning pain boiling beneath an ugly wound.

Slowly, his senses somewhat clearing, he eased back down into the bed and stared up into the darkness, chest still heaving. He tried to swallow but couldn't, his throat lined with sandpaper, his tongue ash. The salty smell of sweat circled his head.

The dreams…

Another tremor of searing pain came slicing through his insides, and he squeezed his eyes shut against it, cursing the dream and his reaction to it. Such sudden movements only served to light the powder keg that his stomach had become. Once it exploded, the agony would roll in as a wave of red (that was how he saw the pain, in colors), erupt like a volcano, and then recede back to wherever it was that pain came from. And then it would repeat. Over and over like the tide it came, only his moon was an earthquake, its aftershocks rogue waves sent in rippled sets with only brief moments of relief between.

But the dreams…

They'd been part of his life as far back as he could remember, always a mystery. Until recently. But why should they be getting worse all of a sudden? Did his understanding of where they came from, of what they meant—of who he *was*—somehow graduate the nightmares to the next level? Now that you understand, here's part two? He didn't know. He'd meant to ask Henry about his own dreams, to get all the nitty-gritty details of his journey through dreamworld, to see if the revelation of his blood inheritance influenced them at all or not. He couldn't ask John or Chadwick because their epiphanies hadn't had time to roost.

Or maybe it was these new angles to his nightmare that led to his self-discovery in the first place? Was it important, the chicken or the egg and all that? He didn't see how it could be. It didn't matter how it started, only how it would end.

He took a deep breath and managed to roll onto his better side. Three weeks had passed since his escape from Osiris, but the internal wounds he'd endured at the hands of the demons were sure taking their good old time healing. He thought he could feel an emptiness inside him, things missing. Or maybe they replaced his organs with animal parts. Perhaps the heart beating in his chest was the heart of a horse. Now there was a thought to wake up to.

Forcing himself to a sitting position, Jackson swung his feet around and placed them on the smooth, limestone floor. Its coldness traveled up his legs and jarred some of the fog from his brain. He blinked. Darkness. He looked to the left, to the right. Darkness all around. He brought his hand up to his face and couldn't see it.

Struggling to get to his feet, he stood there swaying for a moment, taking in the scent of his locale. The dankness of the caves, the feel of the palmetto-thatched bed… There was no doubt where he was. Whether he could see it or not, he'd become more than familiar with his quarters. Which was also why he was confused, because where was the torch that he'd left lit by the door?

He walked through the dark, toward the entranceway, his fingers outstretched and probing. When they made contact with the wall, he moved his hand to the left, brushing the surface of the stone until he found the cedar doorframe. He ran his hand up, up, up…

He frowned in the darkness as he swiped his hand back and forth, looking not only for the torch, but also the bolts in the wall that had kept it fastened in place.

No torch. No bolts. No holes.

Suddenly, a wave of nausea struck him, and he turned his back to the wall, leaning against it, his head in his hands. A sense of vertigo began creeping up on him. He knew this feeling, the nausea. It wasn't from his wounds or the darkness, though. It was something else.

He stumbled back to the bed and reached beside it for his backpack. Finding it where he left it, he unzipped one of the side pockets and took out one of the dozens of matchbooks he'd brought along with him on the *Gegenes*. Most had been exhausted by now, but there were a few complete packs left. He struck one, and a little flame danced to life, casting a faint glow over the small room. As he walked through the shifting shadows and back to the doorway, another tsunami of lava came crashing into his side, doubling him over in mid-step, sending him to his knees. The match burned between his fingers while he fought the urge to scream. Finally, it passed, and he got back to his feet, sweating.

He held the light to the wall, examining the stone's surface where he knew the torch had been, but could find no such evidence of its existence. No burn marks, no scratches, no holes. Nothing had ever been fastened to this wall.

Confusion came and disoriented him for a second. He must be in someone else's room. And that's when he caught sight of the makeshift table beside the bed and the wooden cup resting atop it.

It all came back to him.

Some of the men—Purees, as Paul had come to call the pure-blooded island dwellers—had broken out a case of old wine they'd salvaged from a Graveyard ship years ago. They'd been waiting for a special occasion to drink the hundred-year-old wine, and the night before a battle you weren't likely to survive certainly qualified.

Jackson swore out loud as he limped over to the table, the nausea slapping him in the face. He brought the cup up to his nose but didn't need the proof of scent to verify what had happened. He knew perfectly well what they did, the source of his dizziness.

He threw the cup against the wall and heard it crack as the match winked out. The throwing motion sent explosions popping across his ribs, but he ignored them, too angry and worried now to care about the pain.

Finding his socks and boots, he pulled them on as quickly as he could. He was still in his jeans and an old, dirt-stained undershirt that Michael Jordan endorsed on television. It smelled terrible, years' worth of sweat, dirt, and last night's wine concocting a nice sour stench that Jackson would've never dreamt of wearing into enemy territory, but he had no time to do anything about it now.

He grabbed the backpack, winced as he slid his arms through the straps, and then grabbed the M16 that he'd left leaning against the wall in the corner of the room. There wasn't much ammo left for the thing—for any of the guns on the island, in fact. The Purees had salvaged most from the Graveyard over the years, and their intention to hide from Osiris rather than to engage in conflict had preserved a lot of ammunition to this day. But he knew that it was *this* day that would most likely see the exhaustion of every last bullet.

He headed out into the corridor, the mystery of the missing torch now lost beneath the revelation of what his friends had done to him.

The corridor was empty and mostly dark, only a single torch blinking off in the distance. The stillness was eerie and it fueled the growing desperation swirling in his gut. He forced himself to move faster.

A few days ago, he'd finally talked the others into allowing him the menial chore of sentry duty—which amounted to little more than sitting in a chair with a rifle resting across his lap. The humility of his predicament was maddening. And yet the dynamite packed between his ribs constantly preached the reality of his condition. He understood his limits. He just hated them. He'd spent his days listening to the plans being made by those around him, the attack on the pyramid complex, to be in the mechanism at the exact moment of the summer solstice. He had assumed he was going to play a role in all of it, that he would be there with them when the time came to transport out of this hell. He saw now that his friends must've had different plans for him.

It was impossible to know what time it was—what *day* it was, really—but a sinking feeling insisted he was too late. What that might mean, he couldn't even guess. He'd heard the theories, all the strange ideas concerning what could happen to them if Osiris escaped. Would the island fold up and vanish into nonexistence, its reality no longer sustained by the presence of the one who created it? Would those who used it end up back in the real Bermuda, or some distant epoch where the fallen angels still ruled as gods on the earth? The possibilities seemed as numerous and feasible as one's imagination allowed. But if his feelings were accurate and something *had* already happened, then the lonely passageway offered no clues as to what that something could be. It seemed that some torches were missing, but other than that…

Except that wasn't entirely true, was it? No, he realized. The feeling that he'd missed some important event was actually built upon another feeling. Or rather the absence of a feeling. And he knew.

Grasping a metal railing that had been taken from some victim of the Devil's Triangle, Jackson willed his way upward, one step at a time. When he finally reached the top, he was sweating again.

"Hey!"

The shout rebounded off the limestone walls around him, startling him. He turned, not having a sense of another's presence at all, and squinted into the darkness.

"Where are you going?" a young, squeaky-sounding voice demanded.

"Where are they?" Jackson asked, standing at the top of the stairs, still unable to make out the one talking.

"They left."

"When?"

"I don't know. Five, six hours ago."

Jackson swore. "No one's come back yet?"

"No."

"How many are still here?"

"Ten of us, plus the women."

Maybe he wasn't too late. But no, he knew he was. The solstice had passed, no doubt about it. "Why's it so dark in here?"

"Some of the torches are gone."

"They took them?"

"I don't think so," and the underlying tone to his voice added, *Why would they take torches in broad daylight, anyway?*

But Jackson figured they could've taken them in anticipation of the pyramid's dark chambers. Though that wouldn't explain his own missing torch and the absent holes in the stone that once secured it, would it?

Jackson turned with a grunt and continued topside.

"Where are you going?" the kid called after him.

Jackson kept walking.

* * * *

No one stood guard at the entrance of the cave, and Jackson found that to be a little odd given how strict they'd been with protecting their women. Unless the duty was given solely to the kid he'd just spoken to. But would they leave the purity of the island's femininity in the hands of a mere boy? Maybe. If they truly believed God had sent a handful of ex-Navy SEALs for such a time as this. He pushed it out of his head, the absence of more guards just one less obstacle to slow him down anyway.

Carefully contorting his body around jagged outcroppings and beneath sections of low-hanging ceiling, he continued toward open air. He could've used another exit, one less constricted, but this was the path that would put him closest to his destination.

The darkness turned to a grayish hue, allowing a visual orientation that was growing brighter with each terrible step. By now, however, with the opening in sight, there should've been a ray of golden light ahead. Either the opening had been further concealed, preventing the sun from penetrating the tomb, or it was night. But then a frigid burst of air slithered through the limestone womb, carrying with it a distant rumble and the smell of rain. And when he finally squeezed his way out of the caves, it wasn't night that greeted him, but a raging storm busy thrashing the island.

He was drenched instantly, the rain so heavy that he couldn't even make out the forest around him. Dark clouds blotted out the sun and gusts of wind leaned against him, making him stagger. All he could hear was the rain striking the ground. It was falling so hard that it felt like bee stings on his flesh. Then lightning cut through the sheets of rain and lit the sky, and he could see the forest beyond, bending over beneath the wind. He spit mouthfuls of water as he stood getting his bearings. He figured it was late afternoon, well past the sun's zenith, yet he'd known that already. From the moment he realized the feeling was gone, he'd known what time it was—or at least that it was beyond the solstice. And the boy just confirmed what day it was, so there were enough pieces to construct a timeline and at least one absolute occurrence in its center, but what that occurrence meant for him and everyone else left on the island was the true mystery that remained.

He pressed ahead, pushing against the wind and rain, moving toward the forest, rifle clutched firmly in his hands, pain a bonfire burning inside him.

Having gained some shelter from the storm within the density of swaying evergreens, he found it hard to keep his mind tethered to the task at hand. Instead, it kept asking questions to which there were no immediate answers. Had Henry, Paul, and Hunter drugged him as punishment for his crimes, intending to leave him here in this place for lying to them, for getting Nick and Chris killed? Or were they simply trying to protect him from himself, knowing that he wouldn't survive the mission in his condition but would nonetheless refuse to stay behind? He couldn't bring himself to blame them if it was their lack of trust in him that resulted in his being left behind. After all, he'd been learning not to trust himself lately. The fingers of the puppeteer seemed to slip into his mind at random times, leading him into a darkness he couldn't resist. But at least after realizing Ronald had deceived *him* as well as the others, that the blood of the Nephilim was running through *his* veins too, he could target the cause of such influence and put up a fight. Now, however, even that dark feeling of control was suddenly gone—even the little bit of it that he'd grown accustomed to ever since arriving in Bermuda. And that's how he knew that Osiris was gone.

The forest was thick enough to allow for some relief from the stinging rain, but what little light the dark clouds permitted was swallowed up by that same density. He shielded his face with his forearm, keeping the whirling debris from his eyes. He kept going, watching and listening as best he could.

An explosion of thunder shook the ground at the exact moment he sensed the presence of someone behind him. He swung the 16 around, wincing as the motion wrenched his wounds.

Just the leaning trees and waving branches.

He released his left hand from underneath the rifle and wiped it across his bald scalp, flinging the rainwater to the ground as he studied the forest. Then he returned his hand to the M16, bent low, and peered down its sights. The feeling was still there, like something was about to come bursting forth out of the weather at any moment.

Still nothing.

Trying to shake the feeling, he rose and continued.

A voice.

He stopped, listened. He knew it must be his mind playing tricks on him, that it would be impossible to hear anything over the rain pounding against the canopy above.

But there it was, whispering through the storm and raising the hair on his tattooed arms.

He knew the voice.

Eliot…

He spun to the right, the pain in his side suddenly a distant echo in light of the woman's voice.

Eliot, it came whispering again.

He peered through the rain, knowing it wasn't possible.

Eliot…

This time the voice came from his left, and he was certain that he would find her standing there when he swung around.

But, of course, she wasn't.

Eliot, it's me…

Emotion was flooding through him like a rainbow waterfall, each color a different feeling. But the most predominant of all the colors was that of fear, and that told him all he needed to know of his predicament—which is why anger came as the second widest swathe. He was being toyed with by something that scared the hell out of him, and it was twisting all the other emotions like a rusty blade in his soul. And that pissed him off.

He flexed his fingers around the weapon, ready to fire. A few minutes passed without hearing the voice, and he started moving again.

A hundred yards later, he wondered if he'd really heard her voice at all, or if he was, in fact, starting to crack. In any other place in the world, he wouldn't even entertain such a question, but this wasn't the same world he'd spent his years. Here, in this place, he'd learned that strange was the rule and things normally ludicrous weren't so silly. But her voice… Why now? And he wasn't sure if it was a question for a shrink or for some evil that was out there following him.

The voice called again, and this time when he turned, he found a clearing through the trees. There was something in the midst of the clearing, but the rain concealed it. It stood there, hovering like a blur, a smear of color behind the veil.

Eliot, come to me…

He stepped out from behind the tree line and into the blinding rainfall. Water running down his face and into his eyes, he still couldn't make out what was in the field. He didn't remember anything being there before. He checked his back side before continuing on, making sure there was no army of the Fallen about to fill him with arrows. Despite the violence of the storm, the sense of the island was as still and as empty as that of the caves. He didn't like it.

The further into the field he got, the bigger the bright color became. Soon he couldn't see anything around him at all, just a constant, white sheet of rain.

And a pink, stone house.

He blinked, expecting the mirage to disappear. It didn't. He listened for the voice, for his name. His *first* name, a name not many in his life had called him by. But she had.

A few more moments passed, and still the house stood some fifty yards away. Crouching low, he moved as quickly as his injuries would allow, feeling the crude stitches in his side pulling at his flesh.

He swept the rifle over the pastel cottage, covering the windows and doors as if goblins might be watching him, ready to pounce. *Something* was, of that he was sure. But there was no sign of it.

The low, square building was familiar in that it was identical to a hundred others that sat scattered atop Bermuda's lush hills. What it was doing here in *this* Bermuda, he had no idea. As long as he'd been here, he'd neither seen nor heard of any houses. And one this close to the caves would've been common knowledge for sure.

Turning, he faced back out into the clearing, aiming the rifle at the invisible forest he knew was out there. He wondered if he could be in a henge. He hadn't noticed any monoliths or other megalithic architecture, no gypsum-covered circles… Not that he believed an entire house could be transported through one, but what other explanation was there? And yet, as far as he knew, the henges and portals only transported to different parts of the same island. If they could be used to transport back and forth, from one version of Bermuda to the next, then surely there would be no need to use the pyramid complex at the solstice. Then again…

He looked up through the rain and could just barely make out smoke coming from the chimney on the roof. That was odd. Maybe the goblins were home after all. He reached out to touch the front door, almost expecting his hand to pass straight through it like a hologram. But his fingers touched wood, and the door moved beneath them.

There was that old, familiar voice in his head. Not hers, but his own. It was the voice that saved his life more times than he could ever count and in more places throughout the world than he could remember, and it screamed at him now, urging him to run. But he couldn't. He had to know.

Please, come to me…

He pushed the door open and went inside, pulling it closed behind him. The house was still, silent. The rain beat on the roof and thrashed the windows as his clothes dripped on the tile floor, forming a lake around his boots. He held the rifle steady, aiming it further into the house. The kitchen was to his right, cordoned off from the other rooms by a long counter seating two barstools. To his left was the living room and dining room, visible from his position through an open window that looked through the wall beside him and into the double room. Two large windows shielded by Victorian-style curtains, a brown leather sectional couch, pictures on the wall, a rather custom-looking coffee table resting atop a Persian, a sixty-inch LCD TV fixed above a hand crafted chestnut cabinet, a dark lacquered dinner table set on a wooden floor... There were two candles on the dining room table, lit and dancing. Lightning flashed, shadows creeping up and down the walls, over the floor, across the furniture. Thunder rattled glassware in an unseen hutch.

It was all quite impossible.

He walked forward until he was past the stools and counter and turned into the kitchen. His wet boots made the stone floor slippery, and he placed his steps carefully. The kitchen was on the smaller side, which one would expect in a cottage, but all top-of-the-line stuff. A big black refrigerator, a stove with a microwave above it, wraparound cabinets, garbage disposal, recessed lighting over marble countertops...

But it was the microwave that captured his attention. Or rather its bright green digital display.

2:43.

He turned to the refrigerator and yanked the door open, unsure what he was about to find. Severed heads, giant toes in twelve packs, pots of eyeballs...

Salad dressing. Orange juice. Eggs. Milk. Bread. Lunchmeat. A bottle of Coke.

The light from the fridge sliced down his body and across the kitchen floor as spiders rappelled down his spine.

Standing in the glow of the tall machine, the cool air hit his wet clothes and made gooseflesh of his skin. He shivered first from the cold and then from the spiders.

A carton of milk standing on the bottom shelf had its sell-by date stamped for all to see.

JUN 27 11.

He tried to compute the meaning of this but wasn't exactly comfortable with any of the choices that came to mind. He closed the door and left the kitchen behind, heading back to the hall.

As he approached the living room, he threw the light switch on the wall. He didn't really expect anything to happen, but then again, the light in the refrigerator was working. But nothing did happen.

Eliot...

He spun back, toward the TV.

Eliot...

This time it came from behind him, down the hall and further into the house.

He was pleading with himself, trying to run, yet a more dominant part *needed* to know…

He followed after the voice, his heart pounding in his chest, his emotions a hurricane. A door came up on his left, and he opened it, finger held ready against the trigger.

A bathroom.

After quickly absorbing all the normal details of a nicer restroom, he moved to the sink. Looking down at it, he reached for the faucet. When he turned the knob, water came spilling into the sink. He stared at the flow, his mind unraveling. Plumbing.

He was dreaming. Had to be. This was just a new chapter added to his old nightmare.

The realization brought a strange sense of relief, and as he looked up into the mirror, he felt his muscles relax just a bit.

It was all a dream. In his head and unable to harm him. He closed his eyes, gripped the edge of the sink with one hand, and took a few deep breaths. When he opened his eyes, someone was in the mirror, standing behind him.

He spun so fast that he was certain he'd snapped a stitch or two, but there was only the empty shower stall.

Thunder rumbled, and rain continued hammering the roof. Lightning streaked through the sky.

Sweat and rainwater stung his eyes as he pressed his hand against his side. Blood. He swore and left the bathroom, wanting to find the source of the voice he knew so well, dream or not.

But it *is* just a dream, he told himself, stepping back into the hall. He shifted the weight of the backpack.

Eliot, I'm in here, the voice whispered. It came from behind the closed door at the end of the hall.

"Just a dream," he said out loud, half expecting not to hear his own voice.

He stood facing the door, which lit up every time lightning flashed through the windows.

A deep breath. Another.

He reached a hand forward, grasped the handle, and turned it.

The door opened, and he was greeted by a bright bulb shining from the ceiling of the main bedroom.

"Dreaming…"

The room contained a neatly made queen bed and two antique-style dressers. They seemed to match the hand-crafted signature he'd seen in the rest of the house. A hamper stood to his right against the wall. Clothes were spilling out of it and piling onto the floor. Jeans, shorts, sundresses, bras, boxers, bathing suits… He noticed the framed pictures that lined the walls, and he recognized the background in most of them. Bermuda and its cruise ships, pastel-colored houses, crowded beaches, mopeds and restaurants.

Just a dream. It was the reason he hadn't been able to see the kid in the cave, why there was no evidence for the torch that had been fastened to the wall in his room just the night before. Just a dream, his mind missing certain details in its production of this current episode. He stared at the pictures of this happy, young couple and recalled when, not so long ago, his own house had known such things.

Eliot...

He turned his head to look back over his shoulder, wanting so desperately to see her, yet simultaneously terrified by the prospect of it. The dream, as all dreams do, would have to end eventually, so he might as well try to speed things up if he could, to get to the point, the climax. Maybe then he could wake up and join Henry and the rest in getting out of this place.

But there was only a closet behind him, its two doors open in a seeming gesture of invitation. How he knew this, he wasn't sure and guessed it didn't matter. It was a dream. You know intuitively in dreams.

He turned to face the open closet and lowered the rifle. What power did such a weapon wield in dreamworld? Peering into the space, he could make nothing out beyond the open doors. No hanging clothes, no racks of shoes. Not anything. In fact, as he forced his feet forward, he noticed that the room's light itself failed to seep into the small area, no shadows or even shades of gray. Just a perfect blank space.

Eliot, I'm here...

There was no doubt where the voice was coming from now, and this had to be the end, the revelation. Her face.

He stepped closer.

Closer.

With each step, the air grew colder, as if the closet was a doorway into space.

"Denise?" he whispered.

Eliot...

His boots were an inch from the line separating carpet from void. That close, and still he couldn't see into the closet, couldn't detect any variance of color or reflection that would emanate from a painted wall.

It was a portal to some other place, like the dark circles he'd seen on the walls in the temple, transporters to other spots on the island. His mind was borrowing from recent circumstances and adding them to a more distant past in the creation of this weird vision. She didn't visit him enough in his dreams and, nightmare or not, he needed to see her now.

Slowly, he lifted his left hand toward the blackness, the knowledge of it all being a dream not able to keep his heart from pounding and electricity from shooting through his body. Just before touching the divide, he stopped, hand trembling in the air, suddenly unsure.

And then a chorus of screams came exploding from the closet, riding a rush of wind that moved the pictures and lifted the curtains in the room.

Then it was gone, leaving only the lingering sensation of some sinister presence behind. A presence that was real, crushing. If he *was* sleeping, then something must be hovering over his unconscious body, influencing his mind with its probing fingers.

Wake up, he told himself, no longer interested in seeing her and abandoning all hopes of getting to touch her again.

Starting to withdraw his hand from the darkness, a bony, disfigured arm suddenly shot forth from nowhere and latched on to his wrist. Then it tried to pull him in.

His muscles flexed, bulging, as he wrestled against it. The hand was only bones—phalanges, metacarpus, ulna, and radius—held together by cords of ligaments and tendons—palmaris longus, flexor carpi, radialis, flexor digitorum sublimis—with some rotten muscle and patches of flesh wrapped tight enough to keep it from falling apart. It smelled awful, like sulfur and rot. But it was so strong.

Jackson swung the 16 up with one hand, and the barrel disappeared into the closet. He pulled the trigger.

Nothing happened.

Another hand shot out of the nothingness and grabbed his ankle. He dropped the rifle and planted his palm against the doorframe, bracing himself. The arm attached to the hand gripping his wrist came further out of the closet, revealing itself up to the elbow. Jackson let go of the doorframe just long enough to bring his hand down hard on the bony joint. The grip loosened a little, and he was able to wriggle free from the skeleton. As he turned to run, another hand came out at him and grabbed his other foot. Both the hands gripping his ankles pulled at the same time, ripping his feet out from under him, landing him hard on his side.

The explosion of pain brought with it a white flash that almost knocked him out. Gasping, he reached out, his fingernails trying to find a hold somewhere in the carpet as he was pulled toward the closet.

He spun onto his back, the pack keeping him in somewhat of a sitting position, and his feet crossed as he tried wriggling free of the hands. The hands that had his ankles, however, were not the same hands of whatever burnt corpse had grabbed his wrist, but of some demon. Sharp talons and leathery skin that leaked black, oil-like fluid were clawing at his skin, tearing his jeans. Jackson did not want to go with this thing. He needed to wake up. Now.

He screamed, his muscles bulging in his neck, arms, and shoulders. He was sliding across the carpet, no way to slow himself down. The space was a mere few feet and the time was only a couple seconds, but it felt like a mile and an hour.

When his crossed feet were pulled into the open closet and through the veil, they vanished, crossing the threshold into some other world. He was going in.

At the last second, however, he reached out and grabbed the rifle from off the floor beside him, swung it up, and pulled the trigger. This time, the gun worked, and spent shells rained down on the floor around him as the recoil rocked him back and forth while he screamed. The bullets tore through the clawed hands, and they opened, releasing him with a hellish shout that echoed through the bedroom, over the rain.

He had disappeared up to his thighs before he was able to stumble backward across the floor. Almost out of the bedroom, a creature came lurching out of the closet, materializing out of nothing and reaching for him with open claws. But some dark, liquid-like sheen that had been invisible before prevented the demon from fully entering into the bedroom. It stretched beneath its advances like some kind of slime-based shrink-wrap, refusing to tear loose.

Jackson emptied the remaining clip into the demon, but the holes the rifle punched through its skinny, writhing body only filled an instant later, swallowed up by its oily composition.

The creature's oblong head snapped back and forth, its mouth opening and closing, sharp, needle-like teeth snapping as it roared in frustration. As it thrashed, the pair of ram's horns protruding from its head smashed wildly into the open doors on either side of it, cracking and splintering the wood.

Finally, it drew back, allowing the substance it was wrestling against to relax and disappear again. The creature, which to Jackson seemed like some version of Ridley Scott's *Alien* twisted with the Greek god of the wild, Pan, left with a hollow moan that echoed out from whatever pit it returned to.

Jackson just sat there, holding his breath, his body still, paralyzed, trying to make sense of what he'd just seen. Then he was back on his feet, empty rifle in hand and stumbling through the house. He burst out through the front door and threw himself into the storm.

Sitting there in the grass, beneath the angry sky, he turned back to the pink house and stared.

Whatever was happening, it was no dream.

TWO

21st day of June, 2011. Bermuda. Pyramid Complex.

Paul touched the side of his head and felt a warm river run over his hand, travel down his wrist, circle his forearm. He stood, swaying, trying to gain his senses, to remember what happened. The last thing he remembered was cutting his way through half a dozen savages as the others followed Chadwick to the pyramid. He held his arm out in front of him and tried to focus on his blood-covered tattoos. Everything was still fuzzy, the fog in his head squeezing. The familiar inked python that wrapped his arm multiplied and blurred beneath the streams of blood. A dizzy spell tilted the floor, and he stumbled to maintain his balance. He went sideways and collapsed against the wall, the corridor spinning, forcing him to sit. He closed his eyes and waited for the world to stop reeling.

As he sat there, a swirling image came into his head. The giant lifting Hunter up into the air on his spear and flinging him down off the temple steps. *No.* He swore, putting his left hand out on the floor to steady himself. It doubled and tripled in his vision, and he leaned closer, squinting, trying to bring them all into one. When finally his hand stopped doing its Mr. Miagi exercise (wax on, wax off and all that), his last two fingers came into focus with a shot of pain that may or may not have been triggered by the sight of them. He swore louder, leaned back against the wall, and shut his eyes again.

A few, long minutes later, clarity finally introduced him to the half-naked men that were littered throughout the stone passageway, lying butchered in a sticky lake of blood. He was pretty sure he'd done that, though he couldn't remember it. The only thing he did remember was the clanging chaos that swallowed him up and the sure feeling of finality.

Blood ran into his eyes, and he wiped it away. He looked around for something he could use as a bandage. As he reached out to grab the nearest corpse, he stopped, getting a better look at the fingers on his left hand. He held them out in front of him, examining them more closely. He groaned.

His pinky was dangling sideways, hanging from the second knuckle by a flap of skin, while its neighbor, the ring finger, was cut halfway through. It didn't hurt as bad as it should, but it would. No doubt about that. He turned his attention back to the body beside him and pulled it closer. There was a knife within reach, too, and he used it to cut away the dead guy's loincloth. Once he had it free, he wrapped it around his head, stopping the flow of blood. The material smelled worse than any postgame locker room he'd ever been in, and it had his stomach heaving and turning.

There was a pleasant breeze whistling through the corridor, and if it wasn't for the reeking halo around his head, he might've said to hell with it all and just retreated back to Slumberville. The cool stone against his aching body was also trying to convince him to stay there on the floor. But the smell was too much. Instead, he finished his self-examination, finding a few more red stripes he wasn't in any danger of bleeding out from, and got to his knees.

To his left, down the hall and into the breeze, he noticed what looked like natural light flooding through the intersecting corridor. Fresh air. He used the knife to steal clothing from another body, wrapping his fingers, hand, and wrist with it, and then got to his feet and headed for the light.

As he passed another dead body, he reached out to grab the sword that was sticking up out of its sternum. One strong jerk should free it from the bone without him even having to break stride.

But the sword didn't budge, and it jerked his shoulder back, stopping him dead in his tracks. Letting go of the handle, he studied the crude weapon. The movement wasn't right. Even if the sword couldn't be loosed from the breast bone, the force of his yank should've at least moved the body. That there had been no give at all seemed…unnatural.

Tucking the knife into his belt, he grasped the sword's handle with both hands. He didn't need the sword, there were plenty of others lying around, but he needed to know. He pulled, his muscles swelling from the strain, and the feeling in his two severed fingers came screaming back all at once, splintered bones and shredded tendons rubbing together like a fiddle concert.

The sword didn't move a whisper. And neither did the body it was lodged in.

He let go of the sword and took a step back, his fingers on fire, and started kicking the body.

It didn't move. The head with its wide, sightless eyes didn't wobble and roll on the stone, its toes didn't turn to point in a new direction, nothing. It was solid, the sword, the body, and the floor all one immovable entity.

He knelt and tried slipping his good hand between the floor and the corpse, but there was no space in which to insert his fingers. The two—flesh and stone—were one, as if the floor had melted into a liquid wax and then hardened around the body.

Paul spit, got back to his feet, and decided on another sword that was lying nearby. He hadn't the slightest clue what had happened to the guy, how his body could've sunk into the stone like that, but he left it behind, chasing the light.

When he reached the top of the hall, he found that it ended in a T, light streaming in from the left. He turned into it and stared, not at one of the strange bulbs he'd seen before, but at daylight.

The tall corridor stretched out before him for another fifty yards before meeting sky. He'd found his exit, the wind whistling past him. He looked back over his shoulder to make sure nothing was trying to sneak up from behind. Nothing was coming for him. He went after the opening.

As he got closer to the light, a cool mist came to greet him with the breeze, as did the faint sound of thunder rumbling from beyond. He didn't care, he only wanted out of this tomb.

He was just twenty feet from the end of the corridor when a face appeared from out of the stone wall beside him. Only it didn't just appear. It had been there like some twisted wall decoration, mouth agape in frozen animation, eyes wide and bulging. Paul wondered if the "mighty men of renown" from Noah's day used to mount human faces on the walls of their cities, too, slicing the head top to bottom and hanging it like a trophy animal. He looked at the bearded face, touched it. The flesh was soft, still warm. Drool hung from its lips.

Lightning tore through the sky outside, illuminating the dim hall with a burst of rapid flashes. One of them lit up something else in the wall, about two feet from the face and six inches down.

Four small bumps protruded from the wall.

Reaching out, he touched them.

Fingernails.

He took a step to the left, to the other side of the head, and there found four more fingers, these extending from the wall at the knuckles.

He backed away, flexing his own fingers around the handle of the sword, wanting to be away from the place even more. He turned and covered the last twenty feet, walking through the rain that the wind was driving into the mouth of the opening. By the time he reached the end of the corridor, he was soaking wet.

Almost leaping straight into the storm, assuming there would be a giant step beneath, he caught himself at the last second and saved himself from plummeting to his death—which, he marveled, would've been a ridiculous way to die after all he'd managed to survive. Standing there, the toes of his boots hanging over the edge and into the air, he reached a hand out to steady himself.

Beneath him was no outward progression of ziggurat steps, but the pointed tops of evergreens.

What the hell?

With his wrapped hand holding onto the wall beside him, he leaned forward as much as he dared, hanging out into the air and looking down. He might as well have been leaning out the window of a skyscraper. This side of the ziggurat went straight down before disappearing into a forest he was sure hadn't been there before. Looking up, the side of the temple melted with the fast-moving storm clouds and a sense of vertigo swept over him.

He fell backward into the corridor to keep from swaying out into the sky.

Sitting there, he just stared ahead, watching the storm. It didn't make any sense. He must've been pushed into one of those portals while fighting, because this couldn't be the same temple he'd entered with the others. That ziggurat had been in the middle of the open pyramid complex, not to mention that it was stepped in design while this one was…*what?* An obelisk building? Did they make such things?

Another bolt of lightning branched through the sky right before him, and he could feel its heat. He looked back to the head in the wall, to the fingers.

"What the hell happened?" he mumbled.

* * * *

As he moved through the vast, empty corridors, his mind raced with all the possibilities of what could've happened while he was unconscious. The sun was well on its way to setting, so by now, the complex had either functioned the way Chadwick had theorized or it hadn't. Were his friends still here, or had they escaped? And escaped to where? What about Osiris? Did he take his armies with him? Is that why it was so quiet now? Conversations from their many meetings came flooding back into his memory, all the conjecture about what could happen to the island if Osiris left it. And for a second, Paul saw himself running aimlessly through empty hallways for the rest of time, trapped in a snow-globe universe comprised of only himself and this ancient skyscraper. It wasn't a pleasant thought, but it brought back some of the drivel Chadwick had spouted about the pyramid complex at Giza, the missing capstone that supposedly held the secrets of First Time, the star shafts' stellar orientation, the alignment with Orion and the Milky Way circa 10500 BC, the megalithic geometry used in its construction along with pi and phi, Thoth the Atlantean being the only one privy to its secrets, the prisoner of the pyramid, the acoustics tuned to F-sharp, the pyramid used as a gateway for the gods, Enoch's Royal Arch, the pharaoh's journey to the Duat…

It hadn't made any sense to him then, and it certainly didn't make any more sense to him now, but it did seem suddenly relevant.

A dirty foot was sticking out of the ceiling high above him, further evidence that *something* had happened at the solstice. Chadwick must've had some clue as to what he was talking about, even if no one else did. But *what* happened?

Finally, after what seemed like hours, he found himself standing in the temple's entranceway, and the scene before him on *this* side of the temple at least proved familiar. He wasn't in some giant obelisk temple after all. Nor was he confined to its empty halls forever. Staggered steps stretched down and away from him, leading to the courtyard they'd battled in just hours before. The storm was flooding the steps, turning the whole side of the structure into a massive waterfall. At the base of the ziggurat, the bodies of all those that had fallen on the steps were piled up, torrents of water shooting past them and forming a lake in the open yard. Beyond, Paul could make out the vague shape of the swaying forest. There was no sign of battle, of anything other than the ferocity of the storm, and he wondered if he *was* the only living person left on the island.

He moved through the rain, trying to find the human-sized steps built into the larger, Nephilim steps. He stood no chance of navigating the monster blocks in these conditions, not without inviting a broken back. Locating the stairs, he tossed the sword aside, not wanting to impale himself if he slipped during the descent. He went down backward, one careful step at a time. The cold water pouring over the steps reached to his elbows, and his damaged fingers ached.

The wind whipped around the temple with hurricane force, threatening to carry him away if he didn't keep his body pressed as closely to the structure as possible, all the while the torrent of water trying to flush him straight to the bottom. And half a dozen steps from the ground, he finally did lose his footing. He landed hard on his side, the wind knocked from his lungs. The waterfall carried him over the dead bodies and dumped him into the courtyard, where he found himself floating on his back, rain pelting his face. He lay there for a while, just floating in the cold rainwater, trying to regain his breath without inhaling water at the same time. His ears dipped below the surface of the water, and the sound of the rain striking the lake was actually soothing. If it wasn't so cold, it might even be relaxing, the pool cleansing his skin of blood, sweat, and filth. He spread his arms and legs, trying to let the cold massage some of the soreness out of him, or at least numb him to it.

He wondered, as he often did in such nonsensical moments, how he got here. To this place. What had been the key point in his life that sealed this fate? What precise turn would he have to miss in order to avoid giants and fallen angels and portals to other realities? Or perhaps there was still hope that it was all a dream, that he might just open his eyes at any moment and be—

Be where? He couldn't even remember what he'd been doing before Jackson called him. Or even before the news came of Henry's disappearance. Whatever it was, it obviously had to be better than what he was doing now, floating on his back in a lightning storm at the foot of a Nephilim temple.

He opened his eyes, his thoughts suddenly disrupted, and sat up. He heard something, low and distant, drifting through the rain. He looked back up to the temple and could barely make out its shadow under the weather. Dark skies and lightning were all he could see.

He closed his eyes.

But there it was again. A shout.

Getting to his feet, he looked around the courtyard, blinking the water from his vision. Unmoving shapes of lifeless bodies and the fallen giant fitted in reflective armor that John had ridden down the steps, smashing its head apart. But there was no movement catching his eye, and it was nearly impossible to pinpoint which direction the shouting was coming from, though it had to be close for him to hear it over the rain. He turned to the woods, didn't think it was coming from there, so he started sloshing through the lake, heading back toward the temple. The noise was growing louder, but he assumed it was probably the wind howling through the complex.

And then he heard it clearly. It was coming from the pile of bodies at the temple's base.

"Help!"

He struggled against the flow of water and finally reached the bodies. He ducked beneath the arch of water pouring off the last step and began pulling at the pile.

"Get me out of here!"

He grabbed the first carcass, tugging at it and moving it into the waterfall until the current carried it away. When he turned over the next body, he saw a face he recognized. A young Brit that had arrived on the island with his parents when he was just an infant. The poor kid survived both his parents in this place but would now never get a glimpse of the world he was born in. His midsection was open, organs unraveling and swimming out of his corpse like eels. Paul brought a hand down across the kid's eyes, closing them, and let the water carry him away, too. If he hadn't been so accustomed to death, he might've shed a tear.

He sent two more bodies on their way before finally finding the source of the shouting.

"'Bout time!" Hunter shouted over the water. "I been calling for you for five minutes!"

Disbelief ran back and forth through Paul's mind, and he blinked. He blinked again but still, there was his black friend, his comrade and brother. But it wasn't possible. He'd seen the Nephilim spear go through him, saw him land against the last step. There was no way he could've survived. And yet there he was, staring up at him. "Thought you were dead!" was all he could say.

"Not yet!"

Paul grabbed him beneath the arms. "Gonna let the water carry you into the yard!"

"Can't wait!"

"Be just like your favorite Sesame Place ride!"

"Very funny, you piece of—"

"Here we go!"

Paul pulled, his torn fingers protesting, and Hunter screamed.

The first few feet were difficult because Hunter's heels were dragging heavily through the mud. But then Paul got him beneath the water pouring off the pyramid and he drifted away on his own. Paul followed him.

"I can't move, man!" Hunter called out when Paul came up wading beside him. "Can't even feel my body!"

Paul reached down, grabbed him by the foot, and pulled him through the lake, toward the forest. As he neared the woods, Paul looked back down at Hunter and for the first time got a good look at his wound. The head of the spear that impaled him had been large enough to tear most of Hunter's chest and back apart, and it had. It seemed his whole chest was open, like he'd fallen on a grenade. It didn't make sense that he was alive. And that wasn't to mention the shattered spine he should have sustained from his landing. Regardless of how he was still alive, though, if he was paralyzed, Paul knew there wouldn't be much anyone could do for him. It was only a matter of time. "It's probably a good thing!" he answered back.

"That bad?"

Paul didn't respond, just focused on getting into the woods.

Once he had Hunter lying on solid ground, hands folded atop his wide, gaping wound, Paul sat leaning against a cedar tree, staring out at the ziggurat and the surrounding temple complex as he caught his breath. Except that there was no surrounding complex.

"What happened?" Hunter asked. The rain wasn't so loud now that they were beneath the forest canopy, and they didn't have to shout.

"I don't know."

"Did they make it?"

"I don't know." Paul looked over his friend once more and decided he should probably have his wounds wrapped. Not that it should do any good, but here he was still breathing, so…

Thunder rolled through the forest.

"What happened to you?" Hunter asked next.

Paul stood. "I tried buying them some time."

Hunter coughed, and blood came bubbling from his chest, oozing up between his fingers.

"We gotta get you bandaged up." Paul walked out of the woods and back into the rain. Finding a floating corpse that suited his need, he got to work removing its pants. "Sorry," he mumbled to the dead guy, and left him floating face down without his dignity.

He took the jeans back to Hunter. "This ain't gonna feel too good, though I suppose any feeling should be a good sign." He slid the belt out of the loops, setting it aside. Then he kneeled. "Ready?"

"I was born—" He screamed as Paul rolled him onto his side.

"Child."

"I'm beat up pretty bad," he said through clenched teeth.

"You'll be fine. Quit whining."

He pulled his own shirt off and ripped it in half, then folded both pieces into sopping squares. He put one of them beneath Hunter's hand, over the wound in front, and placed the crotch of the jeans against his back, wrapping the legs around and tying them loosely over the shirt. Then he slipped the other piece of cloth beneath the seat of the pants, against the exit wound in his back. It was ridiculous, like a Band-Aid over a gunshot, but there wasn't much else he could do. Even if a medivac were to airlift him off the island and fly him to the nearest state-of-the-art facility, there would be little, if anything, they could do for him. Not unless they had a bunch of spare organs on hand. He rested Hunter down onto his back again and looked him in the eye, his hands gripping the jeans.

Hunter sighed. "Oh—"

Paul pulled the pant legs tight, and Hunter screamed, lifting his arms in protest. As he double knotted the legs, Paul smiled. "Look at that. You moved your arms." He patted him on the side of the face. "That's good."

"You sonofa—" But Paul's bandaged hand was suddenly clamped over his mouth before he could finish.

Paul pressed a finger against his lips, eyes peering through the trees, searching. When he lifted his hand from Hunter's mouth, Hunter kept silent, his own eyes large and swiveling around, trying to detect what had alarmed Paul.

"Company," Paul whispered. "In the courtyard."

Hunter couldn't turn his head enough to see in that direction. "What is it?"

"Giant."

And sure enough, walking toward them through the flooded courtyard was a glass-armored giant, sword in hand, hatred burning in its eyes. It seemed to be looking for them, as if it could detect their heartbeats but was having trouble locating them through the storm. It was only a matter of time, though.

Paul slapped Hunter on the shoulder and smiled. "Stay here." He stood, watched the giant get closer for another second or two, and then charged out of the forest.

He didn't know what he was doing. He had only the knife tucked into his belt and that sure wouldn't be enough against the armored Nephilim. But he had to keep the monster away from Hunter if his friend had any chance of surviving the next few minutes.

The giant spotted him through the trees and came to a stop. It stood there, tracking him with its eyes, watching him run. Its armor reflected the lightning, illuminating it like a bulb under a darkening sky.

When Paul burst out of the woods and into the courtyard, he was a mere twenty yards away from the giant. But the thing didn't move to chase him. It turned its head away from Paul and looked back into the forest, toward Hunter.

Paul cried out over the rain, "What are you waiting for, you—"

A loud bang of thunder drowned out the expletive, but the giant's eyes snapped back on him as if it both heard and understood it. And then it started running.

Paul kept moving, sloshing through a foot of water, looking around for anything he could use as a weapon. The giant was gaining on him fast, the water no more than a mere puddle under its long strides. Should he turn into the woods? Try to lose the giant in there? Or should he turn to the ziggurat steps? He'd never be able to make it up the waterfall, but then maybe the monster wouldn't either. The steps might be his only weapon. He changed course, heading for them.

But the giant anticipated the move and positioned to cut him off.

Paul swore. There was no way that he would make it to the temple first. *The woods, then.*

He cut right, heading back into the forest. He could feel the giant gaining on him, could feel its breath on the back of his neck. He pushed himself harder, kept his fatigued legs pumping through the water. He kept expecting the top half of himself to suddenly slide away, to topple over with a splash and to watch his legs keep on trucking for the woods without him. But the sword never swung, and before he knew it, he was just fifteen feet from the forest. *Gonna make it…*

Something struck him in the back, lifting him off his feet and throwing him forward, landing him on his face.

It felt like a ninety-five-mile-an-hour boulder struck him in the back, and for a moment, he was stuck lying on his chest, paralyzed. He could see the woods right there in front of him but couldn't make his body do anything about it. *Move.*

Slowly, his body began to respond, and he rolled onto his back. There, at his feet, was the giant's seven-foot sword. It was the hilt that had struck him. Apparently, the beast wanted to have some fun with its prey before eating it. Paul looked up and watched the mirrored armor materialize out of the rain before him.

He tried moving backward, but the giant was already at his feet, bending over and retrieving the sword.

Paul got back onto his stomach and started crawling for the trees. Behind him, he heard the giant start to laugh.

THREE

21st day of June, 2011. Bermuda. Twilight

Jackson could see what should be the Atlantic Ocean through the trees, lying past a mangrove swamp off to his right. He was staying within sight of the shore, following the coast along what was once North Shore Road. His view of Ireland Island, which was growing dimmer and dimmer in the darkening storm, would let him know when to turn into the forest and toward the complex.

North Shore Road.

He looked down at his feet, to the mud sucking at his boots, and couldn't help from being taken back—back to the day he'd walked this very tract of land, her hand in his. He could hear her laughter over the rain, could remember their conversation as they trekked all the way from their hotel to the movie theatre in Hamilton. He couldn't remember what the movie was, didn't remember caring. That was the day before he met Ronald, the day before everything changed.

He tried to concentrate on his surroundings, to let go of the past. That's what everyone said you had to do, right? Let go of the past. Everyone was a psychologist these days. Only problem was, the second you tried putting shoes on the advice, it turned to fog in your hands. Air…foolishness…*words*. That's all it was. Preached by people who had no clue what they were talking about because they'd never been there themselves. Let go of the past, Jack. *Yeah, sure.*

He tried to divorce himself from the two different worlds, the two different times. He had to move faster. It was growing dark, and he was only now turning inland toward the complex. He didn't have a flashlight in his backpack, and he had no intention of relying on split-second flashes of lightning to guide his way through the forest. Not after what he just saw in that house. Giants and flying scorpion creatures were one thing, but whatever was trying to get out of the closet belonged to a whole other league of evil.

He kept going, forcing himself deeper and deeper into the woods, his body telling him to stop. But he didn't dare stop or go back. There were answers awaiting him at the pyramid, and they were answers he needed more than anything else in the world.

A hundred yards later, he took a few seconds to rest, leaning against a palmetto tree for support. Every breath was a switchblade in his side, and he doubled over. He'd been stabbed with a switchblade before, and the feeling was certainly comparable. Stab-stab-stab. Three quick thrusts, in and out so fast it'd taken a few seconds to even register what happened, to see the blood start flowing. That was before the SEALs. Before a lot of stuff. But he never forgot the intensity of the attack, the cold brutality of it. Or the pain. He closed his eyes and tried taking shallow breaths, but his pumping heart wanted more, his lungs begging for gulps, not sips. He thought of a cramp with scissors and started to laugh at the picture of it. *I'm losing my damn mind.* And he laughed harder, the cramp man cutting away with each roll of laughter. But he couldn't stop, and he was laughing and crying at the same time.

A burst of lightning seeped through a window in the canopy and lit up the forest floor. He saw something there, through the rain and his tears. Forms scattered across the flooded soil.

The crack of thunder that followed sobered him up, snapping him out of his psychosis. *Put it behind you, Jack. Get over it already.* He stood straight, trying to hold on to the image the flash of light had revealed. But the scene faded from his mind's eye before he could do anything with it. So he moved forward, curious to find out what was around him.

A body. That's what it was. He knew it before he got within ten feet of it. It was dark in the woods, but it wasn't *that* dark. Not yet. He'd seen his fair share of dead bodies in his lifetime. Had helped many, many bodies make the transition to dead himself, so he recognized death even before he could smell it. There was nothing like it, the dead. The human corpse. He'd discovered early on that a presence tended to linger over it, a heavy feeling like a wet blanket draped over the world, dripping of some great mystery, a clue as to the true meaning and purpose of existence (though the clue never seemed more than a shadow vaguely detected in the periphery of some sideways glance). Or perhaps it was the absence of a presence taken for granted, not detected until it was gone. He didn't know, and after having scores of the dead cross his path, he ultimately stopped caring. Had to if he was going to be the soldier he needed to be. And so the dead lost their mystery, the voice humming of some vague truth about reality having gone silent a long time ago. Meat on bones, that's what they were. That's what they'd been for a very long time now. So he didn't understand why, all of a sudden, stepping near *this* body, all those old virgin feelings were suddenly whispering in his ear again, the mystery of death and its sting all floating through the air here. *Because I'm losing my mind, remember?* Oh yeah, keep forgetting. So he did his best to put the weight of this person's death, the finality of it, out of his head as he knelt beside him—*it.* "Just a bag of bones, dude." That's what Chris had told him once, during one of their first tours together. And Chris knew that as well as anyone could now, didn't he?

Eliot? Her voice cut through the density of his scrambled thoughts but didn't clear them, only added to the chaos of it all. Was it him or was the forest starting to spin?

Eliot?

Just a bag of bones, dude. That's all I am.

Eliot? Are you coming to me?

His head whirled. He was seven again, with his folks in one of those teacup rides at Disney World, his dad turning the center wheel as fast as he could, the world around them reduced to a vomit-inducing blur of color. He'd spent the next hour lying on a bench, trying to keep his intestines down.

Eliot, I need you.

Mom and Dad. Disney World. A funeral. A switchblade. The Navy.

Don't you know who you are? came Ronald's voice joining the medley.

Oh, man. I'm breaking up bad, he thought. He brought his hand to his head. It was warm, but he was soaked by the flood falling from the sky and couldn't tell if he was sweating or not. But he knew he was. Knew it was fever. It was all fever. The whole lot of it was just insane fever, scrambling his brain like eggs. *This is your brain on drugs.* Crack. Sizzle. The old TV commercial, Mom and Dad with coffee and eggs in the morning, with the newspaper and Bob Barker.

No wonder Henry and company didn't want to take him along. *I'm out of my live-long days.* And then he wondered what the hell that meant.

The body was one of the pure-blooded from the caves, he could tell from the clothing. Not from the face, because the face was pretty much gone, swiped off by what looked to have been a lightsaber. Even with all the impossible things he'd seen on the island, he was still pretty certain they were safe from Sith giants. At least they had that going for them. That was another island for another time. *Jedi giants*, and he almost laughed again.

It was one of those fallen angels the Bible and the Book of Enoch talked about. Osiris. It was all his fault. He did this. He killed this kid. Brought him here to this place. *Just like I brought Chris and Nick, right?*

Turning his attention from the fallen Puree, he searched the forest floor, through the giant ferns, and saw more bodies. The feelings darkened, and for the first time he wondered if it was a disturbance in the Force that he was feeling. Was *he* a Jedi? Did he have those midi-chlorianwhateverthehelltheywere things in his blood like young Anakin? Along with the blood of the…Anikim?

This is getting confusing. He closed his eyes and tried to get his dad to stop spinning the damn cup so fast. Couldn't he see that he wasn't having fun? That he was about to send a stream of spinning puke all over them?

A battle had been fought here. The number of bodies made that clear, both Puree and Fallen.

He got up from the kid with no face and started making his way from body to body, corpse to corpse, the disturbance in the Force growing with each contact. But he wasn't making the rounds to make sure the dead could pay the ferryman (or whatever the tradition was; his own tradition had been handed down by the Special Forces and didn't include coins on the eyes but a single playing card). He was looking for a weapon. And the fifth bag of bones he came to had just what he needed. An old 1891 Carcano Modello bolt-action service rifle.

He wrestled the gun from the death grip and checked it over. Examining the machine seemed to bring some of his sanity back, to clear his head of voices and memories. Handling the rifle turned him into a soldier again, the trigger to his other Navy SEAL self. It felt good in his hands, familiar even if he'd only held this particular model once or twice before. It didn't matter, though. It was a rifle, and he was Chuck Connors.

He looked down the sights of the Italian weapon known mostly to Americans for its use in Dallas, when the guy who supposedly fired it sent a magic bullet in and out of President Kennedy. Maybe he'd have the same sort of powers with this one. He checked the modified clip and saw it was still full. The poor dead guy next to him hadn't even gotten a shot off.

Jackson got to his feet, slung the rifle over his shoulder, and concentrated the best he could on keeping the forest still. Then he continued following the trail of bodies—both pure and impure—toward the temple complex, leaving the empty M16 behind.

Twenty minutes later, he could no longer keep the forest from spinning in the fading light, and the sound of the rain was only disorienting him more. Perhaps he wasn't going to make it after all. He wanted to stop, to rest. He could build a shelter, make a fire. He could sleep and surrender to dreams of her. It sounded amazing. But he knew, from that faraway voice that was still his Jiminy Cricket reason, that to do so would be the end of him—which, right now, actually didn't sound so bad. And that was the real test, wasn't it? To find a way—the will—to keep caring. Because he could use a little end of himself right about now, a little peace, a little slumber in the summer. Though if what John's Bible declared was true, his afterlife could turn out to be a real bummer.

He laughed at the rhyme and stumbled forward. He kept tripping, lost in the purple haze debate of whether to surrender to all the fever promises or not, telling himself that it *should* matter that they were all lies. And before he knew it, he'd made it after all.

There was the courtyard, right before him.

Standing tall, he swayed back and forth while the rain lashed his face. Water ran down the ziggurat's steps, turning it into some strange mall fountain from Mars. He blinked, wondering why Mars, when he noticed the bodies floating in the courtyard around it.

It was over. The war was over. Whatever had happened, whatever the result, he'd missed it. Which he'd already known, really. What was it that he expected to find here? What was the revelation he'd pushed for? Osiris was gone, the solstice past. Did he think there'd be a giant sign draped down the side of the pyramid?

> *Thanks for the nightmare. We're out of here. And you should know that things are a bit different now. Portals to hell have materialized. Stay away from them. Good luck, Chuck.*
>
> *-Henry, Paul, Hunt, John, and Chad.*

He sighed, completely lost, no fight left in him. He sank to his knees, suddenly longing for her voice, not caring if it was real or not. "Are you still there? Will you have me now?" he mumbled through the rainwater that spilled over his lips. But then he spotted something across the courtyard, near the opposite tree line. "Wait. Hold that thought, my darling."

* * * *

The giant stood over him, studying him as if he were a dessert dish, whipped cream, cherry, the whole works. There was a smile on its haggard face, its blue eyes full of wild anticipation.

From Paul's vantage point down on his back, the giant's armor reflected the swaying forest behind him and the violent sky above at the same time, making the fourteen-foot creature a sort of confused chameleon, there but not there, a moving mirage, its blond hair hanging below its massive shoulders, matted against the moving scene. Disoriented and in pain, he knew there was no escaping the Reaper this time, this Reaper with six fingers. But there was no way he was just going to roll over and take whatever sick finale had the thing smiling so big.

The Nephilim raised the sword and swiped it downward in a pendulum arc from left to right, aiming for Paul's ankles. He pulled his feet in, and the sword cut through the dirt just inches away from the soles of his boots. Clumps of mud struck him in the face and chest. The giant laughed some more, then swung again, the blade inching closer. Paul scurried backward, but it was no use. The giant was toying with him. It would slowly hack his legs off, working the blade up to his thighs one swing at a time. Then it would take off his arms, starting at the wrists. God knew what it would do then.

"You die." Its voice travelled over the storm. "First I have pleasure."

Paul would have been more concerned with whatever "have pleasure" meant if he wasn't so shocked at hearing the thing speak. He had no idea they could talk, let alone in English. He spit and reached for the knife that was still secured beneath his belt. Before he could pull it out and do who knew what with it, a loud *crack* echoed throughout the temple complex, over the thunder.

The giant turned its head to the side, looking back over its shoulder and into the courtyard.

Another *crack*, and this time the giant's head snapped, long blond hair whipping forward over its face, covering its eyes. It staggered over Paul, trying to keep its balance, sword waving wildly in the air. Blood appeared, mixing with the rain and running down over the glass. It pitched forward, falling onto its chest beside Paul, landing with a muddy splash.

Paul rolled away at the last moment, the giant's sixth finger just inches from his leg.

The giant began to push itself back to its knees, its hair hanging to the ground and hiding its face. More an act of defiance than anything else, Paul reached out and threw a strike with his good hand, knuckles connecting with cheekbone. Paul had put many a man to sleep with that punch, but hitting the Nephilim was like trying to knock out a marble statue.

Its head turned, and one furious, blue eye appeared glaring out from behind parted strands of gold, tangled hair. The river of red flowing down across its armor was thickening, originating from somewhere beneath all that hair. But the hidden wound didn't stop it from reaching out its right hand and grabbing Paul's neck. The blue eye continued staring at him, seething, while its grip tightened.

Paul reached for the knife, but knew he wouldn't be able to get it out and into the giant before hearing the sound of his own neck snap.

Another *bang*, and something other than the rain splashed against Paul's face, stinging him and getting into his eyes even as the grip on his neck fell away. He struggled to catch his breath and cleared his eyes. The giant was on its chest, half its head missing, brain and blood turning the puddles red.

Paul rolled onto his back, chest heaving, tremors racking his body. He didn't know what happened, wasn't sure who or what had saved him. He brought a hand to his face and began picking pieces of bone from it, the cold rain rinsing him of the defiled blood.

* * * *

Jackson slung the rifle over his shoulder as he left the woods and limped into the courtyard. His head was spinning, and he couldn't believe that he'd managed to put the giant down. Maybe the rifle was magic. He was on the verge of passing out, the world a blurry chaos on which he could no longer keep his balance. He didn't know whose life he'd just saved, but it didn't really matter. The person could fill him in on what he'd missed, on what had happened.

He stumbled and swayed across the front of the ziggurat, studying the bobbing faces in the water around him. Some of them he knew; others were too mangled to identify. Halfway across the courtyard, his body finally gave up on him. It didn't come down to a matter of will after all, he thought as he collapsed. As the darkness swallowed him, he rolled onto his back and managed to get his head out of the water. The last thing he saw, besides the rain pelting his eyeballs, was the man he'd saved standing over the giant and hacking its head off with its own, monstrous sword. It was the custom of the pureblooded to follow David's example, the postmortem beheading of Goliath. Whether the practice was a failsafe or a statement, no one seemed to care. As of yet, no one had seen a headless giant get back to its feet.

As the scene faded away, however, there was a certain detail that struck Jackson familiar, something that went back far beyond his arrival on this island. It was the man wielding the giant's sword…

His eyes closed, and Denise came stepping out of the closet, seducing him with promises of sweet, sweet rest.

FOUR

21st day of June, 2011. Bermuda. Nightfall

Noise filtered in from somewhere beyond the veil, indiscernible sounds that could've been the muffled dialogue of another language. And sure enough, as the seconds ticked by, the sounds transitioned into voices—*familiar* voices—and finally morphed into words. Figuring he was still dreaming, Jackson didn't immediately open his eyes. Instead, he lay there (wherever *there* was, floating in the courtyard, he supposed) and tried to find Denise again. Where had she gone? He begged her to come back, but she wouldn't.

Without having to make a conscious effort to do so, he realized that he was actually following the conversation taking place around him. Slowly, his surroundings began to take shape right there in his mind's eye. A fire snapping and popping, the heat of it against his body, the close proximity of those speaking, the sound of swaying trees and the feel of their embracing closeness, the absence of daylight against his closed eyelids… And of course, there was the pain, which told him that what he was hearing and feeling was no dream.

He opened his eyes and squinted into the firelight.

"Well, look who's come back."

It was Paul's voice for sure, dripping with the bitter sarcasm that had been his tone toward him ever since finding out that he'd set them up to come to this place. To save Henry, to help Osiris escape, to get Chris and Nick killed.

A shape materialized from the other side of the fire, and Paul's face came into view, cradled by dancing flames. He could've been a demon himself, with his scars and cold eyes coming out of the fire.

"Guess I should thank you for saving my life," Paul said. But his eyes held the rest of the thought. *I wouldn't need saving in the first place if it weren't for you, though, would I?*

"I didn't know it was you," he responded, wincing as he moved to sit up. "So you can save your gratitude for someone else."

"Oh, please don't start," came another voice.

Jackson turned his head and found Hunter lying by the fire. He was shaking his head, his eyes moving back and forth between them. "I've had enough of the junior high crap between you two. Give it a rest or get over it. Please."

Before Jackson could respond, a bolt of electricity shot through his side like a red-hot poker, and he dropped down onto his back.

"What're you doin' out here?" Paul asked.

"What am I doing out here? Trying to find out what the hell's going on. Find out what I missed while I was out, why my friends drugged me and left me here to rot on my own in this nightmare."

"A nightmare you introduced us to, thank you."

"That why you did it?"

Paul spit. "You would've never stayed behind, and you know it."

"Damn right."

"Exactly."

"You would've never made it, Jack. If you'd come with us, you'd be floating face down in the courtyard right now," Hunter said.

"So it was better to leave me here?"

"You could use the device at the next solstice or equinox."

Maybe, Jackson thought. He looked up into the sky and could make out stars dancing through the gaps in the canopy. It was no longer raining, and the clouds had moved on to wherever clouds go in this strange world. "How long have I been out?" he asked.

"Couple hours." Paul walked around the fire.

"The others?"

"That's the million-dollar question, Jack." He knelt beside him, reached out and took a knife from off a flat stone that was resting in the fire. He held it up, examining it, the flames' reflection dancing up and down the blade.

Hunter spoke up, and for the first time, Jackson caught the pain strangling his words. "Last we saw 'em, they were headed for the pyramid."

"You think it worked?"

"How the hell should we know?" Paul answered, his eyes still on the knife.

Jackson looked around. "Where are we? And why don't you have a shirt on?"

"I used my shirt to dress his wounds. And we're on our way back to the caves."

"You two dragged me?"

Paul shook his head. "I dragged *both* of you."

Jackson managed to sit up, breathing his way through the motion, hand pressed into his side. "What happened to him?" he asked, nodding toward Hunter's prone form.

"Got myself skewered and tossed off a temple," Hunter said.

Jackson studied his friend lying there beside the fire. It was hard to make out any details in the dim light, but he hadn't seen a single movement from him yet. "He okay?" he whispered to Paul.

Paul began unwrapping the cloth from around his hand. "Maybe."

"And you?"

"Oh, I'm all sunshine and rainbows." He held his hand up to the fire and examined his fingers. A blade must've caught his knuckles while his hands were gripped on his own sword. The finger was cut straight down, but the blade hadn't pierced the skin all the way to the handle, so there his pinky hung. He looked at his ring finger, pausing only to ponder the fact that no ring had ever been on it and now never would.

Jackson watched as Paul placed his fingers flat against the rock and set to work with the hot blade. The pinky came off easy, as he needed only to cut through flesh, but his ring finger proved a bit more work since splintered bone and tendon still held it together. He didn't make a noise as the fingers came off, but he growled when he pressed the flat side of the glowing knife against his new nubs to cauterize them. He threw the knife into the ground and swore, then picked up his two fingers. He threw one at Jackson and the other at Hunter.

"One for each of you."

They laughed, and for a second they were back in time, behind enemy lines and dressing their wounds after a conflict. Only they were a few faces short now.

They lapsed into silence, eyes captivated by the fire's rhythmic dance.

After a while, Jackson finally broke the silence. "Something's different."

* * * *

Hunter wasn't sure what Jackson was referring to as being different, but he sure knew there was plenty different about *him.* He could feel it, inside him. He didn't know what it was, couldn't pinpoint it exactly, but… *I should be dead* was the thought that kept going through his mind, over and over on a continuous loop, trumpets and guitar chords and drums and a piano too. *I should be dead, yeah-yeah-yeah. Hey, man, don't you know I should be dead, dead, dead?* But then his mind would veer off and away from the music track, putting away the reality of what had happened to him, focusing instead on how good he felt. Which was absurd, since he'd been run through by a spearhead the size of a shaded lamp. But oh, he felt so…*alive.* He listened to himself talk, and he could hear the pain in his voice, choking his words, but…

He remembered falling through the air, the thoughts that ran through his head as fast as they could, like they needed to all get in there before the window of opportunity closed for good. He'd thought himself dead for sure, was just waiting for the picture to blank out when he finally hit the ground. The sprinting thoughts, many of which were actual memories, seemed spilled from a mixed bag of history, no continuity at all, just selections made at random, a blind, subconscious hand picking out of a hat. There was his mom and pop, some childhood friends he hadn't thought of in decades, Jazz the dog, a few of the women he'd loved, some holidays, particulars from certain missions, a scene from *What's Happening Now*, a giraffe he'd once seen eating from a tree in an African plain… The way time seemed to slow in order to give the thoughts time enough to register was odd. There was once a time when a soldier next to him had been struck by a bullet while in the act of throwing a grenade, and he'd watched the thing fall and bounce and roll while a million thoughts and memories raced around his head in similar fashion as he covered the mere dozen feet and kicked the bomb down a stairwell. What was even stranger than the sense of time being altered was the fact that, in addition to the random memories and thoughts, he'd actually remembered these similar experiences on his way down and had the wherewithal to compare them. The thing that set the falling apart from the other time-stopping event was that in this situation there wasn't a thing he could do about it. Except hit the ground, of course. Which he did. But the impact had registered in his brain as a fact only, because he was gone before he could feel it.

And then he opened his eyes and found himself trapped beneath a pile of bodies. At first he thought the weight of them pressing down on him was preventing him from being able to move. But then he realized that it was his spine, and what a terrifying feeling that was, consciousness trapped in a jar. Hallelujah! though, as feeling began crawling back into his body. At first it brought with it an excruciating pain, but after not being able to feel or move at all, the sensation of pain itself was a beautiful thing.

You should be dead, man! I should be dead, dude! It all hit the fan, man! I should be maggot food! Yeah, yeah, yeah… And yet here he was, *recovering.* How it was possible, he didn't know, but he could feel his body repairing itself, his strength coming back. It was exhilarating, empowering, glorious. But there was a thread of fear slithering through the back alleys of his consciousness, way back there, whispering that something was wrong, that as good as things felt now, he was heading for something rather nasty further on down the road.

He felt like he could sit up but didn't want to reveal his self-healing powers to his friends just yet. Maybe it was that inchworm of fear or something else, but he wanted to hear what they had to say, what it was they'd seen.

He watched as Paul pulled the knife out of the ground. The blade was still hot, but not hot enough, and he put it back into the fire. "What did you see?" he asked him, even though what he really wanted to say was, *Please allow me to introduce myself…* And wasn't that a disturbing thought. *That* was no song he wanted to be singing. No, sir. Not at all.

"A house," Jackson answered.

"We found Henry's wallet in a house," Paul replied, staring at his missing fingers.

"Not a wattle and daub hut. I mean a *house.* Running water, pictures on the wall, a refrigerator."

Hunter blinked. The bizarre was the norm in this place, but the norm from the real world being here would be more bizarre than the bizarre that was normal. He almost sang that out, but bit his tongue. G*oo goo g'joob, man.*

"There was a clearing," Jackson continued, "not far from the caves, close to where Flatt's Bridge should be. The house was just sitting there in the middle of it."

They'd become familiar with the area over the last few weeks and there was no sense in asking if maybe it had been there all along. They would've known. The Purees would've known.

Jackson looked toward the knife. "Ready yet?"

Paul picked it up and nodded. "C'mon over."

Jackson moved close and lifted the side of his shirt, exposing the popped stitches and a few skinny streams of oozing blood.

"Don't cry, okay?" Paul said as he pressed the blade flat against the wound. The skin around the leaking lesion sizzled like a chunk of meat tossed onto a grill, and Jackson hollered.

Paul's grin was lit by the fire, and there was no doubt that he was enjoying himself.

Jackson looked down at his side and swore. "More scars. Denise would love it."

The mention of his late wife struck Hunter as a bit more than strange, and he and Paul exchanged a perplexed glance. As far as anyone knew, Jackson hadn't so much as spoken her name since the accident. Why he'd chosen this particular moment to broach the subject was…*suspicious.*

But Jackson didn't elaborate. Instead, he poked at the tender burn and mumbled, "I had stitches in there." Then he lay back down, trying not to move. "What about you?" he asked Hunter, putting further distance between now and the drop of his wife's name. "You need any mending?"

Oh boy, do I ever. "No, thanks."

And Paul started laughing.

"What's he laughing about?" Jackson asked.

Hunter shrugged. "Not sure." *He's laughing because he knows, yes, he knows that I should be dead, dead, dead. No mending for me, you see, just let me be and I'll be fine to dine on the wine of swine, you see, I've been around for a long, long time…*

Jackson frowned, rolled painfully onto his good side, and came face to face with a giant, blond head mounted on a spike. "This the one I shot?" he asked, failing to be startled by the grotesque sight.

"Yeah," Paul answered, getting his laughter under control. "Next time try taking it down with the first shot. Had me concerned." Then he added, somberly, "It talked to me."

Jackson shot a thumb at the severed head. "This?"

"*Before* you shot it."

"What did it say?"

"'You die. First I have pleasure.'"

Jackson looked back at the spike. "Didn't know they talked." He looked at Hunter and asked him, "He gonna be carrying this around with him now?"

Hunter smiled and knew immediately that his expression came out void of any pain. He wondered how long it would take them to notice. "He always was the sick one."

Jackson grunted an affirmation and picked up the knife. "How you feel?"

Truth be told, I feel quite marvelous, mister. Uh-huh, quite good, as a matter of fact. Should be dead is what they said, but look at me now, you egghead. Goo goo g'joob, dude. That's not what came out, though. The rational side of himself, the one with the trickle of fear rattling around inside, said, "I don't know. Can't feel much." But that was a lie. He could feel everything.

Jackson carefully untied the jeans that Paul had wrapped around his chest and then lifted the blood-soaked piece of shirt. He frowned in the shifting light. "You said he was run through with a Nephilim spear?"

Hunter could tell that his wound was healing itself, but he had no idea how fast. The tone in Jackson's voice could be interpreted in a number of different ways. Surprise at how small the wound was or that he was still breathing. That had certainly been Paul's reaction, even if he'd yet to share it with Jackson.

Paul walked over to the spiked head and yanked the pole out of the ground, exposing its diamond tip. It was over a foot wide at its base, four corners ascending to a razor-sharp point.

"That went through him?" Jackson asked, surprised.

Hunter knew that when the point passed through his chest, the base following should've left a cross, one foot by one foot, in his chest and out his back. But then when the giant flung him off the spear, and the tip passed back through him… There should be entrails, and ribs, and all kinds of things protruding out of him. *Something's wrong*, a voice whispered in his head. Was it his own voice? *I should be dead.* But you're not, so you're welcome. *Who are you?* I am he as you are he as you are me.

Paul nodded. "I sure don't know how he's alive."

But Jackson was now looking at Hunter and seemed confused by what he was seeing. "What the hell are you talking about?"

Paul walked around the fire and, seeing Hunter himself, echoed Jackson's surprise.

"So am I getting better?" Hunter asked, reading the disbelief in their eyes.

Paul tilted his head to the side, studying his friend and brother of so many years. "Yeah, seems you are."

He smiled. "Well, that's good news. Maybe I'll be able to move soon." *You could move now if you wanted to. Hop right to your feet and do the Carlton dance, make them both crap their pants.* He looked up at the sky, to the stars. "Where do you think they are?"

"Who?" Jackson asked.

"You think they made it back to his Golden Age?"

Hunter didn't see with his own eyes the look Jackson and Paul traded, but he knew it just the same. And for some reason, it made him laugh.

* * * *

"What's happening to him?" Jackson asked. He nodded toward Hunter, who'd just gone from laughing to sleeping.

"I don't know. But I saw him take *that* spear through the chest and then watched him fall from the top of the temple. The way he struck his back on the last step…" He trailed off.

"There's barely a scratch on him."

"You saw the shirt."

"It was a lot of blood."

"Looked like a grenade had gone off in his chest. No way someone could survive what I saw."

After a pause, the fire crackling in the silence, Jackson said, "I think you should see it."

"Your house?"

He nodded.

Paul folded his arms across his bare chest, the fire keeping his flesh warm, and added a thought of his own. "The backside of the temple is gone. Like it was sliced in half, top to bottom."

Jackson stared at him.

The fire popped, and sparks showered into the air.

"When I came to, I was alone in the temple, dead bodies all around me. Some of them were sticking out of the walls."

"*Sticking* out of the walls?"

"Like they'd become one with them."

Jackson squinted. "You're not thinking…"

"If you're thinking it, then so am I. Something changed."

"Because of a Philadelphia Experiment?"

"Whatever they did in the pyramid, wherever they went, it changed this place. Altered it somehow."

Jackson absorbed the words, knowing them to be true. After all, there was the case of the missing torches and the house.

"And the pyramid is gone."

"The pyramid is *gone*?"

"Yeah."

"If the pyramid is gone, then…"

"I know."

They fell into a prolonged silence, listening to the crackle, snap, pop of the fire.

Jackson looked over at Paul, the impossibility of their situation a ball circling the rim of understanding, either about to fall in for two points or not. "I'm sorry. For everything."

Paul blinked, but only asked if there was anyone left back in the caves.

"A kid keeping watch tried to keep me from leaving, said the women were still there. He said no one had come back."

Paul nodded. "I've only seen that one giant, but I wouldn't stay out here longer than we have to."

"You think Osiris took his army with him?"

Paul leaned back against a fallen tree branch. The thought of Revelation unfolding back in the real world was an unsettling one, but Osiris and his demonic army could just as easily be pounding on the doors of Tartarus right now. But the only question that concerned him at the present was where that left his friends. "I don't know."

"Well, we gotta figure it out fast."

FIVE

22nd day of June. Bermuda. Morning.

The night passed without incident, and the three of them awoke to a beautiful, red-orange sunrise. A cool breeze swam easily through the woods, carrying with it the many scents of an early, dripping forest. It was a new day—the first day after the solstice—and they stared in baffled wonder at the new skyline the clear morning introduced. The temple complex, rising over the tops of the trees in the distance, was indeed missing what had been its most significant feature—the crystal-capped pyramid they'd first seen back in May while navigating the Sound in that terrible storm.

Hunter watched as Jackson and Paul went about joining three cedar branches together with shoelaces, belts, and strips of clothing taken from nearby corpses. They were making him a sort of MacGyver gurney, two long branches that could be used as poles with a shorter, fatter branch centered between them. Oh yeah, it was gonna be a comfortable journey through Sherwood all right. He wondered if he should tell them he didn't need a gurney, that he could just up and walk with them. But he didn't. Instead, he just kept watching them toil with the branches, amused at the pointlessness of their endeavor. *Strange days have found us, strange days have tracked us down.* He felt the lyrics appear in his head, saw the words. Tasted them. But he hadn't *heard* them. Which was strange, because both Jackson and Paul stopped what they were doing and stared at him.

"Didn't know you were a Doors fan," Paul said.

Nor am I a Beatles fan, but nonetheless, goo goo g'jube, man. Had he said that aloud, too? Didn't look like it. They were still waiting for a response. "Just seemed appropriate is all."

"Can't argue with that," Jackson answered.

But Paul didn't look so sure.

And that annoyed him. He knew their little secrets, had heard them whispering about him last night and this morning. Knew they didn't trust him, that the speed with which he was recovering had them on edge. He began singing about looking for a new town.

This time Jackson's eyes narrowed as he studied his crippled friend.

I'm not crippled, Hunter thought, and was surprised to find a steady stream of venom aimed at his two friends. *I am he as you are me…* The thought, the recitation of the lyric, was his own. Yet it wasn't. It was a message to himself from… From what? What was happening? Why was there this intolerable feeling aimed toward the people he cared for most in this life? Men that he had saved and that had saved him more times than he could count? And this childish, strange behavior, this freakish off-the-rocker act he had going… This wasn't him at all. He was a Navy SEAL, a professional soldier, a survivor. He was loyal and tough and self-sacrificing, and all that stuff that you got medals for when the whole world got sucked into that proverbial fan. This…*this*…was not him.

Yes it is. I told you. I am he as you are me and we are all one and the same.

He was losing his mind.

No, and this thought was his alone, a genuine Hunter-of-old protest. He wasn't losing his mind, not unless an unraveling psyche also tended to repair mortal wounds overnight. *No, I'm not losing my mind. I'm gaining someone else's.*

"Good work, soldier boy."

He looked at Jackson, who was still studying him, but his lips were pressed together tight. Paul had his back to him, tying off the last few pieces of their project. Neither had spoken, and it certainly hadn't been his own voice he'd just heard.

You can't fight it. Not now. Best to just let go and let me.

Who are you?

No answer came through the fog that was barreling through his conscious mind, erasing, copying, modifying, altering, becoming. And then came the opening lines to "Sympathy for the Devil" by the Stones.

Hunter tried to protest, but the sudden clarity was already fading and he was fast sliding back into that other him. The one that was both him and not him. Soul, spirit, body, and…the presence. It was *Invasion of the Body Snatchers*, it was *The Exorcist*, it was MK-Ultra and Count Dracula. It was Jesus Christ and a herd of swine off a cliff. It was the end and it was the beginning. It was wonderful and it was terrifying. He was sorry and he was not, hated it and loved it. And finally, he did let go.

He closed his eyes and let Paul and Jackson finish his chariot.

* * * *

Paul pulled Hunter over the uneven terrain, sweating, hand aching, tired. But it was Hunter's singing that was driving him crazy most of all. At the moment, he was reciting the *Shaft* theme song, and Paul wanted to kick him in the face. Forget the question of his miracle healing and all, what bothered Paul now was how the hell Hunter could be *singing*. Not the Doors and Stones stuff he'd been mumbling before (that at least had been understandably appropriate in a twisted way) but light-humored songs like this. Hunter wasn't exactly Hunter at the moment (that was terribly obvious to both him and Jack), but it was still pissing him off. And scaring him. Scaring him because it reminded him of something else, something from before the Gulf, from an extraction mission in North Burma.

He looked over at Jackson and wondered if he was thinking the same thing. He couldn't tell. Jackson seemed focused on simply clearing their path of debris.

The village. It had been as *Apocalypse Now* as they'd ever witnessed, and a haunted presence (there wasn't really any other way to put it, even when later reporting the incident to command) was immediately sensed hanging over the place. Later, they'd learned that in the Naga Hills, on the northeast frontier of Burma, slavery and human sacrifice had been part of the culture there, that there were rumors it still was.

At the time, Paul hadn't believed in evil spirits, demons, or ghosts. But, undeniably, there had been some overseeing evil there that all the villagers seemed in concert with. There were no pentagrams painted in blood or women stirring baby stew in big, black caldrons. But the eyes, and the way they stared... The way they laughed when asked through the translator from another village about a white woman wearing a cross around her neck and carrying a black book. Hysterical, nonsensical...mocking. And *pleading.* They had done all they could to get themselves mowed down without actually doing anything. They were begging, behind the insanity, to be helped, to have an end put to their suffering; for behind the dead, dancing eyes was the agonizing look of imprisonment. Never would they be able to ask for it, to put their wish to words. Whatever was controlling them would never allow that. But there they stood, laughing, jeering, mocking, and threatening to rush them, to sacrifice their bodies to the Prince of Darkness. It was *Tears of the Sun* meets *Children of the Corn.* Witchcraft or Voodoo or something similar. And Paul remembered feeling, for the first time ever, that there were things in the world that he neither understood nor was equipped to handle.

He looked at Hunter again, looked into his eyes. There it was. Unmistakable. The same mixed look—a dead, flaking sheen over something that was very much alive. Someone was home for sure, but it wasn't the one who'd been paying the mortgage all these years.

Naga Hills was here, in this other Bermuda, powers at work now that hadn't been before. Yeah, Paul was sure of it. Things were different now.

Hunter's melody echoed through the forest's silence, continuing to rub against Paul's nerves like a block of sharp on a cheese grater. But in the back of his mind, Paul had a faint understanding as to why he wasn't kicking him in the mouth. The reason he and Jackson were both tolerating the noise was, in fact, because they actually hoped it might attract the attention of...anything. They'd yet to see more than dead bodies; no giants, no animals, no nothing but the morning breeze and the not-so-good vibrations of Naga Hills. If Hunter's new singsong alter ego could startle a flock of birds into flight, or (god forbid) even send a monster after them, then they would at least have an answer to one of their many questions. And the answer, no matter what form it came in, would be a sort of comfort, wouldn't it? Just about anything that could rule out the eternal snow-globe hypothesis would be welcome. Already, there'd been the giant Jackson killed, the head of which was still on a spike back at their campfire, but the more time that elapsed without running into any other sign of life... Then there was the probability factor, the odds of the three of them being the only ones around. It didn't seem very likely that they should be the sole survivors on the island, and Paul wondered if Jackson, too, was entertaining thoughts of all this being one big dream.

His thoughts came to a screeching halt when Jackson suddenly stopped with a raised hand. They were at the edge of a clearing, with Hunter whistling a Christmas song behind them.

Paul dropped the gurney, and "We Three Kings" came to a jolting halt. "Sorry," he said, and stepped toward Jackson, leaving Hunter behind to moan on his mat.

Jackson pulled down a needled branch and brought the clearing beyond them into view.

Paul stared, then blinked. But the pink house wouldn't disappear. There was smoke rising from the chimney. "Somethin's rottin.'"

Jackson agreed.

There wasn't much on this spinning rock that scared Jackson, but Paul could tell that this house had him in quite a tizzy. It was in his eyes—a wide, astonished sort of terror in place of the trademarked scrutiny that had always been so objective.

Behind them, Hunter sat up.

"I'd sure like to go in," he said, his tone lost somewhere between jovial and mechanical.

They turned and looked at him, more than a little puzzled at his upright position.

"You don't wanna go in there," Jackson stated, staring at him, his hand still on the branch.

"I do," he whispered back, and then he giggled. "I *really* do."

Without taking his eyes off him, Jackson leaned his head toward Paul and whispered, "You thinking what I'm thinking?"

"If you're thinking Naga Hills, then hell yes."

It was impossible that Hunter could be alive, getting better, sitting up. It was also impossible that this Bermudian house could be here now when it wasn't yesterday. They turned their eyes back on the house, deciding they could deal with Hunter later. Big, puffy clouds glided across the blue sky, over the chimney's rising smoke. But the picture-perfect scene was a farce, a mask over the true image, which was odd and dark and esoteric.

"Yeah," Jackson said, "Naga Hills."

"Naga Hills?" Hunter cried out in disbelief. "What're you talking about? C'mon, man, I *need* a Coca-Cola. A nice cold Coca-Cola."

Jackson's eyes slid back in Hunter's direction. "What?"

"Remember those old Diet Coke commercials with Paula Abdul and Elton John?" He laughed, and there was not a trace of pain in it. "I want to see the house, get a drink…a shower."

"You go in there, you might come out someplace else," Jackson muttered.

"Someplace else sounds good to me."

Paul spit on the ground and looked at Jackson. "What'd you see in there?"

Jackson fell quiet.

"C'mon, Jack, tell him what you saw," Hunter said.

And then he stood.

Jackson and Paul could only stare in disbelief at their friend.

"I need that Coke," he said, and walked past them, straight through the tree line and into the clearing.

* * * *

If he was a moth, then the house was a flame, drawing him in like a tractor beam. He didn't fight it, couldn't if he wanted to. Which he didn't, and that was perhaps the strangest part. He was increasingly aware of the other presence spreading its fingers inside him, taking more and more control away from him. But it felt so…*freeing* to just surrender and let the thing reshape him, make him new. Was that wrong? To give in? He thought that maybe it was, yet couldn't seem to care long enough to do anything about it.

As he approached the house through the clearing, he could hear Jackson and Paul calling after him from behind the trees. Were they hiding? From the house? The thought struck him as comical and it turned his lips into a grin. *Why are you so afraid?* But he knew why they were afraid, it was the same reason he *should* be afraid. But of course he wasn't. Couldn't be. Not now. Not anymore.

He made it halfway to the door before Jackson was on him, spinning him around by the shoulder.

"What are you doing?" Jackson shouted under his breath.

"I'm going in."

Jackson looked into his eyes. "You're not right, Hunter. Something's happened to you."

He smiled. "I know." *Oh yes, I do.* He wanted to listen to Jackson, knew he was right, that the last thing in the world he should do was go into that house. But he had to. *Sorry, man.* And the last of all that "band of brothers" stuff, the loyalty and friendship that had been forged over the years, melted away. There was no alliance here anymore. He was alone. *Well, not entirely alone, are we?*

"I can't let you go in there."

Hunter smiled and removed the pants and Paul's wadded shirt from his chest and dropped them to the ground. "Look at me."

But there was nothing to see.

Jackson took a step back.

"Goo goo g'joob, Jack."

Paul was now beside Jackson. "You wanna do this the hard way, don't you?" he asked.

"I want that Coke."

Jackson couldn't seem to take his eyes off Hunter's perfect chest. "How do you even know there's a Coke in there?"

"Does it matter?" Though he wondered just how he *did* know it. *I know a lot of things.* Who are you? *I keep telling you, I am he as you are me.* You healed me. *You're welcome.*

Paul grabbed him, not really sure why Hunter shouldn't go into the house, but believing that if whatever was in there had Jackson scared, then it was probably a good idea for all of them to stay out of it.

"Let me go."

"You know I can't do that. I don't know what's happening with you, but you'll thank me later."

But Hunter opened his mouth and from out of it came an unnatural scream, its decibel piercing, stabbing, sending Paul and Jackson sprawling to the ground in front of him, hands over their ears.

He was vaguely aware of a shooting sorrow, a torrent of his former self bubbling up in protest. It reached his eyes the same as it had in those Burma villagers, a silent plea broadcast through an expression impossible to misinterpret. *Help!* And then it was gone, swallowed by the whirlpool force swirling inside, the darkness rewriting him like a virus. *Help!* The internal cry grew fainter as it receded into the pit forming at the center of his being, a vacuum draining all that he was in order to make room for…*me, man!*

He stretched out his hand, and for a split second he was nothing more than an observer in his own body, watching himself reach out, hoping with the last vestiges of himself that he was in fact signaling for them to help him. But the laughter in his head shattered that hope, kicking it in the pants on its way out the door. Instead, his outstretched hand sent a current of invisible energy that lifted them two feet off the ground and hurled them backward across the clearing.

"Leave me be," he said to them. He turned his back and walked to the house. As he reached for the handle, a passage from John's Bible came from nowhere and struck up a chorus of church bells deep in his soul. At the same time, however, the "I am he as you are me" part of him jumped on it, trying to silence the alarm by distorting the verse with some sort of psychic fog.

Hunter had read the entire book, from Genesis to Revelation, in just a few days, staying up late, unable to put it down (though apparently just reading the Good Book didn't quite translate to being "born of the Spirit" or else he wouldn't be in this predicament, would he?). *And in that same hour he cured many of their infirmities and plagues, and of evil spirits…*

Evil spirits. *Is that what you are?* He wanted to cry out to John's God for deliverance, but he couldn't. It wouldn't let him.

He stepped inside and walked through the house. By the time he reached the bedroom, his conscious self had been entirely devoured by the hijacker. Before him stood the open closet, its blank space reeling him in. He took one last look out the window, saw Paul and Jackson running for the house, felt his lips smile, and then stepped in.

* * * *

Paul reached for the door, but Jackson grabbed him, keeping him from entering.

"Aren't we going after him?" Paul asked.

"You don't want to go in there."

"What?"

"I'm telling you, you don't—"

But Paul was already past him and through the door.

"Hunter!" he called out, looking left and right, absorbing the impossible settings in an instant. "Hunter!" He went room to room, checking closets and even the bathtub, but there was no sign of him.

He came to the bedroom last.

It was empty.

He stepped toward the closet. It was the only place left he could be. His fingers ached, and he clenched his fist, the new feel of it awkward and painful. Then, just before stepping into the small space, chills stormed through his flesh as a cool breeze came blowing out of it, his bare chest erupting in goose bumps.

That's when he noticed the void, the black nothingness of space staring at him where only hanging shirts should've been. There was no closet. No walls. Nothing. It was a hole into the center of the universe, a portal to…

Paul.

He blinked.

Paul, help me.

It was Hunter's voice, echoing from somewhere far away.

I need you, Paul.

Paul swore and thought about jumping in. But then he was being pulled from behind. He stumbled backward, trying not to fall as Jackson yanked him toward the door.

Something came out of the closet.

A little girl.

She stood there, dirty and afraid, staring at him. She looked to be somewhere between seven and twelve. He couldn't tell. Couldn't then and couldn't now.

A tear slid down her cheek, clearing a path through the grime. Her dress was tattered, her shoes worn down to nothing.

Paul shook his head. "No." And the next thing he knew, he was on his back in the grass, Jackson holding him down.

"We gotta go," Jackson was saying to him.

But all Paul could think about was that little girl standing there in the bedroom.

Finally, Jackson was able to get him to his feet and began pulling him toward the woods.

"What did you see?" Jackson asked, out of breath and panting.

But Paul didn't answer.

SIX

22nd day of June. Bermuda. North Coast.

They moved slowly without a word, Jackson sweating and grunting through his injuries, the pain twisting and wrenching his guts all over the place. The distance from the house to the caves was no more than two miles, but because of Jackson's condition, they were miles to be hobbled over rather than sprinted across (as they would've preferred).

The silence was something they'd learned a long time ago, the disassociation. Hunter's fate was unknown, and they had a million questions concerning it, but now wasn't the time to climb aboard that way of thinking. There would be plenty of time to grieve and mourn and question and curse later on, *if* they could keep their focus on getting back to the caves. It had been a long while, but it was by no means the first time they'd needed to detach from a tragedy to complete the task at hand. They fell into it like an old chair, not very comfortable but the shape of their asses still imprinted.

It wasn't until they were halfway there, the ocean in sight on their left, that Jackson finally repeated his last words.

"What did you see?"

Paul took his eyes off the forest for a second and set them ever so quickly on Jackson. Then they were back in the woods, peering intently through the wild network of foliage. What he saw wasn't possible. And yet here he was, practically shaking with fear, expecting the girl to materialize from behind a tree at any moment. Whether it had really been there or not, he knew what he saw. But he wouldn't be talking about it with Jackson. That history lesson was for the vault, and not even a ghost could make him tell of the thing he'd tried so hard to forget.

"What did *you* see?" he answered back.

But Jackson didn't answer either. Instead, he stopped moving and looked up. "Wait," he said. "You hear that?"

Paul stopped moving too. "What?" He pulled the knife, ready to use it. "I don't—"

"Diselo! Diselo!"

Jackson spun.

"Diselo! Diselo!"

Paul couldn't locate the source of the noise, but he recalled Jackson talking about it months ago, right before they'd found barbequed Nick in the ashes of the Nephilim fire. "Shearwater?" It was one of the things that had solidified the truth of their situation, since the shearwater had been gone from the island since 1985 (Jackson then adding that an insect pest destroyed most of the island's cedar trees back in the '40s).

Nick's dead! You tricked him into coming here and now he's dead!

We came to save Henry.

That's when Paul put his pistol against Jack's mouth and demanded the truth. Hunter had broken up the fight.

Hunter…

No time to think about that now.

Jackson shook his head. "No," he whispered. "It's the witch's call."

Jackson had told them that the Spanish believed they were being laughed at by witches, that devils haunted the island. Now it seemed as if he was coming around to the same way of thinking.

Paul tried to put the noise, along with everything else, out of his head. *Birds. They're just birds.* And wasn't that what Jackson had shouted once they'd stopped shooting them out of the sky? No, those had been cahows, hadn't they? Another bird. They'd never actually seen the shearwater that Jackson talked about. Only heard them.

"Come on," Jackson said. "Let's just get back."

* * * *

Jackson couldn't get her out of his head. She'd been there at the house again, calling to him. It was driving him mad, her voice. Its soothing ring and the warmth it spread through him was making him miss her even more, miserably more. He wanted her. Of course it couldn't *be* her, right? It had to be some trick meant to get him into that closet. But what was the closet? He saw what had come out of it, so if he was honest with himself, then yes, perhaps he did have an idea. But taking the time to polish it up wouldn't mean anything good for Hunter. Besides, he had other things to grapple with right now…like unquenchable guilt. Henry, Nick, Chris… The whole thing was undeniably, unequivocally his fault. At least they'd saved Henry. *Maybe.* Truth was, there wasn't any way to know what happened to Henry, John, and Chad. The only thing for sure was that Osiris had left the premises. Oh yeah, he knew that as well as anything. The angel wasn't here. Not anymore. He knew it as sure as a television knows it's not plugged in. The link, the broadcast, the power, the psychokinetic hook his genetic makeup had allowed…was gone. In fact, had it not switched off, he wondered if he would've realized it was ever on to begin with. The change had been too slow and subtle, and without knowing he was the offspring of Titans, how could he have ever identified what was happening to him? He had no secret journal of family bloodlines like Henry did, and his dreams, as far as he could tell, hadn't been all that revealing in that regard. But once he discovered who he was, that Ronald had played him the same as the others, he was able to recognize what was happening inside him. The knowledge was a mirror, and through it he could see himself turning on his friends, working for the fallen ones. Knowing had been torture, feeling their slimy fingers massaging his mind, manipulating him. He'd fought those fingers the best he could, but Osiris had him in the palm of his hand, his own DNA the leash keeping him from escape.

Then it was gone, and he was free. Free to hate the things he'd been used to do, the things he'd allowed to happen. And that could only mean one thing, his

Nephilim blood was no longer being manipulated by the presence of his angel daddy. Osiris was gone.

But... What did his departure mean for them now? Aside from his strings being cut, what else had changed? Paul's story of people becoming one with the temple walls, the pyramid missing, and the presence of the house all verified that some kind of alteration had been triggered by the use of the mechanism. But more than the physical differences, Jackson couldn't shake the feeling of another kind of change. A deeper, darker one. The peace that should've been left behind whenever any evil has departed a place seemed nonexistent. No righteous angels busy making victory laps around the island, and no celebrations being thrown by the surviving Purees. Why? Because, Jackson knew, the void Osiris left behind had immediately been filled by something else.

He continued to follow the half-hidden footprints he'd spotted some hundred yards ago. They led right up to the cave's entrance. Whoever had made them had attempted to conceal them with a tree branch, swiping the ground back and forth as they went.

Reaching the entrance, he turned to Paul. He knew Paul had seen something himself back in the closet and that whatever it was, whether the same creature that tried dragging him to hell or something else, it had him disturbed, too. Maybe Paul would talk about it later, once he'd had time to digest it. Jackson wouldn't keep pressing him for it now. "Some of them came back," he said.

"I figured from the tracks," Paul answered.

The tracks were fresh, made some time since the rain stopped. And it wasn't the enemy because they wouldn't have bothered to hide them.

Jackson navigated around the rocks. "Maybe we'll get some answers." But they both knew what he really meant was, *Thank God we're not alone.*

Once inside the cave, the outside light fading behind them, Paul whispered, "We have to go back for him."

There was no way they could go into that dark void where demons lurked and voices of the dead sang, but Jackson knew Paul was right. They had to do *something*. But first—

A faint *click*, simultaneously paired with a bright circle shining in their eyes, echoed off the limestone walls.

Jackson raised his hand, blocking the light.

"It's you! Thank God!" a voice cried out from behind the flashlight.

* * * *

They were a hundred and twenty feet underground, and torches were hanging from the surrounding walls. A long table split the room in half. It was the place the pure-blooded castaways had first taken them, after rescuing them from the giant that had Nick for its breakfast. That was only months ago, but standing here now seemed to turn those months into years, their acclimation to the island having evolved so much since then. And yet, gazing over the dozen or so men crowded about them, peering into their eyes, they understood that they themselves were still the rookies in this place; still so much they didn't know—*couldn't* know. Not when these men had been born here, had *grandparents* here. These survivors had stories, legends…*history* that had been handed down to them, father to son and father to son. They knew all there was to know about the island, what it was capable of, its laws and how to survive it. In light of their hosts, Jackson and Paul still had only but a *sense* of the goings-on here.

The staring faces began to blink and then look around as the crowd split down the middle, making way for someone bumping shoulders and pushing their way through them.

"You are still here," Samuel said, stepping feebly into the dancing light.

His wrinkled face was drawn, even more serious than before. Morose was perhaps the best word. He was old and frail, his many years in this place taking their obvious toll. All the horrible stories that he could tell could simply be imagined by reading them in the straight, jagged lines that covered his face. His color was dark, noticeable still in the dim light the cave dwellers had become accustomed to. Though neither Jackson nor Paul, or anyone else to their knowledge, had ever seen Samuel take a single step into sunlight, the evidence of such exposure was there, stamped on his skin. What business the old man had out in the hostile forest was unknown to them. Maybe he liked spending Sundays on the beach, reading the Book of Enoch and sipping from a secret stash of Graveyard rum.

"We weren't sure if you would be returning or not."

And of course, neither were they, since the plan had been for them to escape the island through the pyramid, too. But now the pyramid was gone and their friends with it.

"Just us two," Jackson said.

"The others?" His eyes were bright, blazing with an intensity that confirmed the sharpness of his mind, even if it stood in contradiction to his physical frame. But as bright as they were, intense with driving purpose, it was impossible to miss the little dimness that had settled in around their edges since they'd first met him. Back when he was so sure God had sent them as deliverers.

Jackson reached for one of the makeshift chairs at the table. "I need to sit, if you don't mind."

"Of course," Samuel replied, those sharp eyes homing in on Jackson's injuries. "And you"—he looked back to Paul, to his bare, tattooed and bruised chest—"must be cold." He turned to one of the men next to him and ordered a cloak. The man hesitated ever so slightly, a fleeting flicker in his eyes before complying. He didn't want to miss the conversation, which was evident by the speed with which he left when he finally decided to.

Jackson sat at the table and leaned forward onto his elbows, his head in his hands. Everyone else remained standing. "How many came back?" he asked, still avoiding Samuel's initial question for the moment.

"Twenty-seven here, but there may be some still trying to find their way back."

Paul frowned at the statement, at Samuel's word choice, but kept his silence.

"We don't know about the other caves. We plan to unite tomorrow at daybreak, all of us that remain." He paused, and the silence loomed. Then, more pointedly, said, "What happened?"

Jackson closed his eyes, and Paul thought he might've fallen asleep, so he answered, rehearsing all that he'd seen and could remember up to his regaining consciousness. It wasn't much. Nothing at all, actually. He knew nothing, saw nothing. Had no idea what happened to Osiris, his army of giants, or those who were last seen racing the sun to the pyramid.

"But something changed," Samuel said. "Something *did* happen." He stared straight into Paul's eyes, unwavering determination searching for answers that just weren't there. "I've been on this island for a long, long time. Many solstices and equinoxes have come and gone without altering a thing. But yesterday, *something* changed. The device was used, and its usage altered the island."

"Altered how?" Jackson asked, looking up.

Samuel moved his head to the side and nodded in the direction of the man closest to him. It was a man they recognized but didn't know. He stepped forward, and they could see that his beard was caked in drying, sticky blood, presumably from the gash across his cheek. His eyes were exhausted and full of despair, loss and failure wrapped by disorientation. Paul and Jackson knew the look well.

"Returning from the battle, some of us meant to skirt the Lake," he said, his voice a low grumble.

They understood the Lake to be a reference to Harrington Sound and nodded.

"But we couldn't find it," the man continued. "Just thick forest from one coast to the other. The Lake is gone."

Samuel must've expected protest because he preemptively began defending the man's reliability. "These men have been traveling the woods for years. Some of their fathers and great-grandfathers did the same. Their survival, *our* survival, depends on an intimate knowledge of the entire island."

"We know that," Paul answered. He focused on the man with the blood in his beard. "You were there at the pyramid for the solstice?"

The man nodded.

"What did you see?"

"We saw the sun align with the capstone, saw it fill up with rainbows. Then there was a blinding light and a loud noise like a trumpet—"

"Like the sounds you hear in the night before a new pillar is found standing in the morning?" Jackson asked.

"Yes. But much, much louder. And the light was painful, forced us to look away. Even the giants had to turn their heads. Felt like your eyes would melt right out of their sockets." He trailed off, his gaze turning to the ground at his feet.

"Then what?" Paul prodded.

"A great, whooshing gust of wind howled past..." He looked up. "When the light faded, we couldn't see anything but spots, like we'd just stared at the sun too long. When we could finally see again"—he looked around as if seeking support from those around him—"we found that we were no longer at the foot of the pyramid, but in the thick of the forest."

"The pyramid was gone," Paul stated.

"Or they were taken elsewhere," Samuel answered.

Paul realized that, to the Purees, teleportation was probably the most sensible explanation given their familiarity with all the henges and ley line stuff. "I don't think you were transported," he said. And he told them about the men in the walls, the missing half of the ziggurat, and the pyramid no longer on the skyline.

"Has anyone seen any of the Fallen since the flash?" Jackson asked as soon as Paul was finished adding to the confusion drowning the room.

"No," Samuel said. "Only the one you killed. Maybe Osiris did take them."

"Maybe. Or maybe not." Paul took an old, hooded sweatshirt from the man who had been sent to get him clothes. He pulled it over his head, feeling his muscles crying out from the stretching, and thanked the guy. There was a faded, red swoosh set against the gray background. "We need to find out what happened to the island and where the enemy is. We need to find out how many of us are left and take inventory. And we need to do it fast."

"We will gather as one in the morning and determine these things." Samuel looked around the room, to the dirty faces that stared hopelessly back at him. "We have lost so much," he whispered. "But God has not left us yet."

Paul snorted. "You still think God sent us to save you, huh?" He pulled the hood up over his head.

Samuel bowed. "I think we will find out soon enough."

Jackson pushed himself back away from the table and forced himself to stand. He stood swaying for a moment and then asked about the women.

Samuel nodded. "They are all safe." Then he added, "There is food and water for you. Eat, drink, rest, and we will continue this conversation later. I can tell there is still much you are not saying. We will get to all that later. Go for now."

* * * *

Paul followed Jackson into his room.

"Where's the light?" he asked. It was pitch black, and he had to grope around in the dark, looking for the bed while Jackson leaned against him for support.

"Gone when I woke up."

Finding the bed with his boot, he eased Jackson down onto the palmetto mattress. Now, in the privacy of the room and momentarily safe, Jackson let his game face drift away. The activity had taken its toll, and there was no hiding it any longer, no distraction great enough to keep his mind from it. He should've never left the room.

Paul sighed, his own body reprimanding him. "The torches are gone, huh?" he asked, feeling his way back to the door.

"Never there in the first place," Jackson responded, groaning as he twisted his large body on the tiny bed, trying to get comfortable.

Paul didn't know what that meant and didn't care enough to stay and find out, so he just left, closing the door behind him and taking the corridor down twenty yards to his own room.

Room—that's what they *called* it, but these little hollows felt more like cells in an old dungeon to him. He'd yet to take a rock pencil to the walls, counting the days off in scratched sets of five, but he could feel the seed of that desperation, knew it was busy germinating. Down here there was no way to track the hours, and if you weren't careful, you could mistake one morning for the next (or the previous) when stepping back into daylight. With that said, however, despite the disorienting nature of the underground life, the "rooms" did have some advantage that Paul appreciated. Mainly they were quiet, private, and sported beds (sticks and palmetto leaves may not be one's ideal selection, but after spending years sleeping in swamps and deserts, Paul had other things to complain about).

He pushed open the door, stepped into darkness, and didn't even bother lighting the torch that may or may not still be there. The world and all that was falling apart in it be damned, he just wanted to sleep. And sleep he would. No matter what might be happening on the surface, no matter what that house was or where Hunter went, no matter if they were stuck here forever or if Henry was now trapped in First Time, whether there was an army of Nephilim giants on their way to the Crystal Caves right now or not…he was going to sleep. It was something he'd learned to do on command a long time ago, something that survival demanded be mastered. Who knew, maybe he *would* wake up somewhere else (he still couldn't recall where that would be, though, where he was and what he was doing before this mess). It was a pleasant thought, and he let it carry him to the bed. He fell onto it chest first, totally exhausted, practically asleep before his head hit the—

Stone floor.

He'd been able to get his hands under him in that split second of realization that he was still falling, and it might've saved his teeth, but the impact with the ground still jarred him, running the air out of his lungs. He groaned in agony and turned onto his side. Where the hell was his bed? But he didn't really care, did he? No. He was already asleep, the little girl standing in the bedroom, the terrible odor of the loincloth still wrapped around his head, and his two missing fingers waiting for him.

SEVEN

22nd day of June. Morning. Bermuda.

"It's time."

The words drifted into Paul's consciousness, swam around a bit, and finally took root. As they grew into meaning, they brought him out of the dream. Well, not exactly a dream, more like a state of memory, or the feelings of one. It was hard to define because there was no specific remembrance, no visual of anything, just the lingering sense of it. He knew he'd visited a time when he was young, back before blood and pain and death had become his expertise. Back before his first true love was killed in the drive-by shooting that had rattled his hometown to the core. Back before the gangs, before he was kicked off the football team for breaking his own quarterback's hand. Yeah, it was a time before all of that, a tranquil time that he hardly remembered anymore. He wanted to return to sleep, to find those days again, those feelings. He knew the little girl might be waiting for him at the gates, but he'd already gotten past her once and he trusted he could do it again. The brief period of light on a timeline dominated by darkness, before hell opened its gates and drew him in, shutting behind him and swallowing him whole.

"Come," the voice insisted.

He blinked, and just like that, the past and all its feelings evaporated into a yellow-orange light that seemed to be surrounding him. Torches. He sighed. The island. He was still on the damn island.

He sat up, realizing he was on the floor, and remembered the bed hadn't been there to catch his fall. It was missing, as were two fingers on his left hand.

"Time for what?" he asked, answering the first statement. He looked up at the shadowy faces around him and counted five men in the room. Two of them were holding torches. Jackson was in the background standing against the doorframe in the dancing glow, his backpack over his shoulders. He didn't think they were calling him for breakfast.

"Time to gather with the others," the closest said, offering his hand.

Paul took it with his good hand and was pulled to his feet. A dizzy spell came over him, and he touched his head, feeling the loincloth still wrapped around it. The scent was gone, but he figured his poor nose had just gotten used to it. "Morning already?" He pulled the loincloth off his head and walked past the five Purees, pushing the cloth into Jackson's chest and forcing him to take it. "That's for you." He walked into the corridor, pulling the hood of the sweatshirt up over his head, Jackson complaining about the smell coming from his gift. "Where to?"

"To the Council Room," one of them said, walking past him and into the lead. Paul couldn't tell who it was for sure, though it sounded like Arkansas Joe. Joseph wasn't from Arkansas, but his father had been. Joseph happened to be born on the island, the beloved offspring of Arkansas dad and Fort Lauderdale mom (who had come to the island a couple years later). Joseph didn't have an Arkansas drawl or a Floridian twang but one unique to this place and shared by those born here. The island was its own melting pot, and the kiddies here were schooled by teachers from all over the world, each tongue dipped in a unique accent. "It's not far. Just south of here."

"I miss anything?"

The man looked back, his face momentarily illuminated by the light he held in his hand. It was Arkansas Joe.

"Nothing. It's all real quiet."

"Any more of you come back?"

"No."

When they exited the cave, they were met by the light of dawn and a steady, cool breeze. The rest of the Purees were already out and standing around, waiting. Samuel was standing amongst them and leaning heavily on a stick. Most were standing with their faces turned to the forest around them, watching for any sign of the enemy. Paul saw guns in their hands, old relics taken from the Graveyard. A 1956 Swiss SIG MP310 (its long 40-round magazine either empty or half full of 9mm Parabellums) was in the hands of the young Australian. Daniel, the Irish guy who was friends with Patrick, was holding tight a 1983 LAPA FA-03 (an assault rifle produced in small numbers back in the early '80s but still used by a few Brazilian police units), Pete the Norwegian had an Italian submachine gun that had long become obsolete back in the real world, and Theodore the Brit had an Austen, its side clip reminiscent of the WW II-era submachine guns. Most of the others had swords, spears, and knives. Paul knew there couldn't be that much ammo left after the battle. Already most of the guns (any requiring something other than 9mm or 5.56mm rounds, mostly) had used up whatever ammo had come ashore with them years ago and had since become utterly useless. If there remained a stash of ammunition, then the rifles that were compatible with it were most likely scattered out across the forest floor, clutched tight in cold, lifeless hands. If it turned out there was still a reserve of bullets, then retrieving the rifles would be a priority.

Paul looked away from the crowd of islanders and swept his own eyes over the forest. He wondered what was out there. Or what wasn't. He wondered a lot of things. Then he looked at Jackson. "Nice threads."

Jackson was in bellbottoms that were too tight and too short and an army jacket that wouldn't zip or reach his wrists. He didn't have a shirt underneath it, and fresh bandages could be seen hugging his midsection. "Thanks," he muttered, not bothering to turn his own eyes away from the trees. He redistributed the weight of the backpack, trying to hide the pain it took to do so.

Paul stretched his neck, rolling his head in slow swivels, inhaling the cool, ocean air through his nose. "Gonna be an interesting day."

Jackson nodded.

"Okay, let's go," Samuel said, and the party formed a line and marched into the woods.

As Paul watched the Purees slip into the forest without a noise, he realized that, though these people had no official training as soldiers, they had so far survived the island much longer than he had, and had already surpassed the stay of Nick, Chris, and possibly Hunter, all three Navy SEALs that had single-handedly taken on armies in other countries. That was cause for respect. They knew what they were doing, and Paul made a conscious effort to swallow his pride and follow their lead. He felt for the knife still tucked into his belt and wished he had something more.

As if reading his mind, the squirrely-eyed kid behind him (the one they called "Hap") said, "Don't worry. There'll be plenty of weapons for you."

"Good." He held his left hand up, unwrapped the bandage, and examined his fingers.

"Hurt much?" Jackson asked, looking back at him.

He shook his head. "Just tryin' to think how I'm gonna hit those bar chords now."

"Might have to find another gig. No more weddings."

The thought of Paul playing the guitar at a wedding, standing there in a tuxedo and strumming pleasant melodies with a grin on his face, was enough to make Jackson smile to himself. But instead he asked, "XE Services?" calling out the mercenary group formerly known as Blackwater.

"Good band name." And then he answered the real question that Jackson had, for some reason, decided to bring up now of all times. "No."

"Who, then?"

Paul didn't answer, just kept paying attention to their surroundings. "Why you asking?"

Jackson shrugged. "Thought I knew."

"Guess you didn't." His mind grabbed the little girl, slanted eyes filling with water, standing there in that dress, dirty and torn... "You know where we're goin'?" he asked, moving the conversation away from that particular topic. None of the others had inquired about his recent past upon reuniting for their little Henry-rescuing vacation, and he was pretty sure it was because they already had a good idea of it. It would've been an awkward conversation.

"They sent runners out last night to get everyone together from all the caves."

"They make it back?"

"Evidently. Didn't see anything either. All quiet."

Paul thought about turning the tables on Jackson, asking him about Denise and why he was suddenly bringing up her name, but decided against it. Now wasn't the time.

They let the surroundings absorb them into a still, silent embrace as they continued moving toward what they all hoped were answers. Even if they still weren't so sure of the questions.

* * * *

It wasn't a long trek, only about fifteen minutes' worth before they were at a rock cliff that reached twenty to thirty feet in the air. A hole in the middle of it stood gaping at them. Whatever they'd used to hide it in the past had been replaced by two men now standing guard on either side, weapons in hand.

Samuel stepped to the front of the line, and the man on the left side of the entrance acknowledged him with a slight nod before turning into the cave. The other guard took three steps back from the entrance, inviting them past him. Samuel took a long, wondering look around, and then led them in.

They followed the first guard into a large, circular room where men of all ages and nationalities stood lining the walls, waiting for them. Jackson counted fifty-three faces, and some of them he recognized. Above them, an opening in the rock ceiling revealed the morning clouds as they drifted lazily by.

"Is this all of you?" a large, older man asked once the last of them had entered the room. He stepped forward, separating himself from the rest of the group.

Samuel nodded. "We are all that returned."

There was no "official" government among the Purees, Paul knew. No king or president or pope. But that didn't mean there weren't men present who were born to lead and others that were born to follow. This man, who Paul and Jackson both knew as Jared, was this group's voice. He, like Samuel, had no other title. No one called him "boss" or "sir" or "General Jared." They listened to him because they trusted him. And when they didn't, they let him know, which always resulted in some sort of compromise. There were banishments from the caves for those who put their own personal interests above the good of the whole, people who put everyone else at risk for one reason or another, but there were no king's guard or capital police to enforce those decisions. In such extreme circumstances, the rest of the cave dwellers just crossed their arms and said goodbye. No structure. No hierarchy. Just an organic living experience. And if there *had* been incidents in the past, Paul never heard of them. Given the nature of humanity, he was almost positive there had to have been. But then again, they weren't dealing with thousands of people, and with the ever-present threat of being eaten by giants, it was possible they'd never had the time or luxury for power plays and conspiracies amongst themselves.

Jared's voice echoed off the walls, the morning light illuminating him as he stepped into its beam. He wore black jeans and a bomber jacket. His hair was long and black, and a big beard hid most of his face. Like Samuel, his features displayed the hard years spent running from giants and hiding from angels, but it had yet to turn his hair white. Either that or he'd scavenged some Just For Men from someone's schooner. When he spoke, he spoke in a voice barely above a whisper. And yet it seemed to have no trouble reaching every ear. There was power in his voice, and Paul knew why people fell in line behind him. "We remain," he stated, still looking around the room. He just stared, his eyes processing, digesting, planning. Until they found Paul and Jackson. "You." He took a step toward them, leaving the sunbeam. "Where are the rest of you?"

Paul shrugged.

"I'm told they entered the pyramid, that there was a blinding light…and then—" He made a vanishing motion with his hands. "Gone."

Paul cleared his throat and flexed his aching hand. "That's right. Poof."

"And you haven't seen—"

"Only one giant."

Jared held him in unblinking regard for a moment longer and then waved to one of the men against the wall beside him. The man immediately turned his back to them and reached down into the shadows, picking up a ladder that had been lying on the floor. He carried it to the center of the room, where he poked it up through the opening, leaning it against the edge, its last three rungs protruding out into the morning air.

The man stepped away from the ladder, and Jared was halfway up the old rickety thing before any of the visitors even knew what was going on. He was over the edge and gone two seconds after that.

"Pretty spry for an old guy," Paul grumbled.

Then Jared's head popped back into view, the sunrise a glow around him. "Come up," he called down to them.

Samuel nodded to the men he'd led here, indicating that they should follow.

Paul and Jackson waited until the two dozen men from the Crystal Caves were up and over the top before attempting the climb themselves. Every step was agony for Jackson, and Paul supported him the best he could, following behind and reaching up to steady him whenever he needed it. The whole time, the wood groaned and creaked under their weight, and they expected a *snap* and a quick drop. But the ladder held, and they managed to join the others on the top of a lush hill beneath the warm sun.

There was forest all around them, but the men were all staring northeast, none of them speaking, looks of bewilderment on most of their faces.

Paul didn't understand what they were looking at, but Jackson seemed to. He was limping forward, the same puzzled expression in his eyes as they studied the treetops in the distance, morning mist leaking through their countless, pined fingers.

"What is it?" Paul asked.

Jackson raised a finger and pointed in the direction everyone was staring. "Castle Harbor…" He met Paul's gaze. "It's gone."

Jared approached them, overhearing Jackson's statement. "You have a knowledge of the island from the other side?"

Jackson nodded.

"I've never seen the real one."

"You born here?" Jackson asked.

He shook his head. "Shipwrecked when I was young."

Jackson began pointing in other directions. "Nature Reserve should be over there, and Tom Moore's Jungle by the caves we just came from. St. David's Island out there, where the US built the airport…"

"Maybe someday I might get to see it for myself."

Doubt it, Paul thought. "They said that the Lake was missing, too. Replaced by forest."

Jared nodded. "I heard that."

Paul turned his head and spit. "We don't know this island anymore."

Turning east, Jackson studied the watery horizon, wondering if anything out there could've changed, too. Was there a world out there that could be gotten to now? Or were they still prisoners in some giant teardrop? He saw Jared looking at the horizon with him and knew he was thinking the same thing. But instead of commenting on what was or was not a new possibility, the tough old Puree simply turned back to the ladder.

"We have plans to make," he stated.

One by one, the men turned away from the strange land before them and followed Jared back down into the cave, mumbling under their breath. As Paul and Jackson stood watching, Paul asked, "Should we tell them about the house?"

"Not yet."

"What about Hunter? We have to do something."

"What?"

"I don't know."

"Well, neither do I."

They all sat on the ground, knees up and facing the two old, time-beaten leaders, who stood like a preacher duo at some hillside revival. Only there was no field, just the smooth limestone floor of a cave in Bermuda (but not Bermuda), the message being proclaimed one of survival, not sanctification.

"These are the weapons still available to us," Jared said, raising a finger and pointing at a mound of death (or life, depending on how you looked at it). It was a pile comprised of guns, swords, spears, knives, and assorted explosive devices ranging from old dynamite to grenades. Most of the guns and bombs looked as likely to work as the shipwrecked vessels they'd come from.

"There is not much ammunition left for the guns we do have. Only a couple shots for some of them. But just one shot could be the difference between life and death."

Or simply between dying now and in five minutes, Paul thought.

The sun was high in the sky now, the room lit and warm from its energy. Samuel walked into the middle of the room, beneath the opening, his staff *tap-tap-tapping* along with him. When he came to a stop, he leaned on the stick. "Something has changed." He took over, summoning strength back into his voice. "And we can only assume that it was Osiris using the mechanism that changed it. Now the question that needs answering is how *much* has changed." He looked around, finding approval in all the unblinking eyes. "I think one of the first things that should be done is to organize scouting parties. One to travel south and one to go north along the island's perimeter. Once we know our borders, then we move into the interior." He stood straight for a second, looked over at Jared, and then fell back upon the staff. "We need to know where we are, where *they* are. We need to know what's out there. If we still have enemies here, then it would be best if we know before they do."

Jared nodded his consent as did all the others. "Any thoughts?" he asked the group of survivors.

Of course, there were a million thoughts, all swarming in a cloud of static tension one could almost touch. And yet no one spoke. There was no need to. Jared was right, they all knew that. Their survival had always depended on knowing the layout of the land, the barriers and the hideaways, where to find fresh water and food.

"Okay then," Jared said. "Two parties. One north, one south. Avoid contact with the Fallen if possible. Once we have a proper understanding of our surroundings, we'll then have a better idea of how to proceed."

Arkansas Joe spoke up. "What about the dead, Jared?"

An uncomfortable glance flashed between Jared and Samuel. Seemed that was something already decided on.

But Paul interjected before they could answer. "We need any and all supplies we can find. If it's okay, I'll go with a team back to the complex and help retrieve any bodies and equipment we come across."

Samuel raised his stick and pointed its splintered end at Paul. "Any volunteers to go with our new friend?"

Almost every arm in the room went up.

"All right, looks like you have your group. If there's any—"

"Yeah, we'll abort at the first sign of trouble," he answered. "We'll bring back all the bodies along with the supplies we find. Then we'll bury our dead and burn theirs."

Jared nodded. "We will work out the details in a moment. But first"—he turned and began walking toward a spot in the wall being guarded by two men standing side by side—"there's something else you need to see." He motioned for everyone to stand.

Paul helped Jackson to his feet.

"Follow me," Jared called over his shoulder.

The two men standing shoulder to shoulder parted, revealing an opening in the rock. Each of them held spears and had FN 1949s slung over their shoulder. Paul took note of the post-WWII semi auto that was capable of using multiple caliber bullets and wished they had more of them.

The two guards, one a black man with dreadlocks and the other a younger Chinese guy, left the hole in the wall and made their way all the way to the other side of the room, where they took up position at the main entranceway (or at least what they referred to as the main entranceway—the opening used to enter the cave).

Jared disappeared into the hole. A moment later a flame erupted as he lit a torch.

"Where we goin'?" Paul mumbled to the guy next to him.

The guy didn't answer him, didn't even look at him, and for the first time Paul realized that, in light of recent events, his status as Mr. Popularity among the Purees might have changed. In fact, this revelation continued, it was entirely possible that many of the survivors *blamed* them for the deaths of their friends and family members. *Or, depending on how peachy things turned out, the entire Puree extinction*, he thought. He nodded in understanding and muttered, "Right…I got you, Hoss." And, in fact, the guy beside him did resemble the beloved Cartwright. Sort of.

They filed through the small opening one at a time, following Jared's distant flame down one crevasse after another until finally coming to a set of stairs that had either been carved out or blown out (or both). They descended into breezy, colder air, leaving Jared's men behind. Whatever Jared was taking them to see, his people had already seen it and must not care to see it again.

"This reminds me of that time in—"

"Shut up, Paul," Jackson snapped under his breath.

Paul smiled in the darkness. Jackson didn't like talking about that mission, about the watermelon-sized spider that had chased him through a network of caves in South America.

The flickering light disappeared to the right, seeming to evaporate into nothing. But as they approached the spot, Paul saw that there was actually a slit in the wall, running from floor to ceiling. No, not just a slit, but two separate walls, one running parallel to the other. Between them was a narrow passageway that headed back the way they'd come. The men in front of him were turning their bodies sideways and slipping into the gap, following after Jared. "I ever tell you I'm claustrophobic?" Paul asked Jackson, who was having a difficult time getting his large, damaged body to turn sideways with the backpack on.

Jackson didn't answer.

It took about five minutes of slow sidestepping before the gap widened and morphed into another chamber. Everyone gathered around the torch, stretching, breathing the cool air that was suddenly swirling again.

At the other side of the chamber, there stood a steel door.

The torchlight in Jared's hand reflected off its polished surface.

"Must've been a bear getting that thing down here," Paul muttered. It wasn't large, just the size of your standard door. But it did look heavy. Maybe taken from a Navy cruiser or one of the frigates.

Without a word, Jared grabbed the long handle and pulled. The door swung out toward him and revealed to all what was behind it.

Nothing.

Just another rock wall.

Jared lifted a trembling hand and held it out, placing his fingertips against the stone. The motion of it seemed reverent, and he stood there, head bowed as if praying.

"I don't get it," Paul whispered, waiting for a secret door to open or a disco ball to descend. He wasn't the only one missing what was going on, a chorus of mutters filling the air around him. He looked at Jackson, the torchlight dancing in his eyes…eyes that *knew*.

"What?" Paul asked, though traces of the answer had already begun to sprout in his own mind, emerging in the forms of men sticking out of walls.

Jared removed his hand and slowly turned to face the crowd he'd led there. The flickering light in his hand caught the moisture in his eyes, even while his voice remained steady as ice. "Behind this door was where the women, our wives and daughters, spent most of their time in this godforsaken place." His eyes drifted to the floor, sudden shame and guilt visible on his face as he tried to justify the past. "We kept them hidden away so that we wouldn't have to…"

They all knew what he was getting at.

"But now they're gone anyway. We wanted to protect them, but instead we put them in the worst place possible."

"They're trapped behind the rock?" someone asked in horror.

"They're *in* the rock," Paul realized. And out loud apparently.

Every head in the room turned in his direction.

"Maybe," Jared conceded. "But if not…if there's a chance they could be out there somewhere." He pointed up and to his right, but Paul figured it was probably just because he was right-handed and not necessarily indicative of where he thought the women might actually be on the island. "Then I want you to find them. God knows what's going on out there, what happened. And if they're out there alone…"

"If they're out there, we'll find them," someone said. But the voice revealed that it was something hoped for rather than something believed.

"There isn't any time to waste," Jared said, moving away from the wall. He didn't bother to close the door.

As they headed back the way they'd come, once again following Jared's torch, Paul grabbed Jackson's arm. The thing was still like a tree trunk. "Don't even think about it."

"I know what I'm doing," Jackson whispered back.

"Oh yeah? And when did that start?"

Jackson looked away. "I'm not staying here."

"You need to rest. You're all wrecked, man."

"I'm going to the Graveyard."

"You don't think they've picked those ships clean to the bone by now?"

He shrugged, wincing from even that. "Probably, but where else are we gonna find bullets?"

Paul knew it was worthless trying to stop him. "You can't go alone. You won't make it."

"I'll see if I can get a couple guys to come with."

Paul sighed. "Whatever." Then, walking up the steps, he added, "Shouldn't we tell them about the house? What if they come across it? We should warn them."

He nodded. "We'll tell them to stay away from any houses they might find."

That was fine with Paul. "What about the women from the Crystal Caves? What happened to them?" Paul realized that the follow-up conversation Samuel promised hadn't yet occurred. Or perhaps he'd slept through it.

"Still there. They're fine."

"Did you see them?"

"No."

"Then how—"

"I was up early and so was Samuel."

"Oh good, so you can fill me in."

When they rejoined the men from this cave, they had a better understanding of the look permeating their eyes, of the sense of loss and despair they were enduring.

Paul shivered as a swarm of chills raced up his back.

UNDISCOVERED COUNTRY

And therefore God judged them with great judgment, and they weep for their brethren and they will be punished on the Lord's great day.

—Book of Secrets of Enoch 18:4

For owing to these three things came the flood upon the earth, namely, owing to the fornication wherein the Watchers against the law of their ordinances went a whoring after the daughters of men, and took themselves wives of all which they chose: and they made the beginning of uncleanness. And they begat sons of the Naphidim, and they were all unlike, and they devoured one another: and the Giants slew the Naphil, and the Naphil slew the Elijo, and the Elijo mankind, and one man another. And every one sold himself to work iniquity and to shed much blood, and the earth was filled with iniquity.

—Book of Jubilees 7:21-23

"Hear, O Israel! You are crossing over the Jordan today to go in to dispossess nations greater and mightier than you, great cities fortified to heaven, a people great and tall, the sons of the Anakim, whom you know and of whom you have heard it said, 'Who can stand before the sons of Anak?' Know therefore today that it is the Lord your God who is crossing over before you as a consuming fire. He will destroy them and He will subdue them before you, so that you may drive out and destroy them quickly, just as the Lord has spoken to you."

—Deuteronomy 9:1-3 (NASB)

EIGHT

23rd day of June. Afternoon. Bermuda.

There were too many bodies to bury now. And too many corpses to burn. It was a task that would take a couple days, maybe three, depending on how many men were committed to it. But that wasn't their top priority. They'd have to come back for that later. Right now, they needed to finish collecting whatever useable resources they could find and figure out their surroundings. Paul knew that the men scouring the woods around him weren't thrilled with the idea of leaving their brothers to rot among the trees another day, but they didn't really have a choice. There wouldn't be anyone left to bury the bodies if all the surviving Purees were killed trying to transport them through unknown, hostile territory.

He looked down upon another corpse. A single, severed foot in a dirty tennis shoe was lying next to half a man's face. There was no trace of the other half. He leaned down and plucked an old machete from the man's pale hand and put it into the bag with the other weapons he'd found. The bag was getting heavy.

"Russ," a voice whispered behind him. One of the men from the party pushed past him and walked up beside the single-footed body. He put a hand over his mouth, staring down at what had obviously been a close friend or family member.

"Sorry," Paul muttered. "Mark him, and we'll come back tomorrow." He walked on, not wanting to hear the man's muffled sobs.

They were almost to the temple complex, and they'd come across more dead than Paul even realized had been alive in this place. He figured there were about four Fallen dead to every one Puree, which was impressive work for his cave neighbors. Unless the giants had gone berserk and started fighting everyone, in which case there'd just been more bad guy targets for them. He figured that there had been about a hundred and fifty Purees before the battle started (not including the women, since he hardly saw any of them and had no idea what their numbers were). There were just over two dozen left from the Crystal Caves, and he'd counted fifty-three in Jared's cave this morning, which was supposedly an assembly of all the survivors from the entire island. That meant that over half the pure-blooded population had been wiped out in a single day. He had no clue what percentage of Osiris' army had been destroyed. Five percent? All of it? There was still no sign of it anywhere. Maybe they wouldn't need any weapons at all. That would be nice.

So far, they'd only recovered a few guns that had any bullets left in them. If they had to battle again, and Jackson couldn't find a secret stash of firepower in the Graveyard, the battles from here on out would be fought the old-fashioned way. Not a favorable scenario for the pureblooded, and he wondered if Osiris had prevented his armies from using firearms due to their non-sustainability. But then he considered the materials for the complex, the henges, the pyramid… If Osiris wanted to arm his minions with guns, he certainly could've arranged it. Maybe he knew they'd just slaughter each other with them. In any case, Paul didn't want to go up against giants and whatever else might now be lurking on the island with a crappy old sword. He wanted to keep the fingers he had left.

Something deep in the woods caught his eye. Movement, he guessed. But as he stood there staring, slowly slipping an M14 from Jared's remaining stockpile off his shoulder, he thought he could feel eyes on him. Something out there looking at him, staring at him. But through all the plants, weeds, rocks, and trees, he could find no trace of it, only a still silence to mirror his own. Chills crept up his neck as the feeling grew stronger, stronger than Naga Hills, stronger than in the house with the girl. He raised the rifle, knowing that the five bullets it held would do nothing against whatever force was out there. This was no giant, no mere man. This was something else.

"What is it?" someone whispered while stepping quietly toward him.

He didn't lift his eyes from the rifle's sights to see who it was. "I don't know."

"An animal maybe?"

"I don't think so." He sensed the man beside him raise his own weapon, pointing it blindly at the area in question. The rest of the men were moving on ahead, and they were in danger of being on their own. He lowered the gun and moved his head in the direction of the others. "C'mon, let's keep up."

"You sure?"

Now he did turn. The man speaking to him, still pointing a 1972 German HK13 into the woods, was bare-chested, sporting sandals that were half hidden by blue Civil War pants, his face mostly concealed by a low-sitting cowboy hat. A long, straight scar crossed his cheek, and he'd have a few more to match it once the fresh wounds covering his neck and chest healed. "I'm sure," Paul answered, studying the guy. He wasn't a big guy, but Paul could tell he was strong. He was all business, and his eyes, as they peered through the forest, knew the score same as he did. "What's your name?" Paul asked.

"Robinson."

"Crusoe?"

"Ha-ha."

"Where'd the HK come from?"

"This?" The guy finally took his eyes off the trees, giving up on whatever it was (or wasn't) that had first captured Paul's senses. He turned the long Heckler & Koch over in his hands, letting Paul see it.

Paul nodded. "Light support rifle, chambered for NATO rounds. Twenty or thirty-round detachable bow, clip, or straight belt feed." He could see the bipod clipped in place and running underneath the barrel, and it appeared the scope was in working order as well. He so wanted to trade his M14 for it.

"Found it myself, actually. In the submarine."

"No."

He nodded.

"How many shots you have left?"

"This clip is full, and I have half another." He slung it over his shoulder. "Started out with ten boxes of bullets. Now down to this. Everyone's running dry now."

"So how are you with a bow and arrow?"

Robinson snorted.

Paul couldn't place his accent and would've assumed he was like all the other weird-talking people that grew up in this mini smorgasbord if it weren't for the tattoo on his arm. He didn't get a MOM tattoo on this island. Maybe if they were having a beer in a bar in some US base halfway around the world, Paul would've asked some more questions. Or maybe not. Questions had a way of rebounding, and there was no way he would start the "get-to-know-me" game with anyone, much less his friendly neighborhood Puree here. No, sir, not a chance. So he took one more longing look at the rifle and then doubled his pace back to the others, leaving Robinson to wonder what it was that had spooked him. Paul didn't know himself, but whatever the feeling was, whatever had *pinged* on his extrasensory radar, had disappeared.

As he walked on, trying to shake that aftertaste of the psychic contact, Paul's mind began to weave and turn, darting in and out of holes, each one bearing a riddle. He was thinking of Hunter, of the house and the girl, replaying it over and over, trying to find an explanation. When one didn't present itself, he began thinking of the women, both in the Crystal Caves and the ones that had vanished behind a wall of rock. Were they gone? Their bodies like those he'd woken up to? Like the stories of the men involved with the Philadelphia Experiment, becoming one with the ship they were in? How many women were there, anyway? What had their lives been like in this awful place? And then he found himself thinking of Jackson, of his mentioning Denise. What had prompted that? He hadn't mentioned her in years, had said he didn't ever want to talk about it, which was why they'd all left it alone, honoring his request. But suddenly here she was again. Why?

They were coming up to the courtyard. They could see it through the trees. The bodies were still there, no longer floating in water but sticking out of the mud. The ziggurat's fountain was dried up, and the scene was clearer now that the heavens had closed its floodgates.

Stepping into the slop, leaving the forest behind, the rest of the pyramid complex opened up before them. The pyramid was indeed gone, as had already been established, but now they were witnessing firsthand in broad daylight what else was missing…all of it replaced by forest. They stood there, staring in disbelief and wonder at the impossibility of it all.

Paul turned back to face the woods they'd just exited, the *ping* suddenly exploding back onto the radar. The feeling of being watched was stronger than ever. And then he saw her. Standing in the fingered shadows of waving branches. The girl that he'd killed so long ago.

Only she wasn't crying anymore.

* * * *

Jackson took a deep, painful breath and second-guessed his decision to make the cross-island trek to the Graveyard. He needed to rest. And to drink. A lot. His vision was clouding, and he was having trouble staying focused. He leaned against a tree and squinted at the three others as they waded deeper into a sea of ferns. He pressed his hand against his side, where Paul had seared his flesh closed, and there was some relief to his insides when he did so. He couldn't figure out what those bastards had done to him while he was imprisoned in the ziggurat, but he knew what it *felt* like they did to him. Felt like they'd enjoyed playing a game of Frankenstein on his innards. He was still alive, though, and each new day he awoke in this hell testified that they hadn't done anything so dramatic. But they did something, that was sure. He wondered if the UFO nightmares would be starting soon, the bright light, the probing, the cutting… Didn't Chadwick say something about aliens, fallen angels, and ancient gods all being one and the same?

They were almost to Tucker's Town Bay, but Jackson was beginning to doubt whether the Graveyard would still be there. The route they were on now should've taken them alongside Castle Harbor. But there was no Castle Harbor, only more woods. But the bay was in the harbor, so if the harbor was gone, the bay couldn't be there either. And neither could the Graveyard.

Suddenly, Arkansas Joe turned and started waving at him, signaling for him to join them in the waist-high ferns. They were staring at something on the ground, something at their feet.

Jackson sighed and pushed himself off the tree, navigating his way through the dense undergrowth until he was standing in the huge, fan like ferns, too. "What is it?" he asked as he approached.

They pointed down at the forest floor.

A horse. Two tails. Dead.

"A fresh kill," Joe stated.

It was one of the horses they'd seen before, the product of Osiris' genetic manipulations. The horse's ribs were showing, the meat picked off the bone. The blood hadn't dried yet.

Jackson began searching the grounds, looking for any evidence that might reveal which way the hunter (or hunters) had run off in. Drops of blood and bent ferns went southeast, toward where Harrington Sound used to be. Well, now they knew there were still animals and hunters on the island.

"Let's keep moving," he said. "Keep your eyes open."

The Frenchman (Pierre, Jackson thought his name was) nodded and mumbled something in French. Jackson knew there had to be different languages spoken among the Purees but had only heard their attempts at a uniquely accented English. He looked at the man but received no further explanation. The guy simply flipped the collar up on his jean jacket and shivered against a series of chills as the wind swept through the ferns around them. Then he turned with his sword and rifle and pressed onward.

As Jackson hobbled after them, he once again considered the possibility that he might be dreaming. After all, the plant life he was touching had materialized from nowhere, replacing ocean with solid ground. Whatever happened at the solstice, it seemed to have merged two worlds into one. *Or maybe many worlds into one*, he thought. A multiverse overlap? Different, alternate universes existing at once suddenly colliding on the same plane? The Bermuda that the *Sea Venture* shipwrecked on back in 1609, the Bermuda that Osiris had been imprisoned on, and now some other versions of Bermuda being mixed in, too? He looked at the trees, the clouds. Or maybe it was something else. Maybe it wasn't a merger of multiple places or realities, but of time. What was Bermuda like thousands of years ago? What if the use of the pyramid had altered the island in such a way that time itself had been bridged? But then there was the closet elevator to hell.

And Denise.

* * * *

Someone called him, and he turned away from the girl. When he turned back to her, heart still frozen in his chest, she was gone. Paul looked to the right and to the left, scanning the woods. She wasn't there. He stepped back, emotions swirling inside. Guilt, remorse, terror… Was it in his head, or had she actually been there? When he'd seen her in the house, she was as he remembered her, crying, pleading. But this time her face was not one of sadness, but of cold calculation. Paul had never been a fan of the horror genre, had never needed the cheap thrills to make him feel alive, but he'd seen enough previews for them on TV to recognize the girl's expression for what it was. He flexed his bandaged hand around the barrel of the M14, but the feel of the weapon brought little comfort.

"Paul," the voice repeated.

He turned away from the forest, the hopes that he was simply hallucinating fading fast. "What?"

It was Robinson. He was pointing to the temple. "Are we going in?"

Paul stared up at the ziggurat for a few seconds and then turned his attention to the others who were already busy combing the courtyard, examining corpses and collecting every weapon they could find into backpacks, duffel bags, belts, and pockets. He knew they would have to venture back inside the temple at some point. The answers they needed might be in there somewhere. Some clue as to what happened, where the pyramid had gone, where Henry, John, and Osiris had gone. The answers to getting out of this nightmare could be hidden within the corridors, keeping the company of men sticking out of walls and black portals able to transport them to who knew where. Gypsum-covered henges around the island? Different rooms in different structures? Back to the real world? Or perhaps to the dark side of the moon? And then what of the captured women that had been in there? Were they free from Osiris' spell now that he was gone? Were they in there somewhere waiting to be rescued? They would have to enter the mystery at some point, but not right now. The men were tired, hungry, and thirsty. They were emotionally shot and needed time to recover. Entering the temple now, exhausted and unprepared, would be foolish. He hadn't seen a living soul in there upon waking up, but he hadn't explored the whole structure either. He didn't know *what* could be in there.

"No. Not today."

Robinson nodded, continued scanning the grounds. "Just what in the hell happened?" he whispered.

Paul knew he was referring to the absence of the pyramid and the other structures that had made up the temple complex. They were gone, missing, replaced by a full-grown forest that appeared to be hundreds, if not thousands of years old. He thought of telling him about the back end of the temple, how it had been sliced off, but didn't feel like it. "I don't know," he just said. He looked up to the sun, and assuming time was still following its normal pattern, figured they'd been out for nearly three hours. It was time to wrap it up. They'd come back for the dead tomorrow and worry about the temple some other time.

Ten minutes later, they were all standing around him, bags full of salvaged weaponry and equipment.

"Okay," he shouted, "we'll take the beach back. Keep your eyes peeled on the tree line. We still don't know what is or isn't out there."

They nodded their tired approval and began moving. As they walked north toward the ocean, leaving their dead friends in the mud, Paul's missing fingers caught fire. He thought of ice, of Advil. Of the Coke Hunter had gone on about and how he could really go for a cold Coke right now, too. He thought about the kitchen, wondered if he might be able to—

The girl.

She was standing up on a hill, the sun positioned behind her, backlighting her. She was staring at him, dirt and blood all over her.

He froze, and one of the men bumped into him, jarring his attention from her. When he looked back to the hill, there were only trees, the sun casting their long shadows down across the courtyard.

Robinson came up alongside him. "You okay?"

Paul didn't answer, just continued walking.

NINE

23rd day of June. Late afternoon. Bermuda.

Jackson's hopes of there still being a Graveyard were fading with every foot of new forest they covered. They should be in the bay right now, swimming with the fishes. Instead, lavish forest pressed in on them from all sides. And, unlike the twisted island they were used to, this *other* version of Bermuda was teeming with life—chirping birds, tree-swinging critters, even some oinking pigs.

It bothered him, the pigs. He'd stood on St. Catherine's Beach and explained to John how Gonzales Ferdinando d'Oviedo tried getting pigs onto the island back in 1515. Strong winds had prevented him from doing so, and as far as Jackson knew, there was never another attempt. So where the hell did the bacon come from?

The turtles, the shearwater, the cedars…they were here because this Bermuda had never been settled by modern man. And as far as he knew, Osiris hadn't summoned any swine through the Triangle. Horses, yes. They'd seen them. But no pigs. Again he wondered if their time might've been merged with a much older time, a distant age when pigs were as common to Bermuda as its pink sands.

He thought of Antarctica, how they say it used to be north of its present location, before the pole shift, and wondered if the land-mass he was on now was once elsewhere…or part of something bigger. The ancient maps Ronald had hanging on his wall, the ones revealing Antarctica from a time before it was covered in ice, proved that man had charted the seas and populated the islands much longer ago than conventional thinking allowed. The Oronteus Finnaeus map of 1531, Philippe Buache's map of 1737, the famous Piri Reis map of 1513 found in Istanbul in 1929… He'd spent hours talking to Ronald about the older maps that the ones displayed in his house had been based on—maps from the Library of Alexandria that had ended up in Constantinople, maps that were impossibly accurate for a time before the chronometer, how they displayed Upper Egypt as the center of the world… Could portions of this island have been reverted back to some ancient time? And if so, did all its biological life come along with it? Its creatures…its *people*? But then there was the house, which obviously didn't come from the deep, mysterious past. Though similar technologies may have existed (as indicated through Egyptian hieroglyphics), the milk had a current expiration date. And he had a hard time imagining the ancient Atlantians swinging by the local grocery store for a gallon of milk.

He shook his head off the trail to nowhere, forgetting how he'd even ended up there. *Pigs*. Oh yeah.

"I see the ocean," Joe said, pointing through the trees ahead.

Jackson squinted. He could make out pinpricks of turquoise through the density. "If that's the ocean, there is no more bay. No more Graveyard."

"Wait. I see something," the third member of their group called out. He was a tall, sinewy Cuban, but Jackson had still not gotten his name. "There's something out there, in the water."

At first Jackson thought it was just the sunlight glimmering off the surface of the ocean, but then he saw it too. There *was* something out there. "Come on," he said, and forced his aching body to move faster.

The trees thinned out and gave way to a white beach, the crystal waters caressing its cluttered shore. Half-buried planes and boats stretched up and down the coast. Jackson could now see that the thing in the water was the USS *Cyclops*, sunlight reflecting off its rusted bow a hundred yards away.

"It's still here," Pierre mumbled, amazed.

Jackson put his hand up to shield his eyes from the sun and surveyed the beach to the east. Flight 19, the lost WWII Avengers that had done so much to popularize the Bermuda Triangle, were still lined up side by side, most of their wings buried. The hull of the submarine that they'd seen before was rising just five feet out of the shallow surf, its hull like a metal dome separating the frothy waters. There was no way to know whether it was a piece of the whole or if the entire vessel had been buried straight down into the ground. A horde of airplanes were stacked on top of each other, upside-down, some of them moving back and forth with the tide.

He looked west and saw more of the same.

"Where do we start?" Joe asked.

Jackson looked up at the sun. It was getting late and they were running out of time. "Anything you don't recognize?"

The three others looked up and down the beach.

"There." The Cuban pointed. About two hundred yards down the beach sat a Navy warship. "I don't remember that."

Jackson nodded. He was pretty sure he would've noticed a modern-era US destroyer as well. He thought about mentioning the house, whether he should warn them or not of some of the island's new toys, but didn't feel like getting into all that right now. They didn't have the time for it. "Okay. Be careful, though. Anything seems off, you get out of there right away. We'll meet back here in twenty." Not that any of them had synchronized watches, but they all understood the general timeframe they had in which to work.

"Where are you going?" Joe asked.

"We don't have time to stay together. Two of you go to the destroyer, one of you check out that DC-3 over there."

They looked at him with blank, impatient stares.

"The big airplane with the propellers that's sitting next to that old schooner," he explained, pointing.

They nodded their understanding.

"I'm going to have a look in the patrol boat over there." He pointed up the beach, in the opposite direction. "Twenty minutes."

They turned and headed away, navigating through the displaced Graveyard. Jackson watched them until they split up. The Cuban and Pierre continued on toward the destroyer, and Joe veered left toward the plane.

After adjusting his backpack and rifle (a Lee-Enfield Rifle No 5 Jungle Carbine that had been handed to him by someone back at the caves) Jackson headed off toward a US Navy Vietnam-era patrol boat. It was resting on its side and wouldn't be easy to board, but he had a good feeling about it, even though their best bet of finding working supplies was probably in the destroyer. Guns, radios, food, clothes… And why not? The refrigerator in the house had been stocked.

He checked the 1944 UK Rifle No 5 bolt-action again, severely unhappy about it. It had a rubber shoulder protector and a flash hider, but the shortened model was notorious for its excessive recoil and muzzle blast. Its sights also tended to drift out of alignment, which is why the thing was discontinued three years after its introduction. The ten-round detachable box magazine had six remaining shots, which meant he would have to make each one count if it came to that (hoping the thing even fired). He blew sand out of the trigger, then held it ready as he ducked beneath the wing of an old Cessna.

A voice came to him, drifting off the waves, carried by the breeze.

"Eliot…"

He stopped and turned back toward the destroyer. The two men were growing smaller before it, and he almost shouted for them to stop.

"Eliot…"

He whipped his head back around. Her voice, *Denise's* voice, wasn't coming from the destroyer. It was coming from somewhere out in the water, somewhere—

Footprints.

Jackson dropped to a knee, still in the shadow of the airplane's cracked wing. Chills racked his skin as he stayed still, scanning the waterline for any sign of movement. The wet sand down by the water held a set of footprints he could make out all the way from his position. They stretched out along the beach, disappearing every so often in the encroaching surf. He couldn't make out the direction they were headed in, too far away for that, so he rose to his feet and began using the planes and boats as cover, creeping back and forth toward the footprints.

"Eliot," the voice whispered.

He did his best to ignore it, moving closer to the tide.

A broken mast from an old seventeenth or eighteenth-century ship stuck out of the sand in front of him like a telephone pole, no sign of its sail. He leaned against it, aiming the Jungle Carbine into the shadows around him, expecting an Osiris soldier to come bursting out of a nearby vessel at any moment.

He listened.

Nothing but the crashing waves and the gliding surf with a few dozen vessels creaking and moaning in its fingers.

He could make out the prints now. They were heel to toe, pointing west. They were small. Maybe a child, or—

Eliot, please…

This time her voice seemed to originate in his mind, like she was there with him…*in* him. And maybe she was. Or again, could be he was cracking. God knew he'd seen enough in the last few months to fry any sane person's mind. Like the egg. Crack. Sizzle. But he knew better.

He crept out from behind the tail of an old Air Force jet and walked up beside the line of prints. Five toes on each foot. He followed them, the hair on his neck standing straight, his own boots leaving imprints twice as large next to the barefooted impressions that could not possibly belong to Denise. No matter what the whispered voice insinuated.

He tapped his finger against the trigger, ready.

Suddenly, the heel—to—toe imprints changed, abandoning the heel. Whoever was walking the beach had, at this point, begun to sprint, all the weight on the balls of their feet, the distance between them separating drastically.

Thirty yards later, the prints turned up the beach.

He paused, his heart pounding in his chest.

More prints, coming from the forest and heading down to the water, intersected the path of the little feet. Only these prints were bigger than his own boot-clad impressions. Much bigger. Huge craters in the dry sand.

He followed them with his eyes, tracing them into the wet sand ahead of him, where each had become a perfect stamp. And there his fear was confirmed.

Six toes.

He looked out over the ocean, beyond where the giant had evidently walked straight into the water. Where had it gone? For a swim? Or maybe it was moving along the beach, hiding its tracks beneath the water.

He chose to keep after the tiny prints and chased them further up into the dry sand, where they deteriorated into mere divots. It became a challenge to keep on the trail, hard to tell the divots from the hills. The footprints led him past another overturned Cessna and beneath a broken derrick before disappearing behind a plane's vertical stabilizer rising out of the sand like a huge, gleaming shark fin. He went around the fin and, standing in its shadow, spotted the superstructure of a passenger-cargo ship protruding out of the sand just twenty yards away. The footprints went directly to it, leading to a broken window on what Jackson believed to be the passenger deck.

Taking a quick look around, scanning the dozens of vessels littered around him, he moved as quickly as he could. He was facing the front of the superstructure, positioned just about in the center of it, which meant he couldn't see around it to where the stern should be. Seven windows stood just over his head, all lined up in a neat row. Above the passenger deck, the bridge and observation decks loomed. He turned and looked back in the direction he'd come but found no evidence of the rest of the ship. There was no sign of the radar, antenna, exhaust stacks, derricks, or anything else, either, and he wasn't sure if the entire ship was beneath the beach or if the superstructure had somehow been separated from it and dropped from the sky. What he did know, however, was that someone was in there.

He pulled himself up through the broken window and dropped down inside the ship.

He landed in the main lounge, the Lee-Enfield already sweeping back and forth through what was a musty-smelling room. Sunlight streamed through the windows behind him, illuminating the deck with wide, beaming rays. At his back, beneath the windows, a long book cabinet stretched the length of the wall. Some books were still standing in it, but most were spilled haphazardly across the floor at his feet. There were two striped sofas and two arm-chairs around him, as well as an overturned coffee table and lamp stands. Directly across from him, on the aft wall, was a long desk, sofas still sitting perfectly at each end. Behind the desk, there'd been a glass wall looking into the lobby and its descending staircase—the glass now in pieces and covering the soggy carpet.

Jackson looked to his left. A curtain hung half open over a doorway. It was the same to the right. For no particular reason, he chose the door on the left, stepping over books, framed pictures, and broken lamps on his way there. He paused in front of the curtain, listening for any sign of movement from the other side. Nothing. He pulled the curtain open, ready to fire.

The dining room. Most of the tables were on end, and the chairs were toppled throughout the small, oval-shaped room. Curtains were covering some of the windows, but there was enough light streaming in to illuminate the space. Utensils and broken plates were all over the floor, the mounted wall lamps long dark.

He moved back into the lounge and, just to make sure, looked out the window. The waves were crashing on the beach, the Graveyard still present. *Good.* For a second he'd imagined the dining room being some portal to another dimension, one worse off than the one he was already stuck in.

About to head across the lounge to what looked like a bar room on the port side of the deck, he heard a noise. Turning to his left, careful not to step on the broken glass, he studied the lobby and the staircase. Had the noise come from below, or…

He stepped through the doorway that led to the lobby and its staircase and found himself looking down a hallway, a closed door at the end of it. There were seven more doors that lined the left side of the corridor, five on the right. The ones on the left would be staterooms. All of them were closed.

The air was heavy and humid in the hallway, no air-flow at all. It was quiet and musty, and the walls had black mold crawling on them.

Eliot…

The whispered voice sounded off in his head like a trumpet, and he almost squeezed the trigger. *Not now, dammit.*

He could hear movement in one of the rooms. He swallowed, his throat dry, his heart pumping. It couldn't be her. It just *couldn't.*

Forcing one foot in front of the other, he entered the corridor, approaching the first door on the left. As he got closer, he saw that it wasn't closed all the way. A sliver of space existed between the door and doorframe. Looked like the screws in the upper hinge plate had rusted and snapped, allowing the door to pull away from the frame. He peered through the gap. It was a galley, but it was too dark in there to see anything. It didn't matter. He knew no one had gone in there for quite some time since opening the door would result in the bottom hinge plate ripping out of the moldy wall and the door falling into the room.

He moved on, suddenly very conscious of the weight on his back. He squirmed beneath the backpack, his shoulders sore. Sweat dripped into his eyes. What would he do if he opened a door and found her standing there in a stateroom? What would it mean?

The next door was closed and still fastened securely to the wall. He touched the handle, half expecting his hand to pass right through it, the revelation of this ghost ship finally dawning, but the handle turned and the door swung open.

The stateroom would have been considered elegant in its day (and going by the décor, that day seemed to be around 1960). Even with the broken windows, peeling wallpaper, rusted metal, and sun-bleached carpets, Jackson could see it. The salty air, the wind, and rain did its best to corrode what he now knew to be a passenger cargo liner, but the vessel had held up remarkably well. Or at least the superstructure had. The main mast, loading mast, foremast, derricks, crane and exhaust stacks should've all been standing like totem poles out of the sand, reaching higher than the observation deck. Again, that there was no sign of them meant they'd either snapped off, had been salvaged upon arrival, or that the superstructure itself had been separated from the ship.

The curtains were shredded over the two open windows and were blowing into the room on the fingers of a cool, ocean breeze. The room was spacious, eight feet of floor space between two dark timber-framed beds with rusted trim. A desk sat beneath a mirror that was still hanging intact on the wall. A coffee table, sofa, chair, and cabinets also furnished the room. He wondered why all this had failed to be confiscated by the pureblooded. The beds would be far more comfortable than the palmetto-thatched things they were all sleeping on.

And then a troubling thought struck him. What if the boat hadn't been brought here some fifty years ago by Osiris? What if it had only been here for a few *days*? The possibility of that, all the moving parts of time and space and quantum mechanics, the Bermuda Triangle and the Philadelphia Experiment and the Terry Gilliam film with Sean Connery and John Cleese…

Eliot. I am here. Come to me now.

He turned, certain she would be standing in the hallway behind him. But there was nothing.

A crash. From the cabin next door. Shuffling feet. Drawers opening and closing.

Whoever the tiny feet belonged to was in the next room.

Eliot, please.

He caught a glimpse of himself in the mirror, recognized the look in his eyes. Fear. Hope. He also saw how ridiculous he looked in the small jacket and short bellbottoms.

Moving out of the room and back into the hallway, he took a deep breath, aiming the rifle at the next door. It was closed, but he could see shadows moving back and forth beneath it.

His heart felt like a grenade with the pin pulled, about to explode at any second. He frantically wiped the sweat out of his eyes with the back of his hand, the weight of the backpack suddenly nonexistent.

"Eliot."

His breathing stopped, his body frozen. The voice was not in his head. It had come from behind the door.

After a moment to regain his breath, he reached for the doorknob.

And stopped.

Her voice had called to him in the house, too. From behind that door leading to a demon-filled abyss. How did he know this door didn't lead to the same?

The shadow continued to move.

He took a step back. She was dead. She wasn't here. Whatever was behind the door was something else, something that would drag him straight to hell, he was sure of it. No, he wouldn't do it, no matter how bad he wanted to.

He took another step away. And another.

The door opened.

TEN

23rd day of June. Early evening. Bermuda

When they reached the beach, Paul suggested that they take a rest. He got no complaints, but wondered if they resented his taking the lead. After all, they'd been here forever and knew the place better than he did. Or at least, *used* to. It was a whole new ballgame now, a whole new world and all of that. And maybe that leveled the playing field of experience a bit, because they didn't *seem* to mind complying with his instruction. In fact, he could still spot a twinkle of hope in some of their eyes, a last-ditch faith in the American newbies having been sent here by God to free them from this prison. Even after most of the Purees had been wiped out (and despite his earlier suspicions of them blaming him for what had happened), it appeared he was still their Moses. At least for the time being. And maybe because they had no other choices. After all, if the ex-SEALs weren't here to deliver them, then who would be? Especially if Osiris' departure closed the Bermuda Triangle gateway. This was it, the fourth quarter, and Team Paul had the football.

He dropped the bag of weapons into the sand beside him and rested the M14 down on top of it. Then he sat, feeling like every bone and muscle in his body was cursing him as he did so. Most of the others did the same, lying on their backs and closing their eyes against the sun.

The waves crashed against the big rocks that sat scattered in the shallow waters. The water was crystal, the sand pink. Clouds stood still, pinned to a vibrant blue backdrop. He felt himself drifting away, the world around him slipping off into the distance. The voices of the men grew quiet as the sun's warmth massaged his face. Sleep was here, beckoning him with its hooked finger, and he could not resist.

His mind was filled with thoughts of the girl, of what it meant. Was the island haunted? Had the pyramid merged the physical world with the spirit world and now the ghosts were here for revenge? Or was it something else? Some mysterious power the island now had, manifesting guilt over past wrongs? His imagination toyed with such ideas, all the while Jackson's voice repeated: *No, it's the witch's call.*

The sun that was warming his face disappeared, and he frowned, his descent into slumber halted. Forcing one eye open, he found himself in Robinson's shadow. But Robinson wasn't looking down at him. He was looking out into the ocean, eyes trying to work out a puzzle.

"What is it?" Paul asked, making himself sit up.

"A ship."

By the time Paul got to his feet, others had taken notice too, all of them gathering at the shoreline and staring out at the distant shape. It stood like a smudge against the bright horizon, miles away.

"A cruise ship," Paul stated, wondering if Robinson really did wake him up.

"Taken out of the Graveyard by the storm?" someone close by guessed.

Paul shook his head. "You would've known if a cruise ship was parked on your island. This is something else."

"A new arrival…" Robinson said.

Paul squinted against the glare. "Sort of."

Back in the day, he would've been able to make the swim to the ship no problem. But not now. Not in his condition. And how would he even get up onto the ship once he reached it? Could crew and passengers still be on it? They would need to find out for sure. If anything, there should be plenty of supplies aboard.

"You thinking what I'm thinking?" Robinson asked, eyes still on the boat.

Paul turned and looked at him. "I doubt it."

"I'm thinking if we were ever to try sailing off this island, doing so aboard a luxury liner would be nice."

It would be nice. *If* there was anywhere to sail to. But then he understood Rob's point. It might be better to live out the rest of your days aboard a cruise ship, hoping to one day show up in the real world, rather than hiding from giants every day. He nodded. "We'll need rope."

"Not a problem."

But Paul was afraid the ship would be gone by the time they could assemble everything they'd need. "How fast could we get a boat rowed here?"

Robinson studied the exhausted faces of the men around him. "Not sure any of them have it in them to sprint all the way to the boat and then row it back."

He was right. They would collapse halfway back to the caves. Still, they couldn't just let the ship drift away. He looked up at the sun. It was descending, dipping closer and closer to the water. They had a few hours of daylight left and then they could only hope the ship would be there in the morning. He wasn't willing to take that chance. He could tell it was moving even now.

"We're going to lose it," Rob stated.

And for a second, Paul considered that perhaps that would be a good thing. After that closet in the house, who knew what might be on the ship? "Okay, lead everyone back to the caves," Paul said. "Move as quickly as you can without killing yourselves. Take only the weapons you need. Leave everything else here with me. I'll keep an eye on the ship until you get back here with the boats."

"You're staying here by yourself?"

He shrugged, looking around. "Unless you got volunteers."

As if on cue, the witch's cry started up again, echoing through the forest behind them. Paul flinched. Rob didn't.

Whistling, Robinson pointed at two Purees, motioning them over. When they reached him, he said, "You two stay here with Paul and keep your eye on the ship. I'll take the rest back to get the boats."

They nodded, and Rob looked at Paul. "Okay?"

"Fine."

And then Robinson waved to the others, picked up his HK13, and started leading them up the beach.

Paul and the two others watched them go, trying to ignore the birds at their back.

"Get cozy, gentlemen," Paul said. "We're gonna be here for a bit." He sat back down, pulled the rifle across his lap, and turned his attention to the cruise ship.

* * * *

Jackson snapped the shortened rifle up and stepped back against the wall behind him in one fluid motion as the door opened inward, the windows from within spilling light into the hallway around him.

His heart stopped in his chest, and his finger fell away from the trigger.

Standing there in the doorway, one hand clutching a framed picture and the other still on the doorknob, was a woman.

Denise.

The sunlight was swimming through her long, blond hair. She was tall, her eyes a dazzling blue, her skin soft and lacking the typical island tan.

She froze when she saw him, too, a shout of surprise catching in her throat.

It *wasn't* Denise.

Confusion paraded over his mind, stomping his sense of reality. Slowly, things became clear and his heart started to beat again. The woman was not Denise, but she sure shared some striking similarities with her.

Seconds ticked by as they stood there, eyes locked on each other, her hand still on the doorknob, him pointing the rifle at her.

"Are you going to shoot me?" she finally asked, the fear of being startled seeping out of her eyes.

Her accent was island-raised Puree. He recognized it immediately and knew she was one of them.

He blinked and lowered the rifle. "No." It came out in a whisper.

"Who are you?"

"Jackson."

She squinted at him, and her hand fell away from the door. "You're one of the soldiers."

He couldn't be sure whether he was the soldier she was referring to or not but guessed that he probably was. "What are you doing here?"

She shrugged, then looked down at the picture in her hands. "We were sitting around waiting to hear news of the battle and…"

She looked up and waved a hand in front of her face. It was a motion that Jackson first associated with a Jedi mind trick, and he second-guessed his earlier dismissal of island Force. But if she was trying to brainwash him into accepting a story, it wasn't working. Instead, he thought of the naked temple women—and where else could she have come from? With Osiris gone, his slaves would be free from his spell (as he personally knew), allowing them to wander away from the temple to…random ships in the Graveyard? He thought of the intersecting footprints. The giant coming from the forest, her sprinting up the beach.

And then he understood. "You were in the cave…"

She nodded, her hair falling over bare shoulders. She was wearing an old black spaghetti-strapped tank top that was a little smaller than it should be. She was beautiful for sure, just as Denise had been, but her beauty was only confusing him more.

"I was talking to Rebecca, asking if she thought we would be okay, and then suddenly I'm standing in the middle of the forest."

"Just you?"

She nodded.

That may or may not be good news for the other women believed to now be one with the limestone cave. He had a thousand questions for her, and his mind was racing, emotions swirling like a storm. He swore he could still hear Denise's voice echoing in some far off corner of his mind. And she looked so much like her. Her eyes, hair, lips… He wasn't sure he could trust this experience, this meeting. Was it real, or would she suddenly explode into a storm of crows and fly away? Was she actually there in front of him, a pure-blooded woman transported from Jared's cave at the solstice, or was this some terrible deception, attempting to lure him into a trap?

"You started running."

She looked at him questioningly.

"I followed your footprints."

"A giant came out of the forest," she answered.

"Looks like it went into the water."

"It did."

"Did it come back?"

"I didn't wait around to find out."

He let his eyes drift downward, to the picture. "What do you have there?"

She turned the picture around and held it up for him to see. There were two people, a man and a woman, with their arms around each other. They were smiling at the camera, the background out of focus but clearly a backyard. Trees, a fence, a garden… They were higher than all that, though, standing on a deck. "My parents," she said.

He could definitely see her in their faces. He looked above the picture, back into her eyes. So many questions, so little time. He needed to get back, to meet up with the others. Before turning away, however, he let his eyes focus on the room behind her. Drawers were opened, mattresses flipped.

She saw the question in his eyes. "This was the boat that brought them to this place. This was their room."

"How do you know?" His eyes went back to the picture.

"They used to bring me here when I was young. I remembered seeing the picture here on the table."

"They didn't take it with them to the caves?"

"Times were different back then. We had more freedom to wander. The boat was our secret getaway."

Whether the "freedom" she was referring to was associated with Nephilim danger or pure-blooded regulation, he would have to inquire another time. Sound came from behind him.

Broken glass.

Someone was about to step into the hallway.

Jackson grabbed her arm, pushing her back into the room and closing the door behind them. He put a finger to his lips and motioned for her to back into the corner across the room. He didn't know who was coming, maybe just Robinson, Pierre, or the nameless Cuban, but he wasn't about to take any chances.

He moved to the side of the door and got ready.

The handle turned, and the door crept open.

And then there was stillness, the door wide but no one entering. He kept his eyes on the girl's, waiting for that telling moment of contact. There was no way the person in the hall could miss her leaning against the wall in the corner, knees slightly bent, long legs showing in a pair of old khaki shorts. She was in the doorway's direct line of sight.

Her eyes widened. Not a lot, just enough to tell him she'd been spotted. He hoped to God an arrow or spear wouldn't scream through the room before he could do anything. Hoped that, if it was a bad guy out there, that he would want more from the girl than just her blood.

Suddenly, and without warning, a figure exploded into the cabin. It came so fast that Jackson almost missed him, letting the person past and onto Denise (*not Denise!)* with a crude knife. But he managed to get the butt of the rifle around in time, striking the attacker in the face from his concealed position beside the doorframe. There was a *crack*, and one of Osiris' Fallen landed hard on his back, feet lingering in the air for a second.

"Guess they're still here," Jackson mumbled, watching the blood start to puddle from the broken nose and mouth. "We need to go."

She stared at the crumpled body on the floor, watching as the blood spread out and soaked into the old carpet of her parents' stateroom.

"Come on," he urged.

She lifted her eyes. "Is he still here?"

He knew exactly who she was talking about. "No. He's gone."

An ever-present tension released its grip on her face, and the skin across her brow and around her mouth and eyes—for perhaps the first time ever—relaxed. She was free. Imprisoned on the island, and apparently with men still trying to kill her, but she was free. And that freedom was evident in the watery glaze that now filled her eyes.

Jackson was about to say something, probably something stupid, but a noise came from outside before he could get anything out. He forced his gaze off her sparkling eyes and crossed the room to the windows.

What he saw below shocked him. "What the hell?"

He spun away from the sight outside, intent on grabbing the girl and getting out of there pronto, but when he came around, he found another of the Fallen standing in the doorway. The girl (*and how in the blue blazes did she do that?*) had gotten across the room and was now in the same position he'd been in beside the doorframe, reversing their prior roles.

The man was big, bigger than Jackson, and the sword he held was already in the process of being released. He didn't have time to get the rifle up, and could only brace against being skewered to the wall.

But she was already attacking, herself.

As the monster stepped forward into the room (in order to clear the doorframe when he unleashed the sword), the blond woman exploded into action, a knife suddenly in her hand, materializing from nowhere, and *stab-stab-stabbing*. She'd stepped forward, dropping to a knee as her knife flashed silver to red—one, two, three lightning stabs, and the soldier's sword flew from his hand and went straight out the window as he went twisting over from the attack.

She continued to thrust and stab, working around him, administering quick strikes to his legs, sides, ribs, and back. Jackson couldn't keep up with the blows.

When the monster finally crashed to his knees, blood oozing from punctured arteries, she stepped into his back and grabbed his head, jerking it back and stretching his muscled neck. Another red flash and then a line across his neck, opening, opening, opening until it disappeared beneath a waterfall of spurting blood.

She pushed the kneeling corpse in the back, and it fell over with a soggy thud.

The entire thing only lasted a few blinks, and Jackson stood stunned, staring as the girl's chest heaved beneath the tank top, sweat beading her hairline, veins bulging in her forearms and neck.

He didn't know if he was terrified or in love. He did know this was definitely *not* Denise. No matter how much they looked alike.

She took three long strides across the room and went to the window. "What did you see?" But he didn't have to answer.

Running out of the woods and pouring onto the beach all along the tree line was an army of Fallen soldiers. Like ants swarming to candy, they seemed to be heading straight for the superstructure.

She looked back to Jackson, who was just standing there, his mouth open, still staring at the work of her hands. "Well?" she asked.

He blinked. "Huh?" And then he snapped out of it. Even if she was a ninja and he was John Rambo, they stood no chance against a hundred demon-possessed men. Not with just two knives and a couple bullets.

"Let's go." Jackson grabbed her bare arm and pulled her after him again. They ran out of the stateroom, the girl only resisting long enough to grab the framed picture off the floor.

They could hear men dropping into the lounge, walking on the broken glass.

He thought about taking the stairs down below deck but decided against it. Even if the rest of the ship was below them, he had no idea what condition it might be in. They could find themselves trapped in the dark with no way out.

He pulled her in the opposite direction, toward the closed door at the end of the hall. He was hoping for a deck on the other side, one looking out over the sand that they could jump down from or use to climb up into the above decks.

He pushed the door open, and they were immediately greeted by daylight.

They ran out onto a deck that should've been overlooking the rear of the ship, but of course, there was only the Graveyard beneath them.

Hearing footsteps pounding down the hall after them, Jackson slammed the door shut.

"We need to get out of here."

But she was already halfway up to the boat deck, her long, lithe body moving gracefully up-up-up until swinging her feet over the rusted rails. She looked back down at him, hair glowing in the descending sun. "Come on," she urged, looking up at the forest and the men still pouring out of it.

Jackson felt like an elephant trying to work its way through a jungle gym after watching the way she'd simply glided upward. He dropped down over the railing and swung the rifle back toward the hallway door below just as it banged open and the runner came barreling out onto the deck. But before he could send off a bullet, there was a knife sticking out of the person's neck. He went down hard on the deck, clutching at the knife as he died.

Jackson looked at the girl again. "Who the hell are you?"

"Robyn," she said. "With a Y."

"What?"

"My name, it's spelled with a Y not an I."

He continued to stare.

She turned and skirted a sand-filled pool that occupied most of the lido deck, not waiting for him.

"Where you going?" he called after her. The bridge and the observation deck were above, but he didn't know what they would do up there. They needed to get off the boat and into the woods.

Then a shadow fell across them, and he looked up. A bare-chested man with scars and crude tattoos all over him hopped down from the bridge, landing feet first in the pool beside Robyn-with-a-Y. He grabbed the ladder and climbed up out of the sandbox.

Jackson was about to fire, but the guy ran straight past Robyn, grabbed the railing, and threw himself over the side of the superstructure. He never even looked their way.

Jackson lowered the rifle, confused. The look on the man's face hadn't been one of anger or hate, but one of sheer terror.

The Fallen soldier boy wasn't after them. Something was after *him.*

Robyn stopped moving and looked back. "Are you coming?"

He ignored her, turning to the railing and looking down across the beach. The Fallen weren't attacking their position, or even concerned with it. Most were running straight past it, others hiding among the wreckage of the Graveyard.

"I think we need to get off the beach," he said.

"They'll see us," she answered.

"I don't think we're on their menu today."

With Osiris gone, maybe the soldiers, like himself, were free from his influence, too. Maybe they weren't the enemy anymore. Maybe the guy who'd come in after Robyn just wanted to ask her out; the guy coming in after him having just reacted to his friend lying on the ground with his face smashed in. Or maybe not.

He followed the railing along the deck, passing Robyn and the pool, and took the paint-peeled steps up to the bridge and then up to the observation deck, Robyn following on his heels.

Once up top, he raised a hand to shield his eyes from the setting sun. He swept his gaze back and forth over the beach, trying to find Arkansas Joe and the others.

"What are you looking for?" she asked.

"Friends." And then he saw them. "There!" He pointed. He could make out Pierre and the Cuban making their way from boat to boat, trying to stay hidden from the river of what now may or may not be demon-possessed men rushing past them. He tried to find the DC-3 but wasn't able to see it from his position due to a pile of wreckage blocking his view.

"Pierre," Robyn whispered, squeezing Jackson's wrist.

The touch sent a firestorm up his arm and tingled his scalp. *Shoot.* Here he was in the midst of hell, needing to find a way of escape right now, and all he could think about was her hand on his wrist. He yanked it free before it got them both killed, and took the stairs all the way back down to the boat deck.

When he reached the bottom of the stairs, almost tripping over the guy with Robyn's knife in his neck, he came face to face with a frenzy-eyed man with a mohawk. Without even thinking about it, he threw a throat strike with his right hand, fingers stiff like a spear, and rammed into the soft part of the neck between the larynx and carotid artery. It was a move he'd perfected to lethal standards over the years, and it worked the same now. The Fallen soldier dropped dead before he even knew what was happening.

Maybe later Jackson would invite the remaining Fallen army over for tea and crumpets to see where things stood, but right now he would continue operating as they always had in this nightmare. There was no time for anything else. Osiris' men were all running from something, and it wasn't Jesus Christ on a white horse come back to judge the wicked.

He hurled himself over the railing, and failing to complete his perfect landing form, landed with a jolt that seemed to tear his midsection apart. He rolled onto his back and looked up to the railing, making sure Robyn was in the process of joining him. But she wasn't there.

"Are you coming?" Her voice sounded from beside him. And before he could even respond, she was off sprinting toward the woods, bloody knife back in her hand, the picture still in the other.

For a moment, he thought about just lying there and watching her run away in those khaki shorts. Then he cursed himself and got back to his feet. He touched the bandages that still wrapped his waist, surprised to find no seepage, and took off after her.

ELEVEN

23rd day of June. Early evening. Bermuda.

The cruise ship seemed to be drifting further and further away, just a dot against the horizon now.

"We can't wait for them," Paul said.

The other two men exchanged concerned glances, dreading what his next words might be.

"We need to find something that floats and get out there."

Their faces dropped.

"Has to be two miles," the one on his left stated. He was a scrawny man, probably in his mid-fifties, black curly hair, of Italian descent.

"Closer to three," Paul concurred.

"We can't swim that far. And we don't even know if we'd be able to climb aboard once we got there." This from the other guy. Paul hadn't bothered getting either of their names.

He stared at the shrinking ship. They couldn't let what might be their best chance at getting out of this place just slip away. He looked to the forest behind them. "Fine. But you're helping me with my raft."

"You want to build a raft?" the non-Italian guy asked. His bloodline obviously came straight out of the Orient.

He nodded. "Let's go." He went to the straightest cedar he could see standing near the beach. "This should do." Looking back to the others, he saw they were still just standing there, staring at him. "Move, dammit!"

They exchanged another troubled look and then finally began moving, each with sword in hand.

"We're cutting this down and then into four," Paul explained. "Got it?"

They nodded.

"Good. I'll be back."

"Where are you going?" the older one asked.

"I need six long poles and a rope." And then he took off into the forest, happy to hear the sound of metal whacking cedar echoing after him.

* * * *

Just a few dozen feet from the tree line, Robyn pulled up and ducked down beneath a rotting sail that stood pitched like a tent amidst the other Graveyard wreckage. At first, Jackson didn't know why she dove for cover. There wasn't anyone within fifty yards of her. And then he caught the shadow gliding toward them, coming from his left. He looked up at the sky, expecting to find a large cloud moving in front of the sun, but there were no clouds anywhere near the golden ball. Nothing physical blocking it, and yet the shadow came, like an inky tide spilling over the beach, reaching out to them, over them.

He knelt beside her, eyes locked on the pressing darkness. "What—"

And it was upon them.

He grabbed Robyn in a protective embrace, pulling her tight against his large, wounded frame, covering her head with his arms and waiting to experience whatever the dark phenomenon would feel like. A prayer slipped halfway through his mind before…

Cold.

Like ice, tropic warmth shredded by stabbing icicles, freezing, paralyzing.

He couldn't move his arms or his head, his whole body numb. Robyn's heat, her body pressed against his, vanished, just a cold rock in his grasp. His breath hung in front of his face, frozen crystals drifting upward in the dark midnight. He thought of the closet, of its nothingness, a void into another dimension, into hell. Had the protective sheen over the doorway snapped, the black hole within sucking the island into itself? Were they heading into Tartarus, Osiris' absence no longer sustaining the reality of this strange world?

With all the strength he could muster, he tried moving his eyes up and away from Robyn's hair. He managed to peer sideways, to where the shadow had originated, realizing that this was what the Fallen forces had been running from, this tide of cold evil that was targeting them.

In the distance, he could see sunlight chasing the tail of ink. Whatever this darkness was, it seemed to be something passing. He could only hope it didn't kill them as it moved on. He could feel his heart slowing, and his vision began to fade. The icy fingers were pulling him under. *Denise*, he thought. But it wasn't Denise. It was Robyn. *Robyn*… He was confused, his feelings distorted, feelings that died a long time ago, died with her. Who was who and what was what? And where were they going? A shadow that wasn't a shadow, a black river carrying them along…

He was so tired, so cold. He let his eyes close, the puffs of steam from their mouths now just tiny flares.

And then it was past, and the sun's warmth was back.

Robyn managed a choked whisper. "What was that?" She was still cradled in his arms.

He blinked and looked around. They were still under the sail, everything in front of them appearing normal. They both turned their heads and saw the dark streak slither onward until it was out of view, sliding away, sunlight spilling into its wake. Half a dozen of the Fallen were hiding behind broken hulls and snapped wings, but they weren't staring off at the receding ink like they were. No, their focus was still concentrated on where the darkness had come from, their eyes still wide with fear.

"I don't know," Jackson mumbled, releasing his grip on her, trying to ignore her feel. "But—"

And then he saw it, saw what the Fallen army had really been running from. And it wasn't the liquid evil that froze them. That had just been a red carpet and palm branches for the heralding of this new thing.

It was moving its way back and forth along the tree line, weaving—no, *flickering*—in and out of the forest, coming toward them.

Robyn saw it, too. She leaned forward and squinted, as if doing so might help hold the thing still long enough to identify it. But no amount of squinting could bring it into focus, to get it to stop twitching and blurring. There was *something* there, that was for sure; it was only a hundred yards away and impossible to miss in the sunlight. But it seemed more like an apparition, a creature in a vapor-like cloak that blended into the surroundings. It was large (they could at least tell that), and it was moving fast, *gliding* through the trees, in and out of focus. It was maddening, Robyn rubbing her eyes as if the problem was with her bright blues and not with reality's rabbit-ear reception.

Jackson found it easier to concentrate on the thing through a peripheral view. To look at it straight on was like trying to pick out the hidden image on one of those 3D post cards that were popular a few years back. You had to look *through* those pictures for the Christmas tree or dinosaur or teddy bear to jump out at you. But how did you look through a tree line that stretched out for miles, the object of your focus moving rapidly toward you? So he looked away from the tree line, focusing on the beach instead. And in the corner of his eye, he could see what appeared to be a humanoid figure, slightly hunched forward in its movement, an oblong watermelon for a head.

Jackson grabbed Robyn's hand, the feelings that had been distracting him suddenly nonexistent, and pulled her to her feet. "Run!" And he pushed her toward the forest.

"What is it?"

"Just run!"

As soon as they were on their feet and moving, the beach came alive with them, all those hiding suddenly up and running. Some of Osiris' minions ran toward the forest, some continued on down the beach, and a few even started swimming straight out into the ocean.

Robyn's muscled legs pumped like she was after cross country gold, and she kicked sand high up in the air behind her. Jackson again tried to keep up, but every sand-sinking step was a bomb detonating in his side. He clenched his teeth and did his best to press on despite it.

Just before bursting through the tree line and into the shadowy forest, he looked down the wall of cedars to his left and once again spotted the thing. It was fifty yards away. And then it was gone, blurred out of focus, one with its surroundings. He thought of the *Predator* movies but didn't think this thing was some ugly alien just using a camouflaging technology. This thing was…*spiritual.* Other dimensional. There was no spaceship that crash-landed here, he was sure. But there was an open closet door…

Robyn looked back from the thick undergrowth ahead. "Come on!"

Jackson swore, ducked beneath a cedar branch, and caught his foot on a root. He pitched forward and, out of habit and instinct, turned in the air as he fell so as not to lose his face on a rock. But landing on his side wasn't much better, and the impact set off a flash of light through his head. The last thing he saw was Robyn's bare legs coming toward him. They were great legs, like Denise's legs…

The next thing he knew, he was flying, the ground below sliding past rather quickly. Her legs grew closer, her dirty and torn shorts filling his inverted view. And then they turned, and he could only watch her backside as she moved away from him again.

He blinked, shook his head, and felt the sudden stress in his arms and shoulders. He moved his eyes off Robyn's shorts and turned his head. On his right, he saw Pierre, on his left, Arkansas Joe. They were carrying him, his feet dragging across the forest floor. Sound returned—the huffing and puffing of labored breathing, the stomping of sprinting feet, the slapping of leaves, and…

Screams. From behind them, back on the beach. Ungodly, terrified screams. Screams that transcended physical pain and simple death. Whatever was happening back there wasn't just some good ol' fashion killing. No, it was a reaping of souls.

"Where's the Cuban?" Jackson thought he asked. But he couldn't be sure if it left his brain or not. If so, they ignored him, still dragging him away, further from the beach and its sounds of eternal torment. He tried to get his feet working, to run on his own, to at least assist those dragging him, but he was getting no response from his legs.

From that point on, everything was in and out. Hands pulling him, grabbing him, Joe's face looking down at him, Robyn's long hair waving in the breeze, the trees passing by overhead, the sun growing fainter, the sound of a river, the warmth of a fire, pain in his side, unintelligible words being spoken, darkness.

He'd been semiconscious the whole time but unable to comprehend or hold on to any one thought. When finally he did come back, he sat up and saw Denise staring at him from the other side of dancing flames. *Eliot…* His heart raced as a deep-seated terror took root, and he thought, *I'm in hell.* But then a steep pain in his side sharpened his perspective, and Denise's face turned into Robyn's, the flames just the small fingers of a campfire.

He looked around. It was night, and there was no sign of Joe or Pierre. It was just him and Robyn-with-a-Y.

* * * *

Paul knew he needed a rope, and a long one at that. He wasn't sure that what he was thinking was even possible since the ship was too far away to make out its details. If it was impossible, then his only chance of getting on board would depend on the unlikely event that there was someone on the ship that would be willing to lend him a hand. However, if he were to row all the way out there with nothing to use, he might as well sit there on the beach and at least get some rest while waving goodbye to the boat.

The log raft they'd made was crude and simple, but it would get the job done. Six cedar logs fastened to three evenly-spaced poles running crosswise above and beneath them. They'd found enough vine to tie it all together, and he would've put a floor down over the top poles to keep out of the water and provide a flat surface to work on, but there wasn't time. Plus, plywood was hard to come by at the moment.

He tried using vine for what he was thinking but gave up almost immediately. A waste of time and energy. He needed rope, and they didn't have any. Needed something he could use as a grappling hook, too. He tried going back to the pyramid complex, revisiting it in his mind, visualizing the scene. Had there been rope anywhere? Had the giants been wearing any over their shoulders (as they did when hanging severed heads from their necks)? What about *inside* the temple?

He looked at the ship, wondering if he could make it to the complex and back before it slipped away, and swore. There was no way.

"Here."

Paul turned and saw the Asian guy walk out of the trees. The guy took off once they'd started building the raft, and Paul assumed the guy had mailed it in. But here he was, a giant rope wrapped around his shoulder and trailing behind him on the ground. He dropped it in front of him.

Paul looked first at the rope and then at him. "Where'd you find that?"

"We took it with us to the complex. Jared thought we might use it to climb the pyramid."

"Didn't really work out that way, though," the Italian said, rocking on his knees and wiping his palms on his thighs.

The rope man shook his head. "No, it didn't."

Paul didn't know if the rope would be long enough, but if there was a lower deck with a railing, or a lifeboat within reach… But he'd need some kind of hook. "Get me a bow from the sack, will you?"

Little Italy (as Paul had started to think of him) stood and went to the bags they'd filled. Paul went to the rope, picked it up, and handled it. Hemp. Good stuff. Strong. Old. He remembered that the government encouraged farmers to grow hemp back in the World War II days, when they needed it for naval purposes (tow lines, mooring, tackle and gear) because the reserves of Manila hemp were running dry. And he remembered how they torched the fields when the war was over. He began making knots, one every two feet or so. But he still needed a hook. The bow and an arrow, now being handed to him, would be pointless without something that would both catch and support his climbing weight. He looked back to their bag of tricks.

Turning onto his back, exhausted and soaking wet, he held his throbbing hand, still not used to the missing digits.

"Did we make it?" the weary voice asked from beside him. Little Italy (who eventually got tired of being called that and said his name was Eddie) had decided to come with him after all, which meant they had to add two more logs to the raft. Paul didn't mind; it meant another person to paddle. The raft was small and cramped, but it held together and did its job the best it could. As did they.

The raft bumped into the hull of the ship, and Paul reached out, stroking slick metal with his fingertips. "Yeah, we made it."

"Thank God," Eddie whispered.

The three-mile raft ride had been set against a sky on fire with red and orange hues as the sun sank into the ocean and turned it to liquid gold. It was magnificent for about ten minutes before the pain and fatigue made it moot. Their paddles were nothing more than needled branches and less than efficient. Eddie passed out half an hour into the voyage, and Paul had to finish the race alone. He had to admit, though, that without Eddie, he would've never made it. Not before his arms fell off.

Now it was night, and only a crescent moon hung to illuminate their bobbing world. There wasn't a single light shining from anywhere on the ship, and Paul was beginning to have serious misgivings about boarding her. There was an eeriness that reeked of Naga Hills. A familiar feeling lately.

He was so tired, and Eddie was already asleep again. He needed to close his eyes, to rest. But first he had to secure the raft, make sure they wouldn't be waking up alone in the middle of an endless ocean. With nothing but the clothes on their backs, they wouldn't last long, and Eddie didn't look all that appetizing.

When the spasms rocking his back and shoulders finally settled, he rolled onto his stomach. The water sloshing up through the logs smacked him in the face. He forced himself to his knees, wiping the salt water from his eyes, and reached for the coiled rope.

On their approach, with a glimmer of sunlight still assisting them, he'd been able to spot their best chance. The stern, below the first open deck. Ladder rungs were welded onto the hull and led up to the railing. It was their only shot. All the other open decks were way outside his reach. The rungs were above him, barely visible in the moonlight. This wasn't going to be easy. He looked at Eddie, then at the hook tied to the rope.

It was a shark hook, barbed. One of the Purees had taken it from the Graveyard, bent it so that the point didn't curl back up but stuck straight out at ninety degrees, making it more effective as a weapon. Paul curled it back into a hook the best he could. It was all he had for a grappling hook, but he was lucky they were even able to find that in the bag of recovered materials.

He looked up at the white cruise ship. It stretched up into the dark sky like a skyscraper above him. The first welded rung was about forty feet away. He didn't think he needed the bow after all. He focused on the rung, planting his feet in the rolling seas and taking a deep breath. The hook started twirling in his hand. Once, twice. He let out some slack. Three, four. Some more slack until it was almost touching the raft. Five, six. And then, with a shout, he let it fly.

The hook clanged off the hull and came back down.

Paul tensed, waiting for it to land on his head. It didn't. It landed six inches from Eddie's. The Puree didn't wake up, though, and Paul sighed in relief as he reeled the hook back in.

This was like a game he used to play with the other kids in the neighborhood, well before being kicked off the football team. Arrows and Lawn Darts, they'd called it. Standing in a circle, someone would either chuck a lawn dart into the air or shoot an arrow as straight into the sky as they could. The object of the game had obviously been to avoid the thing coming back down into your head. Something that had never actually happened (though Frannie Archibald had one go into his shoulder, forever putting an end to the game thanks to his need to see a doctor and then spilling the beans on what had happened).

He swung the hook again. It wasn't heavy, but after the rowing, it was heavy enough to make his arm unhappy. He let it go again and this time there was no sound at all before the rope began folding down around his wrists.

Uh, oh.

He dove off the raft just as the hook landed where he'd been standing. He spit salt water out of his mouth and swam back over, the rope still in his hand. After pulling himself back on board, he found Eddie sitting up and staring at the hook.

"Sorry 'bout that," Paul said, picking it up again.

"You could have warned me."

He supposed that was true. "Okay. Watch out." And he tossed it again.

The sound of metal clanking on metal. This time, the rope (with two feet to spare) didn't come back down.

They looked at each other. Was it hooked, or just lying across the top of the rung? There was only one way to find out. He pulled. The rope went taut. He pulled harder, satisfied that it was secure. The only problem was that the rope was hanging four feet above the raft.

"Don't suppose you'll let me tie this to your leg," Paul muttered.

"No."

"Fine." Paul started taking his pants off with one hand, his busted fingers on his other hand still holding onto the rope. He would've given it to Eddie if he trusted him. He'd done good paddling, but he wasn't so sure he would remain conscious long enough for him to get his pants off.

Once he had them off, and he was literally butt naked in the moonlight, he tied the end of the pant leg to the rope. Then he tied the other pant leg to his ankle.

"You're not staring at me, are you?" he asked Eddie as he sat.

"Not a chance."

"Good." He rolled over and fell asleep, his foot keeping them tethered to the quiet cruise ship.

TWELVE

23rd day of June. Night. Bermuda.

Blood and dirt were caked to the face staring back at him, but even that couldn't hide its beauty. It was amazing how much she looked like Denise. There was something in her eyes, though, something that Denise's never knew. He wanted it to be keenness, bright awareness and understanding, but he wasn't so sure it was anything other than cold savagery. For now he'd go with keenness, but he had his guard up. After all, there was the way she'd handled herself back on the boat. He'd been around some GI Janes before, but what she did was something he'd never seen from a woman (had only seen it in a few men, actually)—that cold, calculated brutality of a person in "the zone."

The fire crackled, and he turned his attention to his injuries. Someone had cleaned him up and re-stitched where the other stitches had popped. "Where's Joe and Pierre and that other guy?" he asked, again noting their absence. Last he saw them, they were carrying him.

"Chad. They went back."

"Back?"

"To Jared, to let him know."

He shook his head, confused. "They just left you here?"

She smiled. "I am perfectly capable of taking care of myself."

"Yeah, I got that. But…"

"You're confused. Why would they leave me out here on my own after keeping me hidden for so long?"

He nodded, squinting at her. "Pretty much."

"Osiris is gone."

"I know."

"That changes everything."

He forced himself to a sitting position, grimacing. His head was spinning. Questions begetting questions and all. "Do you know what's happening?"

"Yes. And no."

"Yeah, that's about where I'm at, too."

"You should try to sleep some more, get some energy back. Big day tomorrow."

"What do you mean?"

"Pierre found something in the Graveyard. We'll need to go back in the morning."

"By ourselves?"

"They'll be meeting us with others."

He rubbed his head. "What did he find?"

She smiled. "You'll see. Go to sleep."

He laughed.

"What's so funny?"

"Nothing."

She continued staring at him.

Jackson looked away. For some reason her eyes on him made him uncomfortable. Maybe it was his clothes, the short pants and small jacket. Maybe it was the stench of sweat circling him, or maybe it was the way her eyes seemed to be digging through his soul. He lay back down and shut his eyes, keeping her out of there.

"Mind if I ask you some questions first?" he asked.

"Sure."

"How is it you speak English so well?"

"School."

His eyes blinked open. "School?"

"Since we've been in the caves, we've had teachers making sure everyone grows up learning to read and write. English just happens to be the predominate language."

"'Predominate.' You are educated."

She smiled.

"They teach you to fight, too?"

"Yes."

He thought about it, his mind trying to absorb what a castaway education would be like. "So you can read?"

"How else do you think we pass the time in our cave?"

Her tone said more than her words, letting him know she was speaking specifically of the female populace here. He wasn't sure if it was resentment or resignation, but he decided to test the waters. "What's it like being a prisoner among your own family?"

"Nothing in this place is easy." Then she shrugged. "But then I don't have anything else to compare it to, so…"

"Was it necessary? To hide you all away like that?"

"We always had to be extra cautious. Osiris…has a way with us…"

He nodded, recalling the legends, the power that fallen angels supposedly had over the female persuasion.

"We used to be as free as the men, left to our own judgment. Once in a while someone would fail to return. Same for the men. Though he wasn't using the men to breed more giants for him, but it was one of the risks, one of the unavoidable dangers of this place. Only Samuel and the others began to think that it *was* avoidable. And when ten of us were taken in the same week, they insisted that we be kept underground as much as possible."

"So the hiding was new?"

"We've always hidden here. But things started to change. Whether he needed more breeders, or he just wanted to further appease his monsters, we didn't know. Only that he began actively seeking us out."

"And you think that's changed now?"

She looked up from the fire and found his eyes again. "You know that for yourself, don't you?"

"What do you mean?"

"Aren't you one of his offspring? Can't you sense his absence?"

"How do you know I'm—"

"People talk."

He looked up in the darkness, to the canopy he couldn't see, the smoke rising in the firelight. "I knew it as soon as I woke up the other day. It was like—"

"Like your thoughts were your own again?"

"Yeah." Then he wondered what she knew of it.

She read the question in his eyes. "He started reaching out, touching our minds with thoughts and images…*feelings*."

Jackson's own experience with the Fallen Angel's influence was more subtle, more of a body-snatcher brainwashing than what she was describing. She was talking about seduction.

She continued. "The ones who wanted to taste what he was offering… There was no turning back for them. No taste and see and then decide. The moment they dropped their guard, they were his."

"He could do that without being near you?"

She nodded. "But the power he had over our minds was nothing compared to being in his presence."

Though she suggested Osiris began pursuing them more aggressively because he saw the end of his plans in sight and needed more workers bred, or because his subjects just needed an occupation to keep them from boredom, Jackson thought that (based on the literature) there might be more to Osiris' wanting to comingle with the Puree ladies. Or less. The sex was, after all, the entire reason for his fall in the first place. Maybe he saw his wild-oats days coming to a close with the completion of his device, and he wanted to increase his sample size while he still could. He didn't know and wasn't about to ask her what she thought of it.

But she brought it up all on her own. "We read the Book of Enoch and the Bible, and so I guess whatever sexual mysteries, whatever cosmic fascination he has with the daughters of men could've been the only reason he needed to…" She trailed off, not wanting to think about it. She looked down and whispered, "Everything is different now."

"That's a good thing, right?"

"Yes, of course it is." But she didn't sound so sure. She stood up, walked around the fire, and sat down next to him. "What happened back at the caves?"

He stared at her.

"You were shocked when you realized I was from the caves, like I wasn't supposed to be here."

He forced a smile. "You mean it's normal to go from being in the cave one instant to being in the middle of the forest the next?"

She held his gaze, unblinking, waiting.

He sighed. "Joe—"

"Wouldn't tell me."

A moment passed, the fire eating the wood and shooting a spray of sparks into the air beside them. He was trying to think of a way to deliver the news. He was never good at bedside manner, though. He'd never seen the sense in empty promises, at least not on the battlefield. When your guts were lying in a pile next to you, blood squirting everywhere, you had a right to know you were dying. At least that's what he thought. Sometimes people had a message for their wife and kids, some had things to say to God. In any case, there usually wasn't time for sugar-coating the obvious. The mission had to go on. But with Denise he'd learned to lessen the bluntness of his facts, to soften his delivery a bit. Now, as he stared into Robyn's saddened eyes, he was trying to remember how he'd done that. But he was drawing a blank, so he just told her. Told her about the changes to the island, of the room she'd been in with her family and friends now being no room at all, just solid rock. Told her about the pyramid vanishing, the ziggurat's missing side, the lost torches, and the lakes now filled with forest. And about the house.

She just sat there, her blue eyes staring into the fire. Jackson saw a tear glide down her face, holding the light of the fire in its bulbous frame. It was a lot to digest, though he figured she'd had all the prerequisite courses aced by now.

Still staring into the flames, she asked, "Do you think they're out here somewhere?"

He'd already told her about the men Paul saw embedded in the temple walls, so there was no way he could deceive her with statements of positive certainty. "It's possible. If it happened to you, it could've happened to them."

Whatever quantum secrets would deposit her in one place while putting the rest of her company elsewhere were mysteries they couldn't even begin throwing guesses at.

After a few more moments of staring at the flames, she changed the subject. "My parents died when I was seven."

He blinked, considering her again, noting the way the fire shined off her hair.

"My father was killed by them, stabbed through the heart." She pulled her hair to the right of her neck, and it spilled down over her chest. She began combing it with her fingers, eyes still lost in the fire. "My mother lost her footing and hit her head on a rock."

"I'm sorry." It sounded stupid, but what else could he say?

"I remember the stories they told me about home." A small smile pulled at the corner of her lips as she contemplated the details of that foreign word—*home*. "Ice cream, roller coasters, houses with bathrooms…grocery stores."

As he watched her lips move, he wanted more than anything to introduce her to those things. To take her to dinner and a movie, all the things he knew so well and had enjoyed for so long. Things he couldn't help but appreciate after witnessing parts of the world that the 10 o'clock news would never cover. The comforts of the free world were nice, and it was because he didn't take them for granted that he wanted so badly to show them to this girl who had never seen anything but horror, had known nothing but danger and uncertainty. There were kids he'd seen starving in Africa that he wished he could've taken back home with him, shown them something more than pain and hunger, and he figured this was sort of like that. Though there was a selfish reason, too.

"Not all the real world is like that," he said. "Some places are just as dark and evil as this one."

"And even the kingdom of comfort that serves ice cream along with its peace has its own sort of evils, I know," she said, shocking him with the statement. "But I just want to see it. The world my parents were part of. I want to meet my aunts, uncles, cousins…my family. My own blood."

"I'll do everything within my power to get you ice cream."

She smiled, tossing her hair back over her shoulder. "Promise?"

"Scouts honor."

And it was obvious she had no idea what that meant.

"So what's with your name, Robyn-with-a-Y?" He wasn't sure if it was Christopher Robin she was named after or Batman's sidekick.

She leaned back. "I was named after a character in a book my parents used to read to me. And my father's name was Robert."

"What was the book?"

"*Ivanhoe.*"

"Ah." He smiled. "Robin Hood."

She put her eyes on him, surprised. "You know it?"

"Of course. Robin Hood is very popular in the real world. But he spells his name with an I, not a Y."

"I know, but my mother told me it was more ladylike with a Y."

"That it is."

"Have you read it?"

"*Ivanhoe*?"

She nodded.

"Nope. Saw the movie, though. Robert Taylor and Elizabeth Taylor."

"I've never seen a movie."

"Well, that's something we shall have to remedy, then, isn't it?" he said in his best Scottish accent.

She squinted at him.

"*Braveheart.* Uncle Argyle."

She shrugged, and he laughed. Until the pain in his side choked it out.

"Are you okay?" she asked.

He thought so. "You ever kill anyone before today?" he asked instead.

"We've had to defend ourselves before." She picked up a twig and tossed it in the fire.

Jackson continued to be amazed by the girl, by the way she carried herself. There was a wise maturity that emanated from her, one that he knew had been forced upon her.

"You were a soldier?" she asked. "You and your friends?"

"Yeah."

"Did you kill before you came here?"

"Yes."

"Was it different?"

"What do you mean?"

She folded her hands. "We are told that the men we're fighting against here are unredeemable. That the Fallen cannot be saved, that they are demons."

Jackson bowed his head. He'd done more than his fair share of killing and had never once apologized for it. It was his duty, his orders. It was the way of the world. Soldiers killed soldiers. Even though the dispute was between leaders, it was always the soldiers that fought it out. Fathers, brothers, husbands, sons… Everyone had their own story, and not for a moment did Jackson try convincing himself that every person he killed deserved to die. Naga Hills…yeah, there were those places and those people, but there were also others whose only crime was to have been born in a different part of the world.

"I guess it's different," he answered. "We aren't killing giants with six fingers."

"Do you feel guilt?"

Watching the way she'd cut through those men earlier in the day, he'd think guilt would be the last thing on her mind.

"Sometimes."

"It's the burden we carry, though, right? The price we pay to protect those we love?"

He wasn't about to get into the reality of war, of politics and all the other reasons to kill. Reasons tucked neatly out of sight beneath the loud banner of protecting the innocent. Those were headlines that were mostly used to gather public support for wars long in the books. "It can be."

He reflected back on what she'd just said, about her enemy being unredeemable. Was it true? *He* was the offspring of Osiris, so did that mean he was a lost cause, worthy of only a swift stroke from a sharp blade? John's experience in this place, what Osiris had shown him, seemed to prove that his Jesus was able to overcome the tainted blood flowing in his veins. At least for those in the real world, anyway. But what of those born here, direct descendants of Osiris whose blood hadn't been diluted over the generations? Were they redeemable? It was easy to tell yourself they weren't when you were busy fighting them. But was it true?

She interrupted his thoughts with a question. "Did God bring you here to save us?"

And that was the million-dollar Puree question, wasn't it? "I don't know if God brought us here or not."

She studied him with those blazing blue eyes. "Maybe He brought you here to save you."

He paused, looked at her, and wondered what she expected him to say. What she *hoped* he would say. He considered her question, and not for the first time. But before he could think of something to say, she stood.

"I'll be back." And she walked into the woods, head down, dragging a string of thoughts behind her.

Jackson watched her go as his dead wife continued to whisper in his ear.

* * * *

Paul opened his eyes and looked around. The moonlit fingernail had set a portion of the ocean to silver sparkles, and Eddie was standing on the raft and staring up at the ship.

"What is it?" Something had awakened him, and it hadn't been Little Italy getting to his feet.

"You didn't hear it?" Eddie's voice was shaking.

For someone who had spent most, if not all, of his life surrounded by the bizarre, Paul thought Eddie would've been better adjusted to such a climate. "What did it sound like?" He sat up, untied the pant leg from his ankle and removed the rope. It was still taut, secure. He pulled his jeans back on with his bad hand, the waters rolling beneath the raft trying to throw him off balance.

"I knew I shouldn't have come with you," he whispered.

Paul was about to mention something about his manhood when a scream sounded out from above. It echoed over the waters and peeled Paul's flesh. Maybe this hadn't been such a hot idea after all.

"What do you want to do?" Eddie asked.

Paul stared up at the deck. The scream sounded like it had come straight from the pit of hell. He watched, almost expecting a silhouette to pass by, backlit by the moon. "We can't go back. Not now. We don't know how far we've drifted."

A bump beneath the raft.

Eddie stumbled and fell on his butt. They both froze, eyes locked on the cedar poles keeping them afloat.

"You don't think—"

But Paul didn't get to finish his thought. He buttoned his jeans just as another bump struck the raft, this one much harder than the first. Some of the vines snapped.

The logs began to separate, and Eddie swore while Paul scanned the waters.

There, about ten yards out in the glittering swells, right before the ship's shadow darkened the water.

A fin. Streaking toward them.

Eddie shot back to his feet much like Roy Schneider had after getting a close-up of the great white.

"I know, don't say it," Paul muttered, holding the rope out to him. "We're gonna need a bigger boat."

But Eddie didn't respond, just stood fear stricken before the four-foot dorsal coming at him.

"Suits me," Paul said, and he jumped. Reaching up, he grabbed a knot on the rope and swung toward the ship, his feet dragging through the water. He hit the hull and started pulling himself up, hand over hand, wet boots slipping against the smooth metal of the ship. His arms protested, his missing fingers ached, and every part of him wanted to let go, to just let the big drink take him.

It wasn't an altogether unappealing thought, if not for the hungry shark that would grind him to pieces first.

He finally got within an arm's reach of the welded rung and grabbed it with his good hand. He bent his knees and crossed his feet on a knot, pushing himself up and taking hold of the next rung. A few seconds later he was standing on the rungs and looking down to Eddie, waiting for him to start his own climb.

But Eddie never came.

Peering down into the darkness, Paul could just make out the raft. Or what was left of it. The cedar logs were floating off in every direction.

The rope went taut.

"Help!"

Paul leaned away from the hull, hanging onto a rung with one hand. Straight below him, Eddie was holding onto the vine, half his body in the water.

"Pull yourself up!"

"I can't!" There was terror in his voice.

Paul swore. There was no way he could get into a position that would allow him to pull on the rope, not when the hook was fastened to the rung he was standing on.

There was a short scream swallowed by a splash and then silence, the rope swaying back and forth.

Paul's face dropped. *Bye bye, Little Italy.*

He pulled himself back against the hull, rested a second, and then started climbing. Finally, he reached the railing and pulled himself up and over it, collapsing to the deck exhausted and spent.

On his back, he just lay there, listening to the sound of the ocean, the feel of the breeze. The black inky sky was turning gray over the water, and he knew the sun was on its way, thank God. He decided he would just rest here until things got a bit brighter. And wondered why no one had ever mentioned sharks before.

Another scream.

He opened his eyes and sat up. Maybe he wouldn't be resting.

The scream had come from within the ship; there was no doubt about that. He used the railing to pull himself up and stumbled across the deck.

Empty lounge chairs, a hot tub, a mini bar… He stared at the two closed doors behind the bar, expecting them to burst open at any moment. He swung the M14 and all five of its shots off his back as if it could protect him from the forces buzzing about him.

He looked back across the ocean, in the direction he thought they'd come from, and hoped for some sign that reinforcements were en route. But there was nothing. Just water in every direction.

Time to get to work. He put the rifle down.

Seven minutes later, just as clouds began sliding in front of the moon and sealing the ship in dark predawn hues, he tossed a half-dozen bottles of alcohol into a heap of kindling. Life preservers, towels, wooden chairs, pieces of the hot tub, and whatever he could find that would burn.

He lit a match from the matchbook he found behind the bar and held it in his hand. A breeze blew it out. He cursed, dropped the match, and lit another. When he looked up to his pyre this time, the girl was behind it. She was back by the bar, in front of open doors.

His heart froze in his chest, every new sighting more terrifying than the last. He swallowed, not taking his eyes off the little girl he'd gunned down, and tossed the match into the pile. Then, as the bonfire lit up the deck, and hopefully the horizon for any Puree who might be looking for him, he grabbed the M14 and ran. The doors were open. She had opened them. She was more than a ghost.

He couldn't dive off the ship, not without knowing where the island was and certainly not with Eddie-eating sharks out there. But he wasn't about to enter the ship either. Who knew what the inner decks of this derelict boat might hold? So, doing his best to ignore the girl, he slung the rifle back over his shoulder and ran to the bar, leaped, planting his lead foot on the counter, and launched himself up into the air. He reached out, grabbed the bottom rung of the railing on the next deck, and once again pulled himself up and over.

He came down on a jogging track and looked back at his handiwork, hoping he hadn't just set the whole ship on fire. And that the right people would see it.

The girl was gone.

THIRTEEN

24th day of June. Dawn. Bermuda.

After returning from whatever business she had in the pitch-black forest, Robyn had once again settled down across from him. She'd been good for a few hours, keeping alert and ready, watching over him, but then ol' Slumber came a-chargin' and she wasn't up for the fight. Jackson had watched the short struggle, the firelight dancing in her glazed eyes as they went in and out of focus. It wasn't the first time in history that the watchman found himself (or herself) abducted by Mr. Sandman, and Jackson smiled, amused by her effort. He let her sleep, taking over the role of eyes in the dark—though mainly they stayed fixed on her.

Finally, dawn cracked open the edge of the world, and the darkness around them began to fade. Still she slept. Still he studied her. She was attractive, there was no doubt about that, and he would be a liar if he denied feeling something for her. Discovering just what that feeling was, however, was a different matter. Hot Amazon woman on danger-filled island? Yeah, the *feeling* could be a lot of things. Or one. But he tried putting it out of his head for now, instead focusing on her closed eyelids and again trying to imagine all the things she might've witnessed growing up in this horrible place, how it had to affect her.

There was a *snap* that came from somewhere on his left, and he swung his head around, rifle coming up simultaneously.

It was Pierre and Arkansas Joe, their empty hands up as they made their way through the thicket.

Jackson lowered the gun. He didn't see Chad with them.

Robyn stirred, opened her eyes and blinked. Then she stretched.

"How do you feel?" Pierre asked Jackson as they both stepped into the little clearing around the campfire, studying the Navy SEAL.

Jackson forced himself to a sitting position. He felt like he'd been body-slammed by an elephant, and thought he remembered slipping out of their grasp as they half carried, half dragged him through the forest. "Like someone dropped me," he replied.

Their eyes disengaged from his, looking elsewhere and confirming certain pains.

"Thanks for not leaving me behind," he said, his tone reassuring.

Joe nodded. "Are you ready?"

"For your little discovery? The suspense had me up all night."

Pierre looked to Robyn. "How are *you*?"

She stretched again, then pulled her hair back into a ponytail, producing a string from nowhere to tie it off. "I'm fine. Let's go." And she was on her feet.

Jackson peeled his eyes from her face, the pony-tail reminding him of Denise. He had always liked the ponytail, and his wife had appeased him often.

"You wouldn't happen to have the coffee on, would you?" Jackson asked Pierre.

"Breakfast is waiting."

"Yeah, but what about the *coffee*?"

Pierre and Joe both smiled that smile parents give their kids when trying to hide a surprise from them, and some life squirted into Jackson's eyes. "Tell me you're not joking." The subtle tease of coffee had the smell of dark roast wafting through his brain. It was almost enough to bring tears to his eyes.

Pierre didn't respond, just turned and started walking back the way they'd come.

"Don't mess with me, guys," Jackson warned, pulling his backpack on and hobbling after Pierre and the imaginary scent of his favorite brew.

Pierre waited for Robyn to finish collecting herself, and then walked alongside her as the night evaporated into a glorious dawn.

Jackson took note and recognized what was going on. *Poor Pierre*, he thought.

* * * *

The gray turned lighter and lighter, and now there was a sliver of orange breaking over the water. By the time he reached the sun deck, the horizon appeared as a line stretching from one side of the world to the other. And it couldn't have come any sooner. The screams from within the ship had started up again and were quite unbearable. On top of that, the little girl in the tattered clothes wouldn't stop following him. He knew he had no right to complain given he was the one responsible for her current condition (that being dead), but it didn't mean he had to like it. Was this a sort of payback? Her being assigned to his continual misery? Was it punishment? Judgment? Where had she come from? Why now? Was it the closet?

He shook his head. It'd been an accident, a mistake from his recent mercenary days. He'd been engaged with the enemy, heard a noise behind him, spun. Too late, he realized that the little girl was holding a doll and not a gun. And now here she was.

Here. She. Was. In real life. Not the dreams he'd had every night since, but here, on the ship with him. She'd *opened* the doors on the deck below. Whether with her hands or some spirit power, it didn't matter. What mattered was that she was able to influence physical properties in *his* realm of existence. Yeah, she was *here*. And it couldn't possibly be a good thing. Not when considering how much her face had changed since he'd seen her earlier in the day. Then her expression was exactly as it'd been the moment after he'd shot her. Sadness. Shock. Disbelief. Pain. Realization. But now… Now her look was far different. No, this wasn't a ghost come back to offer forgiveness to the one who'd robbed her of life, no "you have to move on" message of mercy from her rotten lips. She was here for an entirely different reason. He just didn't know what the holdup was. He was here, and she could apparently be anywhere she wanted to be, so why not just get it over with?

Because she wants me to suffer first, to feel as hopeless as she did standing there with bullets in her, her blood draining out, soaking the doll still in her hands. Well, if that *was* the case, fine. But in the meantime, he was going to try to stop the ship.

He wasn't exactly sure how to stop the ship, whether he could use a winch to drop anchor from the bow or if he had to go into the ship to activate it. He'd never been on a cruise ship before, but he read an article not too long ago about a drunk passenger who managed to drop the rear anchor of a cruise ship by simply entering a "staff only"-marked door. The guy said he was just curious to see if he could do it since it looked similar to his own boat's anchor system. Paul didn't recall seeing a rear anchor on the starboard side upon their approach, but even if there was one and it was as easy as pushing a button, he wasn't about to go getting lost on all those decks looking for some closet with a sign on it. In fact, there was no way in hell he was going inside the ship at all. At least not until the sun was nice and high in the sky. Maybe that was childish, maybe it wasn't, he didn't really care. He wanted to be able to *see* where he was before deciding on whether it was worth walking down the halls of a ghost ship. As for the anchor… He was certainly familiar with them, but he was no boatswain's mate, and he wasn't sure it would work even if he did figure it out. With no idea where he was, how far away from the island he'd drifted, the anchor might not even reach the bottom (he didn't want to think about that). But he had to try, and he hoped to find everything he needed right there on the open bow.

He was passing windows on his left when the morning light from port spilled up and over the deck, passing through the glass-enclosed rooms. He could see rows of treadmills inside. Massage tables.

He kept moving forward. An enclosed gym. The sauna.

Once clearing the enclosed sports deck, the ocean wind came at him unobstructed, sweeping over the open deck and whipping at his clothes. It was a chilly breeze, though the air was already warming with the red-orange arc breaching the water's surface.

He stopped and looked over his new surroundings. A long pool stretched out before him, the rising sun reflected in the still water that filled it. There were a hundred lounge chairs wrapped around the pool in neat rows, and that Naga Hills feeling started pecking at him again. There was no sign of anyone on the ship, but there was no sign of anyone leaving the ship either. The rowboats were still in place (at least on this side), and so far there was no evidence of the chaos that would've been left behind from having to abandon ship. He squinted, looking to his left. To his right.

The sun was rising on port. Which meant the ship was heading south.

But if the ship was heading *south*…

He turned away from the sun, grasped the railing, and peered into the darker, western horizon.

And snapped the rifle off his shoulder so fast that he almost threw it straight into the ocean.

A rowboat, about a hundred yards out, coming toward him. Oars were moving, dipping in and out of the water.

He squinted, trying to make out a face in the crowded boat. They had obviously seen his fire, but who was *they*? Purees or the Fallen?

A figure in the boat rose, and Paul could see the long shape of a rifle in his right hand. The person began waving with his left.

Paul smiled. He couldn't help it. He'd never been so happy to see a cowboy hat before. He waved back.

* * * *

Jackson stepped out from beneath the evergreens and into the pink sand, finding himself in the relocated Graveyard once again. Everything looked the same as it had yesterday when he and Robyn left it on the run. Except, of course, the body parts.

The sun was rising to their left, coming up over the east end of the island and casting its early hues across the beach. Even in the dim light, it was impossible to miss the carnage. It was everywhere, spinning in the surf.

"The rest of them are gone," Pierre said, standing behind him.

It was hard to imagine any surviving given the number of body parts littered all over the sand. "It slaughtered them."

Pierre nodded.

"Why?" Jackson remembered something from the New Testament, something that Jesus had said when certain people tried attributing His miracles to the Devil's work. *How can Satan cast out Satan?* He'd asked. *A house divided against itself cannot stand.* But isn't that what happened here? The thing from the closet chasing down and butchering its own? But then the Nephilim had always been at war with each other, so perhaps it wasn't as simple as all that. Maybe with Osiris gone (him being the dictator of this hell), there was nothing left to bring order to the evil.

Like Iraq, and the reason they hadn't gone after Sadaam back in '91. You take out the dictator, as evil as he is, and you remove what control and stability does exist. If there's nothing in place to fill the vacancy, you get a whole heap of chaos, every little worm free to do whatever it wants. Cheney had said as much back when he was director of the CIA, explaining to the public why the administration decided against going all the way to Baghdad. Of course, as vice president, he must've changed his mind and hello modern-day Iraq.

Pierre shook his head. Of course, he had no idea why.

Jackson couldn't take his eyes off the dark blood, dried and windswept over the sand. It was everywhere, and splintered bones protruding from torn flesh poked out of the beach. Whatever the thing from the closet was, Osiris' leftovers hadn't stood a chance. Like the angel of death that slaughtered the firstborns of Egypt, this thing had simply swept through the fleeing soldiers, passing through them and dismembering them. But the screams… The screams didn't tell of a quick death, and he could imagine well enough what it would be like to be *slowly* taken apart.

Pierre studied him. "What was it?"

Jackson blinked. "I don't know."

Unsatisfied, he countered, "You may not know, but you *do* know more than that."

Jackson sighed. "Maybe I should just show you." God knew he didn't want to go anywhere near the house again, but Hunter was still in there so going back was just a matter of time. Maybe it was even safe now that the closet demon had broken free and was out and about on the island. Or maybe the doorway to hell was left standing wide open, nightmares passing in and out as they pleased.

The answer seemed to satisfy him, and he didn't press the issue. Instead, he pointed off to their left. "Come on, this isn't what we had to show you."

Robyn and Joe were walking in front of them now, their own eyes scanning the wreckage and tree line, watchful for any signs of a demon creature sequel. Beyond them, Jackson could make out the shapes of people huddled around a fire. Next to them, there appeared to be a train car lying on its side.

As they got closer, two things made themselves clear. First, it wasn't a train car but a shipping container. And second…there was coffee. The smell was unmistakable, and Jackson shook his head. "No way," he whispered.

Pierre smiled. "There was a French press and coffee beans on one of the yachts."

That was one of the best things Jackson ever heard in his life. He put his arm around Pierre's shoulders and gave him a hard squeeze, then slapped him on the back. "I thought you were looking in the Navy ship."

"Didn't need to."

There were a dozen Purees sitting around the campfire, the French press sitting on a piece of metal that straddled the burning wood. Above the coffee was a spit with some sizzling meat hanging on it. He didn't know what it was, but he was starving and it didn't smell all that bad. He looked at the faces of the men and recognized most of them. They acknowledged his presence with nods and waves, but they were more interested in Robyn. They stood and rushed her with hugs, each firing questions at her. Obviously, the group had been updated with news of her status prior to the reunion, but Jackson could tell from the look in their eyes that they hadn't fully believed it. Now they found themselves with proof, proof that perhaps their own kin might be alive and well, too.

Jackson couldn't help smiling. And then his attention went from the embraces to what they were all holding in their hands.

He blinked. "Where the hell did you get those?" He'd seen them without really seeing them, figuring they were old antiques from the pile in Jared's cave.

Pierre motioned for him to come over to the container. It was blue, on its side, one end open with scrap metal spilling out onto the beach. There was a faded and peeling radiation symbol on the outer door. He was familiar with the technique. It was often used to conceal narcotics.

He stepped closer and could see wooden crates in the back as the sun came up over his shoulder and lit up the inside of the long, rusted box. He put down the old 1944 Jungle carbine, leaning it against the container, and walked carefully through the stream of metal (that he hoped wasn't really radioactive) and came before an open crate.

AK-47s. A lot of AK- 47s.

Even after sixty years, the AK was the most popular and widely used assault rifle in the world. Its reliability in harsh conditions, its low cost, and its ease of use made it available in just about every region on the planet. And here were crates and crates full of them. Headed to the Middle East no doubt. From Russia or Iran or the CIA, it didn't matter to him. They were *here*.

He started looking around for the missing piece.

Bingo.

Three crates along the back wall were stacked with loaded magazines—"banana clips" each holding forty 7.62x39mm rounds. There were also seventy-five-round drums stacked in the corners of each box. More than enough for whatever *physical* threat might remain on the island. But of course, the question was whether it meant a hill of beans now that the other threat was roaming free. Jackson had a strong suspicion that guns and arrows would do little against the thing that tried pulling him into the abyss. He recalled the way its inky flesh just swallowed the bullets whole.

"Good, yeah?" Pierre asked, leaning against the door and watching him ram a banana clip into a rifle.

"Oh, yeah," he replied, pulling the slide back. "Oh, yeah."

"We'll start moving them back to the caves."

He nodded. "Good." Then he looked back at the silhouette in the doorway. "You all know how to use them?"

"Of course."

"Then make sure everyone has one, at least two mags per person at all times."

"Do you think we'll need them?"

"I was just about to ask you that."

He turned and set his gaze on the orange ocean, thinking. "Who can say?"

"Hopefully we won't. But there's at least one giant out there. Robyn saw it walk into the water yesterday."

"She told us."

"She didn't see it come back."

"Maybe it didn't."

Jackson shrugged. "Maybe it didn't." He walked out of the container with the AK-47. "Anybody shoot one yet?"

"Not yet."

"Might as well get it over with. No sense in hauling them all the way back if they don't work." With no further warning, he raised the rifle, pointed it out over the ocean, and squeezed off the entire magazine, the rifle rocking back and forth in his hands, his muscles bulging, veins showing in his forearms and biceps. The sound was deafening in the still morning, shattering the tranquility of the sunrise. The *ka-ka-ka-ka-ka* echoed through the forest (and most likely the entire island). When he was done, he ejected the mag and dropped it in the sand. "Have everyone fire at least one shot. Better to be sure now than when your life depends on it."

Pierre wasn't looking at him; he was looking at the tree line.

"Relax," Jackson said. Then he followed Pierre's eyes. "But hurry up."

He went over to the others and passed along the instructions. They looked a little hesitant, as if the shots just turned them into some huge blip on Satan's radar, but they each took their new toy to the edge of the beach and fired off a few rounds.

Jackson watched them as they fired. Watched the way they held the rifle, the way it recoiled in their hands, the way they peered down the sights. Not too bad.

Pierre looked back at him and gave him a thumbs-up. Jackson answered with his own.

"Okay," Pierre hollered. "Now that we woke the dead, let's get out of here. Give me a line and let's get this over with!"

They all responded, those who were still sitting getting to their feet and forming a line from the container to a makeshift cart (its wheels stolen from a Cessna). The AK-47s began flowing immediately, like a stream of metal death through their hands, being stacked neatly into the cart. Even if left uninterrupted, it would take them a good portion of the day to get all the contents of the container back to the caves.

Jackson turned back to the sun rising behind the island. It sliced open a red stripe across the ocean, spilling millions of twinkling sparks from the wound. The warmth of it tingled his skin, and he allowed his eyelids to fall.

A memory exploded like a bomb in his brain. It was the sand. For some reason, this pink sand that he'd been surrounded by for months now was triggering a picture in his mind's eye—that wine bottle of coral sand set up in their home. Denise had put it up with all the honeymoon pictures. It was a physical piece of their island paradise, ever sitting there as a reminder of those special days. Until the accident and his throwing it against a wall. He'd tried to salvage what he could out of the carpet afterward, but his efforts only recovered a tablespoon.

"You okay?" a voice asked from beside him.

He opened his eyes, felt a liquid presence in the corner of one of them, and nodded. It was Robyn. He didn't turn to face her, didn't trust the look in his eyes.

"Here." She handed him a blue coffee mug.

He looked down at it, at the US Navy insignia on its side, and took it with a smile. Fingers of steam twisted and turned from within it, carrying that glorious scent he thought he'd never smell again. He raised it to his lips, savoring his first sip.

"Good?" Robyn asked.

He nodded. It was amazing. "Thank you."

She just stood there next to him, hands empty, staring out into the ocean.

He took another sip and then offered it to her.

"No, thanks."

"You don't like it?"

"Not at all."

He smiled and drank some more. He could see the boat she said her parents had come on, the superstructure sticking out of the sand some five hundred yards away, the sun just stroking its peeling paint. He knew she had her eyes on it even now, and another twinge of sympathy stirred in his gut. He realized that there was no way he could allow her to go to the house with them. He didn't know if Pierre or Joe could convince her to stay, but he couldn't risk taking her to a place that had already stolen Hunter.

He looked down at her. She was tall for a woman, but he was tall for a man. The sun had almost cleared the island now, turning her hair into a gold halo. She was so beautiful, but all he could do was think of Denise. Of that sand-filled bottle. He knew that he was in danger of falling for Robyn but didn't know if he could entirely trust whatever these feelings were for her. How much of what he saw was his projecting Denise onto her? Did their physical similarities present an unfair scenario there was no hope of separating? Did he *need* to separate them?

What was he even thinking? He was stuck on an island from hell with giants and demons roaming free in unfamiliar forests, Henry was gone (transported to who knew where through a pyramid that was now missing), Chris and Nick were dead, Hunter was in the closet, and here he was trying to interpret *feelings* for a girl! He pushed it all from his head.

"We should get back," he said. He took another sip of coffee, remembering the last time he stood on this beach staring out at the sun. That time it had been John who came up behind him, after following him from the Carter House. It seemed like an eternity ago. He walked back to the assembly line, noting that the cart was almost to capacity.

Arkansas Joe came up to him. He had a chunk of charred meat in his hand. "Here," he said, holding it out.

"What is it?" Jackson asked, taking it.

"Shark."

"Shark?" This was the first time he'd even heard the word mentioned here.

"There were four of them thrashing around in the surf, pulling apart the bodies. We got one of them."

"You see sharks often?"

"Nope. This was the first."

Jackson glanced back to the rolling seas. He ripped off a piece of the cooked meat with his teeth, thankful for the coffee to wash it down. Sharks… It didn't sit right with him. Not now.

"You have something to show us?" Joe asked, pushing for the answer to his previous question.

Jackson sighed and then nodded. "But I don't want Robyn to come with us. Send her back with them." He nodded toward the cart.

Joe frowned.

"Listen," Jackson whispered, "I don't know what's going to be there. Could be a whole lot of bad things waiting to rip *us* to pieces, too. I'd rather she not be there for that. And so would you."

He nodded, disappointment fleeing his eyes. "Okay. We'll tell her to go back with the others."

* * * *

Paul was on the aft deck where he'd first begun, the fire he set beginning to burn out behind him. He was glad the planking hadn't caught. The overturned, metal tables he'd started the fire on seemed to have kept the flames from the deck, allowing him to avoid his own funeral pyre. He'd seen people go out that way. No thanks.

He watched as they climbed the knotted rope and helped them over the railing once they reached the rungs. All of them managed to avoid slipping into a toothy grin.

"Where's Eddie?" The question came from the Asian guy who'd been on the beach with them, the one who supplied the rope. Eddie had said his name was Li.

"Slipped off the rope. Shark got him."

Li's brow wrinkled. "Shark?"

Paul wasn't sure if he didn't know what a shark was or if he just couldn't believe one had eaten his friend. "That's right, Jet." He started humming the John Williams soundtrack, made a fin out of his hands, glided it back and forth.

Li looked at him like he was crazy.

Paul ignored him.

Robinson came up next to him. "He was really taken by a *shark*?"

"Yeah. Stay out of the water."

Robinson turned to face the ocean, sadness and disbelief crowding his eyes.

"Hey," Paul said, slapping him on the shoulder. "I need you to help me lower the anchor."

Robinson's eyes came back, though he wasn't done with the grief just yet. Add it to the pile of those to be mourned at a later time. "Do you think it will reach?"

"I don't know. How long did it take you to row out here?"

He shrugged, then took off his cowboy hat. "The ship is heading east and seems to be getting nearer to the island."

"We're being pulled back in," Paul mumbled. That's why the sun was where it was. The island was like a drain, sucking everything back into it, just like the Purees had said from the beginning. Which meant they weren't drifting east anymore but south, and that what should be St. David's Island and the airport would be somewhere off starboard. "Maybe we shouldn't set the anchor just yet."

"Do you even know how?"

"Not really."

Robinson swept his eyes over the open deck, then up to the stairs. Paul hadn't seen the stairs in the darkness. If he had, he surely wouldn't have jumped off the bar in his best Jackie Chan imitation.

"The ship is empty?" Robinson asked.

Paul didn't know. He thought so, but then there was the screaming. And his new best friend, of course. Maybe there were a thousand vacationers all huddled together in the lobby, entertaining themselves with games to pass the time. Maybe the ship was full of dead bodies. Maybe there were faces in the walls, arms sticking out of the hull. "I have no idea."

"We should look, then. Maybe get into the control room and see if we can get this thing running."

He thought about mentioning the screams but decided against it. Maybe the sun chased them away. Besides, if it was something they needed to know, then they would be finding out one way or the other, wouldn't they? "Sure," he answered. There should be a gun safe on board too, one the chief security guy and the captain would've had access to. They could use all the firepower they could get, especially if Jackson's Graveyard search came up empty. "We stay together at all times. No matter what."

Robinson nodded, and then waved and brought the half-dozen Purees together. A couple of them didn't have rifles, just swords and knives. Paul didn't know what good they would do, but he felt better that they had them.

This time, instead of moving upward and staying on the open decks, Paul followed the Purees straight through the big, heavy door, and entered the cruise ship.

FUTURE PAST

And one from out the order of angels, having turned away with the order that was under him, conceived an impossible thought, to place his throne higher than the clouds above the earth, that he might become equal in rank to my power. And I threw him out from the height with his angels, and he was flying in the air continuously above the bottomless.

—Book of the Secrets of Enoch, 29:3,4

In like manner the Watchers also changed the order of their nature, whom the Lord cursed at the flood, on whose account He made the earth without inhabitants and fruitless.

— The Testament of Naphtali 1:27

And the angels, the children of heaven, saw an lusted after them, and said to one another: 'Come, let us choose us wives from among the children of men and beget us children. And Semjaza, who was their leader, said unto them: "I fear ye will not indeed agree to do this deed, and I alone shall have to pay the penalty of a great sin." And they all answered him and said: "Let us all swear an oath, and all bind ourselves by mutual imprecations not to abandon this plan but to do this thing…" And they were in all two hundred; who descended in the days of Jared on the summit of Mount Hermon…

— Book of Enoch 6:2-4, 5, 6

FOURTEEN

24th day of June. Morning. The Ship.

Exiting the empty restaurant, they found themselves in a long starboard corridor. A few open doorways on the right were glowing from the sunlight beginning to fill up the day. They entered the first room, which turned out to be a lounge. Circular tables, chairs…cookies.

White chocolate, macadamia nut, oatmeal raisin, all arranged in circular patterns on silver plates set across a bar in the back of the room. There were pitchers of room temperature coffee and water.

The six Purees scattered throughout the room, eyes wide with wonder. None but Robinson and Daniel had seen anything like this before (Graveyard participants excluded).

"Wow," Robinson remarked through a mouthful of cookie. He held what remained of the chocolate chip treat, stale as it may be, up to the window, examining it as if the chips might be gold. "I forgot…"

"You're not gonna start crying, are you?" Paul wanted to know.

He responded by tossing the rest of the snack into his mouth and pulling the brim of his hat down. Then he turned and helped himself to some more.

The others were shoving cookies into their mouths as well, and Paul thought it might seem rude if he didn't have one too. He took an oatmeal raisin. Not too bad. Way better than what they'd been eating—which wasn't much. He grabbed another and took it to the windows. They stretched the entire height of the wall, slanting inward as they rose. Paul stood before them, staring out over the ocean while the sun climbed the sky on the other side of the ship. If they were circling the island, then out there somewhere was its east end. He tried to calculate in his mind how fast they might be going but decided to just stick with "slow."

Turning his back to the fiery sea, he pulled a chair out from beneath a table and sat, setting the rifle down in front of him. It felt nice to plant his rear end in a sturdy chair for a change. He crossed his arms, leaned forward, and studied the breakfast-eating Purees while keeping an eye on the doorway. There was Robinson and Li from the earlier salvage operation, and he recognized Theodore-the-Austin-carrying-Brit and Daniel-the-Irish-friend-of-Patrick. The other two were only slightly familiar to him. He thought the taller one with the short hair and cavalry sword was Sanders, though it was entirely possible he'd just come up with that on his own since the guy bore a striking resemblance to Colonel Sanders, the KFC guy. And the last of the six was a hatchet-toting black dude named Carl. Again, it could've been his looking like Carl Weathers that formed the assumption, or it could be that was *why* remembering the name came easy. He wasn't sure. All the men, however, looked capable by and by.

He surveyed the room again, taking note of the details. All the chairs were pushed beneath the tables, all their tops spotless. Which meant that whatever happened to the ship must've happened after normal lounging hours and before anyone had a chance to pick at the snacks—so while everyone was sleeping. And he was sure that the ship hadn't come through the Triangle as the other Graveyard ships had. No. This ship was either docked or close to docking in one of Bermuda's ports when, all of a sudden, here it was instead. And without its crew and passengers. Or so it seemed.

"Ready?" he asked them, wanting to get this over with.

They shoved the remaining cookies into whatever pockets they had and filtered back into the hallway. Paul got up and joined them.

The next doorway on their right was to a room full of computers. Most of the men present had never seen a computer, and if they were in working order, Paul would have been delighted to blow their minds with such sorcery. But they were dark, useless without power.

"Come on," Paul said, and nudged them forward down the corridor.

They found only staterooms and darkness ahead of them. Stairs were on their left, in the middle of the deck.

"Look," Robinson said, touching a map on the wall. Paul stepped close and looked it over. Ahead of them were the cabins. Rooms 6001 through 6082. Eighty-two rooms, all their doors closed.

Paul ran his own finger over the plastic-encased diagram, studying the portside of their deck. A studio, library, sushi bar. Below them, on deck five, were showrooms, stores, casinos, clubs. On deck four was the medical center, lounge, and a whole lot of blank space that Paul thought might be what they were looking for. Above them were more cabins.

If anyone else was on the ship, they would have to run into them to find out, because there was no way they had time to search the 500 or so cabins, all the stores, restaurants, clubs, and theatres. But he did want to try something first.

"Hold on a sec," he mumbled, walking past the stairs and into the dark, cabin-lined hallway straight ahead. He tried the handle on the first door he came to. It didn't move, but with the electricity out, the magnetic seal was nonexistent and he was able to push the door open without a key card. He stuck his head in, the light coming from the windows making him squint. There was a hanging lifeboat outside the window, blocking a view of the ocean. The room wasn't messy, but it wasn't spotless either. Not like the computer room or lounge they just passed, which reaffirmed his suspicion that the change had occurred in the wee hours of the morning. The bed wasn't made, there was some trash in the wastebasket, some of the drawers were ajar. Someone was in here, most likely asleep, when suddenly...they weren't. They were somewhere else now, but Paul couldn't begin to guess where. Hoped he wouldn't find out.

He stepped back into the hallway and let the door close on its own. Then he stood there, in the dark, thinking.

He heard something.

It was faint, distant, but he heard *something.*

"Do you hear that?" he asked the others. He could see them in the leftover glow of the computer room, but they couldn't see him.

"Hear what?" Li asked.

That was obviously a "no." He set his back to the dark hallway and began walking back to the others when he heard it again.

Thump. Thump. Thump.

He stopped, the hair on his forearms rising around the painted python. "Now do you hear it?"

The rest of the Purees were only thirty feet away and should be able to hear what he was hearing. Unless it was in his head…

Thump. Thump. Thump. Thump.

It sounded like…a heavy person walking down the hallway. No. Not *walking*…more like stumbling. There was a full two seconds between each sound, and the mind's eye had no trouble conjuring zombies pacing the empty decks around them.

"I hear it," said Daniel.

Robinson nodded.

Paul slowly turned his head, looking back over his shoulder and squeezing the grip of the M14 with his remaining fingers. What else walked that slow and patient other than the undead? Of course, it might not be walking at all. Could be a bumping sound. Or something with a longer stride.

He saw nothing behind him but darkness.

And then two glowing red dots appeared hovering in the void.

His heart leaped in his chest even as his body spun toward the two pinpricks of light, rifle coming up in his hands.

Nothing.

He blinked, and they were gone. Or they hadn't been there in the first place.

"What is it?" Robinson whispered, his own weapon ready.

Paul began backpedaling out of the hallway, toward the daylight glowing out of the computer room and hugging his comrades. Maybe he didn't see what he thought he did. Maybe it *was* in his head.

Thump. Thump. Thump.

Or maybe they were exactly what he thought they were.

Eyes.

"What did you see?" Robinson asked again once Paul was beside him.

"Nothing."

It was clear that Robinson didn't believe it, but he didn't press him. "Down?" he asked instead.

Paul took a breath, moving his eyes to the stairs. It was going to be dark wherever there weren't windows to the outside.

Thump. Thump.

"Yeah. But first we need some light." He went back into the computer room and started kicking over chairs, stomping on their legs, breaking them off. Understanding what he was doing, the others began doing the same. Soon they all had lit torches, courtesy of matches found in a drawer in the next-door lounge and curtains torn from the windows.

"Ready?" Paul asked.

They all nodded, but the affirming movement contradicted the reservation obvious in their eyes. No. No one was ready. But what else were they going to do? Lower themselves back to their rowboat and paddle back to the island, leaving the mystery here unexplored? And why? Because of some noises?

"Let's go." Paul held the torch in one hand, the rifle ready to go in the other. He left the room and went to the stairs, leading them all down to deck five. The torchlight flickered and bounced all over the stairwell, and the sounds seemed to get closer. Louder.

"I don't like this," Robinson whispered at Paul's back.

"No kidding," he answered.

They left the Promenade deck and were now standing on the Tiffany deck below it. It was pitch black at the midship stairs and Paul almost wanted to keep taking the stairs down just to avoid standing still in the dark like this. They huddled together, moving the torches back and forth in front of them, trying to get a sense of their surroundings. Walls and closed doors.

Thump. Thump. Thump.

They all looked back to the stairs they'd just descended, positive that something else was now coming down them.

Li didn't wait for instructions, he went straight for the door in front of them, pushing it open and finding himself in another hallway. Though this one had a ball of light hovering at its end. A door to the outside.

"This way," Paul called to him, leading the others not into the hallway after Li, but to the left of that hallway, into another dark opening. If he remembered the map right, there was a store behind the wall on their right and the atrium lay ahead of them.

Li came back and fell in line with the others as they all moved away from the sounds coming from the stairwell.

"What *is* that?" Daniel asked.

"Is it a giant?" Theodore asked.

That's what Paul was thinking, but it would have to be bending over, wouldn't it?

"Just keep moving," Robinson said.

They came to the atrium. It was a circle in the middle of the ship, light streaming in from the port-side windows. They might as well be standing on the second level of a shopping mall, big carpeted stairs winding down to the main plaza where the reception counter was. Wooden floors, a grand piano, glass elevators, leather couches around finished tables, huge chandelier overhead. If the electricity was flowing, the place would be lit up like Christmas, maybe some smooth jazz playing if the pianist was on break. But now it was silent, still. The rays streaming in from the windows cut laser-like swaths into the darkness, but somehow, they only managed to accent the deck's emptiness.

"What now?" Robinson asked. His eyes were locked on the foyer below as if trying to detect something in its shadows.

"Keep going forward, to the next stairs," Paul said.

"What *is* this?" one of the others whispered, eyes wide with strange wonder.

Paul didn't know how the brains of the island's natives were computing it all, whether they were stuck in wonder or if they were reaching sanity's end, but he didn't really have time to care. He wanted his company fixated on the creepy noises behind them and the possibility of being attacked, not ogling over the floating alien city they'd just climbed aboard.

They moved out of the atrium and soon found themselves in the casino. It was dark in there, no windows to the outside, and they relied on the torchlight to navigate the slot machines and blackjack tables.

Thump. Thump. Thump. Thump.

It seemed to be following them, still coming from behind. Paul turned and faced the entrance to the casino, expecting to see *something* enter in after them. The noise was getting louder. So loud, in fact, that he wasn't entirely sure that it was even coming from the same deck. It could be that it was above them, right on top of them. He looked up.

Thump.

Thump.

Thump.

The noise grew slower, more rhythmic. Paul raised the burning curtain above his head.

"Come on!" Robinson shouted to him.

Paul turned and could only make out the hectic line of dancing flames streaming toward the other end of the room as his company retreated toward the exit. He ran after them.

He burst into the hallway and found them all descending the forward stairs, down to deck five. He didn't know what was on deck five other than the medical center and the lobby, and the map on the wall hadn't included decks one through four—areas off-limits to passengers. Which was what they wanted—the anchor room or engine room or some other, similar room. He had no idea if it was even possible to get the ship running again, but he figured it would be an unmarked location that let them know for sure.

The procession of torches descended in a square pattern, the steps leading to a landing before continuing down to deck five and the medical center. Paul put one foot on the first step and stopped.

Paul...

He looked up.

Paul, help me.

It was Hunter's voice.

Paul, please...

Paul looked down and watched the last of the torches disappear as it moved out of the stairwell. He stepped back.

Thump-thump-thump-thump.

Running. Had to be.

Paul, get me out of here…

He swore, the footsteps (if that's what they were) getting louder, closer, faster. Something was coming at him. He turned away from the stairs and ran through the dark, toward the bow. He tried to remember what was ahead of him, but couldn't.

And then he saw the big doors.

The showroom.

Paul, I'm in here.

It was Hunter's voice, no doubt about it. But was it really *his* voice, or was it in his head with ghost girls and red eyes?

Thump-thump-thump-thump-thump.

He turned his head to look behind him.

And, as if answering his question, there the girl stood. Staring.

He tripped over the incline leading to the lounge and went crashing into the heavy door, dropping both the torch and the rifle in his attempt to control his fall. He stumbled into the showroom.

But it wasn't the showroom.

It was Court Street. And he wasn't facing a stage, but the obelisk in the courtyard of the Cabinet Building. A moped drove past him, almost running him over.

He stood in shock, Bermuda buzzing around him.

FIFTEEN

24th day of June. Late morning. The House.

The clearing stood open before them, the morning breeze rustling the tall grass.

"There it is," Jackson said. There was no need to point or further elaborate on the "it" he spoke of. The pink house stood in the middle of the empty field, illuminated by the invading sun. It appeared as a spotlighted prop on the mind stage of some playwright's stoned imagination—bizarre, out of place, alien. Disturbing.

Jackson leaned against the tree in front of him, his fingers dancing gingerly over his wounded side, pushing, probing, massaging. To his right was Pierre, Arkansas Joe, the kid Hap that had been behind them in the procession to Jared's cave a couple days ago, and Patrick. They were all holding their breath, minds sizzling with overloaded synapses.

Jackson knew Hap and Joe had been born on the island, so there was no telling what was going through their minds. Perhaps they'd seen pictures of houses before, or perhaps not; but here one was. Pierre and Patrick, however, were not born on the island, and the merging of the two realities meant a little something different to them. As it did to Jackson.

Smoke drifted from the chimney, its long gray tendrils slithering through the blue sky like a burnt offering to whatever god was now in charge of the island. It'd been easy to find the house once the smoke appeared through the canopy, and Jackson had been warding off waves of skittish questions ever since, promising his party answers upon arrival. Of course, he didn't really have answers. Only a story. Which he whispered now.

When he was finished, their response came in the way of wide and doubt-filled eyes.

"You can go in there if you want, see for yourself," Jackson said, reading their skepticism.

Their gaze went to the house, up to the smoke, then back to him.

Jackson, himself, wasn't sure what should be done about the house. He didn't *want* to go in there. Not even if the closet was still sealed with that dimensional goo, keeping its monsters in their abode of oblivion nice and well behaved (he was pretty sure that was no longer the case).

But Hunter was in there.

"What do we do about it?" Patrick asked with his Irish tongue.

Jackson realized that he hadn't seen Patrick since he and George (God bless his soul), had taken them to the henge. The henge they just happened to be at when the Fallen appeared out of nowhere to sacrifice a Nephilim giant—

Jackson paused, his thoughts suddenly speeding down another vein.

He tried to remember everything Chadwick had talked about then, what Patrick had said about the Nephilim spirits being freed from their bodies, becoming spirits able to travel back and forth between the two worlds…what the Book of Enoch seemed to hint at. He felt a discovery near, a revelation just on the tip of his brain. But then it was gone.

"What do we do about it?" Patrick asked again.

"I don't know." And that was the truth.

They stood there, studying the house for a few more minutes. It was quiet. Still.

The forest whispered around them. Leaves rustled calmly in the breeze. Some birds chirped far away.

And then a loud noise that was something between a *smack* and a *crack* with a little *boing* gluing them together.

Pierre looked up and saw an arrow sticking out of the trunk he was leaning against, just inches from his head, its long pole-like shaft still vibrating. The tree was almost split in half, bark chipped and missing all around the point of impact.

The next sound that exploded in their midst had a wetness to it. It came an instant before the crack of splitting wood, but it was so fast, there was no way the ear could perceive it as anything other than one sound. The eye, however, could observe the aftermath of the thing that caused the sound and then decipher in retrospect that there were two separate causes for the noise.

Pierre looked down from the arrow above his head and to the one now going through him. It was through his chest, on the right side, pinning him to the tree. He swore in French.

Jackson, Hap, Joe, and Patrick dropped into the thicket, their eyes scanning the forest behind them in the direction the arrows must've come.

"Stay down," Jackson whispered as he began crawling over to Pierre. He had to get him down, because the next arrow would certainly take his head off.

As soon as he reached him, he sprang up, grabbed Pierre's shoulders with two hands (trying to ignore that tingling spot between his shoulder blades that warned of an arrow coming) and said, "This is gonna hurt." And he pulled him away from the tree as hard and as fast as he could, all two feet of the arrow sliding through his chest until he was suddenly free and sprawling forward, both of them collapsing to the ground.

Jackson pushed Pierre off him, his mind again racing back to that day in the henge—Chadwick telling of Narvaez finding giants along the Mississippi, giants said to be great archers, extremely accurate and with force enough to pierce red oaks straight through… Patrick had responded by mumbling, *I've seen that.* And the look on his face now said he was seeing it again.

Giants.

"How far away, do you think?" Jackson whispered to Patrick. Pierre was lying belly-up next to him, hands clutching his chest, blood flowing between his fingers and painting him red.

Patrick shook his head. "I've seen them hit targets two football fields away."

It sounded like "fewt-ball", and Jackson knew he was talking soccer. But he was pretty sure that, though a soccer field was wider than a football field, the length was the same. Which would make the distance 240 yards. That was 740 feet. He thought the world record was something like 650. Not good. Or maybe it was just far enough for them to make a run for it. Even with Pierre.

"We need to get out of here," Joe said, looking back over his shoulder and to the house.

Jackson knew what he was thinking, and it would've been the obvious choice if not for the revolving door to hell in the bedroom. But where else could they go?

Another arrow whistled past them. It took Hap's hand off. The kid screamed, clutching his wrist. It was so fresh and cleanly cut by the diamond arrowhead that for a second or two they could actually see the bone and veins and layers of skin and muscle and all of it. Then the blood began squirting and it all disappeared.

Without even hesitating, Patrick leaned forward and pulled the shoestring out of his left Converse sneaker. Moving quickly, he tied it around Hap's arm. Tied it tight and knotted it. He smacked the screaming kid in the face, twice. The kid stopped screaming, staring at him with those squirrely eyes, wide and full of pain. Shock, fear, some anger.

"You lost your hand, mate. Not your head. You'll learn to live with it. *If* you can pull on your big-boy pants. Understand?"

Conflicting expressions were battling in Hap's eyes. Understanding that the Irishman was right, and the absurd disbelief at what was being asked of him. *I just lost my HAND!* was what the kid *wanted* to say. But he managed to swallow it down, his eyes drifting to the hand now lying in the dirt. He tried to will those fingers to move as he had been able to since birth…but they didn't move. Didn't do anything.

"Don't look. Won't do you any good to look." Patrick grabbed the bottom of Hap's baby blue shirt, ripped off a good piece of it, and wrapped it around the wound. It instantly turned a dark purple, but the blood was beginning to slow thanks to the shoestring.

Movement out ahead of them, between the trees. Maybe seventy yards out.

"You see that?" Jackson asked.

"I think so," Joe whispered back.

Then a giant stepped out from behind a crop of nearby trees, a bow in its hand. It was nocking another arrow.

To the left of it, another giant stepped forth. This one had an axe the size of a lamppost in its hand.

A third giant appeared behind them.

"We gotta go *now*!" Jackson cried. He grabbed Pierre under the arms, pain blasting away at his side, and threw him up over his shoulder. He started running, careful not to trip but moving as fast as he could, still waiting for a crystal arrowhead to come flying out of his chest.

Patrick pulled Hap to his feet and yanked him by his remaining hand. Patrick stumbled a little, and his unlaced sneaker flew off. Joe followed them, bending over and snatching the lost shoe.

They ran out of the woods and entered the clearing. They would be easier targets out in the open, but it was the quickest way to the house.

"Come on, come on, come on, come on…" Jackson was muttering, his footsteps heavy and awkward with Pierre draped over his left shoulder and bleeding all over him. Hap tore away from Patrick's grasp and ran out in front of them, his skinny legs lost in a blur of terror-induced adrenaline. *Almost there.* "Come on, come on, come on…"

The house was getting bigger, closer.

Jackson stole a glance behind them and saw the three giants explode out of the woods after them. *Come on!* His legs had grown heavy, like they were filled with concrete, and now he was beginning to lose feeling in them. Soon they would just turn to jelly and fold up beneath him.

Almost there.

Joe turned and began backpedaling, firing his new AK-47 from his hip. The sound echoed around the clearing, bouncing off the surrounding wall of trees. But the shots didn't seem to be doing anything to their pursuers.

And then a second AK started going off.

It took Jackson a second to see where it was coming from, and then he saw the muzzle flashes in a window on the far side of the house. Whether or not the carefully aimed firepower was hitting its mark didn't seem to matter. It caused the giants to spread out, which bought them a few more steps.

Hap flung the door open to the house and disappeared inside. Patrick was next, and then Joe turned and covered Jackson, allowing him to carry Pierre through the doorway. Then the door was slammed shut and Jackson stumbled into the living room, dropping Pierre onto a couch.

Jackson's chest heaved as he tried to both catch his breath and remain conscious. Swinging the AK off his back, he joined the others in the hallway, all eyes on the closed door, expecting it to be smashed down any second. They all raised their weapons, sweat running into their eyes, Hap cradling his bandaged forearm behind them.

And then a voice startled them half to death.

"Took you long enough."

They all spun and came face to face with Robyn. She was replacing the banana clip in her smoking assault rifle.

SIXTEEN

Bermuda.

At first, Paul didn't know if it was a vision or whether he, like Scrooge, had been spirited back to Bermuda, a phantom standing on the street and observing the tropical hustle and bustle of twenty-first-century normalcy.

And then the light in front of him switched red and a guy on a scooter came to a stop beside him. Paul watched him, unsure whether or not he was really there. Until the guy turned, looked directly at him, and frowned.

"You okay, man?" the guy asked, his accent British.

Paul turned and looked behind him, expecting to find someone else there that the scooter man was addressing. But there was nothing but bushes lining an empty sidewalk.

"You look like you could use a hospital."

He looked down at himself, at his bloodied and torn Nike shirt, at his lacerated forearms and missing fingers. He couldn't imagine what his face looked like. He lifted his eyes back to the man. "I'm fine."

"Sure you are. Hospital's that way." He pointed to his left, down Front Street. Then the light turned green, and he took a right, pausing only to look back over his shoulder at the crazy American who had obviously been mugged and left for dead the night before.

Paul watched him go, but his brain failed to compute it. How was it possible? How could he be here? *Back* here? Of course, the obvious answer was that he couldn't be. He'd tripped while going through the theatre doors, lost his torch and gun, probably hit his head. But would he know all that if he was unconscious?

The air was crisp, about fifteen degrees cooler than the seventy-something the sunrise had just warmed the ship with, the sun itself about an hour behind in its climb. There was no sign of cruise ship activity across the street in Hamilton Harbor and no great flourish of tourist traffic, which was odd even in the early morning hours. He turned around again, looking for a swirling black hole through which he might still see into the derelict cruise ship in the other Bermuda. But unless it was hiding in the bushes, there was only the metal gate surrounding the Cabinet Building. He let his eyes go to the obelisk, and chills pricked his flesh. It could've been the cold breeze off the harbor, but more likely it was the whispered inclination in the back of his mind that the Egyptian phallic icon was actually a kind of cosmic radio beacon connected to the Beyond. The obelisk was the only one on the island he was aware of, and he found it hard to believe dumb luck alone transported him to it.

He moved his feet along the sidewalk, and the feeling of concrete beneath his boots reminded him of other times he'd returned to civilization after long missions spent in the world's blind spots. But this was a return from the blind spot of all blind spots. This was from the Naga Hills of Dimension X, and this time, he could almost get on his hands and knees and kiss the sidewalk.

He was back, baby. Didn't matter how. He had made it. No more giants. No more cave dwelling. No more turtle soup with rainwater. And most importantly, no more dead girl following him around.

He stepped off the sidewalk and crossed Front Street, his eyes taking in all the pastel hues so comfortably surrounding him. And then he stopped and looked back to the buildings of Hamilton. The capital. It was the site of the pyramid complex in the otherworld. The world Jackson was still in. *Screw him*, Paul thought. It'd all been Jack's fault to begin with. He was the one who tricked them into coming to Bermuda, meeting with Ronald and getting on Henry's boat.

But Hunter was still there, too. Somewhere.

A cab honked and swerved to miss him. His spell broken, Paul realized he was standing in the middle of the street. He held up his three-fingered hand in a gesture of apology. The citizens of Bermuda were almost freakishly friendly, and he was sure the cab driver wasn't thrusting a middle finger at him. No, rather he was probably calling the police to report what he probably believed to be an accident victim, dazed and out of sorts in the middle of the street. But even if he didn't report the beat-up American (and the guy on the moped didn't either), how long would he be able to walk around like this? Right out front of the capital? What would he tell them when they asked what had happened to him?

Now across the street, he looked out into the harbor, realizing there was something wrong with the picture before him. It was too…*empty*. At least for the end of June.

He needed a phone. *I need a doctor*, is what he knew he should've been thinking. *Hell, a shrink*. But it was a phone he was looking for. He needed to know.

He waved down a taxi. It pulled over, and the dark-skinned driver immediately flung the door open, stepping out of the small minivan.

"Sir, are you all right?" he asked. He hurried up to him, even placed a hand on Paul's shoulder.

"I'm fine."

"Sir, let me take you to the hospital." He looked down at Paul's hand. "You're…missing *fingers*, sir!"

Paul laughed, finding the horrified and concerned look in the cab driver's eyes quite hilarious. He laughed harder, bending over with hands on his knees.

The guy took a step back. It was that slow, cautious step that people take away from sudden uncertainty.

Paul held up his good hand to the concerned gentleman, signaling that there was no need for him to be scared. But he still couldn't stop laughing. "I'm okay," he finally managed to spit out. And then, slowly, he was able to get himself together.

"You don't look good, my friend."

Paul nodded. "I'm sure of *that*. But I need to make a call."

"Long distance?"

"Yeah. I need to know…"

The islander didn't ask what it was that needed to be known, only reached into his pocket and pulled out a cell.

Paul took his wallet from his back pocket, surprised that it was still there. He hadn't looked at it in some time, and given all it'd been through, he had no idea what he was going to find in it.

This time it was the Bermudian who put up his hand. "No, no, it is fine."

Paul was relieved to find over a hundred dollars in cash still in his wallet. It was damp, and if he wasn't careful, it'd probably fall apart in his hands when he tried pulling it out. "Hold out your hand," he said.

"Friend, I do not—"

Paul grabbed his hand and turned it over, palm up. Then he turned his wallet upside down and wiggled it until the green bills fell out and into the man's hand. "Be careful. They've been through a lot, and you should let them dry before handling them."

The driver just stared at his hand, at the fifties and twenties, bewildered.

Paul snatched the cell out of his other hand. Started dialing. There was no way this would work. Even if they did make it back here, it had only been a few days ago. Surely they wouldn't be—

Ringing.

He held his breath. And then he looked up with a sudden thought. "What day is it?" he asked the man.

The Bermudian looked up from the money, probably thinking of a bill or two that he could now get caught up on, and blinked. "Excuse me?"

Still ringing.

"The *day*. What *day* is it?"

"It's Wednesday."

That meant nothing to Paul. He was pretty sure it was supposed to be Friday, but with the way things were on the island, he could've easily lost track. "What's the *date*?"

Now the driver was looking even more concerned. "The twenty-first."

"*Of?*"

"December…" He took a step toward him, regaining the one he'd previously lost to doubt and fear. This one was all-pro Samaritan. "Please, friend, let me take you—"

December 21st? Paul's head spun. That was the winter solstice…*six months from now!* Or maybe…

But before he could ask for the year, the ringing on the other end stopped.

"Hello?" Henry's voice answered.

Paul needed to sit, or he was going to fall over. Everything was moving. He signaled to the driver to open the side door, which he did.

"Henry," Paul started.

There was a moment of silence on the other end, and then, "Paul?"

"Yeah, it's me!" He smiled, tears welling in his eyes. The driver placed one hand under his elbow and the other against his back, helping him up into the van. He collapsed into the seat. "You made it back…"

"Yeah, of course we did. Where are *you*?"

"Bermuda. I—" He had no idea where to start, so he said the only thing he was certain of. "I'm *back*."

"And Jack?"

Paul could tell Henry was pacing back and forth, quickly. Excitement was overflowing in his voice, his words coming out at light speed but still far slower than his racing thoughts. "Jack and Hunter are still—"

The sliding door slammed shut next to him, and his eyes closed in reflex. He kept them closed and brought a hand up to his forehead. He thought he could hear the guy running around to the driver's side door still hanging open. He would take him to the hospital for sure. That was fine with Paul. He'd go anywhere the nice man wanted to take him. He had Henry on the line. They'd made it back.

But now he was asking about Jack and Hunter. "I don't know how it happened, Henry. I—"

Suddenly, he became aware that the activity on the other end of the line seemed to have ceased. It was still. Quiet. Dead.

"Henry?"

Nothing.

He opened his eyes.

And found himself sitting in a cozy theatre seat, facing a dark and empty stage.

SEVENTEEN

24th day of June. Late morning. The House.

"In *there*?" Patrick asked, pointing to the closet. He had his sneaker back on, but without the laces, the old tongue was flopping down over the plastic toe.

Jackson nodded. He was having a hard time taking his eyes off the closet door. They were standing in the bedroom, him, Patrick, and Joe. Pierre was lying on a couch in the living room. Hap was on another couch, sound asleep after passing out. It was unclear whether his unconscious state was due to blood loss or shock, probably both, but he seemed to be okay for the most part. Robyn was at the windows, going back and forth with her new toy, keeping an eye out for the giants and anything else that might be looking to return home. The giants had come within ten yards of the house before turning and disappearing back into the surrounding woods. No one knew why, but Jackson had a pretty good idea.

"You're sure?" Patrick pressed, taking a step closer.

"I wouldn't."

"And you said Hunter's in there, too?" Arkansas Joe wanted to know.

"Yeah."

"Should we knock?" He was joking, a nervous giggle following the question.

The last time he was in the bedroom, the closet doors had been wide open, the abyss visible beyond, something trying to get out. Now the closet was shut and appeared to be a normal closet, in a normal bedroom, in a normal house. "You might not like what answers."

Patrick frowned. "The thing on the beach, you think?"

"I *know*. I saw it."

"So what do we do?" He looked like he didn't want to be in the bedroom at all.

After Jackson told them the closet stories, what had happened to him, Hunter, and then Paul, they'd just stood in the room facing the closed door. Truth was, Jackson didn't know what to do. He didn't want to open the door, didn't want to go *near* the door, but here he was, in the bedroom, incapable of taking his eyes off it. Ten minutes since they got themselves situated in the house, seven since he'd finished his story.

"I don't know." He paused. "Maybe we—"

"For Pete's sake," a female voice interrupted. Robyn walked straight through them and to the closet, not slowing down, not caring. She reached for the closet handle and, before anyone could object, yanked the door wide open.

"No!" Jackson hollered, but only a closet—filled with clothes on hangers, a small shoe rack with sneakers and high-heeled shoes, flip-flops and sandals—was there to answer him.

Robyn turned, one eyebrow raised. "Your friend's in *there*?"

He frowned, stepping forward. There was no trace of the liquid barrier, the oily sheen that had kept the creature from escaping before. No empty space. No void. No Hunter.

Just a closet.

They all looked at him, their unspoken doubt crystal clear.

"That thing came out of there," he said. He brushed past Robyn and slammed the closet door shut. Then he went to the bed, bent over and grabbed the frame, and dragged it across the floor. He pushed it against the closet.

"What are you doing?" Joe asked.

"Peace of mind." He stood, touching his side, and left the bedroom.

The three of them took a moment to study the closet door one more time, and then filed out of the room.

Jackson went to check on Pierre. The arrow had obviously gone through, and the blood that was bubbling out from the wound said the lung was punctured. Finding gauze pads under the sink in the bathroom, along with petroleum jelly, they'd sealed the pad over both holes. Jackson used some masking tape they'd seen in the kitchen to tape down three sides of the bandage, allowing air to exit the hole while simultaneously preventing air from being sucked in and collapsing the lung. It didn't seem to be working, though. The lung was collapsing anyway.

"I wanted to see the hills where I grew up one more time," Pierre groaned. His breathing was labored, shallow. "I can't even remember the name of the town."

Jackson put a hand on his shoulder. "You'll see it again."

He smiled, appreciating the words but knowing their uselessness. He put his own hand atop Jackson's. "Just make sure you get her out of this place."

Jackson stared at him, his face growing severe. Then he nodded. "Of course."

"She deserves better than all of this."

"I know."

Pierre's eyes grew sad, his game face fracturing for a split second, fear and doubt and a sense of loss shining through.

"Hang in there, will you? We'll see what we can do. Don't quit."

Pierre did his best to nod.

Jackson stood, went over to Hap and studied his wrist for a minute before joining the others in the kitchen.

"Is he going to be okay?" Robyn asked.

Jackson shook his head. He spoke softly, both because he didn't want his words to be overheard by Pierre and because he didn't want to hear them himself. "He needs surgery. The hole is too big for the lungs to repair themselves. I can try to release the air pressure building against his lung, but…that's only going to prolong things."

Her eyes dropped to her feet, the arm holding the AK suddenly growing longer, limp. Tears ran down her cheeks.

"You like him." Did he really just say that? He couldn't believe it and felt ashamed.

"Not in that way, no," she whispered, apparently not taking offense. "He's my friend, has been like a brother."

"He feels a bit differently about you, I think."

"I know." A few more tears fell, landing on her left boot and the tile floor.

Without even thinking about it, Jackson took her in his arms and held her. The boldness of it shocked him, and he realized it came as naturally as if he were hugging Denise after her own brother was killed in that car wreck a month before their wedding. She didn't resist or push away, though. In fact, she pressed against his chest, burying her head in his mass. This was a different side of her than what he'd seen so far. But it was not surprising—someone she'd spent her whole life with, someone who had tried his damnedest to woo her, was dying in the next room.

He ran his fingers through her hair, wondering where the line was. Not that he was thinking about anything beyond offering a shoulder to lean on, but would she know that?

Patrick and Joe looked a little uncomfortable standing there next to the refrigerator, watching the newcomer embracing one of the women they'd done everything within their power to protect for the last number of years. It made Jackson uncomfortable, too. But before he could pull back, she did it for him.

She wiped her eyes, looked around as if for the first time, and said, "So this is what a real house looks like?"

Jackson nodded, looking around, himself. "Find anything in there to eat?" he asked Joe and Patrick.

Patrick was not a native to the island, so the house (as bizarre as its presence was), was not as surprising to him as it was to those who'd never seen the outside or inside of a modern home. "Plenty," he said.

Arkansas Joe appeared mesmerized by everything around him, and he came up behind Robyn. "This is how people out there live?"

Again, Jackson could've explained the various classes, the haves and the have-nots, the poor and the well-to-do, but he just said, "Yeah. Pretty much."

"I'm going to check the perimeter again," Robyn said. She raised the AK-47, the last of her tears now dry, and resumed her window rotation.

Jackson stared after her, wondering what she might be feeling about their little moment. Then he was past it and concentrating on more pressing matters. Like if he would ever find out where Hunter was.

"Let's eat," Patrick said, opening the fridge and pulling out a loaf of bread. He tossed it to Joe and then reached back in for more.

"Help me look for some things first," Jackson said. He gave them a list.

Half an hour later, Robyn was sitting in the open doorway, hugging her knees to her chest, the assault rifle lying at the ready by her feet. A stiff breeze was blowing over the clearing and catching her hair, whipping it over her glazed eyes. They'd managed to take the pressure off Pierre's lung, keeping it from collapsing, but they all knew it was an exercise in futility, just something to *do*. And doing felt better than waiting, even if the end of it was all the same.

It wasn't the first time Jackson had to poke a hole in a man's chest to relieve pressure, but it was the first time he'd used the top of a large soap dispenser to do it. It hadn't been on the list of items he was looking for, but it was all they could find. Pierre was asleep now, having passed out from the insertion of the long tube into his chest.

They'd eaten a full meal from the fridge, and Robyn and Joe found themselves amazed at the taste of a fresh, civilized meal. Grilled cheese sandwiches with tomato slices and onion, grilled on the stove in a puddle of butter and garlic. There were a variety of potato chips in the cupboard next to the fridge, too (barbeque and salt and vinegar seeming to be everyone's favorites), and they had sweet pickles, the soda Hunter had so wanted, and chocolate brownies for dessert. How their stomachs would handle the foreign ingredients would be a different matter.

Patrick was in the living room, looking at the pictures hanging on the wall. "Where do you think they are?" he asked.

Jackson was leaning on the wall separating the living room from the hallway, where he could keep a good eye on Robyn, Pierre, and the closed bedroom door. He'd been wondering the same thing ever since seeing the photos himself. "I don't know." Could be they were still in this house, back in the real Bermuda, going about their daily routine completely unaware that a copy of their home had been transmitted to another layer of reality where strangers now ate their food and gawked at their possessions. Or, they could be in the great nowhere, floating between worlds, lost in the void. And then there were the Philadelphia Experiment stories, the things Paul said he saw in the temple. Jackson hoped it wasn't that. The last thing he wanted to do was open the cabinet under the kitchen sink and find a face from the pictures sticking out of the floor, staring up at him.

Jackson watched Patrick hover over the wall, taking in the pictures of the world he so missed. He began to recall bits of the conversation they'd had the last time he'd seen the Irishman. "When you took us to the henge…"

Patrick turned.

"You were talking to Chadwick about certain passages from the Book of Enoch, about the Nephilim souls becoming spirits or demons."

Now he turned completely, his back to the wall. "Yes."

Jackson wasn't sure where he was really going with it, but he couldn't help thinking there was something about it that was relevant to their present situation. "You said that the giants were being sacrificed in order that their spirits would be free to leave this place. To travel back to the real world and help Osiris bring his offspring here."

"That is right."

He was thinking of the closet, Denise's voice, the darkness that spread over the beach. "After the solstice, after Osiris left, something happened. Some type of merge. We know what it looks like on our end; we don't know if it's the same on the other." He had a hard time imagining CNN covering a breaking story about buildings vanishing, land appearing from nowhere, and people suddenly becoming wall ornaments. "But what if the spirits of the Nephilim, once free to travel back and forth, are now trapped here with us? The Bermuda Triangle, the Doorway to Hell, suddenly shut down without Osiris here to maintain it?"

Patrick looked confused. "I'm not following."

And how could he unless he saw what was in the closet and heard whispers from the dead? "What if…the island really *is* haunted?"

He brought a hand to his bald head and stared at the floor as he considered Jackson's question. When he looked up, there was suspicion on his face. "Because of that?" He pointed in the direction of the closet.

Jackson didn't answer.

Patrick walked toward him, his eyes gliding back and forth between Hap and Pierre. Under his breath he whispered, "What else?"

Jackson should've known the question would be asked. Why else would he assume that trapped spirits were now haunting the island just because he had some experience with a closet portal to hell? It would be more likely that the haunting (if there was haunting going on) would emanate from that open doorway, and not necessarily from disembodied spirits of slaughtered Nephilim giants. And, Jackson figured, that was entirely possible, too. But he wanted to explore all the options, wanted to know why and from where Denise was calling him. If it could *be* Denise. Was it something unleashed on the island, freeing all the fiends of hell into this place? Or was it the spirits of the Nephilim playing games with him?

He stole a glance at Robyn. She was still sitting in the doorway with her back to him, facing the forest, waiting for the giants to return. He looked at Joe, who was in the kitchen, lost in his own thoughts, absentmindedly munching on a pickle. "I'm hearing voices," he whispered back.

"Voices?"

He nodded. "Familiar voices. Of the deceased."

"This just started?"

"After the solstice."

Patrick gave it some thought and shrugged. "Don't know what to tell you about that. Seems anything is possible anymore."

And did it really matter whether it was Nephilim ghosts tormenting them or demons from the underworld? Yes and no. As far as the torment went, it didn't matter. But whether it was ghosts and goblins trapped in their world or monsters from some open portal to hell made all the difference in the world. And there was a portal to somewhere, wasn't there? Otherwise where was Hunter? Where had the Ridley Scott demon come from?

"Since you brought it up," Patrick began, changing the subject, "all that stuff Chadwick was talking about, the giants and all back in history… That all true?"

He shrugged. "It's in the books."

"If Osiris did make it back and is operating in the real world…"

That was something that Jackson didn't want to think about right now. "Let's just figure out how to get back ourselves, okay? We'll worry about the coming New World Order and the rise of the Beast later."

Just then the sixty-inch LCD above the chestnut cabinet blinked on, exploding the stillness with a burst of static.

Patrick jumped, and Jackson came off the wall. Robyn and Joe turned their heads.

The television. Jackson didn't know why he hadn't thought of turning it on before. Obviously, they weren't going to catch the local news or be able to binge-watch the *X-Files* on demand, but...electricity was coming from somewhere, so yes, the TV should power on. But getting reception was a whole different matter, as the loud static confirmed.

Until it didn't.

"*Help.*"

Joe stepped off the barstool, and Robyn got to her feet. Jackson and Patrick just stared.

"*Help me.*"

It came from the television all right.

Joe was in the room now, Robyn walking in right behind him. They all stood there, transfixed by the snowstorm of static.

But it was more than static.

"Do you see it?" Patrick whispered.

No one answered.

"*Please...*"

Then they saw it.

The static began to take shape, and though they might question themselves later, they all knew in that moment that they were looking at a face.

"*Jack, are you there?*"

"Is that—" Joe's voice sounded drunk with fright.

Jackson wanted to say it was. Wanted to say it wasn't. How could he be sure what it was? After all, he'd been hearing Denise, too. But then, he realized, they were *all* hearing the static man.

Hunter.

"*Help me, Jack!*" the static screamed. Then a burst of wind blew through the house, rattling the pictures on the wall and knocking a candle over on the dining room table.

Jackson took a slow, cautious step back into the hallway between the living room and the kitchen. First he looked to his left, toward the front door that Robyn apparently left open (which might explain the burst of wind). But then he turned to his right, toward the bedroom. That door was wide open. And beyond it, in the room, the bed was no longer against the closet door.

And the closet door was open.

"Uh-oh." But before he could say anything else, there was a noise from the front door. Spinning back, he saw a giant stooping down and peering into the house.

EIGHTEEN

24th day of June. Late morning. The Ship.

It couldn't be real, had to be some kind of hallucination. Maybe even a vision. *Something.* But not real. He tripped coming through the doors, probably hit his head, the whole thing a dream. *How long was I out?* And how the hell did he end up sitting in the chair? Depression swirled within him, a deep guttural groan of despair. He was free from this place, this hell. Had made it back. But he hadn't. Because here he was. Back on the ship, the whole experience in his mind alone.

Then he felt it.

His eyes slowly slid down to his hand, almost afraid of what he was sure couldn't be there. But it was. The driver's cell phone.

He stared at it, his mind reeling. He brought it to his ear.

"Hello?" His voice was barely a whisper.

Nothing on the other end.

He looked at the display on the screen. It was backlit, showing a connection and a call in progress. The seconds were ticking by, approaching the three-minute mark. He tried again, leaning forward in the dark. "Hello?"

Still nothing.

He looked at the display again. The time of the call hit 3:06 and then reset to zeros. The backlight went off, and the call was lost. Standing, Paul tried dialing again.

NO SERVICE. OUT OF NETWORK.

He stared at the carpeted floor, thinking. Thinking hard. Thinking fast. He slipped the phone into his pocket, then swore loudly at the room around him, the veins in his neck and arms bulging, a bolt of fire throbbing through his missing fingers.

Hunter's voice had brought him in here. *Here.* Bermuda. The future. The solstice.

It wasn't possible. But he had the phone in his pocket.

Then what brought me back?

If the theatre was something like the closet in that house, a portal to another place, then how (and why) had he returned? And what had happened to the portal? Did it fold up and wink out after use? Relocated to another place, always on the move?

There wasn't time to think it out now, even if answers were possible. The others had gone down to deck five and that thing could still be stalking them. He'd revisit the impossible phone in his pocket later. He went up the aisle and back to the double doors. As he pushed them open, a thought struck him. Not with the force of Thor's hammer, but with a pinprick of sharp concern, the flick of a razor across the canvas of probability.

What if the others *weren't* out there?

What if *that* had been six months ago?

He went out the doors, expecting the same dark, empty ship with the torch and rifle still where he'd dropped them.

But he found none of that.

* * * *

Robyn fired at the giant, the blasting noise filling the house and stirring Hap and Pierre from their slumber. They'd slept through the television, but the reports of the rifle were deafening in the small confines of the house, and no sleep cycle could withstand such concussions.

Jackson, Joe, and Patrick all picked up their own AKs and took positions in the cramped hallway around Robyn. They emptied entire clips into the monster, sending it backward and reeling into the grass some fifty feet away.

They ejected the empty clips and rammed in new ones.

"What is it?" Pierre's weak voice came from the living room.

Hap was up on his feet, holding his wrapped stub and looking around the corner and out the open door.

"Don't move," Jackson said to both of them. He began walking to the door, rifle raised and ready to fire again, the other three on his heels.

He stepped outside, stealing a quick look left and right, making sure there were no other giants ready to attack. It looked clear. He continued walking, stepping down into the grass.

The giant was on its side, blood squirting up into the air from multiple holes like some freak show water fountain dispensing fruit punch instead of *agua*. It was big, probably around thirteen feet tall, dressed in a skirt like the olden days.

"Careful," Arkansas Joe warned, circling around it to the left, weapon aimed.

"Is it dead?" Patrick asked.

They were close now, within its reach if it were to make a sudden grab for them.

Jackson didn't see its chest moving. "Looks like it."

Beside them, Robyn had shouldered her rifle and was now lifting the Nephilim's gigantic sword. Her muscles strained under its weight as she balanced its tip straight up in the air. It was longer than she was tall and almost as wide. It looked ridiculous in her hands. She stumbled over to the giant.

"Stay back," Joe said.

She ignored him. Instead, she shouted, bringing the sword back over her head (this almost made her fall on her butt) and then down again, the weight of the sword doing most of the work. The sword fell onto the thing's neck, slicing through thick knots of muscle, but failed to pass completely through.

She tried to pull the sword from its neck, but she couldn't budge it. So she started stomping on the handle, driving the base of the blade down at an angle and deeper into the Nephilim's neck.

Jackson came around and put a hand on her shoulder. He wasn't sure why he did it, why anyone does it. She was stomping on a corpse, why not let her get it out? If it was still alive, they would be helping her, so what was the harm in letting her finish what she started? He'd seen it dozens of times. Rage and fear boiling over and focusing on a threat already neutralized. And every time there was someone there to try to stop the person from continuing, as if letting them go on would somehow turn them into a criminal or fracture their sanity. It didn't make much sense as far as logic was concerned, just something you did. And even though he knew it, here he was trying to get her to calm down. "It's okay," he was saying. Which, of course, it wasn't. Just that something needed to be said, and what else was there?

But she gave in, leaning into his frame, eyes staring at the thing, chest heaving. He slipped an arm around her, wondering once more at all this woman had been through. Enough, obviously.

He looked down at the giant, half expecting it to rise, again wondering why he'd stopped her when his own inclination was to punt its head over the house just to be sure. He supposed it had more to do with expressing concern for her than anything else. He let go of her, grasped the rifle with both hands, and looked into the surrounding trees, waiting to see what the gunfire might draw.

He didn't have to wait long.

"Look!" Patrick cried, pointing back at the house.

Jackson spun his head around.

There, on the top of the house, was one of the scorpion-creatures from the Book of Revelation. It crawled to the edge of the roof, went over the side, and walked upside-down through the front door.

"No!" Jackson raced back across the fifty feet separating them from the house. But just as he was about to reach the door, it slammed shut. He didn't stop or slow down, just lowered his shoulder.

There was a loud *crack* as something in the door splintered, but it didn't open.

The others were beside him now, all of them ramming their bodies into the door as Hap's screams filled the air.

* * * *

Paul stumbled to a stop, his eyes wide and unbelieving, darting every which way. He was in the lobby just outside the showroom, the elevators and stairs to his right, the dark and empty casino ahead.

Only it wasn't dark. And it certainly wasn't empty.

A woman in a low-cut dress (*elegant* would've been the word for her had her silicone jiggle not been so obnoxiously obtrusive) brushed by him, drink in hand. She smiled at him questioningly as her ankle twisted in her ten-foot high heels and she went staggering sideways. Her free hand went out reflexively, searching for the wall, but her manicured cuticles missed it, instead passing into an alcove. She hit the wall with her face and then crumpled to the carpet, spilling her drink down the front of her.

Paul didn't go to help her, didn't offer his hand or ask her name. He just turned away, looking back in the direction of the casino. If he'd been confused before, now he was befuddled beyond belief.

Music, human commotion, and the sound of slot machines and other beeping things tickled his ears but did nothing to satisfy his brain. And food. There was the amazing smell of food…

He thought he heard the drunk woman call him something mean from the floor behind him, but he just started walking away, toward the casino. Two steps into his journey, the elevator doors opened and a crowd of people hurried out. They were all stumbling and swaying, laughing hysterically about something that probably wasn't very funny. They were wearing dresses and suits, hair done up nice, fancy jewelry sparkling in the hallway lights. They passed right by the woman on the floor (who didn't even seem embarrassed that her booze-soaked mountains had escaped their meager confines). One of the men in the group, however, did steal a glance back at her, muttering something rude and then laughing even harder. He pulled out a cell phone and took a picture of her, though he was laughing so hard, it would be a miracle if the picture was anything but a blur. Then they passed Paul, and all their laughing came to an abrupt halt as they laid eyes on him. They hurried past as if they'd just caught him in the middle of beating up the woman on the floor and wanted no part of it. Once they were a good ten feet away, one of the guys whispered something and they all broke out in laughter again, the guy with a camera snapping a shot of him.

Paul followed them, and they all tried running away, afraid of what he might do to them. They all tumbled to the floor, tripping over each other and landing in a pile there in the hallway. Paul just walked around them.

The casino was packed with drunk couples all eagerly throwing their money away and finding it hilarious. Paul moved through their midst, taking it all in. Occasionally, someone would look up and take him in with their eyes, studying him like some specimen that didn't belong. Paul knew the feeling.

The tables were crowded with women bending over and rolling dice, all other eyes not on the dice. A few circular lounge chairs had couples reclining on them, a few were even slow dancing beneath the chandelier in the center of the room. The scene was alive, energized. Paul walked through it slowly, wondering what was happening to him.

He was back at the atrium, looking down at the plaza from his position on the above deck just as he had minutes ago. Only now there was no sunlight streaming through the windows and casting armies of shadows through the dead deck. It was nighttime, he could see that, and the place was lit up. Someone was at the piano, pounding the keys in an upbeat, lively jazz piece, while flocks of people moved back and forth between the bar, front desk, sales consultants, and then off in the direction of a dining room he couldn't see but remembered from the map.

He walked around the atrium, following its oval path to the bistro, more people passing him and looking him over as if they'd just watched him swim to the boat and climb aboard. Which had pretty much been the case.

He went into the bar, squeezed between two people in shorts and Hawaiian shirts, and ordered a drink. The person behind the counter served him, and Paul downed the stiff drink in one gulp, hoping the force of it would smack his mind back to where it belonged. It didn't. And neither did the next two.

He swiveled on the stool and looked down into the crowd below. Studied faces of people caught up in the moment. People oblivious to what would happen. Or *not* happen, Paul supposed. Was he in the past? A different present? The altered future? He had no idea. He wanted to try Henry again. He took the cell from his pocket and saw that it had a signal. Surprised, and heart beginning to jump a little, he dialed Henry's number. He brought the phone to his ear.

And that's when he spotted her.

The girl. Standing down in the plaza, right at the foot of the winding stairs. She was looking up at him, staring.

He lowered the phone, his heart now a bass pedal thumping away at his heart. It didn't appear that anyone else in the plaza could see her. People were walking up and down the stairs, brushing shoulders with her but not even glancing her way, which was absurd given her unfortunate state.

"Restroom?" he asked the bartender.

The man, now drying some glasses, nodded to the side at a flight of stairs that led down to deck five.

"Thanks." He got up and left his company, who he could hear muttering something about his scent. He lifted an arm and took a big sniff. No roses there. He took the stairs down to the first floor of the bar and found a sign for the bathrooms.

"You okay, sir?" a maître d' rounding the corner asked. He was in typical cruise line attire, name tag reading "Steven" though it was clear his name was really something that would be much harder to pronounce.

"I'm okay. Just tripped is all."

The man could only offer a look of doubt as he studied him from head to toe, eyes settling on the missing fingers. "The medical center is that way." He pointed.

"Thanks. I was just on my way there. After using the little boys' room." He left the guy behind and opened the door to the bathroom.

The lights were out. He ran his hand up and down the wall until he found the switch and flicked it up and down. Nothing. He sighed, opened the bathroom door, and stepped back into the bar. It, too, was now dark.

And empty.

* * * *

The door finally gave, and Jackson burst through the front door, AK-47 against his shoulder, eyes looking down the sights and ready to unload seventy-five rounds of 7.62x39mm bullets from the drum fixed behind his left hand. The screams were coming from the living room, where they'd left Pierre and Hap. Jackson swung the rifle to the left, clearing the wall and entering the living room, the others doing the same behind him.

The creature (of the same sort that had killed Chris) was on the couch, standing over Pierre, its black, scorpion tail curled up over its body and hanging like a pointed wrecking ball just behind its long blond hair. Its face, mostly human looking, was being held back by Pierre's outstretched arms, his hands around the thing's throat. The creature opened its mouth, showing those large, lion like teeth, and roared in Pierre's face.

Jackson ran into the room and realized, just before thrusting the rifle into the thing's side and blowing it up and over the side of the couch, that Pierre wasn't trying to keep it from biting his face off but was trying to keep it *on* him. And off Hap.

The blast tore through the chimera's side, tearing off one of its wings and tossing it onto the floor on the other side of the couch.

Robyn and Joe were already around the couch, shooting at the thing as it tried getting back to its many feet. One of its legs fell off. Then another. It tried crawling, roaring in frustration and pain, thrashing its tail wildly about the room, snapping the stinger like a giant whip. It plunged into the wall behind Robyn and Joe, passing right between them. The wall exploded into the hallway, and when the tail retracted, it brought chunks of sheetrock with it, striking them in the back and knocking them forward.

Now Patrick was coming around from the other side, head on. He fired into its face, and its eyes and mouth vanished into bloody holes. But its tail kept swinging. It flew sideways over its head, and Patrick ducked beneath it.

Jackson jumped up onto the couch, one foot pressed against its back, the other firmly planted against Pierre's hip. He joined the shooting again, and the four of them emptied all their ammo into the monster.

By the time the tail flopped dead to the ground, blood dripping from the ceiling like rain, all their ears were ringing. Pierre was saying something, but no one could hear him.

Jackson lowered the rifle, ejecting the drum, and stepped down off the couch. He looked over Pierre, trying to spot any new injuries. And that's when he realized Pierre was shouting at him, pointing past him and into the hallway.

Jackson followed his finger. There, in the kitchen, was another of the scorpion monsters.

"Reload!" he cried, pulling a magazine from his pocket and ramming it home with the heel of his hand. "Hap, get behind me!"

The kid ran over and ducked behind the couch.

Jackson began firing, quick three-shot bursts, well aimed at the creature's forehead. He stepped forward as he did so, closing the gap between them. The creature's face and neck squirted blood, and when it tried to lunge, its legs slipped on the tile floor.

The others were at Jackson's side, firing. Empty shells were bouncing all over the room, branding their exposed skin, but they didn't notice.

The monster went down without so much as leaving the kitchen, but they were running out of ammo. Panting, they reloaded again.

"Is that all of them?" Patrick asked.

Robyn answered his question by walking back to the open front door. She surveyed their surroundings, then looked up to the roof. All seemed calm.

Jackson was about to tell her to come back in, to get out of the doorway, when something suddenly appeared sweeping down from above the top of the doorframe—some kind of tentacle wrapping around her waist.

And then she was gone, plucked up out of the doorway and into the air.

NINETEEN

24th day of June. Late morning. The Ship.

He froze in the dark. He had the sense that he was still in the bar, but he couldn't be sure. He was fairly certain that he was back, though. Back to the ghost ship, the one drifting clockwise into the island of misfit angels.

Thump.

"Ah, crap."

Thump.

He didn't have the torch or his rifle. He thought they were probably still back up by the theatre doors where he'd dropped them three realities ago. But then the question returned, didn't it? Even if he was back where he started, *when* was he?

He knew when he *wasn't.* He wasn't on the ship's maiden voyage or at any time *before* the island. And if, as he believed, what was happening to the ship was similar to what had happened to the island in the aftermath of the pyramid's use, then he could be right back where he started with Robinson, Li, Theodore, Daniel, Sanders, and Carl still on their way to the medical center without him. *Or*...he could be fifty years into the future, the ship stuck on the island like the ark on Ararat, and the only person left alive in this realm.

Thump. Thump. Thump.

He made his way toward the light coming through the plaza's large windows. The sun looked to be in mostly the same position as it had been when he first heard Hunter calling for him. That, plus the thumping noise still stalking him, had him almost convinced that he was back to the beginning again. Now he just needed to find the others.

Stepping into the long rays streaming through the multicolored windows (blues and yellows mostly), he took care to avoid making any unnecessary noise. He still didn't know what was stalking them and didn't very much care to find out. He took the stairs, passing where the girl had been standing in a crowd of people just a few minutes before. Chills poked his skin. He took two steps at a time. The bartender had pointed off to the right, toward the aft end of the ship on deck five where the medical center was, but he needed his rifle and torch first. He wasn't about to go walking long dark halls with nothing in his hands.

He went quickly and came to the casino again. There were no windows in the casino, and he could barely make out his hand in front of his face. He did his best to avoid the blackjack tables that had just moments ago been crowded with scantily clad women, the couches with groping couples, and the slot machines that had filled the air with that oh-so-popular soundtrack. He bumped into a table, moved around it, kept going.

Thump. Thump. Thump.

It sounded like it was right over him, maybe on the deck above.

Paul…

He spun, but his eyes hadn't yet adjusted to the near total darkness.

Help me.

"Hunter?" he called out. Chasing after the voice hadn't gotten him anywhere last time (actually, it had gotten him back to Bermuda, hadn't it?). "That you, man?" He still wasn't sure if the voice was in his head or not.

I'm here.

Again, he was certain the voice was coming from the theatre, just outside the casino. He continued in that direction—it's where he was heading anyway—retracing his earlier steps, walking into a déjà vu that embraced him entirely too tight for his liking. The sense of it brought back the initial feelings he'd had after first awakening on this side of the solstice—the idea that he was the only one left on the island, trapped and alone in a snow-globe world for the rest of eternity. Now he had the same thought but with another, disturbing ingredient. Had the space-time continuum been so disturbed by whatever had happened with the ship that time itself had been hung up on a repeating cycle? Like a CD that skips-skips-skips then starts over? Was that him now? Walking through multiple universes, skip-skip-skipping, until…reset and repeat? Was he about to follow Hunter's voice into the theatre again, find himself in Bermuda, then back in time to a crowded ship, then back again? And again? And again, repeating forever?

"Shut up, Paul," he whispered to himself. He left the casino behind and came to the elevator the drunk woman had collapsed near. Of course, there was no sign of her or the crowd that came taking pictures of them. But…up ahead, he did see a flickering light. His torch.

He bent over, picked it up, and waved it around. The curtain was almost completely gone, the wood itself now burning. He figured he was down to mere minutes with the flame. He saw the M14 lying at the foot of the theatre doors and picked that up, too.

Thump…thump…thump.

It sounded distant now, not as loud.

Thump-thump-thump-thump.

But it was quickly getting louder, closer, and faster all at once.

He reached for the theatre doors, positive it was coming from *inside.* Was it Hunter trying to pound his way out?

The doors burst open with a *bang!* He stumbled backward, raising the rifle as he went down on his butt, the torch falling to the floor again.

Things were rushing out of the theatre—three, four, maybe five of them. They filled the doorway and were rushing past him, over him, on top of him. He almost squeezed the trigger, sending his five remaining shots into whatever was swarming him. He heard a loud groan, and then intense pressure fell on his chest, chasing the air from his lungs.

He felt grabbing, tugging, frantic movement all over him.

"Robinson!" a voice cried.

"Get me up!"

The voice was right in his face, and he could feel the breath of words against his cheek. The weight left his chest, but then a sharp, crushing force came down on his mangled hand.

He yelled out.

"Paul?"

Reaching for the torch lying beside him (all he'd seen during the last seven seconds was a myriad of hectic shadows flying all over the walls), he raised it above his prone position, struggling to sit up.

The light, as it rose, uncovered Robinson standing there over top of him, Li, Theodore, Carl, and Sanders shapes in the background.

As Paul got to his feet, piecing together what had just happened—them sprinting out of the theatre and knocking him over—he studied their expressions in the torchlight. The looks on their faces, coupled with their lack of weapons and torches, told him all he needed to know about how they'd gotten there. But what he was dying to know was… where they'd *been.* And what had happened to the sixth person in their party.

* * * *

No!"

It was a collective cry, and all three of them took off down the hallway after her.

It wasn't far, hardly ten paces, but it seemed to Jackson like an eternity, every hundredth of a second a moment closer to her—*to Denise?*—being gone. In actuality, it took less than three seconds for him to clear the front steps. They leaped down into the grass, immediately spun back to the house, and saw her body flailing as the black rope thing that was wrapped around her waist carried her back across the roof and out of view.

Jackson swore, still not getting a look at the thing carrying her, and started sprinting around the side of the house. "Go around the other way!" he hollered to the others.

When he reached the back of the house a moment later, Joe and Patrick were already getting there. There was no sign of Robyn. They stood, panting, eyes sweeping back and forth. There was nowhere for her to have gone. The woods were a football field away, too far for the thing to have reached it in the mere seconds it took them to—

A sound, from above them.

"On the roof!" Patrick hollered, lifting his AK-47.

Jackson looked up, too.

Suddenly, Robyn came flying through the air, her body limp and awkward as she tumbled down, down, down…

Jackson lurched forward, running hopelessly for her. She hit the ground five feet in front of him, landing strange, not a muscle in her body ready and tensed for the impact. No perfect landing form, no tuck and roll. She managed to avoid landing on her head somehow, falling onto her side, palms turned out, legs swinging clumsily at the knees. Jackson knew from the way she fell that she'd been tossed off the roof unconscious. He could only hope, as he bent over her, that the ground had been just soft enough from the recent rain to have absorbed most of the shock. If not, if she'd landed on a rock…

He didn't even look back toward the thing still on the roof, not even when both AK-47s started sounding off around him. He brushed the hair out of her eyes and put his hand to her throat. Her neck was strong, slender, and the pulse that beat in it was pounding full. She was alive.

A hot shell struck him in the face, stinging him. He swatted at it, then looked back at the house and saw a dark, fluid like shape go over the side of the roof and twist back into the house, breaking through a window. In the brief moment it was in his vision, his mind attributed its likeness to a squid, or Dr. Octopus. Something with a lot of legs.

"It's in the house!" Joe cried. He looked at Jackson, eyes wide with concern, with hesitation. Hap was in there. Pierre was in there.

But Robyn was out here.

"Go!" Jackson yelled back, waving at him.

Joe and Patrick went back around to the front of the house, leaving Jackson alone with Robyn.

He laid his eyes on her again, afraid to find that her pulse had thinned in the three seconds he'd looked away. But there was more than a pulse, there was a smile.

"You didn't catch me."

Under any other circumstance, Jackson might have laughed. Might have leaned down, grabbed her head with two hands and kissed her hard on the mouth. But people were about to die, he was sure of it. "Can you move?"

She opened her eyes, her crystal blues appearing first in narrow slits, then in big, round awareness. "I think so." She first turned her head, then planted her palms against the ground. She pushed herself to her hands and knees and paused, holding the position. She looked up at him, and blood was suddenly all over her, coming from somewhere he couldn't locate. It was covering the side of her face, her neck, soaking her shirt. "Go," she growled.

Gunfire exploded again from within the house, but he wasn't going to leave her.

"Save them," she said, trying to get to her feet.

"Stay still," he said, resting a hand on her shoulder. Blood ran over his fingers.

She shook off his hand. "I'm fine. Go!"

She was far from fine, in fact—

But then she stood and started limping back to the house herself. She went around to the other side, bent over and picked up her rifle that must've fallen off the roof during whatever it was that had happened up there, and went as fast as she could to the front door.

Jackson couldn't believe it. This island girl was like something out of a movie. She-Ra or Lara Croft or Elektra. Only better looking. He had no choice but to follow her back into the house.

The house seemed still, quiet. They could see the bedroom door at the end of the hall standing wide open.

"Joe? Patrick?" Jackson craned his neck to see around the corner and into the living room. Robyn was still just ahead of him.

Something wet began sucking at their shoes. Looking down, they found a red delta of sticky blood flowing out of the kitchen and into the hall, spreading away from the dead scorpion thing. No one was in the living room either, only the other creature's remains.

A sound from the bedroom.

Robyn took one quick step toward it, but Jackson grabbed her arm before she could get any further.

"Wait."

She nodded, acknowledging the worry on his face and deciding he was probably right. They continued slowly, one careful step at a time, the closet door still open at the end of the hall. Even from there, they could tell that the hanging clothes that were inside before were now gone.

They walked into the bedroom and found everyone there, standing in a line off to the left of the closet, staring into it. The bed that Jackson had dragged in front of it was on its side and up against the adjacent wall.

"I believe you now," Arkansas Joe muttered, not even turning to face them.

The closet was gone, just a dark space beyond the trim that outlined the doorway.

"Where'd that thing go?" Robyn whispered, wiping blood out of her eyes with her forearm.

Little Hap raised the only pointer finger he had left, aiming it at the black void.

A low, reverberating bass line started humming from within it.

"What is that?" Patrick asked.

"Nothing good," Jackson answered.

The sound was growing louder, nearer, the air colder.

"C'mon," Jackson whispered, grabbing Robyn's hand. He took a step back, and she didn't resist.

The humming turned to growls, and they all moved back. But none of them could take their eyes off the Nothing, hearts pounding in their heads, the stillness so tense it seemed the very room could snap in half.

Screams now. Distant and muffled…but screams.

Pierre turned, the first one to break the spell, and looked at them. "You need to go. Now." His hand was over his wound, his breath labored and painful.

Jackson nodded. "We'll make a gurney, carry you out of here."

"No time. Leave now. Before they get here."

Jackson began to turn even as he asked, "Who?" It was the way Pierre's eyes had darted past him, down the hall and back to the front door.

"Them."

And there they were. Six Nephilim giants on their way toward them, halfway across the field.

"Pierre…" Robyn started, her hand slipping out of Jackson's.

He smiled, and an emotional glaze swam over his eyes. "Take care of yourself."

She shouldered the rifle and stepped to him, wrapping her arms around him and squeezing hard. A short moan escaped his lips as he lost his breath. "Sorry," she whispered, and brushed her own tear away. She was tall enough that she didn't have to stand on her toes to kiss his forehead. He closed his eyes, savoring the feel of her lips against his skin, and a few more water drops went sliding down his face. Then, without another word, she moved past him and grabbed Hap's remaining hand.

"Wait. What's happening?" Jackson threw his eyes between them, trying to understand what was in development here.

Pierre looked up, and his eyes were now drowning. "You need to leave."

"Not going anywhere without you."

"Yes, you are." He managed to keep his voice under control. "You know I'm a goner. I won't make it. I'll only slow you down. Hell, I might punch my ticket before they even get here."

Joe and Patrick interrupted, each taking a turn shaking his hand, saying their quick goodbyes through invisible messages exchanged through eye contact alone, each message received and confirmed by slight nods of the head.

By now the giants were closer, and the sounds from the closet were impossible to ignore.

"You're out of time. Go," Pierre insisted.

Joe and Patrick stepped away. There was a window above where the bed was resting on its side, and Joe smashed it out with the butt of his rifle.

Now it sounded as if an army of tortured souls was about to climb its way off the long ladder reaching up from the depths of Closet World and crawl out onto the bedroom floor.

Robyn swept Hap up into her arms and handed him to Joe, who was sitting up in the window frame. He lowered him out onto the ground and then hopped down, too. Next, Robyn climbed up. But before she joined them outside, she looked back at Pierre, the guy who had always secretly loved her (though it wasn't a secret to her or anyone else), and gave him one last, tear-filled smile. Then she was gone.

"Come on, Jackson," Patrick said. The giants were just a couple paces from the front door.

Jackson couldn't believe they were just going to leave Pierre here to die. But Pierre seemed resolved to it. And of course, he was right. He was on borrowed time and would never survive a sprint to the woods anyway.

"Take care of her," Pierre said, staring into Jackson's eyes, a stream of tears breaking free. But though there were plenty of tears, his gaze did not waver. Then, in a lightning-quick move, he reached forward and grabbed the AK-47 from Jackson's hand. Pushing him aside, he ran past, charging down the hallway with trigger held down, screaming with all the air he had left in his broken lungs, as the giants smashed their way into the house.

Patrick grabbed Jackson and began jerking him toward the window. He reluctantly went along, going out the window and landing in the grass together.

Looking up, Jackson was both hurt and pleased to find that Robyn hadn't waited for them (for *him*, really). She was still holding Hap's hand when she disappeared into the trees a hundred yards away, Joe right beside her. She didn't even look back.

As they stumbled to their feet and took off for the woods themselves, they tried to ignore the concert of terrible noises resonating from within the house—the closet sounds reaching their crescendo and their friend being ripped apart and eaten.

Jackson knew his feet were moving. He was slightly conscious of it, but he was mostly in a vacuum, everything around him paused, distant. The noises behind him had stopped. Something, that octopus thing that had snatched Robyn, went into the closet. But something else had come out. It was a revolving door to somewhere. Somewhere dark. Somewhere evil. And for the first time, he was sure he would never see Hunter again.

As the world began to come back to him—things moving again, the wind in his face, the beating of his heart, distance being gained—a new thought came to him. A thought with a face. The face of another fallen brother whispering, *Take care of her.*

* * * *

He knew they'd experienced something similar, a slip into a different place or time. He could see it through the masks of incomprehension covering their faces. He understood it and had no trouble identifying it. He knew the same expression was staring back at them. But there was more. Along with the inability to compute what they'd just experienced, there was also terror. They'd *seen* something—had *been* somewhere—that Paul had not.

He waved the torch back and forth. "Where's Daniel?"

Robinson, Li, Theodore, Carl, and Sanders all stopped, holding their breath, the fear on their faces suddenly on pause as they looked around.

Paul swore. *They came back without him and didn't even know it.*

Robinson turned back to the theatre doors, gripped the handle, and flung it open.

Paul wasn't sure what Robinson was expecting to find in there (wasn't sure what *he* expected to find either), but it obviously wasn't what he was hoping for, because he let out a loud expletive that echoed through the dark and empty showroom.

"What did you see?" Paul asked Robinson as he turned back to face them.

But Robinson ignored the question. "We need to get off this ship." He brushed past Paul, heading back toward the casino.

Paul stuck the flaming end of the makeshift torch into Theodore's face. "Theo. What did you see?"

But even in the dancing half-light, Paul could see that all color had fled Theodore's face. Whatever they'd seen had scared the hell out of them, and they weren't going to talk about it until they were far away from the ship. The rest of them moved past him, hurrying after Robinson down the dark corridor. After stealing one last glance at the theatre doors, Paul followed.

The casino was still empty, and they made their way through it with ease, no thumping noises chasing them down at the moment.

"Where are we going?" he shouted ahead to Robinson, who was moving too fast.

"Off," he called back.

Paul stopped. "Hold on!" he yelled. It got their attention, breaking through their wall of blind urgency, and they huddled to a standstill in front of him.

"We need to get as far away from here as possible," Robinson explained. "Before…" He swallowed. "Before it happens again."

"Before *what* happens again?"

He looked around to the others, almost as if making sure *they* still believed what they'd seen before deciding whether to say it out loud or not.

"What did you see?" Paul asked again. Then he added, "*Where* did you go?"

It was clear to Robinson from the inflection in Paul's voice that he wasn't simply referring to a room on the cruise ship. He hadn't meant the medical center or the bridge, but something else, something that hinted at a similar experience. "You saw something, too."

Paul nodded. "I was in Bermuda. Six months from now. I called Henry."

They all stared at him in wide-eyed wonder. But no fear.

"Then I came out of there," he continued, "and the ship was full of passengers…" He stepped closer to Robinson and looked into his eyes. If he was on his way off the ship, then he needed to know if what they saw might offer a clue as to why he'd heard Hunter's voice calling for him. He set his eyes on Carl. "Now *what* did *you* see?"

"Don't ask them," Robinson said. "They wouldn't know. But *I* know. Of course *I* know."

"*Where*?"

He looked up, his eyes full of the horror again, of realization and dread. "Washington."

The skin between Paul's eyes pinched into stacked Ws. "As in the capital?"

"As in…the Washington Monument."

"And?"

"And it sure as hell wasn't good."

Thump. Thump. Thump.

And now screams. Coming from the theatre.

Robinson turned. "We need to go! *Now*!"

Before it happens again is what he'd said before. Paul began to wonder if there was a link between the noises and the room portals. His mind went inadvertently to a movie, a movie he'd seen with a girl back in 1987, a girl named Maggie Goodwin that he had liked a lot. The movie was *The Princess Bride* and the scene that came to mind was the scene in the Fire Swamp, when the noise—*tsh…tsh…tsh-tsh-tsh*—preceded the *poof!* that exploded from the ground and set Buttercup's dress on fire. Yeah, is that what the thumping was…a warning? Things aligning themselves for an opening into time and space? A countdown? Paul didn't think so. That would imply the ship was a sort of device. Like the pyramid. Or maybe it was the Triangle that was responsible after all. Maybe Osiris' presence hadn't *created* the Doorway to Hell, maybe he'd just learned to control it; and now that he was gone, the Triangle (created by the space crystals from Atlantis or whatever—that was a topic for a much later time) was left to its own random nature. But whatever the case, Paul agreed with Robinson. They needed to get off the ship *now.*

"The boat bay," he said.

"What?"

"I don't think we'll be able to lower the boats from the side. Maybe, maybe not. But we should be able to get out through the boat bay. There should be boats, Jet Skis maybe."

"Where?" Carl asked.

"The marina. Somewhere beneath us. Deck three maybe. All the way aft."

"Let's go, then."

They ran through the window-lit atrium, passing again the winding stairs. Paul glanced at another map on the wall just before the light behind them faded and they were once again dependent on the dwindling chair leg. He decided to keep on past a stairwell, leading them along another theatre on their right and into the photo gallery, the hallway full of framed couples who, in some time past had gotten their photos taken out on the deck. But they were only afforded torch-smeared glances as they hurried past. The people in the hallway were more like ghosts to them anyway, an echo of some in-between where the most recent passengers may or may not be trapped.

The hallway rounded and met with a night club on the starboard side and a saloon on port. The aft stairs and elevator stood amidships. Beyond it was a big club with another stage, and past that an open deck with ping-pong tables and golf.

They took the stairs down to deck five.

TWENTY

24th day of June. Early afternoon.

By the time they stopped to catch their breath, no one was really sure where they were. They thought they were on the north side of the island, nearer the coast. But there was no ocean in sight, so then they assumed they were walking through the new forest, where the Lake (Harrington Sound to those from the Other Side) once was. If so, then they hadn't run west like they thought, but northeast toward cave Jared.

"Let me look at you," Jackson said, kneeling in front of Robyn. Sweat glistened on her face and neck, her shirt damp and sticky. Her hair hung in tangled strands over her eyes, blood streaming from her head and turning some of it red. Her chest rose high with each gulp of air.

She winced when he probed the side of her head, finding a long laceration running behind her ear.

"What was that thing?" she asked.

He shrugged. "Didn't really get a good look at it."

Her eyes were locked in the past, unblinking. "It was slimy, like a worm. Slippery. I thought I'd slip away from it, but…" She wrapped her arms around her stomach, hugging herself. "It was so tight. I couldn't breathe."

Hap seemed to still be lingering in shock, but he managed to comment, "It looked like a squid."

And it had. If he meant a Spielberg interpretation of an Orson Wells Martian squid. "You've seen a squid before?" Jackson was surprised.

"In a book…" And then he retreated into his shock room, determined to stay in there from now until…well, until he was ready to come out, Jackson supposed.

"It had tiny teeth or claws in its arms. One of them caught me."

Joe frowned, leaning forward from the tree he'd perched against. "With its arms wrapped around you so tight, it could've easily ripped you open…"

She nodded. "Its arms were lined with them. They came in and out, like knives." She leaned back and hooked a strand of bloody hair behind her ear. "It wasn't trying to kill me. It was trying to *take* me."

"Take you where?" Patrick asked.

But she closed her eyes, concentrating instead on getting her breath back.

Jackson stood. "It's not too bad. Some pressure should stop the bleeding." He took the backpack off, struggling quite a bit to do so, and then pulled off the small army jacket, stretching his chest and back in order to get his arms out. His upper half was only covered by bandages now, and his huge chest glistened in the sunlight. He handed it to her. "Not ideal, but better than you having to take off yours."

She shot him a look, wondering if he really meant it. She could tell that he did. And that he didn't. She took it from him and held it against her head. "Thanks."

Jackson set his eyes on the others. They looked okay, physically. Emotionally, they were dealing with having heard the horrifying sounds of their friend being pulled apart. "We'll take a minute, but we need to get back to the caves as soon as possible." He found a spot of forest floor that looked okay and sat there, leaning against a fallen piece of cedar. He listened to their surroundings. Beyond the movements of their group, there were birds singing, some small creatures darting back and forth through the underbrush, and a calm breeze moving through the canopy above them. He thought they were okay for now, but he didn't want to be out here any longer than need be. The island was a big question mark now, and not even the people who'd spent their entire lives here knew it anymore.

He closed his eyes, trying not to think of Pierre. Of Nick's head swinging from that giant's neck, his bones found in a campfire. *Take care of her.* He would if he could. If she'd let him. He thought of Paul and his mission, wondering how he was getting along and if they'd found anything of interest at the complex. He had a lot to tell him when next he saw him that was for sure.

He opened his eyes and looked up into the sky, through the canopy and to the sun. He considered it hanging there in space, the means of life and existence. But how many suns were there? Not just throughout the galaxies, but in *this* galaxy? How many tiers of reality were there? How many universes coexisting at the same time all on top of each other? He smiled. The idea was serious enough among the ivory-tower-dwellers, all the books on black holes and quantum physics… But to actually believe that he was, right now, in another universe lying just beneath the surface of the one he'd been born in, seemed utterly ludicrous. And yet, here he was, sucked into a different Bermuda by a fallen angel. He laughed again, chuckling really, but it hurt his side and sent his dark humor into a coughing spat.

Denise. What was she doing here? Whether she was *really* here or not, she was here. In his mind. But why? Was she trying to warn him of something, sending a message from the netherworlds? Or was it ghosts and goblins and spirits and demons all floating about having their fun?

And then there was the thing from the closet. How had it gotten out when before it seemed so unlikely, that protective sheen a force field unable to be breached? Somehow, it had escaped, and now (at least in some capacity) there seemed to be a revolving door to wherever the portal led. Which, he supposed, could be anywhere. First Time, Atlantis, Orion's Belt, Hades, the real world… But he didn't think the thing that had brought that sweeping darkness with it had just stepped off a pleasure yacht in Hamilton Harbor.

He looked over at Robyn. Her eyes were closed, the tears that had cut clean lines through her dirt-streaked face now dry. The sun coming down in wide rays through the trees seemed to be focused on her position, spotlighting her, lighting her up like she was the main character in a Broadway play. His heart fluttered, his chest grew tight, and his throat seemed to swell. Butterflies with wings on fire. She turned her head toward him, her eyes opening and catching his stare. She held it for a moment, then closed her eyes again. He took a breath and shifted his gaze, not wanting anything to do with this right now. And of course wanting everything to do with it. He stole one more glance her way, and then thought of what she'd said, about the thing not trying to kill her, but to take her. He pondered that because it struck him as odd. Why would it try to take her? And to where? Back into the closet? Maybe. Or maybe somewhere else on the new island.

It was this thought that he was stuck on when sleep came and snatched him away.

* * * *

They found a door in the dining room that opened to the galley and then a door in the galley that led to an enclosed stairwell. Following Paul's chair leg, they made the descent down to deck three.

Either the screams were now too far away to hear from their position on deck three, or they'd stopped. No one cared. They wanted off the boat before they ended up somewhere from where there might be no return. Paul wouldn't have been too upset with that possibility, not when considering *his* two trips. But he could tell that wherever the others had been spirited off to (Washington, DC? *Really?*) had not been such a hot time. That was obvious by how fast they were pushing him to go, running up his heels.

Stepping into another hall after skirting a bulkhead, the flickering light revealed a posted sign with an arrow pointing toward the marina. They walked through the narrow corridor, which felt like a tomb, and eventually came to a set of double doors. They paused, looked at each other, the dim and dancing light casting shadows across their faces, big dark spots under their eyes, long drooping smears hanging from cheekbones. Paul thought they resembled walking corpses. And maybe, upon opening these doors, that's exactly what they would be.

"Ready?" he asked, doubtful himself.

Robinson walked past him and pushed open the doors, not wanting to waste another second.

It was dark, cool. Open.

Paul could feel concrete beneath his feet and could sense the vast openness around him. For a second he thought he'd walked straight into the Outer Darkness John's Bible talked about. But then he caught a whiff of oil and other chemicals and knew they'd found the marina. The flame rustled at the end of the stick as it gulped the air, the open doors creating a sudden draft. "We have to open the hatchway." His voice echoed.

He wanted light just as much as he wanted off the ship. He didn't know what was in here with them, or what *could* be in here with them. He felt the little girl's eyes on him and wondered if the two other eyes that he'd seen smoldering like embers could be hers or if they belonged to something else.

He walked around, the torch held out in front of him, the flames tiny, dying. He was looking for—

He found an office door and knew that the controls would be in there, though they'd be useless without power. But he thought there would have to be a way to lower it manually.

"How do we open it?" Sanders whispered, plenty of foreboding in his voice, like if they didn't get it open in the next few seconds something in the dark was going to eat them all.

"I don't know," Paul replied.

Paul…

He spun, the torch exploding with a *whoosh* as he swung it around.

"What?" Li whispered to him.

Paul didn't answer. He stared into the nothingness ahead of him, not able to see anything. But he could feel it.

Paul, please…

It was a voice in his head, he knew. Genderless. Like a thought, but one not his own. He poked the shrinking flame forward, penetrating the black and illuminating a small, spherical area of floor around him. Each step he took revealed another foot of bare concrete. The marina was like a warehouse, its ceiling high and outside the flame's reach.

Paul.

Another step toward the hatchway, and the curved line of light on the ground continued to move with him. More smooth concrete. He didn't know how close he was to the end of the line, but for reasons he couldn't explain, he was sure the origin of the voice was in front of him (and not just *in* him). Another step. More concrete. Another. The same. Another step.

Shoes.

He stopped, his heart lurching to a halt within his chest.

Dirty, tattered shoes. Black, the soles separated and flapping like the loose tongue of a dead animal.

He raised the leg of the chair, and the light climbed up over the shoes, revealing legs.

Higher.

The ragged hem of a dress.

Higher.

The tiny waist of malnutrition.

Higher.

Hands, arms, shoulders…

He held the torch there, hand trembling. He was slightly aware of the others gathering behind him.

Then the left shoe moved forward.

The little girl's face shot into view as she stepped into the glow, her dark eyes and pale face like a ghost, and Paul shouted in surprise, stepping backward onto the feet of someone behind him. He went down, landing on bodies. As he fell, he swung his torch hand down to brace himself, the piece of burning chair slamming off the concrete and shattering into a blast of sparks. The ember-speckled floor glowed for a second and then disappeared.

They were in the dark.

Paul wasn't sure if what he was hearing was his own panicked breathing or the breathing of whoever was under him. He started to get up, frantic to get away from the girl, but the person under him grabbed his shoulder, stopping him.

They lay on the cold floor, silence all around, waiting, eyes darting about uselessly.

"Is she gone?" Robinson whispered in his ear.

And a new series of chills swept through his body, tingling his scalp. "You saw her?" he whispered back.

"Of course."

And so she was here. With them all.

Before Paul could reply, a loud noise clanged out and echoed throughout the marina.

Gears shifting, chains moving, wheels spinning on tracks.

Clank—clank—clank...

Carl and Theodore yelped in surprise. "What is that?"

Then a burst of salty air flew in their faces as a laser line of light appeared at the top of the room. It gaped wider...wider still.

The hatchway was opening.

Water came rushing past Paul and Robinson, soaking their backs, and they hurried to their feet. For a second, Paul thought they were going to have to retreat back into the ship to avoid being sucked out to sea, but the water leveled off at just a few inches.

The morning light from outside flooded the marina, lighting up every corner of the room. They all squinted as their eyes adjusted.

"What happened?" Li asked, sloshing through the water.

She opened the hatchway, Paul thought. But he didn't say it. He knew she was capable of manipulating his physical world, he'd seen her do it when he first climbed aboard the ship. But why would she open the door so they could escape? And where did she go? She was gone, as if never there to begin with. But she had been there. Robinson saw her.

"Look!" Sanders shouted, pointing out into the sea.

A large fin lazily crossed the open hatchway, right to left, as if waiting for them to come in for a dip.

Paul ran through the water, skirting pallets of shrink-wrapped boxes, and went to the boat bay. The boats—kayaks, Jet Skis, and a few Boston Whalers—all stood lined up behind a wire cage, the doors padlocked shut. He raised the M14 and fired a single shot, blowing the padlock to the floor. He swung the doors open and went in, stealing another look back into the ocean, at the huge fin still hanging around.

He considered the man-eating shark (or sharks) and weighed their options. The Boston Whalers were probably their best bet. If they worked. There were three seventeen-foot commercial models with center consoles. The SEALs had used Boston Whalers in Vietnam, and he'd seen the Bermuda Police Service using them back in Other Bermuda. They should work just fine.

"Help me!" he called out, jumping in and out of one, getting to the front and pushing it backward. The others came over and grabbed a side, moving it out of the boat bay and into the center of the marina.

Paul hopped back in and went to the center console. He looked over the controls and was relieved to find the safety clip already hooked on the emergency shut-off switch and the key in the ignition. They were needed to engage the engine, and he was glad they didn't have to waste more time searching the marina for them. He made sure the boat was in neutral, held his breath, and turned the key.

Everything suggested that the boat *should* work. Why wouldn't it? But then, how would he know, really? After all, the cruise ship was a dead and deserted city. The motor sputtered, and smoke filled the air.

Bingo.

He shut it down.

"Help me get another one."

They moved the two of them on their skids and got them next to each other, floating in the few inches of water and pointing out of the hatchway and into the open seas.

"You know how to operate one of these?" Paul asked Robinson.

Robinson looked over the console. "I don't know what all these buttons and screens are, but I'm guessing the wheel to the left takes the boat left, and moving the gearshift forward moves it forward."

"Pretty much." He ran to the back of the boat. "Get in. Two of you get in with him."

Robinson stood at the wheel, and Carl and Li sat in the two back-seats beside the motor.

"Start it," Paul commanded.

Robinson turned the key and got the same result that Paul had gotten from the other boat.

Paul pumped his legs, moving the boat across the marina floor and toward the ocean. When he was about five feet from the edge, he extended his arms and pushed them out into the sea.

"Lower the motor!" he shouted to them, careful not to slip and fall into the waiting teeth.

The motor went down into the water, and Paul turned his back to it, signaling for Theodore and Sanders to get in the remaining boat. They also took positions in the rear seats, and Paul handed them the M14. Then, half-expecting the girl to grab his leg or close the door on them, or for them to pass through the hatchway and find the three of them alone in some other time, he moved the boat out into the ocean as fast as he could, jumping in at the last second.

He lowered the motor into the water and turned the key. But even as he pushed the gearshift forward, moving the boat into the choppy waves, he questioned their situation, wondering again why the girl would let them out. He also thought back to the organic occupants of the cruise ship. Were they still on the ship, enjoying their vacation, only a *copy* of the ship sent to this Bermuda? Or were they about to find the entire hull full of human faces?

He steered the boat around the cruise ship, passing it on its port side. It was even bigger in daylight, a towering building full of empty decks. Robinson followed them, steering his own boat into Paul's wake. Everyone stared up at the ship as they passed, each trying to unravel its many mysteries. Trying to put

Daniel out of their minds. Because, no matter where or when he was, if he was no longer on the ship, then there was nothing they could do about it.

When they sped past the ship's bow, the island came into full view.

And three things made themselves known all at once.

First, it was later in the day than they thought. Second, they were now heading south and a lot closer to the island. And third, they weren't quite sure what island they were looking at.

TWENTY-ONE

24th day of June. Afternoon.

He dreamt. Dreamt of baseball at his house in Charlotte. Right after their wedding. Hunter, Chris, and Henry had come over. It was the playoffs. October. They were drinking beer and placing stupid bets, digging up the past and telling old war stories (though not the ones they didn't want Denise overhearing, the ones that might make her wonder at night). Chris had said something hilarious and they'd laughed for what felt like three hours—through four innings and the post-game. He couldn't remember in his dream what the joke was, or if it was really funny or just the beer, but it was a pleasant memory and a good dream. Until he'd tried calling Paul to come and join them, to see if he was in the area. It'd been a year or two since any of them had seen him, and he wasn't returning their calls.

Nick was out of town doing something the dream didn't recall, but he watched as the conversation about Paul was rehashed, the Giants and the Cowboys coming on in the background. Angry Paul the mercenary. They all knew it, though he'd never said anything, but where else would he be? They were worried about him, worried he was being outsourced to fight in the new terror wars. Denise came in, her blond hair in a pony-tail, a "Bermuda Horseshoe Beach Lifeguard" T-shirt snug as can be, and sat in his lap. The dream didn't seem to forget any details about that moment. The feel of her weight on him, the smell of her hair, the way her fingernails danced lightly across the nape of his neck, the way her eyes sparkled in the light of the TV… And then he noticed the book. It was past her, over her shoulder on the shelf beside the football game. The name on the spine, "Ronald Douglas Carter."

And then it all came back like a flood of wicked spells.

His eyes snapped open and he sat forward, rays of light blinding him. He squinted and shielded his face with his forearm as his mind opened its door and let in the present.

Despite the way the dream ended, there was still a lingering sense of Denise, of the once upon a time they'd so briefly enjoyed. It permeated his brain, stirring old emotions that he couldn't help savoring. But they were slipping away. Possibly forever. There was always that chance that the next time would be the last, and those feelings—the *actual* feelings, not just the vague memory *of* feelings—would be no more.

"You okay?"

He turned his head and saw Robyn standing in the shadow of a tree. He wanted this new girl, he knew that. But at the same time, he didn't want her to replace what remained of Denise. The fact that they were so similar in appearance made him certain that it would only be a matter of time before Denise became Robyn. He wanted that and was terrified of it at the same time.

"Yeah." He got to his feet, stretched as much as his side allowed, and surveyed the landscape. "Where'd the others go?"

"To look for water."

He turned one eye up through the trees, placing the sun. "How long have I been out?"

"Maybe an hour."

"How are you?"

She shrugged. "Fine."

He nodded. There wasn't anything to say to that. But he wasn't talking about Pierre. He was talking about her injuries. "Your head?"

"It's okay. Bleeding stopped."

"Good."

"Did you hear them?" she asked.

"Hear them?" He thought she was going to say something about the giants eating Pierre, and really didn't want to talk about it.

"The giants."

He waited, not wanting to assume anything until he was sure what she was getting at.

"They were talking."

"The giants?" He had *not* heard that.

"Yeah. Before they came through the door, they were talking to each other."

"In English?"

"I don't know. I couldn't really hear with…"

With Pierre trying to get us to leave without him. He walked to her.

"But they were talking, saying words…"

"Paul said one of them talked to him in English."

"I never heard them talk before," she whispered.

Until now, Jackson had thought of the giants as nothing more than mindless ogres following the orders of their master. But he realized that if the legends were true, of Genesis and Enoch and all the mythologies, then the Nephilim giants were the furthest thing from dumb monsters. They were gods. The heroes of old, men of renown. Legends. So it made sense that they would be able to speak in more than grunts and moans.

"Where do you think he was going? The one that walked into the ocean?" she asked, staring blankly into the woods.

Jackson wondered if she realized she'd just given the giant a gender, making a man out of the former "it."

"I don't know."

He took her hand in his and she didn't resist it. They stood there, staring into the woods, silent. Then she moved closer, stepping into him, and leaned her head against his shoulder.

"Hey!" a voice shouted.

She jerked her head away and let go of his hand as if snapping from a hex and coming to her senses.

They turned to see Hap, Arkansas Joe, and Patrick running through the trees.

"Hap's looking better," Jackson muttered.

They came to a stop in front of them, bending over and trying to catch their breath.

"What?"

Patrick swallowed, tried speaking, and finally managed, "A ship…"

"A ship?"

"Yeah…" Another breath. "Heading west. A *huge* ship!"

"Show me." Jackson went back to his spot of slumber and retrieved his backpack and rifle. Robyn did the same. Then they followed the others back the way they'd come.

* * * *

The land before them, big green mountains on the horizon, was not the Bermuda any of them had seen before. They knew it had to be the southwest end, where Paul remembered Gibbs Hill Lighthouse being, but rather than cedar-studded hills, what was before them now was endless forest. It stretched to the west as far as they could see. Paul was almost sure that the girl had opened the hatchway to lure them into another hell.

The two Whalers were resting side by side, idle and bobbing up and down atop the rolling waves. Everyone was standing, staring at the land before them, trying to understand it.

"Where do you think we are?" Theodore wanted to know.

Paul flexed his hand on the silver wheel, trying to move his half-fingers. They still hurt.

A splash from outside the boat drew his gaze.

The shark was thrashing, its tail breaking the water's surface. Under the afternoon sun, they could all see its long shadow gliding back and forth around them. It had to be twenty feet long, most likely with some Eddie in its belly. Which could only mean one thing.

He answered Theo's question. "I think we're home sweet home. Sort of."

"What do you mean?" Robinson called from the other boat.

"None of us has been this far west yet."

"You think the island has changed so much?" Sanders questioned. He pulled a cookie from his pocket and took a bite.

"Only one way to find out." Then he turned and stared at both Theodore and Sanders, lowering his voice. "Tell me what you saw."

Theodore hadn't been born on the island, which was obvious from his accent. If what Robinson had said about the Washington Monument was true, then Theo would be the one most likely to confirm it. Paul focused on him.

Theo's eyes did a little twitch and dance as he remembered the experience. Whatever it was, he didn't like thinking about it. "It was your capital. I remember it from school and TV, back when I was a kid."

"Washington, DC?"

"Yeah. We went into the medical center, but ended up standing under the…" He raised his hand into the sky, indicating something tall.

"The Washington Monument."

"Yes. Like the ones here, on the island."

"Okay…" Sure, that was strange, but when did it get scary?

"It was dark. Not night, though. It was midday. But the sky was red, blood red. There was…ash. Falling from the sky like snow."

Paul stared at him, suddenly wondering what might be going on back home.

"There were…creatures all over. Airplanes were flying through the sky, shooting at them. Bombs were exploding. But there were so many…"

Chadwick's 2012 crap came to mind, as did all their talk about Satan's Golden Age, the one Osiris supposedly wanted to reinstate by releasing his chained brethren from the Underworld. "Do you think what you were seeing was now. Or the future?"

He shrugged, and of course, the whole thing would look like the future to him after not seeing the world since he was a boy.

Paul moved his eyes, setting them over Theo's shoulder, to the ship that was beginning a northwest course. He'd talked to Henry in the future, and Henry hadn't said anything about the apocalypse having started without him. But it hadn't been *that* much in the future, only six months. Theo could've been six years in the future.

He turned back to the wheel and pushed the throttle forward, sending Theodore and Sanders spilling back into their seats. "Sorry," Paul shouted over the engine.

The giant fin fell in behind them.

Robinson quickly got his boat going forward, matching Paul's speed at about three o'clock on his starboard side.

By the time they were moving over the dark spots in the water, where the reefs came close to the surface, three more fins had joined the one already in pursuit.

And, just a few hundred yards from land, close enough to make out the beach and the tree line beyond it, the sun hit its zenith and a flash of light exploded from somewhere deep within the mountains.

If Theo and Sanders were talking about it, Paul couldn't hear them over the engine and the waves crashing against the hull. But Paul didn't need their help in figuring out what it was that just lit up brilliant over the green, jagged tree line. He squinted, the glare piercing his eyes, and smiled. He didn't know for sure why he smiled, but he did.

They'd found the pyramid.

He placed his hand over the bulge in his pocket, making sure it had actually happened. Yup, there it was. The taxi driver's cell phone. Henry had made it back, had said so himself. So there was no reason why they couldn't, too.

Besides, they *had* to make it back. They had to warn the world of what was coming.

* * * *

Jackson and Robyn climbed the ridge after them, using tree branches to help pull them along. Finally, at the top of the ridge, they got a straight shot of the ocean. It seemed to sweep out into an eternal horizon. The sun was high, and Jackson figured it was after noon. There were no clouds, just a deep blue expanse above and a moving, rolling field of aquamarine below. The sound of distant waves crashing against unseen rocks below drifted lazily through the breeze.

"It was right there," Patrick gasped, pointing to the empty ocean.

"No," Jackson responded. "It's over there." And he pointed to the right.

A cruise ship, off the westernmost tip of the island, about to skirt Southampton Parish and climb north around the hook. It was too far away from their position to make out any details, but there was no mistaking it was a cruise ship.

"Where do you think it came from?" Joe asked.

Jackson frowned, squinting across the crystal sea, trying to unravel this new element. Did it mean the Triangle was open now? Could they take a boat out there and find Virginia? Like Sir Thomas Gates and Admiral Somers had done over three hundred years ago? Is this what the giant knew? Was it possible that it could swim that far? He imagined a sea of people frolicking on a beach in the Outer Banks, skim boarding, playing volleyball, napping to music, throwing a football, surfing, having chicken fights in the water… And then, from the depths appears a head emerging from beneath the surface. First a set of eyes, then a nose, a mouth, chin, neck, its massive shoulders and chest, waist, hands with twelve fingers… He saw in his mind's eye those on the beach who would first spot the monster towering out of the water, walking nearer to them. That classic dolly zoom shot of Roy Schneider in *Jaws*…

Or maybe it was just another post-solstice change. It didn't seem plausible that it had been here the whole time, circling the island and waiting to be parked in the Graveyard. Surely one of the Purees would've seen it if that were the case.

"I don't know. But maybe we should find out."

"How? We'll never catch it." Robyn looked back into the woods. "We'd have to cut across the whole island."

And hope we don't miss it by the time we get there, Jackson thought.

Joe nodded, following Robyn's gaze into the great new unknown. "We don't even know what's in there anymore."

They were right. It would take them the whole rest of the day to make the trek back to North Shore Road, then they'd have to find a way to get across the Great Sound and to Snorkel Beach, the very tip of the hook. And they'd have to do it before the ship passed that point (assuming it would pass there and not continue north). "Okay. Then it's back to the caves. We'll rest, catch up with the others, and decide where to go from there." He turned his eyes to the kid. "How you doing, Hap?"

He offered a brave smile and brushed his dark hair away from his eyes with his remaining hand. Jackson knew the kid needed some consoling, but that would come later, when time allowed.

"Okay. Let's go." He motioned for Patrick and Joe to lead the way and fell in behind them as they descended back down the ridge.

Twenty minutes later, however, Jackson ordered them to stop.

"What?" Joe turned, wanting to know what was happening. They all wanted to be back before dark (or before the demons came out to play again), and none of them welcomed another delay.

Jackson stepped out of line and wandered into the thicket off to their left.

"What's he doing?" Patrick asked Robyn.

She shrugged, then went after him.

"Where are you going?" she asked his bare back.

He moved vines out of his way, stepped over knotted undergrowth, but didn't answer.

"Jackson," she said.

He froze. He knew she'd called him Jackson, but he somehow heard Eliot. And again he felt Denise's presence.

She came up beside him, trying to figure out what he was doing. "What?"

He shook Denise's dream hands off his neck, and pointed.

But she didn't see what he was looking at.

"One of their villages," Patrick whispered, standing beside them.

There was fruit—large fruit—hanging from nearby trees. Plowed earth with ordered vegetation sprouting out of it. Rows of huts.

Robyn took a step to her left and saw past the trees that had been blocking her view. It was all there now.

They raised their weapons and stepped through the trees, and, as far as Jackson was concerned, back into Naga Hills.

The air was dead in the village, no noise of any kind to greet them. The atmosphere was heavy, everything still, as if an invisible blanket had been draped over the area.

They walked in a line, rifles ready, Hap secure between Robyn and Joe.

The first hut they came to was empty. And so was the second.

It was deserted. No one home.

But that didn't mean there wasn't something else present. They all felt it. Something moving…watching.

"I don't like this," Patrick whispered.

"Me neither," Jackson agreed, eyes captured by every shadow.

"Let's get out of here, please," Robyn added.

Then they were past the last two huts and at the edge of a small field. Across from them, the grass met a wall of small trees. The bark on all of them was stained red.

Two of the nearest trees weren't empty.

Bodies hung on them. One was a headless child, and the other a grown woman, her chest gone. They'd been hanging there for a while, that was obvious. Some kind of sacrifice, maybe? Jackson recalled the narrative from Second Chronicles, of Ahaz burning and sacrificing his children to every green tree. The works of the Devil. Naga Hills. Demons afoot.

"Let's get the hell out of here," he muttered, and turned away from it.

No one argued or said another word.

They left the village behind, entering back into the woods. A hundred yards later, however, they came to something else.

An obelisk. Positioned within a gypsum-covered henge.

"Hold on," Jackson said, but it was too late. Hap had wandered out in front of them, head down and not looking where he was going. He crossed into the ring without ever even knowing it.

And disappeared.

"Hap!" Joe cried.

They all ran to the phallic symbol that represented the Cult of the Phoenix and the seed of Osiris, stopping short of actually penetrating the circle.

"Any idea where it goes?" Jackson asked.

"No idea."

He swore under his breath, looked down at the gypsum in front of his toes, and then looked over at Robyn.

She nodded, ready.

"On three?" he asked.

But she just turned and jumped in, disappearing after the kid.

Jackson swore again, and the three of them followed.

It was a bizarre thing, to be standing in one spot and then finding yourself in another almost faster than you could bat an eye. Everything within sight altered immediately, like one of those red View-Masters you had as a kid. Pull down on the lever and the cardboard reel rotates, bringing another picture into view. *Click. Click. Click.* A different scene every time. And here Jackson stood, as he had before after using one of these ley line contraptions, trying to keep his sense of reality from spinning away from him. At least those fellows on *Star Trek* had the luxury of the whole beaming process while they dematerialized. Not here, though. Here it was simply *click*.

Before he even had an idea of his new surroundings, Jackson was bringing the AK-47 up, ready for anything. As his brain caught up with the new environment, he noticed a few things simultaneously. They were at a much higher altitude with a heavily forested expanse spread out below them, the ocean was off to their left, and Robyn was in the process of running toward Hap, who was standing idle near the edge of the cliff, staring out over the treetops.

Joe and Patrick were next to him, and there was a shadow coming down over them, extending across the ground like a giant pointer aiming at the ocean. They didn't need to turn around to know they were standing at the foot of another obelisk.

They moved out of the circle and made their way after Robyn and Hap, their eyes locked on the endless green spread out below them, the blue ocean stretching to the horizon in the other direction.

Jackson knew Bermuda well. Had a few maps of it saved in his brain. If this was still Bermuda, then it was either a grossly changed Bermuda, or it was from some time in the distant past when this spot of the Atlantic knew more than a tiny island shaped like a fishhook.

When he came to a stop next to Robyn, she looked at him, and there were all kinds of things in her eyes. A sea of sparkles floating fear, anxiety, hope, affection, excitement, dread… But she didn't put any of it into words. Jackson was about to ask what was wrong, when she lifted her arm and pointed out over the forest.

At first, Jackson didn't see it. The sun was reflecting off something and creating a blinding glare that he couldn't see past. And then he realized that was exactly what she was pointing to.

Joe shielded his eyes with his hand. "Where are we?"

"Has to be the south end," Patrick answered.

"What *end*?"

He was right. There was no end. Just trees and mountains as far as the eye could see. This was more than the Great Sound being filled like the other bodies of water they'd seen after the solstice. This was new land altogether. Risen out of the depths of the sea and continuing northwest for miles.

Finally, a single cloud came drifting through the day sky. It was a small cloud, more of a wisp than anything else, but it crossed the sun's path and momentarily averted a portion of its rays. Just enough for a sliver of shadow to appear moving as a line over the treetops. And as it moved, it headed into the glare, carving a path through it, inches at a time.

Suddenly, the glare was gone, and there was only a crystal triangle peeking up past the canopy.

"The pyramid…" Jackson whispered.

They'd found it.

"Look." Joe pointed. There was a tremble alive in his voice, resonating from some place deep down in his throat.

As the shadow slid beyond the capstone, the glare returned in the form of a prism shooting light in every direction. As the shadow moved on, however, Jackson caught a glimpse of something he'd seen before. It was only a fraction of a second before it was whitewashed by the blinding light, but it stamped his mind like the lingering image on an old projection TV just switched off. He'd seen it a long time ago, back when he was a kid. A scene from a movie.

The Wizard of Oz.

Robyn held her breath for a moment. "Did you see them?" The breeze was magnificent up here at the top of whatever this mountain was, and it blew her hair across her face. When she parted the blond strands (still colored red) away from her eyes, there was new fear circling them.

"Yeah, I saw them."

Monkey devils. Flying around the capstone like vultures, their bat-like wings beating tirelessly at the air. There were no unicycles being pedaled as far as he could tell, but nevertheless, that was the childhood correlation the sight spawned.

"What are they?" Patrick wondered aloud. Apparently they'd all seen them.

Before anyone could come up with an answer, Hap began tugging at Robyn's hand. His head was turned out toward the ocean, his red-wrapped stump raised, an imaginary finger targeting something out in the sea.

They managed to turn away from the pyramid's blinding reflection (and the creatures it now consumed) and surveyed the ocean.

Patrick took a step in that direction, as if a foot closer would identify what they were straining to see. "Is that the ship?"

It was just a dot on the horizon, but closer to shore were two lines of wake cutting through the ocean and chasing after two other dots.

Joe took an old pirate telescope out of his pocket and extended it.

"Where'd you get that?" Jackson asked. He couldn't believe he'd had it the whole time.

He stared through it, his face thoughtful. "I've had it for years." Then he handed it over. "I think you better have a look."

Jackson took it and peered through the scope himself. The ocean leaped forward at him, the waves larger. He moved the instrument from side to side until he found the frothy wakes, then he followed them to two Boston Whalers. They were too far away even with the telescope to be sure, but Jackson was almost certain that Paul was piloting the lead boat.

Joe nodded toward the boats. "I think that's Robinson."

Jackson handed the scope to Robyn. She took a nice long look before concurring. "And Carl. Can't make out the other ones. They're heading for the coast down there."

Jackson couldn't even begin to guess as to how they ended up on the Whalers, but he figured they must've spotted the cruise ship and found a way to get aboard. Maybe they'd seen the pyramid, too. From their distance, however, and their position beneath the treetops, he doubted they could have seen its sentries.

"Change in plans," he announced. He looked at Robyn, took in her face, her beautiful face, hating that he was going to put her in harm's way again. But he didn't have a choice and that was life these days. They needed to stop Paul and fill him in on all that he'd missed. Warn him of the thing that was out there, devouring both pure and impure alike. "Let's find a way off this cliff and see if we can't meet up with them." *Before Paul gets it in his mind to do something stupid.*

Robyn leaned close and whispered that she was worried about Hap, that she wasn't sure he could take any more. She was right.

"We'll meet up with them and then go straight back to Jared," he whispered back.

Joe nodded, overhearing them. "I'll carry him," he said.

"Okay." Jackson handed Robyn his rifle and then turned his back to her. "Can you get it off?"

She slung his rifle over her shoulder, where it clacked against hers, and then gently pulled his backpack down off his shoulders.

"Thanks." He unzipped it, turned it upside-down, and shook its contents out onto the ground. Wasn't much. Clips for the rifles, a knife, some matches, John's Bible. He took the knife and cut two holes in the bottom corners of the pack. "Might not be too comfortable, my man, but should be easier on you." He motioned for Hap to come near. Picking him up, he held him over the open backpack and lowered him in, letting the boy poke his legs through the holes.

All three of them then lifted the bag into the air and helped get the straps over Joe's shoulders. They zipped the bag up as well as they could, and there Hap hung, legs sticking out of the bag. He wrapped his arms around Joe's neck.

"Just don't choke me," he said.

Hap only nodded.

"Okay." Jackson took his rifle back from Robyn and, when he was sure the others weren't looking, planted a ninja-quick kiss on her cheek.

She blushed but didn't say anything.

He felt odd, and for the first time really grasped their age difference. It wasn't an absurd gap, but it was one that could be a deal-breaker. He was going to say something, but she was already moving, navigating this new terrain, trying to find a path that would lead them down and to the coast.

"We need to find some water. And food," Patrick said from the rear.

But Jackson wasn't paying attention. His mind was all over the place as he tried fitting the contents of his backpack into his pockets, his eyes on the back of Denise's legs. *Robyn's* legs, he told himself. *Robyn's legs.*

They found the pyramid. There was still a chance they could get out of here. They had six months until the winter solstice, three until the equinox. Wasn't much time to figure out this new land and develop a plan.

As they descended, he found himself muttering a prayer. A prayer for survival. A prayer for escape. He was tired of this place. He wanted to go home. And the woman in front of him…he wanted to take her with him.

Four days. It had only been *four* days since Henry was here with John and Chadwick. And he'd only just met Robyn yesterday. It felt like a year ago, but he'd known her for a single day. What was he thinking? He traced her figure with his gaze, stopping at her head, noting the way the blood in her hair was growing darker as it dried. He thought back to the thing that took her. *Took* her… He paused at that. Where was it planning on taking her? And he thought of all the other women that were in the cave. Where had they gone? Could they be out there in the new territory? Was it possible that Osiris' army hadn't disappeared, but had just changed addresses? What if everything was still functioning as normal on the island, just in a different part? The things out there hunting down the women, taking them back to the pyramid. *What if Osiris and Henry and John and Chadwick never left the island?* What if they'd just moved with the pyramid? What if they were still here?

Patrick's Irish accent broke apart his thoughts. "Look!" he blurted out, head turned back the way they'd come, up toward the sky.

Jackson's mind was tripping over his thoughts, over the possibility that nothing had really changed at all, but he managed to get his eyes off the blood in Robyn's hair and put them up toward the sky with the others'.

A sea of ink was appearing off in the distance. Like the sky had been opened, the blue separating and revealing the darkness beyond. Only the sliver of black wasn't just there on the outside, it was seeping in. Spreading. Rolling across the sky and swallowing its color like an eraser. It was coming. Again.

They ran.

EPILOGUE

24th day of June. Afternoon. The Ship.

He stood, looking out the window, watching the two Boston Whalers grow smaller and smaller as they neared the land. A tear slid down his face. It wasn't a sorrowful tear, or even a tear of regret. He wasn't sure what it was. Only that he felt...lost. Which was ironic since he'd just come back. He was all better now, physically, and he supposed he had some dark magic to thank for that. But he wasn't complaining. Better than being dead. Or at least that's what he kept telling himself. It depended on what dead was, exactly. If dead was where he'd been to, then forget it. He'd sooner spend every waking hour of this life being tortured with razors, knives, whips, water, electricity...whatever. Because compared to what he'd seen, after where he'd *been*, that would all be like Disney World.

Thump. Thump. Thump.

He ignored it, stuck inside his own head. The other presence was gone now and things weren't as funny as they had been. He was alone, his thoughts and feelings and pain all to himself again. He knew what they did, why they took him. Legion or whatever name they had. Demons were what they were. They'd come inside him like a body snatcher and took him over, from head to toe. They manipulated and poisoned. But also healed. So that they could take him through that door. To open it. So the Others could get out. He had been their key.

He brushed the tear away with the back of his hand, not completely understanding why they'd needed him, how it all worked out there on that Twilight plane, but he was sure that it was his entering the closet that let the other things out of it. Dark things. Gross things. Things that would break your mind in half. And if he hadn't had the fortitude of demons, their company reinforcing his mental aptitude, then he would be no more than a vegetable now. You can't get a glimpse of hell and escape it unchanged. It was too much. The suffering too vast. The Darkness too complete. Even with all he'd seen through the years, of war and evil, it was nothing in light of this Darkness.

For a while, he thought he was resigned to spend eternity as a phantom, calling out to those he could see but unable to make them see him. To touch him. To help him. He had been everywhere all at once. All over the island and on the ship. Moving about through the passageways of time, through reality's back doors. It had been an improvement from the initial entering of the closet. Of that hell. And he wondered if he had become a demon himself, wondered if that was what hell turned out to be for some.

But it changed. For some reason, it had let him go. And now here he was, on the ship, standing in one of the bars. What this meant for him, he wasn't sure.

Was he really here? Was it a trick? Some greater level of torment unfolding…the glimpse of hope, of remembrance, of a chance…only to have it snatched away?

Thump. Thump. Thump.

He sighed, then looked down at himself. He was naked. Wherever he'd been, it had kept his clothes before spitting him back. He wasn't even sure how long he'd been here. He remembered seeing Paul, calling out to him. But of course, Paul couldn't see him. And then, he was opening his eyes to find himself sprawled naked on the floor here.

His self was handed back, but there was damage done before the invaders left. They'd broken the place up pretty bad during their stay. He wasn't sure if the damage was reversible, if his mind could ever completely be made right. He thought he could function, but alone at night when trying to sleep… He had a vivid perception of alcohol and pills. But then, maybe it wouldn't matter. Wouldn't matter at all. The end was near, after all. No, not Chadwick's 2012 Mayan stuff. That wasn't it at all. It was something else. Something…unbelievable. He was sure that the others, Robinson and company, had gotten a tiny glimpse of it when they were ported away into the future. But even what they saw was just a small portion of the whole.

The Golden Age…

Behind him, doors crashed open and Daniel came stumbling into the room, eyes wide with panic.

Their eyes met, and Hunter smiled.

Daniel looked him up and down and almost ran back out of the room.

Thump. Thump. Thump.

"What—" But he didn't get much further than that.

It was okay. Hunter understood. "You just missed them," he said, pointing out the window.

Daniel ran over, slapping his hands against the window. As his eyes found the two shrinking Whalers, his hands closed to fists and slammed the glass. After a moment, he turned his head back to the naked black man. "What are you doing?"

Hunter shrugged. "Just got here myself."

Confusion twisted his face and it was obvious he was trying to figure out where he was. After all, opening doors on this ship had proven to be a bit of a wild card.

"No," Hunter said. "You're here, all right. And so am I."

Thump.

"And so is he."

"*He*?" Daniel asked.

"The giant. He swam to the boat, climbed aboard, and has been wandering throughout the ship for some time now. He's much too big for the low ceilings and narrow halls, so he's making quite a racket." He thought that he was talking rather well, considering his mind felt like Jell-O at the moment. It was almost scaring him how calm he sounded to himself. Here he was standing as naked as could be in front of another man after having just escaped hell, a giant was on the loose nearby, and his heart was as steady as if he were discussing golf.

Maybe...he thought. *No*. They were gone. He could tell. He was his own. Had to be.

"What do we do?" Daniel asked.

Hunter shrugged and walked to the bar. "Have a drink, I suppose." He reached for a bottle. "Then, we should probably find a way to join our friends and see if we just can't help them save the world."

BOOK III

APOCALYPSE RISING

NOT THEM

And against the angels whom He had sent upon the earth, He was exceedingly wroth, and He gave commandment to root them out of all their dominion, and He bade us to bind them in the depths of the earth, and behold they are bound in the midst of them, and are kept separate.

—Book of Jubilees 5:6

To Michael likewise the Lord said, Go and announce his crime to Samyaza, and to the others who are with him, who have been associated with women, that they might be polluted with all their impurity. And when all their sons shall be slain, when they shall see the perdition of their beloved, bind them for seventy generations underneath the earth, even to the day of judgment, and of consummation, until the judgment, the effect of which will last for ever, be completed. Then shall they be taken away into the lowest depths of the fire in torments; and in confinement shall they be shut up forever... Destroy all the souls addicted to dalliance, and the offspring of the Watchers, for they have tyrannized over mankind. Let every oppressor perish from the face of the earth; Let every evil work be destroyed...

—Book of Enoch 10:15-16, 18-20

...And the coast of Og king of Bashan, which was of the remnant of the giants, that dwelt at Ashtaroth and at Edrei, and reigned in mount Hermon, and in Salcah, and in all Bashan, unto the border of the Geshurites and the Maachathites, and half Gilead, the border of Sihon king of Heshbon. Them did Moses the servant of the LORD and the children of Israel smite...

—Joshua 12:4, 5 (KJV)

ONE

September 21, 2011. Morning. Bermuda.

The water moved gracefully, reaching up onto the pink coral sands with liquid, massaging fingers. Bright aquamarine hues shimmered in the near distance as the clear surf rolled its way up the beach before slipping back into itself. Scattered rocks littered the shoreline, and the tide moved over and around them with fluid grace, flinging an occasional white mist into the gentle ocean breeze. Farther out, in the wide space between where the waves swelled and the calmer, darker blues swallowed deeper depths, other, larger rocks stood breaching the surface. They reached for the sky like monoliths left behind by some forgotten age.

It was a beautiful scene in this world, just as it would be in the other. No one could deny that, and surely no one would. But in this Bermuda, the luxury to stop and marvel at such displays came rather infrequently, most of the island scenery met with a passing indifference on the road to more immediate concerns. Just nice pictures decorating the walls of hell.

He squinted as a cloud loosened its grip on the sun, a beam of light shooting between its puffy fingers and exploding a line of living diamonds across the water. It wasn't the first time he'd taken the time to gaze out the windows of his recent prison, but it was the first time he found himself in awe of its splendor.

It was her, of course. Denise. She was in his head, sitting at the controls and manipulating his thoughts. She'd loved the sky, the sunset. Had gleaned all manner of meaning out of it, seeing the ethereal and metaphysical currents in such moments as part of the Grand Mystery, a spiritual echo that stemmed from an existence complimented by perceivable awe and wonder toward what could only be reflections of the Divine. No, he hadn't shared in her optimism back then. Too calloused from the realities of war to appreciate any evidence of a merciful Creator. But he'd never discouraged her from talking about it, had always tried to keep his own bitterness from infecting her soul. There would've been no point in that victory, standing hand-in-hand atop her dashed Hope while forcing her to salute the newly erected flag of his god, Fat Man Futility. The sound of her voice came back to him now, the way her voice resounded with wonder whenever she'd speak of such matters, the magic that lit her eyes… Damn him if ever he'd tried to steal that from her. He had no reason to, other than to make her as dead inside as he was. *God, I hope I never discouraged you that way,* he thought.

Time had begun to stretch thin the memory of her voice, but recent events on the island had served to refresh that part of her person. He imagined just what she would say now, imagined her saying it, relishing the sound of her voice, all the inflections and the subtlest mannerisms that would identify it as hers.

Natural selection doesn't need things like color and beauty… she said.

He smiled, letting the imagined dialogue play out in his mind, the narrative expounding on her conviction that the impact such things like beauty and color had on the human soul was the very evidence of an Artist—the capacity to appreciate the art simply the result of being created in the Artist's likeness, the programmed response being, "Who is responsible, and what does it mean?" All the questions outside of science's purview.

Eternity is written deep within our hearts, she'd quoted.

He sighed and picked up a handful of sand, sifting it through his fingers. He watched it blow away, knowing that her ideas on beauty were only a springboard into more subsequent thoughts. Like love, morality, universal right and wrongs, honor… Other intangibles that didn't *need* to evolve with everything else. She could never get her brain to compute the fact that everything had happened on its own from out of Nowhere and Nothing, and that such transcendent attributes could then, out of the same Nowhere and Nothing, somehow tether the "Great Accident" together in perfect, metaphysical symmetry. It had seemed to her oddly dismissive of all probability and likelihood.

Privately, he'd dismissed her convictions on the basis of all the evil he'd witnessed. Yet, as he looked at it now, if Nowhere and Nothing were the two pillars of his belief, then evil could not exist. With no Purpose, Point, or Paternity, things like morality, right and wrong, good and evil were just illusions conjured up in the human psyche as a fail-safe to keep the species from destroying itself. But with no such thing as intention, the failsafe itself would be an accident. And he realized he'd been using something that didn't exist to disprove the existence of the very thing needed to exist in order to support his case. Furthermore, if there was no sense to the universe, and here he was part of it, how then could he possibly determine it to be senseless? If there was no meaning, then he shouldn't have been able to discover that there was no meaning, should he? And again, if such "sense" and "reason" and the rights and wrongs she'd spoken of had simply evolved from out of nonsense and pointlessness, then the concept of good and evil were nothing more than ideas engineered by Chance. But then that didn't make "sense" because nothing could be "engineered" without intent, and there could be no intent if everything was senseless and without reason.

He blinked. *If only you were here, Denise…*

Here? No. That wasn't what he meant.

Yet, she *was* here. Somehow, in some way, she'd been calling to him, reinvigorating the part of him that had started to forget her. Whether mimicked or real (though it terrified him), it had sparked a flicker of hope in his own soul. Hope that she was more than dust crapped out by Nothing and destined only for oblivion.

Movement drew his eyes down to the water's edge, nudging his late wife from the command chair. It was Robyn. She was walking, ankle-deep, in the surf, staring out at the sunrise. He wondered what thoughts the display touched off in her mind and couldn't keep himself from assuming they would mirror Denise's.

She stopped walking and stood still, facing the ocean, the breeze lifting her hair off her shoulders and sparking a gold fire about her head.

He watched her intently, studying her shape, his mind suddenly switching tracks from one woman to another. He wondered if she knew he was there, watching her. Probably. Then, as if reading his mind, she turned and locked eyes with him.

They stared at each other for a moment, all kinds of things being communicated through the air between them, though all unsure and murky. Finally, she turned and went back the way she'd come.

Jackson swore under his breath.

Scouting and surviving had defined the last few months of daily living in this new version of their Other Bermuda, yet, despite the high tension and uncertainty, a little romance had found room to bud in the recent weeks. Their first kiss was on a deserted Horseshoe Beach under a starlit sky just three days ago. She'd opened her heart to him, sharing thoughts and feelings she'd never really had before and hating how vulnerable doing so made her feel. In response to such vulnerability, he'd looked into her eyes and called her…Denise.

After a moment of awkward silence, she'd taken a single step backward. The movement had only covered a few inches of sand, but in terms of their relationship, it had been miles. That was the last time they'd spoken, and it was a festering wound he couldn't ignore, no matter what else was going on in the strange world around him. The power of love, he supposed.

Love.

It was Denise's favorite piece of transcendent "evidence." Not the selfish, biological "love" that some would argue was necessary to forward humanity, but the self-sacrificing, selfless love that tortured those afflicted by it, that led to the "till death do us part" promise of devotion. Did he *love* Robyn? Or did he love that she reminded him of Denise? Perhaps getting their names mixed up was a clue…

He took his eyes off Robyn and shifted them back to the rising sun, trying to put both women out of his mind for the time being. There were more pressing things that required his attention.

He groaned as he rose to his feet, his body reminding him of the horrors endured at Osiris' hands. He'd recovered remarkably well over the last few months despite a few relapses due to confrontations with Osiris' Leftovers, but there was still that naggings stitch in his side. He reached down and grabbed one of the AK-47s they'd retrieved from the shipping container. Giving one last glance to Robyn, he began making his way up a sand dune. Skirting some large rock formations, he cleared the rise.

"You ready? Or you need some more time with your navel?"

It was Paul. He was standing there waiting for him with his own AK-47 propped up and resting on his shoulder. Shirtless, his muscled and scarred chest covered in mud, he looked as if he'd come straight off a *Rambo* poster.

His cold eyes stared out from the black mask he'd applied, and Jackson couldn't help thinking that they were somewhat haunted. Something had been going on with Paul...ever since Hunter had disappeared in that house. But whatever it was, Paul wasn't one to share.

Jackson shouldered the rifle and walked past him. "Let's get it over with."

"Your girl coming along?"

Jackson sighed. "Shut up."

Paul smiled, staring after him.

Jackson knew everyone was talking about their recent romance, that it was obvious there had been some kind of falling-out. He tried not to care what they thought, wanting to distance himself from the feeling of being back in grade school. "I hope this isn't gonna be your new routine over the next few months."

"Is it gonna take you that long to kiss and make up? Because if so, I can't promise that I'm just gonna sit idly by while there's a beautiful damsel in need of comforting."

Jackson stopped, turning. "That's not funny."

Paul shrugged and spit. "Neither is me being here."

Jackson had nothing to say to that and continued on his way, thinking again about the idea of a fail-safe. It was something he'd been thinking about a lot lately, largely because he saw it as one of the key ingredients to getting out of here. At first, he'd thought that Osiris had brought John to the island despite his faith, but now he understood that it was *because* of it. He'd known from the beginning that John was "the key." Ronald had told him as much (though Ronald's own knowledge of what Osiris was really up to was probably limited as well), but it was more than just Osiris needing one more of his offspring. John had been his fail-safe to ensure that his using the pyramid would not result in the same conclusion as the last time he'd attempted to open the gates of Tartarus. And judging from Paul's phone call to Henry in the future, Osiris' plan had worked. The question was, did the rest of the Leftovers that were hoping to use the pyramid at the next solstice or equinox need a fail-safe, too? And if so, who could it possibly be? Was the faith-infused DNA of the Savior necessary to keep them out of Hades? Or had it just been necessary because a Fallen angel was operating it? Could Nephilim blood condemn the same way Messianic blood could protect? Because he, himself, had Nephilim blood flowing through his veins, and unless one of the others had John's faith (he was pretty certain he could exclude Paul from such consideration), then he might be endangering them all with his presence.

He moved a needled branch out of his way as he made his way back to the cave, trying hard to keep his mind from taking the next logical step down this road of thought. But it was a slippery road, and he lost his footing and slid right into it.

Was he really in a position to deny the basic realities of what his wife had suggested, what John and Henry had come to believe themselves? After being in this place where the question of the supernatural was no longer a question? Fallen angels, demons, things right out of Genesis and the Book of Enoch...

There *was* more. Of course there was more. He was staring it right in the face. The spirit world existed, good and evil, the supernatural, the writings of the Bible so suddenly relevant to his reality. He'd found ways to downplay Naga Hills, but there was no dodging this. Nowhere and Nothing stood no chance against what his eyes had been witnessing here on a daily basis. He couldn't *deny* it like he used to…

But he could *ignore* it.

Even that was getting more and more difficult, though. He knew it was there. It hung on his periphery like a phantasm, but he just couldn't bring himself to turn and confront it. Wasn't exactly sure why. He supposed it had something to do with facing his eternal destination. Yet, on the other hand, that same coin had a side that advertised a possible course correction. So then why was he being so stubborn about it?

Get us out of here, and I'll do whatever you want, he thought. And then wondered why God would be inclined to take such a deal in the first place. *Get me out of here, and then I'll take your hand. Deal?* Perhaps God would just as soon let him fall into the abyss. Would serve him right for being so arrogant as to assume God needed Him more than he needed God. Making deals on the terms of his own salvation after his emancipation had already been purchased…

"Ready?"

Robinson's voice cut through his thoughts, returning them to the back room of his subconscious. "Yeah," Jackson answered, approaching the entrance to the cave. "Let's get your ladies back." He bent over and picked up his backpack.

TWO

September 21, 2011. The New Territory. Morning.

Robyn had remained ahead of them for most of the trek, anxious to reach their destination. They stood back now and watched as she climbed a pile of rocks that was taller than she was and stood occupying the space between two large trees.

Stepping closer, Paul stared at her legs as her faded and ripped shorts rode high. When he finally took his eyes off her, he found Jackson staring at him. Paul shrugged. "Losers Weepers, pal."

Paul saw Jackson's jaw tighten, and then the mammoth of a man moved between him and Robyn, climbing the rocks after her. Paul smiled.

He moved the rifle back and forth, covering the surrounding woods and waiting for Robinson to catch up. "Anything?" he asked once the man in the cowboy hat and Union blues was beside him.

He wiggled his toes and leaned back in his worn sandals. "Nothing," he whispered back. He tilted the brim of his hat upward and wiped a bead of sweat from his brow, striking a line of skin through the camouflage mask.

Paul nodded, and they continued after Robyn and Jackson through the strange, solstice-induced forest.

Last week, while on a scouting mission in the New Territory (as they had since named it), a group of Purees had wandered across a clearing. At the backside of the clearing, they discovered a cave with fresh foot traffic leading in and out of it. Curious, they'd spent the night huddled down in the surrounding woods, waiting to see if whatever was responsible for the heavy foot traffic might return in the morning.

Just as they were about to give up and return to their own caves, they watched as a Nephilim giant came strutting into the clearing, tugging Priscilla and Ruth, two of the missing Puree women, bound behind it. The giant (which they later estimated to be nearly twenty feet tall), was yanking them on a leash, pulling them off their feet and dragging them on their chests through the tall untamed grass of the clearing. Priscilla and Ruth, kicking and screaming and fighting against their restraints, were anything but willing participants. The reported resistance led the rest of the Purees to believe that Osiris' absence now allowed the pure-blooded women to maintain control over their own will, which was a huge development as far as the Puree community was concerned. But, as the report went on to show, the women's struggle to escape only seemed to further amuse and excite the giant. It had taken them into the cave, their echoing screams and shouts left lingering behind for a moment, and then silence swallowed any sign of them.

The tired spies then rushed back to Jared and Samuel, delivering the news to the rest of the community that had survived the so-named "Solstice War" and the subsequent battles since. It was good news—some of their sisters, thought to have been dead for months, were still alive. But, considering all the diverse perversions they'd likely been forced to endure through that time…it was terrible news as well.

The New Territory was still a mystery. Over the last few months, only about three square miles of the fresh terrain had been scouted, and it was still unclear how far it even reached. Paul had attempted to reach its end two months ago by taking the Boston Whaler up along the coast. But he'd only made it two miles before the sky turned black on him, that familiar, inky darkness unfolding like a scroll across an otherwise cloudless sky. There'd been a couple of run-ins with the closet demon since that day on the beach, and it was soon understood that the dark sky served as a warning of the demon's close proximity. Paul had turned around and sped back as fast as he could. The Whaler had since run out of gas.

Accompanying the mystery of the new land were the theories about it, and three months was ample time to come up with all kinds of ideas. A slice of another dimension superimposed on top of this universe, and the pyramid having acted as a time machine, transporting everyone back in time to when the island had been much larger, were two of the more prominent thoughts. And though most of the island survivors were completely ignorant of string theory, quantum mechanics, black holes, and all the speculative science that the rest of the world at least picked up from the Syfy channel, their "ideas" were, in essence, describing the same basic things.

The question Paul had concerning the "Change," however, wasn't so much what the new land *was* or where it had come *from*, but rather what might've come *with* it. Because, if the land did come from somewhere else or from some other time, then wouldn't it be plausible that the occupants of that land (if any) might have come along with it? Case in point: the flying monkey things now circling the relocated pyramid. Had they always been on the island, a creation of Osiris' genetic engineering, or had they flown out of the closet? *Or* had they come as citizens of the New Territory?

Too many questions and no answers in sight.

Reaching the top of the rock pile, Paul stopped and stretched. Resting his fists against his hips, he took in the area ahead of them. It was dense and wild, no natural paths anywhere.

Jackson and Robyn were about twenty-five yards away, wrestling through the thicket and trying to climb over a large rotting tree that had fallen years ago.

Then, suddenly, they dropped, crouching low behind the tree.

Paul's hands fell away from his hips.

Jackson snapped his head around, found him still up on the rock pile, and put out an open hand: STOP. Then he put a finger to his lips.

Paul grabbed Robinson and pulled him down into a crouching position beside him.

Jackson put an open hand behind an ear, indicating that he'd heard something.

Paul responded by motioning that he understood.

Then Jackson pointed at him, then to his own two eyes, and then out in front of him into the woods.

"He wants to know if we can see what he's hearing," Paul whispered to Robinson as he tried peering down from their elevated position and through the thriving maze of forest. There was nothing that—

"I see them," Robinson whispered.

Paul didn't. "Where? You sure?"

"There's three of them."

He looked harder and finally detected motion about thirty paces ahead of Jackson and Robyn's current position. "How the hell can you tell there's three of them?" He didn't wait for a response though, and instead said, "Let's circle around." Then he made a hand signal to Jackson, conveying his intent.

Jackson touched his thumb and index finger together, signaling that he understood.

Moving to their left, Paul led Robinson down off the rocks and into a sea of ferns. The dirt beneath them was moist and spongy, and the pale green, serrated fingers moved lazily out of their way as they army-crawled through their grasp. After forty yards, they turned back toward the three strangers, approaching them from what would be Jackson's nine o'clock. The fanned appendages began giving way to less pliable plant life, and soon they were navigating thorny underbrush, following hard, protruding roots to their large sources. They used the wide, scattered trees as cover, Paul's bare skin now crisscrossed with scratches.

Close enough to see now, Paul peered out from behind a five-foot-wide tree trunk and saw that there were actually four of them—all men. They were in a circle, bent over something at their feet. He couldn't make out what it was, but he could tell from the bobbing movements of their heads that they were eating it—hands to mouths, heads pulling and jerking back away from them. "Can you make out what they're eating?" Paul whispered.

Robinson squinted beneath the brim of his hat, trying to see into the circle. He shook his head.

All Paul could see were flashes of red. He took a slow, controlled breath through his nose and let it out of his mouth. Then he looked at Robinson. "You ready?"

Robinson nodded.

Paul repositioned the AK-47 across his back and pulled a knife from his belt. He flipped it once, grabbing it by the handle so that the blade was pointing down.

Suddenly, the stranger closest to them stopped chewing and became as still as a stone. His back was to them, but he tilted his head as if trying to hear something elusive.

Paul held his breath and Robinson tensed. There was no way the man could have heard the soft smack of the knife's handle against his palm, but…

Then the man began to turn his head, looking back over his shoulder.

But then Paul heard it too.

Without moving any other muscles, Robinson raised his index finger and pointed it up and beyond the eaters, to a ridge that ran up from their right and down to their left seventy yards across from them.

Jack and Robyn had apparently decided to move in from the other side, putting the four strangers between them. Paul detected their movement as they worked their way down off the ridge and into the tangled mess of the forest floor.

The man stood, rising from his crouch as if in slow motion, every muscle in his body attentive. Other than the loincloth, he was naked, but the markings that covered his sinewy frame were akin to Osiris' Fallen order. Blood dripped from his chin, droplets splattering on his marked chest.

Another of the eaters stopped chewing, meat hanging out of his mouth, and stood too. He turned and seemed to stare right at Jack and Robyn's position. Then he made a noise and shook his head, the bloody flesh swinging back and forth from his chin. Now the other two men stopped eating and turned their attention to the ridge behind them too.

Holding his left hand up before Robinson, Paul went to signal a countdown. And then remembered his missing fingers. After three months, he thought he would've gotten used to his discounted digits, but that simply was not so, and his eyes had to constantly reaffirm their loss. Instead, he closed his fist, hiding the haggard and scarred appendages, and nodded his head toward the inked strangers instead.

Robinson nodded, flexing his own hand on the AK-47's grip.

Finally having spotted something that must have confirmed their suspicion, the loinclothed men all retrieved long spears that had been lying, unseen, at their feet. And then they were off like jungle cats, gliding effortlessly through the maze of twisted foliage and converging on the ridge.

Without another signal to Robinson, Paul lurched forward, springing to his feet, and took off after them.

Robinson reacted to Paul's sudden flight by pushing hard off his planted foot, which slipped out from under him in the soil, digging a rut into the ground and sending him forward onto his elbows. Recovering, he got back to his sandaled feet just in time to see Paul raise his rifle. But before he could pull the trigger on the run, the lead stranger suddenly went from a full-out, gazelle-like sprint to violently jackknifing off his feet. He landed on his back with a sword sticking out of his chest.

The other three men, who had begun to fan out in an apparent attempt to surround their prey, suddenly slid to a stop, their spears held cocked by their heads, their eyes frantically searching for the source of the thrown sword.

Then Jackson was in front of them, exploding out of the undergrowth, snapping branches and tearing vines, a floating cloud of debris chasing after him as he raced to confront the three strangers. His massive size and crazed white eyes popping wide from the mud mask gave them all a moment's pause. And then they were launching their spears at him.

All of them missed, flying mere inches past Jackson and Robyn (who no one had been able to see following in the shadow of Jackson's bulky frame). With no more weapons at their disposal, the strangers turned and ran. But it was too late. Jackson was already on top of them.

By the time Paul and Robinson reached him, Jackson had already broken one of the stranger's necks, smashed another against a tree, and was in the process of turning the face of the third into hamburger.

Paul stood beside him, watching with interest as Jackson continued to pummel the unconscious stranger with his blood-soaked fists. He wasn't wearing his backpack, and Paul figured he'd taken it off before charging into battle. He glanced at Robyn and saw that she was staring at Jackson too, the look on her face unreadable. "What a savage, huh?" he asked, getting her attention. Then he winked at her.

Ignoring his sarcasm, she looked back to Jackson. "Stop," she said.

Jackson paused at the sound of her voice, as if suddenly cognizant of what he was doing. He got to his feet, his eyes coming back from wherever he'd been. Blood dripped off his knuckles. He looked away from the mess he'd made of the face beneath him and considered the groaning man he'd left lying still at the base of the tree. He wasn't moving, his spine snapped.

"Take a breather," Paul said. He moved past Jackson and flipped his knife so that he was squeezing the blade between his thumb and forefinger. The paralyzed man tracked him with his eyes. He tried to shake his head in protest, but—

The knife flew from Paul's hand in a silver flash, splitting the man's right eye and entering his brain. He was dead instantly, which in some ways could be considered a mercy. No doubt he would've been eaten alive by the animals that patrolled the New Territory.

Paul looked around, stretched, and then bent over to retrieve the knife. Part of the eyeball came out still stuck on the blade. "Eww…" He flung it into the grass.

"Who are they?" Robinson wondered aloud, staring down at the bodies.

Paul cast a casual look over the bodies and shrugged.

But Jackson looked concerned.

Picking up on his second-guessing, Paul spit. "Does it matter at this point?"

Robyn frowned, unable to decipher the unanswered question that Paul just answered. "What?"

"Nothing," Jackson said.

But it wasn't nothing. Not to Jackson.

Whereas Paul had considered the possibility from the start, it hadn't crossed Jackson's mind until just now. *Oh, well,* Paul thought. Jackson was starting to get a little soft anyway, starting to go the way of John-the-wayward-Ranger.

Paul started walking back to the abandoned meal, curious to see what had been on the breakfast menu. He turned his head as Robinson came up beside him, his eyes settling momentarily on the green MOM tattoo he'd gotten somewhere prior to this place.

"What's wrong?" Robinson whispered.

"Jackson's having second thoughts about killing those fellas. He assumed they were Fallen, but maybe they weren't. Maybe they just showed up as part of the New Territory. Maybe they were starving. Maybe they don't know about Osiris or giants or any of it." He looked back into his eyes. "That possibility bother *you*, Crusoe?"

Robinson let his eyes drift back to the four corpses, thinking how close he'd been to shooting them all down himself. "Yeah, it would."

"Thought so." He veered off to where the first man had died while trying to pull the sword from his chest, his fingers sliced to the bones and still gripping the blade. Placing his boot on the man's bare shoulder, Paul yanked the sword from his chest. Then, taking one glance at Robinson, he slashed the bloody blade in a downward arc and separated the man's hands from the rest of him.

Robinson frowned. "What—"

Paul bent over and picked up one of the severed hands. The dead fingers were partially closed as if still grasping the sword, so he lifted its pinky finger into the air. "This little piggy went to market..." Then he tossed it at Robinson, bouncing it off his chest.

Robinson bobbled it, the lifeless fingers spreading apart and bending awkwardly in his grasp as he tried to keep it from hitting the ground. Finally getting a hold of it, he held it up. "Six fingers," he realized. And then the feel of all those bloody, crab-like phalanges dancing in his grasp made him toss it.

Paul smiled, holding up his own left hand and wiggling his three remaining fingers. "Three more than I got."

"So why don't you just tell him?"

"Jack? Oh, it'll do him good to stew over the possibility. Besides, did I mention he's the reason I'm in this hellhole?" He joined Robyn and Jackson, who were already standing over the meal, and could feel Robinson's wary gaze on his back. He could read all the many uncertain thoughts aimed at him, and knew he tended to have that effect on people. He didn't entirely dislike it.

"Hungry?" Paul asked, stepping in between the two lovebirds. He could tell the kill was fresh, and wasn't entirely joking. It was a horse, or had been—one of the two-tailed varieties they'd occasionally seen throughout their stay here. Since they knew that to be Osiris' doing, this horse must've wandered off the reservation and gotten itself tracked down by a group of Leftover explorers. Its stomach was open, and most of its insides were missing.

They salvaged what was left, shoving pieces of meat into their pockets.

It was all quiet now, the new forest still.

Jackson went back to the base of the ridge to retrieve his backpack.

* * * *

They came to a stop half a mile later. The ground was high, but it dropped off in front of them, racing down to a wide, snaking stream below. They knew from the scout reports that the cave was a mile or so beyond the stream. They were getting close.

"Shouldn't be too much farther," Robyn said, tracking the flowing water with her eyes. A sheen of sweat glistened on her skin as shadows danced across her face, the sunlight fractured by the rocking, bending canopy above.

Paul stood beside her, spit to his left, and then added his gaze to hers. He mumbled something unsavory under his breath, something about their new world.

Robinson slid down a smooth-barked tree until he was sitting crouched against it. He took off his hat and hung it on his knee, then ran a hand through his sweaty hair. He put the hat back on and pulled the brim low enough so that it concealed his eyes. He watched from that shadowed security as Jackson appeared from behind a tree, catching up with them. His face was a mask of self-doubt and exhaustion. Robinson could only imagine what might be going through the American's head—all that *could* be going through his head. From his newly discovered Nephilim heritage to the guilt at having deceived his friends into coming to this place (at least two of them dying as a result), and then all the swirling gusto of being in love… He had a lot going on, and Robinson wondered if—

But his thought was decapitated by Jackson's sudden stare, as if he'd felt his mind being probed and didn't particularly like it. Whether Jackson could see his eyes or not, Robinson averted his gaze all the same. Clearing his throat, he reached into his pocket and took out a piece of raw meat.

Jackson saw Robinson look away, and knew what he'd been thinking. He was thinking the same things himself.

He looked down at the blood drying on his hands and thought about the violence that had overtaken him. It was no mystery, really. He knew what had triggered it. He'd had similar episodes in the past, when he felt that Denise had been threatened. And it was the thought of what these men might've done to Robyn had they managed to get their hands on her that set him off this time—scenes that had quickly nested in his mind's eye the fuel driving his fists. He flexed his fingers, feeling the soreness set in, and was suddenly reminded of one particular time that rage had overtaken him. But he quickly pushed that memory away. He'd spent too long trying to forget that ever happened to stare it in the face now.

He let his eyes drift over to Robyn. She was standing next to Paul, both of them looking out into the forest, their backs toward him.

She'd told him to stop.

Yet he wasn't sure how to interpret the feeling behind the command. Was it disgust that jettisoned that word out of her mouth? Was it fear? Because not that long ago, their roles had been reversed—him telling her to stop hacking away at the dead Nephilim they'd killed outside the house. But these weren't giants, were they? They were men, and maybe even men from some other time and place.

He was still staring at Robyn, trying to figure out her mind, when Paul looked back over his shoulder and flashed a taunting smile at him. Standing arm to arm with Robyn, he moved his hand down, pretending to press it against the small of her back. Then his smile grew, and he moved his hand lower.

Jackson flipped him the finger.

Getting to his feet and walking over to him, Robinson said, "Those guys all had six fingers. Just in case you weren't sure."

The skin around his eyes relaxed, and he felt some trepidation lift from his shoulders.

"Paul just likes seeing you squirm. Guess he's still upset about…" He trailed off. It was none of his business.

"Thanks for telling me."

Robinson lifted the brim of his hat with a finger and squinted, analytic-like. "You alright?"

"Yeah." But after a couple of seconds, he started laughing. He was so far from being alright.

* * * *

"There it is," Robyn whispered.

From their vantage point, the cave resembled the opening of a mine, rock blasted open by dynamite a long time ago. It was held in a frozen embrace by a tree-studded rise on the other side of a flowered meadow.

"Where do you think it leads?" Robinson asked.

Paul pushed past him. "Only one way to find out," he muttered. He walked on through the thinning forest until reaching the edge of the tree line.

The field itself was eerie, its tall grass unmoving, the thousands of red flowers like splotches of blood sprayed from the sky. A hundred yards separated his position from the cave, and covering that distance with no cover wasn't an appealing thought. He saw a worn path stretching across the field, coming from the tree line to his left and leading straight into the mouth of the cave. He had no trouble imagining the two women being dragged along that line, kicking and flailing. "Looks inviting," he mumbled as the others caught up to him.

Jackson kneeled beside Paul, shifting the weight of the backpack, and studied the scene himself. Though the cave was only a football field's length across from them, the length of the field was much greater, and the trees surrounding the meadow were too distant to detect anything that might be waiting for them.

"What do you think?" Robinson asked no one in particular.

"You two go," Jackson said, indicating him and Paul. "We'll cover you."

"Gee, thanks," Paul responded, pushing off the tree and readying the rifle.

"Feels strange," Robyn whispered.

Paul nodded his agreement. It did feel strange, like the house Jackson had found…like Naga Hills. He studied Robyn for a moment, the way her golden hair was pulled back in a ponytail, the way her sparkling eyes seemed to shine from out of the mud mask, the way she stood there with the assault rifle pressed beneath her rising chest… Even covered in mud she was stunning. He kicked the thought away before it could lay eggs in his head, and moved his eyes to Robinson. "Ready, Crusoe?"

Robinson took a deep breath, stealing himself. "Let's get it over with."

Paul knew that Jackson would have preferred to have him stay behind and provide cover with him, but there was no way he was going to put Robyn out there as a walking target. The effective range of the AK-47 was about three hundred and eighty yards, and Paul could pretty much put down anything that walked into that window. But Robyn? He wasn't sure if she could shoot the broad side of a barn if it hiked itself up to its knees and started running at her. Which didn't do much for his sense of confidence as he and Robinson stepped out into the high, still grass.

"Watch to the right," Jackson whispered to Robyn, his own eye peering through the iron sights of the Kalashnikov. Over the last three months, he'd taught her how to zero the rifle, and she'd done a relatively good job learning how to compensate for wind and elevation. "Adjust the rear sight to two." The tree lines to their left and right were over three hundred yards away, but he wasn't going to have her wasting ammunition by trying to hit anything at that distance. He wasn't even sure she would hit anything over two hundred yards, but their main purpose was to provide cover fire, which he felt she could do rather effectively if needed. "Don't shoot at anything until it gets within that two hundred range we practiced with."

She nodded, sliding the rear sight forward to the number two setting. The far end of the field was slightly elevated, so she quickly gave a little twist to the front sight, screwing it down. There was no wind, so she didn't bother with drumming it left or right. She held the stock firmly against her shoulder, her finger resting on the cool steel trigger, her left hand cradling the wooden fore-grip.

Jackson was tracking Paul and Robinson from the corner of his vision, and could see them half-crouched, sweeping their own rifles back and forth.

Naga Hills…

There was an electricity that seemed to be hovering over the field, tingling his scalp, and he knew the cave was an open throat into something sinister. He had a vision of its mouth closing on Paul and Robinson and the hill swallowing them into hell. He briefly flicked his eyes to the sky, half-expecting to see that black cloud stirring above and the closet demon descending.

Nothing but blue skies.

He shivered despite the sweat dripping down the nape of his neck.

They were in the middle of the meadow, the grass brushing their thighs and the flowers staring at them. They were out in the open, the nearest cover back where they'd started from.

"Almost there," Robinson whispered.

Paul knew he was talking to himself, trying to keep from bolting the rest of the way. Which might not be a bad idea, actually. Except, of course, for the foreboding energy that was spilling out of the cave like exhaust from an old muffler.

A sound exploded from their left.

Spinning, they swung their rifles around and saw a cloud of birds come gushing out of the green flesh of the distant trees. The black flock flowed upward like a trail of dark blood in zero gravity, sweeping, spreading through the sky, blotting out the sun. The shadow cast was long and liquid, slithering across the meadow and right over them. They could only watch the birds—

No. Not birds. *Bats*. Thousands of them. Maybe tens of thousands of them.

"Ever seen bats on the island?" Paul asked, watching them with even more unease.

Robinson swallowed, eyes locked on the flapping, vampire-like wings. "Never."

The bats screamed in one unified, nerve-shattering chorus as they raced across the clearing.

Paul looked back to the tree line, wondering what had sent the tree rats into flight.

Jackson and Robyn both swung their aim to the left of the field, picking up the black stream pouring across the sky as Paul and Robinson stood motionless beneath it. *Move*, Jackson thought, looking back to the trees. Something was there, hiding. He could feel it.

Paul drifted to his left, Robinson to his right. Both were leaving the bats behind and proceeding to opposite sides of the cave's gaping mouth. They had their AK-47s aimed straight into its throat, ready for anything that might come hurling out of it. The hole was so dark, Paul wondered if it was a cave at all. Maybe it was like one of those portals they'd seen on the temple walls…or the closet in that house. Maybe they'd step into it only to suddenly be elsewhere.

They positioned themselves on either side of the opening, their backs pressed against the rock, their eyes sweeping the meadow. After another leery glimpse at the bats, Paul gave a big wave to Jackson, signaling them to proceed.

Jackson met Robyn's eyes, and they held each other's gaze for longer than necessary, as if they were both waiting for the other to say something that would break them from the spell they'd been under. But neither said anything. Finally, Jackson just asked if she was ready.

"Yeah."

He reached out and grabbed her arm in what he meant to be a reassuring gesture, a message that they were in this together and that it would all be okay. Her strong, lean muscles flexed beneath his grasp, but she didn't pull away.

He leaned over and kissed her on the temple, the warmth of her skin seeping into his lips and spreading throughout his body. What the hell, right? They were probably about to die anyway.

He left the trees behind before she could react, not wanting to face her protest if indeed that was how she was going to respond. As he walked through the field, her close behind, his heart thumped in his chest. The air was thick with invisible energy, and he couldn't help associating the cave ahead of them with the Dagobah cave in *Empire Strikes Back* (the last movie he'd seen in the theater with his father). In that instance, Yoda had told Luke that the only thing in the cave was what he would take in with him, but Jackson didn't think that would be the case here. The cave was a sort of nexus, he could feel it, but he didn't think it was a metaphoric one like in the movie.

The bats continued to fly overhead, a long and black flowing rope that now connected opposite tree lines, their squeaking cries both irritating and unnerving. Half-convinced he was walking to his death, that the cave was a mouth to eternity, Jackson began to revisit the thoughts he'd had on the beach earlier, and—

Robyn suddenly went streaking past him, sprinting the hundred yards to Paul and Robinson.

Jackson swore, clenched his teeth, and took off after her, his pack slamming against his back every other step. Taking it slow had worked for Paul and Robinson, their movement not seeming to attract any attention, whereas her quick movements would pull on the periphery of any nearby eyes. Then again, maybe she had the right idea. Maybe, in this place, it was more important to get from point A to B as quickly as possible.

They made it across the meadow and past the bats without incident. Leaning against the rock face of the hill, they bent over gasping for air as Paul and Robinson continued to cover them.

Paul caught Jackson's eye and flashed him a "what the hell was that" look.

Jackson shook his head and turned, squaring up with the cave's mouth.

The swarm of bats disappeared into the forest on the other side of the meadow, their shrieking voices abruptly silent.

The eerie silence returned.

Paul spit. "You ready for this?"

A brief, unsure expression passed between them, none of them having any idea of what to expect. They could take one step into the cave and find themselves in the center of a Nephilim war room. Or a plague-soaked Europe, a Nazi concentration camp, or First Time itself for that matter. There was only one way to find out.

Jackson went first.

Ten feet into the cave, Jackson turned back to make sure the meadow was still in view. It was. He stopped and pulled the backpack off his back. Reaching inside, he began removing torches.

Paul stepped past him, his eyes straining to see into the darkness and looking for an excuse to pull the trigger.

Suddenly, the walls around them began blinking to life.

THREE

September 21, 2011. The Cave. Morning.

The blinking lights stopped them in their tracks, emanating from the sides of the cave. When finally the flashing stopped and the light remained constant, they could see that the bright glow was coming from long tubes attached to the walls. They seemed to have flickered to life the same way fluorescents in an empty hospital wing or classroom blink on when someone enters it.

Paul had seen similar bulbs lining the corridors leading to the pyramid, and Johnny had told them of the ones he'd seen in the temple. Paul was sure that Jackson was about to launch into a lecture on Egyptian hieroglyphics and their portrayal of such technology. But it didn't come. Instead, Jackson just stood there in silence with the rest of them. Paul studied him, his features awash in the artificial glow, and reminded himself that this wasn't the Jackson he'd known over the years. *Then who the hell is it?* Was it Jackson on the yellow brick road to Henry's heaven, or was it Jackson the Titan? Jackson in love, or Jackson the human guinea pig of the gods?

"Electricity," Robinson whispered in amazement, breaking the silence.

And here it was. If Jackson was going to snap out of his fugue state and return to his old self, then this was surely the moment. It was the perfect set, and he could easily spike it with all the stuff Chadwick had told them about—electroplating, ultrasonic drills, aluminum… But, no, the ball soared over his head and went into the net. Paul spit and began following the long lightbulbs of antiquity into yet another unknown.

As they walked farther and farther into the cave, the dirt beneath their feet began to give way to rock, and the walls gradually swooped apart. The ceiling was high enough to be invisible, the tubes' light not able to penetrate its height.

"We're descending," Robyn whispered.

Paul looked up into the darkness hovering above them like a starless night sky, and immediately imagined big vampire bats hanging upside down all along the unseen ceiling. Maybe it was best they couldn't see what was up there. He knew they'd been descending from the beginning, that they were getting farther away from the ceiling and not the other way around. After all, the hill the cave was cut through wasn't that tall.

"How far do you think it goes?" Robinson whispered, the concern in his voice suggesting that they might not get back if they traveled too far.

"No way to tell," Jackson answered.

Paul looked back behind them, the entrance no longer visible. "Maybe one of us should've stayed behind as a lookout."

"Maybe," Jackson agreed flatly. "Might as well keep on going now though."

"Might as well."

More rock outcroppings started coming up out of the ground and out of the walls, and the light that struck them cast haunted figures across their path. All Paul could think about was Naga Hills.

Robyn stopped, tilting her head toward the ground. "Wait." She seemed to be listening for something. "Do you hear that?"

Jackson took a step toward her, shaking his head. "What is it?"

She looked at Robinson.

He strained to hear but ultimately shook his head too. "I don't hear anything."

"I do," Paul said, and he walked straight past them. The tunnel continued for another fifty yards and then began turning at a slight bend, the walls narrowing around him. He followed the leftward bend around and around and around and—

He stopped.

The rest of them came around the long bend quickly and stumbled to a stop alongside him.

"What in the world…" Robinson took off his hat, his eyes wide at the sight before them.

The tunnel dipped steeply and then continued to slope down into a scene that seemed straight from *Journey to the Center of the Earth.*

At the bottom of the slope, the walls shot away again, accommodating an enormous space that was filled with giant plant life. A small stream flowed lazily through the center of it, and it was the sound of its trickling that Paul and Robyn had heard. Giant mushrooms as tall as trees stood throughout the bizarre expanse, other tall flowers (red, blue, and green) huddled beneath their caps, staring up at their gills like little boys looking up ladies' skirts. The whole scene was odd, as if they'd just wandered onto the set of a 1966 *Star Trek* episode. There was a luminescence that glowed throughout the alien landscape, lighting it up like midday despite the apparent lack of the bulbous tubes that had accompanied them here.

"Where the hell are we?" Paul muttered, looking up and then turning to see if maybe they'd stumbled through a portal. Satisfied that they hadn't, he began searching for the light source.

Understanding what he was doing, Jackson said, "Has to be some kind of phosphorescent mineral in the rocks…activated by heat."

"Has to be," Paul muttered. Then he led them all down onto the spongy soil that ran like carpet across the ground.

"Listen," Robyn whispered, motioning for them to be quiet again.

Paul tried to hear over the trickling stream, wondering what she'd detected this time. Between Robinson's vision and her hearing, he thought they could give the NSA a run for their money. And then he heard it too. "English."

Jackson cocked his head, eyes squinting as he strained to hear it for himself. He nodded slowly. "Where's it coming from?"

Paul led them to the foot of the stream and beside a mushroom stalk that was as wide as a cedar trunk, its umbrellaed cap hovering like a flying saucer twenty feet above them. The voices were louder here, though still undecipherable. Paul continued to lead them beside the stream, following its current.

It led them to a rock wall, the stream pooling against it and swirling clockwise before slipping through a crevice and descending into a yet another level of the subterranean world.

They could make out certain words now, the voices even louder, but still they couldn't tell where they were coming from.

"Where are they?" Robyn whispered.

Jackson walked up to the wall and began moving to his left, tracing it with his hand. After a dozen feet, his hand disappeared, slipping behind the wall. He stopped, stood back, and motioned for everyone to come over.

There was an overlapping gap in the wall, hidden in the shadow of a mushroom tree. It was about three feet wide and stretched from floor to ceiling.

"You have next?" a deep, harrowing voice asked, though the one that answered seemed even larger.

"Bring me the dark one," it echoed.

"Must be another chamber below," Jackson said.

Once again, Paul took the lead by stepping past him and leaning into the opening.

"Can you see anything?"

He shook his head and moved farther into the darkness. And then he disappeared altogether.

Jackson was about to follow after him, when Paul's face suddenly reappeared.

"There's a turn five feet in. You can see light from below," he explained.

"Can you see who's down there?" asked Robyn.

"No." But he didn't have to see them to know who (or what) they were. He'd heard them speaking before.

Suddenly, the loud sounds of a struggling woman came barreling up the narrow tunnel, passing Paul and echoing into the mushroom forest.

Paul turned back toward the screaming and yelling, the rest of them pressing in after him. Amongst the screams, they could hear the smacking of flesh and saw in their mind's eye the captive slapping at her captors.

Paul looked back to Robyn. The dim light from the lower cavern barely touched her face, but he could make out the emotion burning in her eyes—rage, horror, determination, and hopelessness all swirling in a choreographed dance around her pupils. He moved his gaze to Robinson, but he just looked pissed. Genesis chapter six and the Book of Enoch was being reenacted down there, only this time there was no willingness on behalf of the Nephilim's "choosing." Whatever bewitching power the Fallen had had over the daughters of men, allowing them to "take any of whom they chose," it was certainly absent now. Unfortunately, judging from the tormenting laughs now stifling the sounds of resistance, the Nephilim didn't seem to mind.

Just as Paul was about to confer with Jackson on a possible course of action, Robyn shot to her feet and charged into the narrow corridor, slamming him into the wall and crushing his mangled hand as she squeezed through. He reached out, trying to stop her with his good hand, but she was too quick and slipped past. He swore, shaking his hand, and watched helplessly as she slid beneath the opening ahead of them and dropped out of sight, falling into the lower level below.

A split-second of shock fastened the rest of them to the floor as they all tried to comprehend Robyn's sudden and reckless impulsiveness. But once it passed, the three of them were sliding through the same opening and falling into the light right behind her.

The drop was about ten feet, and they all hit hard, toppling into each other, their rifles bumping heads and elbows.

Recovering, Paul looked around, his eyes sweeping fast. The area here was smaller than the one they'd just come from and contained significantly less plant life. The stream they'd followed here was spilling down the side of the wall in a waterfall before continuing across the room and splitting it into two equal halves. It flowed into the wall on the right side of the chamber and disappeared into another crevice, spilling down into yet more subterranean levels.

There were no bulbs on these wall, the illumination conceivably being generated the same way as in the mushroom forest now above them. And standing there in the light, on the other side of the stream, were three naked giants. Tattoos and branded flesh covered their enormous bodies, suggesting they were part of Osiris' offspring that he'd left behind. They were huddled together, their backs to them.

Too preoccupied with their prisoner to notice the four intruders dropping down into the room, and then even Robyn's careless splashing across the water, they were completely taken by surprise by Robyn unloading her AK-47 on them.

At least they would have been had she fired. Just before pulling the trigger, however, the giants stepped away from each other and revealed the object of their sport. Robyn stopped short on their side of the water, Paul sliding to a knee beside her. By the time Jackson and Robinson joined them, kneeling down at Paul's side, the giants had still not detected them.

The flailing, screaming woman went down hard beneath a heavy blow. As she lifted her head, eyes peering helplessly through sweaty strands of black hair, she spotted the four of them standing there. Her attention became so ensnared by their sudden presence that she didn't even react to the large hands ripping the clothes off her body.

But her sudden indifference made the giants stop and turn their heads, pieces of her clothes still in their hands, and look for whatever had captured her gaze.

Paul knew Robyn wasn't going to wait, nor should she. Now that the Puree was on the ground at the giants' feet, she was out of the line of fire. But the third giant was already bending over and lifting the girl by her hair when the first bullet flew down the chromed barrel at 2,350 feet per second.

Robyn shouted with rage and kept the trigger engaged. The assault rifle jerked back and forth in her hands, shells flying everywhere, the sound deafening.

When Paul, Jackson, and Robinson added their firepower to the attack, the closest two giants disappeared beneath clouds of red mist. As they jerked and bucked beneath the storms of bullets, the third giant, positioned behind its two fallen brothers, raised the girl into the air by her hair. Her body dangled from its massive hand, her legs kicking, her hands trying in vain to pull the six-fingered vice apart.

By the time the closest giant crashed to its knees and opened a line of fire to the third giant, it was too late. Even as Paul aimed for its head, it grabbed the girl's thigh with its free hand. Four bullets left spurting marks across its chest, but they did nothing to stop the Nephilim from flinging its arms apart, the girl's hair in one hand and her thigh in the other.

Her head flew off in one direction, spinning like a ball, her hair trailing like a black, whipping tail, while the rest of her went clumsily in the other.

Robyn cried out with a savage grief that echoed throughout the room, hot tears spitting down her face. Looking down, she replaced the empty magazine with one from the back pocket of her shorts, ramming it home and pulling back the slide. When she looked back up, blinking through the stinging emotion, two of the giants were gone and only the one on its knees was left. It was cradling the contents of its stomach in its hands and wearing a look of uncertain dread on its face.

Three huge swords had been left leaning against the wall behind the scene. Jackson walked over to them, selected one at random, and dragged it back to the kneeling giant, the sound of the blade scratching the stone floor echoing after him. Even kneeling, its rear end resting on its calves, the giant was three feet taller than Jackson. He walked up behind it and lifted the heavy blade, pushing its tip into the base of the giant's neck. Once he had enough pressure applied and the sword wasn't going to fall, he shifted his right hand to a reverse grip on the handle and wrapped his left arm underneath and around the hilt. Then he pushed forward off his toes and drove the sword at a forty-five-degree angle up through the giant's neck. The blade was six feet long, and twelve inches of it slipped out the front of its neck beneath its chin before Jackson ran out of leverage. When he let go of the sword, the weight of the sword pulled the giant backward until the handle was touching the ground and the giant's head was tilted back, its soulless eyes staring at the ceiling.

But that wasn't good enough for Robyn. She walked around the body, used the sword like a ramp, and climbed up to the giant's head. She grabbed its hair and began twisting and pulling, the muscles in her neck and shoulders rippling beneath her skin. The width of the blade had all but severed the head completely, and when Robyn jumped off the sword, still holding the giant's hair, she finished the job, bringing its head with her. With a loud, agonized cry, she swung the huge head in a hammer throw and launched it across the room.

It bounced once and landed in the stream, bobbing along in the shallow water, drifting with the gentle current. It hit the far wall and began spinning in an endless spiral, circling round and round, too large to follow the water down through the opening in the rock.

Jackson stared at her and wondered if there was a difference in what he'd done earlier and what she'd just done now. In degree of savagery, maybe not. But this was a giant that had been abusing her sister and had just participated in ripping her in two right in front of her. The victim of his rage had been a man he wasn't even sure of at the time, a man who had done nothing but defend himself from attack. The fact that they'd all turned out to have six fingers was of little consequence.

Robyn was standing there, her eyes wide and unbelieving, incapable of taking them off her friend's face. It had bounced off the wall and rolled to a stop, tangled in its hair, with one bloodshot eye staring up at her.

Jackson grabbed her shoulder and tried moving her along, but she pulled away from him.

"We need to chase them down before they get help," he said to her.

"We don't have time to wait for her!" Paul shouted, already running after the other two giants.

Jackson knew he was right, and left her standing there.

Robinson, with tears streaking through the mud on his own face, called back over his shoulder for Robyn to follow.

They were running through another tunnel, more glowing bulbs accompanying them. They ran and ran, but like the temple halls before, the tunnel just seemed to go on forever. They weren't going to be able to stop the giants in time. Wherever they were going, they were probably already there. Best thing to do was turn back and try to get out while—

The tunnel suddenly ended, coming to a stop at a huge metal gate.

FOUR

September 21, 2011. The Cave. Morning.

Paul slowed to a jog as he approached what appeared to be a portcullis. Its latticed gate stood from floor to ceiling, standing at about thirty feet and spanning the entire width of the tunnel. Long spikes had been welded into its metal frame, racing up and down the gate and spaced every two feet. The spikes were pointing at Paul, the portcullis serving as an entrance to a place where not everyone was welcome. Huge footprints in the dirt ran beneath his legs and through the giant gate. He spit as Robinson and Jackson came up beside him.

Robinson leaned his head back and took in the medieval-looking gate with wide, hesitant eyes. "I think we need to go."

But Jackson stepped forward, trying to get a glimpse through one of the many square openings.

"Don't think you're gonna fit," Paul said.

Jackson didn't respond, just walked up to the gate, stretching out his hand and running it along one of the huge, three-foot spikes. He put his face into one of the latticed windows and then looked back. "There's another one."

Paul's eyes narrowed. "A killing area?"

"Seems like it."

Robinson shook his head, not understanding.

Jackson explained. "Medieval castles often had two portcullises to the main entrance. Sometimes they'd leave the one in front open and then lower it after their enemies walked past, trapping them between the gates. Archers would then fire arrows through slits in the walls and openings above." He stepped back from the gate, still puzzled. "A kill zone."

Robyn finally joined them, her eyes swollen, her cheeks wet. "How does it open?" she whispered.

Jackson regarded her for a second, then shook his head. "That's just it. Hoisting chains attached to the top of the gates run up to a geared windlass above the gateway. There's all kinds of hoisting equipment up there somewhere." He was staring at the top of the gate again. "Has to be huge for a gate this heavy."

"You ever seen anything like this before?" Paul asked Robinson.

He shook his head. "Never."

"I don't think this was Osiris," Robyn added, wiping her tears with the back of her hand and making pink streaks beneath her eyes.

"Neither do I." Jackson took another step back. "How'd they get through the gate so fast?"

Before anyone could wrestle with the implication of his question, a sudden, unfamiliar voice cut through the room.

"Robyn?" The sound of the voice was so fragile, so thin, that it seemed to drift through the air like a soap bubble about to pop.

They looked around, trying to locate its source. The walls on either side of the portcullis were covered in shadow, the rock pregnant with handfuls of protruding growths that shattered the light and concealed the two corners from view.

"Ruth?" Robyn whispered back, peering into the darkness on the left side of the gate.

A woman appeared, slipping out of the dark as if birthed right out of the wall. Shadowed arms reached out after her as if pleading for her to stay, but they fell away beneath the light.

Her clothes were torn and dirty. Fresh blood painted her neck and exposed shoulders. Her blond hair was a tangled mess, her feet bare and bruised. She limped as she walked, distributing her weight to the outsides of her feet. Her left arm hung awkwardly, probably out of joint. And though her eyes were desperate and terrified, they all saw a spark of hope flicker to life when she recognized that the mud-masked person before her was Robyn.

They ran to each other, colliding in an emotion-filled embrace.

The woman named Ruth immediately began sobbing against Robyn's shoulder while digging her fingers into the flesh of her bare arms. Her body rocked with convulsions, and she crumpled to her knees, pulling Robyn down with her. She buried her head in Robyn's ample bosom and clung to her as if she were a dream that would dissolve if she let go. Robyn held her tight as she cried.

Robinson walked over and placed a hand on Ruth's neck. Her head flew back at his touch, and after recognition dawned in her eyes, she let go of Robyn and stood. She threw herself into Robinson's arms.

Paul stepped forward and cut through the reunion. "Where'd they go?" he asked Ruth.

She considered him for a second, her dripping eyes looking over Robinson's shoulder, and then slowly raised a finger at the wall on the other side of the tunnel.

Paul exchanged a doubtful look with Jackson, and the two of them crossed in front of the gate, walking to the other side of the tunnel.

"Are you okay?" Robyn asked Ruth.

Releasing Robinson from her embrace, she took a step back and stared at Robyn, searching for words that might express what she'd endured over the last three months. But words weren't necessary, if even possible, because her eyes told all. But before Robyn could respond to the horror she'd just intimated, she whispered, "Priscilla… They came and took her."

Robyn nodded and had to bite her lip as more tears spilled from her blue eyes.

"What the hell is this?" Paul's voice echoed.

Robinson released Ruth and looked over to where Paul and Jackson were standing. "What?"

But they didn't answer, just kept staring down at something on the ground.

Robinson walked over to them, and Robyn took Ruth's hand.

"They went in there?" Jackson asked Ruth, pointing.

Stretched out across the ground and running up the side of the wall was what looked like a black curtain. It was extremely dark in the corner, where the wall and the floor met, ripping a line in the rock about ten feet long. The blackness seemed to lighten the farther away the tear extended, growing into a dark gray about seven feet up the wall and four feet across the ground.

Ruth nodded.

"They didn't go through the gate?" Paul asked, confused.

"No."

"Then what are the footprints?" he asked, pointing to the traffic beneath the latticed grille.

"The others," she said, her voice barely above a whisper.

"What others?"

She shook her head. "They bring us here to…impregnate us. But—" she started crying again "—they usually end up killing us in the process."

"Who?" Robyn asked, wanting a list of names.

"There's no time," Paul said, grabbing her arm. "We need to get out of here."

Jackson swung the pack off his back and opened it. Then he ejected the magazine from his AK and used his thumb to slide its three remaining bullets into the bag. He took out a new magazine and rammed it into the rifle before setting it aside. Standing there with the empty mag in his hand, he stared into the dark hole. And tossed it in.

It vanished as soon as it touched the space—just blinked out as if suddenly erased.

He looked at Paul, both of them having seen this before—in the closet of the pink house and on the walls in Osiris' temple. The only question was where it led.

"Have they gone in there before?" Jackson asked.

Ruth shook her head. "It was smaller before, just a small crack in the floor. It's gotten bigger over the last weeks."

Robyn stared at her. "How many times have they brought you here?"

More tears ran down her face. "I don't know."

Hearing that Ruth had been taken here multiple times for the sole purpose of being impregnated, Paul could only curse under his breath. But Robinson began pacing, rage pumping through his veins and wanting an outlet.

"So this could go anywhere, then." Jackson studied it. "It could be like the henges and lead to some other spot on the island, or…it could be like the closet and lead to hell."

"Or maybe neither," Paul answered. "If it's getting bigger, spreading, then maybe it's a glitch. But whatever it is or isn't, unless you're gonna hop in after them, can we please get the hell out of here?"

He turned and faced Ruth. "Is anyone else here with you now?"

"Only Priscilla."

He looked at the others. "Let's go."

"But what about Priscilla?" Ruth cried, Robyn leading her back through the tunnel and away from the spiked gate. No one answered her.

When they reached the dead giant, Jackson and Robinson both used their bodies to maneuver Ruth away from where Priscilla's decapitated body was sprawled. Their efforts worked, and Ruth made it across the stream without incident.

Paul was in the rear, and after Ruth had gotten across the stream and he was sure no one was looking, he reached down and snagged Priscilla's head off the ground. With no time for anything else, he tied her hair through his back belt loop. Her head bounced against the back of his legs as he hurried to catch up with the others.

Ruth led them through a hidden pathway that the giants used (saving them from having to climb back up through the hole they'd fallen through) and had them back in the long bulb-lined corridor in no time. A pinprick of light appeared ahead of them and then continued to grow with each step. A minute later, they were standing at the cave's opening and staring out into the open field.

They stood behind the line of natural light that swept across the ground as if stepping over it might trigger an ambush from the trees across the meadow. They aimed their rifles over the tall, unmoving grass of the clearing, looking for any signs of danger. And although it seemed quiet, Paul had no trouble imagining a nocked arrow with their names on it.

But Ruth mustn't have had any such concern, because upon seeing the open freedom before her, she took off for it, crossing over the line and embracing her emancipation with reckless abandon.

Robyn reached out to stop her, but the girl's movement was too quick, too sudden, and she managed to slip away from all of them. About ten yards into that freedom, however, she realized that she was alone. Slowing to a stop, she turned and looked back to the cave. Confusion pinched her face as she tried to understand why they weren't with her, and then understanding dawned, and she realized her mistake.

"Come back," Jackson whispered, looking past her to the distant tree line.

Her eyes darted back and forth, searching her surroundings. Feeling suddenly vulnerable, she crossed her arms over her chest. She didn't want to go back to the cave. *Couldn't.* But—

"Come on," Robyn urged, her eyes wide with dreaded anticipation.

Paul turned to make sure nothing was coming up behind them.

Finally, Ruth took a step toward them.

"Come on, Ruth," Robinson pleaded, his own outstretched and pleading.

Robyn took off, intent on dragging her back, but she only got two steps away before Jackson's hand clamped on her arm and stopped her in her tracks. "Let me go!" she pleaded, wrestling with him. "Let go of me!" When she realized he wasn't going to, she turned her attention back to Ruth. "Run, Ruth! Come on! Ru—"

Ruth's neck, tall and strong in her tattered V-neck, blossomed into a roselike display of red—petals of flesh peeling back around a sudden, protruding stigma. She blinked as her mind raced to make sense of what just happened. Slowly, her eyes drifted down and focused on the arrowhead sticking out of her neck and hovering in the air before her. She collapsed to her knees as Robyn's scream echoed throughout the clearing. Her fingers danced frantically up and down the arrow's shaft, unsure what to do about it.

Paul and Robinson stepped out of the cave's mouth and sent a volley of cover shots into the surrounding woods as Jackson and Robyn raced out to her. They grabbed her under her arms and dragged her back into the artificial light of the cave.

The lights blinked twice and then went out.

An arrow streaked past Paul's face, carving a deep furrow into his cheek. "Great," he mumbled and pressed a hand against what would be another scar on his face.

Jackson moved Ruth onto her side and quickly snapped the arrow just above the fletching. He knew he shouldn't remove it, but he could tell it was blocking her airway, and it wasn't like there was a hospital anywhere nearby. Besides, he knew she was already dead. The only choice she had was whether she suffocated or bled to death. He thought bleeding would be the more merciful way to go (after all, how many people intent on suicide suffocated themselves?), so he slid the long shaft out of the wrecked hole, leaving a shattered, spurting mess beneath her chin. Arterial bleeding would quickly result in shock, and then she would be gone. With no pressure points available between the neck and heart, there was nothing they could do but watch her life spray out of her.

Robyn sat beside her and took her head in her lap. She rocked back and forth while caressing her hair. "Shhh…" she whispered. "It's okay…" She wiped the tears from Ruth's paling face even as her own joined them.

The arrowhead was so wide that it had left precious little flesh behind.

"Finally…" Ruth whispered. "Finally…leave…this…place…" She squeezed Robyn's hand as her eyes closed and she became still. The stream of squirting blood grew shorter. Then, with one last moment of consciousness, her eyes snapped back open, and she grabbed Robyn's shoulder. "They're not them," she said. And then her eyes closed for the last time, the blood now just a trickle, her body completely relaxed.

Robyn cried and whispered through quivering lips, "'Where, O death, is your victory? Where, O death, is your sting? Let nothing move you…'"

A noise came from behind them, rattling out of the cave.

"We need to get out of here," Paul said.

Robinson crouched down beside Robyn and placed a firm hand on her shoulder. Tears were drowning his own eyes. "Come on," he whispered. "Nothing we can do for her now."

"I'm not leaving her here!" she shouted. Her voice echoed back and forth.

"Robyn," he started to say.

"I'm not leaving them here to be…"

Without warning, Paul bent over, grabbed Ruth's lifeless body under the arms, and swung her up and over his shoulder. Her body flopped awkwardly as he turned to Jackson and Robinson. "Light it up."

"What about Priscilla?" Robyn asked, standing.

Paul turned toward the opening and let Robyn get a glimpse of his back, of Priscilla's head swaying from his waistline. "I grabbed what I could," he said over his shoulder.

Before she could respond, Robinson raised the AK and fired three deafening shots at two men who had just appeared out of the darkness behind them. Lowering the rifle, he took a step toward the crumpled shadows, blinking the tears out of his eyes and trying to make out who they were. "What're they wearing?" he whispered.

A hand jerked him away, Jackson's voice crying out, "Let's go!"

He turned and went for the daylight.

Paul fired the AK-47 singlehandedly, his other hand busy securing Ruth's body over his shoulder. The weapon rocked back and forth in his grasp, veins ripping through his bicep and forearm. He moved as quickly as he could through the tall grass, more arrows flying his way and barely missing their mark, before he was out of the field and back into the woods with the others.

* * * *

Ten minutes later, satisfied they weren't being followed, they stopped to rest beside the stream. Paul set Ruth's body down beside a tree and stretched his aching body. As he laced his fingers behind his head, arching his back, Robyn whipped out her knife and sliced his belt loop in half. Priscilla's head fell from his waist, and she caught it before it could touch the ground.

"Hey, watch it!" Paul protested, his fingers probing the tear in his jeans. Satisfied that the blade hadn't nicked his skin, he spit. "You're welcome."

She pulled her shirt up over her head and wrapped it around her friend's head. Standing there in what could've been her mother's bra, she stared lasers at him.

Jackson found himself staring at Robyn's sweaty body, at all the muscles rippling beneath her shiny skin as she sucked air into her lungs. When she looked away from Paul, she caught his gaze. Their eyes met briefly, and then she turned and took Ruth's head farther upstream.

"Never seen anything like this before," Robinson proclaimed from the stream's bank. The shallow water circled his ankles as he examined the broken arrow from Ruth's neck. Sunlight drifted down through the canopy and reflected off the dark, obsidian-like arrowhead. It was broadhead in its design, but looked like something from the future rather than the past. The head itself resembled a harpoon of some sort, but below the head were eight winglike blades that fanned away from the arrow's shaft, two pairs on each of the arrow's four sides. Robinson pressed down on one of the wings, and it moved in toward the shaft. Springs.

"What the hell?" Paul walked into the water and took it from him, looking it over for himself. "This wasn't made here."

They all looked at each other, thinking of the iron gate, the footprints that didn't belong to the giants, and contemplated Ruth's last words: *they're not them.*

FIVE

September 21, 2011. Afternoon. Bermuda.

Paul stared out over the ocean from the top of the grassy hill and watched as the wind slashed white lines into the blue expanse. The surface seemed alive, a massive living organism—rolling, swaying, breathing. The midday sun accented the horizon with a blinding stroke, but Paul knew what was out there even if he couldn't see it.

The ship.

It'd been weeks since he'd last seen it, but he was sure it was still out there, trapped within the domed borders of this prison just like them. If it was circling the island, then he didn't know when he'd see it again, since they had no idea how big their island was now.

He couldn't stop thinking about the ship or the little girl that haunted it. About Hunter's voice calling out from within the theater. About the guy, Daniel, that they'd left behind there. About all the different doors and all their possibilities…

He continually thought about going back.

He looked down to his hands, at the arrow he was holding. It was something from a fantasy space opera. *Robin Hood 3000* or something. Maybe a steampunk rendering of *Knights of the Round Table*. But it didn't belong here, on this set. Nothing they'd seen before, not even the megalithic technologies Osiris had harnessed, hinted at anything like this. The girl's dying words kept swirling in his mind. *Who* wasn't them?

He looked up and tuned back in to the scene behind him, just catching the last shovelful of dirt landing on Ruth's body. Two fresh mounds now stood side by side in a growing line of others. And despite having only Priscilla's head to bury, they'd gone the whole way, carving out the entire six by four from the earth. Paul thought it was a waste of time and energy, but he held his peace.

Jared stood at the foot of the graves, an old and tattered Bible open in his hands. Paul couldn't hear the words being spoken from the Book, the wind at the top of the hill snatching them away before they could reach his ears, but he didn't care. "Death, where is thy sting?" and all that… He'd seen a lot of death, and no words he'd ever heard ever made a lick of difference when the big wasp of mortality came buzzin'. He understood the reason for believing in the hereafter, the future promise of a better world that made this one bearable, but he wasn't one of those believers. He preferred the truth straight up. Life was a joke without a punch line, an accident without a cause, a story without a plot, and a journey with no destination. You could try to sugarcoat it all you wanted, but he knew in his heart that all that awaited anyone was total oblivion. Or at least that was what he'd thought before the ship. Now there were holes being drilled into his certainty. Power drills in the hands of existential, paranormal operators. This place, the girl…

He studied the faces that stared down at the two mounds of dirt, observing their eyes, their tears. There were sixteen of them standing shoulder to shoulder, most of whom Paul knew from Jared's cave. Theo the Brit, Patrick, Colonel Sanders, Arkansas Joe, Hap, Pete the Norwegian, Li, Charles, Samuel… Their faces were filled with mixed thoughts and feelings. Abject despair at the loss, hope that there were others out there somewhere waiting to be rescued, fear that they wouldn't find them in time, and the horror of knowing what they'd been enduring for the last three months if they were alive.

He looked down at the arrow again. Diamond-tipped weapons were one thing, but this… He lifted his eyes and let them linger west, over what should be Bailey's Bay, and to the distant shapes of new mountains poking into the sky. *They're not them.*

A shadow fell over him.

"That gate," Jackson's voice started.

Paul squinted into the distance and nodded. "When do we go back?"

"Tonight."

* * * *

All the Purees had gathered at Jared's cave for a sort of wake after the burial on the hill. During the later stages of the assembly, Paul and Jackson had secretly slipped away, setting out for the New Territory as the sun sank beneath the earth, leaving streaks of red hues bleeding down the sky after it.

They moved through the familiar forest with ease, gliding like shadows in the twilight. By the time they reached the new land, the moon was a silver orb shimmering on the face of the water.

"Let's take five," Jackson said.

They sat and rechecked their rifles, neither of them overly concerned with the fact that they had no plan.

"You see the guys Robinson shot?" Paul asked.

"No."

"He said they were wearing strange clothes."

"You think they came from the other side of the gate?"

Paul shrugged, and Jackson studied his eyes. "What are you thinking?"

"I'm thinking maybe it's not a good idea to have those bulbs turn on and light us up. That we could get trapped in the kill zone. I'm thinking that I'd like to avoid that black hole that's growing down there."

"So what do you want to do?"

"Let's go around the cave, see what's on the other side."

"Copy that."

* * * *

They were back in the trees that skirted the meadow, the cave on the other side. It seemed more like days had passed rather than hours since they'd been here, but then the events on the island always complicated one's perception of time.

The moonlight shone off the cave's rock face, accenting its jagged edges. The entrance was dark, which could mean that there was nothing currently going on in there if the lights were motion activated. Or maybe someone had just flipped a switch earlier, and now there were hordes of six-fingered goblins crouching in wait for them.

Paul leaned forward, resting against a grassy swell that rose between two of the trees bordering the field. His eyes had adjusted to the scene before him like an old-time sniper in pre-night-vision days, and he set his gaze on the general area the arrows had come from earlier, waiting to detect movement in his periphery. He lay still for ten minutes before he was satisfied they were alone—or at least that there was no one out there moving. He turned his head to signal Jackson, who was a little farther up on the rise, his rifle covering the field. But before his eyes found Jackson, they saw something else off in the distance, up behind Jackson on a moonlit hill. There was no mistaking it. Not with the established context of this place. The silhouette was distinct and sharp, its edges hard, contrasting strokes.

It was her.

The girl.

"Paul," Jackson snapped in a whisper that shot down to him.

He blinked, looked to Jackson and then back to—

She was gone.

"What is it?" Jackson asked, maneuvering down the slope toward him.

He clenched his jaw, making the pain in his cheek flare up. "Nothing. Let's go."

But before he could get up, Jackson grabbed his shirt, fisting the open sleeve above his bicep and yanking on it. "Tell me."

Paul placed his damaged fingers over the hand Jackson was using to grip his shirt and slowly pulled it away. "It's not important."

"The hell it isn't."

"What do you want, Jack? You wanna play counselor? Go ahead. You can start us off with Denise."

Jackson stared into the glint of Paul's eyes.

"Oh, is that subject off the table, Jack?" He shoved him away. "Don't pretend you ain't got your own ghosts." He got to his feet and stepped over Jackson, moving along the inside of the tree line and out of the silver light. His eyes searched the shadows, looking not for the Fallen or alien demons, but for the little girl that he hadn't seen in months. He wondered what could've brought her ashore.

* * * *

Time was illusive, slippery, uncertain. It came and went, rewound and skipped forward. So much so that it was impossible to keep track of what was when and when was what. They'd stopped trying almost immediately, mostly to preserve what little sanity they still had left.

The ship. It was a time machine, a portal to different times and spaces.

Daniel stumbled over to the window. It was the same window he'd found Hunter standing at naked as a jaybird in some other time—past or future, he couldn't be sure anymore. He thought it was his past, but after so many bouts of déjà vu, he'd stopped figuring on anything. It was (or will be) where he had stood (or stands) next to Hunter and watched (or watches) the two Boston Whalers speed back to the island, leaving them behind. But there was no island now, just darkness suffocating the moon.

He turned away from the window and surveyed the room. He had to be careful, keep his guard up. They'd already killed the giant that had somehow managed to climb aboard, but "now" could be before "then." As they'd discovered already.

"I think it's okay," a shadow said.

Daniel jumped. "Stop doing that!"

"Sorry."

He turned and watched as Hunter walked into the silvery light streaming through the slanted windows. His black friend seemed to be approaching the border of normal, but he still had some ways to go. Not that he had a prior disposition by which to compare him since he hadn't really known him before the ship, but the guy he'd found (whenever that had been or would be) had been...something quite different. Lately, however, he seemed to be not so much something different. For example, he'd decided to start wearing clothes again. Yeah, whatever had taken hold of him seemed to be loosening its grip.

"Anything?" Daniel asked him.

"Not what we're looking for."

Daniel swore. "Any idea what—" But he wasn't even sure what unit of measurement to use. Day, month, epoch?

Hunter understood the question. "Seeing that we're both here, and we both know what we're talking about, I'm going to assume that it's now."

"Now?"

"Yessir."

Daniel started laughing, amused at the absurdity of it all.

Hunter said, "I think we've gotten all we're gonna get from the ship. At least for now."

Daniel nodded, wiping his eyes, exhausted and half mad himself. "Amen."

A noise.

"Or," Hunter said, cocking an ear, "perhaps I'm wrong."

It was a sound that needed no guesswork.

Daniel sighed, reaching for the axe. It was still wet with Nephilim blood on it from the last time, but here it was again. Back from the dead, because they hadn't killed it yet. "How do you want to do it this time?"

Hunter thought about it.

SIX

September 21, 2011. Night. The New Territory.

Jackson followed Paul into the strange territory, wading through ferns that at times reached so high they touched his shoulders and tickled his neck. The farther they went into the New Territory, the denser the woods became, trapping the moonlight in its canopy. In the darkness, networks of waterways trickled like background vocals to the louder chorus of nocturnal animals singing nearby. What kind of animals they might be was anyone's guess. The Bermuda they had initially awoken to aboard the *Gegenes* was horrible enough, but at least it had been contained to a small altered geography. *This*… There was nothing to compare this to. No maps, no insight from the island dwellers, nothing. The place was a complete mystery to everyone.

As was the man he was following.

He watched Paul's slippery form continue to move ahead of him and wondered what he'd seen back by the clearing. He knew he'd seen something. Not once in all the years fighting their way in and out of the world's hellholes had Jackson seen such fright in his friend's eyes as he had in that singular moment. Whatever it was that he'd seen had terrified him, though the fact that he didn't want to talk about it indicated something more akin to a personal horror rather than something that presented a clear and present danger to both of them. And his suggestion that they kick off their ghost stories by talking about Denise convinced Jackson that he was as likely to see whatever was haunting Paul as Paul was to hear Denise's voice. And that was good, because he had no desire to meet the ghosts of Paul's past.

Paul climbed a small hill and then disappeared down the other side of it. Jackson went up the hill after him, but suddenly stopped, pausing midstep.

Something was there with him in the darkness.

He moved only his eyes, attempting to detect the thing's presence without giving his away—if it wasn't too late already. He clenched the AK-47 tight, fighting the urge to run. He knew there was something there. He could feel it. Not just in an instinctual sort of way, but actually *feel* it. The hair on his arms and neck was literally standing tall due to some sort of static charge hanging in the air. An electric current, cracking and popping in the cool night air, seemed to be slithering through the forest like a giant electric eel. He wondered if maybe there was another of Paul's so-called glitches around here, since the feeling in the meadow and cave was similar. Could he be one step away from falling through a tear in the space-time-continuum? Or was it something else entirely?

Sweat began to trace his hairline. He still couldn't see anything with his eyes, but his mind had no problems conjuring up images of some long glowing thing swimming back and forth through the trees, looking for him.

Then he did see it.

And it wasn't the slithering, tubelike serpent his mind had suggested, but rather a spherical shimmer. A floating ball at the base of the hill he'd just climbed. And it was growing, expanding. Fractured moonlight swam through its curved edges, accenting it like a giant soap bubble. He could see through the sphere, but the terrain beyond it was distorted, the very reality of the dark landscape being stretched, bent, and skewed until it became so distorted that it was like he was looking through some kind of kaleidoscope.

He tried to control his breathing, to remain still as he studied the phantom circle floating just thirty feet away from him. He wondered what would happen if it popped, and then decided he didn't want to be around to find out. He took off up the hill, pulsating bursts of static electricity tickling his bones.

When he got to the top of the hill, he turned and stole a glance back down at the thing. But there was no hovering circle distorting the forest floor anymore. Instead, there was a silhouette, the silver glow of the moon outlining its humanoid figure.

Jackson didn't need to see the thing all lit up in midday glory to know what it was. He'd seen it before.

He turned and continued running.

* * * *

Robyn held the torch up to the wall, studying the names of the women she'd grown up with. They were etched into the rock that now filled the space they'd last been seen. Where *she'd* been before being transferred elsewhere. Ruth's name was there, as was Priscilla's. She read over the others, praying for each of them.

Tabitha. Sarah. June. Melody. Lilly. Sofia. Fleur. Susana…

She cried until she had no more tears left and then made her way back to the others.

* * * *

Paul turned at the sudden sound of Jackson thundering down the hill behind him, instinctively raising the 47 and aiming past his lumbering form to what he assumed was something chasing after him. But there was nothing to see in the darkness.

"It's here," Jackson gasped when he finally collapsed beside him, hand pressed against his side.

"What's here?"

"The thing from the closet. It's on the other side of the hill."

"What?" Now his finger was pressing against the trigger, eyes squinting back up the hill.

"It just appeared right in front of me."

"Did it see you?"

He shook his head and swallowed. "Don't know."

Paul swore under his breath as his mind started referencing scenes from *Predator.* Schwarzenegger, Weathers, Ventura—Navy SEALs hunted by an invisible alien in the jungles of Central America. But this predator wasn't just some ugly creature from another planet with a cloaking device. This thing was more sinister than that. This thing had climbed out of Hell. "So what do you want to do?"

Jackson lifted his own rifle, doubting that their bullets would do much but figuring anything would be better than just thumbing their noses at it. He shivered, recalling the charred hands that had tried to pull him into the closet—those sharp talons and the leathery skin that had leaked black oil-like liquid all over him. He'd shot those hands, and they'd let go of him long enough for him to slide away. "Sit tight, figure it out at daybreak," he finally answered.

They had wanted to be back before daybreak, to avoid being detected in the New Territory, but Jackson was right. The last thing they wanted was to cross paths with that thing. Better to hunker down and turn into a fixture of the forest until sunup. They'd have more options once they could see their surroundings.

"Fine. I'll take first watch," Paul said.

The cries from Osiris' soldiers as the thing ripped their bodies to pieces and ate their souls echoed in Jackson's memory. "Alright. Let's find a secure spot."

They moved farther into the woods, looking for a defensible position that would conceal them throughout the night.

* * * *

They stood in the cramped staircase, soaked in fresh Nephilim blood. Though it was the same blood. The giant was beneath them again, head on the concrete floor, feet in the air. Just like last time. And the time before that. Its body was twisted awkwardly between the pressing walls of the steep metal stairs, no room for it to even lie down and die in.

Hunter wiped the blood off the sword, adding more dark streaks to the growing collection on his pants. How many times would they have to kill this thing? How many times would their method work? So far, the thing never failed to chase them into the bottom of the ship, to the service stairs. From there, it was just a matter of getting it to lose its balance. Once wedging itself upside-down, arms pinned at its side or over its head (the details varied a bit each time), it became easy work.

Daniel used the back of his hand to wipe the sweat out of his eyes, smearing blood splatter across his face in the process. "How many more times?" he panted, giving voice to Hunter's own question.

"Maybe none, or a ton. Three or more, we'll see a shore with a door, and then we'll be what for." He frowned. He hadn't meant to say that. Wasn't even sure he was thinking it. He ignored Daniel's wide, questioning eyes, and searched within himself. Probing, looking… But as far as he could tell, he was himself and the only one home. He'd just have to try to keep a lid on the fizz. He flashed his best smile at Daniel, but that only seemed to freak him out more. "Sorry, lad. Seems they kicked over some furniture on their way out of Dodge. Know what I mean?"

He didn't.

"Well, in any case, let's get on outta here." He turned and headed back into the hallway.

"I want to leave," Daniel said, not moving. "No more of this."

Hunter turned. At first, they had made it their mission to try to find a way back to that other future, the one where the world ends with Fallen creatures circling it like scavenger birds. The more doors they walked through, the more realities they experienced, but none of them took them back to the apocalypse. "We are," he said. "We are."

SEVEN

September 22, 2011. Early morning. The New Territory.

Paul got to his feet and stretched as the world began to emerge from the predawn shadows and take form around them. The only things that had attacked in the night were bad dreams. The closet demon had apparently been out and about on other errands.

The forest—as much as could be seen by the light of dawn—appeared normal. Birds chirped, insects buzzed, and animals could be heard swinging through nearby trees. Nothing unusual. Except for there being anything here at all.

Paul looked at Jackson. "What do you think the girl meant?"

Jackson forced himself into a sitting position, his face grimacing from the effort. He knew what he meant, because he'd been thinking about the same thing. "Ruth?"

"Yeah. I don't think she was talking about the giants."

Jackson tried to rub the soreness out of his neck, thinking.

"Those giants looked like all the other giants. And they spoke broken English, just like the one I saw in the courtyard."

"So then what was she talking about?" Jackson wondered.

"We both know that gate and whatever's behind it wasn't put there by Osiris."

"The arrow," Jackson mused.

Paul stood. "What if there are other people here now? And what if they've been here for the last three months?"

Jackson nodded, taking a piece of food out of his backpack and throwing another piece to Paul. "And what if they occupy the territory around the pyramid?"

They chewed in silence, and then Paul said, "Well, if we do have new neighbors, it'd be mighty rude of us not to introduce ourselves."

They shouldered their rifles.

"Lead the way," Jackson commented.

They continued into the dim forest and headed toward what they assumed would be the other side of the mystery cave, wondering what they might encounter in that uncharted territory.

Ten minutes later, they came to a steep rock outcropping that essentially formed a fifteen-foot cliff they'd have to scale if they wanted to avoid skirting around it. It stretched as far as they could see in their limited vision.

Paul covered as Jackson carefully navigated the protruding rocks. When he got to the top, he called an all clear down to Paul, taking over covering their position.

Paul reached out and grabbed the first rock within reach, using it to pull himself up. But his grip slipped, and pain shot through his wrecked hand, the jagged surface grating his mending flesh. He suppressed a shout and spun his back up against the hill while cradling his arm. He studied his hand in the vague light and swore he could see lava pouring out of his shortened digits. He ground his teeth, took a deep breath through his nose, and waited for the pain to roll away.

A low whistle fluttered from above, and he looked up to see Jackson's body outlined against the dark blue sky. He shrugged, hands out and palms up. *What the hell are you doing?*

Paul spit, shook his hand, and reached for another handhold.

Three feet from the top, Jackson reached down and helped him up.

"Thanks," he muttered, then took in the scene before them. Mist stood like a wall in front of them, weaving its way through the subtle shapes of trees, its smoky fingers stroking the ground with suffocating eeriness.

"Got a bad feeling about this," Paul muttered.

Jackson stepped forward, and the fog embraced his feet.

A stick snapped, and Paul swung around. But all he could see was white haze. He remained still for a second, studying the way the mist floated on the air, whisking its way this way and that, trying to find signs of something moving beneath it.

Nothing.

"I've been thinking," Jackson said, his own eyes trying to breach the slithering curtain, "about the pyramid."

"What about it?"

He turned and looked at him. "What if we can't make it work?"

"You know, I was perfectly content pretending that all we had to do was be at the right place at the right time—"

"With the right people."

"With the right people," he agreed.

Jackson squinted. "I sure hope you're right."

"That's assuming those flying monkey things even let us close to the thing. Or whoever else might be over there."

They'd spent the last three months working out a strategy for getting all the Purees to the pyramid by the winter solstice. That gave them three more months to figure it out, which was why their little scouting missions into the New Territory were so important. But now, with the possibility of new neighbors afoot, things might be a little more complicated than they'd originally thought.

"Assuming a lot of things." And Jackson stepped through the veil, letting phantom arms embrace him and swallow him whole.

Paul sighed. He opened and closed his hand a few times and then followed him in.

* * * *

Robyn shot upright with a gasp, something pulling her up and out of her slumber. She sat there, her back straight as an arrow, while her heart pounded in her chest. Finally, the muscles in her back relaxed, and she leaned forward, her head dropping and sending her hair spilling down around her face in a damp, tangled mess. She folded her hands to keep them from shaking. *Just a nightmare*, she thought as she came to her senses. But, no, not really. What had happened to Ruth and Priscilla hadn't been a dream, and it was Ruth's open throat and Priscilla's severed head that had chased her through dreamland.

Her body stilled as the panic turned to sorrow and—

Her eyes snapped wide, but this time it wasn't a memory or a nightmare that had awakened her. It was something else. A sense that something was wrong. No, not necessarily *wrong*, but something…missing. Absent.

She sat up to sore muscles and their protests, and rested her head in her hands. She ran her fingers through her hair, surprised to find that it had dried since the nightmare that had awoken her before. She didn't even remember falling back asleep, but apparently she'd passed out for some time.

Rubbing her eyes, she looked around the room and tried to determine if the feeling might've been instigated by something within her current environment. She was still in a room in what Jackson was continually calling the "Crystal Caves." Samuel had walked her back here himself after the assembly, promising her that she would be safe, that Jackson's room was just across the hall.

She swung her feet around, placing them on the limestone floor, and sat there for a few moments, thinking. Was it the strangeness of the new room that was unsettling, or was it something else that felt out of place?

She stood, stretched, and then walked across the dark room to the torch that hung beside the door. Jackson had given her a matchbook the other day, and she pulled it out of her shorts. Only three sticks were left. She struck one, and the bulbous flame sparked to life, burning the wood and creeping quickly toward her fingers. She held it against the torch, and the tiny flame grew into a cloud of fire, shooting sudden shadows across the room. She recalled the light switches in the house and the light-producing bulbs in the tunnels. Technology, Jackson had called it, and he'd told her many stories about it. She'd seen quite a few examples in the house. The "television" (she still wasn't entirely sure what the thing did), the refrigerator, sinks that spilled water… Born on this island, she wanted to see more of the things Jackson told her were out there, and not long ago she actually began allowing herself to imagine just what it might be like to leave this place. To eat ice cream, watch movies, ride in cars…to start a family in a place you didn't need to worry about people wanting to eat you. She knew she had no right imagining such a fantasy, but she couldn't help it. The closer she and Jackson got, the more she found her hope turning to expectancy.

And then there they were, together, staring into each other's eyes. She had made herself vulnerable to him, completely exposed with her feelings unchecked, her heart wide open. And he'd called her *Denise*. Another woman. *That* had been his response to her heart's invitation. And that one word shattered in an instant all those fantasies she'd allowed to foster over the last couple of months. She'd wanted to hit him for hurting her, for deceiving her. But then, as time passed, she began to understand, because though her knowledge of relationships was limited to an extremely small and unique sample size, she knew what it was to be husband and wife. She knew what it was to her parents, and she'd read of them in dusty old books—the Bible even. *Husbands, love your wives as Christ loves the church…* She couldn't blame Jackson for hurting, for still loving his deceased wife. Yet she did. There was no sense or logic to it, she knew that. But her feelings didn't care about knowledge and wisdom and facts. And that was only more frustrating.

She left the room, trying to leave her emotions behind, and crossed the dark hall. She wanted to talk to Jackson. *Needed* to talk to him. She didn't know what she would say. She couldn't ask him to forget about his late wife, and even though he *seemed* willing to let her into his heart (as hard and bitter as it had become over the years), she wasn't so sure he was actually ready to hand over that key. But then, as she hammered her fist into the door, she began to play back the previous night and realized she hadn't seen him since going down to pray for the names on the wall. And that was…

Her heart started to accelerate when no response came from his room, and the lingering aftertaste of the feeling that had awoken her came back with sudden ferocity. She opened the door and was greeted only by darkness. She began feeling around for the torch, but then remembered Jackson's story of its disappearance and gave up.

"Jackson," she said, not quite in a whisper.

Silence.

She stepped in and felt herself to the bed. It was empty and cold. He wasn't there. Hadn't been there in some time.

She left the room and went straight to Paul's, banging on his door. No response there either, and she pushed his door open too. She wasn't exactly sure how the tattooed man with scars would take to her barging into his room, but he wasn't there to show her. She took the corridor to the stairs and left the cave.

Stepping out into the darker, predawn hues, she was surprised to find that it was earlier than she'd thought. The sun hadn't breached the western sky yet.

The man who was stationed at the entrance of the Crystal Caves stepped toward her. "Are you okay?" he asked.

Robyn looked at him. "Yeah, Pete, I'm fine." Then followed up with, "Anybody else up yet?"

He shook his head. "Haven't seen anyone."

"Jackson and Paul, they didn't leave recently?"

Again, he shook his head. "No, not recently."

"What do you mean?"

"Charles said he saw them leave just as he began first watch. Said they had their weapons and were all dressed up in black. Said they disappeared sneaky-like."

She looked off in the direction he'd pointed. Toward the cave Ruth and Priscilla died in.

The Norwegian recognized the look in her eyes. "You're not thinking of going after them."

But she didn't answer. Instead she went back down into the caves, which she knew would satisfy Pete. But she only intended on staying there long enough to change and get her stuff together. Osiris was gone and, as her friends had demonstrated, so was his power over them. If the giants still wanted to capture her, enslave her, rape her, impregnate her…just let them try.

EIGHT

September 22, 2011. The New Territory.

Paul was close enough to Jackson to see his hand go out, signaling for him to hold his position. He crouched low, trying to see through the fog and beyond Jackson's blurred form. He couldn't see anything.

Slowly, Jackson bent down and laid the AK-47 on the ground. Then he slipped a knife out of his black Levi's.

Paul raised his rifle. The air was pregnant with bad juju, and its wispy fingers were tickling the back of his neck. He waited for another signal.

Jackson readied the knife as the mist began to give birth to something in front of him, flowing tendrils of fog bending and swirling, pushing outward and taking on a humanoid form.

Paul could hear it clearly now. One person, maybe two, walking straight at them.

Jackson tensed as the mist opened its hands and let loose a stumbling figure right on top of him. Driving off the balls of his feet, knife flashing, Jackson slipped around behind the person, grabbing him from behind and putting him in a headlock, the cool steel of his blade pressed against the soft flesh of his neck.

"Wait!" Paul said, just in case Jackson was thinking about opening the person's throat before asking any questions.

The man in Jackson's grip suddenly whimpered, crying out, "Please! Do not hurt me!"

Jolted by the man's accented English, Jackson pushed him away and then jerked him around so that they were facing each other. He studied the person before him, knowing instantly that he was staring at a new castaway.

"Who are you?" Jackson asked.

"Ivan," the man stuttered.

Jackson took in his tattered clothes, his dark skin, and chewed on his accent. "Where'd you come from?"

"The lighthouse," he answered, his eyes filled with fright.

"Gibb's Hill lighthouse?"

The man had clearly never heard of Bermuda's 1879, fifty-five-foot, cast-iron lighthouse.

"St. David's Lighthouse?" he tried next. They were the only two lighthouses on the island, but there were no answers in the man's eyes, only more questions. Jackson took a step back and re-examined the man's accent. Revelation swept over his face, but then skepticism chased it away as his mind argued against the possibility of it. He asked the question anyway. "The Great Isaac Lighthouse?"

"Yes. You know it?" A flicker of hope lit his face.

"Where the hell is the Great Isaac Lighthouse?" Paul asked from behind them.

"The Bahamas," Jackson replied. "Twenty miles north of Bimini."

And the hope that had sprouted on Ivan's face was ripped out of the ground with that exchange. He asked, "Who are you? Where am I? What is going on?"

"That's three of the Ws, mate," Paul replied. "You left out the biggest two."

He didn't have the needed context to formulate the big "why" question yet, and no one could blame him for not thinking to inquire about the last W—*when.* So Jackson dropped it on him. "How has 1969 been treating you, Ivan?"

Paul frowned.

"What is going on?" Ivan repeated.

He was sticking with the "what," then. Jackson tried a different approach. "Where's Mr. Mollings?"

The poor man couldn't take it anymore and turned to run. But Jackson grabbed him by the collar, stopping him.

"It's okay, Ivan. We're not going to hurt you."

But it was clear Ivan would need more convincing after almost having his head cut off. His eyes were on the AK-47s now.

"Who are you?" He was repeating all the wrong Ws.

"We're US Special Forces. We're on a mission."

The words introduced panic, and Ivan's eyes began darting to the trees.

"No," Jackson said reassuringly. "This isn't Vietnam." *This is much worse…* "Is Mr. Mollings with you?"

"Yes. He is still sleeping. I just went to get some water…"

Jackson put a hand on his shoulder. "I know you're confused. I know you have a lot of questions. We'll do our best to answer them for you. But first, we need your help."

He nodded, the sense of utter displacement and vertigo subsiding long enough to maintain eye contact.

"How long have you been here?"

"A few weeks, I think. We have been walking through the forest looking for…"

He nodded. *Earth* would be the word Ivan was looking for, but he couldn't know that yet.

Paul fell into Jackson's shadow and whispered, "What's going on, Jack?"

"I'll tell you later," he said. Then he caught Ivan's eyes again. "What have you seen, Ivan Major?"

"How is it you know us?"

"Like I said, we'll explain everything. But right now, we're on a very important mission. What have you seen in the last few weeks?"

"There is a city. Large buildings. A pyramid like in Egypt."

"Where?"

He pointed into the mist.

"Take us."

* * * *

So you wanna fill me in on what the hell is going on?" Paul mumbled, walking beside Jackson. He touched his face and winced, the groove across his cheek just beginning to scab.

The clouds hugging the ground were beginning to thin, and visibility was increasing. Ivan was walking out in front of them, leading them back toward the things he said looked like Egypt.

"The Great Isaac Lighthouse was built in 1852 as a showpiece for the Great London Exposition. It was called Victoria Light in honor of the Queen. Later, it was shipped to the Great Isaac Cay in the Bahamas." He moved his gaze off Ivan's weary shoulders and to the towering trees breaking out of the mist. "A supply ship wrecked while attempting to deliver parts. Everyone survived except a boy. He was eaten by sharks."

Paul cringed, the whole incident with Eddie and the raft still with him.

"There are reported sightings every now and again."

"Of the boy?"

He nodded. "Years later, there was another shipwreck, this one with only one survivor. An infant."

"This story's getting better and better," Paul muttered.

"Legend has it that the infant's mother, called the Grey Lady, wails in despair during full moons."

"A haunted Cay."

"Anyway, in August of 1969, the two lighthouse keepers—"

"Ivan and B," Paul anticipated.

Again, he nodded. "They disappeared. An investigation from Bimini found the islet deserted. They say Hurricane Anna swept them into the sea. Others blame the Bermuda Triangle."

"And now here they are."

"And now here they are," he agreed.

They walked on in silence for a bit, minds grappling with the figure stumbling before them.

"He still thinks it's 1969," Paul realized after rehashing Jackson's conversation with the guy.

"The solstice must've snatched him from the lighthouse, brought him here somehow."

"And for the last few months, he's been here ever since." Paul spit. Time travel always made perfect sense to him. "But he said they'd been here for a few weeks. I know time feels a little ambiguous here, but not enough to mistake a week for a month."

Jackson shrugged, the mechanics behind the solstice incident a complete mystery to him.

Paul let it go, instead moving to another idea. "You don't think this 'New Territory' could extend all the way to the Bahamas, do you?"

Jackson looked at him but had no answers.

* * * *

She ducked and darted through the underbrush, flashing between trees. The AK-47 was strapped to her back, the strap tight between her breasts. She was moving fast and using both hands to swipe the low-hanging branches out of her way. Her hair was tied in a ponytail and snapping behind her. Sweat seeped through the fresh V-neck she'd changed into before slipping out of the Crystal Caves, her jeans tucked into a pair of old boots that tried to slip out from under her more than once.

She hit a clear stretch that was free of obstacles and was finally able to get up onto her toes, sprinting straightaway. In full gait, she came upon a fallen cedar that cut across her path. Without slowing, she brought her right foot up to her buttocks, and then flashed it forward over the tree, dragging her trailing leg sideways so that her shin paralleled the ground as she leaned forward, her left arm bent across her chest, her right behind her back. She'd never seen a track meet or watched a hurdling event, but the form and technique she used to clear the four-foot obstacle would've matched some of the best out there. She ran through (not really jumping over), a few more, all without missing a step or slowing down. Then she hit the stream and splashed across.

She finally stopped running when she reached the tree line that bordered the meadow they'd crossed the day before. The morning sunlight glowed gold off the tall grass and glinted across the rock face of the cave. She slid down against a tree, trying to work the rifle's strap up and over her head. It was too tight—her breasts too big, her shoulders too wide. Her sudden vulnerability put her in a panic as her fingers worked to loosen the strap as quickly as possible. After working a three-inch loop in the buckle, she tried again, imagining a giant stepping out in front of her while her arms were stuck over her head. She pulled the strap tight and felt a little space grow between the gun and her back. It was a tight fit, but she got it over her head and ready before anything had a chance to jump out at her.

She looked around, scanning her surroundings. Everything seemed still, quiet. No giants. No bats. No arrows.

She relaxed. And then began to crash, the adrenaline that had pushed her all the way here departing as quickly as it'd come. Her chest heaved as her glistening skin rained salty tears down onto the leaves beneath her feet. The rifle became slippery in her sweaty grasp, the white shirt clinging to her chest and shoulders while hanging loose over her torso. She slid down to a sitting position, the rifle across her lap, and closed her eyes.

She wasn't sure how long she sat like that, how long it'd taken her to recover, but nothing had revealed itself while she did. The meadow was still quiet, the cave's entrance frozen in an empty yawn.

Second thoughts began to knock against her assumption that Jackson and Paul had come here. Maybe they'd gone back to Jared's cave. Maybe they'd never *left* Jared's cave. Maybe they went to get more food, more supplies. Maybe they went to the pink house their friend had disappeared in.

Suddenly the possibilities of where they could've gone seemed endless. But then something in her argued, *So what if they didn't come here?* She wiped more sweat from her eyes. *I'm here now, aren't I?* And the other girls—Tabitha, Sarah, and all the other names on that list—might be in there somewhere too. Ruth had said that the giants took them there to impregnate them, meaning they were being held somewhere else and only brought there for the special occasion. But what if that was going on right now? And so what if it wasn't? She could just hide in there until they brought the girls to her.

She stood and moved away from the tree, slipping into the field. The morning sunlight hit her skin and sent a wave of warmth rolling through her body. She hoped she was about to join Jackson and Paul, but if not, she would at least make sure none of her sisters were here before going back.

NINE

September 22, 2011. Morning. The New Territory.

"This is where I left him when I went to find water," Ivan said, pointing to a naked spot on the forest floor. They were about a quarter mile away from where they'd met in the fog.

"Probably woke up and went after you," Paul guessed.

"You think he's okay?" Ivan asked.

"You've been here for three weeks. Do *you* think he's okay?" Jackson replied.

He looked around and then whistled.

"I don't think that's such a great idea," Paul said.

But Jackson held up a finger, waiting to see if there'd be a response.

Ivan tried again.

No answer.

By now the mist had withdrawn to ankle depths, and it was clear that there was no sign of B. Mollings anywhere.

"We can't wait for him," Paul said, and took a knife from his own pants. He crouched in the dirt and carved something into the ground. When he was done, he stood back, revealing his work.

"'B, sit tight. Will B back,'" Jackson read aloud. "Cute."

He bowed. Then he looked up to the sun. "It's getting late."

"Come on," Jackson said to Ivan.

Ivan sighed, shoulders slumped, no doubt believing he must be in the middle of a bizarre dream.

Jackson put a hand on his shoulder. "We have a base with plenty of food and a place to rest. Just show us this city, and then we'll take you there."

"I want to go back home."

"We'll do our best," he promised. Though "back" was a relative term.

Ivan led them to another rise, this one not as challenging as the last, but steep enough. Once at the top, they could tell they were on one of the highest points of the island. Stretching out before them was miles of evergreen forest, contorted, arthritic fingers of mist clinging to the treetops even as the day consumed them. The morning sun was bright and set the whole scene on fire with the blazing dawn.

"There," Ivan said, pointing into the red-orange ball.

Mountain ranges raced across the distant horizon, and Jackson shielded his eyes from the glare. Then he saw it. An angled structure nestled in the midst of the mountains, its point poking through the treetops and disappearing in the low-hanging clouds.

The pyramid.

"There it is," Jackson whispered.

"Wait a sec," Paul said, turning his head and taking in the whole panoramic view.

"Yeah," Jackson agreed, realizing the same thing. He took an old spyglass from his backpack.

"Where'd that come from?" Paul asked.

"Stole it from Joe before we left." He extended the scope and held it against his eye.

When they'd last gotten a glimpse of the pyramid three months ago, they'd been farther west—Paul from the Whaler coming back from the ship, and Jackson from the oceanside hill with Robyn, Hap, Joe, and Patrick. Seeing it now from within the New Territory's interior, though it was still a great distance away, they understood that their first assumption about it had been wrong, and that the last three months of planning might have been for naught.

Jackson moved the lens over the pyramid and could tell that the sides were smooth and seamless, its surface reflecting the trees around it. Turning to the west, he searched for the hilltop he'd stood on when first observing the pyramid. He saw a couple of likely candidates but couldn't be sure. He handed the scope to Paul.

"Those aren't limestone blocks," Paul said, the scope now an extension of his own eye.

"Looks like glass," Jackson agreed.

"Mirrored glass." Paul turned, faced Jackson, and spit on the ground. "It's not the same pyramid."

Taking the scope back, Jackson scanned the area around the pyramid. There were openings in the trees where he guessed other structures stood. Maybe houses and fields and whatever else might constitute the "city" Ivan had mentioned. "Maybe that's what's on the other side of the gate."

"Maybe."

"Someone from the other side has been moving back and forth," Jackson said, thinking of the footprints they'd seen running beneath the gate.

"Someone with spring-loaded arrows."

"They're not them…" Jackson whispered, chewing over Ruth's last words. He looked over at Ivan, who was rocking side to side, nervous, his eyes not on the pyramid but on the scattered trees and rocks around them. "How close did you get to it?"

His eyes flashed up. "Not close to *that.* We were on another hilltop over there I think." He pointed northeast. "And could see buildings and streets…" His eyes went out of focus. "Looked like ancient Rome or something."

"You didn't think to go ask for help?" Paul wondered.

"No," he answered without hesitation, his eyes clearing instantly. "I was in a lighthouse. Then in a flash there was a pyramid. And…" He trailed off, his eyes going far away again.

Jackson finished his thought for him. "And you saw something else."

He nodded.

"What was it that you saw, Ivan?"

"I know it's impossible, but…I think I saw a man…like Goliath."

Paul's gaze narrowed. "Where?"

"Down in the city. Or maybe…" He looked back and forth between them. "Mollings and I had been talking about it, and he thought maybe it was like in *Gulliver's Travels*. Maybe the man I saw was a normal-sized man and all the people around him were dwarfs."

Paul and Jackson exchanged a troubled look as everything about their planned escape on the winter solstice began to change.

Ivan looked like he was about to lose it for good now, and he whispered again, "I want to go home," and then, "Where's Mollings?"

Jackson considered him for a moment, understanding that for roughly three weeks he and Mollings had been wandering around these woods surviving on whatever plant and animal life they'd happened to come across. It was a miracle they hadn't crossed paths with any of Osiris' Leftovers in that time, but maybe the Fallen Leftovers hadn't really ventured into the New Territory yet. Though the three men they'd come across yesterday certainly had. Regardless, Ivan needed some food and rest sooner than later. He looked like he was about to pass out, and his concern for Mollings was only driving him madder. "Okay, Ivan. We'll take you back to our base and get you some food. And then we'll explain everything to you, what this place is, how you got here, and how we might be able to get you back."

Ivan's face lighted just a little, and he nodded.

Jackson turned back to Paul. "Let's get him back, and then we'll try to figure out what to do next."

"Fine," Paul said. But the look in his eye said something else.

It didn't go unnoticed to Jackson, but he didn't press it. As much as he wanted to get a look at this city Ivan spoke of, they couldn't take Ivan with them. They were better off dumping him off with Samuel and coming back again at night.

Just then, the sun broke the tree line and filled the glass walls of the strange pyramid with a blinding light they had to turn away from. They'd witnessed such a thing with the other pyramid, the sun reflecting off its limestone surface, but that didn't even come close to this level of radiance.

"Come on, Ivan." Jackson put a hand on his shoulder and turned him back down the hill. He kept a careful eye on him the whole way down, and it wasn't until they reached the bottom that he turned to say something to Paul.

But he was gone.

"Where'd your friend go?" Ivan asked, alarmed, his eyes crawling back up the hill.

"He'll catch up."

* * * *

Having made it across the flowered field without incident, Robyn moved into the yawning mouth of the cave and froze when she saw the dark stain of Ruth's blood on the ground. She closed her eyes, steeling herself against a sudden eruption of emotions, and took a deep breath. Sidestepping the dried, discolored pool, she began down the cavernous throat and toward the huge gate in its stomach.

Five steps later, the bulbs along the walls flickered and then popped to life, washing everything around her with an artificial glow. She used the light to look for signs of Jackson and Paul, but there was only a hurried wash of feet that had taken the place of their own booted prints from yesterday—which meant there'd been a lot of activity here after they'd left. Yet there were no new treaded footprints on top of that, which meant that Jackson and Paul hadn't been here since.

She examined the prints in the dirt more closely. She wasn't as good at reading them as Robinson and some of the others, but she didn't need any special abilities to see that the people who had made these tracks had been wearing smooth-bottomed shoes. She looked farther down the corridor, to where the two men Robinson shot had fallen, but of course they were long gone.

Go back, she told herself. *Go back, now.* She considered just how close she was to finally getting out of this place. Three more months until the winter solstice, when Jackson said the pyramid would be able to transport them out of here and take them back to a world she'd only heard stories of. *Come on, this is stupid. You came here because you thought Jackson was here, and now you know he's not. Leave before it's too late!*

But she couldn't, not until she knew there were no more of her sisters here. *You didn't see any giant footprints or drag marks, so...* But they were out here somewhere. Maybe on the other side of that gate even. And she wasn't going to leave without finding out. *You won't do them any good by getting yourself killed.* She couldn't argue with that. *Besides, even if you do find them, how do you expect this rescue mission to turn out any different than your last one?*

She took a step backward as the full realization of how stupid she was being slammed into her with sudden terror. She'd let her emotion override her judgment, and now she felt strikingly vulnerable. She could feel the electricity in the air around her, buzzing, warning. *I need to get out of here.*

But a sudden voice sounded out from behind her. "It is too late, I think, for that."

Slowly, and without breathing, she turned her head, looking back over her shoulder.

There, at the mouth of the cave just sixty feet behind her, stood a giant blocking her escape.

"Do not fight to spoil body," the fifteen-foot Nephilim said to her. "I would have you unbroken."

Without hesitating, she took off into the cave, racing for the gates and what Paul had called a killing area. If the giant was going to have her, she determined, then it would have to have her in pieces.

* * * *

They stood on the forward observation deck and watched the sun rise over the distant island. There was no way to know for sure how much time had (or hadn't) passed since they'd observed the Boston Whalers racing back to shore. That event could have been years ago. Or maybe it hadn't even happened yet. And that was their dilemma. Because if they were to leave the ship now and then find out that now wasn't the now they thought, they could find themselves stuck on the island in some other then. And Hunter wasn't so sure there could be any coming back from that.

He rubbed his forehead, trying to concentrate on the mysterious power the pit had left him with while at the same time attempting to avoid thinking about his possession back on the island, his body having been apprehended by a dark, spiritual force. The thing from the closet had needed him, so its compatriots had climbed aboard and drove him into that hell, that spiraling chasm into outer darkness. Just thinking about it could send him into a panic. But it was what the experience had left him with (the experience itself unclear and only definable by pain and hopeless anguish) that he was now trying to understand and control. At some point between being dragged into the abyss and his freedom from it, his phantom self had been taken to reality's backstage (there really was no other way he could think to describe it). And from that backstage, he was able to observe everywhere all at once… It came as a combination of sudden revelations and quick glimpses into the corridors of time. And from this combination, he gained a sense of the ages, understanding their comings and goings, of it all…where it had started and where it was heading. And though this insight might be of the utmost importance, it was the information and detail between those two bookends that he was trying to revisit, to hold on to. For in the midst of that mystery, there was a key. A key to the engine of quantum mechanics, a user's manual to the gateway of the gods. But such knowledge was fading, the supernatural hangover left by the demons' exit diminishing even as sobriety restored him.

He closed his eyes, the morning air against his face, Daniel standing at his side. He wasn't sure how to access—

It came as a flash. All of it playing out in real time, as it was in this now, these very moments. Only a flash, but it was all he needed.

He sees Robyn running from certain abuse toward an ancient gate…

Paul on his own in unfamiliar territory, nearing a city from another time…

Jackson with a stranger, making his way back to the Crystal Caves…

Another man, the stranger's friend, being torn to pieces and eaten by two giants…

More pure-blooded women huddled together and thinking of escape…

The demon from the closet, moving beneath an inky sky and carrying out its mission…

The remnant of Osiris' army, gathering…

A pyramid, shining in the morning sun…

And—

His eyes snapped wide, suddenly staring wild at the landmass before them. "We need to get to the boat bay."

Daniel studied him. “Are you sure?”
“Yeah. We’re here.”

TEN

September 22, 2011. Late morning. The Gate.

Robyn rounded the corner, sprinting back through the mushroomed forest and glowing, phosphorous light. She was tempted to stop and hide among the mushroom trees, but she'd seen giants cut down cedars with a single swipe of their swords and knew these fragile stalks would be nothing more than weeds in its path.

She slid through the opening they'd found yesterday and dropped into the lower chamber below. Knowing the distance of the drop this time, she was able to land in a tuck and roll, bouncing back to her feet and splashing across the stream. The giant's severed head was still spinning in circles against the far wall, and the Nephilim blood that had splashed the floor and walls was now dark and dry, mixing with Priscilla's and looking like some grotesque kind of cave art. Robyn ran past it, knowing the giant was taking the other route down and unsure which way was faster. Could be she'd get to the gate only to find it closed and the giant standing there waiting for her.

But no, as she approached the final bend, the giant's heavy footfalls came sounding out behind her. She was still ahead of it.

She flew around the bend and came face-to-face with the huge spiked gate. It was closed, the long pointed nails daring her to get any closer. But an image of the giant grabbing her and tossing her up against the gate, pinning her there as it did whatever it wanted to do with her, flashed through her mind and erased any reserves she had about approaching it. Without looking back, she ran to the gate, maneuvering her body between the spikes and using them as handholds as she climbed up against the iron thatching. The squares made by the intersecting metal were too small for Jackson to fit through, but she was pretty sure she could slip her sweaty body through without getting stuck.

She tossed the rifle through the hole and then stuck her head through. But her shoulders were too wide, and she had to try again, this time slipping an outstretched arm through first and then following with her head while keeping her other arm pinned to her side. She got her arm and head through, but now her full chest was keeping the rest of her from following. She reached up with her lead hand and grabbed the back side of the gate, trying to pull herself through the window and up into a sitting position.

A shadow fell over her, and she stopped straining long enough to see the giant standing there staring at her. It seemed to be enjoying the show.

She pulled with all her might, the ancient iron digging into the soft flesh of her breasts and the strained muscles in her back. Her right breast popped through.

The giant's face changed, its pleasure replaced by worry at the prospect of her actually getting away. It stepped closer to the gate, but its huge frame couldn't squeeze beyond the long spikes. It reached its six-fingered hand through the iron thorns and managed to brush her foot with its long middle finger. It pushed itself against the sharp points as much as it could bear, trying to get closer, to get a hold on her ankle and rip her back into the room with it. Blood began to flow from its shoulder, chest, and stomach where the spikes were sinking into its skin.

Robyn screamed and finally got her other arm and her entire upper torso through the gate. But then her hips caught. Looking behind her, she could see the giant pushing its body against the spikes, the sharp fingers pushing deeper and deeper into its flesh, its eyes burning now with pain but with uncontrollable desire. It was literally impaling itself trying to get her. She pushed against the gate with her two hands, her body horizontal with the floor, her triceps bulging, her back arching. She felt more fingers on the soles of her boots, and she screamed, the flesh on her hips peeling away. But it was more than her hips that was clogging the square, it was her jeans. Bending her knees up and farther out of the monster's reach, she unbuttoned her pants. Then she tried again. Now as she pushed against the gate, the belt loops on her jeans caught, and the sweat on her stomach and waist moved her out of them, her jeans bunching against the metal. More flesh came off her bare hips until finally they slipped through, her jeans bunched down to her thighs. She landed on her neck and shoulder and crashed down onto her back. She pulled her pants back up and then rolled on to her chest, pushing herself back to her feet.

The giant had worked its way so close that the spikes were halfway buried in its body, and now it seemed like it was stuck on them. It grunted at her as blood trickled down the iron spikes and painted the gate. She swung away from it and found that the next gate was open. She picked up the rifle and ran, following the tunnel into darkness.

* * * *

Jackson agreed to stop by Ivan's little campsite on the way back to the Crystal Caves, hoping they'd find Mollings sitting there waiting for them. But there was no sign of him—no new footprints coming or going. Ivan had wanted to stay until his friend showed up, but Jackson knew that might never happen. He got him to go back with him only by promising that they'd come back to look for Mollings after a meal and some rest. He could've told him that they needed to get back to his people before the man-eating giants or the flying scorpion men found them, but he thought that threatening him with more nightmares might finally snap his mind.

They made it back by late morning, and Jackson introduced the newcomer to Samuel. He watched as Samuel worked his magic, transforming to the hospitable island host immediately. As Samuel led Ivan into the caves and to what he said was a set table, Jackson could hear Ivan already introducing himself and opening up to the wise old man. Jackson was glad he didn't have to see Ivan's face when Samuel got around to telling him where he was. And even gladder still not to have to watch him grapple with *when* he was. *Well, you see, my son, it's the year*

2011—we think—and that pyramid you saw...that was built by a Fallen angel and his giant offspring and may be the only way we have of ever getting out of here...but we have to wait until the winter solstice to try to use it because of...well, there are things that just are, Ivan...like you being here, for instance...

Jackson thought back to the world Ivan knew. Back to 1969. A world where Nixon was still POTUS, man had just stepped onto the moon, and the Nigerian Civil War had already claimed over a million lives. Woodstock, and then *Abbey Road* coming out in a couple of weeks. In December, the Vietnam draft would be imposed, the Air Force would close Project Bluebook, and the Charles Manson cult would murder five people... Yeah, 1969, the year ARPANET was created, the Boeing 747 made its debut, the first ATM machine was installed, Sesame Street aired, and the microprocessor, battery-powered smoke detectors, and the Palestine Liberation Organization were all made. Paul Newman and Robert Redford got together for *Butch Cassidy and the Sundance Kid*, and Clint Eastwood joined forces with Richard Burton in *Where Eagles Dare...*

Where Eagles Dare. Jackson had seen the World War Two flick with his best friend, Todd, back at the theater on Washington Street. Cost of admission was three bucks for both of them. They were young, too young to see such a violent movie, their parents said. But that hadn't stopped them. They said they were going to see *The Love Bug* but snuck into the back of theater number two just in time to see the soldiers parachute out of that frozen German plane. There were other war movies Jackson snuck into that year—*The Battle of Britain* and *The Bridge at Remagen* and *Castle Keep* and *The Great Battle*—but there was something about Clint Eastwood behind enemy lines that never let go of him. In fact, it was probably that one movie that sparked the long black-powdered line to enlistment. While the rest of the world was being pulled apart by turmoil and conflict, that movie theater had been forming his destiny—and, by extension, to this place he was in right now. *Thanks a lot, Clint.*

He ran a hand through his growing hair. He hadn't thought about Todd in a long, long time, the movie itself pulled from a dusty box in some forgotten closet in the back of his mind. It was strange to think that while he and Todd were busy reenacting the cable car scene on a flight of steps that led to Todd's bedroom, Ivan and Mollings were being whisked away from their lighthouse. It was even stranger to think that since then he'd grown up, fought in wars, got married and then widowed all the while the two of them had been...where? Here? Ivan thought it was still 1969 and said they'd only been here a few weeks. And his age certainly supported that belief. But then where had they been for the last forty-two years?

Arkansas Joe walked up to him, little Hap trailing behind. "Morning," he said.

Jackson nodded back.

"Looks like you missed a wink last night," Joe commented.

Feeling the crushing sense of fatigue standing on his shoulders, he rubbed his eyes. "All of them," he answered, reaching past Joe and shaking Hap's remaining hand. The kid was tough, never once complaining about losing his arm, and Jackson increasingly found himself wanting to introduce him to a so-called "normal" childhood. But he knew he was superimposing his own youth onto what he imagined Hap's might be in today's America, and realized the two would hardly be the same. Kids didn't spend all day outside with their friends playing soldiers in the woods anymore. Now they rarely left their bedrooms, content to play their video games and update their Facebook profiles all day. It was a different world now, a whole generation growing up with an entirely different experience than any prior. He figured it'd be interesting to see where it all led and the long-lasting effects it would have on society as a whole. But even with that said, any place would be better for Hap than this hell. He wouldn't be too good at video games with only one hand, anyway.

"You see Robyn?" he asked Joe. The first thing he had done when he got back was check the room Samuel had put her in.

Joe shook his head. "No."

Samuel emerged from the entrance behind them. "He's resting."

"That was quick," Jackson said.

"He was very tired."

Joe looked confused. "Who was very tired?"

"Ivan Major," Jackson said.

"Who?"

But before he could answer, Samuel asked if Ivan had said anything about how he got here, if he knew anything about…anything.

"We didn't really talk. He's pretty shaken, worried about his friend."

"What friend?" Joe wanted to know.

"He said they saw a city in the New Territory. Paul went to check it out."

"Wait." Joe looked at him unbelievingly. "Paul's out there by himself?"

"He slipped away while we were bringing Ivan back."

Samuel's eyes narrowed with accusation. "Back from where?"

Jackson looked away from his stare. "We went to see what might be on the other side of the gate."

Samuel tightened his grip on the staff he was leaning on, clearly not pleased but holding his peace. No doubt he was wondering what would've happened to the rest of his people had the two soldiers not returned. "And did you find out?"

"We saw the pyramid. It looks like it might be in the center of the city Ivan was talking about. It's different."

"What's different?" Joe asked.

"The pyramid. It's not the one Osiris built, the one that Henry, John, and Chadwick hopped a ride in. This one is bigger and looks like it's made of glass."

Samuel blinked. "So the other one is gone, then?"

"I don't know."

"Will this bigger one work the same way?" Joe asked.

"I sure hope so." But Jackson had no idea. As he'd discussed with Paul, he wasn't even sure how to work the old one and just hoped that being in the right place at the right time and with the right people did the trick. Because if there was some kind of hidden console in the wall, some mechanism or ancient computer that you had to prefigure your destination in before hitting ENTER, then they were completely screwed. He thought about Paul's story of transporting back to a future Bermuda and borrowing a taxi driver's cell to talk to Henry. If that was true, if that had actually happened, he'd hope that the first thing Henry would say would be something like, "Listen, you have to stand on the red block to trigger the secret pilot's chair in the floor…"

"Who is Ivan?" Joe asked again.

Hap squinted up at Jackson, the sun shining over his broad shoulder and catching his eyes, and waited for an answer too.

So Jackson recited what he knew of the Great Isaac Lighthouse and the legends that had begun circling after its abandonment in August of 1969.

Joe looked puzzled. "So he's been here for the last…" He paused. "What year is it?"

"2011. I think," Jackson said.

He scratched his head. "So for the last few weeks, he's been here for over forty years?"

That was pretty much the sum of it, Jackson thought.

Samuel set his eyes on Hap as his mind raced through a whole new obstacle course. "Once he's rested, we will try to see what more he may know about this new place." Then he looked at Jackson, his sharp eyes full of severity. "We're running out of time. Three months is not long for all we need to do."

Jackson nodded, doubting these Not Thems would go for them showing up the day before the solstice and asking if they could just borrow their pyramid for a couple of hours. *Oh, and if it's not too much trouble, could you show us how to use it?* "We should go look for Mollings."

"We will," Samuel said.

"And Paul shouldn't be out there by himself either," Joe added. "We should go after him."

"Paul is fine on his own. But Mollings…"

Samuel stretched out a leathery hand to Hap, and the boy left Joe's side. Hooking an arm over his shoulders, Samuel led him back into the cave.

Jackson remembered his grandfather doing the same to him. *Come now, boy. Let's leave this boring talk to the grown-ups, and I'll tell you a tale that will knock your socks off!* He thought it strange to be so sentimental all of a sudden. First Denise, then Todd, and now his grandfather? Then all his God thoughts and his psycho episode on the six-fingered guy (that he hadn't known had six fingers at the time) in the middle of it? Maybe he *was* beginning to lose it. "Have you seen Robyn?" he called out to Samuel's back.

Samuel looked back over his shoulder. "No, but I believe Pete may have. I overheard him talking about her."

He looked at Joe. "Any idea where Pete might be?"

* * * *

It wasn't the first time he'd slipped back into enemy territory after a retreat was called for, and again Paul hoped it wouldn't turn out to be his last mistake. Jackson knew what he was doing, of course, the look communicated between them a familiar one, the absence of protest his approval.

Paul flexed his left hand, stretching his two missing digits. His eyes peered out from his newly applied mud mask, his body concealed in the big fanned leaves that made up the underbrush. In black Dickies and a black long-sleeved shirt (that once was a turtleneck but had since been modified and now hung over his shoulders), he was a fixed part of the forest, just a pair of white, blinking dots hovering in the shadows.

He could tell that he was on the outskirts of the city by the way the forest had begun changing in front of him, thinning out and giving way to footpaths.

A noise.

It was low, distant, and he couldn't distinguish what it was exactly. And he then realized it wasn't a noise, but *noises*. He closed his eyes, trying to pull out these new sounds from the forest's ambient background. And then he understood. The sounds themselves were ambient noises, though of a different sort. Not of the forest waking, but of a city rubbing the sleep from its eyes.

Commotion.

He wondered how much of the city Ivan had seen and wished he'd asked him more questions about it. Could be that he was right now telling Jackson about all its terrible booby traps. *Oh well.* He inched forward, determined to set his eyes on the Not Thems, but not forgetting Ivan's description of the giants he'd seen there.

As he slithered his way across the ground, he allowed his imagination to pair the noises with specific functions. The *tink-tink-tink* of a hammer striking metal (a blacksmith fashioning swords or horseshoes), faint, casual voices (good mornings and howdy do's), the bleating of sheep and goats…

Getting to the edge of the brush, he sprinted across the open footpaths until he reached the leafy cover of another grove of huge pines. He lay still on his stomach, careful to let the foliage spring back to life around him, waiting for any sign that he'd been spotted.

He imagined a bell ringing from the pyramid's capstone and signaling an intruder. And wouldn't it be funny if the esoteric treasure kept in the mysterious capstone was just a simple town bell? *Or maybe not*, he thought, suddenly remembering that little bell in C.S. Lewis' *Narnia* book. It was, as far as he knew, the first time in his life that he'd recalled that scene—the two children ringing a small bell in a strange world and animating a witch. The story had been a buried and forgotten part of his childhood that not even the recent Disney adaptations had been able to raise from the pit of lost memories. He thought it odd, and then put it aside before it could form into a key and unlock more memories. Now was not the time to go opening those doors.

Another sound. This one different and from behind him.

He turned his head slowly, careful not to disturb the brush that was hiding him.

The sound…it was getting louder, closer. He still couldn't see anything, but the *clumpety-clumpety-clump* was unmistakable.

It strode into the corner of his vision and stopped beneath a swath of sunrays poking through holes in the canopy above. Its magnificent, black coat shimmered while loose strands of its long mane fluttered gently on the morning air. It was large and powerful, a warhorse—like the ones medieval knights would ride. Or Crusaders or Vikings or the Black Riders of Sauron. It snorted and kicked restlessly at the dirt with its feather-covered hooves. There appeared to be a harness strapped to its back, some kind of hookup with long poles running through loops and connecting it to…

He couldn't tell. Whatever its freight, it was outside his line of sight, and he dared not reposition himself now. Muddy sweat began to drip into his eyes as he waited for the beast to move.

Finally, the mare stepped forward and pulled its cargo into view. It was a carriage. Not a small Ben-Hur chariot where the rider stood holding the reins, not a stagecoach where the driver sat on the top while passengers relaxed inside, nor was it a wagon from the Old West. Rather it seemed like something out of the Dark Ages, a metal-plated battle wagon with large iron wheels. But there was something about the style of the vehicle that bothered him. It wasn't a product of crude, medieval metallurgy. It was something much more precise than that. There was a sophisticated, almost paranormal quality to its design, like its driver might be the Grim Reaper himself.

He could make out the form of a person through one of the long rectangular side windows, but the person was twisting away from him and looking out the opposite window. Then, like a panel van, the side of the wagon facing him slid open on hidden tracks, and the person turned and stepped down onto the running board that extended the length of the carriage, one hand grasping a welded handhold that allowed him to lean away from its dark interior.

It almost would've been more believable if it were Doc Brown stepping out of the wagon in a white lab coat with either Einstein or Copernicus darting between his legs. Christopher Lloyd back from the Wild West in some new time machine fashioned from nineteenth-century spare parts would make more sense than the person Paul was staring at now.

The man seemed to be searching the forest for something, and Paul's heart thundered in his chest. *Come on, pal. Nothing to see here.* The carriage was now positioned in the same cross-stitched pattern of light that the horse had been in before stepping forward, and Paul could make out every detail of the stranger as he placed a booted foot down onto the footpath and stepped away from his ride.

Paul swore in his head as the horse exhaled air from its nostrils.

The man was about six feet five and clad in what seemed like gladiator attire. He wore a helmet with sides that reached beneath his jaw and then swept forward, extending past his mouth. The sun glinted off the polished metal and the long blond hair that was spilling onto his huge shoulders from beneath the helmet. His chest and torso were bare, revealing a bodybuilder's physique. Both his arms were sleeved in chainmail, and his left shoulder was covered with a plate of protective armor. His lower half was girded with a knee-length battle skirt held up with a belt lined with throwing knives. A huge sword was strapped to his back.

They're not them…

Finally, satisfied that there was nothing out there, the man climbed back into the carriage.

Paul exhaled the breath he'd been holding.

And then the taxi driver's phone started ringing in his pocket.

ELEVEN

September 22, 2011. The cave. Late Morning.

She flew through the dark, uneven tunnel, oblivious to everything around her, completely lost in panic. All her momentum was up on the balls of her feet, leaning forward, and her heels didn't touch the ground. A stitch had woven its way into her side, twisting and wrenching her innards, but adrenaline blocked its pain.

Until it didn't, and the anger and fury she'd felt toward the giants that killed Priscilla and Ruth, those monsters that had hunted down and slaughtered so many of her friends over the years, began to give way to fatigue—those feelings suddenly trampled by the charging feet of terror and left for dead.

Faster. Faster. Faster.

Tears of finality began leaking down her face, the air at her face pushing them into her ears. Her mother's face flashed before her eyes. Her father's. And then she was reliving so many memories. She missed them, and in that split second where flashbacks somehow came fully formed and all at once, she realized with striking clarity that she would not allow any of the Fallen to lay a finger on her and that this was the end. *Her* end.

It wasn't as terrible a thought as she'd expected. In fact, she was surprised to find herself feeling a small measure of relief at the prospect of finally leaving this place. Of course, she would prefer to leave it another way, with Jackson holding her hand and heading into a limitless future, but this wasn't so bad, was it? Not if she believed the things the Bible said about heaven, about how to get there. And how could she not after living her whole life in the midst of the supernatural? Jackson had told her that people in the "real world" considered certain portions of Scripture to be far-fetched and unbelievable, that they mostly spiritualized the parts that contradicted the natural order of things in order to make God's word more tangible in an era of humanism. And she found it odd that there were people "out there" making her reality into a metaphor. She wondered how compatible she would be with such people, but now it looked like she'd never know. And that was okay. The peace that passes understanding was flowing, and she knew that she would have no problem putting the barrel of the 47 under her chin if it came to that.

There was a light source somewhere far above, up on the tunnel's ceiling, and she'd been slightly aware of her own shadow flashing ahead of her as she moved beneath it. But now she realized that her shadow was shrinking. Or she was getting shorter. *Or*, said the burn in her legs, *the floor is rising.*

And then a pinprick of light appeared in the distance, hovering above her and confirming what her legs had suggested. She was running uphill, the tunnel taking her back to the surface.

As the light grew larger, the sound of her labored breathing echoed around her, and she slowed to a jog. Then, suddenly, she was overcome with the sickening feeling that a giant was about to grab her ponytail and yank her straight off her feet, that it would have her right there and then eat her alive.

She swung around, ready to send off a swarm of bullets, but there was nothing there. Just the huge empty tunnel. She lowered the gun and stumbled over to the wall, leaning against its cool surface. As she tried to gain control of her breathing and wait out the pain in her side, she thought back to the scene she'd barely made it out of. There was something there in the room on the other side of the gate that she'd seen. Something unimportant at the time but that had latched itself to the back of her mind as she ran past it.

The hole in the corner of the room, the one Ruth said was growing. The one Paul called a glitch. She wasn't exactly sure what that word meant, but she thought she understood his meaning.

She blinked, replaying it in her mind, slowing it down and zooming in, and realized that it *was* bigger. Significantly bigger. In fact, now that she had it paused in the fleeting, blurred motion of her peripheral vision as she sprinted past it, she saw that it had spread over the whole wall. *What is happening?* she thought. But there was no time for searching out an answer now.

She looked back to the small drop of light at the end of the tunnel, then back down the way she'd come. Which way to go… She could go back to the gate, see if the giant had killed itself on the metal spikes (and if not, she could certainly oblige the monster by finishing the job for it). But what if it had not only freed itself from the gate, but managed to open it as well. What if it was coming for her right now? What if more had joined it?

She started to panic again and could almost convince her eyes into seeing the bloody giant materialize out of the corridor below. No, she wouldn't go back that way. She'd continue on and see what was out there on the other side of the cave.

She dabbed at the scrapes on her hips, the flesh stinging from the contact. Blood was beginning to seep through the sides of her shirt. She wiped the sweat from her forehead, redid her ponytail, and went for the light.

* * * *

Jackson found Pete on the beach, fishing.

"Hi," Pete said without turning around. He had a pole in his hand. Not a pole handcrafted from Bermudian cedar, but a large graphite rod resurrected from one of the Graveyard vessels. He hadn't caught any keepers yet. "Do you see those sharks out there?" he asked, indicating a spot out on the water with a flick of his chin.

Jackson took a quick look and did indeed notice a large dorsal fin carving its way through the water about a hundred yards out. But he wasn't here to talk about sharks. "Samuel said you might've seen Robyn this morning."

Pete nodded, his eyes on the horizon. "I did."

"When?"

"Early." He shot him a sideways glance. "She asked about you and your friend."

"What did you tell her?"

"That the two of you were seen sneaking off at first watch."

Jackson swore under his breath, and Pete frowned, putting two and two together. "She went after you?"

"Apparently."

Pete thrust the pole into the sand and faced him, looking up into his eyes. "Have any idea where she went?"

"Yeah," he answered. "I do."

* * * *

The ship was nearer the island now, and Daniel could see the cedar coast from where he was standing—which was ankle-deep in the water sloshing about the boat bay. He recognized the scene before him and knew they were positioned just west of the new Graveyard. He couldn't wait to get off this ship, and if not for the sharks, he would dive into the water and make a swim for shore right now. Turning away from the open hatch, he looked back into the dimly lit bay and watched as Hunter moved a Jet Ski out from one of the metal cages.

"What is that?" he asked, eyeing the blue and white machine.

Hunter floated it over to him, stopping it just short of the open seas. "You're going to have to hold on," he explained. "Don't let go." And as if to emphasize the seriousness of the matter, a large fin sliced its way across the open hatchway.

Daniel took a quick step back.

"Hey," Hunter said, getting his attention. He looked him straight in the eyes. "Hold on."

Daniel nodded.

Hunter straddled the vehicle and found that the key was already in the ignition. When he turned it, a digital display appeared, showing a full fuel tank. "Thank heavens," Hunter whispered. But he wondered how long the Jet Ski had been sitting, and what, if any, effect all the time skipping might have on machines. He pulled the choke and pressed the green button on the handle, filling the marina with smoke and a loud, ratcheting cough. He held the button in for another fifteen seconds before the engine fired and finally turned over. When the display read 1100 rpm, he knew it would stay running. Slowly, he eased the choke back in, shouting to Daniel that they needed to let it warm up for a bit. He swung off and stood beside it. The last thing he wanted to do was take it out and have it stall right above hungry, man-eating predators.

After a minute or so, he squeezed gently on the throttle, giving it some gas. The shallow water behind the ski fizzed and churned in response. He gave it another ten seconds and then pushed it out into the ocean. Without another look back, he hopped on the Jet Ski. "Come on." He held his hand out to Daniel.

Daniel took hold of him, planting a foot on the runner and swinging his other leg up and over until he was seated firmly behind him.

"Don't be shy. Wrap your arms around me and hold tight," Hunter instructed.

Daniel obeyed.

"Tighter," Hunter yelled. "Like I'm your bonnie lass."

Daniel clasped his right hand over his left wrist and squeezed Hunter's waist as tight as he could.

"Here we go," Hunter said, not seeming to mind the pressure. His eyes scanned the moving surface of the water, and then he hit the accelerator, sending a stream of water shooting straight into the air as they lurched forward, the nose of the ski pointing skyward.

Daniel closed his eyes, sure they were going to topple backward and end up head-down in the water. But the nose crashed back down, and they were suddenly skipping across the water. Every ripple across the water's surface was met with a great, colliding bang, and Daniel thought the strange boat would fall to pieces. It went up and then down—*crash!*—up and down—*crash!* But they continued flying forward.

He peeked over his shoulder and saw the cruise ship towering above the water, growing smaller with every spray-filled hop. He'd never imagined anything like it in all his secluded life. It was amazing, truly. But it was haunted, too, and he was more than happy to be leaving it behind. But the way Hunter had stared at it before leaving made him think this wasn't really the end of the floating city, that Hunter perhaps had some future use for it in mind. Some part of a long equation he'd figured out while wandering naked in and out of time.

He looked away from the ship and saw the wrecked vehicles of the relocated Graveyard come into view.

* * * *

Paul shot upright, not even bothering to reach for the phone that was ringing in his pocket. Even if he were able to press a button that was supposed to end the sound—answer, end, dismiss, silent, a text message response like I'LL CALL YOU BACK—he couldn't count on anything working as it should. After all, the battery had died months ago. It was a ghost phone now, and he couldn't just assume that ghost phones worked the same as fully charged phones, could he? That was why he was still carrying the thing in the first place, wasn't it? Because, for some irrational and unexplainable reason, he'd been *expecting* a call. And that expectation inferred an understanding that the device could become operable again under a new set of metaphysical principles—principles that didn't require a network or a battery. So he wasn't about to sit there in the brush attempting to silence the phone while the stranger in the dark helmet drew his throwing knives.

He stepped forward with the AK-47 trained on the driver, ready to paint the carriage with him if need be.

The man turned and locked eyes with him.

The electronic jingle echoed through the woods, a cheap, synthesized rendition of "Lucy in the Sky with Diamonds." It seemed like something from a funny commercial (maybe one selling insurance) or a bizarre dream. Paul's mind couldn't help but match the tin tones with the lyrics. Marmalade skies and towering flowers and rocking horse people.

The man's eyes narrowed into dangerous slits beneath the shadow of his helmet. His gloved hands flexed.

Paul stared back, his own cold eyes daring him to reach for his sword. All the while the jingle played.

And then it stopped, and the forest returned to sudden, instant silence, the tune echoing in their ears for one more fading second.

Paul took another step forward through the undergrowth, keeping the rifle aimed at the guy's center mass. He wasn't sure if the gesture was understood or not, whether the gladiator man knew what was being aimed at him and what it could do. But he must have had some inclination, because he didn't move.

When Paul set a boot onto the dirt path, just ten yards away from the man now, he opened his mouth to say something. But then he thought better of it. Even if the guy could understand him (and what were the chances of that?), he wasn't even sure what to say. But he had to say something. They couldn't just stand there making eyes at each other all day. So he finally asked, "Where am I?"

The man's granite face tensed, his cheek muscles bulging as he clenched his teeth.

"*No hablas Inglés?*"

Still no response.

And then the guy started to reach back into the carriage, to something that Paul could see was resting on the seat.

He stepped forward, stabbing with the rifle and hoping the guy understood the threat. "Keep on reaching, Conan…"

But the man didn't stop. He grabbed the thing on the seat and turned with it.

Paul thought it might be a crossbow, but really couldn't know for sure. It could just as well be a ray gun, a radio, or a Snickers bar. Whatever it was, though, he wasn't going to stand there and wait to find out. He lunged to the right, deciding on quick evasion rather than filling the morning air with gun blasts.

He spun behind a nearby tree, bracing for the sounds of an attack.

But no sounds came.

As he peered back around the tree, he suddenly thought he might see the guy holding up a cell phone of his own. *Hey, man, it was me who called*, he'd be saying. *I'm an interstellar time traveler from the future. Henry sent me to pick you up. This getup is just a costume.*

Only there was no guy holding a cell phone. In fact, there was no guy at all.

What the hell… He swept his gaze up and down the path, but there were no signs of anyone, just the insidious carriage and its restless horse. He swept the rifle back and forth, waiting a whole minute before stepping back onto the road. He spit and then noticed that the driver's footprints were contained within a two-foot diameter beside the carriage. There were no prints leading anywhere else. Which could only mean one thing…

"Okay, c'mon out, He-Man," he called up to the carriage.

Nothing.

"Look, I don't want to kill you, but if you make me come in there after you, that's pretty much what's going to happen."

Still not a sound.

"Have it your way," he whispered and stuck the end of the 47 up through the doorway as he climbed the step and entered the cramped space.

It was empty, and he thought that maybe the thing that the guy had reached for might've actually been a teleporter.

Or maybe…

He spun around, suddenly wary of being struck in the back. But there was only the calm, swaying forest of the New Territory.

The door behind him, on the other side of the wagon, was open too, and he didn't know if it'd been open before or not.

He climbed back out of the wagon, figuring the guy must've climbed back into the carriage and jumped out the other side, taking off through the woods on the other side of the path. It was the only thing that made sense.

Keeping a wary eye on that side of the road, Paul walked around the large, metal-plated carriage. It truly was ghostly. Like something the headless horseman might keep in his garage for drag races down the Strip on Friday nights. It wasn't crude, but he could tell that it had been built to serve a purpose, like an army vehicle that was meant for speed and mobility. Yet there were touches of unnecessary flamboyance up around the corners, around the doors, on the wheel's large hubs—branches of feathers and clusters of arrows artistically engraved into the black steel. Two large wheels were on either side, positioned at the center of the thing like a chariot. They reached up to Paul's shoulders, and their center hubs, from which long spokes spread, were capped with polished bolts. There were two smaller wheels in the back, extending away from the carriage and apparently for added stability. It kind of reminded him of a Hot Rod, though in this case the bigger wheels were in front rather than back.

He crouched before one of the center wheels and could see his distorted reflection staring back. He hardly recognized himself. And it wasn't the mud mask, the beard, or the tired eyes that was unfamiliar. It was deeper than that, as if he was suddenly the younger, boyhood version of himself staring across time and wondering how he could possibly turn into the distortion staring back at him. And then it was gone, the little boy erased like a dream upon waking, its foggy tendrils eviscerated by the brutal now and all that had taken place between. *Yeah, kid. Sorry 'bout all that,* Paul thought to his younger self.

He stood and walked around to the horse. "I suppose you don't talk, do you?"

It wagged its long tail.

"Well, you don't mind if I borrow you for a bit, do you?" He ran his hand over its black, silky coat. It was a glorious animal indeed.

After one more look into the woods, expecting a spinning knife to materialize before his eyes, he climbed back into the sleek carriage. There was a long bench seat covered with a thick black animal skin. If he had to guess, he'd say it belonged to a black bear. But were there bears over here with the Not Thems? He sat down, pleased at how comfortable it was. Then he reached over and slid both doors closed. The long skinny windows allowed him to look out while preventing anyone on the outside from seeing in. That would be good. Ahead of him was a long pedal that he assumed was a brake. The reins came up through the front opening and were hooked on a handle next to the seat. He examined the front opening, noticing grooves running down its frame. It looked like…

He leaned forward and grabbed a handle that was just on the inside of the roof. He pulled on it, and it came down, bringing an armored window with it. It slid down in the tracks like a garage door, closing with a bang. A window about three feet long and two feet high stretched across it at eye level, the reins coming up through horizontal slits that had been built into the armored shielding. "Nice," he whispered. Whoever the Not Thems were, they were serious about their weapons—which could be a bad thing.

Concealed in shadow and away from outside eyes, he took the phone out of his pocket.

The backlight was on, the display screen glowing.

There were climbing numbers. Just like before.

6:14.

6:15.

6:16.

6:17.

He brought the phone to his ear with a trembling hand. He could hear an open line, faint noises coming through the speaker. He wanted to say hello, to see who was behind all this (it was, after all, why he'd kept the phone), but there was a part of him that was afraid that sending his voice through those tiny holes might enable whatever was on the other end to reach out and pull him in.

Sobbing.

He looked out the front window, then out the sides…

The sobbing grew louder, and he pulled the phone away from his face, the cries echoing in the carriage.

It was her. The girl he'd shot. She was crying, saying something in her native tongue.

He looked down at the phone just in time to see it go dark, the connection lost and the phone dead once again.

Trying to ignore the hair standing on his neck, he slid the phone back into his pocket. *Having a bit of fun, are we?* He grabbed the reins and snapped the leather, moving the battle horse forward.

"Let's see what we can see, shall we?" And he wasn't sure whether his words were meant for his childhood self, the horse, or the girl.

He found himself humming about a girl with kaleidoscope eyes calling.

Accompanied by only the rays of sunlight streaming through the narrow windows around him, he let the horse pull him down the path and toward the city, the unknown ahead, his past chasing from behind.

A WHOLE NEW WORLD

"Hear, Enoch, and take in these my words, for not to My angels have I told my secret, and I have not told them their rise, nor my endless realm, nor have they understood my creating, which I tell thee today."

—Book of Secrets of Enoch 24:3

Then the Lord said to me: Enoch, scribe of righteousness, go tell the Watchers of heaven, who have deserted the lofty sky, and their holy everlasting station, who have been polluted with women. And have done as the sons of men do, by taking to themselves wives, and who have been greatly corrupted on the earth; that on the earth they shall never obtain peace and remission of sin…

—Book of Enoch 12:5-7a

And it came to pass after this, that there was again a battle with the Philistines at Gob: then Sibbechai the Hushathite slew Saph, which was of the sons of the giant. And there was again a battle in Gob with the Philistines, where Elhanan the son of Jaareoregim, a Bethlehemite, slew the brother of Goliath the Gittite, the staff of whose spear was like a weaver's beam. And there was yet a battle in Gath, where was a man of great stature, that had on every hand six fingers, and on every foot six toes, four and twenty in number; and he also was born to the giant. And when he defied Israel, Jonathan the son of Shimea the brother of David slew him.

—2 Samuel 21:18-21 (KJV)

TWELVE

September 22, 2011. The New Territory. Late morning.

Robyn paused in the wide opening of the cave's exit, staring out at a portion of the New Territory that she was sure none of her kind had yet to see. Her first impression was that it didn't look much different than the rest of the new land she'd traveled through to get here, but then she noticed that the immediate area must have been cleared of trees some time ago—a precise semicircle was cut out of the forest ahead of her. With the green ceiling peeled back about seventy yards or so, the rising sun shone directly into the cave and washed over her. She savored its warmth against her face.

There was a dirt path that raced out of the cave and cut through the center of the semicircle. The curved tree line parted and allowed the road access into its bowels, where it continued straightaway to who knew where. It was a path though, so it had to lead to something, she thought.

A gentle breeze rustled through the forest's leafy arms as it waved at small birds darting back and forth between its branches. It seemed calm, tranquil. Peaceful.

But she remembered the footprints in the tunnel and could even make out a few before her now. This was a path recently traveled, and she would be a fool to let herself be enticed by such an enchanted ground.

She stepped out of the cave's rear end (that was how she thought of it anyway) and took three strides down the path, the gun in her hands sweeping back and forth, butterflies dancing around her feet. *Go back!* the voice in her head cried out. But she was too enraptured by this new place to leave it undiscovered. She followed the road and couldn't help thinking of the story her mother used to tell her, a story about a yellow brick road that led to an emerald city. She didn't know if this road let to anything quite so fantastic, but she had a feeling that—

She stopped and looked up. The breeze was combing over a side of the canopy's hair, and she could see up through its new part…to the faint shape of mountains peaking across the distant sky. Or were they just clouds? *No*, she thought. And saw, not quite so far away as the mountains but still a far way off, the thing she'd seen months ago with Jackson on that high hill. There was no mistaking it, for it gleamed in the morning sun, and perhaps she was on the road to an emerald city after all.

The thought rolled through her, filling her with excitement and possibility at first, but then settled into a deep foreboding. Her mother's story told of evil monkey creatures that flew on what she'd called "unicycles." And hadn't she seen those same flying monkey things herself from atop that same high hill? Yes, she had. She'd seen them through the spyglass, flying around the pyramid like sentries searching for intruders.

The wind ceased, and the trees' green hair flopped back down into place and hid her view of the distant sky. She stopped walking, sense beginning to find its place once again. But when she turned around to run back, she found that she was no longer alone.

* * * *

He held the *Avtomat Kalashnikov* tight, flexing his hands around it with nervous tension. The easy-to-use automatic rifle was reliable even in extreme conditions, thus its wide popularity ever since the Russians formally introduced it in 1947. The problem (and this was what Jackson was thinking about now) was its inaccuracy. After a hundred yards, the rifle's ability to hit a target reduced significantly. It was the way it cycled its ammunition, a harsh process that threw off the shooter's aim after every shot.

His target was a hundred and *ten* yards away.

Robinson looked up from the sights of his own AK-47 and glanced over at Jackson. He shrugged a "what do you want to do?"

Jackson looked back downrange, to where they'd spotted movement a minute ago, and tried to decide. They didn't know what was out there moving could have been an animal or a person.

There were eleven of them all lined up in a row, lying on their stomachs and staring out over their AK-47s. They represented nearly a third of the Purees that were left, and though Jared hadn't argued against taking so many into unknown territory, he had given Jackson a severe look before relinquishing them into his care. Robinson, Arkansas Joe, Li, Charles, Pete, Theodore, Sanders, Wilson, Carl, and Patrick were all there with him—their destination the cave with the iron gate. He was certain that was where Robyn had gone, thinking she was following after him and Paul. What she would do once she found no evidence of them entering the cave was what he wasn't so sure of. He didn't think she'd just turn around and come back.

He held up a finger: *just wait a second.*

The thing, whatever it was, seemed to have dissolved into the gently moving scenery, gone as if it had never been there to begin with. Which was a thought Jackson would've considered had all the others not seen it too.

They all held tight, eyes trying to peel back layers of trees and bushes, willing the target out of its hiding place.

Finally, after another minute of the stubborn mystery refusing to manifest itself, Jackson stood up. "Probably an animal just scurried up a tree and is swinging through the trees half a mile away by now," he said, annoyed. Every moment that passed was a moment Robyn could be in danger.

The others jumped to their feet, anxious themselves to keep going, each of them holding on to the hope that their search for Robyn would lead not only to her rescue, but just maybe to the discovery of the other missing girls, too.

They all took a collective step forward when a sudden noise sounded at their backs. It was a strange, guttural chirping noise that seemed to echo around them.

Jackson froze. He knew the sound—sort of. It took only a nanosecond for his mind to pull the lone reference file available and open it wide before his imagination.

Steven Spielberg. Michael Crichton. Sam Neill. Jeff Goldblum.

No. Way. In. Hell.

He didn't want to look back, didn't want to verify what his mind just told him was there. But he had to. His brain managed to fire off the right signals, the sternocleidomastoid and the trapezius rotating his skull, moving his chin sideways and down toward his shoulder. It suddenly seemed like an agonizingly slow process, as if time stalled while all the muscles in his neck moved, flexed, worked. The semispinalis capitis, splenius capitis, scalene, levator scapulae—they all responded to his need to see what was behind him, moving his head into a position so that his eyes could identify what his ears had detected. And though the muscles in the neck have an incredible amount of endurance and flexibility, there is only so much lateral movement the vertebrae will allow before snapping.

Having exhausted the head's full range of motion, he rotated his eyeballs in their sockets so that he was peering back over his shoulder and into the space behind him. And what his eyes saw stopped his heart. Until it triggered the hypothalamus into signaling the adrenal glands, at which point amino acid tyrosine immediately converted to dopamine; dopamine oxygenized and produced noradrenaline; noradrenaline turned into adrenaline; adrenaline bound to the receptors in his heart, arteries, pancreas, liver, muscles and fatty tissues, accelerating his heart rate; the extra blood flow increased the oxygen in his muscles as electrical impulses from the nervous system charged them; insulin production slowed, stimulating the synthesis of sugar and fat into useable fuel; his pupils dilated; digestion slowed; respiration increased. The peripheral world around him dropped out of focus as the more immediate area of his attention became a scene of stunning clarity, his mind processing the sight with lightning speed.

Adrenaline rush, his body getting ready to flee or fight. And that was the decision he had to make—that they *all* had to make. Because his initial response to the sound behind him had been right on the money.

It didn't look exactly the way the movies portrayed it, but damn close.

The thing stood there in the grass, about twenty feet away, positioned between two giant trees. It was watching them, its head cocked to the side in seeming curiosity as its reptilian eyes flicked left to right, taking in the whole line of human flesh. Its talons tapped against the ground, anxious. Then it spread its scaled lips, smiling a horrible, needle-filled grin. It was trying to decide which portion of the buffet line to attack first, Jackson realized. And before he could get his body to follow his head around and raise the rifle, the extinct reptile leaped forward through the air, its feet out, sickle claws gleaming.

Carl, the guy Paul thought looked like Carl Weathers (and whose name actually was Carl), took the two horrible feet right in the back, his head snapping with such force that the few who witnessed it thought for sure the impact had broken his neck. The creature landed on top of him with all its weight, chasing the air out of his lungs and cracking several ribs. Not having any idea what had just happened to him, Carl tried to scream, but he couldn't catch his breath, and no sound escaped him.

The lizard creature had him pinned and seemed to be studying the way he was flailing with amusement, taking a lingering moment to quickly study its prey. Then it opened its mouth and lunged. Carl caught his breath just in time to let out a chilling howl as those needled teeth sank into his back and snapped shut, first impaling, then tearing. He squirmed and wriggled as much as his broken ribs would allow, but the raptor's talons only sank farther into his shoulders, keeping him nailed down. When the dinosaur lifted its head, strips of Carl's dark, bloody skin were hanging from its teeth.

It took another moment before the shock of what was happening wore off and everyone was able to raise their rifles. Jackson himself was about to unleash a volley of bullets into the lizard's neck when suddenly another reptilian head poked out of the undergrowth just five feet beside him, its yellow eyes sizing him up.

He held his breath, afraid to move. There was no way he would be able to get the gun around before the thing had his throat torn open, so he did the only thing he could think of and prayed it would work.

He fired at the lizard already in his sights.

The sudden *CRACK!* of the report echoed through the forest, and the raptor beside him instantly disappeared back into the thicket, its tail sticking up like an antenna over the foliage and speeding away.

The bullet Jackson fired penetrated the thick, scaled skin of the other dinosaur just above the shoulder, and it stumbled sideways off Carl. Then more AKs joined in, and the lizard twitched as a swarm of metal wasps stung it all over. It tried to run away but fell hard onto its stomach, kicking up dirt as its claws dug for traction. It took Arkansas Joe getting as close as he dared to its snapping jaws and firing a bullet into its eye to get it to stop moving.

"Are you okay?" Robinson asked, kneeling beside Carl.

He grimaced. "You tell me."

Robinson took one look at his bloody back, then up to Jackson.

"He needs stitching, but he'll live," Jackson said. He felt the adrenaline begin to ebb as relief deep-massaged his bones.

Hearing that Carl would be okay, the others turned their attention to the dead monster lying in their midst.

"You ever seen one of those before?" Jackson asked while staring off in the direction the other raptor had run off in.

Shakes of the head all around.

"What is it?" Carl asked, squeezing his eyes shut against the pain.

Robinson caught Jackson's eye, and the message communicated was exactly what Jackson was thinking already: *We ain't in Kansas anymore. We ain't even in the other place that wasn't Kansas anymore.*

"Can we eat it?" Li asked.

It was a little smaller than portrayed in the movies and had a mane of bright feathers running down its back, but there was no mistaking it for anything else. At least that was what Jackson was sticking to anyway. He was no paleontologist.

"What do you want to do?" Joe asked.

Jackson sighed. They needed to find Robyn, but Carl was in no condition to press on. And the shots fired had just eliminated the stealth factor. "I'm gonna keep going. We need to find her. You can come with me if you want, but I don't blame you if you'd rather go back."

Robinson considered this, looking around at the others. "Anyone want to back out?"

No hands rose.

He adjusted his hat. "Okay then. How 'bout Theo and Pete take Carl back. The rest of us will keep on going."

Pete and Theo nodded and went over to help Carl to his feet. "Be careful," Theodore said. "Only three more months until magic hour. No use doing anything stupid this late in the game."

Robinson only peered through the trees. "Yeah. Who knows what the hell is out there."

All of them stood there for a moment longer, their eyes on the prehistoric reptile as all the brain's pulleys and cogs, pins and wheels worked strenuously to grasp this new reality.

* * * *

They left the Jet Ski on the beach after taking the time to conceal it with needled branches and branches with large leafy hands. Hunter called it a precaution and said it probably wasn't necessary but that it would be better to be on the safe side. Daniel didn't care. He didn't want to go back to the ship ever again. He *hoped* someone would steal it.

Yet, as they continued to walk through this New Territory, away from the Graveyard, he had the feeling that maybe being back on land wasn't so much different. He'd only had a few days to acclimate to the Change before spending however much time had passed since then on the damn ship. So this was all new to him…again. It was disorienting, his grasp of familiarity finding a handhold only to slip upon climbing to the top of the next hill. It was all so different. And now, where there was once water, there were mountain ranges ripping across the horizon.

It was tempting to think that they'd actually drifted to some other island much farther away, or that maybe Hunter was wrong, and this wasn't the present that he thought it was. But no, there was the Graveyard. And even if there was some other island that had a fleet of lost vessels all its own, he'd recognized some of the names. There was the huge ship that had been one of the landmarks of his existence—the one Jackson said was called the USS *Cyclops*. There was *Southern Districts, Polymer III,* and *Bounty*. And he was pretty sure he'd even seen the boat Hunter had arrived in, sitting up off the beach and nestled between two twisted cedars. This was his home for sure, completely redecorated and with some major additions, but it was his home sweet home all right.

Hunter watched Daniel, observing him as he took in the new scenery the Change had installed. He recognized the incomprehension every time they reached the top of another rise and saw only more lush hills stroking the skyline ahead of them. Indeed, it was a whole new world. Or *old* one, as Hunter knew. This land they were traversing now was land that had long since drifted away and sank into the depths of the sea. He understood that intrinsically, just as he knew who it was that had suddenly appeared on their timeline—the person who was, at this very moment, preparing himself for an introduction to Robyn. He also saw Paul heading toward the ancient city, Jackson not all that far behind.

Jackson…

He can suddenly see his friend in a whole new, transparent light, getting a glimpse into the spiritual and metaphysical goings-on that has him so troubled, unsure, and insecure in his mind—his *soul.* And Denise is here, too. But she's not. And then in a flash, he knows what happened to her, that the "accident" was something far less innocent than the way Jackson had portrayed it that stormy night he'd called him, bitter tears and unhinged anger strangling his voice through the receiver. Hunter feels the pain that still haunts Jackson and sees what it drove him to do, and the guilt that has been poisoning him ever since (and perhaps it was that poison that provided Ronald with an open door into his mind). Hunter sees it. Sees it all. Knows what his friend did, and how he got away with it. Knows that Robyn reminds him of Denise. That he's wrestling with the uncertainty of having descended from Titans, the spiritual war raging within as his soul and mind go back and forth in an endless debate over the nature of reality, its author, what it all means, and whether or not Denise had been right about everything. And then there's Denise's voice that he hears in this place, unsure if it's her speaking to him from another heavenly realm, or if it's a sinister trick being played on him by the trapped demons that occupy the air here.

Hunter stopped walking and took a deep breath, the gravity of his friend's inner struggles momentarily his own. It staggered him, and as it passed, he wiped a line of sweat from his brow.

"Are you okay?" Daniel asked, his own voice unsteady from exertion.

Hunter smiled. "Yeah. But we have a way to go, and you need to keep up."

Daniel came up beside him and leaned against a tree. "To where?"

Hunter stared at him.

"Stop looking at me like that." And if he'd been born in the real world, he would've added, *You're freaking me out.*

"Sorry," Hunter replied. He turned away. "There's a city."

"A *city*?"

"An old city. With old people."

Daniel's confusion only increased.

"Look, Danny boy," Hunter said. He moved his piercing gaze back onto him. "I know you're having trouble grasping all this, that part of you thinks it's all a dream and that you'll wake up back in the caves and life as you know it will return to normal. But your 'normal' is not acceptable."

Daniel pushed himself off the tree.

"Maybe this *is* all a dream, I don't know. But what I *do* know is that even if it is a dream, there's a way out of it. And when we wake up from here, we won't be in your 'normal' anymore, but in what was mine."

"You're talking about getting off the island, like your friends did."

He nodded. "Yessirreebob, that is exactly what I'm talking about." He turned and pointed into the woods. "And the key to our escape is that way."

Daniel stared at him with the same troubled look he'd been using on him ever since meeting him back on the ship. "What happened to you?"

Hunter laughed. "Oh, a little hell and high water, I suppose." He took a few steps forward and then stopped, shooting a glance back to Daniel. "But now I can float, so the high water doesn't bother my boat. As for the hell, I suppose there's still some in me, which is why I can see things that are to be. And even some of what has been." He winked at him and continued onward through the thick island forest while a blue sky marked by brilliant white clouds watched over them. He didn't dare tell Daniel that they'd been on the ship for three months. Not right now. His poor mind would probably break.

* * * *

There were ten men standing in a straight line across the entrance to the cave. How they got there so silently, she couldn't fathom. But there they were, and what a sight they made. They were adorned in gold armor that gleamed in the sun, lighting them up as if they were angels from some celestial city. They held round golden shields in their left hands and long spears that pointed up into the sky with their right. Helmets covered their heads, and except two openings for their eyes, they covered their entire faces too. They stood there, motionless, staring ahead with stoic expressions that seemed to stare over her head and into nothingness.

Robyn took a step back, unsure what this was all about. And then the entire formation took one collective step forward.

She stopped, and the rifle began to rise in her hands.

"I would not do that," a sudden voice said from behind her.

She spun back around, startled by the absolute nearness of the voice. Nothing but the empty path leading into the forest. Her eyes scanned the tree line, trying to find the person who had spoken, though how the voice could've sounded so loud from such a distance without yelling was a mystery.

"Take ease, daughter of man."

She turned back to the cave and this time saw a single man standing between her and the line of armored soldiers. He was slightly larger than the soldiers, though without the armor. In fact, he was dressed only in a long, red robe, its hood up and over his head. A thin silver band cinched his waist, his hands folded in front of him. He stood about ten feet away from her, and though the oversized hood had his face mostly concealed in shadow, she could see his blazing eyes staring at her.

"Welcome," he said, his voice soothing and hypnotic.

Only it couldn't have been his voice.

She blinked and looked around, again trying to find the one speaking.

You are scared.

Her eyes flew back to the robed figure, knowing that it was him who had spoken even though his lips had not moved. They were still tightly pressed in silent study.

You do not know who I am or where you are.

"Who are you?" she asked.

And he stepped forward, reaching up and pulling the hood off his head, revealing long silver hair and a neatly trimmed white beard. He continued to take her in with those intense eyes, reading her, dissecting her. *I am of no consequence to you.*

Her eyes widened as her mind tripped and stumbled over what he was doing—talking straight into her head!

You would not understand my language if I were to speak it aloud, I think.

She blinked. *He's not just speaking into my mind, he's listening to my thoughts!*

He squinted quizzically, his head leaning to the side a little as his contemplation seemed to take on an added dimension. *You are surprised by this mode of communication. You are not from these parts…*

She didn't know if he was questioning her or thinking "out loud."

You are with the others.

"What others?" she asked aloud. She preferred to speak her mind into his ears, rather than have him sorting through her thoughts. She didn't know who this person was, but she didn't like him touching her mind at all.

I can understand your reservations, he said.

But he hadn't answered her question. Did he think she was with the giants? Were those the others he was referring to, or…

Come, let me take you to someone who can answer your questions. He held out his hand as if he fully expected her to take it.

She looked at his hand, counted five fingers, then moved her gaze past him and to the glowing soldiers still blocking the cave.

Please, come with me. Our prince would like very much to meet you.

She didn't know what to say, how to even think right now. She'd just run away from a giant that was trying to rape her, and in so doing found herself in an entirely different world. *They're not them*, Ruth's voice whispered to her. But how had she known who they were or weren't? Had she been here too? Were the other missing girls somewhere on this side of the cave?

Without really knowing what she was doing, she slung the rifle over her shoulder and took his hand.

* * * *

Paul pulled back on the reins and brought the carriage to a stop. They were in the hills now, the path leading them not to the sounds of the local, waking population, but rather up amongst large rock formations that came jutting out of the ground like the plates on a stegosaurus' back. What he thought looked like alder trees had accompanied them to this point, holding hands over their path and offering some shade from the rising sun. Ahead of them, the terrain opened naked beneath the sky, and the road turned left, following the ground's gradual bend as it skirted a steep cliff and open air.

He slid the door open across the tracks and stepped down out of the carriage. "Just hang here for a second," he said softly to the horse, reaching up and patting its thigh as he walked by. He went out from under the swaying canopy and into the bright morning light. He took the path to where it began to curve and then departed from it, crossing the grass and to the edge of the cliff. He thought of all those mountain roads in Mexico he'd motorcycled, and as he peered over, he half-expected to see bleached horse bones and busted wagon wheels instead of rusting piles of crushed cars. If the road were any closer to the edge, he was certain that would be the case.

He was about twelve hundred feet high (near as high as the Empire State Building, he figured), and the lazy clouds swimming close to his head through the blue skies were projecting their shapely shadows across the scene below. *Forget Mexico*, he thought, feeling more like Luke Skywalker looking down at Mos Eisley. Only he didn't have two droids and a Jedi Master accompanying him. Just a dead little girl with unclear intentions.

The cool breeze ruffled his growing hair while white butterflies danced at his feet. He squinted at the ground below and couldn't help thinking of Ivan Major's 1969 lighthouse and his own question to Jack as to whether this new land could possibly spread all the way to Jamaica. Because from where he was standing right now, the idea seemed entirely possible.

Below rested a great valley that ran all the way into the arms of distant, snowcapped mountains in the northwest while tracing the wooded hills in the east. A glimmering stream slithered out of the hills and wound through the valley, flowing north toward the crystal pyramid that was standing like a dagger pointing into the sky, held tight in the craggy grip of more mountains.

A large hawk-like bird swooped down in front of him and began circling the air at Paul's feet. Its shadow projected a small gliding check mark on the ground below, passing over what appeared to be a village.

A village.

Paul took a quick step backward, afraid that the bird's shadow might attract upward eyes. He got on his stomach, scattering the butterflies, and crawled forward until he could see over the ledge again. He thought of Afghanistan, where he'd been in similar situations looking down at a village from atop the mountains that concealed it.

A thousand feet beneath him, rows of huts dotted a large clearing. There was livestock contained within long running fences, and two barns stood at opposite ends of the town. Stacks of hay, animal hides hanging from lines he couldn't see, and what appeared to be clothes stuffed in water-filled buckets told of recent activity, though he could see no one moving about now.

His mind reeled at the sight as he tried to find a place for it in history. At first he was certain it had to be a snapshot from the past, a portrait of a life lived long ago by some ancient people. The carriage, the gladiator driving it, and now this… But then he wondered if maybe it could be the other way around. What if the New Territory wasn't from before but from not yet? What if he was looking at something a thousand years into the future, after a nuclear holocaust hit the reset button on civilization? He thought that was unlikely but tucked the idea into his back pocket anyway before moving on to a third theory. Could it be that, rather than a convergence of times and dimensions (layers of the past and present all stacked up on their Now), the current version of Bermuda and all its leftovers had actually been transported back through time? If so, if their little world was ten thousand years in the past (or future for that matter), then the chances of them getting home would have to include the implementation of time travel *as well as* teleportation. And wouldn't that push their situation from "unlikely" into the "probably impossible" bracket?

Then again, he had a cell phone in his pocket that was given to him by a man in the future, so what did he know? In whatever quantum cookery was serving up this stuff, such an added ingredient (time travel or cross-dimensional transportation) might be as easy an add-on as, "oh, and can I get fried onions on that?"

A sudden breeze moved across the face of the cliff. It rustled through a line of bushes to his right and knocked tree branches together behind him. The bird tilted left…right. Then it dove between the currents until swooping gracefully on the next invisible swell. He'd been afraid that the bird's shadow passing over the town would attract attention to his position, but…there was no one down there to look up. He had heard people though; it was what made him commandeer the carriage and follow the path up to this elevated point. *Or maybe that was another village I heard,* he thought. Maybe he'd missed a turn along the way, passed the exit ramp to the nearby town and ended up here, far above it.

A sudden, terrible unease jolted through him as he considered that this might all be a setup, a trap meant to get him a thousand feet in the air. He slowly turned his head back, expecting to find the girl standing there with a big smile on her face as she reached out to push him over. But there was only the dirt road and the horse standing under the trees.

Suppressing a series of chills, he got to his feet, shouldered the AK, and reached into his pocket for the spyglass he'd taken from Jackson's backpack while he was talking to Ivan and not looking. He brought it up to his eye, and the valley below jumped closer.

He could make out spitted meat hanging over glowing embers of neglected fires, tendrils of smoke drifting lazily past the river and the pails of water left half-filled by its edge. He examined the long wooden fences, tracing them to the barns they ultimately originated from, and could just make out a few empty stalls inside. The ground in front of the barns was all pitted with hoofprints, indicating a lot of daily traffic in and out. He moved the scope back to the river and followed it up into the distant mountains, ultimately picking up the pyramid. The sun was catching the crystal capstone, and he had to look away.

He wondered where the villagers could've gone. Had the driver gotten back and reported his presence and was now leading an angry, pitchforked mob after him? Maybe, but that didn't really concern him. He only wanted to get to that pyramid and into the city he believed sat beneath it. He closed the scope and returned it to his pocket. But before walking back to the warhorse, he pulled out the cell phone. If ever a psychic phone needed reception (batteries not required), this would be the place to get it. But the screen was blank. *Of course it is.*

He walked back to the horse and held up the phone. "Strange things afoot, horse. Suppose you wouldn't know anything about it?" And as he climbed up into the carriage, he wondered how surprised he'd be if the beast actually did turn and answer him. Probably not so surprised. After all, you had Mr. Ed, the animals of Narnia, and Balaam's talking ass in the book of Numbers.

He closed the door and snapped the reins.

THIRTEEN

September 22, 2011. The New Territory. Late morning.

Robyn followed the robed stranger down the path and into the woods, the soldiers behind quickly falling into line and trailing them. When they entered the shadow of the canopy, other men and women, children even, began appearing from out of the thick evergreen forest. Some stood completely beside the large trunks, fully exposed, while others stayed behind the trees and peered around them with caution. She didn't know if they were afraid of her or this man and his soldiers, but she counted at least fifty of them that she could see. They wore simple clothes, clothes that resembled the sketches in the *Ivanhoe* book her mother used to read to her.

It appears as though you have recently experienced a great exertion. Do not worry, there is only a little farther to walk.

And he was right. Just fifty more feet, the path turned up a small hill where a dozen more men on horses were waiting. There was a cart of some sort in their midst, three magnificent white horses attached to it. Two bald men in red capes stood in front of its wheels and on opposite sides of two doors. As the silver-headed man led her to the large chariot, the bald men bowed and then opened the doors, swinging them outward and revealing a set of steps.

The strange man took one look at her and then climbed up into the carriage. She stopped and looked behind her to the ten gold figures and then to the men on the horses. They also wore helmets, though their faces were not completely covered. She could see their faces and the beards that covered them. They wore blue tunics, leather armor covering their forearms, elbows, knees, and shins. They had long daggers strapped to their thighs and shields strapped to their backs.

Run, she told herself, but knew she wouldn't get far. How many of these men would she be able to take out with her rifle before they skewered her with a spear or dagger? And what of all the onlookers? Would they run away at the sound of her machine gun, or would they pull out concealed knives and attack?

The man's hands, rings sparkling in the sunrays coming through the canopy, extended out of the carriage. *Come*, he said. *Do not be foolish.*

And for the second time, she took his hand. As she did, climbing up and into the shadowy interior, a trumpet sounded somewhere in the distance.

* * * *

Jackson was watching a little blue and yellow tree frog slowly make its way up the stalk of a big red-petaled flower. They were everywhere around here—the flowers. Huge red ones that reminded him of Ruth's exploding neck. He tried to shake the mental image, but it only reshaped into other horrors he'd witnessed throughout his violent life—bullets sinking into flesh with a red splash. He covered his eyes with his hand. *Come on, don't lose it now!* When he looked back, the frog was gone and—

Robinson put a hand up, signaling everyone to stop.

A fallen, moss-covered tree lay up ahead in a patch of thick eagle ferns. Whatever Robinson thought he saw or heard, it came from behind the decaying tree. He raised the rifle, and the others mimicked him, expecting another dinosaur to come leaping out at them.

The foliage rustled. Jackson tensed.

And then a white wolf hopped gracefully out of the wavy green sea and up onto the tree. It stood there for a second, its eyes taking them in, and then it darted to the left, disappearing over a nearby rise.

"Where are we?" Li asked, lowering his rifle.

But Jackson kept searching the woods, wanting to make sure the wolf hadn't been running away from something else.

Robinson and Joe both turned to Jackson, echoing Li's question. And when Jackson let the AK down and stood up straight, he shrugged. "How the hell should I know?" He thought that they were somewhere close to Ivan's campsite but couldn't be sure. He figured that when Robyn got to the cave and found no evidence of him and Paul entering it, she might have decided, like they did, to skirt around it. Hell, maybe she'd even picked up their tracks and avoided the cave altogether.

He studied the terrain before them and took note of the mountains in the distance as the wind set the ferns dancing like green fire. He sighed. "All I know is that Robyn—"

"She could've gone back once she got to the cave and didn't find you," Joe said, cutting him off.

He was right, of course. Robyn could be in the Crystal Caves drinking from a secret stash of Graveyard coffee and talking 1969 with Ivan this very moment. But what if they acted on that hope only to get back and find they were wrong, that she was still out here somewhere? No, he wouldn't risk that. There was no time for it. In twenty-four more hours, if there was no sign of her, then he wouldn't have a choice, but it was too soon to turn back now. "Listen," he began. "I have to keep—"

A sudden, piercing sound shattered the placid noise of their environment, interrupting him again. It rolled down out of the mountains, echoing across the rock-studded terrain, sifted its way through the trees, and filled the forest.

A trumpet blast.

They all froze, staring at each other as the blast echoed three more times.

"The Not Thems," Robinson said, looking to the mountains himself.

"So it seems," Jackson replied.

The New Territory had come with its people after all.

But what could a trumpet sound mean? Was an event being signaled? Had they heard their gunshots and were on their way with more spring-loaded weapons?

Jackson didn't wait for a consensus, didn't ask anyone's opinion. He just took off toward the mountains and the pyramid he'd seen sharing their company. He could hear the others following behind him, tearing through the undergrowth, and he was glad for the company. Because he had no idea what he was running into.

* * * *

The trumpet sound burst through the jagged trees and roiled up the widening path. Paul pulled on the reins, slowing his speed. He looked out through the window slits, trying to see what the noise might mean. Had the gladiator gotten back with a report of a stranger in their midst, and now the New Territories were being put on lockdown? Was the trumpet really a siren? He had no choice but to assume so. He'd passed multiple streets and even saw three other carriages navigating them, but none were like the armored vehicle he was in. They were simple wooden things hauling meat or drink, and they'd paid him no mind. But now maybe every Not Them would be on the lookout for a hot, armored carriage being pulled by a black warhorse.

He couldn't stay on the road, let alone march straight down Main Street. So he snapped the reins, directing the horse off the path and into the woods beside him. He kept going, the armored plating scraping against trees and snapping branches. Twice the carriage got wedged between trees, and a few more times than that one of the wheels got stuck in a rut or against a rock. Finally, he decided to leave the thing behind. He got out of the carriage and used his knife to cut away the leather straps linking horse to carriage.

"Okay, horse. What do ya say you let me ride you bareback for a little bit?" He shouldered the AK and attempted to climb up onto the horse's back. But without stirrups and a saddle to hold on to, it took him three tries. When he finally did get up, using its long mane as a handle, he leaned forward and stroked the horse's muscled neck. "Thanks."

He rode at a trot through the forest but only managed to get a few hundred yards before the forest became too thick and impractical for the huge beast. He hopped down and wrapped the reins around a nearby branch.

"Hate to tie you up like this, but I may be needing your services again."

The horse stared at him dumbly.

"Look, if I don't come back, I'm sure someone'll find you. Hell, we practically left a trail behind us with all the branches we broke."

It whipped its tail and shook its head.

"Wish me luck, horse." And then he slipped into the thicket, making his way toward the city. He had to see it, had to know if there was even the possibility of reaching the pyramid by the winter solstice. So far, things weren't looking too promising.

The horse stared after him with indifference, watching him move not only through dense evergreens and white-barked birch trees, but also through clouds of buzzing insects that he could only hope weren't carrying some ancient plague he'd be taking back to the future with him.

Imagine that, he thought. *I get back to the real world carrying the Book of Revelation end of days plague that kills a third of mankind.*

He worked his way along the pined slope of the valley, following the road off his left shoulder, and could eventually see the cliff he'd stood on hovering in the distance behind him. The village he saw from up there must be on the other side of the road and beyond the trees filling the valley floor.

He looked ahead, to the other end of the valley, and kept moving toward the mountains, the tip of the crystal pyramid hiding behind a thin veil of clouds.

* * * *

Robyn looked out the windows of the decorated carriage, taking in the scenery around her. There were people everywhere, coming out of the woods and lining the road. They stared at her through the carriage's openings with a curiosity so intense, she wondered if these people from nearby villages might be thinking of her the same way the Purees had looked at Jackson and the American soldiers. Were these people expecting a savior like her people had been? Or was it something else?

She supposed she would first have to know who these people were before any questions could be answered.

Ahead of them, more men on horses accompanied them, and she couldn't help but feel that her arrival here had been expected. She was a stranger in a strange land being taken to the leader, this *prince.* But why?

You will soon know, said the man beside her.

"Where am I?" she whispered.

The man turned his head, one eye staring out from behind a long strand of silver hair. *You are in a kingdom of Atlas, under the reign of the god Turiel, under the light of Thoth.*

She blinked, turned away from him, and stared at the golden figures marching beside her. *Turiel…* She knew that name.

* * * *

Jackson stopped and leaned against a tree, trying to catch his breath. As the others caught up with him, the sounds of birds fluttering through the air drew his gaze upward. The sun peeked through the tall fir trees, and he could tell it was almost noon. *Time's running out,* he thought. And though he had no hard evidence to support it, he knew it in his gut.

Fir trees… And as he looked more closely at the cones hanging from the needled branches and smelled the turpentine-like scent emanating from the tree, he thought more specifically, *Fraser firs…* Which were native to the Appalachian Mountains below West Virginia and considered to be endangered. And he realized that he no longer thought along the lines of "where" they were, but "when" they were.

"Look," Robinson panted once he reached him. He held up a finger, pointing to a steep decline that raced down and away from them.

Jackson peered through the trees and saw it.

A road.

He brought the AK up to his shoulder, sweeping it back and forth as he descended the slope, careful not to lose his footing on the loose, pebbly ground. The others came down after him.

It had to be a road. It was too wide to just be a footpath. He kneeled, examining it with critical eyes.

"All roads lead somewhere, right?" Patrick asked, stepping onto the road himself. The others stayed in the grass and kept their rifles aimed steadily into the woods.

"That's what they say," he muttered, then, "Look." He waved his finger at the ground, tracing a series of wide lines running through the dirt. Between them, hoof marks scored the ground with crescent moons.

Patrick stepped closer. "Tracks," he acknowledged.

The statement attracted the eyes of the other men. "Tracks?" Charles asked, looking back.

"A cart or carriage," Jackson said, standing. "Pulled by a horse maybe."

"Ground isn't that dry, not that wet. Whatever it was had to be heavy," Patrick reasoned.

"What do you want to do?" Joe asked, stepping onto the road now.

"Follow the yellow brick road," Jackson whispered as he stared off to where the road bent to the right and disappeared into the woods.

"What?" Li asked, not understanding the reference.

"Let's see where it goes."

"What about that trumpet?" Robinson asked.

But he could only shrug.

* * * *

Hunter grabbed Daniel's hand and pulled him down beside him.

"What is it?" Daniel asked. They were crouching behind a row of ferns that skirted the edge of a cliff overlooking a large placid lake.

But Hunter didn't answer, just pointed down at the water.

Daniel strained to see through the green, serrated fingers dancing back and forth in front of him and could only see a vacant beach with calm waters caressing its stony shore. The lake stretched into the distance, where, on the other side, it kissed a rock face full of tall trees the likes of which he'd never seen before the Change. "I don't—"

And then something appeared in his line of sight, stepping out from beneath the cliff they were crouching on. It walked out onto the beach, a long tail slithering after it. It went to the water, dipped its head, and drank.

"What…the…hell…is…that?" Daniel whispered. Even a few hundred feet above it, he could tell it was huge.

"In the world I'm from, they're called 'dinosaurs.' Or at least that's what it looks like to me."

"Are they dangerous?"

"Oh, I believe that they are, though they've been extinct for a long, long time."

They continued to stare at the two-legged lizard, fascinated and terrified of what its presence implied.

* * * *

He heard a commotion echoing down in the valley and had clambered down the steep slope to the tree line. Now Paul could see people, lots of people, standing alongside a wide, paved road. From the top of the cliff, he'd figured the valley to be a couple of miles wide, maybe more, and hadn't expected to see the main road come so close to the valley wall, but he was pretty sure this road was Main Street. He took out the scope and followed the road to the right, toward the pyramid. It went up a hill and then dropped out of sight, possibly bending back toward the center of the valley. There were trees on the other side of the road, so he couldn't tell if there was some kind of structure in the middle of the valley that required the road to circumnavigate it. It didn't really concern him. What did concern him was what all these townsfolk were waiting for. They stood in seeming anticipation of someone's arrival down the road. Like a greeting party, they waited, their heads turned to the west, expecting someone or something to be coming down the road at any minute.

They were standing about a hundred yards away from him, and he could see through the spyglass that they were dressed in medieval attire. *Peasants*, he thought. And he revisited the portcullis.

Suddenly, the chatter took on a hushed element as fingers began pointing up the road.

Paul swung the spyglass up the road and could see the tips of spears bobbing up and down. As they got closer, helmeted heads appeared, then shoulders. Soon he could see a whole parade of soldiers marching down the road. Men on horses trotted behind them. Then came something else even behind them—no, it was something they were *pulling*.

It was a large flat cart with four wheels. Chained to the cart, lying on its back and arms pinned to its sides, was a giant. Its head hung off the back of the cart, its feet extending over the front. It was bloody but alive. Its head was moving from side to side, its muscles flexing against the restraints. It was naked except for a loincloth, and dark tattoos marked its body.

One of Osiris' giants…

And walking behind the prisoner was another giant, though this one was walking freely and dressed in shining armor, a huge sheathed sword hanging from its hip, and a blue cape hanging over the left side of its body.

The people began to cheer, throwing mud and stones and other projectiles at the prostrated Nephilim.

Is this a victory party? The spoils of a hunt? Were the Not Thems at war with the Osiris Leftovers? Paul's mind spun, again going back to the metal gate. And the spring-loaded arrow that had killed Ruth.

He began to understand.

But before he could line it up all nice and neat, another wave of soldiers appeared. More gold armor, more spears, more horses.

And a carriage.

He lowered the spyglass and squinted in contemplation. The carriage was ceremonial, it's design hardly intended for any practical sort of use, whether for war or for the transportation of material. This thing, more akin to Cinderella's magic pumpkin before midnight than anything else he'd seen so far, was the equivalent of a limousine. It was transporting royalty. Or at least someone of like importance.

As it grew closer, he moved a little closer—as close as he dared. When the carriage passed in front of him, he tried to get a glimpse inside. The heads of the villagers blocked most of his view, and when he did manage to find a direct line of sight through the crowd, one of the horsemen would trot alongside the carriage and block its window.

And then he got a glimpse. It was quick, only a fraction of a second, but there was no mistaking it. A man in red was on his side, but when he leaned back, he got a fleeting look at the passenger beside him.

Robyn.

"Holy—" He slowly backed away from the tree line. Then he turned and made his way back up the valley wall. Once he was high enough and completely out of sight, he took off running for the city, his mind stuck on just one thought: *oh crap, oh crap, oh crap.*

He needed to get there before she did.

FOURTEEN

September 22, 2011. The City. Noonday.

After what seemed like forever, the carriage finally came to a stop, and the doors swung open to reveal a line of bald men in red capes standing at attention. They were in formation on either side of the carriage doors, the road between them stretching into the distance.

The man with silver hair stepped down onto the paved street (Robyn had never seen such a road before) and then turned back, extending his hand to her for a third time. But she didn't take it. Instead she leaped straight out of the carriage, landing gracefully on her feet beside him. She didn't miss his gaze tracking her bouncing breasts either, and for the first time she felt panic begin to boil way down in the pit of her stomach.

His lips didn't spread, but his eyes smiled with the twinkling anticipation of a predator about to attack its prey.

This way.

She squeezed the handle of the assault rifle and looked up the road. And the sight before her almost knocked her over.

Never in her life had she ever set her eyes on anything like this. Some of the drawings of ancient cities she'd seen in the encyclopedias from her parents' boat bore a resemblance, but looking at a small sketch and standing before the magnificent scope of such a scene were two completely different things.

The road stretched on for what seemed like a mile, a portion of it bridging a gap created by a wide stream or lake—she couldn't tell which from her position. On the other side of the bridge, the road was lined with towering obelisks leading to an enormous building that made Osiris' temple look like a mere tent. The road stretched straight through the center of the crowded city and didn't stop until crossing a wide courtyard and running into a flight of stairs that appeared to be carved into the outer face of the temple's base. The temple itself was of a strange design. The bottom half resembled the ziggurat temples in Osiris' temple complex, but instead of rising into a small point at the top, it ended prematurely in a large flat platform. Protruding from that base was a much different style of art, large pillars circling its perimeter and supporting more stories on top of them. But as large and magnificent as it was, it was overshadowed by the crystal pyramid that stood behind it, stretching so high that it looked like one of the mountain peaks even farther off, its razor tip slicing a line through a passing cloud.

She moved her head left and right, trying to take in the whole city. Buildings of every shape and size seemed stacked on top of each other as far as she could see, from the wooded valley wall to the right to the wooded valley wall all the way to the left.

Come, the robed figure said again, and he started walking down the road, the bald soldiers falling in line beside him.

She hesitated, though she knew she had little choice. Behind her, the horsemen set their beasts at a slow trot and nudged her forward. And behind them, she could make out rows of the gold-armored men. Her rifle was useless now. *Well, except for maybe one purpose.*

She began walking forward.

And that was when she noticed the other group out ahead of them traveling the same road. Because the highway dipped down the other side of a hill about fifty yards out, she hadn't been able to see them before. But now that they were out of the hill's shadow, there they were.

A giant strapped to a cart that was being pulled by men on horses. And there were other giants, clad in similar armor to the men marching behind her, walking freely beside it.

A vague context began to take shape in her mind. She knew that the chained giant was from her Bermuda and that the ones walking with it were not. It was a prisoner. Captured. Being paraded through the city, its citizens crowding the street on both sides and cheering.

But if this giant from her world was their prisoner, then what did that make her?

She continued in the parade, eyes fixed with wonder on the approaching alien metropolis.

They stepped onto the bridge.

You are in a kingdom of Atlas, under the reign of the god Turiel, under the light of Thoth…

* * * *

"Look," Charles said, pointing.

The tracks in the dirt led out of the woods, following the ascending path onto a plateau. The right side of the grassy plain dropped off down a cliff face, its edge nestled against blue skies. It wasn't to the cliff's edge that Charles was pointing though, but footprints.

Jackson took a step forward, noting how the prints appeared all of a sudden like, fully formed and right in the middle of the road. They continued on up the road and into the sunlight, toes forward, before deviating from the path altogether. Then they came back again and vanished to wherever they'd come from in the first place. Which Jackson knew was up in the cart. The heavy concentration of hoofprints was evidence enough that the carriage had stopped here for a bit, the animal pawing impatiently while waiting for its driver. Jackson studied the tread pattern.

Li looked from the footprints to Jackson's feet and back again. "Hmm."

Jackson nodded, confirming Li's observation. His own footprints, made by his combat boots, were identical to those on the ground. "Paul," he said.

"Paul's driving the cart…" Joe muttered.

"He hopped down here, went to have a look over there." Jackson pointed out to the ledge off the side of the path.

They followed the footprints out of the trees and into the clearing. The sun was almost at its peak, and they all stood beneath its heat, staring at the snow-covered mountains that reached up and poked the distant sky miles and miles away.

Jackson followed Paul's trail to the cliff's edge, each step closer revealing more and more of the scene below. A glistening stream appeared, pouring down out of the forest and flowing through—

He dropped immediately to his stomach. "Down!" he hollered.

They all hit the dirt behind him.

"What is it?" Joe asked, crawling up beside him.

"A village." Instinctively, he reached for his backpack but then remembered that Joe's spyglass was no longer in it (he figured Paul had taken it before slipping away on his own).

Robinson squinted into the valley, the pyramid gleaming over the hills. "Is that the same one you saw before?" Robinson asked, adjusting his hat.

"I think so."

"Who are these people?" the man named Wilson asked as they all took in the little village and its details.

"I don't like this," Sanders answered.

An echo of agreement from Li, Charles, and Joe.

"I don't like lying here with our backs exposed either," Patrick added.

Robinson started shuffling backwards so that he could stand out of view from anyone who might be below. He didn't like his back uncovered either. Not after what had happened to Carl. "You think she could be down there somewhere?"

Jackson shimmied away from the edge too. "Someone's down there." And again, he was faced with the decision to keep going or to turn back. But if she *had* already gone back and was now safe and sound at the Crystal Caves, then that part of his mission was accomplished already, and nothing could be lost in going forward (other than his own life and the lives of the others around him, anyway).

Arkansas Joe sighed. "You want to follow him?"

He stood. Now it was as much about getting Paul back as it was Robyn. "Yeah. I have to."

They all stood.

"Well, then let's get going," Li said.

* * * *

Paul skidded to a stop behind a wall of red-flowered bushes. From there he peered through the scope again, picking up the carriage in time to see it turn sideways so that its doors would open with the flow of the road. The bald men in capes formed lines on either side of the road as if Robyn was about to step out of a limo and walk down the red carpet of an awards ceremony. He set the instrument on the doors and watched them swing open. The man in the red robe stepped out, then turned and offered his hand back up to the person still in the carriage. Robyn jumped out. She landed on the road beside the silver-haired man, and he was surprised to see that she still had her AK-47 with her. The look on her face, magnified to his one eye, seemed distressed. They started walking, heading for a large bridge that crossed a river. Or maybe it was a moat. He couldn't tell.

He moved the spyglass away from Robyn and to the city that was surely her destination.

It was something from a Tolkien fantasy. Ancient Rome meets Atlantis with a twist of Egypt for good measure. *It's not a city*, he thought. *It's an empire.*

The boulevard split the valley in half and led straight into a temple complex, towering obelisks accompanying it until the road morphed into the very steps that ascended the front of the massive ziggurat temple. But it wasn't just a ziggurat temple like the ones the Mayans or Incas built (or whoever the hell Chadwick had said erected them), but there was a beautiful Greek-like temple standing atop its flat peak. It looked like the Capitol Building in Washington bent into a cylindrical shape and then raised high on a circle of colonnades. There was a set of huge doors atop the stairs and in the midst of the tall pillars, with two armored men standing guard on either side.

His heart beat faster as he moved the scope up over the peaked temple and picked up the crystal pyramid hovering in the clouds beyond it. Rainbow beams breached the puffy fingers, slipping through their loose grip and setting the noonday sky above the city to sparkles. And then his heart sank. Because up in that refracted light show, he could just make out little dark spots fluttering back and forth between the rays, and knew they were the things Jackson had seen before. Monkey devils, like the things from Oz, he'd said. And he knew for sure, in that moment, that there was no way they would ever be able to sneak their way through this metropolis unnoticed and somehow breach the pyramid.

They were doomed to this place forever.

He set his gaze back to the city itself, moving the spyglass back and forth, sweeping it from one side of the valley to the other. Huge, temple-like structures with glistening steps leading up to porticoes supported by large colonnades stood sprinkled throughout the dense dwelling places of the city folk. The pointed capstones of smaller pyramids poked the cityscape every so often, and Paul thought there could be a million people down there. A million Not Thems…

He turned his head and spit, wondering what they could possibly want with Robyn. The Osiris giant was chained and obviously a prisoner, but Robyn was unconstrained and still armed. Was she a guest, then? Had the Not Thems of this strange kingdom saved her from the captured giant and now wished to welcome her into their fold? Or (thinking of the armored giants that were no doubt Nephilim of ages ago), were their intentions toward Robyn simply different than what they planned on doing to the giant?

He went to move when a voice sounded beside him, taking his train of thought from 110 mph to 0 in an instant and making his heart just about lurch out of his chest. He swore as he rolled away, kicking up leaves and other debris in a startled attempt to flee the sudden presence.

"You are thinking what I am thinking, no?" the voice had asked.

In his frantic state, he tried wrestling the rifle off his back, but it was an exercise in futility, his movements too frantic, the strap getting caught around his neck or arm or shoulder. Finally, he gave up long enough to look through the dust cloud he'd stirred and at whoever had snuck up on him.

The girl.

She was sitting Indian-style beside him, staring down at the city and not even looking his way.

* * * *

Hunter was moving quick, and Daniel had to struggle to keep up. The trees spread apart and gave birth to a patch of chest-high grass that filled the new opening. The wind slithered through it like swarms of invisible snakes, all of which rattled their tails in a chorus of quietude. It would've been peaceful if not for the possibility of a giant toothy grin suddenly lifting out of the grass in front of them.

"'"I see fields of green…red roses too…"' Hunter whispered in song.

"What?" Daniel called up from behind.

"Nothing, Danny boy. Just singing a song. C'mon up here with me, will you? Stay close. There be monsters afoot."

They made it out of the grass without any run-ins with tooth or talon and were now navigating strips of granite that were arching out of the ground. Up ahead, they grew into large jagged formations that cast shadows every which way. Hunter led them through their open, serrated fingers.

Then he stopped and crouched behind two granite arms that were paused in a high five.

"What is it now?" Daniel whispered, ducking.

He motioned for Daniel to come up beside him and see for himself.

Daniel peered around the rock and whimpered.

The rocks continued ahead of them, racing down a small slope and leading to a stony creek bed. Bushes with little white flowers crowded around the flowing water, their lower leaves floating on their backs, massaged by the current.

On the other side of the creek, an enormous reptile stood in the bushes, its head down, yanking and pulling, its jaws chewing. Blood was flowing off the bank and into the water.

"You see them?" Hunter asked.

And as hard as it was for Daniel to take his eyes off the lizard, he did manage to spot the four giants behind it, moving stealthily from tree to tree. "They're hunting it?" Daniel asked.

Hunter raised his hand and pointed to something else. "I think they are."

Daniel followed his finger and squinted, unable at first to see what Hunter was talking about. But then the slightest flicker of movement flashed through the trees…and he saw men. "What are they?"

"Hunters."

Daniel's face twisted.

"Not as in 'more of me,'" Hunter explained.

"Oh. Right."

They watched as the four giants slowly approached the position of the concealed hunters, unsure of who in these three different parties were hunter or prey.

"Maybe they're coordinating an attack," Hunter surmised.

The creature continued to eat, unaware of the situation developing behind it. But then one of the giants must have stepped on a twig or branch (or perhaps its odor had reached those scaled nostrils), because the reptile suddenly raised its head, strips of flesh hanging from its teeth.

If the lizard was indeed the prey, then this would be when the hunting parties attacked, before it either took off or turned on them. But neither the giants nor the men made any advance. The dinosaur took off into the woods, and still neither group moved.

Hunter put his arm out, barring Daniel from moving forward (not that the Puree had any intention of doing so). "Hold on…" he whispered, eyes moving back and forth. "I think they're hunting each other."

And as if on cue, the men exploded from their cover, turning on the giants with crossbows. They were in dark brown and tan clothes that were covered by some kind of leather armor reminiscent of a 1930s football team. They even had similar-looking helmets.

"Leatherheads," Hunter muttered.

"What?"

"Nothing."

The giants hollered out in surprise as unleashed bolts sank into their flesh with bursts of red. Then arrows came raining down on top of them, screaming from the wooded slopes as if the trees themselves were attacking.

The giants desperately swung their huge swords at the arrows, but there was no stopping them. All four of them were walking pincushions within seconds. Finally, one of them took an arrow through the eye and collapsed face-first into the dirt, the force of the impact pushing the arrow out the back of its head and blowing it apart. Brain and bone hung from what Hunter somehow knew to be a spring-loaded arrowhead.

Roaring in frustrated rage, the other three giants turned and pounded down into the water, running away from the hunters.

The leather-clad army came out of the woods like insects, crossbows in their hands and swords strapped to their backs. They chased the giants across the creek bed and disappeared from view.

Daniel's eyes were wide and bugging out of his head.

Hunter slapped him on the arm. "Seems Osiris' Leftovers are unwelcome in the New Territory."

Daniel blinked. "What about us?"

"I think we should go the other way."

"To where?"

"We have a rendezvous, Danny. A ron-dé-vu. Though for me you could say it's more of a déjà vu." He chuckled. "Don't mind me, I'm just trying to get free." He laughed again.

Daniel frowned.

FIFTEEN

September 22, 2011. The City.

For the briefest of moments, walking across the bridge to the chorus of measured footsteps playing against the backdrop of flowing water, she had a sense of peace. Mountains like she'd never seen before reached into the distant sky around the extravagant architectures of these strange people. But the mountains, snowcapped in low-lying clouds, were even more remarkable. Man had not made the mountains. Man had not made the water or the rocks that played its tune. Man had not created the wind that tugged at her hair or the sun that warmed her face. It was an instant of transcendence like she'd never before experienced, and the psalmist's words floated through her mind: *Be still and know that I am God.* The Bible also talked about "the peace that passes understanding," and if this were either of those things, then perhaps she would be okay after all. For didn't the Book also say not to fear what man can do to the body but to fear the fate of the unredeemed soul?

Then more trumpets sounded, echoing through the valley and shattering her serenity like a boulder dropped on a plate of glass. Ahead of her, on the other side of the bridge, hundreds—if not thousands—of people lined both sides of the road. And when the trumpets finally silenced, she could hear them all shouting and whistling as the captured giant passed between them.

Welcome to your new home, the robed man whispered into her mind.

She flinched.

And now her mind reeled as she stared down at her feet, watching them move, one foot in front of the other, as more questions came pouring into her mind, piling on top of each other, suffocating and crushing each other before any one of them could take root and grow. Had they known she was coming? What could they want with her?

She crossed the bridge and entered the city, the temple standing before her as the crystal pyramid behind it cast a long finger straight down the road, pointing right at her.

* * * *

He blinked.

The girl was still there.

He blinked again.

Still she was there, her small frame unmoving, only one side of her face visible.

"Are you not thinking what I am thinking?" she asked again.

Paul watched her mouth move and could tell that the words formed by her cracked, colorless lips had not been in English. Yet that was how he heard them.

"When you killed me, I was on my way home. I was so happy, even despite what was going on around me. It was my birthday, and my mother and father had a surprise for me." She paused, still staring down at the valley. "I cannot stop wondering what the present could have been."

Paul's head swirled, and he felt abruptly drunk, a shot of 192 proof Paranormal downed in the blink of an eye. He was sure he had to be dreaming. Or dead. And it was the latter concern that slipped out of his mouth.

She turned to face him, her head swiveling awkwardly, the dirty skin on her neck not twisting the way it should.

"You are not dead," she said, and then a second later added, "Yet."

He wasn't sure if the pause was meant to suggest that such an end was forthcoming, or if it was just a statement of fact. He wasn't very well versed in ghost. Were the dead allowed insinuation and sarcasm, or was their communication with the living as lifeless as they were? If she'd meant it as a threat, then he was back to wondering why she'd helped them off the cruise ship three months ago.

She smiled a not-altogether-bad smile, reading his confusion. "Maybe I am not a demon, but an angel."

After what Ronald had told them about angels and demons and spirits, the distinction didn't mean all that much to him. He swallowed one of those big self-aware gulps, nearly choking on his Adam's apple, and suddenly realized how scared he was, that he was shaking and sweating and holding his breath. He closed his eyes and tried to breathe. After all the things he'd seen on this island, this shouldn't be *that* terrifying, should it?

Except that it was *her*, and he didn't know what she was doing, whether she was dragging him to hell or just getting some giggles in what was a rather boring afterlife? No, he didn't think that was it. He thought she had something longer reaching in mind, something with a goal. She had a purpose here.

"I'm sorry for shooting you," he said, his voice choked by a dozen emotions. "It was an accident." But when he opened his eyes to see how his apology had been received, she wasn't there.

Just the wooded slope of the valley.

He swore and wondered what the point of such an appearance could've had. *She'd spoken*, he realized. Why had she spoken? Was their relationship escalating, this the next step on his long road to condemnation? He spit. There was no more room for more questions in his cramped brain. Yet there they were, squeezing themselves in and shaking hands with the longtime residents.

He brought the scope back up and moved it to where he'd seen Robyn just a minute ago. She wasn't there. He moved the spyglass to the right, to the bridge, but it was empty. *What the hell...* He got to his feet and scanned the whole valley with his naked eyes.

There.

The procession had gotten all the way to the courtyard, the man in red about to lead Robyn up the ziggurat steps. How the hell was that possible? It should've taken the parade at least twenty minutes to travel through the city, and his encounter with ghost girl had only stolen seconds. He looked up at the sun, second-guessing the latter part of his assumption. Could he have just experienced a form of time dilation? Twenty seconds in the ghost's presence translating to twenty minutes in the world around him? He spit again. He was getting tired of all the questions.

He moved the spyglass up the ziggurat and to the platform its second half stood upon. Where there was before a closed door guarded by two men, there was now an open door and before it a throne. The man sitting on the throne was wearing a feathered headdress. Chadwick's voice hammered away in his head, repeating over and over, *the priests of the Sacred Feather…* But what about the priests of the Sacred Feather?

He couldn't remember.

* * * *

Robyn's legs were on fire after climbing so many steps. The city around her, and much of it now below her, spread out as far as she could see, all the way to the distant valley walls. She couldn't believe how many people were gathered in the courtyard at the foot of the temple. She'd never seen so many people gathered in one place before. The chained giant had been set in the midst of the crowd for a minute or so, and a deafening roar had erupted as all the people clapped and cheered. Then the prisoner was carted off somewhere else, and all eyes turned toward her. When she passed them, crossing the courtyard and taking her first step up the ziggurat, there was only silence. She wasn't sure what that meant but thought she caught a sense of wonder in the eyes of men, envy in their women. And overall, curiosity.

Finally reaching the top of the steps, the mind-reading man in front of her stepped onto the platform and walked across the smooth stone floor, through the outlying pillars and into the shadows cast by the structure above them. His red robe swept the floor's shiny surface behind him. The bald men had stopped before the platform, taking up a fixed, ceremonial position on the steps, while the gold-armored soldiers continued to follow behind her.

There, before a huge set of doors, was a throne. And sitting on that throne was a man. She couldn't really see him yet, the robed man in front of her blocking her view, but she could certainly see the two giants standing guard on either side of the throne. They were fifteen feet tall and clad in a silver armor that held the reflection of the entire city in their breastplates. The sight of them plunged her uncertainties into an even deeper, darker hole. Her steps faltered, her eyes looking for an avenue of escape. These giants might not be the offspring of Osiris, but they were obviously the seed of some other Fallen angel.

The man in red looked back over his shoulder, perhaps reading her hesitation, and said in his telepathic manner, *You are safe, daughter of Eve. Come, meet your prince.*

The line of golden warriors suddenly split into two branches, sweeping from behind her and circling the perimeter of the platform. They stood between the pillars, their shields now reflecting the silver armor of the giants and vice versa. Then the robed man stepped aside, and she found herself before the throne.

It was a large magnificently crafted chair, though small enough to remain portable. It had been carried and set in its spot before the doors. That was obvious from the long poles beside it, running through metal hoops protruding from the chair's base. It had images and designs and characters engraved all throughout its metallic surface, the chair's back fanning somewhat into a dome that she assumed was supposed to signify the rising sun, little jagged points poking out of it, sunrays. The arms were crafted serpents, their fanged mouths open wide.

The man who sat on the chair was wearing white. His face was full of angles as if he, himself, had been crafted by an artist. And for a second, Robyn thought that maybe the entire thing was a statue. But the eyes… Blue, blazing diamonds sat as two round fixtures set within that sculpted face. They were alive, moving, *seeing*. They twinkled as they took her in and consumed her.

With great effort, she broke his gaze and lifted her eyes to the feathered headpiece that rested atop his long black hair. And she saw that there was an actual diamond there, gleaming from its center. But before its sparkling dance could hypnotize her, she averted her eyes, taking in the rest of him. She thought he was—

He stood, and in so doing confirmed what she had been in the process of determining.

He was tall. Not as tall as the giants beside him, but taller than Jackson.

I have many questions, daughter of Eve. As I am sure you have many questions for me.

His lips hadn't moved, but his eyes acknowledged that the words were placed by him. She didn't like this mind communication thing at all.

You are of a beauty rarely witnessed, and I would very much enjoy knowing you, he added.

She looked up at him, feeling small and powerless in his presence, not doubting the "knowing" he was talking about. "You're one of *them*," she whispered. And in her mind, images of Osiris, Fallen angels, the Book of Enoch, Genesis six, and the Nephilim flashed from within that four-letter word.

The tall man in the white robes with diamond eyes and a diamond forehead blinked. His face clouded with some sort of half-revelation, and his brow wrinkled ever so slightly, a subtle wave appearing beneath the headdress.

What is this? he asked. *Where did you come from?*

When she didn't answer, he took a step forward. Her nose was now in line with his sternum, and she could feel his breath on the top of her head.

He put a hooked finger under her chin and gently lifted her head back so that she was looking up into his face. He tilted his head to the side in consideration as he studied her, his other hand running long spread fingers through her golden hair. Then he traced a finger down the side of her face, down her neck, over the swell of her breast, down across her stomach, and then around to the small of her back. He planted his palm there and with a strong, sudden force, he brought her body hard against his.

You were sent to me. For me. You have mysteries not even Thoth knows of. And you will tell them to me. He leaned his head down and put his lips on hers.

She tried to resist him, but there was a disconnect between her brain and her body, as if he'd severed the link between them somehow. It was one of the most horrible things she'd ever experienced, the loss of her faculties while completely subject to someone else's will. She knew now why it had been so imperative for the pure-blooded women to stay hidden from Osiris, and wondered if she'd already missed her opportunity to escape.

His kiss, however, was not one of compassion or even lust, but rather experimental, a test of some sort. As if his lips were able to evaluate whether or not she would be worth his time. The kiss, with his oversized face pressed against hers, wasn't anything like what she'd shared with Jackson—

The man suddenly jerked back, and now there was a new look in his eyes.

Oh no. She'd given something away. She'd tried to keep her thoughts from formulating into something decipherable, erecting a wall around her mind, but then that single idea slipped through, and before she could reach for it, its tail licking the tip of her outstretched finger, it was intercepted.

But he only turned, his white robes twisting and coiling like a snake at his feet. He implanted a single word into her head: *Come.*

With the use of her body back, she stole a quick glance to her right and left, wondering if she'd be able to make it past the soldiers standing along the edge of the platform before they knew what her intentions were. She could just throw herself into them, take a few of them down with her.

She clutched the AK-47 that was still in her hands.

There is truly no need for all of that.

And he walked past the throne and through the doors.

She hesitated, and then the row of soldiers standing along the top of the stairs behind her took one collective step forward. She didn't have a choice.

She passed the chair and walked between the two giants, noticing the golden bands circling their enormous biceps and the black capes that hung like curtains down the back of their silver armor. She stepped out of the daylight and into the temple.

A massive corridor with rows of huge columns erected on both sides stretched away from her, leading into the bowels of the strange building. She had no idea what was in store for her, but maybe it would be better than the giant back at the cave raping her for dinner and eating her for dessert.

Ten paces down the hall, the man stopped and turned. He stared down into her eyes, but she couldn't read his expression.

My servants will bathe you. And then you will come to me.

"What do I call you?" she asked, returning his stare while trying to guard her thoughts.

His eyes blazed with influence and power.

You may call me Turiel.

* * * *

Jackson had managed to follow the fresh wheel tracks to the deserted carriage, and now all of them stood around staring at the strange vehicle.

"What the hell is it?" Robinson asked. He was looking inside the thing, a hand holding open the sliding door.

"These aren't Osiris' people," Charles said, looking through the woods and for the villagers they knew had to be close by.

"No," Jackson agreed.

"So who are they?" Li asked.

"The natives, I guess. Question is, did we go to them or did they come to us?"

"Maybe both," Joe said.

"Maybe both," he agreed. "Whoever they are, they're more advanced than Osiris was."

Robinson looked up to the pyramid's capstone in the distance. "You mean like the ancient technologies your friend Chadwick was talking about?"

Jackson tapped his finger on the rifle's trigger guard as he looked around. "Hell if I know." Then he signaled forward. "C'mon, let's keep going." He jogged after the hoofprints that continued on into the wooded slope of the valley.

SIXTEEN

September 22, 2011. The City.

Paul didn't know who these Not Thems were or where they came from, but they had giants in their ranks, so he had to assume that they too were mixed up in the whole Fallen angel conspiracy of Genesis chapter six and the Book of Enoch. He was positive that the spring-loaded arrow that killed Ruth had come from one of their bows, but didn't think they'd necessarily been targeting her as a pure-blooded enemy. No, he was pretty sure that they were going to shoot whoever or whatever came out of that cave.

In addition to the gladiator he'd commandeered the horse and Carriage from and the local wagon traffic, he'd also spotted armed patrols. And after seeing the Osiris giant chained and paraded through the city, he was willing to bet the remaining three fingers on his left hand that this new Empire was currently operating under a NO VISITORS policy, trespassers shot on sight. *Unless*, he thought, *you're a hot broad. In which case you're taken to the king himself.* Paul didn't really need any help imagining what for, especially given the specific context of this crazy island narrative. Or maybe he was being too judgmental and should give the Not Thems a chance. After all, he couldn't exactly blame them for wanting to keep Osiris' progeny out of their kingdom.

Were there such things as "good" Nephilim? Like white wizards or jolly green giants? Henry and Chadwick didn't think so and believed the Book of Enoch was clear on that point, but then John had supposedly found redemption despite his own Nephilim DNA, hadn't he? Of course, in his case, thousands of years of reproduction might have diluted the bloodline enough to allow for salvation.

The monsters on the temple platform that Robyn had just walked past stood at fifteen feet, indicating that they were much closer to the original seed than John, Jackson, Chadwick, and Henry had been. These were the "heroes of old," as Genesis called them. The gods of mythology right here in the flesh, and he had to consider that they all served the same master of Darkness and for the same purpose. Which meant he couldn't just walk up and knock on the front door and ask for Robyn back.

He looked up at the sun again. He didn't want to wait until dark, but he didn't know how else he could get up the temple steps and past the caped giants. He could spend more time looking for another way in, or he could go back and get the others. But the only certain thing right now was that she was alive, the uncertainty being how long that would be the case.

He got to his feet and continued toward the temple, staying concealed within the thick forest of the valley wall.

* * * *

Robyn followed the man named Turiel across smooth, polished stone floors and through huge pillars that reached up and supported a ceiling she could barely see. Circling her mind the entire time were the words the red-robed man had spoken to her—*You are in a kingdom of Atlas, under the reign of the god Turiel, under the light of Thoth.* Her eyes took in her surroundings, and she couldn't help but feel amazed at the sheer scale of everything. Fires flickered from big decorative bowls positioned in the corners of the rooms she passed through, sweeping staircases winding up and down to other levels. Thick curtains hung in front of walls, and small trees with long bulbous petals stood beneath them.

Two soldiers walked behind her, their footsteps echoing throughout the halls and chambers until, finally, Turiel came to a stop before a set of tall metal doors. They opened silently before him, and the two soldiers behind circled in front of her and took up opposite positions beside the entranceway to this new room.

Turiel bowed slightly and indicated that she was to enter.

She looked into the room and could see light streaming through high windows, their rays concentrated on what appeared to be a pool in the center of the room. But before she could get a better look, women began appearing from the sides of the room and stepping in front of it, blocking her view. They stood motionless, hands folded in front of them, sheer gowns draped over their bodies, as if waiting for her.

Go, Turiel said into her mind. *No harm will come to you here.*

She looked at him, trying to read his intent, and he seemed to welcome the probing.

You will not be needing that, I think.

The AK-47 suddenly fell out of her hand, bouncing off the stone floor.

She looked up at him, unable to hide her surprise, and he smiled.

Then he turned and walked away.

She stood there for a moment, wondering if this might be her best chance at escape. She could reach down, pick up the rifle, and…what? She'd never make it through the city and back into the woods even if she did manage to escape the temple. So she stepped forward, passing between the two soldiers and entering the sunlit room.

The doors closed behind her.

There was a large rectangular pool in the center of the room, the water in its center aglow with sparkling light as all the rays from the windows above converged there. Long tendrils of steam wisped upward from the bath, slithering lazily through the diagonal sunbeams. Beneath the windows, drapes hung to the floor, clustering in linen piles. If they were meant to provide privacy, then the attempt had been a poor one, as the flowing curtains were as transparent as the clothes worn by the women around her.

The girls drifted over to her, their pink dresses whispering gently on the air. There were six of them, and every one of them was beautiful in a way so striking that she couldn't keep from staring. Makeup accented their facial features, their lips different shades of red.

They reached out and began touching her, navigating her body as if trying to detect some sort of deficiency or flaw. It took all her willpower not to squirm, and she turned her attention to the room around her, wondering if this was like the room Osiris' giants had kept her pure-blooded sisters in. If so, if that was what they were doing to her now, getting her ready to bed Turiel like Esther from the Bible had been made ready for the king, then forget it. She'd get him relaxed and then gouge out his eyes. Though seeing as he could read her mind, that might prove to be a bit difficult.

Once their delicate hands seemed satisfied, they began to nudge her forward to the water. Once they had her positioned at the pool's edge, the toes of her boots just an inch from the placid surface, they began to undress her. Strangely, she didn't resist. Instead, she found herself hypnotized by the steam twirling before her in some kind of synchronized dance. She was slightly aware of her shirt being cut off, of the sudden air against her chest. And then she was falling backward, gliding slowly toward the ground on a bed of female arms until she was hovering horizontally above the floor.

Her boots were pulled off. Then her pants.

She flinched when the jeans brushed over her scraped hips and thighs and almost put an end to the whole thing right then and there. But then she was standing again, the women huddled about her, their wispy gowns hanging suspended in the air after every movement. They took her by the arms and walked her forward, her right foot stepping down and into the water.

The sensation was immediate. The warmth took in her toes, wrapped around her ankle, and then swallowed her whole foot. She put her left foot in and found a second step, the water stroking her sore calf. The women followed her in, the light fabric of their clothes floating on the surface of the still water around them.

By the time the steps ended at the bottom of the bath, the water was to her shoulders, her head and neck wrapped and caressed by steamy fingers. She closed her eyes as every muscle in her body began to relax and unwind, a lifetime of tension ebbing away in an instant. She felt as if she could just lift her feet and float away, all her cares evaporating with the rising mist, the constant, searing presence of all her wounds gone.

Leaves, herbs, and flower petals floated in the water around her head, their strong fragrance striking her mind with soft pillow punches of dreamy confusion. Hands began touching her again. Lots of hands. They seemed to be everywhere all at once, so many fingers. All squeezing, rubbing, massaging. Another fragrant odor filled her nostrils as one of the girls placed her hands on her head and gently pulled it back into the water. Her golden hair swam away from her like sunrays as her feet began to rise. Floating on her back, she closed her eyes as all those many fingers washed her hair and worked the discomfort out of her legs.

A minute later, after almost drifting to sleep (or maybe she had fallen asleep, she didn't really know), she opened her eyes, wondering where all the cares that had previously concerned her had drifted off to. And what were they anyway? They'd been so important, *critical* even, yet she couldn't remember…anything. The only thing she knew right now was relaxed, carefree pleasure, and that was fine with her.

She blinked, and the ceiling came into focus through the steam clouds. There were designs up there. But up "there" seemed a long way away. She squinted, and the designs turned to stars.

Constellations.

Was it a painting on the ceiling (like the ones she'd seen in books on her parents' boat), or was she somehow gazing into space? The tight twisting of her skin over her weary bones and the massaging of her scalp seemed to free her mind from its moorings, letting her travel beyond her normal boundaries. Perhaps she was flying through the stars right now, far above this strange earth.

And then the stars were gone, her feet touching the floor again as hands pressed against her back, pushing her upright. She was barely conscious of her feet moving in front of each other, the women leading her across the pool and up the steps on the other side. A cool breeze fluttered over her flesh as she took the last step out of the water and onto the stone floor. A chill raced through her, and she looked back over her shoulder, wanting nothing more than to be back in the pool. Let her stay in there with all those hands on her for years; that would be fine with her.

But part of her mind, a tiny voice far, far away, whispered that perhaps that wouldn't be such a good thing, that this was some sort of trick. Like how Osiris had seduced her pure-blooded sisters, how the Nephilim had taken as their wives whomever they chose. But it was a crumb on the floor of an extravagant world, out of place and awkward, but hardly noticeable.

They took her to a large mirror and stood her dripping wet before it. She blinked, hardly recognizing- herself and wondering if it even was her. Her skin was clean and shiny, the light from the windows sparkling off her, accenting her curves. She almost looked plastic. Her hair was dark from being wet and tight against her head. All the dirt and blood was gone, her cuts and bruises barely visible. She'd never been this clean in her life, and it took her a moment to believe that the woman staring at her was her.

The women stood around with what looked to be expectation, as if they were awaiting her approval. Their own gowns were wet and clinging to their sculpted bodies like a coating of paint. Robyn wondered if shaking her head would get her back in the bath, but found that she was already nodding.

And then a chair appeared behind her, placed there by two of the women. The others pressed down on her shoulders, forcing her to sit in it. She went down without objection, settling into its comfortable embrace. It was lined with a kind of soft animal fur and wasn't completely unlike the chair Turiel had been sitting in out on the platform. This one didn't have fanged serpents for arms or a rising sun cresting around her head, but it was elaborate all the same, if only on a smaller scale.

A golden bowl was set at her feet. It was filled with a white, creamy substance that the women began dipping their hands into. They rubbed it all over her, pairs of hands coming from every direction and massaging the stuff into her pores. She closed her eyes again as every part of her went back into the pool and began swimming through the stars.

Someone started combing her hair.

She never wanted it to end.

* * * *

The crystal pyramid glowed in the noonday sun, peaking above the hills like an alien mountain.

"Is that where your 'key' is?" Daniel asked, struggling for breath and clutching his side.

Hunter nodded.

They'd covered a lot of ground in the last couple of hours, and they were both sweating profusely. But they were almost there now, and Hunter needed Daniel to keep it together. "I know it doesn't make sense to you," he said. "Hell, it doesn't even make sense to me. But I've seen things, things in the in-between."

Daniel just stared at him, his hands on his knees and panting.

"I got a glimpse behind the curtain of this place, Danny boy. These plac*es*. And what I saw backstage was much bigger than any of us imagined. It's more than Osiris being trapped here and trying to escape." He looked up to the pyramid. "A lot more than that."

Daniel didn't really know what that meant, and he wasn't sure if Hunter really knew himself. "Whatever you say. But you do know how to get out of here?" he asked, bypassing the bigger picture Hunter was trying to set before him and going straight to the only thing that ever really mattered.

"I do."

"How?"

"I can't explain it. It's something that's in my head. Some metaphysical force that I can feel sitting up there waiting to be used. Thing is…there's someone else here that wants to use it, too."

Impatience pinched Daniel's face. "I don't understand."

"I don't really get it myself, my man."

"But we need to get to the pyramid?"

"Well, first we need to get to the temple if we want to save Robyn."

"What?" he blurted, standing up tall. "What about Robyn? What are you talking about?"

"These other people, these people from Before… They have Robyn."

"How do you know about Robyn?"

"Right." And Hunter realized that he'd gone into the closet *before* Jack ran into her on her parents' boat, and that he'd actually never met Robyn before. "Let's just say I had a view from the top."

Daniel threw his hands up in disgust, resisting the urge to chase after whatever that meant. He knew it would only lead to some other cryptic half-answer. "Is she in danger?"

Hunter nodded, his eyes going distant. "Oh, yes. Yes indeed," he whispered.

And that did it. However close Daniel had been to giving up, to throwing in the towel and taking a long mental vacation, there was no questioning his resolve to press on now.

Hunter wished he could give him something more, to help him understand, but there were simply no words that could rationally convey that hiding feeling lurking around in his head. That dark vacuum in the closet had taken him backstage, to the set of this strange show called *Island.* And there, he had been introduced to the cast, had even been given a tour of all the mechanisms and quantum machineries that controlled the sets—opening and closing the curtains, how the scenes transitioned from one location to the next… Yet there was no visual concept in his mind, no memory of seeing anything. Just a *feeling.* An instinctual, primeval axiom hiding out in the shadows of his mind.

He'd never met Robyn, yet he knew of Jackson's love for her and her love for him simply because he'd seen their roles in the story. And he knew now that she was with an angel that had landed with the two hundred rebels on Mount Hermon back in the days of Jared. He also knew that, until now, this angel had been completely unaware of his own place within the storyline of this show, that he had a role in the future, yet age-long conspiracy to reinstate Satan's Golden Age on earth. And *that* was the whole shebang. The plot. The script that all the characters were reading from, whether they knew it or not.

And who was orchestrating the drama? The director, of course. And Hunter had met him in that abyss. He was insane, but he had an agenda, and he meant to see the story through. That *thing* that had climbed *out* of the closet…it was moving all the pieces, all the subplots, toward an apocalyptic climax. And when the final score faded out on the credits of humanity, he'd take a bow to *his* applauding master.

"Hunter?" Daniel asked.

He blinked, his mind returning from the invisible support structures of this existence. "But I don't know if Robyn is part of the final act or not."

"What act?"

"When Abaddon is released in the end of days."

"I don't understand what you're saying!" Daniel shouted, his hands balling into fists.

"Come on. They're going to beat us there." Then he smiled sympathetically. "You might say it's not fair. But there it is, so time to share…what I know with the big red demon and get us out of there."

"What?"

"Let's ride."

* * * *

After traversing the valley wall all the way to the back side of the temple, Paul slid down into a concealed position, sure there had to be guards regularly patrolling an area so close to the capital. There were surely guards all over the temple complex, standing around the courtyards and lining the stairs. There were horses and more carriages moving around the small roads like city traffic, crowds of people still gathered and talking excitedly about what they'd just seen. Paul wondered how much they knew of their new surroundings, if they realized that they were no longer in Kansas anymore.

He took in the back side of the complex, noting the soldiers, the peasants and farmers, and the only entrance he could see. It was at the top of the ziggurat steps, on the platform beneath the pillared temple just like on the other side. And of course, there was a pair of giants standing at attention on either side of the closed doors, staring out over the distance and to the pyramid a mile away. If he somehow managed to get through the courtyard and past the ground guards (maybe blending in with the visiting villagers to do so), he knew he'd only make it two steps up the temple before he'd have giants descending from above and guards climbing up from behind. And at that point his little rinky-dinky-do knife would be useless. He'd have to use the AK, and maybe, just maybe, he could put them all down with its bullets. But then what if its echoing reports were to result in that C. S. Lewis bell ringing out, awakening not a witch, but an entire empirical army of Titans? These Not Thems were not the bums that Osiris' ogres were. These, indeed, were the heroes of old, the things of legend and lore, and there would be no surviving an army of them.

His gaze went across the courtyard and all the way to the opposite side of the valley. He lifted the spyglass and aimed it at the wooded slope and could just make out networks of roads. One of those roads in particular had a person pulling a packed mule behind him. Paul contemplated disguising himself as a farmer, but didn't know how that would get him into the temple. The giants were just as likely to lop the head off an approaching villager as they were to grant access into the emperor's presence. Actually, he realized, it was probably *more* likely that he'd just get his head punted out of the yard.

He looked up the other way, to the pyramid, and could see those monkey things circling the capstone. This was as close as he'd been to them, and through the spyglass, they looked even more hideous. They were rats with monkey tails and bat wings. And though they were nearly invisible behind the blinding light of the capstone, he managed a clear glance or two before having to look away and rub his eyes.

He swore, not knowing what to do, only that he was running out of time.

The taxi driver's cell phone rang in his pocket.

* * * *

By the time the massages ended, her hair had been braided into long ropes hanging down over her breasts. They stood her up and placed a gown over her head, its white fabric falling down around her, circling her feet.

Robyn stared ahead, into the mirror. If she hadn't recognized herself before, then the person before her now was even more of a stranger. Makeup had been applied to her face, and her eyes appeared darker now, her lips fuller. For a long moment, she wasn't certain that the girl in the mirror *was* her. She thought she looked beautiful, yet there was something forbidden about her appearance, about how it made her feel. She moved her fingers, and the image in the mirror did the same. She looked to the left, and the girl facing her looked to the right. It *was* her.

"Now what?" Robyn whispered, still mystified by the bath and mesmerized by the mirror. She pulled at the gown, rubbing the material between her fingers. It was soft and seemed to have a little more substance than the pink gowns the women wore. But if she stared hard enough into the mirror, she could still see her nakedness beneath it. And for some reason, she didn't care.

The women blinked and looked at each other, obviously not understanding her words. But then one of them motioned back toward the entrance she'd first come through.

"Oh." Apparently, her time with them had come to an end.

They formed a line, three in front of her and three in back, and led her around the steaming waters, back toward the doors. She eyed the bath greedily as she passed beside it, wanting nothing more than to slip back beneath its surface. But then the doors were opening, and she was passing through them, re-entering the large hall. The two guards still positioned at the doors stepped in front of her. They motioned for her to follow them. Taking one last glance over her shoulder to the women clustered around the pool, she began walking.

Whatever fragrance and lotions they'd used on her were clearly influencing her state of being, creating a bizarre sense of detachment that seemed almost dreamlike, as if she were in a trance.

Finally, they came to the end of the hall and to another large entranceway that was being guarded by two more sentries. They stood in the shadows cast by the masonry decorating the doorway.

A form appeared in the huge doorway.

Hello, my princess.

The voice echoed in her swirling mind.

Come in; be with me.

She found her feet moving beneath her, carrying her toward the voice.

SEVENTEEN

September 22, 2011. The Valley.

Jackson reached up and ran his hand down the horse's silky neck. Then he combed its long dark mane with his fingers. "What a specimen you are," he whispered. It slapped its tail and let out a soft neigh in response.

"So he went on foot from here," Charles said, looking ahead through the birch trees.

Jackson nodded. "The woods get too dense, so he had to leave the horse behind." He looked at the horse. "Right?"

The horse just stared with its big black eyes.

"How far ahead do you think he is?" Li asked.

Jackson shrugged. "I don't know, but I think we should double-time it before he goes and does something stupid."

Robinson took his hat off and pointed it down through the trees, at the village below them. "Who do you think they are?"

The sun came down through the branched fingers above them, spotlighting the grass in swaying, splintered patchworks of light. Birds chirped and darted through the canopy, insects buzzed, and critters scurried.

Patrick shook his head. "Not from here, that's for sure."

"You'll have to first know where 'here' is before you can say that," Jackson responded.

They all stared at him.

"I can't even imagine all the side effects of using the pyramid. Of what it could've done." But within the privacy of his own mind—where a schizophrenic, round table meeting of sorts had been fully under way for some time now—he was trying desperately to come up with a better answer than that. So far he had nailed down the assumption that there were now at least three different but co-existing Bermudas. Whether the overlap was time oriented or plane oriented (as in different periods of Bermuda's physical history mixing with Osiris' metaphysical basement Bermuda, or alternate realities interweaving beneath their feet) was a harder question to answer. Maybe both. Maybe something else entirely. But there was Bermuda with its modern, twenty-first-century house (with a stocked fridge, flat screen TV, and a closet leading to hell), the Bermuda never settled (or the Triangle version Osiris had been trapped in), and now this Bermuda with all that and a bag of chips (namely this village, the upcoming city and pyramid and its people, the cruise ship, the storage containers of AK-47s, Ivan and Mollings, and so forth and so on). But there was something about the idea of this New Territory being a piece of ten-thousand-year-old real estate that was nagging at him more than all the rest.

"What is it?" Robinson asked.

The round table was cluttered with Ronald's ancient sea maps, the conversation now concerning all the different theories of Atlantis—in particular the one about scientists believing that Antarctica was once higher in the Atlantic prior to the pole shift. But if this was a piece of antediluvian property, and the poles had since shifted, wouldn't there be a difference in climate? *No*, his brain answered. *Not if the pole shift hadn't happened yet.* But he didn't say any of this. Instead, he just shook his head, because none of it really mattered. Knowing where they were or when they were wouldn't make any difference in getting Robyn back.

"Come on, then," Joe said, and took off toward the pyramid.

* * * *

Hunter led Daniel down the wooded slope and all the way to the valley floor, just inside the tree line. The hustle and bustle of peasants and merchants sang out in blurred activity just on the other side of the tree line. Daniel had been mesmerized by the sight of the city ever since being able to see it from atop a cresting hill a mile back. Since then, they'd traversed the side of the valley wall, him muttering the whole way, "What is this place? What is this place? What the hell is this place?"

Peering through the trees and down a busy street nestled between rows of stone buildings, Hunter finally answered him. "A place from another time, Danny boy."

"And Robyn's here?"

"She's *up* there." He pointed to the temple that stood in the middle of the valley.

"How are we going to get her?" But his eyes were still transfixed on the people, the *strangers*, walking up and down the streets and in and out of buildings.

"Well—" he looked up at the sun and then across the city, to the opposite side of the valley "—I believe that Jackson and company are just coming into position over yonder."

"What?" He peered over the top of the crowded buildings, but the opposite tree line was almost two miles away, and he couldn't—

Wait. There was something.

"What is that?"

"That," Hunter responded, jumping back to his feet, "is our signal."

* * * *

The hair on the back of his neck standing ablaze with sixth-sense fire, Paul slowly pulled the phone from his pocket. As he brought out the device that had been handed to him in a future, real-world Bermuda, he quickly moved his eyes to the temple's base, afraid that the noise might have initiated an investigation. But the jingle singing out in his hand didn't appear to cut through the ambient commotion of the city and reach the temple guards half a mile away—even if it seemed deafening to Paul.

It was that Doors' song, the one Hunter had been singing before disappearing into the closet. It echoed off the trees, that synth organ and machine-gun drum sounding like the end of the world in a bizarre vacuum of haunted lyrics. *Strange days indeed*, Paul thought. But according to the display screen, the ringing wasn't due to an incoming call but rather a received text message. From NUMBER UNKNOWN. A hovering icon next to the words indicated an attached image.

His thumb moved to tap the message, which was absurd since the phone was (a) long dead, (b) not linked to a network, and (c) most likely deactivated by now (or then, he wasn't really sure which). But why should he have to touch anything? If the paranormal entity behind the message wanted him to see something, why not just have the picture appear on the screen? Why go through the trouble of making it ring at all? Why conjure up a text from UNKNOWN? *Because*, he realized as his thumb wavered over the screen, *this is a haunting.* And a haunting was more effective with a soundtrack and a series of compounding events that led to—

He tapped the screen, if nothing else hoping to put an end to the music.

The song ended abruptly as an image appeared.

A guy's face.

Paul squinted and turned his body to block the sunlight coming through the canopy over his shoulder.

It was the guy from the carriage. The gladiator with the blond hair sweeping down beneath his helmet.

He looked dead, his eyes closed, helmet dented, and blood flowing from his nose.

As he brought the phone closer to his face, trying to make sense of it, the Doors song suddenly rang out again. He swore, almost dropping the phone, his heart a rocket launched in his chest without the benefit of a countdown.

Another message from UNKNOWN.

Another picture.

No, not a picture. This one had what looked like a cassette tape attached to it. It was a video.

He tapped it. And watched as two bare-chested giants first tore the guy apart and then ate him. They only paused to throw pieces of his body to hidden shapes crouched in the background.

The video played for thirty seconds and stopped. He almost touched the screen again, curious if the video was stored on the phone, accessible again and again, or if having seen what he was supposed to see, it was now gone. Before he could find out, another text came.

HERE THEY COME, it said.

And then: ;-)

The phone went dark, returning to its natural state.

Paul looked up, his eyes scanning back and forth for whoever "they" were, and noticed movement at the temple. He dropped the phone back into his pocket and whipped out the scope. The guards were running away from their posts, circling around to the front of the ziggurat.

"What the hell?" he whispered. He continued to watch as the back side of the temple transitioned to the front, leaving the back entrance unguarded.

Without another thought, he jumped to his feet and broke out of the trees, sprinting into the clearing of the rear courtyard. Maybe it was a trick, a ploy to get him into the open where he could be picked up by these Not Thems, but it was a chance he had to take. There would be no other. And besides, his mind tried to reassure him as he ran, if it is the girl communicating through the phone, then why would she set him up for destruction now after helping him escape the ship?

And the unwanted answer shouted back, *Because she wanted to bring you here for a fate far worse.*

No! He would make it! He had to! A surge of emotion broke through all the old levees he'd spent years fortifying and flooded his mind, pushing him across the near half mile in under four minutes with a battle-charging insanity normally reserved for all-or-nothing, save-the-world, we're-probably-all-going-to-die-anyway, blaze-of-glory antics. And in the center of that adrenaline rush, every hostility he felt toward Jackson was swept away by the raging torrents of desperation. All the blame for bringing them here, for Nick and Chris…it all drowned beneath the crushing reality of their position.

Flashes of Denise standing in her glorious wedding dress suddenly propelled into his mind's eye, her hands in Jackson's as she said the sacred words, *till death do us part.* Then they were putting her body into the ground as Jackson held him, convulsing tears from his shattered soul.

Jackson was his brother. Robyn was Denise.

He wouldn't let her die again.

But just as he reached the stone steps, oblivious to the fire in his legs, a trumpet sounded. It was deafening, and the sound of it actually took him off his feet, a sonic wave slamming into him and tackling him across the grass. He'd been in the front row of a concert before, with a row of speakers lined up beneath the stage in front of him. When the show's opening bass line hammered from the stage, the entire crowd had taken a giant startled step backward. This was like that, only a hundred times stronger. And, unlike the last trumpet that had seemed to signal a type of victory throughout the kingdom, this one was more foreboding, with plenty of that deep, nauseating bass. It reverberated through his body as he stumbled back to his feet. He couldn't tell where it was coming from, if it was originating from the top of the temple or from the pyramid behind. He opened his mouth wide, trying to alleviate the pressure building in his head, and stumbled for the steps.

Everything was shaking, his vision blurred, and he needed to use his free hand to steady himself as he climbed the stairs, his other hand pointing the AK at the entrance above him.

A bald-headed man, his head splitting into two and then melting back together again, came out of the temple with a spear in his hands (two spears…*three* spears?).

Paul squeezed his eyes shut, trying to get everything to stop moving. And then…it did. He immediately pulled the trigger, and the man's left shoulder punched backward, the force of the impact twirling his body as it went limp and fell crashing to the stairs. He tumbled crazily downward, coming to a sprawled stop halfway between the platform and Paul.

The shot rang out on the wings of sudden silence, the trumpet blast having ended a mere second or two before he fired. The *crack!* rebounded off the temple and echoed through the valley behind him, and he was sure that a hundred more men would come pouring out of the ziggurat at any second. *Though*, he thought, *that was assuming they knew what the sound was.* Maybe they'd never heard a gunshot before. Maybe the loud bang on the heels of the horn would only result in a few curious heads peeking out of nearby windows and entranceways, wondering if one of the distant mountains might have split. Although, if these were the same Not Thems that had fired the spring-loaded arrow at Ruth, then they'd already gotten their firearm education.

Before anyone else appeared coming out of the temple though, something else happened.

The sound of more gunshots. *Other* gunshots.

From the front of the temple, in the city.

AK-47s.

When he finally reached the platform, the text message was playing back in his head, and he wondered if the "they" could actually be Jackson and the remaining Puree army. Who else would have AK-47s?

His spine tingled as he raced for the entranceway. Though he believed the commotion had to be his pure-blooded friends, the Doors song that had ushered in the message of their arrival suggested something else…

* * * *

Jackson, Robinson, Joe, Charles, Li, Patrick, Wilson, and Sanders all beheld the city sprawled out before them, their collective mind reeling at its presence. They could see the ziggurat temple at the city's center and could tell that the main road splitting the valley in half went straight up its steps and through a set of doors being guarded by two armored giants. The crystal pyramid towered above it from the back of the valley a mile away.

Wilson turned to Jackson, his black hair pulled back into a ponytail, revealing the big white scar running across his forehead. It looked like someone had tried to get a brain snack out of him. "This is…too much."

Jackson nodded. "It does mock the mind, doesn't it?"

Wilson shook his head like there were a few loose parts up there that just needed to fall into place before everything would make sense.

"Don't try to understand it," Jackson whispered. "You'll only make yourself mad."

Wilson turned his head and exchanged an unsure smile with Robinson before returning his eyes to the anomaly beneath them.

"So what now?" Joe asked.

But Jackson didn't have a clue. They couldn't just walk down Main Street and take the steps up to the temple doors and knock. *Hello, we're looking for a couple of friends of ours. You haven't seen them, have you?* And why would they want to? There was no evidence that Robyn was even here. She was just as likely to be back with Samuel, Jared, and Ivan, eating lunch and wondering where the hell everyone had gone off to.

But Paul *was* here. Definitely.

He looked down from their elevated position. They were about a quarter of the way up the valley wall, concealed behind a row of twisted trees and dense undergrowth. The city was teeming with activity, people filling the tight streets that were carved between rows of stone buildings. To their left, back where the valley began, he could see a steady flow of villagers crossing the long bridge on their way back to the woods. He figured they were most likely the inhabitants of the empty villages they'd passed on their way here. Whatever had brought them to the city, whatever event the trumpet had signaled, must have ended. *Show's over, folks, time to return to your sheep and sh—*

He looked back to his right, to the ziggurat, and wondered if its interior would be anything like Osiris' temple.

"Do you think she could be in there?" Arkansas Joe asked, following Jackson's eyes.

"I don't think anyone could get in there without an invitation."

Robinson adjusted his hat. "Which begs another question, doesn't it?"

Jackson looked at him.

"How the hell are we going to get into the pyramid at the winter solstice?"

"Dude," Jackson said impatiently, "one problem at a time." But the truth was, he'd been thinking the same thing.

"Well?" Li asked, still waiting for an answer to Wilson's initial question.

Jackson sighed. "Let's circle around and get a look out back. Paul's here somewhere, even if Robyn isn't."

They nodded and began to move.

"Wait!" Sanders snapped.

They all paused, trying to discern what had alarmed him.

"Do you feel that?" Sanders asked.

And just as they realized the ground was vibrating, they heard the noise of approaching footfalls. Running.

"Get down!" Robinson shouted in a whisper.

And no sooner had they hit the dirt than a swarm of men and giants came exploding down through the forest above them, stampeding down the valley wall and heading straight for them.

They lay perfectly still as the familiar foes passed straight by them, some of them coming within ten yards of their position. The Leftover army continued on down the sloped terrain and exited the woods, entering the city.

Then, before anything else could happen, a sound blasted through the length of the valley. It seemed to shake the entire city, and every winged creature in the surrounding woods took flight.

Jackson and the others covered their ears, the sound kicking them in the gut and stealing their breath. The charging army must've felt the same way, because more than a few of them went sprawling. Even the city folk stopped what they were doing to put outstretched hands against fixed objects in order to steady themselves. The villagers that had already been leaving the city began to run.

And then it stopped. As quickly and abruptly as it had come, it vanished, returning everything to an eerie silence that—

A sharp crack sounded in the distance and echoed through the valley in a hollow rebound that seemed insignificant on the heels of such a furious alarm.

But Jackson knew what that sound was, and his head shot up. *An AK!* And there was no doubt in his mind who had fired it. It had to be either Paul or Robyn. No one else had assault rifles. At least no one else that he knew of... He supposed it was possible that another contingent of displaced people could've—

More AKs went off. But the sounds of these shots were much closer, coming from the Fallen remnants of Osiris' army themselves as they sprayed the startled city folk with stolen bullets. Because unless there was another stash of AKs that happened to wash ashore somewhere, there was only one place those rifles could've come from.

* * * *

Robyn stared up at the ceiling. No, *through* the ceiling, for there was a circular opening—*a window!* she realized—positioned directly over the bed she was lying on. A few clouds swam through the blue sky-ocean, their shadows gliding over the walls of the room and wiggling across the floor like phantom fish. The sun was a golden ball behind the clouds, inching its way toward the window's center. She could feel its light on her body, fingers of warmth caressing her skin. Even more so when the clouds split, and she had to close her eyes against its brightness.

Her mind was full of fog, a labyrinth of fleeing thoughts all lost and unable to be caught. She was in a dream, and the dream had her. She tried to sit up (or at least she thought she had), but her body didn't respond. For some reason, this struck her as amusing, and unable to help it, she smiled.

You are beautiful.

She managed to move her head to the right, her eyes dragging slowly behind, the room a blur. She could make out the form of a person standing beside her, next to the bed, but she couldn't bring him into focus. *Who—*

It was the tall man in the funny hat who could read her mind...

She almost giggled as she recalled that hat, with all its strange feathers and the diamond that sat there like a third eye in the center of his forehead. She tried to find that diamond now, recalling its alluring gleam. But though she couldn't bring her eyes to focus completely, she was sure there was no hat on his head now.

Then came a fleeting glimpse of what he was going to do to her, and she found the image that it conjured to be both enticing and horrible at the same time.

You will love it. The man's voice (what was his name?) slithered through her mind. *You will love…me.*

And then his huge hands were on her legs.

From deep beneath the surface of comprehension, her mind associated the hand on her right leg with pleasure, while the hand on her left was horror. And they kept switching back and forth, like he was crossing two gloved hands while somehow continuing to slide them up, up, up…

I want to know where you came from. How you got here. I want to know so much about you, because in ways that I do not yet fully understand, you have been sent to me. For me. For this moment and the child it will produce, but also, I think, for something much greater still.

His hands paused beneath the hem of her sheer dress, and she could feel his eyes consuming her. He was on the bed now, too, his shadow cast over her, his head blocking out the sun.

And then she remembered what she was going to do to him.

His hands began moving again, and her mind lost hold of that thought; it spun away into some far-off place deep within the fog.

You have secrets that I will extract. But right now, daughter of Eve, my princess, let us be one.

He lay on top of her, his body large and crushing. She felt his breath on her face. His hands seemed to be everywhere.

No, she thought. And the word broke forth from the fog like a bolt of lightning. Yet, she couldn't *do* anything.

Yes, his voice answered back.

This was the moment! This was when she was to gouge out his eyes or rip his throat out with her teeth! This was her chance!

You can certainly try, my dear.

His hands clamped her bare hips as her mind seemed to detach from its anchorage, a hurricane of conflicting emotion swelling to an incomprehensible wave she couldn't withstand.

He—

A sound.

A deafening, roaring sound that served as the cosmic soundtrack to this angel's defiance of God's universal order, of a violation so great that it transcended her physical body and profaned reality itself. Her mind seemed to break open as the earth itself shook with his lust. Her mind drifted away, leaving her until…

Until she realized that he was no longer lying on top of her, but now kneeling over her. And even from so great a distance, she could see the wide uncertainty in his eyes.

The noise was something else entirely, and as it blasted through the room, reverberating off the walls and causing everything to hum, she found that its deafening, shaking power was actually reeling her back in.

The man (*Turiel—that's what his name is!*) took his hands off her and leaped off the bed. He said something that she didn't understand, and then raced out of the room, leaving her on her back and staring up through the skylight at the blinding sun.

The sound stopped, and the room quit shaking.

Thank you, she thought. *Thank you, God...*

And then, in the sudden stillness, what sounded like cracks or pops began echoing around her. There was something vaguely familiar about the noise, but her mind couldn't hold on to its weaving tail. She closed her eyes. She needed to get up, to leave, to go back to...*who*? There was someone there. She could make out his form, but couldn't see his face or recall his name. All she knew was that she loved him and that she needed to find him. She needed to...

Spread out on the huge bed in Turiel's private chambers, she fell asleep.

* * * *

Paul ran across the platform, passing through massive pillars that stood supporting the glorious architecture above it. As he reached the entranceway, the doors left open by the man he'd just shot, three more bald men came rushing out right in front of him. He barely had time to squeeze the trigger before colliding with them, but he managed a short burst in the ten feet that separated them. And though all three of them were dead on their feet, their momentum continued propelling them forward, and Paul had to sidestep their collapsing corpses.

He moved past them and into the temple, looking down the smoking barrel of the AK and sighting the long, tall corridor he found himself in. It seemed to dead-end about half a football field away, huge Greek-like columns lining both sides of it. He looked up to the ceiling and was surprised to see all manner of artwork decorating it. Images that worked to construct a timeline, or maybe the sacred events of some mystery religion... The work seemed to transcend yet somehow weave together the styles of native cave paintings, Egyptian hieroglyphics, and Michelangelo's work on the Sistine Chapel. But even more impressive than the art was the sheer volume of the room itself. The ceiling must be fifty feet high, he thought, and the pillars... The first few pillars on either side resembled Corinthian columns, but then they became caryatid-like—support pillars sculpted into the figures of women. They were giants, nude statues that were so lifelike Paul half-expected them to start moving. Their eyes seemed to be on him, watching him, their long hair wrapped around their bodies nets to be flung at him.

He swung the rifle to his left and then to his right, finding that he was standing in the middle of an upside-down T, long empty halls continuing past the pillars on either side of him. He stayed straight, passing between the caryatid's, swearing that their stone eyes were tracking him. He found it hard to believe that he even knew what the statues were called, and could only think to blame Jackson for one of the times they'd been in Athens. No doubt his running dialogue had included such details, and for some reason that specific description had gotten stored in some unused closet within his brain. There was something else that Jackson had said to them months ago too (or maybe it had been Chadwick), something about bald men... But those details weren't kicking free and remained as an annoying itch in the very back of his mind. He hoped it wasn't important.

The columns towered over him and cast long crisscrossing shadows across the smooth stone floor. He continued to look left and right, past the women giants, and could see a wall beyond them. But when he got to the end of the hall, he found that he hadn't been at the top of a T, but rather an I. However, this end of the I was not simply another straight corridor, but a shorter one that led to opposite flights of stairs, both of which went up into the palace and down into the ziggurat.

He paused and considered his options as sweat ran down his face and stung the sliced side of his face. The guy with the headdress was most likely the king of this territory, and didn't all bosses dwell at the top of their castles, where they look out over their kingdom and feel the rush of power and gloat in their arrogance?

So up it was. But to the left or right? He looked back and forth, unable to decide. He thought that they might both lead to the same floor, but couldn't be certain. Perhaps one led to the penthouse and the other to the barracks…

And then a shout came echoing from his left. It came from a man, and it was a woman he was looking for, so—

Words.

He paused, tilting his ear toward the voice. It was shouting, someone was shouting. And though he couldn't make out the sentences, he could pick out a word here and there. And they were English words.

He ran left, and as he approached the enormous stairs (they were fifteen feet wide), he could tell the voice was coming from below.

He swore, hesitating for a second. Now he could understand everything the man was shouting, and there was no missing the accent projecting the words. He was pretty sure who it was down there, but it wasn't Robyn. He wouldn't be with Robyn. Robyn was up. Robyn was with the boss man, maybe about to be raped. But the man below sounded like he was being tortured.

Paul looked up the stairs, then looked down the stairs.

Robyn or Mr. Mollings?

Denise or the poor soul interjected from 1969?

He swore again…and took the stairs up.

* * * *

As the Fallen Leftovers stormed into the city like an avalanche spilling down the valley wall, Jackson motioned for the others to begin moving back the way they'd come. Getting mixed up in this wouldn't do anyone any good. They'd find a nice, concealed spot up on the hilltop somewhere and wait out the attack. Depending on how things unfolded, they could sneak back down and look for Paul in the aftermath.

But just twenty feet into their ascent back up the steep terrain, another wave of soldiers suddenly came pouring over the rise above them. There had to be almost a hundred, way more than Jackson thought would still be alive after the closet demon had devoured so many of them on the beach months earlier.

There were scores of giants mixed into their ranks too, and they were all coming straight at them. There would be no evading them this time.

Jackson put his back to the charging army. "Run!" he screamed and ran down the hill, trying to keep his legs from bicycling crazily out from under him. They needed to get onto the city streets.

* * * *

He raced to the top of the stairs and entered another pillar-lined corridor that led to yet another staircase fifty yards away. He sprinted down the hall and reached the next set of stairs just as a robed man appeared at the top of them. Hot shell casings spat out of the assault rifle as Paul squeezed the trigger, the blasts echoing deafeningly around him. The shells bounced off the stairs even as he continued to mount them. The man in the red robe flew sideways, bouncing off the wall and then tumbling headfirst down the stairs. Paul jumped over him.

He cleared the steps and slid to a stop in an enormous room filled with large vertical windows. They lined both sides of the wide chamber, and rays of light entered from either side, intersecting like laser Xs over the long velvety carpet that stretched from Paul's boots all the way to a raised platform against the distant wall a hundred yards away. A large throne sat positioned atop the platform. Huge rectangular windows were carved out of the stone wall behind it to form a string of vertical bands stretching from floor to ceiling. Clouds floated by them as the throne gleamed in the sunlight. This wasn't the chair the guy had been sitting in outside. This thing was a permanent fixture. And even at this distance, Paul could tell that it was a work of craftsmanship unequaled. Its back stretched up and fanned out, intertwining with sculpted designs carved into the wall between the windows.

He began walking, swinging the rifle back and forth, waiting for someone or something to materialize out of the shadows cast by more caryatids—though these were not sculptures of women holding up the next floor with their heads, but bare-chested men straight off the pages of Greek mythology. Telamones. They were holding the ceiling up with their hands, biceps bulging, their eyes hidden behind visored helmets.

A noise from above drew his eyes, and he looked up, swooping the AK skyward.

Big chandeliers hung from golden chains fixed to crossing oak rafters that spanned the ceiling left to right every twenty feet or so. They sat hovering twenty feet in the air. Only they weren't your ordinary castle-variety chandeliers. These were hollow globes fashioned from gold bands, candles fixed on their outsides like orbiting moons. They all seemed to be spinning in lazy slow motion from the crossing breeze blowing through the room. And then he saw something hanging out of one of the globes and realized that they weren't globes at all. They were round cages.

A leg was sticking through the bottom of the next one, and as he got closer, walking until he was directly under it, he saw that there was actually a person in there.

The figure moaned.

Paul swore, startled that the person was still alive. How he was still alive he wasn't sure. The person was all bones. He followed the carpet to the next hanging cage, and there was no doubt that the person in that one was dead. He went to the next.

A girl, malnourished and dehydrated, well on her way to becoming like the ones hanging before her. She stared down at him with eyes that weren't really seeing.

He continued on, each cage he came to occupied by someone a little more alive, and he began to get a sense of what this was. He'd heard of Ashurnasirpal, the Assyrian king, flaying his enemies alive in his presence and then using their skin as wallpaper, their heads as crowns, and he thought that this might be something along the same depraved lines. From his position sitting on the throne, the feather-headed king could entertain himself with watching his victims slowly transform from fresh, attractive bodies to decaying corpses. From the pattern observed, Paul guessed the newest ones were stripped naked and hung up directly in front of him. Once their skin lost its lively tones and they began to shrivel with weakness, they were moved farther back so a new body could take its place before the king's eyes. And all the prisoners had to do, of course, was look down the row of hanging cages to see their own hopeless fate.

As if to confirm his suspicion, a healthy voice began crying out from the other end of the room, from above the throne. Paul didn't know whether there were other kingdoms that this one had been at war with, or whether the guy simply had his own citizens rounded up from time to time to satisfy his sordid appetite for death. Either way, these were not good people, and Robyn was not safe here. There was nothing he could do for the prisoners hanging from the ceiling, but there was still a chance to save Jack's girl. *But Mr. Mollings is going to end up in one of those cages*, a voice inside his head argued. He shoved the voice aside and sprinted down the carpet, ignoring the echoing cries of those still alive and their frantic movements that had set the cages to swinging. And he realized that was exactly what they were probably encouraged to do. With the candles fixed to the outside of the balled cages, it would make for one hell of a nighttime show—them swinging back and forth in flickering light like nude acrobats screaming hopelessly for their freedom.

About halfway through the room, another carpet came sweeping out from between the statues, cutting the room into a cross. He stopped at the velvet intersection and saw that the new road led to more stairs both on his left and on his right. He could see the city out the windows to his right and figured that to be the scene the emperor's private chambers would overlook, so he ran in that direction, passing through two enormous sculptures that he hoped wouldn't lift their stone legs and stomp him like a bug.

He made it past and to the bottom of the next set of stairs when he heard steps clacking off the floor behind him and turned just in time to see a spear leave the outstretched hand of a bald sentry. He moved his head at the last possible second, and the spear flew past him, bouncing off the floor twenty feet down the hall. He fired the AK from his hip and stitched the guard from beneath his right pectoral up to his left eye. Paul ejected the magazine and slammed home another one in its place. He turned back to face the stairs just as a fury of descending feet came trickling down at him. He threw himself to his right and scampered back behind one of the columns. He hid in its shadow and hoped the army of soldiers would turn down the long carpet and just pass right by him on their way to defend the city streets from whoever was attacking it on the outside.

But no footsteps rebounded past him.

Stealing a glance around the column's stone calf, he saw that the soldiers had taken up a guarded position along the steps, intent on protecting whatever was on the next floor. Spears were held ready, arrows were nocked, and a wall of shields had been erected.

He was close.

Taking a deep breath, he poked the rifle around the pillar and squeezed the trigger. The rifle bucked in his arms as bullets ricocheted in showered sparks off whatever metal the guards' shields had been forged from, deflecting into the heads of those standing farther up the steps. Other bullets did manage to punch through the shields, finding flesh on the other side, and blood sprayed the staircase walls. Bodies began to tumble down, rolling into the backs of those still standing.

Paul stepped out from behind the enormous leg and put the rifle to his shoulder, picking off the few guards left standing with precise headshots. He lowered the rifle and ejected the mag. His ears were ringing, and he couldn't hear it hit the floor. He replaced it with one of the few left in his pockets.

As the ringing subsided, distant sounds from outside came wafting through the windows. Gunshots, screaming. But there was another sound. A strange sound that might still be from his ringing head. It was there and then it wasn't, drowned by the gunshots outside. It was familiar though, a—

Realization dawned, and he thrust his hand into his front pocket, pulling out the cell phone.

Another image had been sent.

He tried to work it with his limited hand, almost dropping it in the process. Finally, his thumb hit the appropriate buttons and the image opened.

The picture was a snapshot of a girl lying on a bed. She was in a dress that seemed more ceremonial than anything else. Like a honeymoon outfit. He squinted at the picture, looking closer.

It was Robyn.

The image was a bird's-eye view that seemed to be looking down through a hole in the roof. There wasn't much else in the digital image, the edges of the bed nearly marking the four corners of the phone's screen. He set the rifle down and worked the cell with both hands. He tapped the keypad, zooming into the bed and navigating its edges, looking for any clues that might give away her surroundings.

The phone chimed again, and the image was replaced by words.

BEHIND YOU.

He turned, but there was nothing there.

And then watched as a person stepped out from behind one of the statues, a crossbow aimed at his head.

* * * *

Jackson made it to the valley floor with Li, Charles, Wilson, Patrick, Joe, Sanders, and Robinson on his heels. They'd managed to stay ahead of the landslide, but now found themselves between both waves. The first ahead of them, shooting their way onto the city streets, and the second behind them, heading for the city streets.

"You know where those rifles came from!" Robinson called out to Jackson as he sprinted beside him.

Jackson did, but the only thing they could do right now was try to survive this moment. They'd have to worry about the other thing later. He pointed to a row of buildings that sat off to their right, sitting tall on the outskirts of the city. There looked to be a small alley between them, set apart from the wider streets that intersected the crowded city like a network of veins. "Over there!"

They ran through the field that spanned the distance between the valley wall and the heart of the metropolis, coming at it from the side. Twisted dirt paths flashed beneath their feet as they hurdled obstacles left behind by fleeing peasants. Abandoned carts, wagons, and livestock littered the outlying roads and actually served as a sort of cover from the army pressing in behind them.

As they got closer to the city's exterior, they could see the first wave of Fallen soldiers sweeping their rifles back and forth, firing without even aiming. Most of their bullets seemed to strike buildings, chipping away stone and spraying fleeing citizens with shrapnel, but due to the high volume of people crowding the streets, there were plenty of bodies falling too.

One of the giants grabbed a man that had tried making a break for the woods, and ripped him in half, tossing his body in two opposite directions. A group of people who had contemplated a similar dash for the hills suddenly turned around and ran back into the city, hoping the giant hadn't spotted them first.

"Look!" Charles hollered from behind Jackson, pointing to their right and up above the buildings. A steady stream of gleaming soldiers came spilling out of the temple and descended the front of the stepped ziggurat.

They were too far away to make out, but there was no doubt in Jackson's mind that this was the city guard assembling for a counterattack. He knew that his merry band of pure-blooded castaways would be mistaken as part of the invading army and put down on sight. Hell, even if they weren't mistaken as part of the invaders, they could still be executed on suspicion. Or maybe it was simply a matter of policy that illegal immigrants and trespassers were welcomed with a swift blade to the back of the neck. Either way, he didn't want to cross paths with the city guard. They needed to find a place to hide until they could get out of here.

An arrow came screaming down from the wooded slope they'd left behind, exploding out of the forest wall like a missile. It flew alone, twirling unseen through the air until its tip caught the sunlight and it began to twinkle across the sky. It descended onto its target, sinking into flesh, tearing muscle and tendons, severing nerves.

Charles took a few more strides forward, and at first it appeared that he might not stop, that he could keep on going despite the arrow in his neck. But then his body finally registered the damage…and shut down. He was dead when he hit the ground, palms turned out, face sliding across the grass just twenty yards from the shadows of cover that had been cast to them like lifelines by the stone apartments.

Jackson watched Charles slide across the ground in front of him, his head bobbing awkwardly as the earth resisted his lifeless momentum, a thousand blades of grass, stones, and divots trying to bring him to a stop. Sliding to a stop and swinging back around to face the woods, Jackson scanned the hillside. Even with Charles' body spurting blood out across the grass and turning it red, he had no problem identifying the arrow that killed him. And it wasn't any Leftover who had launched it. Which meant that the hills were already filling with reinforcements from what had to be a nearby instillation responding to the alarm. Or maybe it was just a patrol or two returning to find their city under siege. The latter would be preferred.

Without any prodding, Robinson and Li turned back and grabbed Charles' body, dragging it to an abandoned cart left resting beside a footpath. They flipped the cart up on its side and sat Charles up against it, ducking themselves as more arrows came screaming out of the hills. A group of them punched into the wood with thwacks and thunks, and one penetrated all the way through, sinking into Charles' left shoulder. The spring-loaded metal shot through his shirt and snapped open like a blooming hook, pinning his body to the cart.

"C'mon!" Robinson yelled, grabbing Li and pulling him away from the splintering cart. The others had just made it to the buildings, taking refuge from the arrows in the alley between them. Robinson and Li joined Jackson and ran after them, arrows pegging the ground all around.

They made it into the narrow alley and took a moment to catch their breath as crowds of people poured past the city end of the opening. They watched men and women, even kids, fall to the ground and disappear beneath stampeding feet. Everyone was screaming. Machine guns echoed like sonic booms.

Suddenly, a Fallen soldier appeared standing at the end of the alley behind them. He was staring at them, his eyes saturated with a bloodlust that carried him forward between the two buildings and into the shade of the cramped lane. He held a rifle clumsily in his hands but wasn't firing it. And then Jackson realized that he was *trying* to fire it, but without taking his eyes off them, he was having trouble getting his finger to the trigger. Jackson spun, dropped to a knee while simultaneously bringing his own AK to his shoulder, and squeezed off two quick rounds all in one seamless act. Blood sprayed the left wall as the Leftover went down. But behind the corpse, in the grass, Jackson could see more coming.

"Go! Go! Go!" Jackson cried, pushing Li in the back and shoving them all out the other end and into the river of stampeding flesh.

They fought their way through the frantic mob and to the other side of the street, trying to get a fix on where the rifle reports were originating. They seemed to be going off everywhere.

"This way!" And Jackson led them down another street, taking them toward the center of the valley and to the main boulevard.

A few blocks later, they jogged onto the main street, turning left and right, getting their bearings. The wide road led to the bridge at the beginning of the valley to their left and all the way up the temple stairs half a mile away to the right, the pyramid's gleaming capstone hovering in the low clouds beyond it like the ever-watchful eye on the American greenback.

Big obelisks lined the road, and people in bright, smart clothes were darting back and forth between them, looking for someplace to hide. A hundred yards up the road, a giant stepped out into the street and cut one of them in half with a single sweep of its sword.

"Where do we go?" Robinson asked, his eyes touch and go off their many surroundings. They were vulnerable out in the middle of the city like this, the seven of them forming a circle, rifles pointed out.

Even from half a mile away, they could see that the city guard had taken up a defensive position around the temple and that another wave of them was now pouring into the city, splitting into smaller units and dispersing down side streets.

Before Jackson could answer, more Leftovers from Osiris's army stumbled onto the main avenue in front of them, their guns firing haphazardly from their hips and striking more stone than flesh. These intruders were only a hundred feet away from them, and Jackson spun the contents of his AK's magazine into them, getting them to dance and twitch in rhythm to the rifle's bucking back and forth in his arms.

"Look out!" Joe cried, pointing to their left when Jackson's rifle finally went silent.

Three armored giants came bounding onto the street ahead of them, running straight for the Osiris giant that was still ripping city folks in half. As the near-twenty-foot Titans took fighting positions around the lone bare-chested and tattooed giant, a division of bald men in capes turned onto the street right in front of the band of Purees and raised crossbows.

Patrick and Wilson fired while Joe led the others down an adjacent street and back into the rioting city. A few bolts whistled by their heads as they passed by short buildings with wooden porches, sides of beef hanging from their posts. Baskets of fruit lined the sides of this road, and small farm animals were tied up and caged in the alleys between the buildings. They were in the market district.

Scattered bodies lay face-down in the road, sprawled on the short steps leading up to cashiers' tables, and crumpled in doorways. They were all marked with bullet holes.

Jackson ran through a bunch of chickens, feathers exploding and drifting chaotically through the air at his feet. With great commotion, they tried to fly away from him and jumped into the next intersection, where crowds of fleeing pedestrians smashed them into feathered jelly.

On the other side of the intersection, Jackson could see a giant running straight at the masses. It plucked two men out of the human river like fish out of a stream and threw them both into the nearest building. Their bodies were pulverized against the unyielding stone, and they landed in a pile of broken bones while their wives and children shrieked.

The near-naked Nephilim then went back into the flow, swatting its hands at random, sending people up into the air and flying over the heads of their compatriots.

"This way!" Jackson yelled and turned right, throwing himself into the current.

But just as they reached the next intersection, another giant stepped out in front of them. This one had no clothes on but held two hatchets the size of street signs in its hands. It swung them back and forth, chopping and slicing into the mob. Blood went everywhere.

With the pressing crowd at their backs, Jackson knew they couldn't retreat. He raised his rifle, the others doing the same, and fired over the heads of the people around them, flipping burning casings at them.

They struck the giant's head and neck region, the reports deafening to the frightened and confused city dwellers, eliciting another volley of screams in their scramble to escape the valley.

The giant looked down, ignoring the rivulets of blood squirting from its flesh, and lunged past the people at its feet, reaching instead for the men with guns.

Li went to the ground in a suddenly empty section of street and rolled into a kneeled stance, firing steadily into the creature's eyes.

Joe and Robinson swung around to the giant's left and punched bullets into its right ear as Li continued shooting its upper body head-on. It went crashing down like a felled tree, smashing at least two people beneath it. The ground shook and puffed dust into the air.

When the dust cleared, Jackson found himself separated from the others. He was about fifty feet away from them on the other side of another intersection. "C'mon!" he yelled to them. And then a colossal sword crashed into his chest, taking him off his feet and hurling him backward across the street.

Robinson looked up just in time to see Jackson disappear beneath the crowd. And then another giant stepped out onto the street, swinging a massive sword back and forth in wide swathes of carnage. More blood rained down.

Grabbing Joe by the shoulder, Robinson signaled for him to continue up the street a block and then cut over and double back. Joe nodded his understanding and took Li with him. Robinson, Patrick, Wilson, and Sanders ran straight toward the swinging blade.

* * * *

Paul blinked, wondering if the guy had been there all along or if he might've stepped through one of those dark holes that had been so prominent in Osiris' temple. Not that it mattered how or when he got there, because here he was, dressed in the same fashion as the gladiator he'd taken the carriage from, his eyes twinkling with disdain beneath his helmet, yet rounded with confusion. And Paul supposed it was the confusion that had kept him from pulling the trigger already. His chest muscles squeezed the strap that held the sword to his back as he adjusted the crossbow's aim, the mail sleeves covering his arms no doubt heavy. Sunlight glittered off the throwing knives that circled his waist. And though he hadn't fired yet, Paul knew that the guy was going to as soon as his mind grasped the connection between the weapon in Paul's hands and the pile of bodies at the foot of the stairs behind him.

"They were like that when I got here," Paul said when he saw the man's eyes drift over his shoulder to the scene behind him.

The man's eyes shot back to him, and his trigger finger began to tense.

Running out of time, Paul-o. He was too far away to make a move for the crossbow, words meant nothing, and he'd be dead before getting the barrel of the rifle up. He could pull the trigger anyway, shoot the floor and just hope the blast startled the guy enough for him to make a move, but the guy's reflex might be to pull the trigger rather than to cower. He could try to use the phone, bring up the picture of the other eaten gladiator and turn it around so the gladiator could see it. That might throw his attention long enough for him to get a shot off. But that would take time he didn't have, and without dropping his eyes to the phone still in his hand, he couldn't even be sure it was still on.

So in that nanosecond of weighing his options, he determined there was only one thing to do.

Very slowly, he began bending his knees, raising his phone hand in the air while lowering the rifle to the stone floor with his other hand, hoping the guy understood the body language of surrender.

The gladiator didn't fire. And if he was still going to, he'd waited too long. Paul was in the position he'd wanted, his legs bent like a stressed coil beneath him and ready to spring. He shifted his body weight onto the balls of his feet, lifting his heels off the ground.

The crossbow followed him down.

He launched straight at it, exploding off his feet and twisting slightly as he rose. He raised his left arm over his head, protecting his face and neck from the bolt he knew was coming.

And it did come, the razor-sharp tip piercing his arm, tearing between the biceps brachii and the brachialis before passing through and burrowing into the frontal bone of his skull. The bolt's long shaft was a skewer pinning his arm to his head, and he continued to fly through the air like that until crashing into the bow's stirrup and then into the muscled gladiator holding it. The force of the impact sent them both to the ground, and the bolt ripped free from Paul's head.

Wasting no time worrying about the extent of the damage done to him, Paul threw himself atop the bowman. He'd struck his helmeted head against the floor with a loud crash, and Paul needed to take advantage of whatever disorientation might have momentarily scrambled his brains. He punched the man in the face, careful to avoid the helmet's sharp sides that came swooping outward around the mouth, and his scarred knuckles sent the back of the helmet off the stone again with a metallic *clunk* that echoed off the stone statues around them. The bowman's eyes clouded, and Paul reached for his belt. But the man must've picked up on Paul's intention because he shot his own hands down to his belt, trying to keep Paul from extracting one of his knives. After a momentary hand struggle, however, Paul abandoned the knives, instead reaching down and taking a bolt from the quiver strapped to the man's thigh. And just as the gladiator pulled one of his knives, intending to slip it into Paul's stomach, Paul rammed the bolt into his left eyeball. The cornea shattered, and the optic nerve severed as the bolt drove straight into his cerebrum. His arms went limp and his hands flopped lifelessly onto the floor beside him, the knife skittering across the floor.

Paul rolled off the gladiator and stared up at the ceiling, his rapid heartbeat making a kick drum out of his head. Warm liquid spurted in sync with the hectic beat and ran down his face. He rolled back onto his stomach and managed to get on all fours. Spread out on the floor beneath him, his hands blurred and duplicated, his lost fingers magically restored. He blinked, blood dripping from his head and splashing on his dancing hands.

C'mon, Paul-o, there's still a maiden that needs a-savin'. He got to his knees and wiped the blood out of his eyes with the back of his right hand. Then he raised his left arm, squinting to keep everything from moving, and stared incredulously at the twenty-inch bolt that was sticking through it.

"Well, crap," he muttered.

He wouldn't be able to lower his arm without the tip hitting his side, so he couldn't just leave it like it was. There wasn't too much blood leaking from the wound, so he knew the bolt had missed his brachial artery. And since there was no white-hot electricity pulsating up and down his arm, he knew it had somehow missed the median nerve too.

He was going to pull it out. But first he needed to snap off one of the ends. Pulling from the nock and bringing the bolt's winged tip back through his arm wasn't an option, and he didn't want to slide the four feathers through the hole for fear of nicking a nerve or artery. So he got to his feet and stumbled over to where he'd dropped the rifle. He picked it up and held it with his right hand, pressing the barrel against the arrow right below the head. He pulled the trigger and blew the hand off the statue in front of him. It fell to the floor under a cloud of dust.

He swore, closing his eyes. *Concentrate, Paulie boy.* Sweat ran down his face. He walked over and reached out with his skewered arm, leaning against the wall, the bolt pointing at the ceiling. He rested the AK's cleaning rod retainer (that would hold a bayonet in place) on his wrecked bicep, holding the rifle so the barrel was touching the bolt at sixty-five degrees. If he flinched this time, he could blow his arm off. But at least the barrel wasn't moving all over the place. He fired.

The bullet sheared the shaft three inches beneath the head and ricocheted off the ceiling. Taking a deep breath, Paul set the rifle down, leaning it against the wall. Then he took another deep breath and gripped the bolt around its fletching. He counted to three and, with a groan, he pulled the thing out of his arm. He threw it across the room with a shout and leaned his head back against the wall, squeezing his eyes shut. He could feel the blood trickling down his arm, two streams converging at the bottom of his bicep and flowing down the inside of his forearm.

He blinked, pushed himself off the wall, and walked back to the gladiator. He ripped a length from his battle skirt and wrapped it around his arm, knotting it and then pulling it tight with his teeth.

He touched his head, feeling where the bolt had struck him. There was a hole above his left eye, just below the hairline. He stuck his finger in it and was satisfied that it hadn't penetrated the skull. Another scar to accompany all the rest. But blood was pooling from it and running into his eyes, so he took another piece of cloth from the bowman and wrapped it around his head. "I gotta stop doing this," he mumbled. But at least this one didn't smell as bad as the last.

He looked around and spotted the phone a few feet to his left. When he bent over to pick it up, he could feel the blood rush to his head and pulsate behind the wound. He stood up and slipped it back into his pocket while fighting off a wave of dizziness. He hadn't even bothered to see if the phone had broken when it hit the ground. Because how could you break a phone that worked supernaturally? If metaphysical forces could communicate with him through a dead phone, then they certainly didn't need it in working order to keep using it, did they? "Thanks for the heads-up," he said, addressing NUMBER UNKNOWN. Though whether "they" were helping him or just toying with him was still an open debate.

He spit and then kneeled beside the gladiator. As quickly as he could, while keeping his eyes on the stairs and the empty hall, he moved the quiver of bolts from the corpse's thigh to his own. Then he took off the belt of knives and wrapped it around his waist too. Next he took the sword and crossbow. Standing straight, he adjusted the weight of all his new weapons while listening to the gunshots rebounding throughout the city. He had the crushing sense that he was almost out of time.

Ready to move, he reached down and grabbed the bolt sticking out of the guy's eye. He might not need it, but "better to be looking at it, than for it," as they say. The man's head lifted off the ground when he pulled, not wanting to let go, but gravity ultimately won and the bolt ripped free. Paul held it up and examined the eyeball that came with it. "Gross." He snapped his wrist and flung the jelly ball off the arrowhead. It smacked against the wall with a gelatinous *splat!* Sliding the bolt into the quiver, he ran for the steps, swaying like a drunken sailor the whole way.

I'm coming, Denise…

* * * *

AK-47s echoed through the valley.

"It sounds like a war," Daniel said, sloshing through the water beside Hunter. A wide stream snaked along the foot of the valley's north wall, and they were presently in the middle of it, the water reaching their stomachs. They could see the people fleeing, most running west and for the bridge, but handfuls of people were also splashing across the stream on either side of them and heading straight up into the wooded hills.

Daniel had said that the noise from the city sounded like a war, but his knowledge of "war" was limited to his experience—mainly swords, spears, arrows, and rifles, all used in cedar forests and across island beaches. But the fighting coming from within the city was something that the island-born had never seen before. This was the chaos of urban warfare.

Hunter could see the city in his mind, all its streets and alleys mapped on something akin to a cerebral HUD. He could also see the AK-47s in the hands of the Fallen. A cloud settled over his face.

"What?" Daniel asked.

Not only did he see the assault rifles being used by Osiris' Leftovers, he saw where they'd gotten them from. He turned in the water and faced Daniel. "Those are AK-47s."

Daniel shrugged, the words meaningless to him since he had been on the ship with Hunter when the containers of rifles had been discovered by the others.

Hunter blinked, trying to make sense of how he could know it. "Rifles. Being fired by Osiris' men."

Daniel shook his head in denial. "They don't use guns."

"They do now, Danny boy." He looked to the stone walls and the people running back and forth to a soundtrack of screams and gunshots. "They do now."

EIGHTEEN

September 22, 2011. The City.

The AK-47 rocked back and forth against Robinson's shoulder as he ran for the intersection ahead of them. The giant, standing on the other side of the cross street, turned from its bloody reaping and narrowed its eyes at him. Explosions of red dotted its towering body, and it flinched with annoyance. It threw back its head and roared. Then it charged.

Robinson knew that the giant's long strides would carry it through the intersection before he could reach it, which meant they wouldn't have the space of the junction to battle in and that the giant's long sword would be nearly impossible to avoid between the buildings squeezing them along this portion of the cramped street. But just as the charging Nephilim stepped into the intersection, a large blur came screaming into its blind side and took it off its feet.

Robinson skidded to a stop just short of the four converging streets. He was slightly aware of the others coming up beside him as he watched in stunned fascination as another giant—this one fitted in silver armor with a black cape flowing off its shoulders—straddled the near-naked monster it just took to the ground in a spectacular, neck-breaking tackle. It began raining punches down, but the Osiris Nephilim managed to get its hands up and deflect enough of them to avoid severe damage. It brought its knee up into the attacker's crotch, and the city giant doubled over. The half-naked giant rolled away, grabbed its sword, and got back to its feet. When it turned back to face its attacker, it found the armored giant already standing with its own sword in hand. Their metal blades met in a clash of sparks.

The city giant spun on the toes of its high boots, its cape whipping through the air behind it, its huge sword dazzling in the afternoon sun.

Jackson blinked, unsure if he could trust what he was seeing. His head was ringing, and his vision was blurred. He could see his feet (sometimes four of them) stretched out in front of him and covered with rubble. He took a deep breath and cringed. His chest…

He'd been slapped with the broad side of a Nephilim sword and sent flying across the street, striking the building he was presently propped against. He tried to move his arms and feet and was relieved that they obeyed. His backpack had probably saved him from a severed or crushed spine.

He moved his eyes off his toes and focused again on the unfolding scene across the street, in the intersection. *Clash of the Titans*, he thought. It was like a comic book version of Thor versus Conan the Barbarian, and Jackson was sure his mind had crossed the Rubicon.

The two Fallen ones battled hard if only for a short time, circling, and deflecting blows into the nearby buildings. Chunks of the stone masonry exploded upon each errant swing, dust filling the air and rubble spraying the streets. But Osiris' progeny was no match for the well-trained "hero" of this particular "old." and the city giant of the Not Thems executed a maneuver that culminated in the point of its sword sliding up beneath the chin of Conan and exploding out of the mangled hair of its head.

With a sudden jerk, the caped giant withdrew the sword, leaving the Leftover to sway for a second before crashing to the dirt.

"You okay?"

Jackson moved his eyes from the large victor and to the source of the question. He found Robinson kneeling beside him.

"I think so." He extended his hand to him, and Robinson grabbed it, pulling him up with him as he stood.

"Anything broken?"

He wasn't sure how his ribs weren't cracked to pieces, but he thought that everything was still intact. He'd have the mother of all bruises, but he figured he'd fared well considering what had hit him. He shook his head.

"C'mon, then," Robinson urged, pulling him along and up the street toward the temple. The others came alongside, weapons sweeping back and forth as the city giant disappeared behind taller buildings.

* * * *

Standing at the top of the stairs, Paul swayed, almost falling back down them. He leaned against the wall and steadied himself while waiting for the dizziness to pass. He squinted down yet another long corridor, stumbling forward, continuing to use the wall for support. As the end of the hall grew closer, he began to make out a huge decorated entranceway. *This is it*, he thought. The king's bedchamber.

He was so entranced by the blurred masonry that he almost mistook the two giants standing on either side of the opening for more stone pillars, hidden in the shadows of the overarching stonework above them. They were holding spears that were taller than they were.

Paul froze, wondering if his slow movement along the wall had somehow managed to keep him out of their sight. But then they crossed their long weapons in front of the entrance with a loud *clang*, forming an X in front of it.

It was clear these Nephilim warriors, dressed in the same silver armor and black capes that he'd seen on the others in front of the temple, were prepared to die before letting anyone past them. That was fine with Paul. He raised the rifle and fired.

* * * *

She heard the shots but couldn't register their meaning. The little *clicks* that echoed so far away, *tap-tap-tapping*…

But the tiny clicks had grown into clanks, and the clanks into clunks. And soon it wasn't a distant echo at all, but a loud and obnoxious reverberating hammer that was slamming the atmosphere all around her. Each *bang* punched her brain, rattling it from its fogged moorings. She managed to roll onto her stomach and lift her head, her eyes focusing on the light pouring in from the open balcony. The light danced and jittered in her vision, obscuring everything around her. She tried to see beyond it, through it, but it was no use. She tried to move her legs, but they just stared at her, dumb. She tried harder, and they just laughed. *No!* she screamed to herself. *Move!*

Her left leg obeyed by sliding slightly across the sheets. She reached beneath her and grabbed it with her arms, pulling it up to her chest. Stuck in that awkward position, she then tried again to move the other one.

A voice sounded behind her.

She froze. Had she actually heard a voice, or was it the man in her head again? She thought the voice sounded familiar, and she was slightly surprised that the subtle emotions it stirred were not those of trepidation but rather hope. Who could it be?

One of the glass panels of her brain cage cracked.

With great mental effort, she repositioned herself by rolling sideways and flopping onto her back so that she was facing the entranceway again. There, at the foot of the bed, stood a blood-soaked man with a rifle in his hands. A sword and crossbow hung on his back. His mouth was moving, but she couldn't hold on to the words. She could hear him speaking, but his lips weren't synched with the sounds coming from them. She blinked, so confused.

The man stepped closer, putting the rifle down and taking the sword and crossbow off his back, setting them all down against the bed. Then he pulled his black shirt off over his head.

Able to interpret the gesture, a herd of convulsions stampeded down her spine. But no…

He was coming around the side of the bed, holding out the shirt to her. His words finally reached her brain.

"Put this on."

And then the cracked pane of glass shattered. "Paul…" she whispered, her mind reaching for a handhold. Even through the smeared remnants of the mud mask, she could tell that it was Paul.

* * * *

Hunter climbed out of the water and up the grassy bank, Daniel right behind him. People were running past them in frantic flight, leaping into the stream and splashing toward where they'd just come from.

"Stay close," Hunter said.

Daniel nodded, his head whipping back and forth, trying to take in everything all at once.

They worked their way through a field and climbed over a stone fence before sprinting down a small street that took them, block after block, through intersections of confusion. Finally, it led them to the main boulevard, the bridge at the beginning of the valley to their right, the steps that ran up the front of the ziggurat temple to their left.

The scene up and down the main street gave them pause, and they stood trying to make sense of it. The half-dressed Leftovers were running around like cockroaches armed with AK-47s and shooting fleeing families in the back. The city guard was firing bolts and arrows back at them, but for the moment, the bullets were winning.

Hunter watched as a Fallen soldier ran out of ammo and returned to his sword-wielding ways. He ran to the nearest armored guard and quickly discovered that he was no match for these Not Them soldiers. So rather than engaging with swords, the other Fallen began tossing their empty rifles and running away from the fight, taking every opportunity to strike down women and children in their retreat.

Also battling through the streets were what seemed to be two different breeds of giants engaged in an epic clash of mythological proportions. Huge twenty-foot giants in loincloths and covered in tattoos were swinging swords at giants that were fitted in bright gold armor, their helmets covering most of their faces. As they moved back and forth, flying bullets and whizzing arrows struck them but did not deter them. Masses of people were hurrying to get out of their way, but the Leftover giants, when not engaged with the Not Them Nephilim, were grabbing them at random and tossing them through the air.

"Tell me there's another road," Daniel said.

Hunter looked past the crowds, the Fallen foot soldiers chasing them, and all the individual battles between the Titans, and lifted his gaze to first the temple half a mile away and then to the crystal pyramid behind it. And then he was suddenly looking *through* it all, seeing all the other things unfolding that no physical eye could possibly detect. He saw Jackson, Robinson, and the other Purees moving toward the temple. He saw Paul up in the bedchamber with Robyn and Turiel.

Turiel…

A scene flashed through his head, coming from nowhere and instigated by nothing more than being within proximity to the angel. Or at least that was the best he could figure it. He'd stopped trying to understand the ins and outs of what happened to him and all its lingering effects. But somehow time had just folded back on itself, and his mind was now processing images thousands and thousands of years old. He saw this so-called "Turiel" descending with the rest of the angels that had "left their first estate" in the times of Jared, descending upon Mount Hermon.

And behold, the names of those angels: The first of them is Semyaza, and the second Artaqifa, and the third Armen, and the fourth Kokabiel, and the fifth Turiel… Book of Enoch. Chapter 69, verse 2.

But there was something else, a presence that superseded the Fallen angel's. Something behind the flowing forms of causality, of time and space and all the lines of reality that intersected it. There was a form there, an entity filled with personhood. And it was both Now and Then, its hands pulling the two together.

It was almost too much for Hunter to process, and he felt his mind expanding to psychological boundaries he dare not cross. And yet another chapter of information suddenly flashed in his brain. It played out like a memory, though that was impossible. Nevertheless, he watched in an instant as Turiel, one of the three hundred rebels, moved through antiquity as a priest of the Golden Age, and then as a missionary leaving the Atlantean hierarchy to spread its forbidden knowledge among the sons of Adam.

A priest of the Sacred Feather. Here. Now. But not now, not really.

He blinked, dumbfounded by the backstage pass that granted him access to all time's various floors. If only he could control it somehow instead of being shuttled around as a spectator. Because he knew that the means to fix all this and to get his friends back home was inside him somewhere. The knowledge was on a hidden bookshelf, but it had no title. It was behind a locked door, but he didn't know where the door was let alone have a key to open it.

And then he understood.

As that mysterious presence emerged from the fog, standing defiantly on the present while holding both the past and the future in its hands, Hunter realized that the Darkness hadn't cast him off completely. It still had a little worm in his brain, using him.

"Is there?" Daniel asked again.

Hunter blinked. "What?"

"Is there another way to the temple? I don't think we're going to make it past that." He pointed at the chaos of what could be a million people trying to escape the city via the main street.

Hunter grabbed him and spun him out of the street and back into an alley. "Listen," he said, holding him against the back side of a stone building and staring vehemently into his eyes. "You need to get out of here right now." He pointed to the wooded valley wall on the other side of the stream, the same hill they'd just come down. "Back up there."

"What?"

"Get up there and just hide. This'll be over soon, and then Jackson will be heading back to the caves. You need to intercept them." He spoke the words even as his mind continued connecting dots that were flashing as blips on the radar of his awareness. But this new strain of information was different. There was no dark fingerprint on these. This was all Hunter.

Or maybe even something of a higher nature…

Images flashed upon the big screen of his mind. A helicopter, the ship, the pyramid, Turiel…

There was no time to explain it all in a way that Daniel would understand, so he just blurted it out. "Tell them there's a working helicopter at the foot of the temple Paul woke in. The one that was sheared in half."

Daniel looked at him as if he'd finally lost his entire mind.

"I know it's crazy, but just tell them! They have to get to the cruise ship as fast as they can!"

"What are you talking about?" Daniel cried.

"I'm not sure how it's going to work exactly, but, Danny boy…I think I can get everyone home."

"Home?"

"Back to the real world."

"But the solstice—"

Hunter shook his head violently. "No, it was never going to work. They were just fooling themselves thinking they could use the pyramid again. Only Osiris knew how to operate the mechanism, and now his pyramid is…" He trailed off, his eyes losing focus as another piece of information fell into his head. "They think it moved."

"What moved?"

"Osiris' pyramid. They think it moved, but…" He shook his head again. "It doesn't matter! Listen, Thoth knows the mysteries of the pyramid, and Turiel knew Thoth. And now they need me to free Abaddon…"

Daniel blinked, his mind drowning in Hunter's compounding delusion.

"It's not a delusion," Hunter snapped as if reading his mind. "We're only going to get one shot at this, and, Danny, it has to be *tomorrow*, on the fall equinox!"

"Tomorrow?" Daniel whispered, the gravity of Hunter's revelation beginning to hit home.

Hunter nodded. "But—and, Danny, this is so *very* important—you *need* to be off the island when it happens."

"When what happens?"

"There's no more time! Just go!"

"But what about you?

"I'm gonna have to stall him…" His eyes rested on that idea for just a moment before snapping back to him. "Don't worry about me, and don't come after me! Just get everyone to the ship!"

"Who are all these people?"

"Antediluvians, a slice of pre-flood civilization transposed across other layers of reality, ours included."

"And using the pyramid did this?"

"Yes. But not by chance. Tell Jackson that none if this is chance. The things you saw on the ship, it's Ronald and Osiris and the spirits of the Nephilim unlocking the doors of Tartarus." He closed his eyes as another piece of the puzzle was connected to the forming whole. "They need Turiel…"

Then, suddenly, a blast of cold wind came howling down the alley, tearing at their clothes. They stepped back into the street, the battle now only fifty yards away from them, and looked up to the pyramid. Dust and other debris whipped down the street, and they shielded their eyes. Up around the pyramid's capstone, the sky was an inky black. And it was spreading like spilled oil, reaching out toward the city, eating the afternoon sky and its clouds.

"Go! Now!" Hunter hollered, and he took off down the main boulevard, heading straight for the crowds, the battling giants, the temple, and the coming dark.

* * * *

After emptying the rest of the magazine's contents into the two towering guards and blowing their heads apart (it was quite obvious they didn't know what a gun was because they just stood there daring him to charge), Paul crashed through the big doors and found himself standing before the very bed that had been in the picture on his phone. Robyn was on top of it, lying on her stomach and trying to get to her knees.

Now he was trying to get her into his shirt.

"C'mon, girl," he said, trying to keep his eyes on hers. It was an exercise of the will, trying to keep from staring at her beauty. The dress she was wearing did next to nothing to conceal her nakedness, and he could only hope that her innocence was still intact. The dress, the bed, the makeup applied to her face, and the sensual scent coming from her skin told him what the plan had been, but he hoped there hadn't been time for any of that.

He guided her arms through the sweat-stained and bloody shirt and pulled it down over her head, where it gathered around her neck. "Sorry about the smell."

She stared back at him with empty eyes, and he knew that she'd been drugged with something. Her mind was racing but getting nowhere.

"You don't want to be running around giving all these animals a free show now, do you?"

Blank.

"I didn't think so." He grabbed her under the armpits and lifted her to her feet. His hands incidentally cupped the swell of her breasts in the process, and the contact made her entire body go suddenly rigid. She gulped a startled breath of air through her nose as the sensual nature of the touch (though unintentional) set off a warning bell to her fuzzed brain.

"Sorry," he whispered. And then he pulled the shirt down over her chest and stomach before any indecent thoughts could tempt him with anything else. The shirt reached the top of her thighs, the gown flowing beneath it like a skirt.

She stood almost eye level with him, her braided hair like ropes of gold gleaming in the sunbeams piercing the room. He could stare at her all day if she were his, but of course she was not.

"Ready?" he asked her.

But though the accidental touch had triggered a response from her, it hadn't been enough to break the spell. He wondered if touching her more intensely would help, then chased the thought away. Instead, he slapped her across the face.

Her head snapped to the side, her braids whipping around after it. She blinked and shook her head.

Paul saw a spark of recognition.

So he slapped her again.

This time when she turned her reddened face back to him, there was anger burning in her eyes.

"That's it, girl. C'mon back." He swung at her again.

Her hand shot up and deflected the strike. "Stop."

Paul smiled and almost kissed her. He stepped back to the foot of the bed and slung the rifle over his shoulder. Then he hooked his arm around her waist and moved her to the open balcony at the other end of the room.

They stepped into the open air and were greeted by both the sun's warm light and a hundred different sounds of battle. A five-foot stone railing spanned the edge of the balcony, its architecture matching the Greek-like designs Paul had witnessed throughout the temple's interior. As they approached it, the scene below began to take form. In the foreground, the ziggurat steps stretched out and away beneath them. There were people lying all over the stairs, and one would assume them to be drunks passed out after an epic banquet the night before if not for the blood flowing like so many rivers down into the courtyard, where they met to form a red lake.

At the foot of the temple steps, the main boulevard stretched through the courtyard and raced all the way through the center of the city until exiting the valley a mile away. On either side of the wide road were all the city's prestigious buildings, its network of avenues, its shops and markets, its houses and apartments. And it was all consumed with violence, the outlying urban neighborhoods already completely destroyed.

"What's happening?" Robyn stuttered. Her mind was slowly covering ground.

Paul stood in stunned fascination himself, watching the Leftover soldiers, half-naked, running through the streets and firing assault rifles at the fleeing crowds while the city guard tried desperately to strike them down with bolts and arrows. "I think the Osiris family is trying to sack the kingdom."

She grabbed his hand. "They're using guns…"

"Yeah." And though their aim was piss-poor, they were learning on the job, compensating by tracing their wild shots into their targets. But he knew it wasn't their sudden ability to use firearms that had her concerned. He looked over at her and could see the horrible answer trying to sink in. But there was nothing they could do about that now.

He turned his attention back to the chaos below. It was obvious that the Not Thems stood little chance against the guns (inaccurate as their aim might be), but he also knew that the bullets down there were finite. If any of the Not Thems were left when the last rifle clicked empty (and he thought there would be), then the battle would quickly swing the other way. And even as this thought struck him, he watched as a caped giant made six pieces out of three Leftovers with one sweep of his sword.

His.

He didn't miss the gender assimilation he'd instinctively made and wasn't at all surprised by it. It wasn't the first time he'd been tempted to assign personhood to one of the Nephilim. But these giants, these Not Thems from some other time and place, were of a different ilk than the more savage, barbaric offspring of Osiris—

But his thought went unfinished as something to the left side of the city, up in the sloped hill of the valley, caught his attention. He leaned against the railing, his chin just over its surface, and stared with wide eyes at the swaying, breaking trees. "What in the—" He let go of Robyn's hand and quickly pulled the scope out of his pocket, swinging it up to his eye. Setting it on the valley wall, he was able to catch flashes of…something through the trees, moving quickly down the hill. He looked closer and then dropped the spyglass away from his face, collapsing it back into itself. He stood in shocked horror, staring at the faraway hill with his naked eyes.

And then Robyn caught sight of it, but instead of taking a step forward like Paul had, she took a step back. "What are those?" she whispered.

"They look like…dinosaurs." And now the trees covering the right side of the valley were moving too. "A lot of damn dinosaurs."

He was half-convinced that what he was seeing had to be a hallucination. There couldn't *actually* be dinosaurs here! Giants, yes. Closet demons, sure. Flying monkey men, of course. Scorpion men with lion's teeth, why not? But *dinosaurs*? Yet they continued charging down the sides of the valley, exploding onto the valley floor.

"Look," Robyn said, raising a shaking finger to the right and pointing at the lizards pounding across a section of stream that was visible over the tops of the buildings.

It was clear, even from their position, that the scaled monsters were making a quick snack of the people who were trying to cross the stream and flee the city. But Paul was more interested in what was going on to his left, as the creatures he was sure were *T-rexes* (or something similar—they seemed to be straight from every Hollywood representation he'd ever seen) stomped across the field on their two massive legs and entered the city…where they immediately began feasting without prejudice. He watched as a few tiny specs he knew to be Osiris' men turned and started shooting at the charging predators. But it seemed as though their bullets did even less against the lizards than they were doing against the giants. Paul counted eleven of the dinosaurs before grabbing Robyn's hand and turning away from the view.

"C'mon. Let's get the hell outta here!" He led her back through the chamber and was halfway to the doors when the tall man in the white robe suddenly appeared walking through it, two more giants in his company. The giants were helmetless, their large foreheads standing out, their long brown hair pulled back into ponytails that hung between their shoulders. They held long spears and were fitted with lighter armor than the other Not Them giants Paul had seen.

Robyn froze and dug her manicured nails into Paul's arm as the two giants took up positions on either side of the doorway. "Turiel," she whispered with dread.

Paul looked at her but didn't say anything. He recognized the guy as the one who'd been sitting on the throne on the temple's platform, though he was no longer wearing the headdress. This was the boss, up close and personal. He had a sword in his hand, blood running down its edge and dripping onto the floor.

"We're a little busy here, *amigo*," Paul said impatiently.

Move away from the woman.

Paul blinked, confused. He'd heard the request, yet no one in the room had moved their lips. And then the man smiled, and there was no doubting where the command had come from. *Telepathy?* Paul wondered.

I do not need to use my mouth to communicate, Paul, the voice answered.

He raised the rifle, aware that he was on his last mag. "That's not cool."

Step away from her.

"I think you should get out of my head." And then he added in his mind, *Before I twist your demon head off. You get that part, hombre?*

It would be a mighty feat for sure, he said, the words echoing in his skull.

You're not gonna like what you find in here, Paul warned.

The man smiled and spoke something Paul didn't understand. But the two Titans obviously did, because they both leveled their spears at him and took a step forward.

Paul pulled the trigger and unleashed a firestorm of 7.62x39mm rounds into the giant that was coming at him from his left. Its head opened as three of the bullets, traveling at 2,330 feet per second, punched it between the eyes. The rest of them tracked a line down its nose and mouth, leaving gaping red holes in its face. It crashed to its knees.

Twisting, Paul swung the rifle at the other giant. He had it all lined up just as the Titan was about to release a spear at his head, its arm cocked back behind its head and already starting to come forward—

Click.

He pulled the trigger again. *Click.*

And the giant's spear was away, cutting through the air at a downward angle straight for the top of his head.

Paul moved at the last second, ramming into Robyn as he lunged out of its skull-splitting path. She went to the ground at his feet, and he stumbled over her, trying to keep his footing while readying for another attack. The spear struck the floor behind them and ricocheted back up into the air and over the side of the balcony.

"Go!" Paul screamed to her, finding his balance just as the giant produced another spear (*like a weaver's beam*, Paul recalled involuntarily). The giant charged, and he tried the trigger again. Nothing. He dropped it just in time to dodge a long thrust that would have ripped his torso in half had he been half a step slower. Instead, its sharp blade claimed just a thin layer of flesh from his side.

Robyn stumbled to her feet and went for the open balcony.

Turiel, never taking his eyes off her, shouted something to the giant.

That the giant understood was only evidenced by its immediate obedience. Forgetting its present battle, it ran straight past Paul, going for the girl instead.

With only a nanosecond to decide on a course of action, Paul simply reacted. He launched himself into the giant's feet as it ran by.

The maneuver didn't send the Titan sprawling to the ground, but it did steal a step from it, allowing Robyn to remain just outside its six-fingered grasp. Its fingers just grazed the back of her baggy shirt. She was in full stride by the time she made it onto the balcony, and she wasn't about to slow down. This was her only chance at escape, and if it led to her death…well, wasn't that something she'd already resolved to anyway? She leaped forward and planted her hands on the five-foot railing. Lifting her knees to her chest, she vaulted herself straight over the side.

The giant went to the balcony after her but got to the railing too late. As it looked over the side, Paul pulled a bolt from the quiver still strapped to his thigh and charged the giant's back. Turiel shouted out a warning cry, and the giant turned around at the last second. So instead of ramming the giant in the back and sending it toppling over the railing (it reached just beneath its groin), Paul's hands instead found a hold on its chest plate, which he used to pull himself up and ram the bolt into the side of its neck.

The giant grabbed him with one hand, pulling him away and tossing him back into the room. He hit the ground hard, rolling and tumbling across the unforgiving stone until slamming to a stop against the side of the large iron-framed bed.

He struggled to get to his hands and knees, his vision blurred, his body aching. His headband had fallen off, and the hole beneath his hairline was bleeding down his face again. Looking up through the blood, he watched the giant rip the bolt out of its neck.

Guess this is it… he thought. Sure, he could make a grab for the sword leaning on the other side of the bed, but even if he managed to kill this giant, there was still the man in white to deal with. And he was pretty sure the man in white was just standing there like Emperor Palpatine, getting a kick out of watching Vader go at it with Luke when all he had to do was shoot blue lightning out of his fingers.

But he wasn't ready to die. He thought he was, thought he had been for some time, but now he could see the girl flashing before his eyes and knew that what was awaiting him on the other side was no picnic.

But then Turiel said something in that strange tongue, and the giant, blood spilling down over its armor, just walked past him and out of the room.

Paul struggled to his feet, gripping the bedpost to keep himself from swaying, and turned to face—

His AK-47.

It was floating in midair, hovering in front of him like some kind of magic trick. There was no waver to it, no shudder or swaying of the barrel. It sat there, perfectly unmoving, staring at his forehead.

You took her from me.

He swallowed, unable to take his eyes off that metallic tunnel. It hadn't worked the last time he'd tried it, but he was pretty sure that had been the guy's doing. Finally, he lifted his eyes from the hole and looked over the top of the front sight, focusing on the man himself. He was still standing in the doorway; his eyes were crystals of ice. "Yeah, well, she's kinda spoken for, so…"

So now you will answer my questions and please me in her place.

Please you in her place? His lips twisted into a grin. "Sorry, man. Not my scene. No offense."

Now the gun did move. It swung ever so slightly to the right, just about half an inch or so, and barked twice. The rifle didn't recoil but stayed completely still as it sent off one round right in front of the other, carving a layer out of Paul's cheek.

Paul swore, wiping more blood from his face with the back of his hand. "You're really not helping my chances of someday wooing my fair lady."

The barrel re-centered on his forehead, and Turiel smiled.

Again Paul found himself staring death in the face…and no closer to being ready for the hereafter than he was thirty seconds ago.

NINETEEN

September 22, 2011. The city.

The roar that echoed down the street was indicative of a monster different than all the other monsters he'd experienced thus far, elevating the paranormal skyscraper that was this island to yet another new height. And though it was new, Jackson had no problem identifying it. He'd hoped that the creature that attacked them this morning had been the result of Osiris's experimenting and not representative of a transposed population from some previous or alternate and of the lost. But the roar that was now echoing off the buildings around them and shaking the ground beneath their feet shattered that hope. As he continued to run, the pain in his chest and ribs suddenly disappearing beneath a surging flow of adrenaline, he threw a glance over his shoulder.

And saw it.

The legendary reptilian head, so similar to all the preschool cartoons, books, museum replicas, and the latest Hollywood movies, rose above the buildings a few blocks to his right, its beady yellow eyes tracking the commotion at its feet. Then its head lunged down toward the earth, disappearing behind the stone structures for a second. When it reappeared, there was a thrashing figure in its teeth. The lizard's jaws locked shut with a sudden, furious clamp, and the flailing man instantly turned limp.

"Did you see that?" Robinson screamed, running beside him.

"Yeah," he panted.

And then came more roars, blasting like trumpets from both sides of the valley. Jackson continued leading them up through the side streets, trying to pick the roads less occupied, knowing that if they hoped to survive this strange war, they needed to find cover. And the temple was that cover.

Two blocks ahead of them, a woman came sprinting across the street only to be mowed down by the Leftover chasing her. The Fallen soldier took a moment in the middle of the street to examine his kill, completely unaware of the seven AK-47s being aimed at him. But before Jackson or anyone else could put him down, a scaled leg the size of a tree stepped onto the road between them.

Jackson slid to a stop, Robinson and the others doing the same. They stood there staring in unbelief at the prehistoric monster suddenly towering above them. But it was the Fallen soldier on the other side of the dinosaur that got its attention by shooting at it first.

The monster turned toward the shooter, its massive tail whipping through the intersection and smashing the surrounding structures into clouds of debris.

Jackson ducked and shielded his face and head with his hands.

The reptile's gaping mouth descended onto the shooter, and for a mere fraction of time, its serrated mouth stood like an erected tent over him. Then it snapped shut, the rows of jagged, two-foot-long teeth closing just above his shoulders with a loud crunch. His head was gone, and as the dinosaur chewed on it, his body stood swaying, questioning its own sudden death. And then another, larger bite left only his feet and removed all doubt.

"This way!" Robinson screamed. He turned right and headed down another street, just hoping to keep the buildings between them and the dinosaur.

But Jackson saw three more reptilian heads rise over the tops of the surrounding buildings, and when they passed through another intersection, he was able to catch a glimpse of a Not Them giant swinging its sword at one of them while two other giants launched spears at its back.

They turned east and fought their way through more crowds of screaming and yelling citizens, and once they were a hundred yards from the temple's courtyard, they cut back over to the main boulevard, the temple now directly in front of them. The steps were littered with bodies, indicating that the Leftovers had already been there. The fact that they couldn't see any of them now probably meant that they'd run out of ammunition and had since retreated into the confines of the city.

Behind the temple-palace that stood atop the pyramid was a darkening, swirling sky that all of them recognized as—

An arrow whistled by Jackson's face and skipped off the obelisk next to him.

"Look out!" Li cried, the spreading darkness lost to more immediate concerns.

"Over there, between those two buildings on our right!" Joe added, pointing.

They all ran for cover as more arrows started coming at them from a dark alley across the street.

"Light up that alley!" Jackson cried after taking position behind one of the obelisks lining the road. He could see more dinosaurs and giants coming up the road, and now men on horseback were galloping up and down the streets. They needed to get up the temple steps fast.

They fired in the direction of the launching arrows, their bullets chipping away at the stone buildings concealing the sniper.

"Behind us!" Patrick screamed, turning and shooting into a line of city guards that had just turned down the street behind them. They flew backward as bullets punched holes straight through their armor.

Jackson swore and made a dash through another mob of stray chickens and to the nearest stone structure. It was a house on the corner, the last building along the main boulevard before the courtyard. It had a wooden porch that faced the temple, and he ran up its steps and ducked behind a row of stacked crates and barrels. The porch was covered, and the roof leaned out past the steps, casting a shadow across them. Joe came up and knelt beside him, his rifle pointing at the open doorway to their backs.

Jackson could see Robinson and the others taking positions behind the obelisks and shooting across the street still. He wondered how much ammunition they had left.

"Did you see the sky?" Joe asked.

"I saw it."

"What's going on here, Jack?"

"Damned if I know."

And then Joe tapped him on the shoulder and cried out, "Look!" He was pointing up at the temple.

The porch roof blocked Jackson's view of the temple's peak, but he could see what Joe was referring to, and it wasn't the sky. There was a balcony jutting out from the palace portion of the temple, above the stepped architecture and its pillared platform. And though the railing that wrapped the balcony was high, he could see between the baluster and noticed two people standing against it.

"It's her," Jackson whispered. Even from just a quick glimpse at such a distance, Jackson knew it was her.

"And Paul," Joe agreed.

And then the two forms turned away from the railing and disappeared back into the temple.

Unexpected hope crashed into Jackson's soul and flooded his veins. So consumed by relief, he got to his feet and leaped off the porch without even thinking. The soundtrack of clashing metal, firing AK-47s, and all the corresponding wails of agony went suddenly mute as he sprinted with abandon for the ziggurat steps.

He raced through the courtyard, completely unaware of three bolts that just missed his head. He didn't know if Joe or any of the others were with him, and he didn't care. Robyn was here, and she was alive! And that realization filled him so completely that it was the only thought occupying his mind…until, as he passed two columns that straddled the entrance to the courtyard, he heard gunshots explode from above him. He looked up to the balcony, manicured grass flashing past him on either side, and watched as a form suddenly appeared flying over the railing.

It was Robyn, and she seemed to be falling in slow motion, her braided hair chasing after her, the black shirt she was wearing bunching beneath her armpits, her legs bicycling, arms swimming, a white dress floating like a comet's tail behind her.

"No…"

The balcony jutted out over half of the ziggurat's width, which meant it was about a hundred-foot drop from the balcony to the steps' midpoint.

There was no way she would survive that fall.

He was still twenty feet from the first step when a giant came running out of the temple and down the stairs at him.

* * * *

Hunter sprinted along the stream, following the outskirts of the city toward the temple. On his right, he half-noticed the blurred alleys and passing streets full of the hysterical masses still trying to find a way out of their unexpected nightmare. The roars from the dinosaurs rocked the ground, but he barely noticed. He was focused only on the black vortex beginning to twirl around the pyramid's capstone.

He could see the courtyard ahead, and the stream he was following ran straight to it.

A sudden flash in his mind.

Robyn falling through the air, the ziggurat steps rushing up to meet her, just as they'd rushed up to meet him three months ago. And something else, some large lifeforce moving down the steps. He couldn't tell exactly what it was, the "reception" not so good.

And then he had it.

It was a giant…running down the steps toward…Jackson.

No.

And then he was past the stone buildings and all their intersecting streets and could see her falling with his physical eyes now. She was just a small flailing shape against the backdrop of the temple.

No!

He would not let her fall to her death right in front of Jackson.

And in the blink of an eye, he was suddenly through a door marked "employees only" and in some metaphysical backroom where he could all of a sudden feel within him the power to influence. He didn't question the feeling or the place his mind had stumbled into—there was no time for anything like that—rather he simply reacted to this new instinct. He threw out his hands, and the giant all the way on the other side of the courtyard and bounding down the pyramid steps was shoved to its right. Then, at the last possible second, he raised his right hand and caught Robyn in midair, catching her on a cushion of air and cutting the speed of her fall in half.

She landed on the giant just as it veered beneath her, her feet finding its huge shoulders. The impact sent the giant forward, and she rode its back all the way down.

Hunter was yanked out of that back room so fast that he didn't get to see what happened next, but he thought he'd just saved Jackson's girl and thanked God for it.

* * * *

Robyn's entire timeline unwound across her mind as the steps of the ziggurat rushed up to greet her. Time slowed to an impossible speed, allowing her to meet with her parents one last time in the state room of their wrecked passenger-cargo ship. She saw her friends and said hello and goodbye to all those that had been lost over the years. It was a parade of memories that led to Jackson and her hopes of a new future, but her last thought was one of surrender, of peace. At least she'd be gone from this nightmare and reunited with those she'd just visited.

A blur beneath her. A giant charging down the steps suddenly cut to its left, running right under her. And then something incredible happened—somehow, she slowed down. She could feel it, like big invisible hands had suddenly caught her and were simply lowering her onto—

But as slow as it might have felt, she still hit the giant like a missile, her bare feet striking the padded armor on its shoulders and sending the Nephilim forward and off its feet. It had already been leaning forward in its downward run, and with the impact to its upper body, it was sent flying headfirst down the steps.

She ended up rotating backward and riding the giant down, sitting on its back until it struck the jagged stone with outstretched arms. Her head whipped back and struck the armor that wrapped the giant's waist.

And everything went black.

* * * *

Jackson had made it to the third step when his eyes went from Robyn, falling through the sky, to the giant running down the stairs to meet him. It seemed to cover space at an impossible speed, cutting the distance between them in half almost instantaneously. But the giant wasn't Jackson's main concern, and he lifted his eyes back to the flowing figure just in time to see her strike the stone steps…

Only that wasn't what really happened. The giant, for some reason, took a crazy step to its left, and in that split second between happenings, Jackson could tell from the giant's puzzled face that it hadn't taken the step voluntarily. Rather it was like it had been shoved by some invisible force. And then, instead of hitting the ground in front of the giant, Robyn suddenly…*paused.* Or perhaps paused wasn't the right word. Maybe she *hesitated* in order to allow the giant to get beneath her, but that was impossible too. Yet, as he watched her land on the giant, pushing it forward and down the steps, he couldn't deny what he'd just seen.

He ran around the dead bodies that were draped across his path, and finally reached her with burning legs he didn't even notice. "Robyn!" he cried, dropping the rifle. The giant was inverted, its chin resting on a step, its eyes open and gazing sightlessly at the road below. Its neck had struck the pointed corner of the stairs and snapped. Its arms were stretched out in front of it like tree limbs, and Jackson had to climb over them to get to her. She was lying on the giant's back, her eyes closed, and her face turned toward the darkening sky.

Jackson called her name again, running his hands over her face and head. But she didn't wake up. He put two fingers to her neck and felt a strong pulse, the relief that had been stolen from him rushing back tenfold. And then he noticed that Robinson and the others were surrounding them and shooting at a line of Not Them soldiers that was wrapping around the side of the pyramid.

"Is she okay?" Joe hollered.

Jackson didn't know for sure, but he thought so. He scooped her up in his arms and carried her behind the six Purees who continued to lay down cover fire. "Grab my rifle!" he called out as he made his way to the north end of the ziggurat.

Li picked up the gun and followed him, turning and firing to keep the bowman ducking for cover on the south corner of the temple. The rest of them did the same until they reached the north face and began working their way down to the courtyard.

"You seeing this?" Robinson asked Jackson, pointing to the sky.

Jackson looked up, trying to ignore his screaming muscles, and saw the inky fingers clawing away at the blue atmosphere. A cold wind was beginning to blow through the streets, pushing debris and dust into little tornadoes. It was coming.

The closet demon was coming. And the fact that it was coming with all the fanfare of apocalypse rather than simply stepping out of some bubble, as he'd seen it do last night, told him that the demon wasn't here to investigate, but rather to feast on souls. The hair on his arms began to stand.

Robinson looked down at his own arms. "You feel that?"

"We need to get out of here now!" Jackson screamed. The air was filling with static electricity. The show was about to begin.

They hopped off the temple steps and ran as quickly as they could across the courtyard and to the surrounding wall. The five-foot wall seemed more ceremonial than obstructive, and it didn't take too much effort to climb over it. It was a little challenging getting Robyn's unconscious body up and over, but they were on the other side and running for the stream in no time.

Jackson's body was refusing to obey him, his muscles cramping under Robyn's weight. He passed her over to Wilson, who easily took her up in his arms. They crossed the stream without incident, turning back occasionally to see the black curtain closing over the battling giants and feasting dinosaurs. The sound of AK-47s no longer echoed from within the city, meaning that all the Fallen Leftovers had either been killed or had run out of ammo and were now being killed. Most likely, seeing the coming darkness and knowing what it meant themselves, they were making their own escape back into the woods.

Jackson wasn't sure they were going to make it, and again his hope dipped into despair as they tried to tackle the incline that was the north valley wall. The darkness was almost over top of them, and the wind was howling.

* * * *

Paul wiped the blood off his cheek with the back of his hand as he raised his arms in surrender. "Okay. You got me," he said, staring into the barrel of the floating rifle.

Then the rifle flew backward, racing across the room and landing in the man's hands. He held it out in front of him, taking his time to look it over, and then snapped it in half, dropping both pieces to the floor.

And that was when Paul turned and made a dash for the balcony, intent on going the way of Robyn (and in a flash of madness, he wondered if she, like the bird she shared a name with, had wings and could fly too—he knew of no flying creature that had his name). Just before reaching the open air, however, his feet were suddenly snapped out from under him. He hit the stone floor hard, the air chased from his lungs and his head bouncing like a bowling ball. Invisible hands reeled him back across the room and slammed him into the side of the bed again. Sharp flashes of pain exploded like fireworks all over his body, and his head grew foggy. He groaned, spit, and looked up just in time to see Turiel wave a hand at the wall. And of course, that was where he went, flying up off his hands and knees and across the room, crashing into the wall four feet off the ground. He landed in a heap, his eyes bulging, veins surfacing. *What the hell?* Now he was in an *Exorcist* movie? *If he could just wave his hand and throw people around like a Sith lord, why all the theatrics?*

Because, came the answer inserted in his head, *as much as I would have loved to have the daughter of Eve, I'm starting to see the bigger picture here. And you, Paul, I think might have been sent to me for an even greater purpose.*

"I told you I'm not into that." He spit blood onto the floor, wondering if this "purpose" he was talking about could be why ghosty girl had been helping him this whole time. If, in fact, she hadn't been helping him, rather just helping get him to this place at this time. *But for what?*

And that was when the Fallen angel noticed the swirling shadows sweeping through the room. He looked up at the skylight and saw the darkness eating away at the afternoon, and Paul thought he detected a subtle look of confusion pinch his brow. The Fallen angel then dropped his gaze to the balcony, looking out at his ruined kingdom. As he walked toward it, he said, *Your friend is almost here, and then we can proceed.*

"What friend?" Paul growled, trying to get back to his feet.

He squinted while he moved as if trying to discern the answer telepathically. And then his eyes lit with the answer. "Hunter," he said aloud.

Paul's eyes shot up, and his mind spun. Then he was flung up against the wall.

* * * *

Hunter veered away from the stream, climbed the city wall, and slipped into the chaos. Immediately, one of the Leftover giants began chasing him up one of the wider east-to-west streets. He looked back over his shoulder just in time to see the head of a dinosaur, as big as an SUV, swoop down into the street and grab the giant in its mouth. It ripped its arm off at the shoulder with a jerk of its head. The giant howled, blood squirting across the street and splashing the houses lining it even as it swung its sword at the lizard's throat.

Hunter set his eyes back ahead of him, not bothering to see which creature won the battle, and raced for the courtyard.

By the time he reached the temple, Robyn was gone. He could see the giant lying on the steps, and he began climbing toward it. A quarter of the way to the platform and the temple's entrance, he looked to his left, to the north, and saw Jackson and the other Purees making their way across the stream he and Daniel had just crossed minutes earlier. They had Robyn with them. His little magic had worked; he'd kept her from plunging to her death. He stood for a second watching them. It was the first time he'd seen Jackson with his actual two eyes since being drawn into the closet. He wanted to go after them, to be part of the team again, but he knew those days were gone. History. Things had changed, and now he needed to do something that only he could do. He watched them climb out of the stream and head up into the woods.

That's right, kiddo. You got some things to get done. Don't know how it's gonna work, but I suppose it's gotta be sung. We'll just figure it out when we get there, won't we? Because some serious stuff is going down, ya see. And if we don't get our pals back to planet Earth with the warning, it's game over, lights out, the fat lady done singin' her song next morning. Of course, it could all be a trap, the Devil using us to set the stage for what he's got on tap. And we *release the plague by issuing a warning that it's comin'. And wouldn't that be a kicker, a real self-defeating hummin'!*

He shook the nonsense from his head and looked up at the churning vortex opening in the sky.

And saw something else beneath it.

There, perched on the roof of the temple like some gargoyle statue, was the demon. Its alien eyes were tracking him while its long, slithering tongue flicked in and out of its needlelike teeth. It shifted, flickered, blurred, and blinked up there as if not quite in tune with the proper frequency, making it hard for him to stare at without rubbing his eyes. But Hunter knew that this thing was the true puppet-master, the one sent by Lucifer himself.

And just like that, he saw the plan. It flashed in his mind like so many more puzzle pieces falling into place. The orchestration that had been directed throughout the ages, the pieces being set in careful order. Ronald had seen it in part, but Osiris had no clue. The first pyramid wasn't just used to free Osiris from his prison. No, it had a much bigger purpose than that. It had served to merge multiple realities, times, and realms together onto one single plane, the past and present joined by a trapdoor in a closet that Hunter himself had unlocked when the disembodied spirits of Osiris' slain Nephilim had entered his broken, dying body, turning him like a key in the keyhole of time and space. The pyramid had opened windows and merged timelines, bringing together Turiel and his slice of antediluvian real estate with the house and its portal, but it was his entering the closet that set it all in motion by freeing the director of this horror film. And now the dark quantum-technicians were ready to introduce one of the original two hundred back to earth.

Hunter ran for the platform, keeping his eyes locked with the demon's as best he could as he ascended the stairs. It was getting darker and darker, the sun blotted out of the sky, and he was waiting for the alien to sweep down and carry him back to the pit. Yet he was confident that wouldn't happen, because it still needed him.

"That's right, you bastard, you still need me, don't you?" he huffed.

And then movement between them as a figure stepped out onto the balcony.

Turiel.

The angel that left his first estate, that had ruled as a priest of the Golden Feather, a god of mythology, a missionary of the forbidden Atlantean wisdom-religion, and polluter of the human gene pool. Though he hadn't actually completed all that yet, had he? Because he wasn't *then* but *now*. Here. Standing beneath its puppeteer like a boy on a string.

An image of Paul fastened to the wall jumped in front of his mind's eye, and he saw what Turiel had in store for him…

The angel looked up to the sky as thunder rolled through the exploding clouds, his black hair whipping around his face.

And then, with a dissatisfied expression, he spun back into the room.

Hunter could hear a song playing from up there, the words drifting out into the static air like a supernatural battle cry.

He smiled.

He wasn't alone.

Racing across the platform and through the open doors, he entered the temple.

REVELATIONS

And we did according to all His words: all the malignant evil ones we bound in the place of condemnation, and a tenth part of them we left that they might be subject before Satan on the earth.

—Book of Jubilees 10:11

And they said to me: These are the Grigori, who with their prince Satanail rejected the Lord of light, and after them are those who are held in great darkness on the second heaven, and three of them went down on to earth from the Lord's throne, to the place Ermon, and broke through their vows on the shoulder of the hill Ermon and saw the daughters of men how good they are, and took to themselves wives, and befouled the earth with their deeds, who in all times of their age made lawlessness and mixing, and giants are born and marvelous big men and great enmity. And therefore God judged them with great judgement, and they weep for their brethren and they will be punished on the Lord's great day.

—Book of Secrets of Enoch 18:3,4

They did not destroy the peoples, as the Lord commanded them, but they mixed with the nations and learned to do as they did. They served their idols, which became a snare to them. They sacrificed their sons and their daughters to the demons; they poured out innocent blood, the blood of their sons and daughters, whom they sacrificed to the idols of Canaan, and the land was polluted with blood. Thus they became unclean by their acts, and played the whore in their deeds.

—Psalms 106:34-39 (ESV)

He opened the shaft of the bottomless pit, and from the shaft rose smoke like the smoke of a great furnace, and the sun and the air were darkened with the smoke from the shaft. Then from the smoke came locusts on the earth, and they were given power like the power of scorpions of the earth.

—Revelation 9:2, 3 (ESV)

TWENTY

September 22, 2011. The Temple. Afternoon.

Paul spit more blood onto the floor at his feet. His hands and feet were outstretched and held against the wall by an invisible force. He was a bare-chested, bloody X plastered against the smooth, cold wall, the psychic shackles not giving an inch.

Hunter…

Could it be true? Could Hunter still be here? Had he managed to somehow free himself from the ghost ship? If so, how could this clown possibly know it?

He watched the angel as he stood out on the balcony, his hands gripping the railing, the wind whipping his hair all over the place. Something had taken him by surprise, and Paul had no idea what it could be. He'd seemed pretty sure of himself even while the offspring of another Fallen angel was attacking his empire, certain that this was all part of some bigger scheme that would end in his favor. So what changed? Was it the darkness? Was he afraid of the closet demon?

A sudden gust of wind howled through the room and blew the sheets up off the bed. Like a sail, they drifted across the room before fluttering to the floor at the foot of the open doors. Then the hair on Paul's arms stood as the room filled with a static charge.

"Uh-oh," he muttered. He knew what that meant, and it didn't have anything to do with what they'd felt in that cave with the black hole and portcullis. Nope, this was something he'd run from months ago and that Jackson had encountered more than once without him. The demon was here now, and here he was stuck to the wall like a mouse on a glue trap.

He tried to move his hands, but the pain in his pierced arm sent flashes of searing heat into his brain. *This is it, Paul-o. The fat lady is belting out your last lines.*

Thunder shouted from the angry sky.

That was it, buddy. The last note, its echo fading…fading…fading…

Another sound. This one…*singing.* It echoed loudly throughout the chamber, getting louder and louder. And it was coming from…his pocket.

"Through many dangers, toils and snares—"

Turiel's head snapped away from the chaos engulfing the city and spun around so fast that it looked to Paul as if he went from one position to the next in a single, time-rejecting instant.

"We have already come—

T'was grace that brought us safe thus far—"

Turiel stormed back into the room, his eyes a cocktail of rage and uncertainty. He flew to Paul, sticking his long fingers into his pocket and pulling out the dead cell phone. He stared at it as it continued to sing in his face.

"And grace will lead us home—"

Paul thought he could feel his bonds loosen as the man's forehead wrinkled, those all-knowing eyes suddenly lost in a sea of uncharted territory.

Paul noticed something behind Turiel, a figure standing on the other side of the room against the far wall.

The girl.

She winked at him and disappeared, again leaving him to doubt what his eyes had seen.

Turiel threw the phone against the wall with a shout, and it shattered into two pieces.

Yet the song continued.

"Amazing grace, how sweet the sound..."

* * * *

They got halfway up the valley wall before they had to stop. Wilson's arms were numb from carrying Robyn's dead weight up the steep incline, and even after setting her down, his arms remained stuck in a curled position.

They hadn't been able to outrun the storm clouds due to the steep degree of their climb, but the inky, soul-snatching darkness was still between the pyramid and the temple. They had some time left, but not much. Though they would never make it if they had to carry Robyn the rest of the way. Jackson thought about sending the others on ahead, and perhaps that was what he would end up doing in the end...taking her in his arms and holding her as tight as he could while the Midnight swept over them and took them from this life together. But he wanted to try waking her up one more time before resigning himself to that fate. He went to her side, ordering a perimeter set up around them.

The trees were bending in the howling wind, leaves and pine needles whipping through the air like stinging wasps. A blizzard-like whistle sang out from the moaning wind as it reached a crazy, swirling crescendo, and Jackson swore a funnel was about to spiral out of the sky and rip through the valley. He could make out the forms of fleeing bodies climbing up through the trees around them. Some of them seemed to be holding spears, others children. He even saw a handful of dinosaurs making a mad dash past the easy prey as if somehow aware of what was coming too.

Jackson ran a hand over Robyn's head, her hair still pulled tight against her scalp and tied into braids. "Robyn?" he asked, praying that she would wake up. Yes, it was a miracle that she was even still alive, but the miracle would be short lived if she didn't open her eyes and come to her senses right now. "Robyn, wake up. Please."

Her eyes opened.

His eyes suddenly stung, his heart thumping with relief, and he cradled her in his arms, burying his face in her sweet-smelling neck. "Thank God," he whispered. Then he let her back down so he could look into her face.

Her eyes were open, but he could tell that she wasn't seeing him.

"How is she?" Robinson called out over the wind.

But he didn't know yet.

Then she reached out her hand, first finding his face and then moving it around to the back of his neck. She squeezed, and tears spilled from her eyes.

"Jackson," she whispered.

"I'm here," he whispered. "I'm here."

She blinked, and her pupils finally responded to his presence. Then she sat up and threw herself around his neck.

"It's okay. I have you," he said.

She pulled back, and before he knew what she was doing, she had her lips pressed against his. Her lips tasted like wine, and the intoxicating effect was immediate. He didn't know what had gone down up in the temple, why she looked the way she did and was wearing what she was wearing, but her skin, her lips… He thought they could get drunk on each other right here and now, the reality of the outside world floating away, the danger about to crush them suddenly silly and insignificant.

And then a branch struck him in the head and snapped him out of it. He pulled away from her and could only think to say, "We need to go! Now! Can you—"

"I'm sorry," she said, cutting him off. "For—"

He put a finger to her lips. "Later! We need to go!" He stood and took her hand, lifting her to her feet. She swayed a little and leaned against him for support. And that was when she looked down at herself and saw the white material wrapping around her legs and blowing in the wind.

She immediately withdrew from him, pulling the oversized and bloody shirt down over her hips as her eyes drifted away, rehashing the events that had led her here. Then, like a shot, she suddenly snapped to attention again, her eyes sober and sharp. "Paul's up there," she said. And she turned about, trying to get her bearings for the first time.

"Where?" Jackson asked, gripping her shoulders.

She found the city through the trees and pointed to the temple. "He came for me. Saved me from…" She trailed off, her brow crimping at a blank spot in her memory. And then she had it. "Turiel."

The others had closed in, and Li asked, "What's a turiel?"

But it was Jackson who answered. "Turiel is a Fallen angel."

"The Book of Enoch," Robinson remembered.

Robyn whispered the words she'd heard the silver-haired man in the red robe say to her. "You are in a kingdom of Atlas, under the reign of the god Turiel, under the light of Thoth."

"What did you say?" Joe hollered over the wind.

Her hand went to her temple. "He could…read my mind." She looked up. "He talked to me *in* my head." And then her other hand went up the inside of her thigh, probing for other memories.

Jackson noticed what she was doing, what she was trying to figure out, but there wasn't time for any of it now. They'd wasted too much time already, and the Black was now covering the back side of the temple. He turned her so that she was facing it. Thus far she hadn't registered the coming storm. She was still disoriented and trying to catch up, but there was one thing Jackson knew she would understand right away. He pointed at the spreading Dark and all it was erasing.

When she saw it, her body went instantly rigid. She'd lived through the combing of that thing once before, and she had no desire to do so again. She spun away and looked back into Jackson's eyes with a dread so complete that it was clear she needed no extra prodding.

She started to run.

* * * *

Hunter ran through the stone corridors of the palace's main floor. He knew, the way that he had come to know most things he had no business knowing, that there were multiple floors beneath him—passageways, chambers, rooms...and a secret, subterranean tunnel that led straight into the crystal pyramid at the end of the valley. He knew they would get there eventually, that it was their ultimate terminus, but not right now. First, he had to figure out a way to save Paul—that part of his plan hadn't yet presented itself.

The temple seemed empty, most of its occupants having left to defend the city. There were a few remaining priests, the chambermaids, and a handful of sentries roaming about, but he was aware of their locations and knew they wouldn't interfere with him reaching his destination.

He was only slightly aware of the décor of the ancient site, huge pillars carved into statues of men and women, gods and goddesses, passing by him in blurs as he made his way from one stone hall to another. And then he came across the bodies. They were sprawled haphazardly, their flesh and bones obviously chewed by bullets, and he knew he'd finally found Paul's trail.

He followed the trail of corpses into an enormous hall, where a throne fixed to a platform stared at him from the other end of the room a hundred yards away. Behind it, long vertical windows carved into the stone revealed just how dark it had already gotten outside, and the wind was howling through the windows that lined the high walls to his left and right. Above him, balled cages swung back and forth from the ceiling, their occupants either dead or dying. The sight of them filled him with such horrid revulsion that it was all he could do to keep moving.

He ran down the long velvet carpet, and just before reaching another carpet that formed an intersection in the middle of the room, he spotted a dead sentry, bullet holes running from his chest up into his eye. The man's head had been shaved bald, and Hunter knew in that secret way that this was a Mesniu soldier from the army of "metal people" depicted on the walls of the Edfu temple—the first men, Egyptian tradition said, to be armed by the gods with metal weapons, and the first enlisted men to fight in a war between gods. Only these men hadn't been trained by Horus in Egypt, but by Turiel here, in this place.

Sure, Thoth would build Horus his winged disk to fight Seth, he would have custody of the secret plans of the Great Pyramid, and he would ultimately replace Horus on Egypt's throne, but first he had to leave Atlantis. And, Hunter thought, wasn't it said of *this* kingdom that it was "of Atlas, under the reign of Turiel, under the light of Thoth?" So, he wondered, what would happen if the Priest of the Sacred Feather never made it to Egypt to begin with? What if something were to happen that would cause that Feathered Serpent to bypass most of human history? Would the foundational work set down by one of the three hundred still hold true? These were questions that, as enlightened as Hunter might be from time to time, he had no business knowing, and he threw it all out of his head.

He kept going, stopping when he reached the intersecting carpet to look left and right. On the left he saw nothing, but on the right there were stairs between the caryatid-like pillars of bare-chested men holding up the ceiling. The steps were full of bodies frozen in an upside-down dance, and Hunter continued to follow the breadcrumbs between the stone giants. He walked over a bloody, broken bolt and an empty magazine before noticing a trail of blood connecting the steps to a corpse lying on the ground to his right. Either the dead man (who was missing an eye, he noticed) had stumbled, bleeding down the stairs and had met his end down yonder, or Paul had left him there and, himself bleeding, then went up the steps. Either way, he was close.

Halfway up the stairs, a howling wind came crashing down at him, almost knocking him backward. It whistled and screamed like a chorus of ghosts, and the stone walls began to vibrate.

The swirling blackness that was the closet demon's net was being cast over the valley. The demon, still perched on the temple's apex, was about to partake of its blood sacrifice, drinking the energy from all that it would ensnare in order to obtain the power needed to fulfill its destiny as director of this mad plot.

Hunter lowered his shoulder and fought his way up the stairs, the humming stone tickling his feet. He hoped he wouldn't be too late, that his friend would still be in a condition to be saved.

The words of the old Gospel tune that came echoing down the staircase around him, hijacking the wings of the evil wind, suggested that he had just a little more time.

Hold on, Paul-o! I know what the fat lady don't know…

The walls shook, the screaming so loud, and his breath frozen clouds before him.

The soul feast had begun.

* * * *

They made it over the crest of the valley and onto level ground, but the liquid Black was rolling toward them quick. Robyn paused only to look at her bare feet, which were now bleeding. Jackson wished they could carry her, to put her on their backs and run, but there was no time. She'd have to fight through it and hopefully avoid any missteps that would render her immobile.

"Keep going!" he cried out. And just before they continued on through a field of large rocks and knee-high grass, something came riding across the wind and to their ears.

"You hear that?" Patrick cried.

Before anyone could respond, however, a figure appeared from behind a large rock outcropping that poked out of the earth like a fin about sixty feet away.

They all raised their rifles, a mere millisecond from putting the person down, whatever it may be. But the hands held high over their head gave them just enough pause to allow the person a single, life-saving line: "Don't shoot, it's me!"

Li readjusted the rifle against his shoulder, nervously flexing his fingers while trying to shield his eyes from the debris whipping through the air. "Who's there?"

"Li, is that you?" came the answer.

"Who are you?" Li asked again.

"It's Daniel." And the figure took a step toward them. "Don't shoot me, dammit!"

Li lowered the gun.

"Get over here, now!" Robinson shouted, waving him to them. "Hurry!"

Daniel sprinted over to them.

"Where the hell did you come from?" Joe asked.

"There's no time!" Robyn yelled.

Daniel looked at her. "You're here!"

"Let's go!" Jackson said, pushing them all away from the icy hand coming for them. "We'll talk later!"

But Daniel grabbed Jackson's shirt. "Wait! I have to tell you this in case something happens to me!"

"Later!"

"No, now! I was with Hunter! He's back!"

The temperature was dropping fast.

"You saw Hunter?" Jackson asked, suddenly all ears.

Daniel waved him off. "He said he's getting us all out of here now! But he said we have to be off the island! He wants us to get back to the ship!"

"What?" Li screamed, doubting every word he thought he just heard.

"Where did you come from?" Jackson asked.

"The beach!"

"Can you lead us back there?"

"I think so!"

"Then go!"

Daniel nodded, turned, and ran back the way he and Hunter had come.

Jackson threw the rifle over his shoulder, next to his backpack, and hooked his right arm around Robyn's waist. He lifted her high enough so that her feet were off the ground, and he started running. He looked back over his shoulder and could no longer see the pyramid or the temple. They'd simply been erased along with every particle of light on that side of the valley, a black void from eternity below to endless space above.

* * * *

The walls seemed to be alive, moving. Screams came shrieking from the city outside, echoing throughout the room and competing with the song that was still playing from the shattered phone. The screams were like nothing Paul ever heard before. It was the sound of pure anguish and utter, mind-breaking horror on a massive scale. Jackson had tried to describe what it had been like on the beach the day he'd met Robyn, but nothing he imagined had come anything close to this.

Turiel was troubled by the music, though Paul had a feeling it was because he couldn't understand its meaning or its origin. If this was a Fallen angel, a Titan from old, then he doubted if he understood exactly what the "Amazing Grace" was that was referenced. Still, perhaps on some spiritual level he was picking up on other forces that were suddenly at play here, forces that had tossed Lucifer from heaven, that had sentenced to Tartarus all those who had left their heavenly state and took for themselves human wives, that destroyed their world with a flood…

Paul's mind spun with the lyrics, with the vision of the girl. She'd said that maybe she was an angel, and maybe she was. Maybe the song was for him.

I think the time has come, Turiel's mind-voice said, cutting through all the noise.

"Time for what?" Paul hissed, still stuck to the wall.

And then, as if a black shade had been pulled down over the balcony entrance and across the skylight, the outside world was now a light-consuming black hole. Like the closet Hunter had walked into…

The cold was instant, and Paul's teeth started to rattle, his breath turning to clouds in front of him.

Turiel looked to the doorway. *It is time that I learn the meaning of all of this…*

"Y-yeah? And wh-who is gonna t-t-tell you that?"

And on that note, the song stopped…and Hunter walked through the door.

TWENTY-ONE

September 22, 2011. The New Territory. Afternoon.

Daniel lost his footing and stumbled again as the wind carried the screams from the valley through the air around them. Sweat was dripping into his eyes, but he hardly noticed. He looked behind him to make sure everyone was still following. They'd made it across the field and were now running alongside a river that might or might not be connected to the stream he and Hunter had crossed at the foot of the valley (though the current was flowing away from the valley, so he thought it unlikely). He didn't recall this river from his travels with Hunter and could only hope he was heading in the right direction. They were all following him, and if he were to lead them all to a dead end, then outrunning the teeth of the consuming void would end abruptly. And as that wall of dark continued pressing in behind them, getting closer and closer, the crazed panic he felt only intensified.

He became half-aware of other people sprinting through the woods to his left, on the other side of the river. It didn't matter who they were. Like animals of all sorts fleeing a forest fire, both predator and prey, they were all in the same boat, everyone just trying to stay ahead of the abyss.

A blast of cold struck him in the back and sucked the air from his lungs. He looked back again and saw the others trying to keep up. Robyn was running beside Jackson, Robinson and Joe and Li were right in front of them, and Sanders, Wilson, and Patrick were in the back.

"Go!" Robinson screamed at him, catching his eye. "Don't look back!"

Obeying, Daniel whipped his head around just in time to see a huge pair of scaled legs cut across his path, shaking the ground and snapping the smaller trees in their wake. He threw his hands over his head to protect himself from the falling debris and watched as the thing Hunter called a dinosaur stomped across the river, the water reaching its massive thighs. Then he looked forward again and saw what had made the lizard cut across their path.

Nothing.

There was nothing ahead of them. The forest simply ended and turned to air.

The wind was so loud that he hadn't been able to hear the waterfall, but now he could see it. The river beside them ran about fifty yards ahead and then slipped through a row of rocks, plunging out of sight. The river was moving fast, and it was too wide to cross. He'd led them to a dead end after all. With crushing hopelessness, he turned and looked back into the Dark just in time to see the wall of oblivion overtake two Fallen Leftovers that were thirty yards behind Sanders. He watched the dark curtain pass over them, and for a second, he could still see them there on the other side of the veil, dim and fading but still running. And then invisible hands snatched them backward, ripping them off their feet and sucking them up into the void. Before disappearing completely, they came apart.

And though it seemed instant, Daniel knew that the men had suffered. The way their faces twisted and contorted just before being expelled at every joint, the way their eyes popped with horror and their lips stretched thin over bared teeth… Somehow, in that single moment, they'd comprehended their end and saw their damnation.

Then they were gone forever.

He ran faster, knowing there was only one chance at escaping the black wave. He angled right, jumping through tangled bushes and weeds, and sprinted across the river's stony bank. Without another thought, he threw himself into the wild current and let it carry him to the teeth ahead. As he tried navigating through some rapids, not wanting to get hung up on any rocks, he turned and saw the others splash into the water after him, the Nothingness right on their heels and seeming to consume existence itself.

He bumped into one of the teeth before slipping through, and then he was falling.

* * * *

Jackson watched Daniel slip over the fall and disappear. The rest of them were quickly approaching the same end, the current moving them fast, and he could only hope they would get there in time. There was no guarantee that the Darkness wouldn't reach them down below or that there weren't a pile of jagged rocks waiting for them at the bottom of a hundred-foot drop, but it was the only chance they had. He squeezed Robyn's hand as the Black swept toward them from behind, and the final row of teeth rushed to meet them ahead. The water split around one of the rocks, pulling Jackson to the left of it and Robyn to the right, breaking their hold on each other. The roiling water splashed with white fury and swept them over in a horizontal thrust that cleared contact with the bedrock, jettisoning them out into the open air.

Falling.

Falling.

Falling…

As he bicycled in midair, trying to get a glimpse of the water below (he hoped it was a nice big plunge pool, because it was the only chance they had of surviving this), he tried to gauge how long he'd been dropping. He figured it could be a hundred feet. Certainly not a thousand. Probably not even three hundred, but that was no consolation considering a hundred and seventy-seven feet was the current high dive record, Niagara Falls just a few feet taller at a hundred and eighty, and how many people had survived that leap? A dozen maybe? The Golden Gate Bridge was a key suicide spot at about two hundred and fifty feet, most victims suffering from broken rib cages puncturing lungs and livers, blood vessels and hearts rupturing from the sudden pressure change, and brain damage…and then there was the drowning if you somehow managed to survive the impact. But then again, he knew there were twenty-foot waterfalls that would kill you because the size and shape of the pool it emptied into was too small to compensate for all the water, leaving no way for a swimmer to escape the force of the boiling water—

His thoughts were interrupted by the surface, which he did survive by entering feet first and wrapping his arms around his head while covering his nose with the crook of his elbow. He pressed his legs together and closed his eyes and mouth, falling through the boiling water at just the right angle. Then he was pushed down into the depths of the plunge pool by a tremendous, smashing force. But even as he spun head over heels in the surf-like chaos beneath the chute, he could only be thankful that he'd landed in a pool rather than a shallow riverbed, that he made it through the surface, and that so far, he hadn't found rocks or other debris to batter and puncture his body.

But he still had to avoid drowning, and the turbulence roaring around him coupled with the bubbles blocking out sunlight was disorienting, making it impossible to know up from down. He was trapped in a vortex, unable to swim or break free. All he could do was hold his breath and hope the vortex would slingshot him out the other side and push him away from the waterfall in time.

Finally, the waterfall let him loose and he stopped tumbling. With perhaps a minute left before he would pass out and begin inhaling water, he began looking for lighter hues of blue. Finding them, rays of light stretching down out of a blinding, shimmering sun, he righted himself and discovered the riverbed just a foot beneath him. He could get a good push off it and reach the surface in no time. Then he remembered his backpack, suddenly aware of its weight. He thought he could still make it even with the weight of all the magazines, the AK, and his boots pulling against him.

And then the light disappeared as darkness swept over the water's surface, transporting him from the bottom of a pool to the middle of space in an instant. The temperature plummeted, and he wondered if he'd be a juicy center in the middle of an ice pop.

He moved his arms, stretching out into the void, and felt something brush his numbing fingertips. He explored the contact and found it to be a hand. He followed it to an elbow, then to a shoulder. Next, his probing hands discovered a large breast, and he knew he'd found Robyn. He reached out with both hands and pulled her toward him. Her body floated without resistance, limp and unmoving. Panic began to make his heart beat faster, which increased the need for oxygen. But it was still dark, the demon feasting above them.

His lungs began to ache, and he prayed.

Hang in there, Denise (Robyn)…

Still total blackness.

Her braids were slithering over his face.

Please, God!

He couldn't wait any longer. Darkness or not, he needed air, and she needed resuscitation. He wrapped his left arm tight around her slim waist and pushed hard off the bedrock. Moving his legs in powerful, scissored thrusts, he fought Robyn's weight and his cargo, climbing slowly and laboriously toward the Nothing above.

The water was getting warmer, and thank God, light was appearing!

C'mon! He climbed with his right arm, kicking and kicking and kicking, his backpack and gun like dead weights trying to pull him back down, and Robyn's lifeless body flopping awkwardly against him. He looked down and saw that the bottom was just eight feet away. They weren't going anywhere. As darkness began to creep into the corners of his vision, he let go of Robyn and wiggled out of his backpack, leaving it and the rifle behind. He could come back for them later.

The light was brushing the surface now, beams of light stretching down like ladders around them and illuminating the pool. Jackson positioned himself at Robyn's dangling feet, turned so that his back was to her, and then swam up and through Paul's big shirt that was spread out like a dress around her. He put his arms through the sleeves and his head through the wide, cut neck, his back against hers, his arms and head against hers. He was wearing Robyn on his back and could now use both arms and legs.

He thrust his arms and legs, climbing closer and closer to the light, his chest heaving, the urge to breathe overwhelming. Twice when he was a SEAL he'd passed out and had to be revived by his teammates, and he knew he was only seconds away from blacking out now.

His outstretched hands looked as if they could just grab the surface, like they were right there, yet they just couldn't seem to get there. He let the remaining air out of his lungs, a trail of tiny bubbles following them up, up, up…

Jackson's head broke through the liquid barrier just as he felt himself begin to slip away. With the last ounce of strength he had, he'd managed to breach the surface and inhale a huge gulp of glorious air that brought life back into his bones.

He continued to breathe as his heart hammered in his chest, and he got horizontal, keeping Robyn's head out of the water. He saw the edge of the pool ten yards away, and began swimming for it, praying the whole way.

A head exploded out of the water in front of him as Daniel emerged from below, gasping for breath and flailing against the water. After recovering and getting his bearings, he swam over to help Jackson.

"Tilt her head back. Keep her face out of the water," Jackson panted. The bank was just ten feet away.

When he finally stumbled up onto the bank, Daniel helping to work him out of Robyn's shirt, he found Robinson, Li, Joe, Wilson, and Patrick standing there waiting. They all jumped in to help separate him from her and got Robyn on the ground. There was no time to consider what had happened to the Darkness, where they were now, or if they were still in danger. There was only time to think about Robyn.

Jackson went to his knees, coughing and gagging, his muscles cramping. He looked over and saw Robinson leaning over Robyn, lifting her chin and blowing air down her throat. The others were gathered around her, waiting for their turn if needed. Jackson met eyes with Daniel, who was also on his hands and knees. The look communicated was less hopeful than Jackson would have liked.

"C'mon, Robyn," Joe said. He had his palms pressed against her chest, pushing down hard through the rib cage and to her heart. When he stopped, Robinson covered her mouth with his and blew.

They repeated this for what seemed like forever, and Jackson's eyes filled with tears as realization began to sink in.

"C'mon, Robyn!" Joe was screaming now. "Come on, dammit!" He pushed harder, massaging her heart, not caring if he broke ribs in the process.

Her lips were blue, the color draining from her face. She looked dead.

Jackson got to his feet and stumbled over to them, looking down at Robyn's body. Numbness began seeping through him as his brain engaged a self-defense mechanism meant to preserve his sanity. He looked on with an empty stare, watching without really seeing Robinson and Joe trying to will life back into Robyn.

But it wasn't to be. They were only beating her body at this point. He tried to tell them to stop, that she was gone, but he couldn't get his mouth to work. He took another step toward them, reaching down past Li and Patrick, intending to grab Joe's shoulder, when Robyn's body suddenly arched off the ground and water came jettisoning out of her mouth like a geyser.

Robinson and Joe jumped back, their tear-streaked faces all eyes.

Jackson blinked, unsure if he could trust what he was seeing. Robyn coughed violently, turning on her side and vomiting water over the stony bank. She wheezed long and hard, her fingers clawing through the little rocks and carving ruts into the moist soil beneath them. Then she coughed some more, heaving. Slowly, she got to her hands and knees, Paul's stretched and soaked shirt hanging to the ground beneath her, the white dress she was wearing beneath practically invisible. Doing their best to avert their eyes until she could reposition herself, the men all exchanged quick embraces, thankful that their sister was somehow alive, Robinson and Joe fighting to catch their own breath.

It was a miracle, Jackson knew. And at least the second one since he'd seen her up on the balcony. God had answered his prayers.

They gave her space, confident that she was going to be okay, and for the first time noticed that Sanders was not with them. Robinson and Li walked to the bank, searching the waterfall and the surrounding pool, while Joe looked in the other direction downriver.

Jackson knelt beside Robyn, placing a hand on her back. "You scared me," he whispered.

She reached up and squeezed it. Then she got to her knees and turned into him, wrapping her arms around his neck once again. This time she couldn't hold back the tears, and they came in sobs.

He held her shaking body even while scanning the cliff above them, looking for any signs of the closet demon, giants, soldiers, or dinosaurs. Everything was still, quiet, and the air was warm again.

Then Daniel's voice cut through the sound of the pouring fall. "Look!" he cried. "Over there!" He was standing knee-deep in the water and pointing to the plunge pool.

The others gathered around him, trying to get a glimpse of what he'd seen.

"Oh no," Patrick mumbled.

They all saw the severed arm pop out of the churning water.

"Down there," Li said, now pointing to a group of rocks gathered in a half moon on the river's edge. A head was spinning in circles, unable to escape the current, its hair white with a matching beard and mustache.

Sanders.

"He must've come up too soon," Joe whispered.

They bowed their heads.

* * * *

Hunter knew the demon's net was full, that the lifeforce consumed was enough for what it had in mind…for what it intended to do. And so the sun was shining once more, though thunderclouds were mounting. He knew what the valley looked like, and in some mysterious, yet awful way, he could sense the pain of all those souls that had just been eaten.

The demon, this orchestrator of a cosmic conspiracy so grand, was now licking its lips, savoring the lingering taste of all that energy on its black, forked tongue. It had required a meal of immense proportions, so it had arranged for a three-course setting, each warring with the other beneath its hanging net. But it had also worked its magic to ensure an after-meal meeting with the Three—itself, Turiel of the two hundred, and Hunter, who had acquired the key.

Hunter knew all this as he stepped into the room, though he didn't fully understand it. There was so much he didn't understand, only seeing things in glimpses and fleeting sidelong glances.

"I'm here, Fallen one," he proclaimed, traversing the chamber while laying his eyes on what his mind had already seen. "Let him go and deal with me now."

Turiel's lips curled into a smile as his mind reached out ahead of him, probing, searching…

Not just yet, Hunter projected, answering the ancient priest with his own sudden telepathy.

Turiel blinked and tried to hide his surprise.

Let him go, and then we will discuss what it is you need from me.

Turiel stared at him, holding him with unblinking consideration. *Have it your way.*

The wall released Paul, and he fell onto his hands and knees.

Hunter walked over to him and placed a hand on his bleeding head.

Paul lifted his eyes as realization took root and filled him with purpose. "I'm not leaving you here," he growled, allowing Hunter to pull him back to his feet.

I will be along. He put the thought into Paul's head, tucking it away and out of sight from Turiel.

Hunter could see a million different questions burning intensely in Paul's eyes, but he understood that now was not the time or place.

Later, Hunter said. *Now go.* But he touched him again and managed to transfer a series of images and data into his mind.

Paul looked to Turiel then back to Hunter, wrestling with the knowledge just imparted to him. Then he shook his head and mumbled, "Have it your way, then." He got to his feet. "See you soon." And he ran out of the room.

Hunter turned and faced Turiel. *So where shall we begin?*

* * * *

Paul ran down the stairs as quickly as his injuries would allow, navigating through the dead bodies he'd left sprawled across them. He hit the floor running, sprinting straight into the throne room and following the carpet out the doors at the end of it, not once stopping to look up at the hanging ball cages.

But when he got to the bottom of the other staircase, where he'd heard Mr. Mollings calling from the floor below, he hesitated. He had no weapon other than the bolts in the quiver that was still strapped to his thigh, and he had no idea what else might be down there. But he couldn't leave him, could he?

He swore and kept to the stairs, grumbling the whole way down. He had to get to the horse was what he had to do. That was what Hunter had instructed when he'd placed his hand on his head. And just how was his old buddy able to do that, anyway? He'd implanted all these images into his brain, too—the message behind them both crystal clear and confusing as hell.

Hunter was going to try something tomorrow, at the equinox. And if what he had in mind actually worked, then the bubble that was this reality was going to burst, and everything part of it would implode into oblivion. That black hole in the cave would tear open, ripping across the island and sucking everything in before swallowing itself. The "get out now" part of his message was loud and clear, and Paul did not doubt it. The "why and how" of what Hunter was attempting was beyond confusing.

How Hunter had known about the horse, how he knew anything at all, had been slightly addressed by a vague, over-encompassing arc of impression that left Paul with only enough confidence to believe in Hunter's claims.

Hunter. His friend. Closer than a brother…

He hated leaving him, but Hunter had included the revelation and certainty of that fact along with everything else. He said he would see him again, but Paul wasn't so sure that was the truth. Yet there was more to do on the other side of this strange nexus, for this was only the beginning, the agelong conspiracy now up on its toes and ready to run full tilt to its end. They had to get back, had to stop it if they could. And Hunter was willing to sacrifice himself to ensure that chance.

Paul replayed the images as he reached the bottom of the stairs, descending into the ziggurat portion of the structure. It was if Hunter had injected LSD into his eyeballs, or switched out the normal reels of imagination with some crazy Rob Zombie post-apocalypse picture. It was the scene that Robinson and the others had described seeing on the ship as they went in and out of time, arriving at a Washington Monument that poked a red, ash-filled sky.

The future.

Zep-Tepi, the return of Satan's Golden Age, ushered in by the unlocking of Tartarus and the introduction of Abaddon…

There were other things, more personal things that Hunter had transferred into his consciousness, but there was no time to dwell on those things now, especially if he was going to take this detour to—

The stairs ended in what looked more like a medieval dungeon than something reflecting the grandeur of a past Golden Age. His arm throbbing, Paul thought it strange that a place like this would be in such close proximity to the throne room. At least until he considered the hanging cages that entertained this mad king. Perhaps, rather than having some shepherd boy strum him soothing notes on a harp, he preferred the screams of the tortured filtering up through the floors below him.

Cages lined both side of a hall that Paul thought could be as long as the throne room above him. He wondered about the villagers he'd seen in the New Territory, the townsfolk and the city dwellers, and wondered if they knew about this place. If this world was anything like other governments on earth, then they probably didn't. He doubted that anyone unfortunate enough to discover this place ever made it out to tell of it.

Moving down the dark hall, he peered through the iron bars around him but could see no evidence of occupancy. "Mollings!" he called out, his voice echoing back to him.

No response.

Was it possible that the guards could have released the prisoners? Given them a fighting chance at escaping the invaders? He didn't think so, but…

There, near the back wall, fourth cage from the end, he spotted a crumpled form leaning against the bars. He hurried to the shape and discovered that the exact opposite must've been true. They didn't let anyone go, they'd simply killed them instead.

He tried the door, and it swung outward, the body leaning against it falling into the hall at his feet. Was this Ivan's mate? The second lighthouse operator that disappeared in 1969? Paul kneeled, his aching body protesting, and rolled the body onto its back. Lifeless eyes stared up at him, eyes that did not belong to this realm. If it wasn't Mr. Mollings, then it was some other castaway claimed by the Triangle; his dirty and tattered clothes made that clear. He frowned, wondering if his presence had resulted in Turiel's order to kill him. Had Robyn and Paul, and now Hunter, satisfied a curiosity that Mr. Mollings hadn't been able to? "Sorry, mate," he said, and left him there on the cold stone floor.

* * * *

They were all warming themselves around a large fire not far from the river. After nearly freezing to death and now soaking wet and physically exhausted, they needed to take a half an hour or so to rest. The way the sky was looking, there wouldn't be another chance later. They would dry out, recharge, and get back to the caves pronto. And now Daniel was saying something about needing to get off the island and to the cruise ship…

The fire popped and spewed a shower of sparks into the air. Their eyes followed the tiny embers up into the trees until they turned to ash and disappeared, their minds heavy with the loss of Sanders and Charles and the prospect of many more.

Robinson had been catching Daniel up to speed on everything he'd missed while playing hide-and-seek with Hunter on the ship. The AK-47s, Ruth and Priscilla, the closet demon they'd just escaped from, the Not Thems, Ivan Major and Mr. Mollings, and the cave with the black hole and portcullis. Perhaps the list would have been longer, but at the mention of the black hole, Robyn chimed in, sharing her most recent experience at the gate and informing them all of just how much that black whole had spread since the last time they were there.

After she finished her tale, they sat in silence, not only appreciating all that she'd been through, but what a growing rip in their space-time could mean for their future.

"It shouldn't really matter," Daniel said at last. "Whatever Hunter is planning on doing, he's doing it tomorrow. We just need to be back on that ship when he does it."

Jackson had his arm wrapped around Robyn, trying to keep her warm. All the men had their shirts off and laid out next to the fire for drying, but Robyn was trying to preserve her dignity and still had Paul's soaked shirt over her. After what she'd just been through, he figured the last thing she wanted to do was take her clothes off in front of anyone. He would give her his shirt once it was dry. She had her head against his side, and he looked down, watching her rub her chest. She hadn't stopped rubbing it since being brought back from the dead. It didn't appear that Robinson had broken any ribs, but she was going to be sore for a long time. "Tell me again what Hunter said."

Daniel took a deep breath and then tried to put himself back on the ship, recalling all the bizarre things Hunter had gone on about. He'd given them a brief, disconnected and rambled synopsis before, but now he wanted to be more thorough with it, even mentioning things he'd been convinced were just the mumblings of a madman. And as he spoke, Jackson seemed to hang on every word, especially during the part about none of this being random and that their hope to use the pyramid at the next solstice had been a fantasy.

"What does he mean that this isn't random? *What* isn't random?" Robinson asked.

Jackson looked up. "The house, the closet, this Not Them kingdom, Ivan... He's saying there's a deeper plan at work."

"What does that mean?"

But none of them knew.

"So this whole time we've been assuming we could use the pyramid like John and Henry—"

Jackson shook his head. "John and Henry didn't use the pyramid. Osiris did."

Daniel nodded. "Hunter said that only Thoth knows the secrets of the pyramid and that Turiel knows Thoth." Then he said, "He said he knows a way to get us out of here. He thinks he has some sort of key to unlock a mystery or something. I don't know, it was all pretty confusing. But I think he's planning on activating the pyramid tomorrow, on the equinox. And when he does…" He shook his head.

There was no point in any of them even asking just how Hunter might accomplish that. From Daniel's story, it didn't sound like Hunter himself even knew. Daniel went on until he came to the helicopter again.

"A helicopter?" Robinson asked, doubtful.

"That's what he said. Said it's working and right beside the temple Paul woke up in. I'm assuming you know where that is."

Jackson nodded.

"What are the odds of a working helicopter magically appearing right when we need it to get off the island?" Li wondered, doubting it himself.

"Okay," Robinson said. "Assuming he's right and there is a helicopter that—" He looked at Jackson. "You can fly it, right?"

Jackson nodded. "If it's there and it's fueled, I can fly it."

"Okay," he continued, "so we all climb aboard, but how do we find the ship? It could be on the other side of the island. When's the last time anyone saw it?"

"Well, I just came from it this morning," Daniel reminded him.

"Yeah, but isn't it still moving, circling?"

Daniel thought about it. "You said that this New Territory could stretch all the way to the Caribbean or something."

Jackson shrugged. "It could. We don't know where it ends. You saw all those mountains."

Daniel nodded. "Yeah, but if you haven't seen the ship in a while, it's probably because it was circling a much larger island. I mean, Hunter still called it an island, so—"

"Yeah, but Hunter hasn't been here in a while. He didn't see all this."

"Didn't you hear what I said? Hunter's seen a lot more of this island than is even possible. He's been…somewhere. If he thinks it's an island, then *I* think it's still an island."

Joe waved his hands. "Whatever. The point is, how are we going to locate the ship once we're in the air?" Having been born on the island and never seen one of the Graveyard's flying machines at work, he seemed both excited and frightened at the prospect of actually using one.

"We'll figure that out when the time comes," Patrick said. "There are other things we have to do first." His eyes were locked on the flames, and everyone knew he was talking about getting back to the caves to see if the Leftovers had indeed gotten their stash of rifles from their home.

Robyn looked up. "You really think they would attack the caves?"

"They got the guns from somewhere," Wilson said.

"We don't have much time," Jackson muttered, looking up to the pressing clouds.

And then Joe asked the question that had been nagging at the back of everyone's minds, skirting the periphery of their consciousness but never breaching it. "Just how long do you think we were under water?"

The question should've been absurd in its implied context, but they all looked up to the sun as realization dawned. The ink curtain had been retracted from the sky before they came up for air (which certainly couldn't have been more than five minutes, not with only one of them losing consciousness), but it had left the sun a little out of kilter. The sky was the sky of late afternoon and not the midafternoon sky they'd gotten a good look at while going over the fall.

"I think we lost a couple of hours," Robinson whispered. "I don't know how, but dammit, it's almost evening."

Jackson knew he was right. The storm clouds had shielded the obvious, but now that they were all looking at it, there was no denying the sun had moved a significant distance, the demon's dark virus stealing time along with the light. That left even less time to get back to the caves, find the helicopter, and get everyone onto the ship. If everything Daniel had just told them was true, then there wasn't must sand left in the hourglass.

"Ready or not, I think we need to get going," Robinson said.

* * **

Paul finally found his way out the front entrance and stumbled drunkenly down the long ziggurat staircase, jumping over a giant that looked as if it'd been chopped up with a cosmic meat cleaver. There was no sign of Robyn's broken body, but then Hunter had implied as much. Shell casings were all over the place, and he almost slipped on a few of them. There were body parts scattered up and down the steps, throughout the courtyard, and filling the obelisk-lined boulevard that stretched to the bridge a mile away. It was a scene from hell. And while Paul had no love or concern for any of these people, whether Osiris Leftovers, Not Them soldiers, or the local villagers, the manner in which they'd been annihilated moved even him.

The *power* of the thing…

The story from the Old Testament—he didn't remember what book or who the characters were or even when he'd heard it—where the angel of the Lord killed 185,000 soldiers in one night… That was what came to mind. Either that or the aftermath of a bombing raid.

He hopped off the bloody steps and crossed the courtyard, careful to avoid the terrorized stares coming from so many severed heads. He stepped on a hand. He stepped on toes. He stepped on an ear and a nose.

He didn't miss the rhyme, and he spit.

The obelisks rose up beside him now as he went down Main Street, the same street he'd seen the procession lead Robyn up just an hour or so before (he looked up at the sky and thought that couldn't be right). He saw broken obelisks where either giants or dinosaurs had crashed into them—there were pieces of both across the road ahead. Blood, guts, bones…

He looked down every intersection he came to and saw more of the same down every street, in every alley, spilling out of every door. He walked past the head of what he assumed was a *T. rex*. It was leaning against a building, practically matching its size. Its mouth was open wide, as if frozen in a scream before its head had been separated from its body (there was no sign of the rest of it), its teeth enormous. Paul could see right down its throat and out the back of it, like it was some playground prop.

He came across a large, three-foot claw and picked it up, slipping it into his belt. Then he found a sword and grabbed that as well. He found three AK-47s too, but they were all empty.

He turned left down a side street, heading south and back toward the woods he'd come from. Lifeless homes accompanied him all the way to the city's perimeter, their blood-streaked walls obscene arrows pointing him toward his destination.

The silence disturbed him. He could hear his own footsteps and felt a stiff breeze slithering through the alley at his back. A raindrop landed on his face.

The place was haunted, a ghost town now. Just like that.

Like the ship, he thought.

Gaping skulls, the flesh stripped below their noses, lay sideways in the dirt ahead of him. The jawbones were polished white, rows of teeth still intact within their skeletal grins. They were tongueless and gumless, but their noses, cheeks, eyes, ears, and hair were all still intact, as if they had started out as skeletons and had been in the process of pulling skin masks down over their faces only to find them unfinished. *Or*, he thought insanely, *like Batman's mask, or Iron Fist, or the Flash, or…*

He stopped.

Oh god…

There were children. And though he knew the kids in Osiris' camp were little demon suckers, he wasn't convinced that was the case with the New Territory village kids he'd seen walking with their parents earlier, attending chores, and playing games with one another.

Dead kids… *Why the kids?* Why the little girl he'd shot? Why the drive-by that took his first love back in his hometown? Kids always seemed to be the collateral, the blood sacrifice required for the sins of their parents and leaders and adults at large…

He turned away from the little legs and little hands, but knew it was too late, that their images would be so many more extras strolling the streets of his nightmares.

He stepped over a long Nephilim vertebrae, stripped and polished like an ancient beached whale, and thought back to Naga Hills—how those people (and all people, he supposed) were prisoners to the evil they served. And that this was the end of it all. Slaughter. Death. And he knew that the reaper was laughing, that the Devil was alive and well and feasting on the blood of the innocent served up by all those in his employ.

Am I in his employ? The thought struck him like a thunderbolt. He had always considered himself one mean son of a gun, embracing the identity of an elite killer (albeit one who killed within the parameters of war—mostly), but now, walking this museum of true meanness and callous disregard, the very notion of associating with such violent madness (to any degree) was enough to make him sick. Suddenly, after getting a glimpse of the one who personified meanness, being mean himself didn't seem so cool. In fact, it seemed rather disgusting.

He reached the end of the road and found himself facing a field of grass that ran all the way to the tree line. Another rifle, a finger still curled around the trigger, lay at his feet. He picked it up, shook the finger away, and removed the magazine. Two rounds glinted in the sunlight. He didn't have time to empty the mag for an ammo count, so he just rammed the banana clip home and shouldered the rifle.

Thunder rumbled, echoing through the dead city streets behind him. He crossed the field, which was full of dead horses, overturned carriages, and bones…bones everywhere. He could only pray that his horse was still where he'd left it. He thought it probably was or Hunter wouldn't have implanted instructions to get it into his brain.

He spent the time it took to cross the field to analyze the strange things Hunter had shown him. Things that stretched and tortured his reason.

* * * *

He knew that the demon's net had bent the hands of time, that its casting had trapped minutes, perhaps hours along with its prey. Hunter wasn't sure if that was a fact that would benefit his friends or lead to their undoing. They were on their way to the ship, he knew that much, but how long it would take them to get on board was something outside his periphery. It could take hours (at least hours) or it could take more than a day. It was possible that they might not make it at all. They had until tomorrow, the equinox. Until then, Hunter would have to do his best to occupy this Fallen angel of antiquity, keeping him occupied in his head without giving away his true intentions. Tease him with glimpses of what he wanted without giving it to him. He would have to fill his mind with traps and switchbacks, detours and false road signs.

As Turiel stepped forward, his eyes examining Hunter's dark complexion, he spoke into his mind. "So you have been behind the veil and have come back with their secrets…" He tilted his head. "Secrets that are to be used in reinstating our former glory."

Now Hunter smiled. "You're a little behind on world events, which I gather you perceived from your interaction with the people more or less from my time, so let me catch you up to speed. First, the judgment you know is coming, the reason you left what we call Atlantis to spread your father's lies, has already come. A long, long time ago, in fact."

The angel's eyes narrowed, believing everything Hunter said.

TWENTY-TWO

September 22, 2011. Late afternoon. The Beach.

They'd followed the river for a while, leaving it only when it suddenly turned back into the New Territory, Daniel then leading them through the forest the rest of the way.

Robyn followed the men out onto the beach. It was starting to drizzle, and she could tell a storm was on its way, coming off the ocean. Thunder had been playing softly for the last forty minutes, the rain only teasing. But it was coming.

The trek through unknown territory and back to this beach Hunter and Daniel had supposedly arrived at early this morning—*only this morning?*—went without incident. At times, she hadn't been sure Daniel really knew where he was going. He seemed lost, a delicate panic that fluttered in his eyes whenever he came to a crossroad.

But here they were. Now they could just follow the sands south, and they'd sooner or later end up in familiar territory. Which, oddly enough, was a comforting thought.

Robyn stared at the crashing waves as she walked, her mind continuing to surf the day. Some of the psychological waves, however, were too much for her, and they sent her crashing into the bottom of her comprehension, dragging her over coral implications and tumbling her into a dizzying cycle of vertigo. She was pretty sure Turiel hadn't violated her, though he had certainly intended to. But so much of what had happened was a blur, whatever they'd rubbed into her skin loosing her mind from its moorings (she recalled the sensation of floating through the stars). The thought of being so pliable in his hands reviled her now, and she hated herself for being so weak. If not for Paul…

She wondered what might've become of her rescuer. Was he dead now too? She looked down again at what she was wearing, at the shirt he'd put over her. Jackson had offered her his shirt, but his shirt was even bigger. And in a strange way, she felt like it would be wrong to give Paul's shirt away. He had sacrificed himself for her, changing forever how she felt about him. No, she would keep this bloodstained shirt as a keepsake, a reminder. The dress thing beneath it, however, was clinging to her body like a net, suffocating her, entangling. She wanted nothing more than to get out of it. Robinson had given her his sandals when they came across a dead Not Them soldier whose boots fit his feet. The relief the worn-out and oversized leather brought to her bruised and bleeding soles was immediate. And then they'd stripped the corpse and portioned her out some pants, Jackson tailoring the brown animal hide with his knife so she wasn't tripping over them.

The sound of gulls captured her eyes and she tracked them gliding over the waves.

More thunder. Closer this time.

They were walking at a brisk pace, needing to get back to the caves. Back home. Something had happened there. They all knew it. But then they had to fly a helicopter and get on a boat before Hunter used the pyramid…tomorrow? Her mind was still dizzy from the events of the day, and she hadn't really been able to focus on what Daniel had been saying back at the fire. Everything was a blur, like she could still be in Turiel's bed having this dream while he…

She set the thought to flight before it could spawn a mental image, instead focusing on the fact that she was still alive. She'd jumped off the balcony and somehow lived. She'd gone over the waterfall and somehow lived. And she'd drowned and somehow came back. She was grateful, and she thanked God the best she could in her state of mind. And then she thought, *Dinosaurs? Maybe I really am dreaming…* But if she wasn't, all she wanted to do was climb out of these clothes and crawl into bed and go to sleep for a very long time. But she knew that wasn't going to happen. Not the way the men kept urging her to keep up while casting furtive glances into the forest. Sleep was still a long way away.

A bolt of lightning ripped across the horizon, and clouds collided above the water.

* * * *

Paul found the horse right where he'd left it and, as Hunter had suggested, it was still alive. He staggered over to it, mumbling, "Hello, do you remember me?" and put his hands on its nose.

The battle horse snapped its tail and repositioned its feet, perhaps a little annoyed at being left tied up here so long, no idea how close it had come to being ground meat.

Paul untied it, walked around to its side, and with just about all the energy he had left, pulled himself up onto its back. The effort almost blacked him out, and it took him a minute to recover. He blinked, his head swimming, blood running down the side of his face. He could feel it pooling in the crevice between his clavicle and trapezius, could feel it overflowing and running down his bare chest.

He managed to get the horse back down into the valley and steered it west, going for the bridge. He held on the best that he could while the black beast galloped beneath him, racing for a hidden Jet Ski.

* * * *

The dance began as an awkward sort of mental waltz, both of them circling, evaluating, looking for a chink in the other's armor that would serve as an avenue of attack.

Hunter's mind blazed with a sense of things otherworldly. Or *otherdimensionally*, rather. Where such an ability was originating, he couldn't say for sure, but he felt that it was in opposition to the Fallen angel's own psychic ability…and that was a clue in and of itself, was it not? Perhaps his powers were more than just residue left behind by his former occupants. He wondered if Turiel recognized the demon's helping hand for what it was—

And just like that, they were in, crawling through each other's eye sockets and rappelling down into other realms, leaving their bodies behind like motionless statues as their minds reached out for one another, intertwining over a metaphysical bridge leading through—

Hunter found himself crawling around in dark tunnels. And then he was darting and dashing through cerebral corridors, trying locked doors, not really sure what he was looking for. Until Turiel's timeline began to emerge before him, and he was suddenly seeing back through the ages…and even further still.

* * * *

Now that they were on the beach, Jackson knew they just needed to follow it back into familiar territory. They were making good time, but "good" was relative when all the time they had left might be contained within a single, final grain of sand. Still, barring an incident, they should be able to make it to the caves before dark. But then what? According to Daniel, Hunter had some crazy plan to somehow activate the glass pyramid on the fall equinox, which was tomorrow. But when tomorrow? At around noon when the sun reached its zenith? Like when the Change took place during the Solstice War he'd slept through three months ago? Or could whatever formula Hunter had in his mind be applicable as soon as the clock struck midnight and the calendar flipped? And just how in the hell could Hunter know anything about this new crystal pyramid that came as the capital of this other Fallen angel's empire?

Hunter…

Even now, he was trying to come up with a plan to go back and rescue him. Paul too. But not knowing when the buzzer would go off (assuming it would), made planning anything impossible. He had to get Robyn and the others off the island first. Then, once they were safe…

The wind was picking up off the ocean, and rain was beginning to fall, but he knew the storm itself was still a good hour away. It was coming though, that was for sure. And it was going to be a doozy. Like the one they'd rowed through the first week they were here. If the storm lasted through the night, then that would take care of the midnight scenario since there was no way he'd be able to fly in the storm at night while trying to find a ghost ship somewhere out in the ocean. Again, that was assuming there was a helicopter *and* that it worked—the latter a much bigger miracle than the other. If the storm lasted longer than that… Maybe their only hope was to go straight to the helicopter and go to the boat now. He didn't think there was enough time for that, but if that was their only chance…

The beach they were traversing was still part of the New Territory, but other than the mountain ranges stretching like a giant backbone overtop the inland pines, it was like Bermuda's own coastal topography. The sand was pink, the water turquoise, and rock formations jutted up out of the surf, cutting across the shoreline.

He looked back at Robyn, glad that he'd decided not to turn back earlier. Even with Paul helping her escape, and the miraculous way the giant had broken her fall, she wouldn't have made it away from the Darkness on her own. She noticed his stare and gave him a smile. His heart jumped.

Please, God... Get us out of here...

And for a split second, he allowed himself the possibility of escape, letting the thought germinate in his imagination. Would this be *the* day that he would make it out of this hell, back to his house...to his life. To Henry. The prospect of only having hours left to endure this nightmare seemed too good to be true, and he knew that it probably was. Still, he allowed that brief daydream.

And then, like reality rebuking such a fantasy, a noise came from beyond the tree line, shattering the imaginary scene into a million melting pieces.

Before starting the fire back by the waterfall, Jackson had dived back into the pool and recovered his backpack and rifle. Then he'd handed out the remaining magazines to the others. Now, they all raised their freshly loaded weapons to the swaying forest beside them.

The noise again, climbing above the sound of the crashing waves.

"What is that?" Robinson asked.

Li took a single step toward the tree line as if a foot closer would identify it. "Sounds like..."

Eliot...

Jackson spun his head around, thinking his whispered name had come from behind him. But there was only Robyn standing there next to Joe.

Eliot, hurry...

It was Denise's voice. She was back again.

The sound in the forest was growing louder, getting closer, and now after hearing Denise's voice again, the sound struck up a corresponding memory. A month before her death, they'd gone to the zoo, and the sound coming from the forest sounded a lot like the sound they'd heard a lion making—Denise even commenting that she could feel the bass-filled moan all the way in her bones from the other side of the park.

"C'mon," Jackson said, heeding her voice (if indeed it was her voice—it was good advice either way).

A hundred yards down the beach, a large rock wall stretched out of the trees and cut across the sandy hills, sloping down into the shallow surf and dividing the coast. Natural windows sat within the slanted strata, and Jackson could see only the blue hues of water through them. Which meant the beach must take a turn inland on the other side.

"Hurry!" Robinson said, breaking into a sprint.

The treetops were beginning to shake now, and it was clear that it wasn't from the wind. Something big was moving through them.

"We need to get on the other side of that rock," Jackson said to Robyn, holding out his hand to her.

Robinson, Li, Joe, Patrick, Daniel, and Wilson raced for it, and by the time Jackson got there with Robyn, they were already climbing up through the largest window.

Getting into the window first, Robinson looked back down to the others. "It's about an eight-foot drop into sand. Should be okay." And then he disappeared.

Joe went next. Then Li.

Daniel turned back and offered a hand to Robyn as Wilson jumped next.

Usually, Robyn would've been the last one in need of a helping hand, but her mind was still distracted, and the big clothes she was drowning in (while simultaneously being strangled by the dress under them) made climbing awkward. She climbed up into the large opening and stepped past Daniel. Patrick and Wilson followed, and then Daniel helped Jackson up.

Jackson looked across the distance they'd covered, a river of backward footprints racing north, and then a scaled creature the size of an apartment building blasted out of the forest and onto the beach. It seemed to stumble a bit when its feet hit the sand, its momentum instantly slowed by the sinking terrain. But its long thick tail trailed behind it, snaking through the sand and helping maintain its balance. It whipped its massive head back and forth, a caped giant its chew toy.

Jackson nudged Daniel forward, and he jumped down to the other side.

Go now, Eliot!

Thunder rolled across the water. He jumped.

* * * *

Paul rode the horse as hard as he dared, his body bouncing off its muscled back, his fists buried in its long mane. His arms were aching, and his legs were beginning to cramp, his ability to hold on slipping away. It was raining pretty good now, and he knew he should probably take it slower, but there was no time for slower.

The horse raced up a hill, turned onto a narrow path, and bolted south. Thick coniferous trees lined the left side of the foot trail, their branches reaching out and swiping for Paul's bobbing head, while a steep decline swept away from the animal's kicking hooves immediately to the right. Paul was just waiting for a branch to crack his skull or for the horse to take one ill-placed step and send them both down into the rocks that were everywhere poking out of the declining bank.

And then, just like that, the path emptied into a field, and tall grass was whipping Paul's legs. Ahead of them, a flock of long-necked cranes took flight as the thunderous hooves shook the ground and chased them from their lodging.

Paul recognized the field, though how the horse had gotten them there so fast was something of a mystery. Must've taken a more direct route than the one he and Jackson had taken, skipping the mountain path and cutting straight through the forest. But was this the way to Hunter's Jet Ski? Paul thought he'd been directing the horse, but now he understood that the horse was on a heading all its own. *Maybe not all its own*, Paul thought, wondering just how much Hunter's new abilities were capable of.

It was the field where Ruth had died. He could see the entrance to the cave up on the right even through the curtain of rain. And then there was the *feeling*... That electricity they'd felt around the cave before. It seemed even stronger now, and he swore he could hear it hissing and snapping in the rain. The hair on his arms, even soaking wet, was standing tall, and he thought of that black hole inside the cave.

He tried to bring up a map in his mind, but before he could conjure up a you-are-here arrow, the horse came to a sudden, violent stop, almost vaulting him through the air over its head.

Trotting into a tight turn, the magnificent battle horse began shaking its head with agitation and pounding the ground with its hooves. Then it snorted and stood up on its hind legs, kicking at the air.

Paul's missing fingers flared as he held on. Turning his head toward the distant trees and across the field, he wondered what had made the horse stop so suddenly. Had it felt the electromagnetic—

A face looked up out of the tall grass, about thirty yards in front of him, its eyes blazing and staring right at them.

The horse wouldn't stay still beneath him, and he had to keep whipping his head around to keep the strange face in front of him. He squinted through the rain, trying to make out who the person could be. He couldn't let go of the horse's mane to pull his sword or work the rifle off his back, because if he got tossed, he'd have to stumble, half-conscious, all the way to the Jet Ski. But then it hit him, why not go back to the Crystal Caves instead? He knew how to get there, and it wasn't so far away... Hunter had installed the instructions he'd given Jackson via Daniel into him too, and he knew that there was no way Jackson would bypass the caves and go straight for this mysterious chopper. Not without checking for survivors first. He could meet up with the others there—

The flashing thoughts came to an abrupt halt when the man's face in the grass began to rise, revealing a head of long black hair and swollen cheeks.

Paul frowned, the features oddly familiar.

And then the man grinned and revealed his lion's teeth.

Paul swore and quickly cast his gaze to the cave. He knew what this thing was, had watched one of them kill Chris. Had seen it sting him with its tail, rip his arm off with its bare hands, and then fly him up into the sky and drop him on his head.

Large spiderlike legs teepeed out of the grass around its head. Then they straightened and lifted the monster's body above the grass. Its scorpion tail curled forward, the stinger poised like a wrecking ball over its head. It had two human arms, and their hands were clutching a long spear.

It unfolded its wings.

Paul swung the AK around so that it was hanging across his stomach rather than his back. The cave was to the right and behind the chimera, but if he could hold off the creature with the rifle (assuming it had more than two rounds left in the mag), then he might just be able to beat it to the cave.

He sent the horse after it.

* * * *

They followed the beach around a bend and found themselves at the starting line of another long run of beach that stretched all the way to the cloudy horizon. But there was something oddly familiar about the scene.

"Are we..." Arkansas Joe began to ask, looking around.

Jackson thought so, and Daniel was nodding his head with relief.

And then, in the distance, a tall form (almost as tall as the trees skirting the shore) emerged out of the woods.

"Get down!" Jackson snapped.

The eight of them dropped to their stomachs, weapons aimed out in front of them.

Nephilim.

It was walking through the sand, taking slow, deliberate steps toward the water, leaning into the wind blowing off the ocean. But it seemed to be struggling a little too much against gusts that weren't that strong yet. It was almost as if...

And then the forest gave birth to a boat, its bow breaching the wooded divide and slipping into the path made by the giant's sandy footprints.

The giant was *pulling* a large yacht! And though they were too far to see the rope being used, it explained the giant's struggling diagonal figure.

"What the hell?" Robinson muttered.

"Look!" Li said, pointing down the beach.

Another leaning giant came out of the woods, another boat following.

And then another. And another.

"They're trying to leave?" Robyn wondered.

Jackson looked at Daniel, but he was looking out across the water. Jackson followed his gaze, expecting to find the cruise ship out there, but he could see only rough waves beneath a dark sky. "How would they know?" he asked him.

Daniel looked over to him, but his eyes held no answers. He shrugged, then added, "Are they fleeing the island to escape that Dark, or could they know the island is running out of time?"

Jackson thought about it. He'd seen evidence of a Nephilim giant trying to get off the island already, just before he met Robyn. And he'd just overheard Daniel telling Robinson about a regenerating giant on the cruise ship that he and Hunter had had to continuously deal with. Yet the urgency with which these giants were trying to flee, willing to risk being stranded forever on the water, suggested something more than a final intolerance of their habitat.

No, Jackson thought, *this is an exodus.*

More Leftover giants pulling boats out of the Graveyard's new location appeared.

"What do you want to do?" Joe asked.

Jackson nodded toward the tree line. "Use the trees for cover. We need to get past them."

Robinson shook the rainwater from the brim of his hat (he'd found it hung up on a rock in the river downstream from the waterfall). "Should we try to stop them?"

Jackson didn't know if there was any chance of the giants making it back to the real world—if Hunter's instructions (according to Daniel) to get to the ship meant that the ship itself was to be their saving grace, or whether being away from the island was enough to make the transition. If distance and time were the only relevant factors, then it was indeed possible that these boats, piloted by giants, could show up on a tourist beach one day. "We don't have the means," he answered. "Or the time."

Robinson nodded his understanding and began army crawling toward the trees.

One of the giants got its boat into the water, a 110-foot-long yacht from the '90s it looked like. It was unclear just how the monster planned on navigating the boat, but Jackson thought it stood a better chance of sitting on top of it and using a tree as a paddle rather than attempting to fit inside.

Jackson and Daniel watched as it moved the boat past the breaking waves, the water reaching its chest, while the others followed Robinson to the tree line.

"Watch," Daniel said, his eyes on the boat in the water.

Jackson didn't have to wait long to find out what Daniel was waiting for.

The giant, attempting to climb the side of the yacht, suddenly jerked back, whipping its head down at the water in surprise. Then it let go of the boat and began throwing its fists into the ocean like sledgehammers. The water roiled, something beneath it thrashing.

"Shark," Daniel said.

The other boat-pulling giants stopped just short of the water, watching through the rain as their kin struggled with the predator's razor teeth, waiting on the outcome to decide whether or not to continue themselves.

Jackson tapped Daniel on the shoulder. "Let's go."

Daniel nodded and began crawling, but he kept his eyes on the giant as bloody water started splashing up against the boat's white hull. For a moment he was hopeful that the sharks would prevent the Leftovers from getting any farther, but then the giant got its hands around the shark's tail and yanked it up out of the water, swinging it against the boat over and over again. He could hear the impacts over the surf and thought maybe the giant would sink the yacht, but it stopped and tossed the dead fish up onto the deck.

Daniel turned away and quickened his pace to catch up with Jackson.

"This where you came ashore this morning?" Robinson asked Daniel when he reached them. They were just inside the tree line, huddled in a circle beneath some cedars.

Daniel nodded. "We hid the Jet Ski over there somewhere." He nodded down the beach, past the giants.

"Alright," Jackson said, "let's keep going." He took the lead, guiding them through the dense plant life, the raindrops against the canopy masking the sound of their travel. Ahead of them, however, they could see flashes of movement through the trees as more giants struggled to move more boats from the new Graveyard and into the open seas.

But as they grew closer, hoping to sneak past them and continue down the beach to where the derelict vehicles of the Triangle scattered the coast and shallow tide, they saw something more. Six Leftover soldiers pointing spears at a group of huddled women.

"Holy—"

Jackson put a mouth over Joe's mouth and pulled him behind a tree.

They'd found the missing girls.

TWENTY-THREE

September 22, 2011. Late afternoon. The Cave.

The abomination swiped its tail at Paul as he rode past it. He ducked, the crane-like wrecking ball with a hooked blade whooshing over his head, nearly decapitating the horse as well. He fired the AK with one hand, striking it in the shoulder and stomach and causing it to recoil in surprise. There were indeed more than two rounds remaining (*thank you, Jesus!*), and they gave him all the space he needed. By the time the chimera recovered, Paul was already racing the horse through the opening of the cave, the lights flickering to life all around him.

He rode the horse deep into the corridor, stopping briefly to look back and see if the thing was coming in the cave after him. Sure enough, its silhouette stepped in front of the opening, blocking the light and appearing like some insane wall shadow cast by a collection of action figures on a young boy's dresser.

But it just stood there, watching him without entering.

And that was when Paul finally noticed just how strong the electricity felt now. If it was palpable out in the field, you could almost cut it with a knife in here. His whole body tingled. And was that what was preventing the monster from giving chase? Was it afraid of what was in here?

Regardless, Paul wasn't about to go back out into the thing's waiting human arms. He urged the horse forward, the sound of the pounding hooves echoing off the walls and making his head throb, and watched behind him as the scorpion thing scooted on its insectile legs, gliding out of the cave's gaping mouth and disappearing.

Paul turned back around just in time to see bodies piled across the tunnel in front of him. The horse leaped, catching him off guard, and his grip slipped. He went backward, tumbling off the horse, and falling…falling…falling.

He landed on his back and struck his head on the rock floor. The artificial lights around him started to fade. His last thought before it went totally dark was that he didn't have time for this.

* * * *

Hunter's floating in existential animation, suspended in some in-between world outside physical boundaries. He's aware of his body standing off to the side somewhere while his mind simply absorbs the display before him. A display that takes him back to the beginning. Not the beginning that has no beginning, but the beginning of events that have led to this here and now—Turiel's history as seen through his eyes. The sensation is half like viewing a movie and half like living it. It's almost too much, the majesty of what he's witnessing overwhelming.

He's slightly aware of Turiel seeing his own past as well, though he's sure there can be nothing of interest there…not before the closet, anyway. Because the key the angel is searching for came up out of that room.

But no, that's not right, is it? Because Turiel is not from his timeline. Turiel is antediluvian, a priest of the Golden Feather spreading that Golden Age gospel before the Flood. So there is *plenty* he can glean from entering Hunter's mind—world history, in fact. And in discovering what is in store for his race of Fallen angels, he can begin to understand the reason this is all happening and what role he has been destined to play in it.

But he'll still need the key once he discovers his purpose. Hunter will do his best to keep it hidden from him, of course, but given the fact that he himself doesn't know just what it is will make it rather difficult. Sure, he can sense the general area it's in, which is why he's erected a false wall to conceal that section of his mind, but he knows it won't last. And doesn't *want* it to last. Not forever. He just needs it to buy some more time. And as Turiel's angelic existence in a pre-Fallen universe continues to hook Hunter's mind with both awe and absolute wonder, he's dimly aware (like a distant echo from far, far away) of Paul lying on the ground somewhere, unconscious.

He needs more time, needs to stretch this out until the equinox. It's what Turiel will want, too, once he's understands, but letting him come to that realization will require precise timing.

But now Hunter is totally enveloped in beforetimes, when the sons of God sang for joy, Lucifer led creation in worship of the true, holy God…and it's, oh, so wonderful! And in the reality of that ageless moment, he forgets everything else and glides through the heavens, mingling with angels, and even catching a glimpse of the godhead three-in-one.

He begins to cry before such beauty, where the cosmic fabric of existence is fully contained and completely satisfied within that eternal, relational expression.

And then, suddenly, there is war in heaven, and its ferocity reaches throughout the cosmos, destroying the universe.

He's expelled from glory, a shooting star falling…falling…falling…

* * * *

Jackson's mind raced through options, but nothing satisfactory emerged. Robyn was trying her hardest to remain calm, the sudden sight of her sisters still alive clearing her fogged state of mind in an instant. They couldn't leave the women behind, they all knew that. But how could they rescue them and not get dead in the process? There were at least fifteen Leftover giants and a score of foot soldiers. They didn't have enough ammunition left to even consider confronting them.

"We have to keep going," Joe offered. "Get back to the caves and come back with more people, more weapons."

But Jackson shook his head. "I don't think there's time for all that, even if there are people still at the caves to bring back."

"We can't leave them," Robyn added.

A giant, clothed in animal hides and wearing a wooden helmet, plowed its way through the forest just twenty feet away from them. It didn't see them crouched behind the large rock formation and the fallen tree leaning against it, but it was too close and only a matter of time before they were spotted.

"We can't stay here," Li said.

Jackson didn't know what to do. And then he did. He hated it, but there it was. He turned to Robyn and put his hands on her shoulders. "Joe's right. We have to go—"

She began shaking her head in protest. "You just said there was no time," she whispered over the rain.

"Listen," he said. "If we stay here, they'll find us and kill us. If we try to save them now, they'll kill everyone. We'll come back with a plan. We won't leave them."

She looked at him with a steely, fiery intensity that sent shivers down his back. "We can surrender," she answered.

"And what? Grab the girls and run when they're not looking?"

"Assuming they don't just eat us anyway," Wilson interjected.

She shook her head. "Then I'll stay with them, and you come back and get us. I won't go without them."

"Robyn," Jackson started, but he didn't know what to say. She'd already made up her mind on this matter, and no amount of reason was going to talk her out of it. He had a mind to tap her on the chin and just knock her out (something he knew she would never forgive him for), but before he could do anything, a new noise captured his attention, drawing his eyes.

It was barely noticeable over the growing storm, but Robyn detected it immediately, her own eyes searching for its source. A whistle accompanied by a small blur flying through the trees, whacking leaves and tiny branches and leaving a shower of debris fluttering in its wake. Then the giant that had just walked past them suddenly arched its back and howled. When it turned to look behind it, bending its arm and trying to get a hold of the thing, Jackson saw a huge arrow sticking out of its back.

And then another whistle pierced the air—more leaves falling—and a second arrow buried itself into the giant's bare chest.

It hollered again, pulled its sword off its back, and took a step in the direction the arrow had come from. But then a third arrow thudded right through the wooden helmet, shattering its wood to splinters and splitting the giant's skull. The Leftover sank to its knees and collapsed onto its chest.

Jackson peered into the depths of the forest, trying to catch a glimpse of the attacker. He knew who it was, the size of the arrow making it quite obvious. "Get ready," he whispered, and they all raised their rifles (except Robyn, whose rifle was still back in the temple somewhere).

The giant's wails got everyone's attention, and now the Fallen soldiers were turning their backs on the women, aiming their spears into the woods surrounding them. The giants on the beach were starting to come back, their swords drawn.

Another whistle, and this time a soldier's head disappeared right off his neck. His body stood there for a second or two, just a headless corpse, spear in hand, blood squirting like a fountain into the air. Another whistle, and the person standing beside him lost his leg at the thigh. He screamed, clutching for his leg and grasping only air.

Then the forest opened wide and spewed an army of charging Titans.

There had to be twenty of them, all over fifteen feet tall. Their muscled bodies were covered in black armor, and their faces were concealed by horned helmets. Sheathed swords hung across their backs, while they held huge, double-bladed battle axes in their six-fingered grasps. Dark capes flapped behind them in the rain, making them seem like giant storm phantoms or wraiths not running, but rather gliding like black mist through the trees.

Behind the charging line, another row of giants stepped forward. They were fitted in gold armor and had bows in their hands, arrows nocked and ready to fly.

"We're trapped," Li said, turning to watch as the black giants split, flanking around them.

It was true. They were right in the thick of it, grasshoppers beneath the stampeding feet of monsters.

"Wait until they engage; then we'll cut across," Jackson answered.

One of the attacking giants ran by the soldiers guarding the women and whipped its axe at them in passing, almost as if an afterthought on its way to a bigger and better challenge. The arced blade, probably three feet across, sliced at an upward angle, cutting through four of the soldiers and sending pieces of them twirling up into the trees.

The rest of the Leftover soldiers turned and threw their spears after the dark giant, but none of them struck their target, the Titan not even bothering to turn around and give them a second look.

Taking advantage of their captors' distraction, one of the pure-blooded girls picked up a loose rock that was by her feet, hoisted it over her head, and smashed it into the head of the nearest Leftover. There was a loud crunch, and blood sprayed across her face. The man's comrades were so fixated on the black-caped giants that they didn't even notice him falling to the ground or the girls slipping away.

Robyn saw the girls, about fifteen of them, make a run for it, and she jumped to her feet.

Jackson grabbed her arm again.

"Not yet."

"I have to go," she answered while bending her arm at the elbow and twisting until she broke free. And then she went.

Jackson swore as he watched her leap over the fallen branch and dance through the jagged rocks in Robinson's sandals, almost tripping in her oversized pants. She then sprinted through the trees and went straight at the Leftovers, no weapons on her person.

No, Jackson thought, getting to his own feet now.

But before she could bend over and pick up one of the spears that was still clutched in lifeless hands, another whistle screamed past her and cut two more of the men in half.

She was past them even before their stomachs toppled off their waists, snatching a spear out of their hands on her way.

By now, the Titans in black were fully engaged with Osiris' giants, and their swinging weapons were clanging in loud echoes, slicing through the crowding trees with every missed swing and deflected blow.

Robinson's eyes went up to the canopy. "Uh-oh," he muttered.

Hearing him and then seeing his wide eyes, Jackson looked up, too.

A falling tree.

Its pined branches waved through the air like green arms fighting gravity. It fell in slow motion, and all of them followed its descending arc as it crashed its way through the surrounding trees and met the ground with a ground-shaking kiss.

Then another one fell, landing just ten feet away from them and sending clouds of debris up into the air.

"We gotta go. Now!" Jackson climbed over the rocks, following Robyn's route, and the others scrambled after him. They made it off the rocks and ran against a soundtrack of pounding rain and clashing swords, weaving around rocks and bushes and dodging falling trees.

A caped giant, entangled with a half-naked Leftover giant, crossed Jackson's path, forcing him into a skidded stop before the battling duo. The Not Them giant ducked beneath a swinging sword that had targeted its head, and the serrated steel caught a nearby tree instead, exploding its trunk into dagger-sized splinters that flew at Jackson's face like shrapnel. He felt at least two projectiles rip into his flesh, but he was more concerned with the Titan's counter-maneuver to care. The armored giant was spinning on its pivot foot, and its enormous cape was whipping around, coming at them like a ten-foot black wave.

Before they could get out of the way, it swept over them, engulfing them and rendering them completely blind. The heavy fabric slithered over them, wrapping their arms and legs as if alive and probing, almost knocking them over.

And then it was off them, continuing its rotation and whipping down in a graceful arc that ended with it gathered at the boots of the Titan as it finished its move, its axe coming up in an underhanded swing to meet the Leftover's chin. The surprised giant threw its head back, looking up to the sky at the last possible moment, and the blade missed its face by half an inch.

Turning away from the engagement, Jackson led the others around the battle and to where he'd last seen Robyn leading the women out of the forest like Moses leading the children of Israel out of Egypt. He could hear another tree falling, its creaking, moaning decline getting closer as it made its way to the ground.

It landed right behind them, and they were thrown to the ground by its many branched arms and all their pined fingers.

Rolling onto his back, Jackson untangled himself from the network of branches pinning him down.

"My leg!" Arkansas Joe cried.

Jackson got up and joined Robinson, Li, and Wilson, who were already trying to lift the tree enough so that Patrick and Daniel could slide Joe out from under it.

They pulled him free and got him to his feet. Joe scooted away with them, his leg trailing limp behind him.

"Can you walk?" Li asked, his eyes not on Joe but on the forty or so giants now locked in an epic battle along the tree line.

"I don't think so."

"You have to," Jackson said and wrapped his arm around his waist.

"I think it's broken," Joe answered through gritted teeth.

"Doesn't matter at this point. We gotta get out of here now."

Robinson came around on Joe's other side and ducked beneath his arm.

"Look up there!" Li shouted over the rain and another falling tree (this one farther away). He was pointing up through the foliage ahead of them and to where Robyn had just reemerged with the trail of women behind her. She was leading them up a rocky hill and heading back toward the beach.

Together, Jackson and Robinson carried Joe through the thick tangles of undergrowth while the others covered them, eyes looking for that next arrow that would cut them all down.

* * * *

Robyn stood perched between two sandstone rocks near the top of the hill. She could hear the waves crashing behind her, on the other side. The rain was coming down harder now, and the wind off the ocean was whipping loose strands of hair across her face. She watched as the other girls climbed up after her, navigating the rocks in a single-file line. She couldn't believe they were still alive…that they'd just happened to come across them while on their own path of escape. *Thank you, God.*

She reached out her hand and helped Tabitha, the oldest of the group, up beside her and then past her. The sixty-something-year-old woman, whose great-grandmother had arrived here so long ago, crawled over the top of the hill and started working her way down the other side. Robyn watched her, wondering why the giants had kept her alive. Usually they just killed the women past child-bearing age. She thanked God for sparing her, this woman who had been like a mother to her ever since she became an orphan.

Next was June. She, in contrast, was the youngest, only fourteen, but she was a fighter and wise beyond her years. She navigated the rocks like a grasshopper, stopping only to give Robyn a hug before moving on to assist Tabitha down the other side of the hill and through another network of rocks.

A dozen more moved past her, Mary coming up last. "Thank you," she said, one side of her face still covered with blood from when she crushed the soldier's skull.

Robyn nodded. "Are there more? Sarah? Melody?"

She shook her head. "Not with us. We were together and then just—"

"I know," she said, cutting her off. "Just keep to the beach. We're not far from home." Though what they would find once returning was a different story and not one she was about to bring up.

As she helped the others up over the hill, she looked past them and down into the woods, waiting for any signs of the men, but all she could see were glimpses of the battle being fought between the giants.

She turned in the beach grass that covered the hill and looked down at the beach. Tabitha and June were already down and on the open sand, fighting against the wind. They had a clear shot for about four or five hundred yards before they'd have to skirt another rock formation.

"Hey," Li said, coming up beside her and trying to catch his breath.

"Where are the others?"

"They're coming. Joe's hurt."

She nodded behind her. "Go with them," she said. "I'll cover them."

"Okay." He handed her his AK while taking the spear from her hand. Then he slithered his way down the other side.

Bringing the rifle up, she stared down its sights, making sure none of the Fallen were thinking of giving chase, and watched as Jackson and Robinson appeared, Joe hanging off their shoulders between them. Daniel, Wilson, and Patrick were on their heels, their rifles sweeping back and forth.

Thunder clapped, and then a long nearby roar answered it.

* * * *

As he falls to earth, Hunter looks back on the conflict that took place in the heavenly places and the expulsion that followed—though he hadn't been able to see it outright and is unable to determine why Lucifer and his rebel angels sought to defy God in the first place. Pride on behalf of Lucifer perhaps, but what was the ill-content that led the rest to follow? Was the world Lucifer had promised so much more favorable to their present existence that a third of the angels risked damnation with their usurper to attain it?

These are things Hunter does not have access to, though Turiel, being part of the third, certainly knows. But just as Hunter has locked certain cerebral doors, so has Turiel, for whenever Hunter tries to get a glimpse of it, to hold the answer before his eyes, it slips reflexively into the shadows of his periphery. The lost Golden Age of Lucifer's reign in which Turiel served is also elusive, there but concealed within an irksome haze.

The stars strike the earth, and the repaired creation groans at their impact. And, oh yes, he realizes, it is certainly *creation*, for he now understands (in part, of course) the metaphysical history of all things *ex nihilo*. Because man once thought the cell was the smallest unit of a living creature, it was believed that such life could be explained within the probabilities of so-called "evolution."

But now Hunter sees what the present scientists have only begun to scratch the surface of, and his mind is pulled thin over an infinite landscape. From his shared perspective with the angel, certain aspects of reality come into focus, and it is...*undoing*. The distances between atoms suddenly appear as endless deserts and oceans, with proton and electron moons orbiting intersecting highways and byways of more subatomic particles and the even more complex avenues of tachyons...all paved on the bedrock of dark matter (there is no other word in his vocabulary for it).

The support apparatus of reality, in all its subatomic, clockwork-like precision, is, in fact, a universe all its own, held together by...

The Logos.

The quantum underpinnings of a divine will. And if Hunter's mind was undone by a deeper look into the seeming endlessness of physical reality—of that *design*—then the sense (for that is all his finite mind is capable of) of the Creator who stands transcendent of it all, yet sustaining its existence, is too much indeed. For if he were to comprehend the One in which all things, including time itself—infinite beginning to infinite end—are contained, his mind would surely break.

And then, just like that, it's all gone, replaced by a linear timeline that he rides like a train, looking out its windows and observing the passing ages as certain of the Fallen angels take their rebellion to an even greater level, Turiel front and center among them.

* * * *

Jackson left Joe in Robinson's care and ran out to the front of the line. Even over the crashing waves, he could still hear the sword-play coming from the other side of the rocks behind them. He could also see, looking back, that Osiris' giants had managed to get three yachts out past the cresting waves somehow.

The Graveyard wrecks they'd seen after the Change were just up ahead on the other side of the next rock wall, so the boats the giants were pulling out of the forest either had to be new additions like the cruise ship, the house, Ivan and Mollings, and this supposed helicopter, or the Graveyard had been split up over multiple locations.

Flaming arrows suddenly started streaking through the sky, originating from the beach and targeting the three escaping boats. They left trails of smoke behind them as they sizzled in the rain, and Jackson wondered if the Not Them giants were only trying to keep the Leftovers from escaping as retribution for attacking their city, or if they might be trying to escape the island themselves. Two arrows hit one of the yachts and quickly set it ablaze. Even from so far away, Jackson could see the form of the giant as it abandoned ship, throwing itself into the water and to the waiting teeth of sharks.

Reaching the next rock formation, Jackson stopped and helped everyone through a small opening that led to the other side. The rain made it slippery, and he advised caution to every person he helped up into the opening. Robyn leaned up and gave him a quick kiss as she passed, and he could see that hope had been reborn in her eyes, no doubt the result of having freed so many of her sisters thought to have been lost.

"How you doing?" he asked Joe as Robinson helped him over.

"Hurts," he said, and his face was a sheet of white.

"Almost there." He grabbed his arm and led him up and through the small passageway.

When they got him to the other side, everyone else already standing around waiting for them, they were presented with a new stretch of beach littered with an assortment of vintage planes and boats. And there, right out in front of them, lying upright in the sand, was the *Gegenes*.

"That's Henry's boat," Jackson whispered. "The boat I came on," he explained.

But no one seemed to care. Instead, Daniel was pointing past the *Gegenes* and into the blurred background beyond it. "Look!" he said as thunder cracked, and a bolt of lightning ripped the sky in half over the ocean.

It was hard to make out through the rain, but they could tell that there were people moving back and forth among the vehicles.

"More Leftovers looking for a way off the island?" Patrick asked.

"Looks that way," he answered. He looked back at the fifteen women and for the first time noticed what they were wearing—which wasn't much. They were all huddled together, shivering in the lashing rain. "We'll go ship to ship, using them as cover. Maybe we can make it without being seen."

Robyn shot him a doubtful look.

"If they do spot us, though…" He trailed off. They didn't have enough ammunition left to make a stand, and they wouldn't be able to lose them if they gave chase. He offered a lopsided grin. "Well, let's not get spotted, okay? No guns if possible. Hopefully they care more about getting out of here than coming after us, but let's not find out."

They all nodded, water dripping off their faces.

"Wilson and Patrick, can you two help Joe? Robinson needs a break."

They nodded and relieved Robinson, who was then finally free to stretch his aching back.

"Follow my tracks," Jackson ordered, and he moved away from the rocks, running bent over for the boat he'd used to bring his friends to this place. The guilt of it flashed through him like a wave of hot lava. But then Robyn was squeezing his hand, and he thought about what would've happened to her if they hadn't come. Was it worth Chris' and Nick's lives? To rescue these people? He supposed he couldn't answer that and so threw it out of his head.

TWENTY-FOUR

September 22, 2011. Late afternoon. The Temple.

Hunter stares out at the moving terrain as it hurls past the window beside him and sees the obsession the Fallen angels have with the daughters of Eve…with sex. And he sees certain of them step into the physical realm, breaching earth's tangible plane of existence—not as spirits, but by wrapping themselves with bone and tissue and joining the world of humankind.

He watches through Turiel, who has become a sort of looking glass back through the ages, and sees the Fallen commingle with man. He sees them take women as their wives and explore the many sensual mysteries of their beauty.

Their offspring are half human, half angel and are worshiped as gods on the earth. They introduce the mystery religions, secret arts, technologies, and forbidden knowledge to their subjects, altering the natural course of creation. They build monuments and machines that synchronize with their former celestial estates in the heavens, harnessing power and energy that natural man still knows very little about.

And, having altered humanity's gene pool, they begin working to reestablish their master's former kingdom and to prevent the fulfillment of the Messianic prophecy that foretells the crushing of his head.

But then comes the coming Flood that will wipe out their work, so they send forth their priests, taking their forbidden knowledge to the ends of the earth, building their esoteric codes into shrines they hope will survive the coming cataclysm. They center their shrines on specific locations, locking them into the stars and dead center upon the electromagnetic intersections that wrap the world.

And here Turiel builds his empire…unaware of what is to come, of what *had* come.

Until now.

* * * *

Paul opens his eyes and finds himself in a land of funhouse mirrors where everything is distorted, and everything…

Only he's not waking, is he?

What am I—

But there's no time to think. In fact, he has the sense that there's no time *at all.*

Now is then, then is now, and we are all together one—buddum-dum-dum.

He's slightly aware of a distant beacon climbing its way up through the depths of his subconscious, its jettison triggered by his falling asleep. It's a bright, strobing light flashing and *pinging,* trying to alert him that he's entered dreamland.

—he's thirteen and skipping school with Karen Harper to sneak into a dirty R-rated movie—

—Karen Harper lifts her shirt and invites him to touch her forming breasts—

—Karen Harper is pregnant by sixteen, knocked up by…well, the list of possibilities is long, but he's not on it, thank God—

The beacon rises higher, the darkness turning to a murky gray. Even as he lives through those Karen Harper days, there's something in the back of his mind that tells him something's off center. He's talking to her in the hallway, trying to sneak one last look down her shirt (or something more if she's game). It's her last day here, her parents homeschooling her in order to spare her the unpleasant experience of carrying a baby to term in the hell that is high school.

"If you get bored," he says, "give me a call. Maybe we can catch a movie."

She smiles. "A rerun?"

"I love reruns."

And then she's gone, the hallway and everything in it sucked away into a distant pinpoint of light, leaving him suspended—

No, he's sitting on tattered shingles and looking up at a distant star. *Sirius*, he thinks. *The Dog Star.* His mom is drunk again and fighting with Dad, so he'd climbed out his window and up onto the roof. He pulls a long drag on one of his dad's cigarettes and blows smoke up at the star, wondering if there's anyone up there that gives a damn about him. Movement from across the street catches his eye, and he finds himself staring into the neighbors' bedroom window. They'd left the blinds up and the light on, and now he has a front-row seat to what will bring baby Deloris into the world nine months later. The scene fascinates him so much that he feels awkward and slightly dirty when waving to Mrs. Neighbor two days later, unable to meet her smiling eyes. I mean, the *things* she had been *doing*!

"Mrs. Peggy?" he says.

"Yes, Paul?" she answers with a polite smile.

"You should really close your blinds at night."

And as her smile drops, he drops with it.

Straight down and into Darla Hapney.

—the beacon breaks the surface and broadcasts its signal loud and clear. *This is a dream*, he realizes. And, like a dream, it somehow makes perfect sense, everything all over and inside out, but all the same and right-side up—

Darla Hapney is standing there in the same tweed, earthen-toned skirt that he first saw her in. In fact, this *is* the first time he saw her—her impossibly long legs sheathed in long white socks, her hair pulled back in a braided ponytail with a pink bow tied off at its tip.

God, I never forgot about that damn bow, he thinks, his self now joining the past and the future in dualistic, dreamlike fashion.

Her eyes…

They are big and bright and endless, and he's suddenly pulled off his feet and floating toward them. Each one is a universe, her crystalline irises blue galaxies wrapping around magical, dark orbs. As he nears the different worlds that are her eyes, he comes upon the beautiful mountain range that is her nose, and he wonders if it will dash him in two, sending him in opposite halves into each eye.

But then her eyes are one, and he's lost in the center of its blazing ring. Stars swirl all around him, diamonds shimmering in an ocean of blue light. Her pupil is an open portal, and it draws him in, sending him into…

Their first kiss.

It is a moment that seems to last forever. A piece of enchantment that transcends both time and space and fills his soul with certain of its intangible properties—like love, hope, purpose…

As love's light washes over his meaningless black-and-white world, animating his senses to living color, surround sound, and the dimensions of touch, his future becomes suddenly, amazingly bright.

Then she's in a box and being lowered into the ground—

—flashes of light—

—explosions in the distance—

—machine-gun fire—

—sand—

He relives the pain all over, and its cruel fingers melt the carnival mirrors of this reality into a pool of silver water that not only distorts his memories but intertwines and grafts them all together. The pool grows into a lake, the lake an ocean, and he's sinking in its depths, looking for the surface—or rather consciousness. *I'm dreaming,* he tells himself. *Wake up!*

But he doesn't wake. Instead he's watching Mom leave a bottle of Jack on the kitchen table to walk out into the rain, her bathrobe, pink bunny slippers, and disheveled hair a perfect commentary on her present state. There's a big black snake that has slithered into her vegetable garden. And though nothing edible has grown out of that soil for years, she is struck with the sudden, irresistible urge to defend it now. She bends over, intent on squeezing that scaled serpent to death with her bare, wet hands.

No! Mom! Don't! Paul cries out. He can't help it.

She grabs the fallen wire…and fries herself.

No!

—screaming—

—blood—

—smoke—

The fights. Jeff Riggins, Lance Hopper, Tommy Vance, and Mark Johnson are the ones that flash around him now in this acid-like hallucination that he knows is a dream but can do nothing about. His knuckles break bones, the rage a growing monster inside that both perpetuates and feeds off the violence.

Dream, he says. But it's not just a dream, is it? It's his life. And he wonders if he's dead. If this is his reckoning, all his sins rolled out before him just prior to the elevator down into the fire.

Now the girls. Julie Simpson, Abby Toons, Kate Watson, Shelly Brady… He resents them all, for they are not his darling Darla, but he uses them the best that he can, the monster inside revealing its second head.

* * * *

Robyn was following close behind Li, the women all on her heels, Robinson bringing up the rear behind Wilson, Patrick, and Joe. So far they'd made it without being spotted by the Leftover forces scavenging the Graveyard, but with plenty of distance still to cover, Robyn was half convinced that her pounding heart was going to give them away. She winced with every beat that slammed into her bruised ribs, but it was a reminder that she was still alive, so she embraced it—fed off it.

Looking to the ocean, she could barely see the huge boat hanging suspended on the reef. Not the cruise ship Daniel said they had to get to, but the massive boat that had been here long before her parents arrived, the one Jackson called *Cyclops*. Ahead of them, behind a dome-like rock that stuck out of the sand, the line of planes he'd also called "Flight 19" rocked back and forth in the wind. The planes had been here before her parents, too.

Wet sand was piling up in the rolls of her oversized pants, trying to pull them down off her waist and trip her up. She ran with one hand holding them up. Until Jackson, barely visible ahead, stopped when he reached the rock (which she now realized was not a rock), and put a fist in the air. Li stopped, and she dropped into a crouch, waving for everyone behind her to do the same. They all sat motionless, squinting through the falling water as they waited for Jackson's next signal. Then, appearing out of the liquid curtain, a blurred form could be seen walking around the side of the large dome that Jackson was leaning against.

Jackson was leaning against the rusted hull of the submarine (it was still protruding like a giant dome out of the beach) and facing the crashing waves. He motioned for Daniel to come stand next to him, and flexed his fingers on the rifle, bringing it up next to his head as Daniel crossed in front of him and got out of the way.

The six-foot soldier, dressed in animal skins and covered in tattoos, came walking around the towering hull, but his eyes weren't ahead of him. He was looking up the beach toward the Purees hiding amidst the rows of Avengers. And just as he saw them, stopping dead in his tracks, Jackson came around the cylindrical hull, charging straight at him and bringing the rifle's butt crashing into his head before he could turn around.

Robinson saw the man drop face-first into the sand. Then Jackson was bending over and dragging him by the ankles and back around the submarine and out of view. When no other soldiers came over to inspect the missing scavenger, Jackson waved back to the planes, signaling the others to join him.

"Ready?" Wilson asked Joe.

Joe nodded and put his arm back around his shoulder. Patrick went under his other arm.

"I'll stay with you," Robinson said to them and led them to the next plane.

After two more planes, Robinson looked back at Joe and saw that all the color had gone from his face. He looked like a ghost. "You okay?"

"Are we almost there?"

"We're almost there."

He smiled. "Oh, good. Then let's keep going."

Patrick and Wilson nodded, but it was clear that they were getting tired too. They went to the next plane, and by then all the others were already huddled around the submarine's hull, waiting for them.

Robinson shouldered his AK and then turned so that his back was toward Joe. "Get on my back."

Wilson and Patrick exchanged a look of relief and then gladly moved Joe into position. But when Joe wrapped his arms around Robinson's neck and his knees bent over Robinson's forearms, he screamed. And everyone ahead of them suddenly whipped their heads around.

"Oh, that's not good," Robinson mumbled. If they could hear Joe's scream over the storm, then…

He started moving as fast as he could, stumbling through the wet, clumpy sand and almost spilling Joe twice. He looked behind him but couldn't see anything through the rain. *Good, then maybe they can't see—*

But then, just as he left the cover of the planes and was out in the open sand, six Leftover soldiers pushing and pulling an old motored raft came sprinting across their path just twenty feet in front of them.

Robinson froze.

He didn't know how it was possible the soldiers hadn't spotted them, as it seemed to him that they were in their direct line of sight. Maybe they had seen them, he thought, standing there supporting Joe's weight and holding his breath. Maybe they'd seen them and dismissed them, the need to get off the island greater than a confrontation with the Purebloods.

"Don't they see us?" Joe whispered in his ear.

But then one of the men in the rear of the pack suddenly turned his head so fast that his long black hair whipped around and slapped the other side of his face.

Their eyes locked, and the man stood still, breaking rank with the others and dropping his corner of the raft. The sudden shift in weight pulled at the arms of the others and sent them stumbling. They looked around, trying to determine what had caused the sudden imbalance.

When they spotted Robinson standing there with Joe on his back, fixed like a statue in the rain, they too dropped the boat. And though they carried no weapons, they were still going to try to claim a couple more Purees before leaving.

But just as the one who had first spotted them took a step forward, thunder cracked and exploded his head, a trail of blood, bone, and tissue striping the sand all the way to Robinson's new shoes.

Knowing which direction the shot had come from, Robinson looked beyond the startled men and could just make out a kneeling form farther up the beach. The figure flashed, and there was another crack as another of the Fallen went flying forward and into the raft.

Robinson knew it had to be Jackson. No one else would be able to strike a target so precisely in this thrashing rain now blowing sideways off the ocean. Still, he didn't need to complicate his line of fire, so he put Joe down and stayed still. "Don't move."

Joe's foot touched the ground and he screamed again.

More thunder sounded, and two more dead men filled the raft.

Those remaining abandoned the raft and the two Purees and sprinted back to where they'd come from, seeking cover in the clutter of the Graveyard.

"Okay, come on!" Robinson yelled, knowing they had mere seconds before every Fallen scavenger dropped what they were doing and came for them.

Robinson was practically dragging Joe, his bad foot trailing limply behind them and carving a rut through the sand. Joe was screaming, and when Robinson looked down at him, he understood why. A shiny flicker of white was sticking out of Joe's leg, and he knew it was the bone. Robinson swore.

When they passed the raft, Robinson looked up and saw Jackson approaching. "Thank God."

Jackson hooked his arm around Joe's right side, and once again they lifted his feet off the ground, speed walking as quickly as they could toward the submarine.

Robinson stole a quick glance behind them and saw a tide of tanned skin begin to sprinkle out of the wrecked vehicles and onto the beach. "Faster," he said urgently. But they couldn't go any faster, not with a hundred and eighty pounds of dead weight hanging between them.

After getting a glimpse of what was coming at them himself, Jackson stopped moving and yelled, "Turn!"

Robinson continued to move, swinging left and completing a half-turn by using Jackson's fixed position as a pivot point. They finished turning just in time to face their attackers, the front line of them, completely naked except for the swords and spears in their hands, exploding through the liquid curtain like rabid dogs. The crude tattoos covering their faces only made them more frightening as they opened their mouths in a collective, demon-crazed battle cry.

Jackson fired the AK from his hip, the rifle rocking violently against the crook of his left arm, his bicep bulging, veins tearing at his skin. Empty shells spun through the air, sizzling in the cool rain.

The first two men jerked wildly as the bullets punched through them, and they went tumbling forward, arms and legs flailing.

Robinson fired from his hip too, but he wasn't as strong as Jackson and had nowhere near the level of success in keeping the barrel level. Most of his shots flew over the heads of their pursuers, though he did manage to strike two of them. When their rifles clicked empty, there were still over a dozen Fallen coming for them. They dropped the rifles, pivoted back around, and started running again, Joe hanging on with what little strength he had left.

Ten feet later, Robinson glanced at Joe and noticed that his head was hanging down, his chin resting on—

"Jack!" he yelled.

Jackson looked over and saw right away what Robinson had noticed.

Joe's head was hanging down, his chin resting on the wooden shaft of a spear, its chiseled tip sticking out and pointing ahead of them. Joe's head swayed limply back and forth on top of it.

"Drop him!" Jackson cried.

They let go of Joe's body and let it fall to the sand behind them as they took off down the beach, running as fast as they could. They came to the submarine only to find it deserted, tracks leading down the beach and into the storm. They kept going.

An arrow flew between them and sank into the wet sand. And then another. And another.

Expecting a wild, naked man about to bring a sword down across his back, Robinson risked another look behind...and saw something else entirely.

The Fallen army was no longer chasing them. Instead, they were fighting other men that had come out of the forest, men in black tunics and gold arm bands.

Robinson again shouted to Jackson and pointed behind them.

Jackson looked back and saw Not Them soldiers cutting through the naked Leftovers. Turning, he settled into a slower backpedal and watched in amazement as the assassin-like men in black made easy work of their relatives from an alternate world.

A huge wave crashed into the shore between them, the flying mist blocking the battle from sight and breaking up the path their tracks had made.

"C'mon!" Robinson yelled.

Turning, Jack raced him to the Crystal Caves, following the footprints left behind by their friends.

TWENTY-FIVE

September 22, 2011. Late afternoon. The Cave.

Paul drinks, smokes, swallows, and shoots up. And he watches his life slip away from him…again.

The gangs. The violence. Knives and chains and broken bottles.

It's still a dream. He knows it, because his two fingers are still standing over yonder, following him around like roadies hooked on a rock tour. But still he can't wake up.

And then he's in the mud, exhausted and freezing, wondering what in the hell he's doing. He wants to quit. Wants to ring that bell…that Narnia bell. Signal the witch, bring her back, he doesn't care. Just make it stop. Let him close his eyes. Let him get warm. Let him take a sip from that bottle. Let him swallow those pills. Let him. Let him. Let him.

But he doesn't. Didn't. He'd made it through their so-called Hell Week, made it onto the team.

Yet he's still so tired, his mind walking a tightrope over a fault line.

—bombs exploding—

—more blood—

—the Day of the Rangers, Somalia—

Everything spins…

Into Naga Hills.

* * * *

Hunter knows that Turiel is using his mind to catch up on history, seeing the future through his 2011 eyes just as he's seen the past through the angel's. Still, he has managed to guard the part of his subconscious that holds the mysterious key Turiel is searching for. He himself has yet to find it, but he's aware of the general area. Eventually, he'll need to let Turiel find it if he's going to use the pyramid to get them all out of here, but he needs to buy more time. The equinox isn't until tomorrow, and he needs to reveal it at the last possible moment. Otherwise, the angel might figure out a way to use the knowledge without him and just kill him.

Hunter can see Paul sitting in an empty, borderless room, unconscious. He can see Jackson and Robinson meeting up with the rest of the Purees at the Crystal Caves. And he can see the storm brewing over the island, perhaps the work of the Prince of the Power of the Air—or at least his alien closet demon. He needs to keep Turiel occupied with other things. So he dials up the distractions, planting images of twenty-first-century technology across his path and leading him away, down other more distant corridors of his mind. History, movies, war, science…whatever he can think of that might fascinate this Fallen angel that has yet to see Noah's Flood.

Noah's Flood.

Yes, that's right, your kind was just about wiped out…all of you who rebelled in that first rebellion, who took on human flesh, have been confined to Tartarus until the last Judgment.

But then a sudden, foreign thought that was not his comes blasting through his mind.

Abaddon.

Hunter can feel the clawed hand of the demon on his mind, knows that it is inside the temple and walking its halls beneath them. And he knows that it has just used him as a transmitter to relay a large piece of the puzzle to Turiel.

It is only a matter of time now.

I need to hold on! Please, Jesus, I know they're using me, but I think you have your own plan in all this. So, please, help me to hold on!

* * **

Jackson and Robinson managed to catch up with the others just as they made it to the caves. When Robyn, Li, Daniel, Patrick, Wilson, and the girls noticed that Joe wasn't with them, they began to sob, though the urgency of their situation only allowed the briefest display of emotion. There would be time later for mourning all their losses—or maybe not.

The rain was coming down so hard now that it was stinging their flesh, and the thunder that had begun over the ocean now felt and sounded like bombs being dropped from the heavens.

Jackson shielded his face with his hands, trying to keep the leaves and other swirling debris from his eyes as he looked for any sign of Jared, Samuel, Theodore, Pete, Charles, and all the others. But it was getting on into early evening now, and the clouds were so dark, the rain so dense, that he could barely make sense of anything but the vague, phantom shapes of their looming surroundings. The ground itself was quickly becoming a pond, so it was impossible to get a picture of what might have happened here. If there had been a struggle outside the caves, all evidence of it had been washed away. He signaled Wilson, Patrick, and Li, who had the only rifles left, to come forward and lead them into the cave.

As Li led them into the darkness, they were greeted not by torchlight, but by an empty, eerie silence.

Eliot…

Jackson squeezed his eyes closed and put a hand out, grasping Robyn's shoulder. She probably thought he was just trying to stay close in the dark, but he knew it was something more than that. He needed to touch her, to feel her presence. Because though Denise couldn't be here, he suddenly needed reassurance that she was.

In his head, he answered her voice. *If it's really you, Denise…please forgive me.* And though his apology could've been directed at any number of things, he knew it was more aligned with the skeptical way he'd related to her faith coupled with his developing feelings for this other, younger woman he was now touching. Denise had spent her short, married life unable to share with him the most precious thing in her life, and now here he was finally coming around to believing and looking to share it with someone else. He'd robbed her, so how could he enjoy the very thing he'd neglected to give her?

No, Eliot… Don't you see, baby? I am so HAPPY!

He blinked at that…that voice. That voice that couldn't possibly belong to Denise. She was supposed to be in heaven, not in this place!

I'm not in this place, my love. I am waiting for you in glory among all the saints from all the ages. And oh, baby, you wouldn't believe what it's like! But there are no words that can express the infinite, so just come to me. Come to Him! Please! I miss you, Eliot. Oh, if that's even possible here, I miss you.

Leaning heavily against the limestone wall beside him, his fingers slipped off Robyn's shoulder. He stood there, his eyes staring down at the floor but not seeing it, as everyone moved past him.

Robinson grabbed his arm. "You okay?"

He looked up, and had it been lighter, Robinson would've seen tears sparkling around the faint traces of a smile. Before Jackson could reply, however, a voice sounded out ahead of them.

"Who is it?"

The voice echoed off the rock walls and filled the corridor, and there was no mistaking who it belonged to.

"It's us!" Robyn cried out.

"Robyn?" Samuel's voice questioned.

Jackson heard running, and then the subterranean space began filling with a flickering glow as torches came to life around where Samuel's voice had originated. Robinson pulled him away from the wall, and Jackson followed him.

"What happened?" Li's voice echoed around them.

Pete and the scrappy teenager George were holding the torches behind Samuel. Their faces were a portrait of despair.

"They came for us," Samuel said. His voice was flat, defeated. "After all this time, they finally came for us."

"They came for the guns," Robinson said.

"What?"

Now that Jackson was closer, over a head taller than most of the women standing in front of him, he could see that whatever had happened here had taken its toll on the old man. His eyes were heavy, unfocused, and seemed to confirm their fears.

Robyn stepped closer, placing a gentle hand beneath Samuel's elbow. "It's a long story that we have all night to tell." Though everyone she'd just entered the cave with knew that wasn't necessarily true. "But look who we found." She pointed to the girls.

"Oh my!" Samuel cried out, a spark of life flashing back in his eyes if even for a moment. He stepped forward and embraced each one. "How…"

"Later," Patrick answered.

Then Samuel noticed Daniel, and even more questions filled his surprised eyes.

"Samuel," Jackson called out before the old leader could get completely swept up in the reunion, "where is everyone?"

Samuel stepped away from a girl Jackson had never seen before, and the heaviness immediately filled his eyes again. "They came in so fast. We weren't ready. We put down the first wave, but they just kept coming."

"Jared?" Tabitha asked.

He shook his head, and a series of gasps filled the dark corridor, Tabitha's elderly frame crumbling.

Jackson saw sparkles appear on most of the faces around him, their tears embracing the torchlight. "How many are left?"

"Twenty."

And a sudden, collective scream was emitted from the group, all of them turning and holding on to the person next to them.

Jackson wanted to go to Robyn, to hold her, but he would have to work his way through the crowd, and she was holding onto another girl anyway.

"What about you?" Pete asked. "Where are the rest of you?"

Robinson looked up. "We're all that made it back."

"Paul is still out there," Robyn whispered.

"And Hunter," Daniel added.

Samuel looked at Jackson questioningly as Pete and George groaned at the loss of Joe, Charles, and Sanders.

Jackson answered the unasked question. "It's a long story."

"Where are the others?" a crying woman asked, though it was clear she really meant "who are the other seventeen?"

"They are out there, burying the others."

"They're on the hill? In *this*?" Li asked, incredulous.

"They went out before the storm got bad. I imagine they should be back any moment. I thought you were them."

"Did you see the Darkness?" Wilson asked.

But it was clear from their eyes that they didn't know what he was talking about.

Jackson was about to turn and head back into the storm when a soaking crowd entered the cave behind them.

The two groups flew into each other's arms, crying.

Jackson stood back and watched, hoping that Daniel's message from Hunter was sound, that there was a way out of here, and that they'd all live long enough to realize it.

* * * *

He can no longer describe what he's seeing, where he is. The vague and dreamlike history of Turiel's journey, from angel to god to priest, has dissolved into a sort of metaphysical fog, and he's floating through a semiconscious reality with no windows. He knows his body is still standing without him, and when that closet demon, who worked all this madness together by using the disembodied spirits of the slain Nephilim, gets here there's no telling what it'll do to him once Turiel has what he needs from his head.

But no…

Realization flashes. Turiel needs him present *during* the activation. He isn't able to transfer the key into his own mind and can only hope to turn it from within Hunter's mind when the time comes.

Stuck in this borderless ocean of otherworldliness, Hunter reaches out with his mind (which suddenly seems like a limitless arm capable of going anywhere and connecting with anything) and searches, breaking through the bubble of this island's reality, and feels for a familiar presence.

He finds it. But the connecting point is not only in a different place, but a different time.

Henry, he calls out. *Henry, are you there? Can you hear me?*

And Henry, convinced he is dreaming (and in a way he is), answers back. *Hunter, is that you?*

Henry, I don't have much time, and there are things you need to know. Things you need to do.

What things?

Listen.

The dark demon steps into Turiel's chamber and stands between the two motionless bodies. Its serpentine eyes narrow on Hunter as if it has somehow gotten a sense of what he's doing. It flexes its long black fingers and snarls.

* * * *

After the survivors had assembled in one of the cave's larger chambers, they spent a good four hours talking amongst each other while the storm ravaged the island above them. The missing girls answered all the obvious questions, explaining how they'd gone from talking to each other in the cave one second to suddenly standing in the middle of the woods the next. They cried as they shared the fate of their other sisters—Ming ending up inside a rock with only her nose and fingers sticking out of it, and Tara appearing standing bent over and leaning into the other side of the same rock, everything from her stomach upward swallowed whole. And then there was the story of their capture…and subsequent abuse. It was hard to listen to, even with the edits that were so obviously being applied.

They all cried, the women that were lost family to all. And then Robyn told them about Ruth and Priscilla, who had apparently appeared somewhere else, because none of the girls had seen them since the Change. More tears.

Robyn was then talked into telling her story, which started with Jackson finding her on her parents' boat and ending with Paul fighting the giants and allowing her time to make a leaping escape off Turiel's balcony.

That was followed by a tag-team account of what Robinson and Li had witnessed in the New Territory, from dinosaurs to gold-armored giants to a city they could hardly describe.

Then, once everyone's different curiosities seemed to ebb for the time being and exhaustion started to take its toll, Daniel cleared his throat and told them about the ship, of what he'd seen there, and what Hunter was planning to do.

And all the while, Ivan Major sat in the corner, believing the whole thing to be a dream.

Then they all went to sleep, understanding that, one way or another, it would be the last night they closed their eyes on this island.

Jackson was sitting on the floor in his room, his back against the palmetto-thatched bed, Robyn beside him and leaning into him. He ran his hand through her hair while he stared at the dancing fire blazing on the floor in front of them. She had changed out of the oversized clothes and finally gotten out of the dress Turiel's chamberlains had put her in, now wearing a pair of khaki shorts and a 1983 Redskins Super Bowl T-shirt. The change of clothes seemed to do wonders for her mental state, and Jackson spent about twenty minutes trying to explain who the Redskins were and what the Super Bowl was while he built the fire. Now she just lay in silence, dancing her fingernails across his bruised chest.

Jackson thought about inquiring as to how her own chest was doing, but he thought better of it. He wasn't exactly sure why. Typically, he would've jumped at such a suggestive conversation with a beautiful island woman. And it wasn't like he didn't want her. God knew he did. But something was different now. Something inside him had changed, and he realized that he was actually becoming a different person. He thought Henry, and especially Johnny, would love to hear that. But did he deserve to change? After all he'd done?

His mind spun such thoughts into a white flag and then waved it in surrender at the fire. And he let himself slip away, the flames taking him into the night—perhaps the last night of his life.

"What was she like?"

Robyn's voice startled him awake, and he wasn't sure if he'd been asleep for a second or for an hour. Judging by the size of the fire, he'd slipped into dreamworld for only a minute, but he must've slipped hard, because it took him a moment to gather his senses. He blinked and once again began moving the hand that had gone still atop her head.

It's okay," she said reassuringly. "And I apologize for how I reacted before..."

He swallowed, knowing the conversation would have to be had at some point. "She was..." He searched for a word that could summarize her person, but couldn't find one.

Robyn moved, shifting her body so that she could see his face. "You loved her a lot."

He nodded.

"Do you miss her?"

He tried to swallow the lump growing in his throat. *Denise...*

She leaned her head against his chest, careful not to press against it too hard. "I understand," she whispered. "I didn't before."

He stared into the fire. "You're a lot like her," he said. "So I wasn't sure if that's..." He trailed off. He was never good at this, and Denise had practically been able to read his mind, so he never really had to be.

But Robyn nodded. "You weren't sure if I just reminded you of her, or if you actually did like me."

"Yeah. But you're so different, too. And I love those differences. Not because they're better than hers, but...I don't know. I can only compare it to what I imagine parents feel toward their kids, how they're able to love them all the same even when they're all so different."

"I get it."

"And you're okay with it?"

She smiled. "I am."

"I just don't see how it's fair, to be with someone who will always be missing someone else at the same time."

She didn't say anything for a moment, and the sound of the fire crackling was amplified by her silence. Then she said, "I know what it's like to lose people you love and have to move on."

He sighed, feeling the pain in her voice. "I know you do," he whispered. And he almost asked her to marry him then and there. But before he could get around to actually considering it, she asked *the* question. Not how they met or where they lived or if they had children or anything like that. No, she asked the one question he was scared to death of, and his heart slammed into his ribs, aggravating his chest.

"How did she die?" she asked.

He swallowed, and the night came back like it was yesterday, all those dormant feelings resurrected in an instant. Not knowing how he would get through the story (he'd tried so hard to forget that night), he stumbled into it, knowing he'd have to tell her eventually (if eventually survived the equinox, that was).

"We were driving home from a movie," he began and then realized that he was going to have to explain a few things from his world if she was going to understand the story. Three months of conversation and the encyclopedias she'd read would certainly help, but... He swallowed again, his eyes watery glass. "The whole world is basically connected by big roads, right? You've seen pictures in the books?"

She nodded.

"Well, there are highways—big, wide roads that just go on forever. And sometimes there are bridges that pass over the highways."

"I've seen pictures of those," she said.

He sighed. "We drove under one, and there just happened to be some guy up there with a cinderblock." He stared into the fire, seeing the flames bend into the car's interior. "It's a big brick."

She didn't say anything, but he could tell she was holding her breath.

"This guy thought it would be fun to see if he could hit a passing car with it." He paused, tears rolling out of his eyes. "Denise was leaning against me, just like you are now. We had a sunroof in that car, and it was a cool spring day, so...she insisted we kept it open. She loved the wind blowing through her hair."

"Sunroof?"

"It's a retractable window in the roof."

"Oh," she whispered.

"Well, he timed us up just perfect. We weren't going that fast, on account of her leaning against me and all… And the block came right on through the opening—" he choked "—and landed on her head."

Robyn threw her hands to her mouth, her own eyes wet.

"I was able to keep the car from crashing. But…" Denise's wrecked, caved-in face stared at him from within the fire.

But that's not where I am now, honey. Or what I look like.

"I sped to the nearest hospital." Tears were hanging off his jaw now, and it took all his self-control to keep from weeping. He'd suppressed these memories, imprisoned them in some psychological black site just so he could go on to the next day. And now he was reliving them, one detail at a time, the squeezing despair gripping his chest choking him. "She mumbled things all the way there. Her…face…" He looked away from the fire and squeezed his eyes closed, sending groups of salty tears into Robyn's hair. "She said she loved me. Started saying stuff about heaven…" What he couldn't say, however, what he would not look at, was what those words had sounded like, coming slow and hard through the blood bubbling from her twisted lips and severed tongue, her damaged brain trying to force coherency in her last moments. Her nose was shattered, the corner of the pale gray block resting between her bloodshot eyes… "The block…" he gasped. "I had to… I couldn't carry her with it stuck like that… It was too heavy, but it was…stuck… I…"

Robyn squeezed his hands, her own eyes now lost under a flood of tears, and she seemed to be begging him to stop.

"I just watched her slip away, there in the car, parked right in front of the emergency room entrance. And all I could think the whole time was that it couldn't be real…because we were going camping the next day. She'd never gone before and had been begging me to take her for so long. I'd been planning the trip for months. We were going to sleep in, give the house a quick clean, grab lunch at a new restaurant our friend just opened, and then drive to the mountains. And so, I'm looking down at her, and I just keep saying to myself that it's not happening, that it's the wrong script. Someone got the scene mixed up, and they'll fix it just as soon as they realize the mistake. We were going *camping* tomorrow.

"I don't remember much after that. I have a vague memory of people shouting and pulling her off me."

"I don't know what to say," Robyn whispered, sniffling.

"I hear her voice," he said.

"What do you mean?"

"In this place, I hear her talking to me. In my head. At first I thought it was a trick, demons playing jokes on me or something. But now, the things that she's saying…"

"What is she saying?"

He looked at her, into her eyes, and tried to lose Denise's destroyed face in them. "She's telling me that she's happy now. That she wants to see me again."

"Like she's in heaven?"

He nodded. "She wants me to be there too. Not now, necessarily. But when the time comes..."

"You don't believe?"

"*Didn't* believe. But now... I don't know how I can't. I've seen too much."

She seemed to think about that. Then she asked, "What happened to the person on the bridge?"

And there it was.

And suddenly, he felt his entire future (if there was to be one) hinging on this singular moment. Her reaction to his answer, to the secret he'd kept even from himself (to the extent that it was at all possible), would either reinforce the bridge between them, or blow it up like the bridge over Kwai. He wiped his eyes and cleared his throat. "I found him." The finality in his tone should've answered her next question too, but she wanted to hear it all, apparently.

"And?"

"And I took him back to the bridge."

She was holding her breath again.

"I showed him the spot down on the road where his brick killed my wife. He was young. Stupid. I just wanted him to *know*. To make him *feel* it."

"What did you do?"

"I grabbed him by his scrawny neck and held him over the bridge, his feet hanging and kicking out in space. I wanted to see remorse in his eyes, that twinkle of realization that he'd messed up, that he'd do anything to make it right if he could. And if he'd begged, said he hadn't meant to kill anyone, I'm sure I would've let him go."

"He didn't?"

Jackson's face twisted into a snarl, the firelight raging in his eyes. "He smiled. *Smiled!* Then he spit in my face." The muscles in his arms tensed, as if he were holding him in the air right now. "He would've done it all over again if he could, the little demon child. I've seen evil in the world, Robyn, like the wickedness you've seen here, and this kid had a bad case of it for sure." He ran a hand through his short hair. "So I dropped him. And he flew through the air like his cinder block...and landed on his own head."

How much of the social context she understood, with all society's civil and criminal laws and due process and so forth and so on, he could never know. Her experience with society had been a secluded one, played out within the intimate confines of family life—with every other person trying to kill or rape her. Maybe she wouldn't see anything at all wrong with what he did, though how she applied a New Testament understanding to her Old Testament surroundings was another puzzle he'd never tried to construct. "They called it suicide," he concluded. And then he whispered what she'd already known. "I never told that to anyone before."

"You feel guilty about it."

He shrugged. "She wouldn't have approved. And it certainly didn't take the pain away." There was an understanding shining in her eyes that affirmed that such vengeance might not only be acceptable in her world, but expected.

Then she said the last thing he expected to hear. "I've seen you kill a lot of people, Jackson. I don't know why you think this would be so different."

Because in this world, there are only people and the damned…

"What's the last thing you heard her say to you?" she asked, moving anticlimactically away from the biggest confession of his life. "I mean, since you've been here."

"That she's not in the fire. Or maybe she meant the car, I'm not sure. And that she doesn't look like she did after the brick smashed her face."

"Do you believe her?"

If it is her… "Yes." And he wished he had a drink. Coffee from that French press they'd found if nothing stronger.

"Do you think she'd mind us together?"

After a moment, he smiled sadly. "I think it's what she would want."

She laid her head against him again.

"Oh," he said offhandedly, "I should tell you that my *last* name is Jackson. Not my first."

"What?" she cried. "You mean I don't even know your name?"

He laughed gently, and the pain of it turned his smile into a cringe. "My name is Eliot, Robyn-with-a-Y. It's nice to meet you." And then he did ask her to marry him.

TWENTY-SIX

September 23, 2011. Morning. The Temple.

In what has developed into something more akin to a fever dream, Hunter has lost all sense of boundaries, limits, anything quantifiable. Time, distance…it's all floated away. And though ideas and images make perfect sense in his tumbling unconsciousness, they have no translation in the waking world.

Even still, one fact cuts through the haze. That thing—*what is it?*—has finally found what it was looking for. But he can't recall what it was that was being looked for. He only knows that its discovery means the time now is short.

What time?

The thing—the *angel*—now knows it all.

Angel?

Knows what the future is…and what it can be.

Future?

Abaddon.

Abaddon…

His sleeping mind grasps an outcropping of consciousness, and though the edges are sharp and hurt his hands, he begins to pull himself up.

* * * *

The storm that Jackson had traveled through after he Change three months ago must have paled in comparison to the one that ravaged the island all last night. For though they could see little more than a jagged outline of black pressing against a slightly fainter black, they could tell that the cedar forest before them had been destroyed.

"Must've been one hell of a hurricane," Robinson said, trying to translate the predawn landscape.

Jackson didn't answer. He was thinking about the helicopter and the chances of it surviving such a storm—*if* there ever was a helicopter in the first place. He found himself growing more and more skeptical of the whole "Mission Hunter" thing the closer it got to showtime. And he could tell that Robinson felt the same way.

There was a light, lingering rain hanging on to the tail end of the storm, and clouds still hugged the island. It was going to be hard going trekking to the site of Osiris' temple complex, which was why they were going alone. If they found the helicopter in working order, then Jackson would need someone to help him navigate, but any more passengers on an unproven aircraft could be problematic. And unless it was an airbus, they'd need to make multiple trips anyway.

"How much time you figure we have?" Robinson asked, adjusting his hat.

Jackson shrugged. "I'm thinking noonish if it works anything like Osiris' pyramid."

"But maybe before that?"

"Maybe."

Robinson looked behind him, at the cave's entrance. "Guess we better hurry, then."

They each had an AK-47, and Jackson's backpack was restocked with magazines that Osiris' Leftovers hadn't taken. They hoped they wouldn't need them, that the storm would have kept the enemy too preoccupied to track them. Or better yet, that the storm had killed them all.

They set off, quickly finding plenty of obstacles throughout the shattered terrain. Jackson hoped to reach the house by the time dawn's early light cracked open this new day—their last day.

* * * *

Naga Hills had bypassed the rest of his military career, dropping him off at the start of his private contractor gig. Paul followed himself through the various Middle Eastern conflicts he'd been employed by, unsure where this road would ultimately end. Probably not anywhere good considering the lack of yellow bricks and the overwhelming sense of crushing darkness ahead.

Suddenly, he spotted her. The girl.

No!

She was above him, half hidden in a sweeping rainbow of light that came dipping before him. He recoiled as she stepped down from the brilliant arch as if it were a staircase, and he couldn't help thinking the girl might be Dorothy, Toto in tow. But when she emerged from the light, he saw that it was, indeed, the girl he'd shot. And was this his eternal fate? To relive this one mistake over and over? He couldn't bear it. And then figured that was probably the point.

Please! He didn't know what he was begging for. Forgiveness maybe? To be left alone? To wake up? For mercy? For another chance?

Maybe all.

His stomach lurched, and there was the sudden sensation of falling. He looked down and was surprised to find himself standing on the top of a tower, his feet dropping through its roof. Beneath his sinking feet, he could see through the roof and through all the floors below as if the tower were holographic in nature. From his vantage point, all the floors transposed on top of each other like he was looking through so many panes of glass, each floor one of the experiences he'd just revisited. The tower, which he understood to be his life, was imploding, collapsing into itself. A pit of boiling tar surrounded the tower, consuming his past…and him along with it.

He looked up at the girl, and for the first time in his life felt real, absolute fear. Oh, he'd felt fear before. Felt it acutely at Naga Hills and scores of other times in which he'd almost died. But this *was* Death.

He began to cry, the revelation of his own damnation fully realized.

But then the girl, watching from the foot of the rainbow stairs, stretched out her hands.

He covered his eyes from the shimmering heat of the boiling liquid as it quickly ate up his past like a burnt offering to Darkness, and wondered what she was doing.

Her hands reached down, somehow appearing right in front of his face, palms out as if wanting him to take hold of her. He didn't understand. Was she trying to save him? Why would she want to do that? But then, as he reached for her, he noticed the holes in her wrists.

He frowned, because he was sure he hadn't seen them in any of the visions before.

She smiled.

Take my hands, Paul.

He did. He wrapped his battered fingers around her frail wrists, covering what he knew to be nail holes, and let her pull him up into the air as the slurping, churning pit consumed his past and licked the soles of his boots.

She lifted him up through the air, through dreams and songs and stories of redemption and forgiveness.

He felt the heat of his burning past fade beneath him as he ascended into a cooler, freer atmosphere. Tears welled in his eyes, though no longer tears of terror and remorse, but of thanksgiving and humility. There was a brilliant light ahead, the girl's hands pulling him into it.

But it wasn't the girl that was holding him anymore.

Looking back to the hands that had lifted him from the pit, Paul discovered that a pair of large masculine hands had replaced those of the little girl's. The open wounds between ulna and radius, where the nine-inch nails had been driven, seemed to glow.

And then there was a voice…

Come to me, all who are weary and heavy laden. And I…

—everything rolls back on itself—

…will…

—the death and pain, both experienced and caused—

…give…

—it all becomes a swirling drink—

…you…

—that the man with the holes in his hands takes and drinks—

…rest.

And then he's surrounded by a warm, glowing light, and he's never felt peace and contentment like this in his whole life. He wants to stay there forever and thinks that he will.

But then there's something pressing against the side of his face, sliding from his jaw up to his temple, and the pain of it across his wounds makes him blink.

The quality of the light changes.

Blink.

A sense of surrounding seeps into his consciousness.

Blink.

There's something staring at him, standing over him. He realizes that he's lying on the ground, and his eyes begin to focus.

Two huge nostrils are palpitating over him, sucking the short hair of his head like an alien probe.

He squints, finds that the nostrils are fixed to the end of a long snout, two black bulbous eyes blinking from either side of it.

Awareness comes rushing back, and Paul can make out the shining lights lining the cave walls. The horse nudges him again.

He's finally awake.

* * * *

It was still dark when Jackson and Robinson reached the field that circled the house, and the rain continued to fall. They pushed through the open area, traversing strewn trees and wading through hip-deep puddles until it became obvious the house had been destroyed. It just wasn't there, its silhouette against the graying sky clearly absent.

"This is where it was?" Robinson asked.

"Yeah. Probably all in pieces in the woods now," Jackson answered, pointing east.

But a minute later, they were crushing glass under their feet.

"And this is where Pierre died?" Robinson crouched and found a square tile in the mud, which Jackson recognized as part of the kitchen. Robinson turned it over in his fingers before tossing it away.

"It is," Jackson said.

"Joe said he was eaten alive by giants."

Jackson nodded and then realized Robinson couldn't see him. "Yeah," he muttered.

Robinson stood. "Then I guess there were worse ways for Joe to go." There was no missing the brokenness in his voice.

"I'm sorry for all the people you've lost," he replied. "It seems if we hadn't come—"

Robinson cut him off. "If what you said is true, about that other angel in Bermuda working with Osiris, then if it wasn't you and Henry and John and Hunter and Chadwick—"

"And Nick and Chris," he interjected.

"—then it would've been someone else. Maybe someone that wouldn't have helped us at all."

"Maybe you would've been better off without our help."

Robinson sighed. "Everybody dies, Jack. Whether in this world or yours. But you've given some of us a chance at getting out of this hell."

Jackson considered the man next to him for a moment and recalled that he hadn't been born here. Or at least he didn't think he'd gotten his tattoo here, though it was a crude enough job to be sure. "Your tattoo. Where'd you get it?"

Robinson looked down at his arm, barely able to see the old three-letter mark in the darkness. "Ain't too pretty, is it?" The Ms were in cursive, but the O between them looked more like a zero.

"She die?" Jackson asked gently.

"Yup." He took his hat off and ran his hand through his hair. "Cancer."

"Where?"

"Boston."

"Really?"

"Don't talk like a Bostoner, do I?" He laughed a sad sort of laugh. "Got the tat three days after she passed. Some friend of a friend did it for five bucks. I was only thirteen at the time."

"How'd you get here from Boston?"

They continued walking, slowly, careful not to trip over anything or fall into any more large puddles.

"Seems I ask myself that same question every day," Robinson answered. "What was the one thing that set me on the road to this place? Was it my dad leaving us when I was four? Was it the cigarette smoker who blew cancer into my mom's lungs ten hours a day at her job? Or was it less complicated than all that? Was it just the misfortune of picking the wrong day to set out for Ireland?"

"Ireland?"

"Yeah. My mom was first generation. Her and my dad came over from Ireland in the early '70s. I don't know for sure, but I think they were trying to get away from the Conflict."

"The IRA and all that?"

"Yeah. So when she died, I had no family left here. I didn't know what happened to my dad, if he was still alive or not, and after not hearing from him in ten years, I had no way of finding out. I wanted to find my grandparents, aunts and uncles. It seemed the only way I could keep my mom alive was to find out more of who she was. And this." He held up his arm.

"Boston to Ireland doesn't take you through the Triangle."

"No. My foster parents moved to Florida when I was fifteen, took me out of school and away from the only few people I had any connection with. They weren't exactly a holiday, my foster parents, so I found a ship that was going to Ireland and jumped aboard."

"So you were a fifteen-year-old stowaway. I'd love to hear how you managed that."

"Obviously, not too well, huh?"

They both shared a laugh as they closed in on—

"Stop," Jackson said, putting his arm out.

Robinson raised the 47. "What is it?"

Jackson squinted in the darkness, unsure he was actually seeing what he was seeing. But he knew that it was there, that it *would* be there. Why else had he taken them on this route? "You don't see it?"

"No. What is it?" He moved the rifle back and forth, ready to shoot.

Jackson stepped forward slowly.

Robinson followed. And then he saw it too. "What the hell, Jackson," he muttered.

The last vestiges of moonlight broke through a sudden gap in the clouds and lit the field with a wet, silver glow. It shimmered through the falling drizzle and off the sitting water surrounding them, making the field look more like a swamp. And there, still fixed within in its frame, stood a single door in the middle of it.

Robinson started to circle around it, giving it a wide berth. There was nothing on the other side of it but grass, yet they both had the impression that if the door were to open…

"Is that the infamous closet door?" Robinson asked.

"It sure is."

Had the door been sticking out of the mud at a severe angle, they would've simply concluded it had been tossed there by the storm. But there was no such angle. Rather, the door stood perfectly intact and level, not even a splatter of dirt across its bottom. In fact, as they got closer, examining it more intensely, there didn't appear to be any dirt on the door at all.

"I dare you to open it," Robinson said.

Jackson stared at the door, recalling Denise's voice inviting him through it. Had that been the same Denise he was conversing with now? If so, had she been trying to trick him into falling down the same demonic rabbit hole that Hunter had jumped through? Or could there be another reason his dear departed wife would've wanted him to go through the door? "Hunter went in there and came out on the ship."

Robinson frowned. "You're not suggesting we all line up and take a trip to the other side, are you? Doesn't sound like Hunter is all himself anymore."

"Hunter wasn't all himself before going in." He looked around, happy to find the faintest hint of dawn tickling the horizon. If the helicopter didn't work out, would he dare try the closet? He tucked that possibility into his back pocket. "Come on, let's keep going."

"Yeah," Robinson agreed, and the trepidation that carried his voice suggested sooner would be better than later.

They hurried on, moving across a tract of land that Jackson once knew to be North Shore Road, the memories of his Bermudian honeymoon revisiting him once again. *Denise…*

Eliot, her voice answered.

* * * *

When Paul sat up, he was greeted by a torrent of clashing cymbals banging in his head. He brought his hand up and felt a lump under his hair, figuring it was the reason for his little nap and why he had to look away from the lights on the walls. He looked down at himself and saw just how wrecked he was. His head, face, arm, side, back, and hands… *I could use a nice stay in rehab, I think.*

The big black horse nudged him again.

"Okay, okay…" His head spun in agony to a backbeat of thumping madness as he stood, then swayed, and finally went careening for the wall. He found it just in time, using an outstretched arm to brace himself before collapsing. He knew that if he were to fall down, he might not be able to get up again.

The horse brayed, impatient.

"Yeah, I know," Paul responded, his head in his hands. He looked up through the gauntlet of lights that were like daggers into his eyes and saw the cave's exit in the distance. He noticed that it was dark outside. *How long have I been out?* And was that scorpion thing still out there waiting for him?

He recalled how strong the electricity had felt upon entering the cave and didn't think it was so potent now—unless he'd just gotten used to it while he slept. Either way, he guessed that was what was keeping scorpion man out of the dry cave.

He looked back the other way, also recalling the black hole. Curious, he took a step in that direction, hand outstretched and patting against the wall for support.

The horse snorted.

"Hold on a sec." He followed the path he'd taken with Jackson and Robyn but only had to go as far as the mushroom forest, with its strange luminance, to get his answer. He stumbled through the spongey soil and came to the trickling stream that still divided the huge chamber. He looked around, found the wall with the overlap that led into the chamber below, and saw that there was no longer a wall there at all. Instead, there was a big black void. It seemed to consume the light, sucking it in and erasing it completely. Only it wasn't just the wall that was gone. The dark hole had begun to eat up the floor and ceiling too.

Paul took a step back. If that little crack had opened so wide as to consume the entire portcullis area and the next level above it in just a day…time indeed was short. The island was going to disappear whether Hunter's plan worked or not.

He turned and hobbled as quickly as he could back to the horse, and as he went, he became aware of a dream that he'd had. It trickled down the front of his brain, feeling like a soothing, hot shower as it stimulated his memory and brought back to mind the man with the holes in his wrists that had lifted him out of his sinking past. Tears welled in his eyes as peace like he'd never known flooded through him, from the soles of his feet to the top of his head. Yes, it was a dream. But it had been so much more than a dream. When the tears fell, they seemed to take his headache with them.

"Thank you," he whispered, not sure he understood what had just happened but knowing that it was more real than anything he'd ever experienced before. Yet, he couldn't remain in this state of reflection. As much as he wanted to rest in this new experience, he knew there was still work to be done.

Wiping his eyes, he approached the horse. He took a moment to stroke its long nose, then turned it toward the exit and began walking it out.

When they got within ten feet of what Paul recognized as a cloudy, predawn sky, they stopped. It seemed to be raining a little, and Paul tried peering into the field to see if he could spot the face of the flying lion man. But though the sky was growing lighter, it was still too dark to make out anything that might be hiding in the field.

He stepped back and, with a twinge of remorse, slapped the horse on its rear, crying, "Yah!"

Without question or pause, the horse took off out of the cave, free.

Paul watched as it left the glow of the artificial light behind, its black, shimmering coat disappearing quickly into the rain.

He waited.

A sudden noise from above him, coming from outside—a flapping sound, like bedsheets being shaken out or a flag snapping in the wind. A winged figure swooped down in front of the opening, its horrible silhouette chasing after the galloping horse, its long tail curled and ready to strike.

Paul didn't waste a second. He shouldered the rifle and moved as quickly as his broken body would allow, setting out on the quickest route to the nearest woods. Hunter had managed to implant the image of the Jet Ski, hidden amongst the Graveyard, in his mind, and he knew that was where he needed to be and as soon as possible.

A roar split the air, and the horse's cries echoed around him as he reached the tree line. He felt bad for the animal, but it was fated to die today one way or the other.

The trees, he found, were strewn all over the place, and he had to navigate them in the dark, climbing over, ducking under, and weaving his way in and out of so much wasted land. He'd slept the night away, and that through a hurricane. But what effect would such an event have on Hunter's plans? Surely, he couldn't have foreseen this. *Right?* What if the cruise ship had sunk, the helicopter was crushed, and every boat dashed to pieces?

Maybe they were lost here after all. *Maybe*, Paul thought. But at the same time, he knew that he had finally been found.

* * * *

The darkness was fleeing upward like a rising stage curtain, revealing an alien world mostly shrouded in fog. Visibility was only about five feet, with dark, chaotic shadows crisscrossing behind the veil, their extremities poking through and stabbing at them. It was apparent even from their limited perspective that the devastation was awesome. And as the morning continued to add inches to their fogged periphery, the destruction only became more apparent. Just about anything that was standing seemed to have been uprooted, snapped, or bent to the ground. Jackson had seen similar landscapes on the news in the aftermath of large tornadoes, hurricanes, typhoons, tsunamis, and even earthquakes, but he'd never walked through them himself. It was haunting, the soft pitter-patter of rain unnerving. Both Jackson and Robinson walked carefully, their weapons moving back and forth, half-expecting some monster to materialize out of the fog and snatch them away.

By the time they reached what was left of Osiris' temple complex, dawn's early light had turned the moon away and lit the horizon with deep purple hues they could just make out through the thinning fog. But as illumination grew, their hope of finding a working helicopter in all this mess shriveled. They could make out perhaps a dozen trees standing where just yesterday a thick forest had dominated. The ground was beaten bare, the trees strewn in piles of tangled carnage as if a tsunami had combed the island and then a category five twister tried to blow it dry.

The stepped ziggurat stood out of what looked like a giant funeral pyre, the wind and water having gathered the felled forest around its base. The back half of the structure was still missing due to the Change, but now a substantial portion of its upper level seemed to have cracked and fallen over too.

"Guess we should climb up there and see what we can see," Jackson said unenthusiastically.

"Sure."

It took them valuable time to climb the pile of muddy cedars. They were slippery, covered in mud, and wanting to roll out from under them. When they finally reached the top, after dodging tumbling poles, balancing on teetering limbs, slipping and sliding in the mud, casting aside debris that cluttered their way, and escaping shifting foot traps, they were exhausted. And to keep from falling into the middle of the temple (which had opened like an elevator shaft when the top fell away), they grabbed on to each other in order to retain their balance.

Looking down from the top ledge, it appeared as if the ground had swallowed the temple…and then regurgitated it.

Dark clouds still moved across the sky, but the rain had stopped, and now there was enough light to make out the surrounding scene below. The damage was even more breathtaking from this vantage, the trees that hadn't been uprooted now only four feet tall and splintered into sharp, ragged points.

"You see it?" Robinson asked, turning in a circle while remaining conscious of his footing.

Jackson shook his head. "No." There were piles of shattered wood everywhere, and he supposed the helicopter could be at the bottom of any one of them.

Then Robinson started pointing. "What is that?"

But all Jackson saw were long snakes of knotted foliage stretched across the ground. "I don't see anything."

"No, in the distance. Where the pyramid used to be."

Jackson adjusted his gaze and saw a muddy rock protruding out of the ground where the polished limestone device used to be.

No, not a rock, Jackson thought. Or at least not a natural one. It was too large, too angular, and though it was hard to tell from his position, he was sure the object had to be about ten feet tall, all its sides and angles equal.

"It's the pyramid, isn't it?" Robinson asked. "That's the top of Osiris' pyramid."

And though Jackson couldn't quite understand it himself, he nodded. It had been there the whole time, buried beneath the ground.

Robinson's eyes flashed with a sudden, horrid realization. "You don't think that—"

And for a terrible second, Jackson thought that maybe it was possible. *What if Henry and John and Chadwick never went anywhere but straight down into the ground?* "No…" he whispered. "Paul said he spoke to Henry."

"Future Henry?"

Jackson nodded. "Future Henry."

They continued looking around for any sign of a helicopter.

"I don't see anything," Robinson said.

"Me neither."

Then Robinson started moving around the perimeter of the ziggurat, stepping over rubble and watching his footing.

"What are you doing?" Jackson asked.

"Just want to see something." He stepped on a limestone slab that shot out from under him. It went flying into the center of the open temple and shattered on the exposed floor below. Robinson waved his arms in big swinging loops trying to regain his balance. He was up on his tiptoes and looking back over his shoulder.

Jackson watched, helpless, holding his breath.

Finally, Robinson found his balance and leaned forward. He lifted the brim of his hat and wiped a line of sweat away. "That was close," he said, flashing a smile.

"What are you doing?"

He continued to the back side of the temple, to where it had been sheared off by the Change. "I just have a feeling." He got to the other side without falling and carefully leaned over the edge, looking down to the ground. When he turned back to face Jackson, he was smiling even bigger. "Found it."

Jackson's heart spiked, and he realized that he hadn't actually believed it would be here. "Does it look damaged?" His voice echoed through the temple below him.

"I can't tell," he hollered back. "It's covered with debris. But it looks like the temple shielded it."

"Can you work your way down from there?"

Robinson looked around. "Yeah, I can get down over here." He pointed to his left.

"Then I'll see you there," Jackson shouted and began backtracking down the familiar route. He wasn't about to slip on a mud streak and land on his head like Robinson almost did. Not when they were this close to the finish line. But as he went, he slipped in the mud anyway and nearly flew off the temple's side. *Oh, Jesus,* he thought after recovering. He took a deep breath and tried to stop shaking. *Though I walk through death's shadow…*

Working his way down through the slick chaos the storm had swept against the temple's base, he wondered how much time they had left. Exhausted, he reached the outer perimeter of the wreckage and crawled onto even ground. He stumbled around the base of the temple until it abruptly stopped, the second half of it missing. He looked in wonder at what Paul had tried to describe to him, thinking it truly was like a giant, cosmic guillotine had come down out of the heavens and sliced it right in half. Only it wasn't sitting there in two halves. The operator had taken one of them with him, it seemed. Now all the levels, chambers, and corridors stood exposed. Leaning against the back side of the flayed structure was the top section that had fallen off. It was the size of a house, and Jackson knew the helicopter must be behind it.

The debris on the back side of the temple was considerably less due to the direction the wind had been blowing, and he saw what Robinson meant by the temple acting like a shield protecting everything behind it. As he got closer,

Robinson suddenly appeared, standing atop something that was still blocked by the leaning apex.

"Here it is!" he yelled, waving his arms.

Jackson hurried to him, reaching the fallen temple top and skirting around it.

And behold…

A Huey. UH-1B, he guessed. Olive green, outfitted as a gunship. And he was half-sure it had been taken straight from Ivan's 1969. It had been the jeep of the Vietnam War.

"Unbelievable," he muttered, jogging over to it. It seemed impossible that it could have survived the beating the island took, but there it was, as if it had been intentionally set right inside the east shadow of the temple, where it would be sheltered from the winds and driving rain. It wasn't even that dirty.

Robinson walked across the top of the chopper and removed some large palmetto leaves that were hanging over the two-bladed rotor. Then he hopped down and stood next to Jackson, studying the flying machine. "Can you fly it?"

"If it works." He'd only piloted the newer versions of the UH-1, including the civilian Bell 204 and 205, but he knew it was designed to be an easy fly under difficult conditions. He didn't think he'd have a problem. Other than the fact that its fuel had been sitting in its tank for over forty years, of course. Or however it worked—Ivan hadn't aged forty years in his trip to the future, so he supposed there was no reason to believe the helicopter had.

Jackson stepped in front of the rocket launcher's seven tubes and M134 Minigun and grabbed the big M60 machine gun that was set up outside the cabin. There was an ammo belt stretching from the gun to a large box sitting on the cabin floor. He looked through the cabin and saw the same setup on the other side. He swiveled the machine gun around, thinking.

Robinson noticed the concentrated expression on Jackson's face. "What are you thinking?"

"I'm thinking we could probably fit a few more people in here without these guns…"

"But…?"

"But I'm wondering if they're here for a reason."

Robinson nodded. "Like someone might be helping us out behind the scenes the same way that demon is orchestrating things for Turiel, or the way that guy Ronald helped Osiris?"

Jackson didn't answer, just chewed it over. Could Hunter have arranged all this while he was "backstage," as Daniel said he called it? Not if the helicopter had come at the same time Ivan and the cruise ship and the house and the Not Thems came. Which would mean that either they were insanely lucky, or that there was, indeed, another force working behind the scenes on their behalf. That was actually a rather pleasant thought.

He moved his hands over the crew door, his finger dipping into a few round holes, the paint chipped around them. The helicopter had seen action in Asia. The red and white peace symbol on the side of the gun mount and above the six-barreled rotary machine gun was a symbol of sarcasm targeting the "peaceniks" back home. It meant "peace through firepower."

He stepped onto the near eight-foot skid and climbed up behind the M60. The panel doors were already open, and he ducked into the cabin. He gave the inside a quick inspection, making sure both ammo boxes on the floor were full and lifting the ammunition magazine and checking the feed chutes. It looked like everything was hooked up okay and that the helicopter was fully loaded for battle. He found that both comforting and troubling. He was hoping for an easy transport mission, just pick up the Purees and drop them off on the ship. But if there were angels assisting them (which he assumed had just been Robinson's implication), and they had determined in their otherworldly wisdom that a fully loaded gunship would be most appropriate for such a task, then perhaps it wasn't going to be so easy.

"Well, all aboard, then," Jackson said, stepping out of the cabin and up onto the cockpit step. He opened the pilot's door and slid into the chair. He was in the right seat and signaled Robinson to walk around to the left side. As he waited for Robinson to climb into the copilot seat, he looked over the control panel and tested the pedals. Everything looked good.

Robinson climbed into the seat beside him. "You've flown something like this before, right?"

"Yessir."

"And it's like riding a bike?"

"Like riding a bike."

Robinson's eyes danced over all the gauges, dials, switches, and buttons, not understanding any of it. "Okay then…"

Jackson took a deep breath, exhaled it, then started flipping switches on the control panel above his head, in front of him, and between them. The helicopter started making noise. He looked over at Robinson, and they exchanged a lingering *can you believe this?* expression.

"You ready?" Jackson asked, anxiousness accenting his voice.

Robinson swallowed and then nodded.

"It's gonna get loud and a little shaky." He pushed down on the lever beside him and hit one of its buttons.

As the turbine engine came to life, it seemed to scream from a distance, the rotors beginning to move, crawling in a lazy circle. As the whine of the engine gradually climbed, reaching deafening levels, the rotors picked up speed. The helicopter started shaking violently, and Jackson could tell it was taking every ounce of resolve Robinson had not to jump out and run.

"You okay?" Jackson shouted.

"Whaaaaat?" Robinson called back.

He smiled as the whine of the turbine engine transitioned to the more familiar whop-whop-whop of the slapping rotor blades, and the shaking evened out. He stared intently at the gauges, making sure everything was okay.

He twisted the throttle while accelerating the engine to 6,600 rpm and the rotor to 324 rpm. Then he slowly raised the collective stick while applying some left pedal pressure. The helicopter grew lighter, and Robinson reached down and grabbed the sides of his seat. Jackson raised the stick a bit more, and the copter pulled up into a hover. Then, saying a little prayer, he dipped the nose and climbed, still doubting that this was really happening.

As they rose into the air, the temple fell away, and the horizon flashed pink, the dawn greeting them with a sparkling kiss off the canopy window. As they continued to rise, the battered island appeared through the downward-vision windows at their feet.

Climbing at about 1,210 feet per minute, they were at ten thousand feet in about twenty seconds.

"Unbelievable," Robinson moaned.

Whether he was talking about the destroyed island, the working helicopter, or just the day in general, Jackson wasn't sure. And as the sun broke through the bottom of the western sky, Jackson flew them out to sea.

HOMEWARD

"In the latter part of their reign, when rebels have become completely wicked, a fierce-looking king, a master of intrigue, will arise. He will become very strong, but not by his own power. He will cause astounding devastation and will succeed in whatever he does. He will destroy those who are mighty, the holy people. He will cause deceit to prosper, and he will consider himself superior. When they feel secure, he will destroy many and take his stand against the Prince of princes. Yet he will be destroyed, but not by human power. The vision of the evenings and mornings that has been given you is true, but seal up the vision, for it concerns the distant future."

—Daniel 8:23-26 (NIV)

And he had power to give life unto the image of the beast, that the image of the beast should both speak, and cause that as many as would not worship the image of the beast should be killed. And he causeth all, both small and great, rich and poor, free and bond, to receive a mark in their right hand, or in their foreheads: And that no man might buy or sell, save he had the mark, or the name of the beast, or the number of his name.

—Revelation 13:15-17 (KJV)

The spirit clearly says that in the latter times some will abandon the faith and follow deceiving spirits and things taught by demons.

—1 Timothy 4:1 (NIV)

Let no one deceive you in any way. For that day will not come, unless the rebellion comes first, and the man of lawlessness is revealed, the son of destruction, who opposes and exalts himself against every so-called god or object of worship, so that he takes his seat in the temple of God, proclaiming himself to be God. ... And you know what is restraining him now so that he may be revealed in his time. For the mystery of lawlessness is already at work. Only he who now restrains it will do so until he is out of the way. And then the lawless one will be revealed, whom the Lord Jesus will kill with the breath of his mouth and bring to nothing by the appearance of his coming. The coming of the lawless one is by the activity of Satan with all power and false signs and wonders...

—2 Thessalonians 2:3, 4, 6-9 (ESV)

Just as it was in the days of Noah, so also will it be in the days of the Son of Man.

—Luke 17:26 (NIV)

TWENTY-SEVEN

September 23, 2011. Morning.

Hunter came to his senses in midstride—dreamless sleep one moment, walking in a corridor the next. He blinked, looked around, confusion swirling through his brain like a hangover. The dreams…the visions… *How long has it been?*

Oh, it's been a little while, a voice answered in his head. *It's morning.*

He turned his head and saw the large man walking beside him. Turiel. One of the original that would one day be chained in Tartarus. Except now he would be skipping that little trip, wouldn't he? Because he'd bypassed about ten thousand years.

That is right. I spent the night in your head, reading every book you ever read, watching every "movie" you ever watched, listened to every lecture you ever heard. It is fascinating how much knowledge you have forgotten.

Hunter's head pounded, and he rubbed his temples. "Where are we?" He said it aloud because it hurt less than to think it.

We are on our way back to your world. Now that you have brought the key, we can use the machine this day to travel through the stars and break out of this prison.

Hunter shook his head, grappling with the angel's words. The prison he wanted to break out of had been created when Osiris tried to break Turiel and the other flesh-wrapped angels out of Tartarus.

I understand it is confusing for you. But your understanding is limited in these things. Even compared to my day and age. He turned his head and looked down at him. *Your "science" hasn't even brushed the surface of the universe, and what little you do know has been built upon knowledge handed down to you.*

The dialogue wasn't helping his headache, but things were beginning to explain themselves as he watched his feet traverse a black, polished floor. They were in a long granite tunnel, long bulbous lights shining overhead. Looking ahead, he could just make out a pinprick of light far in the distance. "We're in an underground tunnel that connects the temple to the pyramid." It wasn't a question. Things were starting to come to him again. "There's water around us," he muttered.

Turiel kept walking, taking those long strides, his robes dragging on the ground behind him.

"Aquifers." Hunter's headache was abating now. "Aquifers beneath the pyramid to produce an electrical charge." He frowned, thinking hard on things that seemed to be materializing from nowhere in his mind. "We're at intersecting ley lines, or what the Chinese called 'Dragon Lines.' Strong avenues of electromagnetism run through here, just like all the other megalithic sites of the past. Just like ancient Egypt and the so-called Band of Peace." He remembered

Chadwick talking about some of this but didn't know if it was a heightened sense of memory that was recalling the information, or if this was the leftover ability from wandering backstage still at work. "The blocks used in the lower levels have high magnesium content, just like the dolomite in the lower limestone blocks of Giza. For conducting electricity, the rest of the pyramid was sheathed in a whiter, zero-magnesium limestone that acted as an insulator."

You are trying to understand by comparing what you know of your science with our magic, or what you would call "technology." But your science is based on experience with explosive energy, and that makes a horrible interpretive lens. If you hope to understand, you must first appreciate what you would call "implosion" energy.

Something in Hunter's mind blinked, and he suddenly recalled a book he'd read about Tesla and Edison. He'd forgotten about that. Perhaps Turiel had left it out on the table of his mind after pulling it from those dusty shelves and reading it himself.

"These granite shafts are radioactive and maintain an electrical charge. Between the electromagnetic currents, moving water, granite, and the dolomite, the whole base of the pyramid is electrified. The charge from the ground works its way up through the pyramid and to the capstone." And then, in his mind's eye, he saw the sixty-seven ancient constructions along the bank of the Nile, all connected and energized at a time before the mighty river shifted so many miles away. They were like nuclear power plants that had gone offline, perhaps due to a global flood, the forbidden knowledge used to run them, and what they'd even been run *for*, lost to history forever.

Not forever. We will bring back the glory of his kingdom, and we will once again rule. We will free Abaddon from his chains, and we will retake the earth.

"You've processed all the information that has ever entered my head?"

Yes.

"So then you know the theories about the Sphinx predating the pyramids, and the underground passage that leads from the Sphinx to the Great Pyramid. I'm guessing you have a similar setup here."

A small grin pulled at the corner of Turiel's mouth. *I cannot wait to get to your world.*

Hunter recalled Chadwick saying that there were legends about the laws of physics being modified at ley line junctions and mystical experiences that enabled the viewing into different realms and times and was pretty sure he was on his way to experiencing something similar right now.

For a second, he put all the parallels between this past world and the future world of ancient Egypt out of his head and thought of his friends, wondering if they'd managed to get to the ship yet. He reached out, almost like he envisioned Luke Skywalker doing with the Force, and felt for—

There!

Paul. He was on his way to the coast, to where he and Daniel had hidden the Jet Ski. Only…there'd been a storm. And the Jet Ski was gone. People on his tail, tracking him.

He blinked, found the surviving Purees and Ivan huddled in the Crystal Caves, waiting for—

Jackson and Robinson. They'd found the helicopter! They were *flying* it! They had it over the water, looking for the ship.

The ship...was it still there? He projected his metaphysical senses outward, searching...

Before he could find the ship, however, he found something else.

The demon. It was on its way back to the door.

"What's it doing?" he whispered.

What happens to you and your friends is of no consequence to me. But my compatriot is intent on keeping your friends from escaping. For some reason, it feels threatened by that prospect, though I cannot imagine why.

"It's going to open the door."

And let the spirits out.

* * * *

Paul's physical body was growing weaker and weaker with every step, yet he'd never felt so light or free in his life. The effect that was having on him, however, was rather interesting. His desire—his *need*—to escape death had begun to ebb away; it was no longer such a grave matter of importance. The great Nothingness had always been there with him, haunting him. Never was there a day he couldn't feel its presence behind him, standing over him, the shadow of its scythe across his neck. But then, after Naga Hills, he'd started to think that maybe it might be a bit more than just Nothingness that awaited the dead. And maybe it wasn't hell, but maybe it wasn't something so great as heaven either. Maybe it was some strange half dimension sandwiched between two realities that was incompatible with the human soul. Maybe the afterlife would be like the Philadelphia Experiment, and he'd be stuck inside the hull of a marooned ship for all eternity. Such thoughts (and there were thousands like them) had always consumed him.

Until now. Now it was all gone. The Reaper had turned and walked away, the eternal void filled with a hope he couldn't explain but could feel with every part of his being. He wasn't scared of death anymore. It had lost its sting. And so the fierce determination to avoid it had waned and, in fact, seemed almost desirable in such a condition as his.

Rest, he thought as he climbed through the wreckage. *I can rest.* And oh, how his body rejoiced at such a prospect. How his spirit sighed with relief after fearing eternity for so long. He was no longer haunted by the girl, by his sins. He'd been forgiven, and he was free.

But still, he felt that to give up would be irreverent. Sure, he could die now. That would be easy. But perhaps, being redeemed, he owed it to God (to Henry, Jackson, and Johnny) to live.

He stumbled from fallen tree to fallen tree, the tangled debris wrapping around his legs and slowing him down. His head ached, and his arm throbbed. But he was almost there.

He climbed the top of a rise, and the ocean came into view below him. The sun was rising behind him, in the east, so the watery horizon was still smeared in dark hues, but there was enough light to know that he was in the spot Hunter had suggested. The Jet Ski should be just down there among the other Graveyard occupants.

Only there was no down there.

The entire tree line was a row of uprooted logs sliding back and forth in the surf, and either the Runner had been swept out to see, thrown inland, or was buried beneath the debris. Either way, he didn't think he had the time or energy left to do anything about it.

He sat on the grass and stared out at the ocean, all the ships that had made up the Graveyard washed away from the apocalyptic shore…and no more.

He slipped the rifle off his shoulder, took the sword out of his belt, and lay down. He should try to make it back to the Crystal Caves. Maybe Jackson and whatever Purees were left were still there. Or maybe they'd figured out a way to get on the ship themselves by now. He was still having trouble believing he'd slept all night long. Yet he was still so tired… If he could just close his eyes for a minute…

The sound of the waves crashing against the empty beach took him away.

* * * *

Jackson flew the helicopter out over the water. "You see anything?" he shouted above the noise.

Robinson craned his neck, looking down beside him. "Nothing!"

Jackson continued flying for another mile before banking west and putting the island to their right, following the coastline.

The water was calm now, placid, the commotion the storm must've raked across the ocean's bottom settling so that they could see clear to the bottom.

"A lot of sharks down there!" Robinson hollered.

Jackson nodded. There sure was.

Then Robinson pointed out the canopy and shouted. "You see that?"

Jackson followed Robinson's finger and saw what appeared to be a large disc-like object beneath the water, half buried in the sand. One of the gods' flying discs? Or the starship *Enterprise*? "Storm must've uncovered it!" he yelled back.

"What is it?"

"No idea!"

"Looks like a flying saucer!" Then he was pointing elsewhere.

An airplane, one of its long wings and its entire back side rising out of the white sands, shimmering in the current.

"Looks like a B-52!" Jackson exclaimed.

Then other objects began to appear, some rising out of the ocean floor and others resting completely uncovered atop it.

"They're all over!"

And as Jackson turned north, getting parallel to what was once the hook end of the island, they passed over a fleet of old wooden shipwrecks. He didn't know if they were all victims of the Bermuda Triangle, Osiris having summoned them through his portal over the years, or whether these were newer arrivals that just transitioned here at the Change.

More planes and boats beneath slithering shadows cast by circling sharks.

Jackson continued flying at three thousand feet, cruising steadily at ninety knots. The Graveyard flew past to the right, but even at a mile away, they could tell the storm had completely cleared the beach of all vehicles. Maybe some of the wrecks beneath them had been from the Graveyard, carried out to sea by the hurricane.

"Guess none of those giants made it too far!"

Jackson thought of their attempted escape from the beach yesterday and nodded. "Good."

Soon they were past the tip of the hook, but instead of the island angling northeast toward its original tip at St. David's, it went straight north as far as they could see.

Only it was no longer a dense forest but a flattened wasteland, the mountains standing naked in the distance.

"We have about two hours of flying time," Jackson said, eyes scanning the water.

"If the ship is still circling the island like it was, then it could be on the other side!"

That was true. But depending on how far the new coast stretched north, they might not have enough fuel (or time) to make it all the way around. In fact, it would be quicker to fly straight over the island and to St. David's. Of course, that was assuming the topography of that side of the island hadn't changed too much. No one had ventured that far east in the last three months.

They kept flying, hoping that when they finally did spot the ship, it wouldn't be staring at them from the ocean floor.

* * * *

Paul's dream was a good one and his sleep peaceful, so he was slightly annoyed when a loud thumping sound grew gradually nearer and nearer to his dream, ultimately shaking it from its reel and spilling it across the floor, waking him up. He opened his eyes, looked up into the thinning clouds, and squinted.

Whomp-whomp-whomp.

There was something out there over the ocean, a tiny black smudge against the brightening horizon. It was moving from his left to right.

And then it was past him.

What was that? He closed his eyes, not really caring, and placed the reel back on the projector, picking up the dream where it'd left off.

* * * *

There it is," Robinson yelled, pointing frantically.

Jackson leaned forward and saw a mark in the distance ahead. Relief rushed through him like a cool breeze on a sweltering afternoon. Hope still had a pulse.

The ship came up fast, and they could see the charred planking on the aft of the ship where Paul had made his fire. The top deck that had been cluttered with a hundred deck chairs was completely bare, the jogging track surrounding it spotted with puddles. The pool was overflowing from the storm.

"Can't believe I'm getting back on this thing!" Robinson grumbled.

The stories that Paul, Robinson, Li, Daniel, and the others had told about their time on the ship were less than comforting, and Jackson had to admit that the thought of being stranded at sea on the thing was a bit unnerving. But that was just the next level of this game, and they'd deal with it when they got past the current one.

He brought the Huey in low, slowing to a near hover. The downwash pushed rings of frothy veins into the water beneath them as he swung around the huge cruise ship. The reflection of the Huey stared back at them through the big windows of the upper decks.

"Looks like she made it through the storm without a scratch!"

Robinson nodded, then said, "The marina door is still open!"

Jackson took another pass around the ship, trying to see through the windows. He was going to be setting down on the top deck and unloading people, and he wanted to be as sure as he could that there were no giants or dinosaurs or closet demons waiting on board for them.

Robinson reached over and grabbed Jackson's shoulder. "You want to leave me so you have another seat?"

Jackson shook his head. "No! I may need you on the guns!"

Robinson shot him a thumbs-up, relieved that he wouldn't be stranded on the ship alone, but equally perturbed by the possibility of maybe having to use the helicopter's large machine guns. *Against what?* He knew the island would have one more trick up its sleeve. It wasn't just going to watch them leave.

Instead of following the coast back, Jackson took them on a straight line over the island.

* * * *

Again, that sound brought the reels of Paul's dream movie to a grinding halt.

Whop-whop-whop.

Only this time…

He opened his eyes and rolled onto his back, looking over the leveled forest behind him. And there, coming back the other way now, was the unmistakable figure of a UH-1. It was flying in and out of the circling mist like a serial killer stalking London streets, and Paul sat up. He watched it until it disappeared, confusion wrestling his mind into a pretzel and trying to tap him out. This was a dream within a dream, right? No way could there be a working helicopter on the island. And even if there was, who could possibly be flying it? Had the storm brought with it new arrivals? He supposed Hunter or Jackson could fly just about anything, but…

He stumbled to his feet, the will to live suddenly jolted back by a shot of curiosity. He followed the helicopter, thinking he knew just where it was heading.

But was there enough time left?

TWENTY-EIGHT

September 23, 2011. Morning. Crystal Caves.

Jackson set the helicopter down as close to the caves as he could get. It'd been a pretty quick trip back, but he had the growing sensation that they were running out of time.

"I'm not shutting down," he said. "Go bring back seven people as fast as you can. Tell them there's no time to take anything with them. If they hesitate, just grab the first seven people you see."

He nodded, opening the door. He stepped out, ducking beneath the blades, and ran off, disappearing into the broken trees.

Jackson reached back and grabbed the AK off the floor behind him. He held it ready while he waited for his first group of evacuees to fill the cabin. As he waited, looking for any sign of movement, he wondered again about the storm the night before. He was pretty sure Hunter hadn't known it was coming, or he wouldn't have insisted on them getting onto the ship right away. And that raised questions about what else Hunter might not know.

Hunter…

Was he even alive? If he wasn't—*please, God, let that not be the case*—they would still have to get to the ship. There was that black hole by the portcullis that might or might not be spreading, the closet demon, Osiris' Leftovers, and Turiel's empire of Not Thems. They couldn't hope to survive all that. Not unless they were able to work out some kind of peace treaty with the Not Thems, though that seemed rather unlikely. Haunted or not, the ship was their best shot at staying alive whether Hunter's plan worked or not.

And then there was Paul. How could he possibly leave without knowing if he was still out there somewhere? Not only had the man saved his life more times than he could count, but he'd saved Robyn's too.

I can't leave him. Or Hunter.

Though he realized he might not have a say in the latter matter.

Eliot…

He turned his attention back to last night, to his marriage proposal. It certainly wouldn't make anyone's top-ten list of engagement stories (he didn't even have a ring), but given the circumstances, it had all the needed magic. In fact, he thought, how many other people could boast of popping the question in an alternate reality where the mythological gods of antiquity roamed about beside the lost vessels of the Bermuda Triangle? Of course, that was a story they wouldn't be able to share with anyone lest they find the rest of their lives spent in padded rooms. But even as the memory brought a smile to his face, there was that little voice in the back of his mind insisting that there was someone else better suited for her, that he was robbing her of a greater joy. He had no answer to that voice, for part of him agreed.

"What do you think, Denise?" he whispered, thinking back to when he'd asked her to marry him.

She didn't answer.

Five minutes later, Robinson emerged from the woods with Robyn, Li, Mary, June, and two of the other women on his heels. A few of them had rifles.

Robinson motioned for them to put their heads down as they approached the deafening helicopter. Then he helped them up, one by one, into the cabin. They stepped around the ammo boxes and crowded on top of each other along the bench seats, their eyes wide with anxious panic.

Jackson got Robyn's attention and signaled for her to come around and get in the seat beside him. As she went around the front of the Huey, Robinson stepped toward the pilot door.

"Man one of the machine guns!" Jackson hollered over the rotors.

Robinson's eyes darted to the M60 behind him.

"Just have to pull the trigger!"

He nodded.

"Keep them all tight! No one falls out!"

He gave a thumbs-up and climbed up into the cabin behind him, taking a moment to pivot the big machine gun, testing its mobility and range of motion.

"Hi!" Jackson said to Robyn as she climbed into the seat and shut the door.

She looked at him with eyes full of amazement and uncertainty. She was clearly intimidated by the deafening noise—they all were—but there was the underlying hope that it was going to save them.

"Pretty incredible, huh?" he asked.

She leaned over, careful not to touch any of the buttons, and kissed him. "Take me home!" she yelled.

He smiled and then called back to the others, "Here we go!"

The helicopter lifted off the ground, hovered for a second, and then dipped forward as it climbed, the ground beneath them racing past, and everyone inside holding on for dear life.

* * * *

The tunnel seemed endless, and as Hunter continued walking beside Turiel, he began receiving flashes of the other happenings on the island. They were incontrollable, as they were before, and he couldn't help but wonder if his mind was a sort of broken radio picking up random signals, or if some other outside influence was tuning him into specific channels. In any event, he was now seeing the demon's form approach the door that once opened to a closet. It stretched out its black hand, talons scraping the doorknob, and pulled the door open.

But instead of seeing the storm-battered field on the other side of the freestanding door frame, there was another landscape present.

The demon stepped into it, leaving this world and entering another. Once through, it turned to the side and walked out of the frame, leaving the door wide open behind it.

Hunter looked over at Turiel, curious to see if he'd received the same vision, if he was still in his head and sifting through his thoughts. But the angel didn't show any sign of knowing what was happening above them, only an intense desire to get to the pyramid and free his brother, Abaddon from Tartarus.

* * * *

The helicopter came again, but Paul knew they wouldn't be able to see him amongst the mess of the forest. As it raced by overhead, he waved to it, his arms and shoulders crying out in protest. When it passed, not showing any sign of having spotted him, he collapsed with fatigue. It felt like he'd just shoulder pressed three hundred pounds. Figuring they were making trips back and forth to the cruise ship, he tried to think of a way to attract their attention before running out of transportees.

* * * *

Jackson brought the helicopter down between the radar tower and the tall funnel, the skids hovering just inches off the deck, the nearby pool spraying the air with mist. He held it steady while everyone jumped off and ran, bent over, away from the beating rotors. He blew a kiss to Robyn through the glass. She already had both her arms wrapped around the young girl, their hair whipping about their heads and tangling together. She returned his gesture with a bright smile as he took the Huey back up into the air, stealing a last-second, furtive glance at the closed doors on the sun deck, hoping everyone would still be okay when he got back.

Robinson waved from the cabin as they raced back to the Crystal Caves, the sun peeking up from behind the island and shining through the canopy.

A few more trips, Jackson thought, feeling the full weight of time standing on his shoulders. *If you're still with us, give us a little more time, Hunter! Just a little more, buddy!*

But at least he'd gotten Robyn off the island. That was mission number one accomplished.

He stared out the lower window at his feet as the blues below transitioned to pink sand and then to forest, looking for any signs of—

"What the hell?"

Flashes that at first seemed like reflections caught his eye, but when he looked over at the top of the hill it had come from, he saw a man standing there waving a rifle. He was shooting up into the sky.

Jackson banked to the left a little so that Robinson, who was still behind him on the 60, could get a line of sight on the man.

"You see that?" Jackson shouted back to him.

Robinson stepped away from the gun and leaned up into the cockpit. "Is that Paul?"

Jackson shrugged. "I can't tell! I'll get as close as I can, but I don't want to get too near that rifle in case it's not!"

Robinson went back to the gun as Jackson swung the chopper around, descending at a cautious distance from the bare-chested figure waving his hands. Then Robinson burst back between the pilot chairs. "It's him! It's Paul! I can see his tattoos!"

Jackson smiled. "Unbelievable." But Paul was on a hill that was surrounded by snapped trees, and there was nowhere to set down here. He began climbing again, looking for the nearest place he could use to rescue his friend.

* * * *

Paul watched the Huey rise back into the air and turn so that the figure manning the M60 could wave to him. He couldn't tell who it was, but it was all the assurance he needed. They'd spotted him, and now they were looking for a place they could set down.

"Oh, thank you, Jesus," he whispered. And it was the first time he'd ever mentioned that name with any sense of reverence.

The helicopter flew southwest for about a mile before it stopped and began a series of stationary circles, marking out an LZ for him.

He took a deep breath, shouldered the rifle and repositioned the sword, and started making his way in that direction.

The Vietnam era helicopter then continued east, continuing toward the caves.

* * * *

Hunter gasped when he saw the demon step out of the doorway and back onto the island, leading an army of invisible spirits behind him. At its command, the army took off like a swarm, darting through the trees and searching for hosts.

Hunter blinked, knowing that time was short and praying that his plan would work. The ground in front of him began to rise. They were approaching the machine.

He projected what was happening outward, finding Jackson as he piloted the helicopter, and planted it right in his mind.

* * * *

Just as Robinson jumped out of the Huey, a bubble of knowledge burst in Jackson's brain. Implanted from nowhere, he clearly saw the demon at the closet door, saw it step through and then come back out with an army of ghosts.

The ghosts…

Jackson blinked. *Oh no.* He started tapping his foot impatiently.

Two minutes later, Robinson was back and helping another group of Purees up into the cabin. Daniel was with them, and they both helped the older woman, Tabitha, up into the copilot's seat.

"We have to make a quick detour!" Jackson yelled to Robinson. "Get on the gun!"

Robinson nodded without question and told everyone in the cabin to hold on. And like the last group, all their eyes were wide with apprehension. As the helicopter climbed into the air, their eyes grew even wider.

Jackson put the UH-1B on a setting back toward where they'd found it and in just a few minutes was hovering over the clearing where the house had stood. The door was standing there all alone like the monolith from *Space Odyssey*, only instead of a monkey there was a demon.

It looked up to the sound of the helicopter, its eyes narrowing into slits, its thin lips spreading across a line of sharp teeth.

Not really knowing what to expect, Jackson hit the rocket release button and watched a rocket scream out of its tube and cover the three hundred feet in a streaking instant. It struck the ground right in front of the door. The ground exploded.

Holding the helicopter steady, with the passengers crying out in startled surprise behind him, Jackson waited for the smoke to clear. When it did, the door was still there, standing open, a large crater in the ground before it. The demon was still there too. It looked up and roared. Part of its black, insectile arm was on fire.

"*Hasta la vista, baby*," Jackson muttered, and he sent four more rockets at the door.

Right before the rockets struck their target, the demon turned and slipped through the door. It should've just stepped out the back of it, still in the same field, but instead it simply vanished. The entire area exploded. Fingers of fire stretched up into the air and threw clumps of earth, falling like rain, all over the field.

But then something inside the fire…blinked. Like a shimmer.

Spotting it, Jackson frowned. He wasn't sure if it was the heat from the explosion contorting the air, or something else. He fired one more rocket, and this one soared straight through the open doorway.

It didn't explode, at least not in this world, but it definitely resulted in a series of shimmers that distorted the flames crawling over the door frame.

And then came a full-blown glitch.

The door began appearing and disappearing, flickering back and forth as if a jammed projector was trying to get to the next slide but couldn't. The air around the door seemed to fold on itself, with a gash ripped through the smoke above the door causing the area above it to swing down and over the door. It was a dance of mirrors, and no matter how much Jackson blinked, his eyes couldn't make sense of it. A portal to another realm trying to keep from caving in on itself, it appeared to be reaching out and grabbing hold of whatever fixtures remained in this world. As a result, the two different worlds shimmered and shook in an uncoordinated dance as reality skipped on a broken track.

Until something that looked like a soap bubble consumed the door, refracting the fiery colors in its spherical constructs.

The door winked out, and the bubble popped—a giant rippled shockwave spreading outward in a ring pattern, its force blasting the surrounding area with supersonic energy.

The invisible wave hit the Huey, and Jackson had to fight with the controls to keep it steady. Its tail swung back and forth, but it was just a single passing wave, and Jackson was able to get the helicopter back under control.

"Everyone okay?" Jackson yelled back over his shoulder.

Robinson took a quick survey of the cabin, noting that the two girls, the teenager George, James, and Daniel were still all present. He gave Jackson another thumbs-up.

Jackson nodded and looked back down to the field, but all there was to see was pockmarked and smoldering earth. There was no sign of the door, the house that once stood around it, or the demon that had climbed out of it. It was as if it had never been there to begin with.

Jackson swung the helicopter around and headed back out to sea.

When they spotted Paul working his way through the forest and toward the designated LZ, Robinson started hitting the cabin wall, trying to get Jackson's attention.

"Look!" Robinson yelled, pointing east.

Jackson looked over to his right and spotted a line of people making its way through the forest. The line had to be half a mile long, end to end, and he figured there had to be two hundred people down there. They were moving fast and in one direction.

Toward Paul.

Jackson knew what they were. The vision of the demon had come with such details. The spirits unleashed from the doorway had found their hosts in the surviving men and women of Turiel's kingdom and whatever Osiris Leftovers remained, and they were all—men, women, children, giants, and every other abomination—tracking Paul's scent. Like zombies, they were completely unconcerned with their own fate and well-being, needing only pure-blooded flesh to feast on.

Paul had maybe a mile on them, but they were moving faster. It would be close.

* * * *

Paul watched them fly by, crossing in front of the climbing sun and casting its shadow over the remaining treetops behind him. The song from the phone came back to him then, and he began to whistle it as he labored for the LZ.

Amazing grace, how sweet the sound…

To his left, about a mile or so east, birds took flight.

* * * *

Jackson was relieved to find the ship still floating right where they'd left it. He was still expecting that last-minute curveball from the island. Maybe a whirlpool or tidal wave, maybe that Poseidon manifestation he'd helped spawn in the storm three months ago. But so far, other than the possessed army tracking down Paul, and the unknown shot clock winding down, it had been fairly simple.

As he lowered the helicopter, he saw that Robyn, Li, and the others were still on the deck, none of them having ventured into the ship's interior yet. Well, that was fine with him. He'd prefer to be there with them when they descended into those haunted decks. Because maybe that curveball he was waiting for was actually waiting for them, out here on the open water, in a floating prison from which there would be no escape.

The skids touched the vacant surface, and Robinson, getting used to the deafening helicopter and its sudden movements, quickly helped everyone out. When it took him and Daniel an extra minute to get Tabitha down out of the copilot's seat, Robinson exchanged an impatient, worried glance with Jackson, himself about ready to jump out of his skin.

Come on!

Jackson watched Daniel run across the deck and reunite with Li, both pointing down at the deck as they shouted over the rotors. Whatever they'd seen here, they were not too happy about returning.

Once Tabitha was huddled with Robyn and the other girls, Robinson climbed back aboard, and Jackson took them back up into the cloudy sky.

Tick-tock, Eliot…

* * * *

Hunter fell in behind Turiel's taller form as they finally approached the end of the long granite corridor and were greeted by a large flight of stairs. They were here. They were in the pyramid. This was it. Soon, Turiel would have him in the appropriate room and turning him like the key he was.

Tick-tock, Jack, he thought.

* * * *

Jackson was surprised to see how much ground the possessed army had covered. They were moving even faster than he thought and were going to overtake Paul well before he reached the LZ if they didn't do something about it.

Paul looked up and waved to them as they flew overhead.

"He's never going to make it!" Robinson yelled.

"I know! Hold on!" And instead of continuing straight to the Crystal Caves, he banked east toward the approaching army. If he could slow them down and alert Paul to their presence at the same time, then maybe Paul could find a way to put a little pep in his step.

The army was like a horde of mindless insects moving through the shredded forest, with only one thing on their collective mind, and Jackson brought the Huey as close to them as he dared.

Time to test the M134 Miniguns.

He hit one of the red buttons on the steering stick and brought the pair of rotary machine guns to life. Their six barrels spun, spitting six thousand rounds per minute at the wave of bodies below. Empty shells rained down in a glittering gold stream while trees splintered and then shattered, geysers of dirt shot into the air in long tracing lines, and bodies flailed in wild dances as blood exploded from torn flesh.

Gently nudging the Huey back and forth, Jackson continued spraying the possessed with the Gatling-style guns, left to right and back again. The devastation was incredible, and he could only wonder what kind of impression it was making on Robinson, who had never seen anything like this before. Body parts flew everywhere and, had this been Iraq or some other real-world mission, neither Jackson nor Robinson might ever sleep again without being haunted by the distant faces of women and children being punched into pieces by the twentieth-century killing machine. But this wasn't the real world. This was an Old Testament world full of demons and monsters, the offspring of Nephilim, all of them tied to the same fate as the island.

Spotting a giant in the crowd, Jackson fired a rocket, exploding its top half.

Robinson shouted his approval, cheering the direct hit while anxious for a chance to use the 60. He apparently had no qualms of conscience about their targets.

Then, just as Jackson got ready to fire another rocket, the biggest giant he'd ever seen stepped forward from the dispersing crowd and launched a spear up at the helicopter. It covered the distance between ground and chopper so fast that Jackson barely had enough time to jerk his head away much less maneuver the UH-1 out if its path. The beam went straight through the canopy and through the seat beside him.

As he swung the helicopter away, Jackson looked back and saw the spear's tip sticking out of the seat and protruding two feet into the cabin. Robinson was still there manning the machine gun behind his seat.

"That was close!"

"No kidding," Jackson mumbled. And he turned back just in time to avoid another twenty-foot pole. He banked, and the spear flew past, just missing the rotors.

Jackson fired another rocket, and this one exploded right beneath the thirty-foot giant, blowing both its legs off.

He swung the Huey south, and Robinson crossed the cabin, ducking under the spear, and grasped the other M60 door gun. He pulled the trigger, and shells started flying as the ammo belt fed through the weapon. He swiveled the gun, firing into the crowd as long as he could.

* * * *

Paul watched as the olive green UH-1 hovered less than a mile away and fired its miniguns into the forest floor. It swung back and forth, indicating a wide target area, and sent rockets screaming to the earth. He could feel the ground shake beneath his feet as smoke started climbing into the sky.

Uh-oh, he thought. Because he knew exactly what they were doing, letting him know that he had company and that he'd better pick up the pace.

The Huey started banking in what he interpreted as defensive maneuvers and then flew off toward the caves again, the door gun firing on its way out.

Great. Given the wide attack pattern and the length of the attack, Paul could only assume that a rather large army was heading his way. The fact that the pilot—who he was certain had to be Jackson—had to take defensive measures told him of the army's capability.

He pushed forward, still singing that old tune, knowing he needed another miracle.

TWENTY-NINE

September 23, 2011. Morning. The Ship.

After picking up Theodore, Pete the Norwegian, and four more girls, Jackson once again set the helicopter down onto the ship's open deck and let them loose. He again waved to Robyn, who was now standing in the middle of the growing crowd (still no one venturing belowdecks), and when she saw the twenty-foot spear sticking out of the cockpit's fractured glass, she began to make her worried way to the chopper. Jackson didn't have time for that right now, and he was off again. He figured two more trips would just about do it. But first they had to get Paul.

"Wait!" Robinson yelled, and slapped Jackson on the shoulder.

"What?"

"Set her down again!"

"What? Why?"

"Just do it! There's a rope!"

"Where?"

"Just set it down!" he cried.

Feeling the hands of time squeezing around his neck, Jackson brought the Huey back down. Robinson was out of the helicopter before the skids even touched the deck, and Jackson watched him sprint to a set of stairs and disappear to a lower aft deck. He picked him up again when he ran to the side of the ship, swung his leg up and over, and disappeared again.

Where the hell is he going?

Then a silvery object came flying up and over the side, clanging off the deck, and Robinson reappeared climbing up after it. There was a rope attached to the hook, and Robinson turned, reeling it up, hand over hand, as fast as he could. When he finally had it all in a neat spool between his feet, he picked it up and tossed it over his shoulder, running up the steps and back to the helicopter.

"This should work!" he yelled, tossing the rope into the cabin.

Jackson smiled. It was certainly better than nothing. "Find something to tie it off on!"

And they rose back into the clouded sky.

* * * *

Paul figured fifteen minutes had passed since the helicopter's attack on the unseen forces. Since then, the Huey had flown off in the direction of the Crystal Caves and come back again, heading out to sea once more. He knew now that he wouldn't be able to get to the LZ before being overtaken by giants, flying scorpion men, Not Them gladiators, or whatever else was heading his way. But still the words to the song wouldn't leave his lips. In fact, his mouth was getting adjusted to the strangeness of them, growing more and more comfortable with their depth.

...that saved a wretch like me...

He was ready for whatever was to come, death here and now, or rescue and the chance to live again. Either way a miracle would take place.

...when we've been there ten thousand years...

He could see the rise ahead of him now, poking like a pregnant stomach up through the rigid tree line. It seemed so far away.

Whop-whop-whop-whop...

He turned and looked up into the morning sky behind him, seeing the locust-looking helicopter coming at him against the thinning rain clouds. It slowed on its approach, and when it was just a hundred yards away, it swung its tail around so that it was facing the other direction. The grass flattened, debris scattered, and the remaining trees bent beneath the downdraft as the helicopter hovered just above so many pointed, cedar fingers.

Its guns blazed, and two rainbows of twinkling brass began falling from either side of the Huey.

Just before Paul turned back for the hill, something exploded out of the trees to his right. He spun, bringing the AK around, and watched three men, all naked and all with a savage sort of blankness in their wide eyes, come sprinting straight for him. He fired two bursts from his hip, and the jerking rifle seemed to set his whole body on fire. He screamed as spraying holes opened in the charging Leftovers, and they went down. He tossed the empty gun and drew his sword, but no more followed. Turning his back to the helicopter, he struggled to climb over a fallen tree, resuming his course to the LZ.

* * * *

They were everywhere. Like ants swarming to a lone crumb on a barren parking lot, the possessed army had gotten to within a hundred yards of Paul's position. If they'd taken any longer getting back to him, Paul would've been dead already.

Robinson worked the M60 while Jackson swung the Huey into better positions to use the miniguns. Blood, bone, dirt, and wood were flying everywhere, but still they kept coming.

More giants stepped forward, and Jackson was forced to climb higher lest one of them thought about reaching up and grabbing the chopper's tail, snatching it out of the sky and slamming it into the ground. No longer fighting each other, the Leftover giants and the Not Them giants were now united by a common, indwelling force. Naked, muscled monsters covered in tattoos were firing arrows at them while their armor-clad cousins from another era were launching spring-tipped spears. It was only a matter of time before one of them either hit the rotors or cut Jackson in half.

A rocket took the head off a helmeted giant and exploded in the chest of the caped giant that was behind it. Shards of bone struck the helicopter, cracking the glass at Jackson's feet. He banked right just as three arrows *thunked* into the Huey's belly.

"Toss the rope!" he called back to Robinson.

But Robinson was busy with the M60 and couldn't hear him.

Scanning the ground for signs of Paul, Jackson found that another line of people had separated from the main group and was streaking through the woods from a different angle. Paul was only twenty yards in front of them. Jackson set the miniguns on them, well aware that there were more women and children down there. But there was no time for remorse or guilt or moral consideration right now. There was only Paul being hunted by the residents of Naga Hills.

"Throw the rope!" he hollered again.

This time Robinson did hear him, and he let go of the machine gun in order to toss the rope that he'd tied off to a leg on one of the rear seats.

The bent shark hook he had taken off the welded rung of the ship snapped twenty feet from the ground. "Careful not to catch a tree!" he screamed, watching the glistening hook pass dangerously close to snagging some immovable objects.

"Just cover me!" he replied.

Robinson went back to the M60 and resumed putting down crazies.

* * * *

Paul saw the rope shoot out of the cabin and watched as it snapped taut twenty feet above the ground. He could make out a hook dangling at the end of it and recognized it immediately. It was the hook he and poor Eddie had used to scale the side of the cruise ship three months ago. "Oh, this is gonna be fun," he mumbled to himself.

The Huey hovered over him, the door gunner firing into the woods as a line of charging people suddenly appeared just thirty feet away from him.

While he might not mind the prospect of shedding his mortal coil anymore, being eaten alive by a demon-possessed mob wasn't exactly what he'd had in mind. He could see Robinson at the M60 and waved for him to come lower so that he could reach the rope.

The chopper dipped, and the hook bounced off the ground ten feet away from him. He ran for it, but just as he got there, the helicopter lifted, and the hook went slicing up through the air, nearly hooking him like a fish. He jumped out of the way and chased after it, the crowd ten feet away.

It hit the ground and he dove for it, dropping the sword in the process. But it skidded out from beneath his hands and slid across the grass, out of reach.

A body landed on top of him, and the air was chased from his lungs. Then arms were wrapping around his neck, choking him, hands grabbing his ankles, teeth and fingernails scraping and clamping all over. A knife plunged into his buttocks.

Paul cried out. His vision disappeared beneath a flurry of hands and feet and blood. He could hear the rest of the crowd approaching, ready to join in. He was going to be eaten alive after all.

...I once was lost, but now am found...

He moved his hand to his belt and managed to extract the dinosaur claw. He thrust it upward, felt it puncture flesh, and pulled it back. He did it again. And again. Stabbing. Ripping. The weight on top of him quickly subsided, and the sky reappeared as the men who had jumped on him now stood with their hands covering their stomachs, trying to keep all their intestines from falling out.

A silver flash.

Turning his head, Paul saw the hook skittering across the ground and coming straight for him. Summoning the last of his strength, he reached out and grabbed it when it passed. He slid across the ground, out from beneath the feet of the bleeding soldiers, knocking a few of them over as he went. The helicopter was right above him, dirt and debris flying everywhere, and he closed his eyes, holding on as tight as he could while the chopper lifted him off his stomach, off his feet, and up into the air.

A hand grabbed his foot, nearly pulling him back down for the last time. He managed to hold on, the hole in his arm screaming, and kicked the red-robed man in the nose, sending him away.

Looking down as he climbed, Paul watched the rest of the army congregate beneath him. They all stared up at him through frenzied, blazing eyes, screaming in demonic decibels.

He pulled himself up on the hook, praying his old knot would hold, and reached for the rope. Wrapping it around his forearm, he pulled himself higher, reaching with his left arm for an even higher handhold. Bringing his foot up, he was able to plant it in the curve of the hook and stand straight.

Fractured trees stood pointing at him like ready spears, waiting for him to slip so they could impale him. But he would not slip. He had the rest of his life to live.

He watched the island fly past beneath him.

...through many dangers, toils and snares, I have already come...

* * * *

Jackson set the Huey down gently, allowing Paul enough time to step off the shark hook and clear the area before the skids met the ground. Robinson jumped out of the cabin and gave Paul a wave and smile as he sprinted for the caves. Paul ducked beneath the rotors and opened the copilot's door. With painful effort, he climbed in next to Jackson, maneuvering around the giant spear that was occupying most of the seat space.

"You look awful!" Jackson cried over the noise.

"I feel worse," Paul responded. "Cuttin' it close as usual!"

Jackson smiled.

Paul put a hand to his head. The deafening, rhythmic thudding was trying to tease his headache back out of its hole. "Where's Robyn? Did she get out okay?"

"Yeah, we got her. She's on the ship with the others."

He nodded, surveying the helicopter. "Nice ride! UH-1 gunship..."

"I think it came with Ivan."

He frowned. "Nam? But how'd it get in the Triangle?"

"I've been wondering that too. Maybe a doorway opened on both ends of the Triangle…"

"You mean it got swiped off an aircraft carrier in the Indian Ocean back in 1969?"

He shrugged.

"Where was it?"

"Right next to your half-temple."

Paul recalled rather vividly his toes hanging out over the open space and looking down into a forest that hadn't previously been. He hadn't seen any helicopter. "How'd you find it?"

"Hunter told Daniel."

Paul nodded as if it made perfect sense. "He's in the temple with that Turiel guy. Or at least he was yesterday. I was up there about to meet my maker when he showed up and talked the bastard into letting me go." He didn't know how much Jackson knew about the Not Thems, but the drums were starting their thing in his head, and shouting over the noise was only making it worse. But there was something else he did want to know right now, so before Jackson could respond to the news of Hunter being in the temple (which he might or might not have already known), he said, "The AKs…they were using AKs."

Jackson nodded, somber. "There aren't many of them left, Paul."

Paul looked away, sadness filling his eyes. Then he asked how many trips they had left.

"One more after this one, I think."

"I don't know what Hunter is planning on doing, but I imagine he's doing it soon if he's still able."

"The equinox."

Paul nodded. "But I was just at the other cave, the one with the black hole. And, Jack, it's spreading fast. No matter what, we need to get off the island."

"Oh, we're getting off the island for sure."

And as if on cue, Robinson came running out of the woods with the last of the women, a person he didn't recognize, and Hap behind him.

Jackson shot a thumb back over his shoulder. "I think you should get on the door gun with Robinson."

Paul nodded and climbed out, pausing to help Hap up into his seat. He ruffled the boy's hair, glad he was still with them, and then climbed up behind the M60 on the left. He gave a little wave to the crowded cabin. No one waved back. They looked too terrified to do anything more than pray for deliverance as the earth fell out from under them.

* * * *

Hunter followed Turiel up flights of stairs and through corridors that led through large, empty chambers. The experts said the pyramids were tombs, but he remembered Chadwick scoffing at such a ridiculous and unfounded theory. There were no decorations in the pyramids. They were empty, barren. None of the things that marked the other tombs were present. Rather, the construction of the pyramids suggested its use as an instrument. After all, you wouldn't decorate your oven or the inside of your refrigerator. And as Hunter looked around him, at all the impossibly smooth stone, he swore he could feel the energy buzzing in the walls, in the floor beneath his feet, and in the air around his head.

We are almost there, Turiel's voice proclaimed.

He thought about stretching his psychic fingers back out into the island to get a glimpse of how his friends were progressing. But he didn't dare. Not now. Not this close to the main event. He was going to need every ounce of energy he could muster to pull this off. Besides, there was nothing more he could do for them now anyway. They were on their own.

"How much farther?" he asked.

Turiel turned and looked down at him, considering him. *Are you scared?*

"I'm anxious."

Turiel nodded as if understanding. *We are mere moments from the appropriate room.*

"Will it hurt?"

I do not think it will hurt you physically. But when I take out of your mind the knowledge that Thoth has hidden…that might hurt.

"Can't wait." And then a sudden, foreign thought slammed into him from nowhere, shaking the foundation of his very being. *What if I'm wrong? What if this isn't going to work at all?*

Turiel chuckled, his low, rolling laugh echoing off the walls.

* * * *

Jackson began making adjustments to their altitude and speed, steering toward the long cylindrical form lying lazily in the ocean's cradled embrace. It was truly a miracle. The ship, the helicopter, Hunter's going into the abyss and coming out with a plan to get them home… All the working parts, each one looking so dismal on an individual basis, actually worked together to form their escape. There was a Bible verse that Denise used to quote that came to mind now. *All things work together for the good for those that love God…*

Something caught the corner of his eye, a blur of movement off in the distant northeast. He turned his head and stared in that direction, straining to spot it again. He thought it must've been a bird. There was nothing there but an audience of gray clouds watching the sunrise.

He turned his attention to Hap and noticed that the boy, missing arm and all, seemed to be enjoying himself rather immensely. His eyes were full of excitement and wonder as he stared down at the blue waters, watching the sharks swim around all the wrecked vessels. He also noticed that he had a framed picture resting on his lap.

There was a tap on his shoulder. He turned to see Paul leaning over the sitting Purees and pointing out the side of Jackson's window; his free hand was clutching his butt.

Jackson followed his finger to where he thought he'd seen something, and this time he *did* see something. Saw a whole lot of something. "Get on the guns!" he yelled.

They were still far off, just tiny shapes against the distant clouds, but there was no mistaking what they were. The way the wings flapped, the long tails trailing after them…

The flying monkey creatures.

They'd abandoned their posts around the pyramid and were now coming straight for them.

Jackson thought he might be able to unload the present passengers and get back in the air before they were on them, but it would be close. He looked over at Hap and flashed a reassuring smile. "Hold on, kid!"

But all of a sudden, Hap didn't look so thrilled. His eyes were no longer on the water below but on the flock of flying rodents heading their way. He knew what they were. He'd seen them three months ago just after losing his arm.

Jackson brought the Huey down on the ship's deck for the fourth time, and Paul and Robinson hurried everyone off. Thirty seconds later, they were back behind the M60s and Jackson was climbing into the sky. He swung the helicopter around and raced the devil monkeys back to the Crystal Caves. The things had gotten closer while they were unloading, but the Huey was faster, and they'd have no problem beating them to the caves. The problem would be getting back to the ship. That was when they would be in position to do something, when they were between the Crystal Caves and the ship.

* * * *

Robyn turned her gaze from the helicopter when she felt someone tugging on her sleeve. Looking down, she saw Hap looking up at her.

"Hi," she said, and gave him a hug. "How did you like the ride?"

He smiled. "It was neat. Did you see all those boats under the water? And the sharks?"

She returned his smile. "I did."

He then lifted the picture he'd been holding, offering it to her.

She took it from him, immediately knowing what it was.

"I hope you don't mind; I took it from your room. I thought you might want it," he said.

"Oh, Hap!" She hugged him again, staring at the only picture of her parents she had. She knew that he understood the significance of the image, having lost his own parents a long time ago, their faces now an unrecognizable smudge in his memory. "Thank you so much." When she finally released him, she knelt and looked him in the eyes. "Will you do me a favor and keep it safe for me?"

He took it back and held it close to his chest. "Yes."

A tear slipped from the corner of her eye. "Thank you," she whispered.

* * * *

For the last time, Jackson set the Huey down on the island, and once more, Robinson took off for the Crystal Caves again.

Jackson looked around, contemplating what had been his home for over three months, understanding that this would be the last time he ever saw it. *Good riddance,* he thought.

Robinson came running back with Samuel on his back and the rest of the Purees right on his heels.

"Hurry up! Hurry up!" Paul shouted, waving his arm. Patrick, Wilson, Chad, and a confounded Ivan Major jumped into the cabin while Robinson helped Samuel get situated in the copilot seat.

"Ready?" Jackson asked Samuel after Robinson closed the door on him.

Samuel's sharp eyes, though hopeful, were dulled by a measure of sadness. He nodded, but it was clear he was feeling guilty at having outlived so many of his people.

Jackson understood those feelings (wasn't he feeling them himself?). He reached under the spear and gripped Samuel's shoulder. "You kept them alive for two generations. The fact that any might make it out of here is a miracle."

He nodded, conceding that it might be true, but his eyes didn't brighten any.

"Ready!" Paul shouted once everyone was in position. He was looking up at the sky for rats.

"Copy that."

They were about fifteen feet off the ground when the helicopter suddenly jerked sideways. Paul reached out and grabbed one of the Purees, keeping them from flying out the open door.

"What the hell!" Jackson cried, fighting the controls.

"Something's grabbed us!" Robinson yelled.

Paul looked down and could see something wrapped around the rear skid. He pushed through Patrick and Wilson, reaching between the two front seats, and grabbed Jackson's AK-47. Then he went back to the cabin door and stepped out onto the skid, crouching down while holding onto the M60 with his free hand. Down on the ground beneath them was a squid-like creature, one of its long tentacles reaching up and fixed around the right skid. It was trying to pull them back down to the ground, but the helicopter was too strong, and the bulbous creature was being lifted into the air. But then it shot one of its other arms out to a nearby tree, anchoring itself.

The helicopter lurched again.

Paul leveled the rifle across his lap and pulled the trigger. But with the helicopter swaying back and forth, he couldn't get a steady shot, and he missed the slimy arm. He tried again, knowing their time was running out, and that at any moment the chopper would be diving straight into the ground. He missed again.

Across from him, Robinson was trying to get the door gun on the thing, but it was directly beneath the helicopter, and he couldn't get it in his sights.

It threw another long snaking arm up at them, and this one went into the cabin, wrapping around the leg of a seat.

"Get it off!" Jackson screamed, starting to lose control of the gunship.

Patrick pulled a knife from his belt and stabbed the alien cephalopod's suckered arm that was fastened to the seat between his legs. Black liquid oozed from the leathery hole, and he started sawing back and forth frantically.

The creature howled and let go of the chair, the many suckers lining its arm suddenly filling with sharp daggers. The arm snapped, and a row of the tiny knives caught Patrick on the arm, slicing deep. Patrick screamed, and Wilson grabbed him to keep him from falling out.

Ivan started screaming.

As the creature's arm left the cabin, another one came swinging at Paul. A large tentacular club whooshed through the air, just missing his head, and slammed into the side of the chopper, denting it. Paul nearly lost his grip on the M60 but recovered in time to press the barrel of the AK into the club and pull the trigger. Pieces of it flew everywhere, and again the creature screamed in agony, a giant black beak emerging from its center and opening wide. It released the helicopter and fell to the ground, arms writhing and whipping about until it hit the ground and bounced, still tethered to the tree.

Jackson got the Huey under control just in time and got them out of there. "That was the thing that tried taking Robyn back at the house!" Jackson screamed when Paul climbed back in.

Paul caught his breath, his arm all pins and needles. "How much fuel we got?"

"We're still okay."

"Should we circle around the other way? Come at the ship from the north?" He drew a diagram on his palm.

It made sense. If the monkey demons were waiting for them, they could just circumnavigate them all together. But there was still the matter of time. He looked around, searching for any sign of the things. "You see them anywhere?"

"No."

Tick-tock, Jack. He increased speed, tilting the Huey's nose forward. "Let's go for it. Might not have time for anything else."

Paul didn't protest, and he set his gaze to the upcoming beach, where the trees ended and the water began.

Next to Jackson, Samuel wrapped his arms around the large spear and rested his head against it as if it were a pillow, his lips moving in silent prayer.

Then, just as they were about to clear the island, a cloud of huge bat-like figures burst out of the last line of trees.

Jackson swore, banking hard right and pulling back on the control stick, as Samuel shrieked beside him, throwing his arms over his face and lifting his knees to his chest.

The monkey bats filled the air around the Huey like an incoming swarm of locusts.

Jackson set both miniguns spinning, and half a dozen of the grotesque, ratlike men were instantly ripped to shreds. Jackson and Robinson fired the door guns as they flew past, sending more hairy corpses spiraling down onto the beach.

Jackson got a good look at a few of them as they flew by the cockpit, and he thought that they did indeed bear a striking similarity to those unicycle-riding monkeys from *The Wizard of Oz*—all covered in brown, matted hair, faces like rhesus monkeys with sharp needlelike teeth in their mouths. Some of their faces looked more like baboons, or even mandrills with their colorful faces and huge incisors. Their wings were bat-like, black leathery skin pulled taut like canvas over skeletal frames. And their tails… Their tails weren't the hairy tails of a monkey or a jungle cat or a dog, but of a rodent. Long, pink, hairless.

A few of them had managed to grab on to the skids and were now trying to wrestle their way up inside the cabin. One of them got its claws on the deck, and Paul, along with everyone else seated in the cabin, noticed that its hands were humanoid. Pulling itself up so that its chin was resting between its hands on the cabin floor by the ammo box, it set its yellow, reptilian eyes on everyone. It opened its mouth, exposing four tusklike teeth, and hissed in Ivan's face.

Wilson, sitting across from it, lifted the barrel of the AK he was holding and blew its face off.

Three more rats found themselves caught in the helicopter's rotors when Jackson suddenly dropped a dozen feet and banked right. There was a sickening *chink-chink-chink* sound as the Huey shuddered through the hairy flesh. Blood splattered the windows as pieces of the monkey devils went spinning crazily out of the blades, splashing into the water below.

Two more came at Paul, and he punched holes through them with the 60. One of them spun off, falling out of sight, but the other flew past him, crashing right through the cabin between everyone's feet and out the other side, a streak of blood left across the metal floor. As it passed, however, one of its wings caught Wilson across the forehead, nearly scalping him. It ran across his old scar and formed an elongated X on his brow.

Jackson continued firing the miniguns, and as they consumed the rat flesh, seared clumps of bloody hair and chunks of meat continued to fall, turning the crystal water red.

"Holy—" Paul swung his head around to Robinson. "You see that?"

Robinson nodded and looked again. A convoy of huge sharks were en route from the west, heading straight for the blood. "Must be thirty of them!"

Paul flashed him a nervous grin. "Don't fall out!"

* * * *

Robyn stood leaning against the railing, Li and Daniel beside her, and strained to see the air battle unfolding in the distance. It felt like someone was squeezing her chest, because she could hardly breathe, and her stomach was all in knots. There were so many of those bird things in the air, and the flashes coming from the helicopter were sending a steady stream of them down into the water.

"Come on," Daniel whispered. "Come on…"

Robyn looked at him and saw that he was even more nervous than she was.

"They don't have much time left," he explained, looking at the sun.

She didn't fully understand what it was that Hunter was planning on doing, but she knew that Daniel believed they all needed to be on the ship when he did it. She glanced quickly at the others, noting all the emotion in their faces as they sat huddled together next to the pool. They were happy to be leaving their prison, but they'd heard the stories of the ghost ship. And then there was their destination—a world they knew nothing about. She knew how they felt, but as she looked back to the sky, she wondered once more if it would ever really come to that.

* * * *

Rather than attempt to engulf the helicopter in a suicide attack, the monkey demons were now trying another approach, hanging back at a distance and firing arrows from long bows. So far, the projectiles just bounced harmlessly off the green metal.

Robinson cut two more of the creatures in half before his M60 clicked dry, the belt running all the way through, the ammo box empty. "I'm out!" he screamed, and he took Wilson's AK from him. With all the blood running into his eyes, he wouldn't be able to see anything to shoot anyway.

Jackson called back, "Miniguns are out, too!"

Robinson fired low, then swung the machine gun upward, taking the wing off an attacking baboon. He threw his eyes back to the ammo box, wondering how much more ammo he had left, and when he turned back to the swarm outside, he was greeted by a streaking arrow. It struck his leg, and he was thrown to the floor. He landed on his back just as the helicopter banked, and he slid through the blood on the floor. Both Chad and Patrick leaned forward to stop him, but their hands never found a hold. His head and shoulders shot into the open air on the other side, and he thought for sure he was going overboard.

But Paul reached out and grabbed his belt just in time. When Jackson leveled out, Robinson was able to sit up and grab Paul's arm.

Paul screamed, and his vision went black for a second as his arm seemed to explode and lava leaked from the knife wound in his butt and ran down his leg, but he managed to get Robinson back inside. "Try not to do that again, Crusoe."

Despite the pain in his leg, Robinson nodded. "Copy that."

And then they both noticed the bat monkey that was standing in the doorway of the unmanned door gun. It stood with its feet on the skid, its human hands on the machine gun and gripping the door frame.

Before anyone could react (all of them having been distracted by Robinson almost flying out of the cabin), the thing reached in and grabbed Chad, yanking him out of his seat and falling backward off the skids with him in its embrace.

Before reaching the water's surface, the monkey devil unfolded its wings and flapped into a hover. Then two other creatures flew over, and the three of them pulled the Puree into pieces. The sharks below were feasting on him seconds later.

"No!" cried Patrick and Wilson, leaning over and watching in horror.

Ivan had his knees pressed together and his hands over his eyes, praying that he would just wake up already.

"We gotta get out of here!" Paul shouted to Jackson, nursing his bleeding arm and barely holding on to consciousness.

"Hold on!" he answered back, and he dropped the Huey until they were racing feet from its rolling surface. At least the monkeys wouldn't be able to come at them from beneath now.

Paul climbed over Robinson and got on the other 60, firing at the trail of creatures following them.

"Look!" Patrick screamed, pointing back toward the coast.

All eyes shifted to the right. There, standing across the beach, was a crowd of people. Hundreds of them, all representing everything the strange island had cultivated over the years—from the first people Osiris had brought through the Triangle to those brought here by the Change and every abomination between. They were all standing as one, staring out over the water. At the ship.

"They know," Samuel said.

"Tick-tock," Jackson mumbled. Then he turned and hollered for Paul.

Paul's wounded head appeared between the two pilot seats.

"I'm not setting down!" Jackson explained. "I'm gonna tap the deck! Get as many off as possible! We'll do it more than once if we have to!"

"Got it!" He leaned back into the cramped cabin, careful not to slip in the blood. "Listen up! Those things aren't going to let us land on the ship, so we're going to set down and take off like this!" He motioned with his hands, skipping his right off the palm of his left. "I want Patrick and Ivan on this side—" he pointed to his left "—and Wilson and Robinson on this side with your feet on the skids! As soon as the skids are a few feet from the deck, you jump off and away from the helicopter!" He looked around at their faces. "Understand?"

They nodded, everyone but Ivan more than ready to get out of the loud machine. Paul put a hand on Ivan's shoulder. "Hey, buddy…"

Ivan took his hands away from his eyes.

"You want to wake up? You gotta jump. Understand?"

Blank stare.

"If you don't get off the helicopter, you will *never* wake up! You will be here *forever*!"

His eyes widened to accommodate even more horror, and he shook his head.

"Then jump!"

He swallowed, looked at Wilson and Patrick, who both nodded their reassurance back at him, and finally nodded himself.

"Good." Paul slapped him on the shoulder and then helped him into position as the Huey's shadow chased them across the water. The creatures, unable to match their speed, had fallen back, and Jackson was beginning to climb.

Once the other three were sitting with their feet out of the chopper and planted against the skids, Paul yelled into Jackson's ear, "Ready!"

Jackson flashed a thumbs-up and then looked over at Samuel again. "Can you jump out?"

Samuel nodded. "I'll certainly try!" Then his eyes narrowed. "What are you going to do?"

"Don't you worry about that!" Then he turned back to Paul. "Make sure Robinson goes, too!"

Paul nodded and turned his attention to Robinson. "Time to jump, Crusoe!"

Robinson growled. The arrow was lodged against his shin, the point sticking out the back of his calf.

"Want me to snap it?" Paul asked.

"Yeah!" He swung his leg back up into the cabin.

Paul tore the old Union-blue pant leg up its seam. It was so old, it barely took any effort at all. He ripped off a long strand and wrapped it around Robinson's leg, crisscrossing around the arrow so as to secure it in place and keep it from moving. He tied it off tight, and Robinson grunted. "Nice shoes," he said, commenting on the boots he'd taken from the dead Not Them soldier. Then he snapped the arrow about three inches from the leg.

Robinson screamed.

* * * *

Robyn watched as the helicopter began descending toward them. She could make out a long tail of those flying things chasing after it, but they were a good half mile behind now. She turned to Daniel and Li. "We might need to cover them."

They quickly agreed and went about gathering everyone with a rifle and moving them to the side of the ship. "When they land, those things are going to be coming fast behind them," they explained. "We need to cover them until everyone can get inside the ship!"

Inside the ship…

Neither Daniel nor Li wanted any part of that, but they'd have to face the ghosts again if they didn't want to be snatched off the deck by flying rat men.

* * * *

Hunter followed Turiel into an intersection, turning right and entering another long corridor that continued to incline toward what he assumed to be the central chamber, where the transition would be triggered at the equinox with the appropriate alignments.

THIRTY

September 23, 2011. Late morning. The ocean.

Jackson could see the Purees positioned up against the railing and aiming their AK-47s up into the sky. He thought they meant to cover his landing, but there would be no landing.

He came in as fast as he dared, aiming for the vacant spot between the radar tower and the stack, beside the pool. Samuel was standing with the door open and his foot on the step, everyone in the cabin ready to go.

"Go! Go! Go!" Paul cried when the gunship was still five feet above the deck. By the time they jumped, it would only be three feet. They all went, though Paul gave Ivan a little added incentive by pushing him out with his foot.

Concentrating on the controls, Jackson saw Samuel fade out of his periphery as he let go of the seat and fell to the ship. Then the skids brushed the deck, and he was pulling back on the stick, climbing back into the sky. When he turned back to make sure everyone had made it out, only Paul was still there.

Swinging the chopper around and making for another pass over the ship from the other direction, he shouted to Paul, "Get out!"

"What?" he asked, standing and leaning toward the cockpit.

"Jump!"

"What are you talking about?"

"I have to try to find Hunter!"

"Jack, he's in the pyramid! You can't—"

"I'm not leaving him!"

"Jack—"

"Take care of Robyn for me!" With that, he reached his left hand across his chest and up over his right shoulder, indicating a handshake. When Paul went to grab it, Jackson banked hard left, and Paul, the rifle still in his other hand, went spilling out the cabin door.

* * * *

Robyn watched through a frozen window of time as Paul fell out of the helicopter. He seemed to be falling in slow motion, his legs kicking, arms wheeling. He'd let go of the AK-47, and it was falling with him. But instead of landing in the ocean or striking the deck, he landed in the pool.

Snapping out of her paralysis, Robyn took off for the pool. Just before she dove in, Li right beside her, she couldn't help but take a quick look behind her, noting that the helicopter was heading back to the island.

* * * *

Paul sat, unmoving, suspended in space. There was a pressure in his head, and he couldn't focus on anything. Light was shifting around him, rays of it bending and flaring, hurting his eyes. He tried moving and noted the liquid resistance that responded, the way his jeans were clinging to his body.

He was under water.

Must've blacked out when I hit the surface, he realized. But what water was he under? He twisted, trying to see into the water around him, looking for sharks.

Hands. Not the nail-pierced hands that had pulled him out of hell, but hands that belonged to a feminine body—and not that of the malnourished and fragile little girl either. This was a figure of beauty, an angel with a halo of gold drifting about her head.

It was Robyn.

And then Li was swimming down beside her, reaching his arms out too. Had they jumped off the ship to rescue him? He hoped not. He didn't want to take anyone with him when it was his time to clock out.

Robyn must've noticed the confusion in his eyes, because she began pointing down.

He followed her finger and looked down, his lungs starting to make their request for air. About four feet below him was a white, circular drain. He looked back at Robyn and Li, then reevaluated his surroundings.

He was in the pool!

Somehow Jackson had timed the move perfectly, dropping him right into the deep end of the pool. He smiled and swam for the surface.

"What's he doing?" Robyn asked as soon as their heads broke the surface.

Paul swam for the side, and his body protested every stroke. "He's going back for Hunter," he said, grabbing onto the ladder.

"What?"

"He was never going to leave here without all of us."

She looked up at the fading helicopter and watched the man she loved fade out of her life with it. She started to cry.

* * * *

The monkey demons shifted like a flock of birds as Jackson flew straight at them. Like a flock of geese, they all maneuvered into a new formation as if responding to some unheard command. Jackson could tell that the rat monkeys were unsure whether to attack him or ignore him and continue for the ship. Finally, as he began flying above them, the formation split. Half of them kept course for the ship, and the other half turned after him.

At least I can take some of them with me, he told himself.

Arrows and spears started *dinking* and *clunking* off the bottom of the Huey, and he banked for the pyramid. He realized there was no chance in hell he was going to be able to rescue Hunter, but he had to try. It was his fault Hunter was even here. Then again, it wasn't hell that Jackson was hoping on.

He flew over the crowd of demon-possessed survivors…saw them all standing there, gnashing their teeth like zombies. They looked up and tracked him as he flew past. Then they turned…and followed him.

* * * *

Standing beside the pool and dripping wet, Paul watched the distant shapes divide, half of the creatures following the Huey and the rest continuing toward them on the ship. "Everyone inside!" he yelled. He stumbled toward the nearest door, by the radar tower, and ushered them all inside. When Daniel came holding Hap's hand, Paul pulled him aside. "Take them to the casino and keep them away from the windows. Don't let anyone open any doors. Keep everyone together."

"Where are you going?"

"I'm going to make sure none of those things get inside the ship."

Daniel nodded, took a deep breath, and went in.

* * * *

The corridor led to a vast chamber, and as Hunter stepped into it, the first thing that struck him was its sheer emptiness, as if it were a giant gallery, hangar bay, or an empty stone warehouse. It stretched outward a hundred yards in every direction. The ceiling stood a hundred feet above them and was covered in astronomical configurations. This was it. They were in the center of the pyramid. The control room, as it were.

Erect in the center of the room was a thirteen-foot obelisk. Spread out in a star pattern around its base were what appeared to be seven sarcophaguses.

As Turiel walked across the chamber, his footsteps echoing around them, Hunter noticed four shafts on opposite sides of the room, up near the ceiling.

Star shafts, he thought. And he was hurled back to the day Chadwick had found the giant sword off the beach…when he'd actually asked the archeologist what star shafts were.

He recalled Chadwick's description of the Giza pyramid, how the Giza shafts had been aligned to *Sirius* and *Zeta Orionis* in the south and *Beta Ursae Minoris* and *Alpha Draconis* in the north, and he wondered just what these shafts might be aligned to. *And when.* Hadn't Chadwick said the Giza shafts lined up with their stellar counterparts circa 2500 BC? Even though it was in 10500 BC when the Sphinx was locked into Leo, the three pyramids were aligned to Orion's belt, the Nile reflected Milky Way, and the belt stars were at the beginning of their 12,960-year processional journey back up to the top of the meridian and up through the ages?

And that had been one of the points of the conversation—that the pyramids could have been built under the skies of 10500 BC to look forward 8,000 years or built in 2500 BC and meant to look back 8,000 years. Chadwick had mentioned that the temple complex in Angkor was built between AD 802 and 1220 yet was perfectly aligned to the skies of 10500 BC…

Remembering the details of that conversation on the beach made Hunter's head spin as he attempted to apply its finer points to his current surroundings. Were they still in the Atlantic? Was this pyramid "synced" to the same celestial properties as Osiris' pyramid had been? Or had the Change moved them to another location altogether? Perhaps it wasn't Ivan and Mollings that had traveled so far… Just which hemisphere did this pyramid represent?

Turiel looked back over his shoulder, reading all his confused thoughts, but Hunter couldn't stop himself.

First Time…*Zep Tepi*… Chadwick said that some believe First Time reoccurred at the start of every Phoenix cycle, which was the 12,960-year half-cycle of the Great Year that ends with cataclysm. And they were supposedly in the period of the Fifth Sun, about to make the transition into the Sixth and into a new age. The previous Sun had ended with a global flood. *Noah's flood?* If so, that would've been about 9600 BC, the date Plato gave to the sinking of Atlantis.

Hunter stared at Turiel, trying to place him within such a context. He'd watched him rebel against God as part of the Third. Watched him set aside his first estate and step onto Mount Hebron in the days of Jared. And God would (had) destroyed the world with a flood because of what he and his minions would do (did) to creation. So when was *this*? It was obviously prior to the Flood, because Turiel hadn't seen it yet. But he knew it was coming, and he'd set out as a priest of the Sacred Feather to accomplish what the hermetic text of *The Sacred Sermon* declared—*And there shall be memorials mighty of their handiworks upon the earth, leaving dim traces behind when cycles are renewed.*

But which cycle was this? Where did Lucifer's rebellion correspond to the different Suns? Did it? When was his Golden Age? When, as the Book of Ezekiel suggests, did he rule the earth as God's high priest? Chadwick said some believed the Fifth Sun would end on December 21, 2012, at the end of the Great Year. And could that be the Apocalypse described in the Book of Revelation? Could the Fifth Sun end with the fifth angel being given the keys to the bottomless pit? If so, the Bible spoke of a Tribulation period the likes of which the world had never seen before, followed by a thousand years of God reigning in peace.

But…

Wasn't this whole demonic conspiracy to free Abaddon from Tartarus at the end of the age meant to trigger a war that would no doubt *be* the Great Tribulation itself? A war that would initially seem to be won by the forces of Darkness when the angel of the bottomless pit, "whose name in the Hebrew tongue is Abaddon, but in the Greek tongue hath his name Apollyon" who "once was, now is not, and yet will come" shows up as the returned Apollo? If that was the case, then Hunter was in the midst of a struggle between what the Bible prophesied to be the story's end and Satan's attempt to rewrite it.

Turiel walked to the obelisk, running his fingers against the smooth surface of one of the coffins. Only they weren't coffins, Hunter realized. They looked more like the hibernation pods portrayed in sci-fi movies. Ones astronauts would spend years sleeping in suspended animation in while their vessel hurled them through space.

Something began nagging the back of Hunter's mind. There was something about the number of them that was bothering him. Seven. Seven. *Seven…*

Seven Sages.

And then the Emerald Tablet of Thoth the Atlantean came crashing through his brain, Chadwick explaining that it told of Thoth's escape from Atlantis in a pyramid-shaped spaceship at the end of the previous cycle and how he then returned through a portal once the cataclysm was over.

His eyes shot up to the stars, constellations, and planets. *No…*

Turiel raised a hand and beckoned him with a finger. *Come and fulfill your destiny as the key that will unlock the pit and release Abaddon from his prison.*

"You catch on quick for an antediluvian," Hunter mumbled, hoping that what the angel just said wasn't true. Yet, even if it was true…that part of the end had already been written.

He stepped forward, approaching the gold-plated pods, refusing to believe that they belonged to the Seven Sages.

As he approached the obelisk, thin bands of light began to seep out of the four star shafts.

Showtime, he thought.

* * * *

Paul was positioned in the starboard stairwell on the landing between decks eleven and thirteen. Mary and another girl named Julia were next to him, the three of them aiming their AK-47s back up at the door they'd used to enter the ship. Paul knew Robyn, Li, and Patrick were in like position on the port side, the six of them waiting, hoping the rat demons wouldn't find alternative points of entry.

They didn't have to wait long.

The first creature swung the door open and stepped across the threshold. Its vampire wings were folded, and it wiggled itself through the doorway. That was when Paul pulled the trigger, the girls doing the same.

The hairy demon flew backward and landed out on the deck.

They stopped shooting and held their breath. They could see shadows shifting around the door and could hear grumbling noises outside as the creatures decided who to send in next.

It was of the mandrill-looking variety. It stuck its long colorful face into the ship's darkness, and it was clear that flying over the sparkling water for so long had rendered it momentarily blind indoors. Paul blew the top of its head off. It collapsed in the doorway, its body keeping the door from closing again.

Muffled reports from Robyn's team on the opposite side of the ship began going off as the horde of winged monkeys began pressing in through both entranceways.

Paul and the two girls put down every rat man that tried coming down the stairs, and soon a there was a pile of tangled, bloody hair clogging the doorway. Opossum tails slithered out of the mess like pink snakes, and baboon faces peered out of it, locked in gaping, big-toothed howls. Blood was running down the walls.

Paul slammed in his last mag and hoped they had enough ammo left to avoid hand-to-hand combat. He'd seen how easily they'd torn Chad apart, and he wanted no part in getting that close to them.

The assault stopped, and all they could hear was the ringing in their ears. Empty shells were scattered around their feet and down the stairs behind them.

"Are they all dead?" Mary shouted, her voice echoing in the stairwell.

"I don't know," Paul answered.

Either they'd stopped coming because they were all dead, or because no more bodies could squeeze through, or because those remaining had decided on a different approach.

Paul looked at the two girls and blinked, his vision swaying. He leaned against the wall. "Good job," he said. "I'm gonna go have a look-see. Don't shoot me, okay?" Then he stopped. "Do you have any more magazines?"

Mary pulled one out of the back pocket of her pants. "Last one," she said. "It's all they had left."

"What about you?" he asked the redheaded Julia. "Whatever is left in this one—" she tapped the side of the banana clip "—is what I have left."

"Okay." He stumbled up the steps, his boots kicking empty shells into a tinkling melody. He walked around the monkey devils that were hanging inverted on the steps, noting their stench and stepping on leathery wings that had come unfolded in death. He approached the pile in the doorway and tried to see around it or over it but couldn't. He sighed, took one look back down at the girls, and started climbing.

He had to keep himself from vomiting as his hands dug into clumps of knotted hair looking for handholds. His butt screamed as he climbed up on top of the mound, his bare chest rubbing against slimy tails and sharp talons that poked out of the wings. When he was finally on top, he aimed the rifle out onto the deck. There was nothing. He sat there for a moment, letting the ocean air sweep over him.

"Are there more?" Mary called up after him.

"No." He worked his way back down off the pile of bodies and descended the stairs. "Let's go see how the others made out."

Julia picked a clump of bloody hair off his back when he walked by.

"Thanks," he said, really seeing her for the first time. He thought she was rather gorgeous.

He led them into the ship and found Robyn, Li, and Patrick running out of the other stairwell ahead of them.

"You okay?" Paul asked.

They all nodded.

Li asked, "Do you think we got them all?"

Paul shrugged. "I didn't see any more on the deck. How much ammo do you have left?"

"This mag."

Everyone else nodded in agreement. They were down to pocket change.

Paul sighed, his head now a pounding symphony after all the shooting in the confined stairwell. "Guess we should go up on top and make sure. If we're going to be here for a while, we don't need any of those things nesting in a ventilation shaft somewhere."

* * * *

Daniel couldn't keep his eyes from darting to the doors. They were in the casino, listening to the distant reports of gunfire, wondering if the monkey demons would be coming in to get them. But that was only part of Daniel's concern. He was thinking back over the last three months. Of when this ship had been a prison, he and Hunter its prisoners.

Yesterday, he thought. *That was only yesterday morning…* And, suddenly, as it time finally caught up to him, he felt the sudden, dizzying weight of all he had endured. He fell into a seat and rested his head in his hands. How was it possible that they'd spent three months on this ship? It just wasn't possible. Not unless one of the time skips they'd experienced had jumped over a few rows on the calendar. And why not? Hunter had said this was the present, but maybe he'd been looking for September 22 all along, the day before the equinox. In fact, the more he thought about it, the more certain he was that that was exactly what had happened. So how long had he actually been on the ship? There was no way to know.

When he looked up again, he saw Hap wandering near the doorway to the hall.

"Hap!" he called, motioning him toward him. The boy didn't need to step out the door and enter that future world he'd seen with demons circling an obelisk under an ash-filled sky. Having been born on the island, he didn't know what that place was, but when they were around the fire yesterday, Robinson said it was the Washington Monument in Washington, DC. The way they were talking about it, it must've been the end of the world or something. All he knew was that a strong sense of evil had been in the air, and he never wanted to go back there again.

Hap came over to the round table, the framed picture under his good arm. "What is it, Daniel?"

"Sit with me, will you?"

He planted his misshapen, boyish body in the chair beside him.

Daniel noticed the picture. "Did you go back and get that for Robyn?"

He nodded.

"I bet she appreciated that." He looked over the boy, wondering what had happened to him. He hadn't caught the whole story yet, of what had happened to Pierre in that house that came with the Change. He wasn't about to ask Hap about it though. "Did you miss me?"

The boy smiled. "Of course. We all thought…" He trailed off.

"I thought so too." He looked around. "I was here. On this big boat the whole time." He thought of the giant they had killed over and over. Wondered if it had regenerated again, or if time on the vessel had continued linearly since they'd left yesterday morning and it was still dead in the stairwell. He didn't think Hap needed to know about that just yet, and hopefully not at all. "This new world we're going to… I hear it has all kinds of things like this."

Hap's lips spread into a courteous smile, but it didn't manage to convince his eyes.

Samuel pulled a chair out from beneath the table. "Mind if I join you?"

Hap shook his head, and Daniel gestured at the open spot.

"How are you doing?" Daniel asked him. He'd never seen him looking so old and weary, and this at what could finally be the hour of their salvation. But he supposed he knew what his leader was feeling. In different ways and on different levels, they were all feeling it—the price of admission.

Samuel blinked. "It is a lot to take in, isn't it?"

Daniel didn't know if he was referring to the ship or their overall circumstances and the sudden speed at which events flung them here. He looked back to the hallway, thinking back to all those rooms. He ruffled Hap's hair. "You really have no idea."

* * * *

Jackson was over the New Territory and retracing his journey from the day before. It looked so much different at a hundred feet, and he could see all the footpaths, roads, and villages they'd passed by unbeknownst. The storm's devastation was awesome, and most of the settlements he saw had been flattened. Stray animals were wandering about everywhere, unsure what to do amongst all the debris. He saw more fortifications, temples, monuments, and broken-down carts and wagons. It was a whole other civilization, imported right on top of them. But from where? From when? Was this Turiel really one of the original Fallen angels, one of the witnesses of First Time, of the so-called Golden Age? Was that Atlantis? Were the Not-Thems really Atlanteans?

He didn't really care at this point. Whatever interest he had in such things had dissipated rather drastically once Osiris had left the island and his hold over him was broken. Yeah, he might have Nephilim in his blood, and that blood might have naturally attracted him to such things, but as exhibited by Johnny, the power of God was greater. He only wanted to get home and had been more than ready to take that trip. But in the end, when push came to shove, even with Robyn standing there on the deck, he knew he couldn't leave Hunter behind.

Raindrops began splashing against the canopy as more rain clouds drifted in. Looking behind him, he could barely make out the monkey demons. They couldn't keep up with him, and they had to be tired by now.

He flew toward the mountains, still uncertain of what might be on the other side of them. Perhaps an even greater city from some other place or time. Had the Not Thems explored north beyond the mountains the same way they'd tested their new southern borders?

A piercing sparkle caught his eye like a lighthouse laser. It came through a break in the clouds, slicing open the darkening sky from the northeast. He turned the Huey toward it and soon could make out the crystal capstone protruding up into the clouds, two mountain peaks standing to attention behind it.

* * * *

The seven cryogenic chambers (if that was what they were) were bigger than they looked from the other side of the enormous room. They weren't so large as your typical Nephilim giant, but they were certainly larger than your average Joe. Like Turiel.

Hunter wondered who the other six chambers belonged to, but before he could take any guesses, the thin bands of light slipping out of the four shafts grew into bars. They shot across the room and struck the obelisk on its four sides.

It began to glow.

Either some sort of light-activated chemical or heat-induced charge began to shine up and down the sides of the device, running like water through the engraved characters of some ancient language.

Turiel stepped up onto a small platform that was positioned on the north side of the obelisk, and reached out his hand, placing it in a shallow groove.

Suddenly, the capstone exploded with blinding light, and Hunter had to shield his eyes. When he next looked, there was a beam of light flowing out of the capstone and reaching up to the ceiling. Other, smaller lines moved off the cap as if it were a disco ball. But as Hunter looked at the points of light and the celestial images they were touching, he knew the lines were not random reflections.

The ceiling came alive.

The light reacted with the designs and turned the whole display into a holographic presentation of the galaxy.

Hunter stared in awe at the celestial map that filled the top half of the chamber.

Son of Adam, Turiel called for him.

He turned in time to see the angel reach out his hand toward him. And then he was flying across the remaining twenty or thirty feet, the toes of his boots dragging across the smooth surface of the floor.

When Turiel caught his forehead in the open palm of his hand, Hunter closed his eyes, first feeling the pressure of his fingers squeezing his temples and then feeling his brain being pulled open with the psychic extension of those long fingers. This was it. This was when the key would be extracted and when he would need to do that thing. That thing he couldn't even put to words, but somehow knew exactly how to do it.

The room started to hum.

The floor vibrated.

Other noises from all around him, shafts opening and closing, the room turning…

He opened his eyes and looked up through the spread fingers and saw the ceiling rotating. All those stars and planets… They slid up and down meridians, rotated on their axes, tilted through precessions, and orbited the sun as a certain time and date was calibrated for a specific location.

The noise grew so loud that it was soon deafening, and everything shook. The covers on the capsules sprang open, revealing seats inside.

Hunter screamed.

* * * *

Jackson flew over the valley. What hadn't been destroyed by the battle and the dinosaurs had been toppled by the storm. There were piles of rubble everywhere, and he could only see one obelisk still standing along the main street.

He saw a two-legged dinosaur standing at the edge of the valley wall. It was reaching down through a thatching of fallen trees and picking at a giant that had gotten buried beneath. When the chopper's shadow fell across it, and the sound of the blades echoed throughout the valley, the lizard lifted its head and roared.

Jackson took the Huey closer to the ziggurat temple. Bodies lay scattered all around its base, as if the wind had picked them all up and swept them into the courtyard. Or maybe the closet demon had done that. Scores of smaller velociraptor-type dinosaurs were ripping off limbs and yanking out intestines.

Other than a few cracked columns that traced the ziggurat's base and upheld the palace section, the temple seemed to have made it through the storm unscathed. He hovered in front of the balcony that he'd seen Robyn jump from. He hadn't had a chance to talk to Paul about the whole ordeal, and his mind sifted through all the possible things Paul might have saved her from. He could see the form of a large bed through the opening behind the railing and shuddered.

Everything looked still, quiet. So he banked left and circled the structure. No signs of activity—other than extinct reptiles chewing on ancient antediluvians. He looked up to the pyramid, knowing that was Hunter's final destination. And judging from the sun's position (if noon was even a target time), then his friend should be well on his way there by now.

A road ran out the back of the temple, pointing to the pyramid, and Jackson followed it.

The mile between the temple and the pyramid turned out to be more like two, their previous calculations grossly underestimating its enormity. It was at least twice the size of the Great Pyramid of Giza. And if it weren't for the slightly distorted image and another Huey flying straight at him, he would've flown straight into the mirrored image of the world behind him.

The surface of the pyramid wasn't glass either but sheathed in a more metallic substance. Jackson absentmindedly compared this pyramid to the ones back home, noting that Egypt's pyramids had been stripped of their sheathings during the Middle Ages by mosque builders. But he knew this sheathing was different, and he wondered if he was staring at *oreichalkos*—the shiny metal Plato said the Atlanteans used.

I don't care, he told himself, peeling his eyes from it. He looked to the ground and could see the stream that ran down the left side of the valley disappearing into the base of the pyramid. *Aquifers*, he realized. And again, he told himself that he didn't care. If he made it out of here (which was growing more and more unlikely), he'd be happy to never see another megalithic structure again.

He moved the Huey laterally, looking for an entrance while marveling at the stupidity of his mission. If Hunter was about to beam out of here like Henry, John, and Chadwick had, then all he was about to accomplish was being the only one left behind (though according to Hunter there would be nothing left behind this time). But how could he leave without knowing? And he suddenly wondered if he was subconsciously trying to kill himself. Because there was no reason to think that Hunter wouldn't transport out of here the same way Henry had. And what if he did find him, ran into him just in time to destroy his plan? Maybe his presence would disrupt the escape formula Hunter had figured out, and so damn them all to this place forever.

Is that what I'm doing? Trying to die, because I can't live with the guilt of what I've done?

"Piss on that," he said aloud, and started to swing the helicopter around.

The pyramid began to glow.

Squinting, he could see the reflections in the surface trembling as the structure began to reverberate. The water in the stream was sloshing.

This is it, he thought. It was happening. Even over the rotors, he could hear a resonating, high-pitched hum. The brightness was intensifying, blinding.

He worked the stick and pedals, pulling back into the air. There was no time left. He took off for the coast, certain he wouldn't make it back to the ship.

And then there was a crash, and the world heaved in front of him, spinning uncontrollably as alarms blared in his ears. He fought the controls as best he could, but he was so dizzy, and the chopper was shaking so much that he couldn't even determine what direction he should be trying to go. Then, as the mountains, trees, and pyramid streaked past the canopy in a sickening medley of smeared, whitewashed color, he caught a fleeting glimpse of the biggest giant he'd seen on the island thus far. It had to be thirty feet tall, the sword in its hands another twenty. And he knew what had happened.

The giant had sliced the chopper's tail off with its sword.

Without the tail rotor, the helicopter had no way to fight against the torque being generated by the propellers. If he had been flying at least sixty knots, he might have been able to keep it straight via weathervaning, though he didn't know if this particular UH model was capable of that or not. And depending on how much of the tail the giant had swiped, it might not have made a difference. Regardless, he was going down. All he could do was go into idle and try to control his descent as much as possible by using the twist grip to steer the nose.

The mountains flashed by the canopy every half second as the trees below got closer and closer. Would he hit the trees or the mountain first? It'd be a close call, but either one was going to kill him.

And then the trees were past, their splintered points scraping the belly of the spinning Huey, and slate gray and craggy granite were the only things he could see now.

Jesus, forgive me…

Denise—

A flash of brilliant light filled the cockpit as a powerful shockwave tore through the air. The light left him blind, and the energy slammed into the old helicopter, hurling it into the side of the mountain.

* * * *

Paul followed Li back up the stairs, navigating the mangled bodies of the monkey devils. When they reached the door leading out to the deck, they worked at dismantling the pile blocking the doorway. They pulled the bodies away and rolled them down the stairs. They tumbled awkwardly, limbs cracking and bending in unnatural positions, their wings snapping beneath the weight of the corpse coming down behind them. When the doorway was finally clear, they were both sweating, and Paul's headache was near unbearable.

"Ready, Bruce?" Paul asked.

Li looked at him, still not understanding his nickname. "Yeah."

They stepped onto the deck and into a light rain, rifles sweeping back and forth over the pool area and the radio tower beyond. Then they raised their rifles, spinning around and aiming them up at the funnel behind them.

Nothing.

Just the sky and the hangover clouds from the night before drifting gray and black in a lazy slide across the sky.

"You hear that?" Li asked.

All Paul could hear, other than the soft pitter-patter of rain on the sundeck, was his screaming headache. But he followed Li to the side of the ship and looked over the railing.

Four or five of the bat-winged monkeys were thrashing about in the water below as large fins sliced the water around them. Li and Paul could clearly see the long bodies of the sharks attached to those fins as they circled their prey.

The monkey men tried getting away, but their wings were spread out like flotation devices, and they weren't strong enough to fold against the water. That left them hanging in suspension, helpless.

Li turned his head and faced Paul. "Did you really see Eddie get eaten by those things?"

"More like I heard it," he answered.

But before Li could grow sad or inquire further into the events of that night, one of the sharks below took a quick, experimental bite out of a hairy thigh. The monkey's face dipped beneath the water, its human hands slapping at the surface. Blood flowed out of it in red clouds.

Then another shark took a bite. And another.

Soon, the entire area was a frothing, maniacal bloodbath.

Looking up, Paul set his gaze on the island. He could just make out the mountain peaks of the New Territory. He wondered if Jackson had a plan or not. Wondered if he'd ever see him again. He never did get to forgive him.

A flash.

It appeared at first like an explosion—that split-second point of origin stamped on the retina and held up in the mind's eye. The instant, blazing whiteness that followed consumed everything, and Paul threw his arm up over his eyes, turning away from the horizon. An instant later, an invisible wave of energy struck the side of the ship and sent Paul and Li sprawling across the deck.

* * * *

He was still screaming. The machine whined and whirred with power all around him, the high-frequency pitch seeming to peel his head open like an orange. His brain hurt, and he thought his eardrums might have exploded. And then, having found the secret that his earlier occupants had buried, Turiel's hand fell away from his head.

They key, whatever it was, was being turned.

Turiel's hand on the obelisk moved as he imported the missing components on some megalithic control panel, and the sky map began to shift again. And just as Turiel hit the quantum ENTER button, setting the astronomical clock so that now was later, Hunter reached out with all the energy he'd been saving, found the metaphysical control board that wasn't a control board and hit a button that wasn't a button. He was operating in that other realm now, where human understanding and all its words fell short. He reacted, on some other plane, according to what had been put in his mind to do—what he was sure the Light had given him to do.

With his mind, he nudged a portion of Turiel's celestial calendar, tweaking just a tiny fraction of his formula, and just as intense light filled the whole chamber, there came a slight shift on the ceiling.

Turiel's eyes grew wide with the sudden realization of what Hunter had done, but it was too late to do anything about it.

Hunter stumbled and fell to one of the pods, everything a moving blur. It felt like they were in a capsule falling through the atmosphere. With all the concentration he could muster, he grabbed the side of the open pod and pulled himself in. Rolling onto his back, he looked up.

The last thing he saw as he wondered if this was a spaceship or a time machine or a gateway, was four beings standing over him. They shone brighter than the room, wings spread out and forming a barrier around him. They were holding out flaming swords, their tips overlapping and forming a cross over him.

And then everything was gone.

THIRTY-ONE

Noonish.

Jackson opened his eyes to find that he was still spinning. But instead of gray granite filling the canopy, there were only brilliant blues.

He was crashing into water.

But how could that be? He forced his eyes to focus as he spun, trying to get a full sense of his surroundings. Had he somehow flown straight through the mountain and was now crashing into a lake on the other side?

No. In every direction there was only water.

There was no mountain.

No pyramid.

No island.

The UH-1 slammed into the ocean.

* * * *

Paul peeled himself off the deck, his head not faring any better after the concussion blast that almost threw him across the ship and over the other side. Struggling to his knees, he tried to find Li, to make sure he hadn't been blown over.

"What was that?" Li's voice asked.

Paul turned and saw him standing behind him, staring out over the ocean toward the island. He was about to say something smart when Li's face screwed into bewilderment.

"What?" Paul asked, standing tall and feeling his head swim off his body as the world vanished into vertigo. He took an awkward step forward to steady himself and somehow managed to keep from falling. When the dizzy spell finally left him, he followed Li to the railing they had been standing at just a minute earlier. Before an invisible shockwave had slammed into the ship.

"Look," Li said, pointing to the horizon.

"I don't see anything."

Li nodded. "Right…"

And then Paul understood.

He scanned the waves, the sky, and everything seemed to be normal. Except that there was no sign of the monkey devils and the sharks that had just been feasting on them. No floating clumps of hair. No pieces of buoyant wings. No blood in the water.

He looked up at the sky, wondering if the blast had rendered them unconscious, the ship drifting away from the island while they slept. But the sun seemed to be in the exact same position.

"The island is gone," Paul muttered.

Li's narrow eyes snapped to his. "You mean it worked?"

If Paul could've shrugged, he would have, but the pain in his arms and shoulders was too much for even that subtle gesture. "I don't know… Did the island leave us, or did we leave the island?"

"Maybe both?"

Paul thought about it, his scarred brow wrinkling. "But if we're back, we should be able to see the real Bermuda." And then he remembered what Jackson had said about the Huey. "Unless…"

"Unless what?"

Unless they were thrust out the other end of the Triangle. But then it wouldn't be the same time of day. It would be the middle of the night in the Indian ocean. Unless he believed they could've been out for twelve hours. None of this he said to Li, but what Li hypothesized next was far more disturbing.

"Maybe there is no real Bermuda here."

Li's words struck Paul's heart like a torpedo, sending it spiraling down into the depths of doubt and fear.

No.

Could it be true? Could the pyramid have sent them to some other alternate reality where there was no island east of North Carolina, trapping them in a water-world reality the same way it had trapped Osiris so long ago? Or maybe the black hole in that cave was torn wide enough to swallow the island whole, leaving them stranded on a ghost ship for the rest of their lives.

Li turned away from Paul, reading everything he needed to know off his face, and headed back to the stairs, his shoulders slumped in a posture of surrender.

Paul scanned the skies one more time, hoping against hope for any sign of Jackson. Nothing. Maybe he had made it. Maybe Hunter and Jackson were standing on Front Street right now.

He turned his back to the horizon and followed after Li. His pants were still soaking wet, and his skin was pricked with gooseflesh from the cool breeze and icy raindrops. He needed a cabin with a bed where he could sleep undisturbed for a month or two.

* * * *

When he opened his eyes, he saw nothing but sky. But then water splattering the foreground of his vision forced him to focus.

Raindrops—he was looking through glass.

Disorientation reeled through him as he tried to gather his senses and figure out where he was. Which became rather obvious as soon as he turned his head. He was in a helicopter.

But what had been the mission? Where? Had he been shot down over the Mediterranean?

Then he noticed the huge spear coming through the canopy and penetrating the copilot's chair. *What the hell…*

Denise's face flashed through his mind. But it wasn't Denise, was it? It was someone else…

Robin-with-a-Y.

He blinked, knowing he didn't have the time to figure it out now. He looked behind him and—

A mountain.

That was the last thing he'd seen. He was about to crash into the side of a mountain when—

When what?

But water was bubbling up through the cabin, its frothy fingers reaching for him, and he quickly grabbed the backpack and AK-47 that were beside him. He threw the door open and was struck by his surroundings.

Water.

In every direction and as far as he could see.

What is going on?

A shadow fell across him.

He looked up and saw two creatures from *The Wizard of Oz* circling above him.

And it all came back, months' worth of memories clicking into place instantaneously.

Without another moment of hesitation, he raised the rifle and shot at the monkey devils, the one closest to him jerking sideways and then plummeting. It splashed down fifty yards in front of him. Adjusting his aim, he fired at the other one and finally hit it with his final bullet. He tossed the empty rifle aside and dove into the water and away from the sinking Huey.

* * * *

Robyn met Li and Paul as they entered the shadowy room, and though the expressions on their weary faces were nearly impossible to read, the elation of victory it was certainly not.

Paul stumbled, and she reached out to steady him. His weight almost knocked her over as her hands slipped over his wet skin, looking for a place of purchase that wouldn't aggravate his many wounds. She could tell he was teetering on the brink of consciousness.

Once she had him steady, she blurted out, "What happened? What was that light? What struck us?"

He collapsed onto a chair that was positioned at one of the round tables and put his head in his hands.

She sat down in the chair next to him. "Did it work?"

He didn't answer.

"Jackson?" She looked to Li.

"I don't know what happened," Paul answered. "But the island isn't there anymore." He put his forehead down on the table.

She stood and turned her head toward the windows, staring out across the empty water and trying to decipher what it might mean. A tear slipped down the side of her face.

Then, mustering some resolve, she turned back to him. "We need to get you warm and dress your wounds."

But he was already asleep.

* * * *

He took the knife out of his backpack and began cutting. The wings were like leather, and he cut through their thin and taut composition with ease.

After he had both wings separated from the body, he kicked the bobbing corpse away. For a brief moment, he wondered if perhaps he should keep it as a source of food. There was no telling how long he'd be adrift. But starvation wasn't his concern right now, and the thought of eating the hairy rat disgusted him.

Unfolded, each wing spanned about five square feet; and pulling one on top of the other made it buoyant enough for him to climb aboard. It dipped in the middle beneath his rear end, and water rose over his pants. But it didn't sink.

Two more wings would add to its sturdiness, so after a brief rest, he slid back into the open water and swam for the other monkey.

Once he had the body back to his raft and its wings severed, he added them to his vessel, making it twice as sturdy.

He scanned the horizon but saw only water in every direction.

He lay back and closed his eyes, letting the raindrops land on his face. Had Hunter accomplished his mission? Might he even have made it back? He thought about Robyn and Paul on the ship and wondered if he might be stuck in a world in which Bermuda had never been birthed out of the sea.

* * * *

When Paul next opened his eyes, he found that he was lying in a bed. Lifting his head off the soft pillow, he looked around and knew that he was in a suite on one of the upper decks. *Guess they started trying doors*, he thought.

The room was big, open. There was a row of floor-to-ceiling windows standing across from the bed and looking out over a balcony and the ocean beyond. No rain clouds smudged the sky in that direction, and the sun was resting far lower than the last time he'd seen it. That meant he'd been asleep for hours. Maybe days.

He dropped his head back to the pillow, surprised how much he'd missed such a simple comfort. Then the aches throughout his body began to speak, letting him know they were all still present. He sighed and pulled the cover he was under off to the side. He was wearing a clean undershirt and shorts. Bandages wrapped most of his body.

He closed his eyes and again tried to pray. *Lord, I don't know you all that well yet, and I'm not quite sure how to go about any of this, but if that little girl is there with you, which I suspect she is since I think you sent her to me—either that or you had an angel pretending to be her—can you please thank her for me?*

Then he rolled onto his side, sat up, and swung his feet onto the floor.

A knock at the door.

"Come in," he answered.

The door opened, and Robyn walked in with Daniel behind her.

"How are you?" she asked, looking him over.

He shrugged, which he found he could do now. That was an improvement. "Thanks for tucking me in." She turned her head, gazing out the window, and he could tell she'd been crying. "How long have I been out?"

Daniel stepped forward. "A few hours. I've been keeping everyone from exploring."

Paul nodded. "No sign of land?"

He shook his head, his eyes drifting sorrowfully to Robyn as he did so.

Looking down at his missing fingers, Paul mumbled, "I guess we should at least be glad we're off that island."

"I'm not giving up on Hunter yet," Daniel answered.

"Neither am I, Danny boy."

Robyn faced them again. "So what do we do now?"

Paul stood, stretched as much as his body allowed, and then slid his feet through the carpet, skiing his way to the dresser. He pulled open the middle drawer and found it to be full of clothes, once again prompting the question as to whether the ship had come without its biological occupants, or if it had been vacant at the time of its transition. Grabbing a pair of jeans, he held them up to his waist. A little short, but they'd do. "How is everyone?"

"Fine. Amazed by the ship. Glad to be off the island. Wondering what's next. Grieving our losses…" Then she repeated her question. "What do we do now?"

"Look for food."

"And then?"

"Then we go over the ground rules. Maybe the ship isn't haunted anymore, maybe it is, but we shouldn't take any chances." Yet, even as he said it, he wondered if that was exactly what they *should* do. Maybe present-day Bermuda was behind one of its many doors, just like before when he'd stepped into the theater and onto Front Street, almost getting hit by a cab.

He followed them out of the suite and back to the casino.

* * * *

Jackson shot upright. Something had bumped his raft. He looked around but saw nothing, only the water lapping up over the edges of the wings. He noticed the sun's position and guessed he'd fallen asleep. The rain had stopped, and the sky had cleared. He reached over for the backpack and—

Bump.

He flung himself away from the source of the impact, landing on his hands and knees, eyes frantically searching for a fin.

After a minute passed without any sign of sharks, he moved his hand over the spot he'd been lying on and felt a bulge beneath it. Whatever it was, it was bobbing up and down on the water and tapping the underside of his raft. He pushed down on it, and for a moment it disappeared. Then it floated back into the raft, only this time it wasn't concentrated in a local area the size of a basketball, but rather it was stretched out like a piece of wood, spanning the entire length of the raft. Jackson reached beneath the wings and yanked on the thing, sliding it out from under him. The body of a monkey rat floated out from beneath its own severed wings, bobbing in the water next to them.

Jackson sighed with relief and sat back down. He scanned the horizon, looking for any sign of…anything, and just as he was about to give up and close his eyes again, something in his periphery drew his gaze. It was far away, but it was catching the sun, and he had to squint against the flashing glare.

The cruise ship.

Sudden joy flooded him as everything he'd just put to rest came roaring back to life. He was not stranded alone. Collapsing onto his back, he cheered up to the sky. "Thank you! Thank you! Thank you!"

He got back to his knees, wiped the tears from his eyes, and started to think how he might get himself to it. It had to be three miles away, and there was no way he could swim that far in his current condition. Then an idea struck, and he began folding the top two wings into themselves, following their natural creases. When he had them in a long and firm two-foot-wide length, he took the laces out of his boots and tied them together, making a different kind of raft—one he could straddle like a surfboard and paddle like a kayak. He tossed his boots and rolled up another wing for his paddle.

It would take a long time, but he thought he could reach the ship by nightfall.

He began paddling, the sun racing him to the horizon. *I'm coming, Robyn.*

Half an hour later, the ship had doubled in size. An hour after that, he could clearly see it without squinting. But the sun was beating him, and if it went down completely before he got within screaming distance and there was no moonlight to illuminate the night…

He paddled harder, his arms and shoulders throbbing, his side agitated from twisting.

When the sun finally dipped below the waves, turning the water into liquid gold, the ship was only two hundred yards away.

He looked up to the deck, through the windows, but couldn't see anyone. Maybe they were on the other side.

Or maybe this isn't the same ship…

He was so exhausted, he almost didn't care. This close, he could close his eyes and resume worrying about it in the morning. *If sharks don't get me, or another storm doesn't come up.* It'd be a shame to get this close just to drown at the doorstep. *And wouldn't you rather sleep in a bed tonight?* He pressed on, aiming for the open marina.

The moon did come out to watch him, and in its silver light, he pulled himself up into the shallow water of the boat bay, greeted by the smell of oil and grease.

Stumbling through the darkness, he found the door to the stairwell.

I think I made it, Denise. Guess maybe I won't be seeing you right now after all. And he was surprised to feel a certain sadness ping inside him. *I love you. And you were right about everything. I wish I would've listened to you then. I'll see you again soon.*

He climbed the steps.

* * * *

Paul was sitting at a table beside a slanted floor-to-ceiling window, staring out at the moon, his ankles crossed on an empty chair. He had grown weary of trying to make sense of it all. And not just the last couple of days, but all of it. The whole impossible thing.

Candles lit the room, and he could see them dancing around his reflection in the window. Everyone else was occupying tables farther away, their faces blurred in the dim mirror. But he could tell who most were without turning his head. They were playing games, talking, praying, and some were sitting in silence like he was, eyes distant, trying to make sense of the world.

The whole room made up all that was left of the Purees, and as he watched the old lady tend to Hap while Robyn braided the young girl's hair, he felt compassion for them. The relief of having been saved from the giants was mixing with the conflicting grief of all their losses, making their current situation a hard drink to swallow. Throw in a pinch of an entirely new world they wouldn't be able to relate to or understand… Even now he could see tears sparkling in the candlelight, perched in the corners of sad eyes. And poor Ivan. He looked catatonic, staring at his feet, rocking back and forth. Paul wondered if his mind would ever be able to recover, or if reality had become so unsure and fractured that he'd forever be lost in some psychological purgatory. At some point he would have to pull him aside and tell him about Mollings, about his capture. It would be hard to hear, but Ivan would never be able to move on if he went on believing he'd left his friend behind.

Amazing grace, how sweet the sound… Paul closed his eyes and prayed again, the words coming to mind clumsy and ignorant, but so natural.

When he opened his eyes, he found himself staring at the reflection of a figure standing in the doorway on the other side of the room, the moon superimposed above his head.

He grabbed the AK-47 that was leaning against the window and spun around, raising it at the figure, ready to put it down before it could fly into the room and kill the survivors. But it was no bat-winged creature standing in the doorway.

"Someone should really turn the lights on." Jackson's voice echoed.

Everyone in the room turned toward the voice. Robyn was halfway across the room before most of them even recognized who it was. She threw her arms around him, tears of joy and relief streaming down her face.

"How?" she stammered.

He stroked her back, asking himself the same question.

Paul couldn't keep the smile off his own face as he watched everyone in the room rise to their feet and move to greet the stranger that God had indeed sent to rescue them.

Well, I'll be, he thought.

THIRTY-TWO

The Ocean. Two days later.

Robinson moved across the open deck on the crutches he'd gotten from the infirmary. He and Daniel had been spending most of their time out in the open air, eyes glued to the horizon. Partly because they still had misgivings about the ship's interior, despite no such experiences having been reported since being dropped off by the helicopter two weeks ago, and partly because they still expected Hunter to come through in some way.

A beautiful sunset in a cloudless sky was already in preproduction.

"Maybe this was all Hunter had in mind," Robinson mused, leaning against the railing. "Getting us off the island before it disappeared."

Daniel squinted. "Maybe."

And would it be so bad if that were so? They were already in the process of turning the boat bay into a fishery and water station, trying various methods to produce drinkable water. They could survive for a long, long time. They had a lot of gas and oil that they could even use to run freezers for making ice. The accommodations were comfortable, and there was no longer the fear of being eaten by giants. The girls in particular were just beginning to enjoy a peace they'd never known before. No, it wasn't too bad.

They stood staring out at the dipping sun for another hour, not saying much, just enjoying the ocean breeze and the colorful display. But just as they were about to turn in, Robinson leaned forward and placed his hand over his eyes, shielding the brilliant light.

"You see something?" Daniel asked, trying to track Robinson's line of sight through the crystal flames rolling off the sea's surface.

"I don't know," he whispered. He lifted a pair of binoculars he'd found in one of the staterooms and set them against his eyes.

He stood up straight and stared uncertainly into the distance, the binoculars coming away in his dropping hands.

"Anything?"

Without a word, Robinson took the binoculars off his neck and handed them over.

Daniel took them with quiet curiosity and looked through them himself. It took him a few seconds to find it, but when he did, he too dropped the instrument from his eyes in order to verify that the thing was actually out there and not just in the binoculars.

"You see it?" Robinson asked.

He raised the binoculars again and watched. "A boat."

"I think we should probably get Jackson."

* * * *

Everyone went to the sundeck and lined the starboard railing, looking over the side and watching the yacht approach. It was clear from its long wake slithering through the gold water behind it that this wasn't just a chance crossing in open water. The yacht had been on a straight line with them since it had slipped out of the horizon.

No one spoke. No one knew what to say. The presence of another boat came as a revelation they didn't know how to interpret. But they had half a dozen AK-47s leaning against the wall in front of them just in case.

The yacht was big and futuristic looking, its silver surface reflecting the setting sun and turning it into a gliding flame. It moved alongside the huge hull of the cruise ship with purpose, as if its occupants were surveying the derelict ship for any sign of life. Then it turned and motored aft, toward the open boat bay.

"Grab the guns," Jackson said to Paul, Robyn, Daniel, and Li. Then he turned to everyone else, the expression in their eyes matching his own. "Stay here," he said, handing the last rifle to Patrick.

Samuel nodded, and everyone took a step toward their old leader. Even Ivan, who seemed to have improved a little since Paul told him about Millings, placed a reassuring hand on Hap's shoulder.

"We'll be back," Paul said in an Austrian accent no one else appreciated.

When they reached the marina, they found a motorboat parked in the middle of the bay, the streamlined yacht in the background like a floating bullet. Standing on the concrete surface off to the right of the shallow water were four silhouettes. Their outlines were traced by the orange glow of the sinking sun, their faces concealed in shadow.

"There's no need for those," a voice echoed, and eight open hands went into the air, showing that they themselves were unarmed.

"Where'd you come from?" Paul asked.

"South Carolina," the same voice answered.

Paul and Jackson exchanged a look.

"And where are we now?" Jackson added.

Another voice answered this question. "Right now, you're about two hours from being boarded by UN patrol boats."

Jackson frowned. There was something vaguely familiar about the voice.

"Please, we don't have much time."

Paul chuckled. "Time's all we got, hoss."

But Jackson stepped forward. "Time for what?"

The figure matched his step. "To get you back home, Jack."

Jackson squinted. "Who are you?"

"It's me." And the figure took another step closer, the shadows slipping away from his face.

It was Henry.

Jackson lowered the rifle and blinked. "Henry?" But his mind was tripping over it, refusing to believe his eyes.

Henry went to him and embraced him as if back from the dead. But even in his arms, Jackson couldn't compute his friend's presence. Before returning the embrace, he had to look over to Paul and make sure that he was seeing him too. But Paul was already there, throwing his arms around both of them.

"How are you here?" Jackson whispered, his voice shaking.

"Can we come in?" Henry asked, pulling away and pointing toward the door.

"Who's 'we'?" Paul asked, and he stepped toward the other shadows.

"I think you remember Chadwick," Henry answered.

The archeologist stepped forward and extended his hand. "Good to see you guys again."

"What the hell?" Paul whistled, shaking his hand while trying to get a glimpse of the others.

"This is Frank," Henry said. "He was a police officer in Bermuda, but he can tell you his story later."

"Nice to finally meet you guys," the Bermudian said.

"And this…" Henry motioned for the last person to step forward.

A black man came out of the darkness, and his baritone voice echoed off the walls around them as he waved. "Hello, fellas."

Confusion swept through the five hosts and tethered their minds together in unified paralysis. It was Daniel who finally broke their stunned silence.

"I don't understand…" he gasped.

"Is that you, my Danny boy?" the man answered, his head leaning to the side so that he could see past Paul and Jackson.

Then Paul's tongue was loosed. "But—"

Not letting him finish, Hunter embraced them both.

* * * *

Henry stood looking over the remaining Purees, the sun kissing the surface of the water behind him. He couldn't believe this was all that had survived, and emotion choked him as he shook hands and embraced those he'd known. When he came to Samuel, he could find no words to give the man who had given him protection and sustenance when he'd first appeared on his island so long ago.

"It worked? You made it back?" Samuel asked.

Henry nodded.

"And now?"

"Now is a little hard to explain. But we'll have plenty of time for it later." Then he gathered everyone together, addressing them as a group, Hunter and Chadwick standing beside him. "Friends, I know that you have many, many questions. Believe me, we will do our best to answer them. But right now, this ship is about to be intercepted by—" he searched for a word that they might understand "—the authorities. And unless you want to spend the rest of your lives trying to explain to them where you came from, then it'd be best if you aren't here when they find it. We have everything you need on the boat." He motioned to the yacht below. "So if you would follow Hunter and Chadwick, we'll get you guys back to the real world once and for all."

And as they began leading everyone down to the boat bay, Paul got close to Jackson and whispered, "You notice anything different about our friends?"

"Yeah. They look about ten years older."

"I was thinking fifteen, myself." Then he went and grabbed Hunter's arm just as he was about to follow Daniel off the deck.

"What's the deal, Hunter?" he asked. "I mean, you were just here with us two weeks ago, and now you look like you and Samuel could be the same age."

"I have a lot to tell you," he said. "But what I said was true. The ship is about to be picked up by satellite, and all manner of government agencies are going to be crawling all over this thing, taking it apart. With no sign of the original occupants, and our crunchy bunch here with AK-47s, their homecoming isn't going to be a pleasant one. As I'm sure you can imagine." Then he smiled. "I'm glad you made it."

Paul's eyes grew wet. "Dude, whatever you did back there…"

Hunter put a hand on his shoulder. "Later."

"Okay, on your super expensive yacht, then."

He nodded and walked through the doorway, but before he reached the third step, Jackson called out after him.

He looked back.

"What year is it?"

Hunter just smiled.

* * * *

The horizon was a fire of reds and oranges as the night chased the sun into the ocean's depths, the sleek pleasure yacht heading straight for it. By the time they reached their destination, however, the sun would be rising behind them.

Paul was standing behind Henry, watching as he piloted the hi-tech boat. "This the *Gegenes II?*"

Henry shook his head. "No. I'm done with all that."

Paul nodded, understanding completely. "How's Johnny?"

"He's doing good."

"I owe him an apology."

"For what?"

"Let's just say the blinding light knocked me off my horse, too."

Henry turned.

"Yeah, yeah, I know what you're thinking. Not a guy like me. Whatever." Paul shrugged. "What can I say? Even a wretch like me…"

Henry's smile stretched ear to ear. "He'll be overjoyed to hear that."

Paul scratched at the stubble on his neck. "So was that really you I spoke to on the phone three months ago?"

"It was."

"That was a pretty strange day."

"Hunter told me what he could, but—"

"But he spent most of those three months wandering through different dimensions? Yeah, Daniel told us he'd gone a little cuckoo for Cocoa Puffs."

Henry's face grew somber. "The thing is, Paul…for me, it wasn't just a few months ago."

"Yeah, I've been getting that feeling."

"Hunter will explain all that. As best he can, anyway. I sure as heck don't understand it."

"Right." Paul sighed. "So…Ronald? Osiris? What happened to them?"

"We came back right at the obelisk in Bermuda, and Ronald was there waiting for Osiris. It was quite a scene."

"And you haven't seen them since?"

Henry ran his hand through his silver hair, studying his friend, who was suddenly not as old as him. "Go get cleaned up. We'll talk about all this later. It's a lot."

Paul smiled, wondering how anything could possibly be stranger than where he'd spent the last three months. "Okay." He turned and headed to the back of the boat, where he suddenly took a seat out in the open air and decided to watch the sun set on the weirdest chapter of his life.

* * * *

Hunter sat at a table with Paul and Jackson while Henry continued navigating the pleasure yacht away from the derelict ghost ship. It was nighttime over the Atlantic now, and the Purees were all in line for showers and new clothes. It was the first time most of them ever had a hot shower, and it was all the rage this night. That and the hot tub. And the buffet.

"So it's been two days, you said?" Hunter asked, sipping from a glass of water.

Jackson nodded. "Since the island disappeared."

Hunter stared at his hands for a moment as if trying to determine where to start. "After I was skewered and tossed off the temple steps, I believe I was possessed."

"That would explain the way you were acting," Paul said. "I almost punched you in the mouth with all your singing."

Hunter grinned. "My new occupants led me into the closet, which was…" He shook his head. "Let's just say, if hell has sewer lines, they used me to pry open the manhole cover."

"Gross," Paul mumbled.

"Osiris thought they were freeing him, but that was only part one of the demon's plan. Having John in the pyramid when Osiris used it at the solstice was what allowed for part two."

Jackson leaned forward. "Turiel."

Hunter nodded. "What you called the 'New Territory'…as well as a few other needed ingredients."

"Like the house," Paul added.

"Exactly."

"What about Ivan?"

Hunter shrugged. "As far as I can tell, your friends from 1969 were just collateral. Either that or Ivan's role in all this hasn't been revealed yet."

"Wait." Paul held up his missing fingers. "How do *you* know about them? You were playing sea cruise with Danny when we met."

"Let's just say strolling through those sewers left some residual effects. It's how I knew about the helicopter and how I saved Robyn when she jumped from the temple balcony."

Both Paul's and Jackson's eyes grew a little wider at that one.

"It's how I knew who Turiel was, and what the closet demon was attempting to accomplish. It's how I found a way off the island for us."

Jackson asked, "And what exactly was it trying to accomplish?"

"The demon, or Satan himself, whoever it is orchestrating things on this end of the spectrum, needed one of the original Fallen angels here in today's world."

"Why?"

"To unlock Tartarus and free Abaddon, also known as Apollo, who will lead the world into a new, Luciferian Golden Age."

They frowned, trying to process what Hunter was telling them.

"Why did they need you?" Jackson finally asked. "I mean, Osiris needed John as a fail-safe, but why did Turiel need you? Daniel said that we couldn't use the pyramid, that only Thoth knew its secrets. But if Turiel is one of the originals, then he predates Osiris who just stole the real Osiris' name. Why would Osiris be able to use the pyramid and Turiel wouldn't?"

"Osiris had his helpers too, but he was making a straight shot from one realm to another. Turiel needed to cross time."

"And you just happened to have the right coordinates?"

"In a manner of speaking." He tapped his temple. "Not only did I let the demon out of the closet, they put the information into my head. Turiel took what he needed in order to make the journey."

"So Turiel wasn't in our time?"

"And I don't think we were in his."

Paul leaned forward and asked his question again. "What year is it, Hunter?"

Hunter looked them in the eyes as he answered, "In this reality, it's been sixteen years since we were taken through the Triangle."

Paul and Jackson sat back, their minds whirling.

"It's 2027?"

"It is. We've been waiting for you, preparing."

Jackson leaned forward again. "How did you know when we would be back?"

"The demon didn't want anything leaving the island, didn't want anything else coming back that could jeopardize the agenda, including unwanted attention their way. Everything on the island that wasn't in that room with me and Turiel was consumed as the reality that sustained that dimension collapsed on itself. Being off the island, you would survive the transition back into the real world. But if the cruise ship just appeared out of nowhere right off the tip of Bermuda, then not only would you have to explain yourselves to the officials, but you'd be studied and questioned and monitored by the Philadelphia Experiment crowd. And Ronald's forces would hunt you down."

"So *you* put us in the future?" Paul squinted, feeling a headache coming on.

"I don't know how to describe what I did. After Turiel plugged in his coordinates, I reached out somehow with my mind and altered a portion of his formula that allowed for the immediate area to…fold forward onto a later date while at the same time allowing us passage to Turiel's destination."

"Which was where?"

"Front Street, in front of the obelisk. Same place Henry, John, Chadwick and the five Purees appeared with Osiris. And like then, Ronald was waiting for Turiel with a running car."

"But I talked to Henry on the phone—"

"We showed up on December 21, *2012*."

Jackson held up a finger. "The AK-47s, the helicopter, *you*… All of that was a coincidence?"

But Hunter smiled, and lines and wrinkles that Jackson had never seen before stretched at the corners of his eyes and around his mouth. "Hardly. There's an old quote that says, 'God can use the wrath of man to praise Him and the enmity of Satan to serve him.' And whereas this plot seems to have been hatched in hell, there was another purpose beneath it all, and believe you me, there were angels unseen all around us in that place."

"2027," Jackson muttered, trying to let it sink in. "Why that date?"

"Think of it like a half-court shot. I was aiming for a general area but trying not to overdo it. I had a general idea of when you'd show up—again, don't ask me how—but not the exact year."

They had so many questions, they didn't know which to ask first, and figured they'd be spending the next few months going over it all, but Jackson had one more question he needed an answer to right now.

"I'm guessing the Mayan prophecy didn't come true."

"Depends on your interpretation of the prophecy. If you thought it would be Wormwood and the Great Tribulation, then no. That hasn't happened yet. But if you were with the New Agers expecting a transition into a new age of enlightenment…" He shrugged and held out his hands.

"What do you mean?"

"Let's just say that 'world consciousness'—if you want to call it that—has changed a lot since you've been gone. There seems to have sparked around that time a sudden, global sort of harmonious yearning for—"

"A Golden Age," Jackson finished. "And right when Osiris made his entry back into the world."

Hunter nodded. "Oh, they've been busy fanning that flame into a raging fire. The world is practically begging for what Chadwick calls the Masonic Christ and what I believe the Scriptures call the anti-Christ."

"Apollo."

"The New World Order is on the horizon. Globalism is the new Gospel, nation-states associated with racism and bigotry."

Paul shook his head as if trying to get the idea to fall through a hoop of comprehension.

"There is no more United States of America," Hunter said, watching his friends closely for a reaction. "There is now the North American Union."

They both blinked.

"In less than a year, the entire world will be cashless, the World Bank controlling the global economy."

"No more Wall Street?" Paul asked.

"Wall Street was destroyed by a dirty bomb five years ago. There is only one currency now, and it's all tied to a sort of DNA-laced QR tag."

"In your skin?"

"Not yet. Right now it's part of the identification card everyone is required to have on them at all times, but they've been talking about inserting it in the forehead or in the right hand for some time."

Jackson looked horrified, no doubt wondering what all his years of service had been for if this had always been the goal. "They call this enlightenment?"

"Like always, it was delivered as a Trojan horse, slavery draped in the beautiful colors of freedom, tolerance, and equality for all. Of course, there were propaganda campaigns and disasters taken advantage of…"

"Problem-reaction-solution."

"Terrorism, identity theft, hate crimes…"

Jackson looked out the window, realizing that he and Paul would be as much a stranger in this world as the Purees. "You said you've been waiting for us. What does that mean?"

He smiled. "It means we've been busy. We have ID cards for everyone ready to go, fabricated histories to memorize just in case. But we have obtained a facility that they'll all be safe at. Think of it as Professor X's School for the Gifted. Only it's for the survivors born on an island that never existed in this reality. They'll be taken care of and won't have to worry about giants looking for a midday snack."

A cloud fell over Jackson's face as he realized that all his promises to Robyn had just turned to dust.

Hunter knew what he was thinking. "The world is a different place for sure, but it still has all its illusory trappings that can be enjoyed. Just be careful not to offend anyone, and you can go out to dinner, see a movie, go to a football game. The NAU is the heart of the new technocracy, but the crushing fist of Orwell's vision hasn't completely fallen yet. What Robinson and Li and Daniel saw on the ship, their vision of a Washington Monument standing beneath an ash-filled sky…that's still future."

There was something in Hunter's voice that made Paul ask, "And you're trying to stop it?"

"We have what you could call a little underground movement working to expose the true agenda of this rising one world government."

"But you said yourself that it's already written. How can you hope to change it?"

"The *Titanic* will sail no matter what, so it's more about how many people we can keep from boarding it."

Paul stood. "I think I need a drink."

"Help yourself," Hunter said, motioning to the bar.

Jackson stood too. "I need to talk to my fiancée about our honeymoon plans." But before he stepped out of the room, he looked back at Hunter. "Thanks for saving us."

Paul nudged Hunter's side. "He went back for you, ya know."

Hunter looked back to Jackson. "Why would you do that?"

Jackson smiled. "I realized just in time how stupid it was, that I could've messed up your whole plan. A giant swiped the tail right off the Huey, and right before I crashed into the side of a mountain—*poof*—no mountain."

"You shouldn't have come for me."

"It was my fault you were all there. I couldn't just leave you."

"But it wasn't your fault," Hunter answered. "Don't you see? We've been chosen to fight this battle. All you did was introduce us to the enemy."

Jackson tapped his knuckles on the tabletop, toying with the idea of accepting Hunter's words.

"Besides, God wants you focusing on forgiveness, not fault."

Paul laughed at the irony of that. "What happened to us?" he asked. "We all became little Johnnys."

Hunter then turned to Paul and handed him a folded piece of paper. "I think you're supposed to have this."

* * * *

Paul woke up, and for a moment couldn't figure out where or when he was. When he looked over to the nightstand next to the bed, he saw the folded piece of paper Hunter had given him the night before, and it served as a hook that reeled him back to the present. Which was sixteen years later.

He sat up and swung his feet over onto the floor. Reaching for the paper, he unfolded it and read it again. The words meant a lot coming from Hunter, who had no doubt carried the words of King David around himself for the last sixteen years.

Where can I go from Your Spirit?
Or where can I flee from Your presence?
If I ascend into heaven, You are there;
If I make my bed in hell, behold, You are there.
If I take the wings of the dawn,
And dwell in the uttermost parts of the sea,
Even there Your hand shall lead me,
And Your right hand shall hold me.
If I say, "Surely the darkness will hide me
and the light become night around me,"
even the darkness will not be dark to you;
the night will shine like the day,
for darkness is as light to you.
For You formed my inward parts;
You covered me in my mother's womb.

He brushed a tear from his eye and walked over to the mirror. As he studied himself, he looked back over his life and realized that he'd never been alone. Those nail-pierced hands that had pulled him out of his past had been there the whole time.

When he stepped into the living area, he found Jackson and Robyn talking with Chadwick. Samuel was talking with Henry. Everyone else was either still sleeping or, he could see through the window, fishing with Hap.

"Hey there," a voice said behind him.

He turned and found Frank, the Bermuda cop, standing there with two glasses of orange juice. He held one out to him.

Taking it, Paul nodded. "Thanks." He took a sip. "So how do you figure into all this, Frankie?"

The man smiled and gestured to an empty seat at the bar. "I think we have another hour before our destination."

Paul took one last look over his shoulder, wondering over the miracle of their salvation. Robyn turned her golden head and caught his eye. As he leaned against Jackson's large frame, she smiled a smile that spoke a thousand words of thanks. She was alive because of him. Paul smiled back.

"So," Frank began. "The night I met John..."

As he spoke, Paul looked out past Hap's windswept hair and to the horizon, curious as to what was awaiting them. He slipped his hand into his pocket and felt the paper, and for the first time in his life, he wasn't afraid of anything.

EPILOGUE

December 20, 2028. The Carolinas, NAU. Evening.

John kissed Kristen, then embraced his son.

"You watch over your mother and sister, you hear?" He kissed the top of his head, which he barely had to look down to do now.

"Yeah," John Jr replied, but his mind was on the M16s, obelisks, and gaping skulls covering his father's skin. Even at sixteen, he wasn't used to them.

John knelt in front of Mercy, and she threw herself into his arms.

"Don't go, Daddy," she cried, her blond pigtails whipping back and forth as she shook her head. She, unlike her older brother, never seemed to notice his inked flesh.

He kissed her forehead. "I won't be gone long."

"Promise?"

"I'll...be home...for Christ-mas," he sang as he stood and grabbed a shirt off the dresser, pulling it over his head. He kissed Kristen again and whispered something in her ear that made her blue eyes sparkle.

She grabbed his hand. "Remember, you're fifty now. And the others are all pushing—"

"—wheelchairs, I know. We're all old men now. But Moses was eighty when God called him to lead the Hebrews out of Egypt."

"And is that what you're going to do, honey? Set captives free?"

"In a manner of speaking," he muttered. "I'll be back in a few days." He crossed the bedroom and stopped in the doorway, turning to take one last look at his family. The three of them stood there staring at him, the expressions in their eyes running the full gamut of emotion—from five-year-old uncertainty, to a young man feeling the sudden reality of his responsibilities, to a wife wondering what she'd do in this deteriorating world if her husband didn't come back this time.

Just before turning, the car horn honking again, John studied his son, recalling Osiris' words some seventeen years ago. *Take care of that boy of yours.* And then his offhanded implication that, like the anti-Christ, he would forsake the God of his fathers. But he had given that over to the Lord, believing that it was just the Deceiver's attempt to sow fear and doubt throughout the gardens of faith.

"I love you," he said.

"Johnny, we gotta go!" Paul said, suddenly behind him.

"Hi, Uncle Paul," Mercy said, waving.

Paul stepped past John and gave her a quick hug. "Don't you worry, little angel, I'll make sure Daddy brings back a special Christmas present just for you." His stubbled face scraped her soft cheeks, and she giggled. "Kristen," he acknowledged, tipping his head. Then he pointed his three fingers at John Jr. "You're in charge, sport."

He nodded.

Then Paul grabbed John's shoulder and pulled him out of the room.

John waved goodbye, his eyes burning.

Beneath the dim streetlamp, Paul opened the door and John slid into the backseat next to Henry.

Chadwick turned in the SUV's front passenger seat. "Cutting it close, John. If we don't make it back out in time, Mercy isn't gonna have to make another Father's Day card."

John nodded as he looked back to his house, knowing Chadwick was right. They only had a moment of satellite blackout in which to work, and they were pushing it as it was. He could see the three people he loved most in the world waving in the window. He blew them a kiss as Jackson pulled the black Suburban away from the curb.

When they turned off his street, John leaned past Henry and shook hands with Robinson. Then he asked, "Where's everyone else?"

On cue, a pair of headlights swept through the back of the vehicle as a matching Suburban pulled off a side street and began following them.

"Li, Mary, Patrick, and Frank are in that one," Jackson said, looking up into the rearview mirror.

"Hunter's not coming?"

"He's staying back with the others this time."

In case we don't come back, John understood. With Robyn four months pregnant, and their secret facility's cover constantly facing exposure, it was a good move leaving one of them behind.

Jackson made a left instead of a right at the next light.

"Where are we going?" John asked, confused.

"Just a little detour," Chadwick said.

Paul leaned over the seatback and started going through their gear.

Twenty minutes later, they pulled into the parking lot of a run-down, but servicing motel. It was an establishment they used when wanting to meet with other members of the Resistance incognito. The owner was a sympathizer, and the private security detail that patrolled the grounds helped keep suspicious eyes at bay. That, and the NAU's integrated surveillance system constantly going offline for "routine" maintenance.

Jackson had the Suburban's front tires up against a crumbling parking block. A peeling red door stood in front of them, its brass numbers illuminated by the glowing headlights. 104, and the 4 was hanging upside down.

John asked, "We picking someone up?"

"Yeah," Chadwick said, and Jackson flicked the high beams three times.

The curtain in the window responded as two fingers pulled it aside. Ten seconds later, the door opened, and a man that looked about ten years younger than John appeared beneath the flickering sodium lights that ran down the open hallway.

Then a woman stepped out behind him, a little boy riding her hip. The three of them exchanged hugs and kisses. As the man turned and walked to the SUV, John watched the woman's unblinking eyes as they tried to will the man from leaving. John knew the look. He'd just seen it in his own wife's eyes. It was a unique expression, a deeper, more complicated look than those shared by women sending their husbands off to war for the first time and wondering if they'll ever see them again. No, this look told of previous chapters in which this woman had already seen those fears realized. There had been a time when this man had *not* come back. And now here he was leaving her and their child again, and she was left hoping there was another miracle card in the hand she was dealt.

It was a reenactment of what John had just gone through with his own family.

The man walked up beside Chadwick's window as it lowered.

"They'll be okay?" the man asked, his voice trying to hide the agony he was feeling.

Jackson leaned over and answered, "As soon as we're in the air, someone we trust with our lives will come by and take them to the facility. Until then, the security detail will make sure they aren't bothered by anyone."

The guy looked around, contemplating this. "You know there are a lot of people looking for us. For what we have."

Chadwick nodded. "They'll be fine at the facility. But *we* won't be if we don't get moving."

"Okay."

He stepped away from the window, and as he walked to the other vehicle, he passed John's window, their eyes locking for the briefest moment. But that was all John needed to read this guy's story, and he realized that he was looking at himself some eighteen years ago.

"Who is that?" John asked.

Chadwick answered, "His real name is Joshua Cavanaugh, but now he goes by Matthew Scott."

"And what is it that he has that 'people' are looking for?"

"You wouldn't believe me if I told you," the archeologist said.

"Okay, then why's he coming?"

Jackson put the vehicle in reverse and backed out of the parking spot.

"He's the one who told us about the God Hoax. And what he has…" Chadwick turned to look at him. "Let's just say it's one of the missing puzzle pieces to what they're trying to dig up down there."

They pulled out of the motel's cracked parking lot, and John watched the woman wipe her eyes, the little boy waving frantically to his dad. John's heart broke for them, and for his own family. But this was the price of admission for a front-row seat to the opening acts of the Mystery of Iniquity Paul the apostle wrote about almost two-thousand years ago.

Jackson screeched to an abrupt halt next to the private luxury jet, killing the engine and shutting off the lights. They wasted no time opening the doors and jumping out into the chilly air. In fact, it had started snowing. December in what used to be South Carolina wasn't the same as it was even just a few years ago.

John snatched the large duffel bag Paul tossed him and threw it over his shoulder. As he ran for the running jet that had just lowered a boarding ramp from its backside, he cast a cautious eye over the vacant hangar around them. He ran up the plank and into the warmth of the plane. He dropped the heavy gear and turned to take Mary's load, tossing it on top of his. Then he helped Frank, pausing only to give him a quick embrace.

It took just five minutes for everyone to get seated in the leather chairs and the jet to begin rolling down the runway. John watched Jackson check his watch, look out the window, and whisper, "Right on time."

John turned and looked out his own window and saw a car pulling up beside the empty Suburbans. Before the plane's wheels even left the old runway, all three vehicles were turning out of the abandoned airport.

When they reached cruising altitude, they unfastened their seatbelts and gathered in front of the television screen that Henry had just turned on at the end of the room.

A press conference. The UN logo behind a group of men standing around a podium.

"What is this?" John asked, stepping forward between Li and Frank.

Chadwick turned it up.

"This is them setting the stage," Jackson mumbled over his shoulder.

And as the man behind the microphone began speaking, thanking this agency and that agency, John whistled. "Well, I'll be. Look who it is."

The man standing behind the speaker was a familiar face. A face that never seemed to age.

"Ronald Douglas Carter," Henry acknowledged.

"Or Dr. Grigori," Chadwick added.

"Look!" Paul suddenly shouted, shouldering his way through the group and pointing at something in the top right corner of the screen. "It's him!"

There was a crowd of people standing around the podium, none of them but Ronald recognizable to anyone else.

Jackson squinted. "Who?"

Paul jumped in front of the screen and put his finger on a person standing behind those gathered in front of the blue and white banner. Behind the podium, off to its right, was a hallway. Paul was touching a person that was half-concealed in its shadow and seemed to be watching the scene from a distance.

"It's Turiel!" he yelled.

"Are you sure?" Robinson asked, taking a step forward with everyone else.

"I never forget an angel," Paul answered.

The man had traded in his white robes for an Armani suit, and his long black hair was now styled in a short-cropped fashion that made him look like a movie star, but his blue eyes still blazed, and he was still the tallest man in the room.

Everyone stood still, holding their breath.

Then the Fallen angel, one of the original two hundred, turned and stared directly into the camera. He stared so intensely, that Mary and Patrick both took a step back.

And then a sly smile lit up his face, and the TV went blank.

"What the hell," Chadwick whispered, trying in vain to get the picture back.

Frank looked around the cabin. "Do you think he knows we're coming?"

No one answered.

Then Hunter cleared his throat and ushered everyone into the next room. He hit a button on the wall and a long conference table began rising out of the floor, the leather chairs by the windows sliding toward it. At the far end of the room, another doorway led to more forward-facing seats, the cockpit just beyond that.

Everyone took a seat at the table, the idea that the mind-reading angel might know what they were up to unsettling.

"Listen," he said as he tapped on some keys that lit up on the table's surface, bringing a holographic image of Antarctica hovering over the table's center. "If God be for us, who can be against us, right?"

John looked over at Matthew Scott, who had just nudged him.

"Your brother?" Scott asked.

"Yes. And no."

Scott squinted.

"Turns out I was adopted."

"Oh."

"You're the one that told Chadwick about the so-called 'God Hoax'?"

He nodded.

"How'd you stumble across that?"

Scott sighed. "That's a long story."

"We do have another nine hours before we're over the Southern Ocean."

Before Scott could reply, Chadwick tapped the tabletop, and a red light appeared over a top right portion of the continent. "For a long time now," he began, "there have been a lot of theories put forth about what this dark hole just might be. A UFO, an old Nazi base, an extinction asteroid, the Garden of Eden, Atlantis, or a portal into the center of the earth." He paused. "Truth is, I have no idea what it is. All we know is that the melting ice has opened the door to the last great mystery on earth, and there is right now a massive military excavation taking place to uncover what has been buried there for as long as we can remember. And whatever it is, they're setting the world up for its presentation." He pointed back to the room with the TV, referencing the UN conference.

Then he pointed at Matthew Scott. "Matthew has shared with me certain intelligence that he's acquired since going off the grid in Canada. Information that compelled him to move his family from the safety up north and to risk everything in trying to find us. Whatever they're planning on revealing, whether the Royal Arch of Enoch, the pyramid's capstone with the secrets of First Time and the forbidden knowledge the sons of God altered the earth with…or if Turiel has just located his own lost crystal pyramid that you guys used to transport off the island last year, we have no clue."

Paul's lips stretched into a thin smile. "What if it's the New Territory they're digging up?"

"What's the New Territory?" Scott asked.

Robinson laughed. "I don't think you'd believe us."

John studied the faces around the table. They'd all been through so much, each one having their own story to tell. He wondered if the man beside him had a story that could match the others and saw that he was sketching something on a tiny pad of paper he'd pulled from his chest pocket.

Henry took over where Chadwick left off. "Whatever it is they find down there, we're going to be there to document it. And we're going to get it to as many people as we can. We're going to shed light on the Mystery of Iniquity and see just how many people we can wake up to the truth before it's too late."

Paul frowned. "So you think the end of days deception the prophets talk about will be coming out of the ice in Antarctica?"

"I think it's a piece of it," Chadwick answered.

"And this piece has something to do with this 'God Hoax' Mr. Scott here knows something about?"

John stared at Scott, waiting for him to say something. But all he did was tear a piece of paper out of his little book and slide it across the table to him.

John picked it up and unfolded it. It was a crude sketch, but there was no mistaking it. He stared at the man, his brow wrinkled into a series of Vs. "What does the Ark of the Covenant have to do with this?"

But again, before Scott could answer him, Jackson spoke up. "If what has been buried under two miles of ice is, in fact, the gate to Tartarus, then this might be the event by which Turiel and Ronald release Abaddon from the pit and unleash tribulation on earth."

And then John found himself muttering the words of Jesus. "As it was in the days of Noah, so it will be at the coming of the Son of Man."

"Then the fifth angel sounded his trumpet, and I saw a star that had fallen from heaven to earth, and it was given the key to the pit of the abyss," Henry added.

Then Jackson whispered, "…and shall show great signs and wonders, so that if it were possible, even the elect would be deceived."

At which point Mathew Scott pulled a leather-bound diary out of his pocket and placed it on the table. "You've got to read this."

The jet streaked toward the bottom of the world, racing the melting ice, the winter solstice, and the repositioning satellites. And at some point, before disembarking into the frozen landscape, Paul took a folded piece of paper out of the C.S. Lewis book he was reading and handed it to John. When John opened it, he smiled. It read:

Where can I go from your presence?

A SELECTED BIBLIOGRAPHY

Bauval, Robert, and Adrian Gilbert. *The Orion Mystery*. New York: Three Rivers Press, 1994.

Berlitz, Charles. *The Bermuda Triangle*. New York: Avon Books, 1974.

Book of Enoch as Translated from the Ethiopic (in 1821). Ed. Richard Laurence. Artisan Pubilshers, 2007.

Fleming, John. *The Fallen Angels and the Heroes of Mythology, the Same with "The Sons of God" and "The Mighty Men" of the Sixth Chapter of the Fifth Book of Moses (1879)*. Kessinger Publishing.

Glover, Lorri, and Daniel Blake Smith. *The Shipwreck that Saved Jamestown: The Sea Venture Castaways and the Fate of America*. New York: Henry Holt & Co., LLC., 2009.

Hall, Manly P. *The Secret Teachings of All Ages: An Encyclopedic outline of Masonic, Hermetic, Qabbalistic and Rosicrucian Symbolical Philosophy*. New York: Penguin Group, 2007.

Hapgood, Charles H., *Maps of the Ancient Sea Kings: Evidence of Advanced Civilization in the Ice Age*. Kempton: Adventures Unlimited Press, 1996.

Hancock, Graham. *Fingerprints of the Gods*. New York: Three Rivers Press, 1995.

Hancock, Graham. *Heaven's Mirror: Quest for the Lost Civilization*. New York: Three Rivers Press, 1998.

Hancock, Graham. *Underworld: The Mysterious Origin of Civilization*. New York: Three Rivers Press, 2003.

Hancock, Graham, and Robert Bauval. *Keeper of Genesis*. New York: Three Rivers Press, 1997.

Hancock, Graham, and Robert Bauval. *The Message of the Sphinx: The Quest for the Hidden Legacy of Mankind*. New York: Three Rivers Press, 1996.

Heron, Patrick. *The Nephilim and the Pyramid of the Apocalypse*. New York: Citadel Press, 2004.

Knight, Christopher, and Alan Butler. *Before the Pyramids: Cracking Archeology's Greatest Mystery*. London: Watkins Publishing, 2009.

Knight, Christopher, and Alan Butler. *Uriel's Machine: Uncovering the Secrets of Stonehenge, Noah's Flood and the Dawn of Civilization*. Gloucester: Fair Winds Press, 2001.

Pember, G.H. *Earth's Earliest Ages*. First published in 1876 by Hodder and Stoughton.

Platt Jr., Rutherford H. "The Forgotten Books of Eden." Sacred-texts. 1926. <http://www.sacred-texts.com/bib/fbe/index.htm>

Quasar, Gian. *Into the Bermuda Triangle: Pursuing the Truth Behind the World's Greatest Mystery.* New York: McGraw-Hill, 2004.

Sitchin, Zecharia. *The Wars of Gods and Men.* New York: Avon Books, 1985.

Wilson, Colin, and Rand Flem-Ath. *The Atlantis Blueprint: Unlocking the Ancient Mysteries of a Long-lost Civilization.* New York: Dell Publishing, 2002.

Zuill, William Sears. *The Story of Bermuda and Her People.* Oxford: Macmillan Education, 1999.

If you enjoyed the Progeny trilogy, then you may also enjoy *The Solomon Key*, of which the main protagonist, Matthew Scott, made a special appearance in the epilogue of *Apocalypse Rising*.

Also, keep an eye out for more stories from the Progeny world. Please visit www.shawnhopkins.com and get on the mailing list so you can be informed of special offers, new releases, and other fun stuff. You can even get a free book just for signing up!

And lastly, if you enjoyed this book, please consider leaving a short review. And if you do happen to leave a review, I would love to hear from you! You can contact me via the website. I love interacting with readers! Thanks again! And I look forward to bringing more stories to you in the future.

-Shawn Hopkins

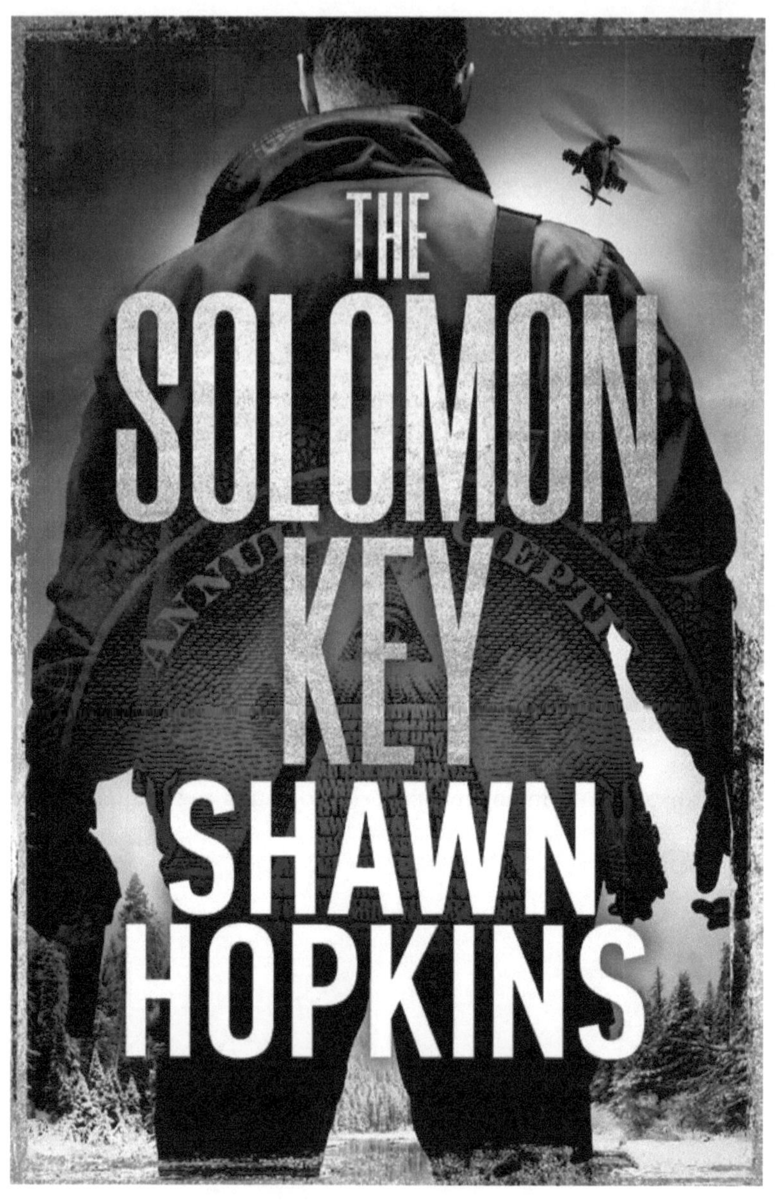
THE
SOLOMON
KEY
SHAWN
HOPKINS

Also by Shawn Hopkins

Nephilim Island: Progeny Book I

Principalities and Powers: Progeny Book II

Apocalypse Rising: Progeny Book III

Progeny: The Complete Trilogy

*Brotherhood of the Beast: A Progeny Story**

The Solomon Key

The Judgment Key

*Thanks For Nothin': The Eli Diaries Book 5***

Enemy: The Eli Diaries Book 10

The Eli Diaries: Volume One

*forthcoming
**get it for free when you get on the mailing list at www.shawnhopkins.com

www.ingramcontent.com/pod-product-compliance
Lightning Source LLC
Chambersburg PA
CBHW020303030826
48979CB00027B/2012/J